THE DIARY

**EDWARD E. STAMBAUGH II, PH.D. AND
J. CONRAD STAMBAUGH**

outskirtspress
DENVER, COLORADO

615402745

*To all those who recognize that hope is the
most powerful force in the human character.*

ACKNOWLEDGMENTS

The authors wish to extend our thanks to Ms. Brandi Pummel whose patient, insightful and thorough editing prowess crafted this work into a readable narrative.

We also wish to extend our profound thanks to Mr. Jeff Herndon for his long suffering patience in translating a concept into cover art of exceptional quality.

Doctor Nathan Forrester's recall for the day that he gave up on the whole psychotherapy enterprise was crystal clear. Bright sunshine speeding through clear autumnal skies brought with it a chill in the air that made breathing easier and life feel worth living. It was the sort of day he had loved since childhood. In the memories of this farmer's son, the cold air meant that the humidity of summer had been dispatched, while the fall colors heralded the end of the hard work of harvest. Soon four feet of soft white fluff would dress out the landscape, leaving only the sentinel evergreens to watch over the hills until spring.

It was nine o'clock and he was seeing his first patient of the day. A well dressed and attractive woman in her late thirties sat down and announced quite simply and directly, "I have the me-disease." A unique event in over ten thousand patients and twenty years of service in hospitals and consulting rooms, it left Forrester speechless. As she related it, everything in her history of interactions with others confirmed her narcissistic self diagnosis including her current difficulties with her husband and children. More from habit than a need to know, Forrester administered his standard battery of neuropsychological screening procedures. They confirmed what he already suspected. The candid lady's perceptions were governed by a strong right frontal lobe, complemented by a clear weakness in the left frontal-temporal area of the brain. Despite the evidence of left brain weakness, the assessment revealed no indications of neurological disease or trauma. This forthright woman was simply another representative of the neurology that drove the majority of the human race.

With some reluctance, Forrester launched into an explanation of how his patients' perceptions and thinking style created both feelings of entitlement, and an inevitable disappointment with a world and its inhabitants wherein her childish demands went unfulfilled. He didn't have to watch her eyes track left as her right hemisphere dismissed his words, he knew his interpretation was a pointless exercise. Most of what he said would be gated out by her genetically engineered way of looking at, thinking about, and emotionally reacting to, the human tribe of which she was a member. He could spend months, perhaps years, hammering away or solicitously pleading with her to entertain alternative perspectives on herself, her family and the world in general, but the only certain outcome of this effort would be a modest fee for service. Consistent with the research proven immutability of his own neurological makeup and that of the others he had evaluated over the decades, this self-centered lady was firmly rooted in the niche wherein evolutionary genetics had planted her.

At the very root of his soul, Forrester felt spent. He was tired of fighting a losing battle with the evolutionary inertia of his native species. He could no longer justify taking money from those in whom he knew he could work no significant change.

His ten o'clock appointment canceled. He dictated a report for the 'me-disease lady.' By the time he completed the dictation it was nearly eleven. It was a good report, seven pages of clear, concise and practical recommendations for getting more of what she wanted by being less of who she was. She'd read it, get angry, set it aside and come back to it over time. She might even try to implement some of what she saw there, but in the end it would make no difference. She was who she was.

At 11:02 he decided to quit the profession for good. In a moment of honest self reflection, he felt compelled to take the advice he'd given to a whole generation of graduate students in psychology. How often he had intoned, "human problems will be solved through biochemistry, genetics or in the ponderous, but inevitable course of evolution, not by talking to people." Like all left hemispheric thinkers, he felt like a helper, but now, after all these years, he knew that he wasn't. The majority of the human race, like the me-lady, was right hemispheric and a left hemispheric thinker was not sufficiently tuned into the tribal pulse of the right brain to participate in the chants and dances that helped that hemisphere feel better.

He felt like a man who had spent his whole life spitting into the wind. Now with a face full of spittle, he wanted nothing more than to drift with the high pressure front of evolution. He'd do the only thing he had ever done well, think about how things work, and hopefully come to some small measure of soul quieting understanding. He would begin at his point of intended departure, namely the data he had so lovingly collected.

Evaluating over ten thousand individuals over thirty years had provided Forrester with an overview of the human race. Seventy percent were significantly more influenced by the right than the left half of the brain, while thirty percent relied exclusively on the left hemisphere. Parsing out the particulars, the thinking and problem solving style informed by the posterior portions of the brain revealed that 57% were right hemispheric, and 43% were left hemispherically energized. Of that total, 55% used their right frontal lobes to line up the bits and pieces of experience for digestion by the problem solving post frontal hemisphere that nature had designated as dominant for a given individual. Of the remaining individuals, 32% picked their way meticulously through the complexities of reality using the left frontal lobe and 13% flipped back and forth between the two frontal lobes as though involved in some cerebral tennis match. His own particular group of thinkers, left hemispheric with left frontal guidance mechanisms, represented only five percent of the population. Individuals in this group tended to get lost in an endless morass of 'why' ruminations.

For a second time that day, Forrester decided to take his own advice. He'd exorcize his helping compulsion and do what nature had crafted him to do, pose why questions. Why these particular proportions of brain configurations in the genetic pool of humanity? Why did the right hemisphere govern the preponderance of the human race? Why should there be left hemispheric thinkers in the mix at all? For the first time, Forrester recognized that these questions could not be answered using the tools of his profession. Only the history of the species could provide clues and intimations relevant to questions of such breadth. Written history was an unlikely candidate in his search for meaning if the goal was understanding anything other than the political bias of the writer. He'd have to start at ground level. The metaphor, concrete as it was, seemed compelling. Perfectly wedded, the combination of dirt and overarching ideas was called archeology. Resolved in that moment, either out of existential desperation, or as an epiphany of insight, he could not say, the decision was made. He'd throw himself into a course of graduate study in the basic science of the past.

⁂

After five years of laborious study in the fundamentals of archeology among kids half his age whose interests were more focused on the hormonal present than the historical past, Forrester achieved one more Ph.D. Still new to the discipline of archeology, it was more than apparent that Forrester had come to the field from decades of work as a neuropsychologist. His approach to locating and studying ancient cultures was unorthodox to say the least, guided as it was principally by the application of his research in brain-behavior relationships to the investigation of the past.

Perhaps it was the screwball bent of Forrester's ideas that forged the relationship between himself and a fellow elder student in the program, Arthur Wendover. Arthur had come to archeology from the business community where he had pursued a successful career in marketing. Arthur's verbal creativity had both fueled his career, and been his undoing. Arthur referred to his demise as a marketer as a derivative of the one-one-one principle: One wrong word spoken at one party to one important person and the money and good times went down the toilet. Arthur's interest in archeology was driven by the challenge of raising money for projects that had absolutely no day to day utility. Forrester's constant companion, Arthur shared, even if he didn't comprehend, the neuropsychologist turned archeologist's raving enthusiasm for investigating the course of the brain's evolution by digging holes in the ground.

Arthur's extraverted showmanship and knack for developing sources of funding was a perfect complement to Forrester's plodding introspection. Schmoozing was second nature for Arthur. This singular talent produced funding for Forrester's craziness. In truth, Arthur didn't want to know the particulars of Forrester's research model. Although he listened patiently as Forrester rambled on, Arthur only wanted to formulate a marketing strategy to sell the idea to bored and lonely corporate wives who desperately desired a sense of mission in their lives. He finally hit on the phrase, 'digging the brain out of the dirt.' What that verbiage lacked in technical precision it more than made up for in financial drawing power. Adequate funding assured, both Arthur and Forrester were loosed from all academic constraints. Finally free to disappear back into his head, Forrester could now work out the specifics that would make possible the practical implementation of his vision.

Informed speculation based on Forrester's research and vast amounts of coffee resulted in a model that would guide their investigations. Forrester reasoned that the human race had begun as right hemispherically activated simians. However, for reasons which eluded his model of brain development, a small proportion of the race had begun declaring themselves as fully left hemispherically activated somewhere between 500 B.C. and 500 A.D.

His own neuropsychological research over the past thirty years showed an increase in the proportion of right hemispherically directed individuals at the expense of the lefts. It appeared that the three thousand year old activated left hemispheric perspective on life was being junked by mother nature. Three thousand years was not even a half a breath in evolution's respiratory rhythm, and yet in that gasp the left hemisphere's moment of life was expiring.

One third of Forrester's life had been spent in attempting, not only to understand the individual patient seated before him, but the species of which both he and that suffering person were a part. What for him had begun as a longitudinal neuropsychological research effort focused on assessing thousands of individuals from a broad sample of racial and ethnic groups over three decades culminated in a series of summary findings in 2994 A.D. Based on this analysis, it was clear that the number of individuals in the general population whose perceptual and cognitive functioning was principally characterized by a right hemispheric bent was increasing rapidly. No matter how many times he ran it through the computer, the results were the same. The 57% right hemispheric plurality had become a 70% majority, gutting the left hemispheric thinkers from 43% down to only 30% of the species. Forrester's analysis suggested that what mother nature had seemingly required untold eons to generate , namely, a 43% left hemispheric proportion of the race, was now being shrunk. Mother nature appeared to have changed her mind and was culling the lefts out of the herd. He had to know why.

To be sure, his small patch of research was nothing in the vast expanse of evolutionary time. However, the trend over the decades was consistent and incremental. If the left hemispheric thinkers were going the way of the Dodo in a span of time that amounted to no more than the blink of an eye, perhaps they had emerged in a similarly brief biological burst. Using a regression algorithm derived from his own research, Forrester pinpointed the full emergence of left hemispheric thinkers in the millennium bracketed by 500 B.C. to 500 A.D. His retrospective evolutionary analysis of the proportionate representation of right and left hemispheric processors in the human species seemed to confirm a significant neuropsychological shift to left hemispheric activation had occurred during this epoch. Given the apparent current trend back to right hemispheric exclusivity in the human species, he wanted to know if the archeological record offered any clues about the period during which the left hemisphere's voice first underwent a significant nonlinear increase in volume.

The historical record from 500B.C. to 500A.D offered support for a thousand year flowering of cognition that bore the telltale earmarks of left hemispheric symbolic abstraction and transcendental vision. This was an epoch of spiritual experimentation in which the birth of new religions revealed the closed character of the systems of belief that had spawned them. Transcendental giants such as Buddha in 483 B.C., Confucius in 479 B.C., Jesus of Nazareth in 6 B.C. and Muhammad in 632 A.D. each revealed their own personal vision of a path into the future leading beyond the constraints of systems that revered the past. During this millennium of thought, the left hemisphere's characteristic 'why' and 'what if ?' vision declared itself with a quiet fervor no other recorded epoch could boast. This did not surprise to Forrester as magnetic imaging studies of the brain had already declared that the left half of the brain was the 'God hemisphere, or put in terms that non-believers could stomach, the left frontal lobes mediated religious experience. The left half of the brain devoted to routine tasks in other species, had clearly found a new calling in man.

Forrester felt at home with thinkers of this historical mind set. As with most full left hemispheric reasoners, he had always been fascinated with the way beginnings inevitably determine endings ... well, most of the time anyway. And if beginnings didn't foretell finishes, that meant you didn't understand all the 'whys' embedded in their inception.

According to Forrester's algorithm, the left hemispherically directed segment of the human race, had gradually increased, from a small beginning, to a level representing approximately forty-three percent of the general population by the year 2000 A.D.. It appeared that the percentage of lefts had remained stable at that level until Forrester's research began in 2964 A.D. Over the course of his data collection effort, the percentage of left hemispheric perceivers in the population had begun a gradual, but alarming, decline.

Choosing an appropriate site for a dig required more intuition than years of archeological scholarship. His own Judeo-Christian upbringing doubtless informed his choice of a starting point. The Middle East was literally pockmarked with holes sunk in the Earth, most of them yielding little more than wages for native hires. Satellites, armed with technologies devoted to finding mineral resources, had, inadvertently revealed many ancient sites while scanning through the Earth's surface to astounding depths.

The selection of a specific site for excavation had been based on two speculative inferences. First, Forrester was intent on finding evidence in the archeological record that corroborated his belief that a minor shift from a right to left hemispheric perceptual bias had begun in the historic past. This meant that he must look at communities that were thriving between 500 B.C. and 500 A.D. Second, he decided not to devote his efforts to sites that other archeologists had previously investigated.

Over the course of his last six years of graduate study, Forrester had cobbled together a map representing all the digs in the middle east in the past two thousand years. He was particularly enamored with sites that had appeared interesting to investigators in the past, but for one reason or another were never excavated. From among several untouched plots, Forrester selected a site in what can only be described as an intuitive process. Strangely, each time he looked at the untouched sites on his map one circled area consistently appeared to reflect more ambient light than the others. He had examined that area of the paper repeatedly but could find no rational explanation for its superior reflective property. Basing his selection on this inexplicable experience was offensive to every logical tenet he held dear, yet, he felt inwardly compelled by this experience to choose that site above all the others. Forrester's degree of discomfort with this event informed his decision never to tell anyone but Arthur the real reason behind his selection.

Mentioning the whole scenario to Arthur, Forrester discovered to his surprise that Arthur wasn't aghast or even particularly interested. Arthur was the paradigmatic example of the axiom that social reality always takes precedence over the factual physics of living. Arthur was only interested in what he could sell to their patrons, logic and facts be damned. If it brought in money, it was the unimpeachable truth. The incongruity drove Forrester crazy, but he took the money. He and Arthur were shortly caravanning into the deserts of Biblical history.

⌖

The dig became a three year nightmare. Forrester and Arthur had moved almost as much of their patron's money as sand. Huge excavators had inhaled, chewed and blown away mountains of dirt from around the remains of a small village located forty meters below the desert's surface. One Sunday, as he watched the mounds of sand grow and the bank balances shrink, Forrester feared this would be the last stand for Arthur and himself. If nothing exceptional showed up here, it would be the salt mines of small college instruction and sucking up to the dean for the both of them.

Late in the day, the shadows were long at the bottom of the huge pit. Forrester prepared to start the arduous climb out of the excavation and return to his hut to await Arthur's return from a libation run to the closest town. Arthur wouldn't be back until after midnight. His trip required time for him to purchase spirits, but also to sample the wares of every bar within staggering distance of his vehicle. Starting up the long ladder, Forrester chanced to glance over his shoulder, and there, illuminated by an oblique ray of the setting sun, he saw what appeared to be a right angle in the sand. Scrambling back down the ladder, he ran toward the patch of sand where he had spotted the odd shape. Never taking his eyes off the target as he stumbled through the dust toward the shining object of his excitement. A stone edge protruded out of the dirt. He knelt down and carefully brushed away the sand revealing part of what appeared to be a large stone slab about eight centimeters thick.

Catching the attention of several native laborers, Forrester began to organize the removal of the slab. The job turned out to be a considerable one as a twelve centimeter grove was cut into the perimeter of the slab on its underside. The groove was about five centimeters from the slab's margins and had to be lifted off a tongue formed by the walls upon which it rested before it could be slid aside.

Arms strained and levers bowed as workers raised the ponderous slab off its foundations. The instant the tongue of the stone foundation cleared the groove in the slab, two rather startling events transpired. First, there was an audible whoosh of air as it was drawn into the vault below, immediately followed by an upwelling of air from the uncovered chamber . The inward rush of air was, in and of itself, quite startling, suggesting that whatever lay below existed in a partial vacuum. However, the upwelling of air from the vault was even more noteworthy as its odor suggested ionization of the atmosphere in the sealed chamber. The effect was so remarkable that, for a moment, Forrester was transported back to childhood and the clean smell of the air after the lightning strikes of a thunderstorm.

Pitching in, laborers soon slid the slab about one third of the way off four supporting walls that extended deep into the earth. Forrester called for lights that were quickly rolled into place and directed down into the subterranean chamber. Cones of illumination penetrated the dust, revealing a room holding what appeared to be a large pedestal holding a stone casket at the far end. At the near end of the chamber, carved steps originated at the topmost edge of the wall and led down to the stone platform. It was clear from the depth of the cavity that even when the parts of the village already uncovered had been above ground thousands of years ago, this chamber had been set into the earth far below the surrounding structures.

One of the most energetic laborers, Abdul, a graduate student in archeology who had been with the project from its inception, bent over the lip of the chamber, peering intently into its dusky recesses. A local, Abdul had approached Forrester with an offer to work for free at the dig's beginning. However, Forrester had since found the funds to hire the enthusiastic young man as a student assistant. Swayed by the unreserved passion in Abdul's eyes, Forrester, out of nostalgia for that feeling in himself, decided to concede the honor of being the first to enter the chamber to this fresh young mind.

Abdul, excitement and curiosity burning in eyes too young to have been dulled by the mechanical disappointment of living, looked hopefully at Forrester.

Forrester nodded and motioned to the stone steps. Abdul grinned and quickly clambered into the shadows, perhaps too quickly. The grating sound of splitting sandstone filled the air. Forrester gasped and leapt forward as one of the supporting walls gave way. The capstone tipped, slid and fell. The eager young archeologist to be disappeared in an avalanche of dust and thunder.

Although Forrester was moving quickly, he already knew what he would find in the dusty shadows. The only part of the crushed body visible in the rubble was the young man's face. Arriving just in time to see the light fade from his eyes, Forrester stared at young man's face as the seconds treked into eternity. The light fading from that kid's eyes seemed to be taking the future with it. Suddenly, native workmen surrounded him, helping to clear away the shards of stone. Among the murmurings, Forrester instantly recognized one voice, still in the distance, that of the excavation foreman, the boy's father.

Hands were everywhere. Bare arms reached out of the darkness as members of the crew helped Forrester carry the boy's broken body through ten meters of choking dust to the head of the stairs. Arriving out of breath at the edge of the excavated chamber, the foreman's eyes widened. He looked at his son, the stairs, the broken stone and finally at Forrester.

Eyes passionately articulating what his heart knew at once, the man was no longer a foreman, just a father. His only son whose devotion had been meted out in lesser measure to him than to Forrester was gone. A dagger produced from beneath his jacket appeared instantly in his hand. He lunged at the foreigner who was responsible for his son's death. Only a few martial arts moves dimly recalled, but automatically executed, saved both Forrester and the grieving father.

Unstained by the blood of righteous revenge, the knife fell on the dusty ground. None of the native laborers would touch it for the sake of its intended purpose in slaying another man. Sinking eventually into the sand, it would become the prize and puzzlement of some digger a thousand years hence.

Quickly enveloped by a cloud of laborers, the now vacant eyed father was escorted to his tent. Others of the crew members remained, gathering around Forrester to offer culturally appropriate excuses and unnecessary apologies for their foreman's actions.

As his eyes stared at the blood stained stairs and the casket on its pedestal below, Forrester saw only life's light fading from the boy's eyes. There would be no official inquiry and no investigation into the young man's death. The corporate sponsor of the dig would issue a certificate of accidental death and pay off the boy's father. It was a swift and unceremonious end to a promising life.

Less than thirty minutes after the young man's body was removed, scientific curiosity overcoming reverence, and Forrester ventured down the stairs, careful not to tread on the still damp blood stains. Standing amidst the dust of thousands of years, he walked slowly to the pedestal and began the painstaking task of brushing sand from the lid of the small stone casket. The care he exercised in removing the ages of silt was that which might have been reserved for preparing a body for burial. Perhaps the tiny receptacle was an ossuary holding the meager remains of another father's son. A bitter poetic justice might dictate that the stone box concealed evidence of another pointless and painful loss three thousand years ago. Forrester would be careful lest he disturb the echoes of one death calling to another from the depths of the pit and across the millennia.

An inferior sandstone, the lid showed wear as though someone had often caressed its surface. Aramaic characters carved into the face were only faintly visible. Some had been entirely worn away. Bringing his hand lamp closer, Forrester read one barely discernible etching, 'blessed ... ... peace makers.' Another at the foot of the cap stone read 'the meek shall inherit the ..... Earth.'

Anxious to help, one of the laborers who had stayed with Forrester moved a tripod mounted spotlight closer to the pedestal. The laborer's attempt to focus the spotlight's beam jarred the casket lid. As Forrester watched helplessly, the stone cover disintegrated into powder, attended by the rasping, scraping sound only crumbling sandstone produces. Through the dancing particles of settling dust, the light clearly revealed a smaller, but much higher quality polished stone casket resting within its larger cousin. Oval in shape with a sheen mimicking white alabaster, the lesser casket appeared translucent resting among the fragments of the disintegrated capstone.

Stepping back from the casket, Forrester was suddenly inundated by fatigue that washed away whatever was left of the scientist in him. Unannounced, images of the boy's death had overtaken him in the midst of this extraordinary discovery. What, at that moment of discovery, seemed an honor conferred on a promising student had in fact been a death sentence. Like some kind of macabre price tag, Abdul's lifeless face hung in Forrester's mind, suspended next to the shining oval. Set in the balance, Abdul's life was too great a sacrifice for unearthing this great treasure. In the face of a find that should have guaranteed his career, Forrester wanted to hide from the terrible price paid for his discovery and everyone who had witnessed the payment.

Contrary to all of his training, Forrester instructed the laborers to transport the entire casket containing the oval to his hut. Failing in his attempts to dispel the image of the light fading from Abdul's eyes, Forrester wandered off into the night not even certain he could find his way back to his desert abode .

Making his way to the hut seemed to take hours as he stumbled through the desert darkness. Upon arriving, he found that the casket and oval had preceded him.

Workers had set the stone casket to one side and placed the oval on a large table in the center of the hut. Not really proper procedure, but if Forrester could wander aimlessly for hours among the dunes, the laborers could demonstrate a lack of focus in their own way. Forrester sat staring vacantly at the translucent oval, for a very long time not really seeing it, his mind wandering in his own personal desert of imageless, wordless desolation. Then, as if summoned from his bleak reverie by an outside force, his eyes fixated on the moving shadows playing over the walls of the hut.

The generator was guaranteed for one hundred years as was the illuminator globe, but the light seemed to flicker all the same. Technically speaking, the light couldn't vary, but something had to account for the changing shadow shapes on the wall.

"A head thing," he said aloud.

He looked about reflexively, but no one was there to hear him talking to himself. Self-talk, he mused, a personal characteristic he shared with those whose strength resided in the left cerebral hemisphere. The practice was only a problem if someone walked in on one of these externalized internal dialogues. How often he had lectured on the tendency for those with strong left brains to verbalize the visual confusion produced by a weak right brain in order to make sense of what they saw. If his research had taught him anything, it was that everything of consequence in personal experience occurred within the confines of the cranial vault. Reality was just the empty white card in Rorschach's ancient projective test. The tissue of individual experience was little more than a movie projector playing each person's personal history on the blank screen of so-called external reality. Rorschach's insights were dead on. People saw the inside of their heads in the outside world, but not because of their childhood. They saw what the inbuilt structure of their brains allowed them to see and spent the rest of their lives looking for hidden meanings. Inkblots were a better measure of brain structure than emotional conflict. This was not the first time that thought had tramped its muddy boots through the spotless hallways of his mind . The shadows dancing on the hut's walls might be inkblots projected by the guilt generator in his head.

With some effort Forrester wrested his attention from his internal ramblings to the sturdy table before him and the polished stone oval that rested upon it. The oval's surface was smooth, but covered with the dry, nose clogging dust of the desert. Its shape was amazingly symmetrical, a perfect alabaster oval about one meter long and half a meter in height. Its color was a translucent white that seemed all the more dazzling as he blew away the fine dust of ages with the minicompressor nozzle.

Stepping back from the table to retrieve the analytic scanner from his expedition pack, he was suddenly struck by the beauty of the tableau before him. The glowing oval framed by dark moving shadows that shouldn't be there, seemed for a moment to be the center of his personal universe. He knew the feeling, it was wonder. Here was the only feeling he had ever experienced that seemed to define man's experience as different in kind from that of the other forms of life with which humankind shared the planet.

✎✦✦✦✎

Then, as he knew it would, the Socratic dialogue in his brain began. He was journaling inside his head again, just as he had done since childhood. It was like keeping a diary of your own thoughts, but a diary that talked back to you. As a full left hemispheric processor, he shared this characteristic with Asperger's Syndrome children. Like the youngsters so diagnosed, much more talk went unspoken than was ever heard by the those who inhabited the right hemispheric world outside of the craniums of left hemispheric thinkers.

Wonder, he scoffed to himself. He had always been a 'wonder junkie' since he was a kid. First, it came in the form of a love affair with nature before he ever heard the word 'biology' or invested in its formal study. Later, he had pursued the wonder of ideas for their own sake with degrees in philosophy and theology. Years of study satisfied his need for the transcendence of symbols and abstractions, but not for wonder. If illumination was the reward of religion, then science was the purveyor of wonder. Infatuation with science, by everyone so entranced, represented an attempt to recapture the wonder and fascination evoked by a universe older than time, but new to each child who first beholds a star.

Crucial to the definition of wonder was that it be an event embedded in the real world of objects, circumstances and living systems. Neuropsychology was the next entry on the scholastic menu, the ultimate blend of phenomenology and tissue. Decades of research provided an almost daily wonder 'fix,' but netted only a sense of depressing technical certainty about the evolutionary infancy of his native species. Scientific research and years of clinical experience had convinced him that the lesson great lives taught, the tragic sojourns of Da Vinci, Schweitzer, Ghandi and King, was that the hand of evolution cannot be forced. Great ideas, poetic truths and scientific insights were but wisps in the wind when confronted by the challenge of summoning fundamental change in the human condition. Enter archaeology, representing not an infatuation with the past, but rather Forrester's search for some physical evidence of transcendence secreted in its recesses.

✎✦✦✦✎

After fumbling a bit through the expedition pack, Forrester's hands finally hit upon the analytic scanner. A marvelous little instrument, it could evaluate and analyze the interior and exterior of any object up to a two meter cube and tell you everything you'd want to know just short of the meaning of life.

Flicking it on, he played the scanner's blue light over the oval. The readout's first entry indicated that the oval was hollow. That was no surprise based on the size-weight discrepancy. Contents: Vegetable matter in layers, probably papyrus. Condition of the contents: Optimal moisture levels, no fungi. Pressure differential of the internal chamber: Approximating a hermetic seal. Now that was interesting! Carbon decay age of contents: Approximately three thousand years.

No dig in which he had ever participated, or read about, had ever found a vacuum sealed stone vessel, much less one housed in a sealed chamber itself enveloped in an atmosphere of ionized gases. The most startling scanner entry was the age approximation of the oval's contents. Three thousand years old would place age of the casket between 500 B.C. to 500 A. D. Whatever was sealed within the oval had undoubtedly originated during the era in which he speculated that left hemispheric activation first flowered.

Enamored with the phenomenon of the oval, Forrester once again set aside every bit of methodology laboriously pounded into him over six years of graduate study in archeology and followed the muse of wonder. Inspection of the oval revealed no obvious seam, but the hissing spray of the minicompressor's nozzle revealed a hairline score that traced its way around the longitudinal axis of the translucent vessel. Closer inspection revealed no obvious keying notch or any evidence of tooling that might point to a way of opening the glowing receptacle.

Feeling the familiar edge of frustration all hands on puzzles created in him since childhood, Forrester stepped back from the table to compose himself.

He admired any well engineered contrivance, from the simple Norwegian genius of the paper clip to the teutonic complexity of the analytic scanner he held in his hand. However, any time these minions of progress didn't instantly divulge their mode of operation, he progressed rapidly from anger with the machine to recriminations against the idiot who couldn't grasp its functioning.

If the oval had been closed, he reasoned, it could be opened. It was that simple. What a joke for a visual-spatial simpleton like himself! Stepping up to the table, once again Forrester's hands moved across the smooth surface of the oval. His touch never registering a seam. A number of destructive scenarios ran through his head, more out of frustration than by way of realistic plans for opening the oval, he dismissed them all. Then, as it had happened a hundred times before, the puzzle resolved itself the instant he gave up the search for a solution. He felt two barely palpable indentations carved to accept the heel of a man's hand, one above and one below the hairline scoring found at opposite ends of the oval. Resting his palms in the indentations, he applied pressure towards the center of the oval, his palms guided by the contours of the indents.

He felt the seal give and saw the upper portion of the oval move.

He heard only the faint hiss of air entering the oval's inner chamber as the heavily ionized air expelled from the oval's partial vacuum. Again, he experienced the smell of high places and lightning as in the underground vault.

The upper half of the oval was lighter than he had anticipated and lifted off with surprising ease. The absolutely smooth, blemish free inner chamber contained a number of papyrus scrolls each sheathed in its own leather quiver. The analytic scanner had accurately read the casket's moisture content, the quivers were soft to the touch and flexible.

Occurring almost as a mental footnote, he noticed that the upper half of the oval, set now to one side on the table, had lost the translucent quality that the bottom half continued to exhibit. Even more remarkable was the absence of the moving shadows on the wall that had appeared in the hut with the oval's arrival.

Forrester cast a glance at the lamp that was guaranteed to produce a steady source of illumination for a century and noted that it continued to flicker. Indeed, the still quavering light seemed somehow brighter. Despite the lamp's apparent increased output, no shadow was evident anywhere within the hut. It was as if the lamp was no longer the sole source of illumination. Instead, every surface within the hemisphere of the structure seemed to luminesce. Try as he might, no matter where he stood, Forrester could not cast a shadow, nor did any other object he could see.

As he lifted the scrolls from their resting place within the stone, he witnessed the translucent quality of the bottom half of the oval dissipate. Almost parenthetically, he detected a growing sense of well being traveling from his hands, coursing through his body and finally stationing itself in a 'Y'-shaped configuration inside his head. He palpated his head in an attempt to localize the feeling within. The two capital points of the 'Y' seemed to terminate in the left and right frontal lobes, while the tail disappeared into an area where he knew the limbic system was situated.

Suddenly, streaming through his head was a cascade of thoughts that mixed technical and poetic ramblings without regard to sequence, all prompted by the 'Y' shaped configuration in his head. As the flow of cognition slowed and conformed to a single thought, he beheld what seemed to be a reconciliation of the most recently functional and the most ancient evolutionary constituents of the brain perfectly synthesized within the 'Y' shaped sensation. Then, in a moment of transformation, his own internal soliloquy was cut short by a feeling of open clarity perfectly interwoven with some unspoken and inexplicable directive that forced his attention back to the scrolls.

Carefully withdrawing the first scroll from its quiver Forrester instantly noted that although the shafts and capitals were plain and worn, the papyrus unfurled as if it had been freshly made. The characters on the sheets were clear and bold, and the language unmistakably Aramaic. Forrester, who was not the world's greatest linguist, read the first entry with the ease that only a native speaker's familiarity confers. That fact astonished him.

> JAMES, BROTHER AND FRIEND, ALWAYS
> QUIETLY THERE. THESE WORDS, FOR
> YOUR EYES ALONE WILL BE DELIVERED
> UPON MY DEATH. WRITTEN IN THE
> VANITY OF SOLITARY PAIN AND AS
> SERVICE TO THOSE YET TO BE BORN,
> I COMMIT THEM TO YOUR KEEPING.
> SHOW THEM TO NO OTHER. BURIED IN
> THE SHIFTING DUNE OF TIME THEY
> WILL BE REVEALED BEFORE EARTH'S
> MANTLE IS SHED.

There it was, wonder. For an infinitely long moment, he was a child again, seated in the shade of the wise old trees of the family farm, drinking in the mist of the early morning meadow. Existing now only in memory was the innocent peace of plants that make all life possible and demand nothing from those they serve. In that very moment, he recognized this botanical model of service as the stout arbor on which he had hung decades of theology, philosophy, science, art and music. These words, penned on parchment so long ago, revealed, in both their meaning and soulful ring, that their author, like the botanical servants of Forrester's childhood, was one who had pursued a life of service and suffering.

A soft murmur of wind stirred the hut and drew him from memory's refuge back to the tangible wonder of the scroll before him.

> I SET DOWN THESE WORDS, TRAPPING
> THEM IN THE SCROLL, EVER IN THE
> HOPE OF BANISHING SPECTERS FROM
> A HEART AND HEAD THAT LIKE A
> NOISY MARKET PLACE OVERWHELMS
> THE EYE AND EAR. LOOSED FROM A
> FEVERISH BROW, I YIELD THEM UP
> TO AGES BEYOND THE HORIZON OF
> THESE TIMES.

Reading the entry instantly transported Forrester to an alien mental landscape.

The scroll's author experienced his internal life, not as a refuge from a world of strife, as did Forrester, but as the center of the storm's fury. Forrester reminded himself to breathe. There was no arboretum of peaceful plants in the head of this writer. The writer wanted out, but to what other refuge?

Outside the hut, the wind was rising and the sand would run in haste before it tonight. Listening to the wind, the contrast abruptly registered on him. Stillness, that was the quality embodied in the light that enveloped the hut. It was not an oppressive hush, but a lucid silence, that made the words of the scroll toll with even greater resonance in his head. The quiet was companion to the light.

> THE NIGHT IS THE WORST, A TIME OF HALF
> DREAMS AND VISIONS. WITHIN THE
> FIRMAMENT MOVE SHADOWS CAST BY
> MESSENGERS WITHOUT NAMES WHOSE
> CHARIOTS FILL THE HEAVENS. SPECTERS OF
> PEOPLE AND PLACES COME, WHICH NOT
> OF NAZARETH, BRING FIRE AND FURY EVEN
> THE ROMANS CANNOT CONJURE RENDING
> THE CLOAK OF DARKNESS.

As a neuropsychologist, Forrester had listened endlessly to hallucinatory narratives, paranoid reconstructions of the cosmos, and most frighteningly of all, the real and unrepentant horrors that man visited upon his birth place and fellow travelers. In all the listening, it was always the voices and not the words that pointed to either infirmity or health. The voice of the scroll pointed to health, but also to pain. The agony painted upon these pages was not that born of a need to see the world in travail as punishment for its rejection of the writer. This was a disturbing vision of some future holocaust set down by his own hand to free the writer's mind from its power.

Years of theological study pointed unswervingly to the author of this ancient and very private journal. Here a familiar voice spoke quietly and passionately, not to the multitudes, but to an audience of one. This was one man's private record, characters etched on flats of reeds watched themselves think, feel, suffer and despair. Unmistakably evident between the letters, the shadow of a man cast upon his own resources was visible. Here was a very mortal heart and soul weighing prescience against fantasy, fear against denial of the angry terror of the human heart, and steadfast horror against faltering hope.

Reading further, Forrester heard in the writer's voice no compulsion to persuade, no need to appease culture or custom, only a compelling desire to reconcile the life within with the world without.

CRAFTING THE WOOD BUSIES THE
HANDS AND FREES THE MIND TO
WANDER. PERHAPS MINE WANDERS
TOO FAR, TOUCHING ON LIFE WHERE
IT CANNOT OR WILL NOT CHANGE. THE
BOUNDARIES SET UPON THE SOUL BY
THE BODY IN WHICH IT DWELLS ARE
KNOWN ONLY TO ITS CREATOR.
SECRETED IN THE TWINKLING OF ALL
BEGINNINGS, A RECEPTACLE ONLY,
THE CLAY CONFINES THE RANGING OF
THE SOUL NESTLED WITHIN.

Breaking into his enrapt study, Forrester heard a faint, yet familiar sound carried on the wind. Its clattering source was still far away across the face of the desert. Forrester heard Arthur's old hopper limping and carping its way through the night. Arthur loved that wreck. It was slow, unreliable, noisy and bedraggled, but Arthur wasn't about to part with it. He carted it with them to every dig. It was more than an antique conveyance, it was a love affair.

Arthur was as close to a friend as Forrester had or very likely ever would have. Acutely feeling the depth of the attachment to his old friend, Forrester quickly distanced himself from the rush of emotion with distracting internal chatter. Arthur and I are left frontal lobe perceivers, he thought, so we see and express the same phenomenology. Arthur, a right hemispheric processor, sees the big picture, grasps the practical, and rushes forward through life with the rhythm of ageless tribal drums driving his pulse. Arthur was the archetype of a life lived in and for the moment. The distillation of Arthur's trial and error history of experience was practical wisdom. That pragmatic wellspring was a resource that Forrester sorely needed and could draw on at any time.

In contrast to Arthur's 'let's give it a go' approach, Forrester understood the world exclusively through the left hemisphere of his brain. As a result, he lived one step removed from the sweat and tears of mundane reality. Forrester grasped the world around him through a sieve that sifted away almost everything but ideas and the governing dynamics of what he understood to be a larger universe.

Watching the two men eat a meal was an ongoing revelation of the neurological differences between them. Arthur, whenever possible, ate dessert first and polished off the balance of his repast in engulfing chunks. Forrester, in contrast, ate his way through one course after another consuming each in small bites. Often, he never achieved the goal of dessert. Arthur summed up his view of Forrester's approach to dining as eating in installments. Forrester knew that it wasn't personal choice but his brain's hardwiring that accounted for the differences between them.

Forrester was the model left hemispheric thinker. He didn't analytically piecemeal ongoing experience. He experienced life piecemeal. Endless curiosity was the stitcher's hand, pushing hope, the red thread of living, one more step forward as the needle of rigorous analysis led the way, punching holes in the fabric of living. Experiencing life in this sequential, analytic fashion left only loops of stitching, moments of transient wonder - separated by yards of emptiness as a meager excuse for memory. Despite a relatively poor return on investment, Forrester's curiosity drove the analytic needle forward moment by moment over the course of his life.

Staring down at the table, Forrester's gaze focused on what might be the most illuminating or devastating document to visit this or any other human epoch. Centuries of digging in this arid land by countless earnest archaeologists had yielded nothing to compare with the record he had stumbled upon.

Having not yet fully considered the responsibility that would come with a find of this magnitude, Forrester fell back on past experience. Once before he had faced the double-edged sword of a significant finding that had required him to weigh its importance as a contribution against the damage that might be done were the results generally known. His decision, then, was not to publish the results of a quarter century of neuropsychological research despite its obvious value. Had his findings been just another footnote supporting another researcher's work, that would not have been a problem. Instead, the effort had produced a powerful neuropsychological tool. Using his method in only thirty minutes, the patient's execution of a few simple tasks produced a configuration of cerebral strengths and comparative weakness that had enormous predictive value. He paled when imagining the uses and misuses such a tool might be put to were it to fall into the hands of those who would perceive the methodology as another stepping stone to wealth and power. The decision that confronted him now had much in common with that one made so long ago.

Forrester had experienced more than his share of soul eroding disappointments, all of which confirmed aspects of human behavior that his own research had long since conceptually revealed. Those experiences and a blindingly clear understanding of his own makeup, had taught Forrester that he didn't possess the tooth and claw mentality required to hold his own with the meat eaters in his tribe. First and foremost, individuals with his left brain configuration were not endowed by nature with the 'dominance at any cost' drive that characterized those who ascended to wealth and power in his species. Second, those with minimal dominance needs like himself were involuntarily attracted to those with greater requirements for power who were themselves destined to abuse everyone in their sphere of influence. Third, those devoted to the exercise of power expended the vast majority of their time and energy to retain their status. It was a life style that interested Forrester not in the least. Fourth, individuals with Forrester's neurological makeup were prone to negotiate with themselves, rather than reflexively defending their rights against encroachment by the desires of others. Fifth, those endowed with Forrester's constitution focused more on the future than the present or the past. This fact was of surpassing significance as a tendency to look down the long corridor of cascading consequences into the future made for a poorly equipped warrior in conflicts with those who lived in an eternal present. The right hemispheric majority, whose limbically charged view of life as one eternal present tense allowed them to do whatever it took to win, won. In short, relative to the simple majority of his species, Forrester was born a loser.

A rational critic of Forrester's carefully systematized ravings would point out that the law exists to sort precisely the kinds of inequities that he had delineated. Forrester knew better. The law is not some adolescent's dream of justice, it is just business. A publicly funded, privately held enterprise, the law was structured to benefit attorneys, and to maintain order in society by upholding the status of the wealthy and powerful who stood in the shadows behind all governmental edicts. This was a threadbare mental rant. One all too familiar for having tramped through his thoughts many times before. The unchanging fatalistic chant always ended with the same coda, nothing much changes about the human condition, but the names and the places.

A whisper of wind interrupted the perfect silence of the light and drew him from his self-indulgent and self-pitying revery to the scroll before him. The ionized emanations in the air increased as he traced the individual characters on the papyrus with his finger. Reading the words was now automatic and the sound of them in his mind was so loud that he imagined that a person standing next to him could hear them resonating in his head.

THE MALLET AND CHISEL CANNOT
TAKE BACK WHAT THEY HAVE DONE,
NOR CAN THE WOOD, ONCE STRUCK,

BE WHOLE AGAIN . IF CERTAINTY IS
ACTION, IS DOUBT THE CHIPS ON THE
FLOOR THAT ARE SHORTLY SCATTERED
BY THE WIND?

AT LIFE'S ENDING WILL I HAVE
CRAFTED SOMETHING OF VALUE
OR WILL ALL THAT I AM BE BUT
SHAVINGS TRODDEN UNDER
COUNTLESS FEET IN TIME'S
RELENTLESS MARCH?

Struck by a sense that the document was reading his mind rather than he deciphering its characters, Forrester began to see the entry's relevance to his current situation. The mallet and chisel were in his hands, and the wood was before him. Whatever he did now could not be undone. He knew that if he showed the scrolls to Arthur, the result would be their publication. That was Arthur. He was the embodiment of manifest destiny and letting the chips fall where they may.

Arthur's belief system and action orientation was a simple function of the strength of his right hemispheric processing. Arthur's mindset celebrated the unified tribal expectancy set, namely, whatever I do will amount to what most people would do in similar circumstances. Conveniently, this mindset almost entirely obliterated individual responsibility. For Arthur, conviction was more than a comfort; it was an imperative to action. Forrester didn't buy into manifest destiny. Such overweening self-infatuation was a morass of denial and arrogance. For Forrester, this right hemispheric aberration of logic and compassion amounted to little more than the belief that conviction and the power to enforce that conviction compelled its application. He knew that to reveal the journal to Arthur was a commitment to its publication that Forrester could never undo.

On the other hand, to consign the scrolls to the earth from whence they came would be to deny an audience of readers the opportunity to view a revered figure as fully participating in the uncertainties and foibles of their common humanity. At the same time, Forrester could not see himself as the executioner of what might possibly be the last vestige of transcendence remaining in a world devoured by technology and ruled by the brightest and most profoundly psychopathic elements the race could spawn.

Arthur was a the right hemispheric thinker whose left frontal lobe directed his behavior. As such, he experienced difficulty fully embracing the most pervasive of human ethos, namely, the ends justify the means. However, Arthur didn't run the world. Those who fully embraced this completely 'human' ethos, were right hemispheric thinkers whose guidance came from the right frontal lobe. With an ever increasing right hemispheric majority in the population, society no longer extended even lip service to standards other than those entailed in the ruthless acquisition of profit and power. From Forrester's own fully left hemispheric perspective, this translated into a straightforward and unquestioned endorsement of rapacious narcissism on the part of the entire gene pool. The heroes of this epoch were those who achieved great wealth and power by means fair or foul. Success granted complete absolution to those who achieved it. Crowned with the laurels of wealth and power, no one dared to inquire of the successful about the body count accrued in their ascendance. Perhaps this was no different than at any other time in history, but the burgeoning human population and the manorial discrepancy between the rich and the poor had become so dramatic that no one who was not born to power could ever hope to achieve it. Arthur understood all these things, and although he may not have liked it, he knew how to work within the system.

A more tightly focused and utilitarian version of technology had made it possible for a small number of people to economically or physically devastate populations of millions with a single computer algorithm. Vast armies were no longer necessary to control the suffering and disenfranchised, making a revolt of the masses against the inequities of the system no longer feasible. Even terrorism had been quashed with draconian efficiency. As soon as the geographic point of origin of a terrorist faction was discovered, that area and everyone in it was summarily obliterated. Needless to say, such pacifications encouraged local populations to act swiftly against anyone who expressed dissenting sentiments.

Assisted by a surfeit of Rhine wine, Forrester had bewailed these injustices with Arthur on more than one occasion. Arthur always listened quietly and then said, 'you got somewhere else to live?' He had a point.

To be sure, there were still elections, still courts, still corporations, indeed, all the trappings of a thriving, democratic culture. The principal difference was that no individual or group remained an effective force in government, the courts, or corporate life unless they subscribed to an agenda set by the unseen and incestuous cabal of the wealthy. The new Jeffersonian ideal read, 'that group governs best that governs least visibly.'

A shabby sense of discomfort crept over him causing Forrester to stand back and evaluate his own description of the world. An objective appraisal of his own sentiments left no doubt, they reeked of self-pity and fatalism. His was a mindset born out of an inability to 'play the game' and a fundamental aversion to coming off the bench to participate in the bloodletting. Try as he might, he could not dismiss a view of reality in which only those who made the rules didn't have to play by them. For many years, he sat in the consulting room listening to the rich and powerful share their perceptions and secrets to believe that society was anything more than the strong preying on the weak. In apparent response to his fatalistic mood, the next entry in the scroll seemed to verify the longevity of mankind's addiction to power.

> DOES THE LION BIRTH A LAMB OR
> THE JACKAL SUCKLE A GOAT? THAT
> WHICH IS OF THE WORLD IS
> BLOODIED BY FEEDING UPON
> ITSELF.

> MAN IS BOTH LION AND LAMB
> UNTO HIMSELF. NEVER LORD OVER
> HIS OWN PASSIONS, HE SEEKS
> POWER OVER HIS FELLOWS AS
> RECOMPENSE FOR HIS WEAKNESS.
> EACH FAULT COMMON TO THE FLESH
> IS SEEN BY EVERY MAN IN HIS FELLOW.
> JOINTLY DISCERNING EVIL WITHOUT,
> THEY EACH AND ALL STEP BACK INTO
> THE DARKNESS WHERE UNBEKNOWNST,
> SAVE AS ENEMIES, THEY SLAY ONE
> ANOTHER.

The pattern seemed clear, that having fulfilled the most basic of his survival needs, man's natural prey was himself. Consciously retreating from his wholesale wallowing in the social injustices of reality, Forrester knew that if he didn't suppress this extraordinary find, then, very likely, someone else would for reasons that fell under the general rubric of social control. Even the few entries he had read seemed manifestly at odds with the social order as he had come to know it. Dominance was accepted as the systematizing principle of the universe. Any voice to the contrary was likely to be silenced. Worse yet, some corporate jerk-off would find a way to splice selected entries from the scrolls into self-serving fortune cookie platitudes useful as endorsements for any number of short-lived advertising campaigns. He could see it now: 'Has the stress of living buried you waist deep in the chips of doubt? Take brand X and be at one with the world.' Better buried than turned to shit, he intoned to an audience of one.

Listening to himself reason through a situation before instantaneously shifting gears to an analysis of his own internal commentary had been an annoying habit since childhood. It sounded very much as though he had already reached a decision and now the automatic intellectualizing program had kicked in. The perils attendant to Forrester's full left hemispheric processing were more than fully manifest in this tendency to bequeath to its owner more questions than answers.

Right hemispheric reasoners were blessed with reflexive conviction and knee-jerk denial when things went wrong. They were always right regardless of the facts or the consequences. It looked like W.B. Yates was right thousands of years before Forrester's research respectively confirmed the difference between left and right hemispheric thinkers: "The best lack all conviction. The worst are full of passion and intensity." Well, it wouldn't be the first time that poetry achieved insight before science.

He felt his eyes returning once again to the scroll without any conscious intention to do so.

> THE TREE WILL BE HEWN TO A YOKE TO
> CARRY WATER TO THE THIRSTY OR TO
> PRESS DOWN THOSE WHO FALL TO THE
> WILL OF CONQUEST.
>
> THE PURPOSE OF ITS LIFE IS FULFILLED
> IN THE TREE'S GROWTH AND FLOWERING.
> THE INVENTION OF ITS CARCASS REVEALS
> THE CRAFTSMAN'S INTENTION FOR GOOD
> OR EVIL.
>
> CUT INTO EACH SOUL'S GRAIN IS A
> BROAD CHART OF ITS TRAVELS. YET,
> IN LIFE'S JOURNEY, NONE CAN SAY I
> AM OBLIGED TO THIS PATH OR THAT
> BYWAY.

Denial was not Forrester's strong suite. Yet, he knew he was part of the same hypocrisy that allowed corporate and governmental entities, as if there was a difference, to reap obscene profits while extolling their actions as serving the public weal. He and Arthur dug in the sand because it amused the neurotic wife of a mega-industrialist. Forrester was a whore to his own curiosity, no better than the gougers who paid for his habit. He recognized that, for him, as for every other barely evolved simian on this tiny blue world, the source of human depravity dwelt within. The uncompromising mandate of individual survival, often at the cost of others' lives, could not be dismissed, or by being made to be tautologically true, be generalized to all living organisms. The common wisdom held that transplanting personal malevolence to the next guy solved the problem. As a psychotherapist, Forrester knew that this sort of relocation of the abode of evil didn't really work for the individual, despite its historically unchallenged utility as a political maneuver.

The raucous clamor of Arthur's hopper grew more clearly audible. Its sputtering and coughing indicated Arthur was making progress toward the camp. Now, almost reflexively, Forrester looked back to the scroll, desperate for some shred of guidance.

> I FEEL LIKE A MAN AFOOT WHO HEARS A
> CHARIOT IN THE DISTANCE, THAT HE KNOWS
> WILL OVERTAKE AND CARRY HIM WHERE
> HE WILL NOT GO. I AM NO LONGER THE
> CARPENTER, NOR EVEN THE PLANE, I AM
> BECOME THE WOOD.
>
> FIBER AND GRAIN, READIED FOR THE
> CUT, I AM SET UPON THE BENCH OF LIFE'S
> TRIALS. YET TO BE SHAPED TO A PURPOSE,
> I AWAIT THE CRAFTSMAN'S HAND.

Becoming the wood was not an idea that set well with Forrester, anymore than it had for the scroll's scribe. He could not embrace Arthur's, whatever works, fuck the consequences, unified tribal expectancy set, nor could he simply walk away from the decision. Forrester was stuck with a moment of truth. The discovery of the scrolls, indeed, what appeared to be a personal diary, put him in the same quandary as he had experienced in deciding the fate of his own research. Both represented powerful tools, that given humankind's history were more likely to find application in supporting the status of those already in power, rather than in bettering the condition of the many. The promise of great power had always attracted more of those whose interest was in consolidating it under their control than the few who desired to disperse its benefits among the masses.

In the metaphor of the scroll's entry, it was Arthur who would be driving the chariot hell-bent across the sands. He would reach down and scoop up Forrester and the scrolls at a full gallup. Then, in a charge of perfect conviction, Arthur would carry these powerful private sentiments off in a campaign to destroy transcendence. In that moment, Forrester knew he could not be the messenger who heralded the demise of transcendence for his species. His faith in his own kind did not include their ability to rise above the need for power. His fear was one he clearly shared with the author of this ancient diary as the next entry caught his eye.

THE MESSAGE WITHIN IS CLEAR AND
WILL NOT RELENT. THE FAULT IN MAN
IS DOMINION, BUT NO ONE LISTENS
UNLESS I SHOW POWER. I FEAR THE
LOCK OF HUMAN LONGING ACCEPTS
ONLY ONE KEY.

The racket of Arthur's hopper grew closer reverberating through the canyons that lay five kilometers from the dig. Forrester would have to act quickly. Removing the scrolls from their quivers, he unfurled each one completely on an adjoining table. In one slow sweep, he passed his personal journal scanner over the entire text of the diary. As he reached down to roll and sheath the first scroll, his eye was caught by another entry.

OFTEN MY WORDS, OPENLY SPOKEN,
ARE WELL AND TRULY RECEIVED. THE
LIGHT IN THE EYES OF THOSE WHO
HEAR PLAINLY MARKS A QUICKENING
OF THE MIND AND SPIRIT WITHIN.
YET, WITH ONE SUN'S SETTING AND
RISING, THEY ARE LOST LIKE A SOLITARY
KERNEL AMIDST THE CHAFF IN THE
NOISY RUSTLE OF LIVING THAT SIGNALS
THE MORNING.

LIKE DUST FROM THE DESERT, FAITH
CAN BLOT OUT, IN A MOMENT OF
RAPTURE, ALL THAT IS FAMILIAR. YET,

WHEN IT SETTLES EVENLY ONTO THE
BOWL OF STRIFE AND CUP OF FEAR
THAT COME TO HAND EVERY DAY,
IT PASSES FROM SIGHT.

Pausing a moment, he mused over the passage ringing in his head and tasted the scribe's feelings of futility. Hurriedly rolling up the scroll, he replaced it in its quiver. Carefully sheathing and gathering all of the scrolls into a permapack, Forrester placed the bundle into a DNA secure case keyed to open only to his hand. The oval was a bigger problem. Too many of the workers had participated in its excavation and Arthur would want to know what was inside. Forrester quickly scanned the hut, his eye falling on the remains of the large, rough hewn sandstone box in which the oval had rested.

"The light," he said aloud.

Perception by omission had always been an area of weakness for Forrester. He had just noticed that the light within the hut had changed. The illuminator globe now emitted a steady light, casting shadows in a wholly conventional way about the hut. The every point illumination as well as the lucid silence that companioned it had vanished. Now, the small steady sounds of the desert sifted into the hut with the sand. His eye falling on the secure case, he smiled. The encompassing illumination and lucid silence had returned to the confines of the secure case with the scrolls.

Moving quickly to the large sandstone receptacle, he noticed a small irregularly shaped rectangular box among the broken bits of the casket lid that had shattered during the excavation. Made of the same material as the casket lid, the box had gone undetected among the shards. Retrieving the small roughly hewn box from the debris of the casket, Forrester pried off the lid with relative ease and was greeted by the pungent odor of slightly rancid herbal oil.

Four carved wooden figures spilled out of the box. Each measued about ten centimeters in length. Grabbing a cloth from the table, he gently wiped the excess oil from the figures. Although the bodies of the figures were identical, each of the purposefully enlarged heads bore a different expression. Early in his career Forrester had done some research into facial expression, split-half redundancy and the like, but he considered himself no expert in the field. Examining each figure in turn, he noted in passing that the fundamental features of each face were the same.

Etched upon the face of the first figure was an unmistakable grimace of pain. Whether the torment was physical, psychic or both was too fine a difference to foist upon the carver's art. The next figure plainly portrayed sadness, however, the face demonstrated not an expression of momentary grief, rather, it mirrored a quiet cosmic sorrow. The third face seemed; on initial inspection, to exhibit surprise, but on closer examination it seemed more that of fascination or wonder. The head of the last figure exhibited was noticeably larger, and more than the other three difficult to categorize. It expressed an almost buddha-like in its serenity, but not quite. The lines around the eyes, particularly those carved in the involuntary area of control served by the orbicularis muscle, suggested knowing and patient acceptance. These features expressed neither a benediction flowing from superior knowledge and control, nor a condemnation arising from fatalistic resignation. This was an expression Forrester had never seen in the tens of thousands of faces he had peered into over years of professional consulting.

The noisy clatter of Arthur's hopper, ricocheting off the rocks surrounding the camp, announced his arrival within the larger confines of the dig. Whatever Forrester felt he must do, he had to do now. Gathering the four figures he replaced them in the stone box. He then put the box in the bottom basin of the oval. He successfully reset the upper half of the oval to its mate with relative ease and was reassured by a barely audible click as it locked into place. The oval no longer emanated its translucent glow, but since Arthur hadn't witnessed the aura, he wouldn't notice its absence.

With its signature cough and sputter, the hopper came to rest just outside of the hut. Almost in the same instant, Arthur burst through the door. He exploded through all portals in the same fashion, a veritable blur of motion and speech.

"Hey Nate," he shouted, his arms burdened with two large cartons.

Arthur never called Forrester 'Nathan' or 'Forrester', or in fact anything other than 'Nate' even though he knew Forrester hated that abbreviation.

"Got some of the good stuff. No pussy this run, but the next best thing," Arthur said, obviously having sampled some of the good stuff during his stay in, and on his return from, town.

Nothing in Arthur's demeanor suggested that he even noticed the oval resting on a table in the center of the hut. He was the sort of fellow who was first and foremost a man, and then almost as a footnote, a professional. He emptied the contents of the first carton on a side table as bottles of Piesporter Michelsburg and Black Tower tumbled out.

"There's that pre-teen grape juice you like, and some real spiritus fermenti for me," he remarked, yanking an eighteen year old Glenlivet from the second carton and downing a quarter of the bottle in one toss.

"You dig up anything sand shaking?" Arthur asked after swallowing the hefty jolt.

Arthur loved his little puns, but in truth they didn't typically merit even a low moan.

Pulling the cork on a bottle of Black Tower, Forrester knew that this was when the face to face lying to his best friend began. He also knew that he had never been a very good liar. Lies always cluttered his head and made it nearly impossible to think clearly about anything. Avoiding deception was not so much a moral decision as it was an exercise in cognitive efficiency. He had to choose his words carefully or not speak at all. Two entries that had caught his attention while rolling up the last scroll leapt to mind.

> TOO MUCH SAID IS OFTEN TOO LITTLE
> HEARD, WHILE ONE WORD WRONGLY
> GRASPED CAN UNDUE A GREAT WORK.

> UNBIDDEN, WORDS COME SPILLING INTO
> MY HEAD. THEN, FALLING FROM MY
> LIPS, THEY ARE NOT MY VOICE, YET THEY
> RING OF TRUTH MOST HARSH. I MUST BE
> WARY.

A timeless admonition, Forrester thought to himself. As Arthur set down the Glenlivet, Forrester cast a glance over his shoulder toward the oval resting on the table and Arthur followed his gaze. Arthur was on his feet immediately. He moved so quickly to the oval that Forrester saw it as a single step. His hands were on the oval and with one motion, it was open. Forrester never ceased to be amazed by the facility of a good right hemisphere.

"What have we here?" Arthur asked gleefully as he opened the box containing the figures. With analytic scanner in hand, he confirmed the age of the figures as three thousand years.

"This will get us a corporate bonus for sure and a little video coverage. We might even land another five year grant, or a desk instead of this sandbox," Arthur said excitedly as he turned each of the figures over in his hands.

That's what Forrester liked about his old friend, he was never overwhelmed by the numinal, everything was instantly translated into the meat and potatoes menu of everyday living.

"This will make the old lady happy. She can rub this in the stretched skin faces of her cronies at cocktail parties now and forever, Amen," Arthur exclaimed ecstatically.

The 'old lady' was, of course, their corporate benefactor and judging by what Forrester knew of her, Arthur was probably correct.

"I can see it all now, the four faces of man, kind of like the four horseman of the apocalypse. Statuettes, T-shirts, the whole nine yards," Arthur said, framing each phrase with broad gestures. "We'll have to be sure we get the distribution rights on this stuff. Nate, we could retire!"

What more could be said. Arthur was Arthur, and as always, fully immersed in the business of living. Forrester was more convinced of the correctness of his decision at this moment than he could ever imagine being in the future. Arthur was his yardstick of humankind. A good man. No. More than that, all men, wrapped up in one package. A trustworthy and essential companion, Arthur was a constant reminder of how bizarrely different Forrester's own perspectives and beliefs were from those of his fellow creatures.

Forrester decided not to share the death of their prize student with his partner. There was no compelling reason to cast a shadow on Arthur's ebullient mood. Besides he knew what Arthur would say, 'damn shame, bright kid, but the past is beyond reclaiming.' Arthur likely felt a great deal more than that, but his words would reveal only that much.

Busying himself with wrapping the figures in eterna-seal, plans for the good life were written all over Arthur's face. Careful not to move his head, Forrester cast a self-satisfied glance at his secure case in the corner of the hut. The case, like everything else in the hut, was already sifted over with the fine dust of the desert. Good, he thought to himself … good.

Chapter 2

Twenty five years older, Forrester felt fifty years more spent. Resting on a well cushioned bench, his medium frame slumped over until he appeared half his actual size, he felt old. His rumpled white uniform had the nose of two consecutive shifts in the infirmary and hung on him as though he were a ambulatory clothes tree. In a moment of fatigue induced distraction, he mused about how his research had demonstrated that the brain was fundamentally a motion detector that had evolved into a motion initiator. Like reams of his other findings, he had never published that finding. Well, he wasn't detecting or initiating much motion right now. He was dead tired. He was only susceptible to reminiscence during periods of exhaustion. Likewise his toilworn condition was also the only circumstance that refocused Forrester's attention from his internal reveries to his surroundings

Seated in a corridor, well a tube really, that bent away and around gently curving corners in both directions, he took a moment to carefully examine his environs. Punctuated with regularly portholes into the blackness of the void, walls crafted of polished steel and carbon fiber alloy seamlessly met the floor and ceiling . The stars shone more brightly here than they ever had beneath Earth's protective blanket of atmosphere, but out here they also seemed colder.

How different this setting was from a dusty dig in the Middle East a quarter of a century ago. Prompted by the memory, Forrester fumbled in his pocket to retrieve the small personal storage scanner on which he had recorded the contents of the scrolls during that momentous time. He didn't activate it. Its contents were an obligatory part of his living recall. The scanner now served only as a link to a moment of decision obsessively worked and reworked over the years. Driven relentlessly by the mills of uncertainty, the pivotal decision that life had handed him had been ground to powder by logic, theology, and neuropsychological second guessing. Dropping the scanner into the half torn pocket of his smock, he felt its weight as the small unit struck the pocket's bottom. The thump it made seemed consistent with the way he felt, sorta at the bottom of his resources.

Events over the intervening twenty-five years had changed more than just Forrester's personal life. Many of the world's trappings had also been altered.

The atmosphere had been run through the wash and rinse cycle so that global warming was only a historical footnote and there was food for all.

A precipitous decline in the world's oil reserves had been greeted by the marketing of full blown safe and practical nuclear fusion technology. Not surprisingly, the oil companies held the patents. Molecular biology merged with quantum physics in something called a transubstantiator that could convert common materials into edibles, although the power costs were high. The consumable conglomerates held those patents, but, in keeping with man's endless fascination with monopolies, the old oil companies indirectly managed the conglomerates because the oil companies controlled power production. The petroleum multinationals also retained the rights to the remnants of world's oil caches, significant, because oil was the easiest material to convert into food.

Forrester took little interest in these matters. However, Arthur kept Forrester up on every new development through his many contacts in the corporate community. Many of Arthur's confidants held posts within the United Nations. This ensured that he was party to a steady stream of gossip about clandestine matters of international importance. Although not a player of any significance, Arthur used the information he received to grow a considerable investment portfolio. Carefully planned leaks made his friends wealthy as well. People just told Arthur things. Something in Arthur's manner encouraged people to confide in him. That something plainly said here is a confidant and father confessor at large.

The United Nations was now a large multi-corporate consortium. This cabal of power brokers represented the interests of its corporate member states, each of which controlled a portion of the planet's land mass. Within these marble halls, decisions about the direction of the world economy were made. The Security Council, representing the world's principal stockholders, adjudicated disputes between corporate entities and served as a planetary board of directors and court of last resort.

One of Arthur's oldest and closest friends, Yuri, was secretary to the U.N. council of extraterrestrial affairs. An affable fellow, Yuri had leaked information about a forthcoming antigravity technology patent to Arthur. However, before Arthur could arrange to purchase shares in the company, Yuri disappeared. Arthur took this as a sign and never completed the stock transaction. Several days later, Yuri's lifeless body was found in Central Park, his death written off as an attack by a homosexual rape gang. The death of his friend hit Arthur pretty hard. Although he maintained his contacts at the U.N., he always steered conversations with them away from matters with financial significance. Yuri's death signaled the end of Arthur's investment activities and cast him back into the legions of the salaried.

Space travel became the industry of the millennium once corporate and national treaties had carved the planet into well defended zones of exploitation. After all deals were signed, sealed and delivered, the New York-Swiss financial consortium published the patents covering anti-gravity technology that made space flight both efficient and economical. Earth orbits were well segregated, but crowded with stations that represented some arm of what the man on the street now referred to as 'Natcorps.' The Natcorps entities encompassed corporate control so completely that they mirrored, and in many cases improved upon, the reign of the ancient nation states.

Transforming governance of the planet from national to corporate control had its seeds in the multinational conglomerates' historical dissatisfaction with national governments. Despairing every time their profit margins dipped because of territorial, political and religious squabbles among nation states, the conglomerates decided to do something about it. Corporate rancor came into pinpoint focus through a series of wholesale mergers of multinational businesses that resulted in the consolidation of the reins of commerce into the hands of a small group of individuals. This anonymous panel of oligarchs met secretly at regular intervals to air their grievances against the ills of political rule and to plot ways to rid themselves of nation states.

Forrester had not only lived through, but was party to, some of what the history books now referred to as the capitalization of the Earth. Angelica, one of his most promising students kept Forrester apprised of her rise to power in the unfolding corporate takeover of the planet. Forrester never could understand her attachment to him, but he accepted at face value her explanation that he was someone who could be trusted with whatever was on her mind. Angelica was true polymath, a veritable Mozart of the melody of money and the harmonies it evoked in the human mind. Through the momentum of her brilliance, which Forrester could appreciate, and her reflexive business savvy, which Arthur admired, she ingratiated herself into the cabal of power brokers who ran the planet. The fact that she was a beautiful young woman probably didn't impede her upward progress. This tiny group of god-like oligarchs, the existence of which was such a closely guarded secret that even the most tenacious investigative journalists had only suspicions of its existence, instigated the capitalization of world government.

The epiphany experienced by this conclave of the powerful took the form of a surprisingly simple truth. In order to ensure consistent profits, multinational companies should not be competing with each other, but with nation states for the loyalty of the population. Forrester, never mentioning it to Angelica, could see her hand skillfully guiding this simple and insightful alteration in the political history of the planet. Insidiously, nation states were organized as marketing entities that fell under the control of the corporations who provided employment for their constituents. Taxation revenues to national governments were voted down as corporate entities provided more and more services to their employees. Taking their cue from the Roman empire, the multinational corporate entities left indigenous populations to their own customs and identity rituals and concentrated solely on commerce, utilizing only those controls required to ensure continuing profits. Forrester knew, without ever asking, that Angelica's Jeffersonian philosophy of minimalist intervention lurked in the shadows behind this masterful stroke.

In less than a decade, the transition was complete. History texts, published under U.N. supervision now proclaimed the demise of nation states as but another step forward in civic evolution. Social organization, which had begun with the tribe as extended family and later progressed to the territorial tribe (nation states), had become an enlightened tribal structure founded on planfully apportioned supply and demand.

Each Natcorp derived authority from its economic stranglehold on some sector of the world economy and its private autonomous armed 'defense' force. The Natcorps' computer complexes, through which each company controlled its enterprises and portion of the planet, were located on space stations that occupied extreme orbits about the Earth. These stations monitored all activities on Earth and were, without question, the most heavily armed and secure platforms anywhere in the solar system.

Forrester clearly recalled Angelica's first unannounced visit to the small college at which he and Arthur were gentlemen professors. On this occasion, her rambling references revolved around the theme that conflict was endemic to the human condition. Forrester's sad agreement with her premise seemed to encourage her. Angelica hesitated before offering a solemn but oblique statement that war needed to be removed to a theater where investment property would not become a casualty of corporate confrontation. Frankly, Forrester was not certain about what Angelica had in mind until months later, when the U.N. passed a resolution that all corporate wars would hereafter be fought in space. Smart girl, he thought to himself. It was the sort of simple intervention that called on parental admonitions everyone had heard growing up: 'If you're gonna fight, take it outside.'

The capitalization of the solar system was a natural extension of the philosophy that had worked so well on Earth. Vast numbers of Natcorp bases had been established on the moon, and on Mars' and Jupiter's satellites. The resources necessary to supply the juggernaut of technology having long since been exhausted on Earth, exploring and exploiting other solar satellites became an absolute requirement of doing business. The big four Natcorps: MM (mines and minerals), PP (power provision), CC (choice consumables) and FF (finance and funding) were all represented by installations in space and on the ground throughout the solar system. Corporate wars commonly occurred after a breakdown at the negotiating table, but were fought by large corporate fleets in the uncapitalized spaces between the planets. These armed conflicts tended to be brief as none of the four Natcorps wanted destructive expenditures to significantly impact the bottom line. The price of goods and services to the general public remained fairly stable as the four Natcorps never allowed profit taking by a single corporate entity to overburden the common consumer base.

Law enforcement and its judicial arm functioned neither better, nor worse under independent corporate jurisdiction than it had under national and local administration. After all, only the flags had changed, not the nature of man. The business of the law still attracted the same kinds of people, namely, those who enjoyed the exercise of power under the guise of meting out justice. The rules really changed that much and were the same for everyone. In short, the more money or influence you had, the more 'justice' you could purchase.

Even though planetary regions retained their ethnic heritage and some sense of their old national borders, in truth, the world had been carved into corporate sectors. Each sector was strictly governed by a Natcorp that held the territory by treaty with its corporate neighbors. There were no border conflicts as Natcorp governance was directed to profits not territory. The United Nations made certain that the quality of life for the general population remained the same regardless of geographic location, in order to minimize emigration across Natcorp boundaries. Large scale shifts in the population were bad for business. Migrations across corporate borders disassembled supply and demand algorithms that delineated the consumer base by corporate planetary sector. These computer models made servicing the needs of the population predictable profit centers and were therefore sacrosanct.

Memorable in several ways, Angelica's last visit with Forrester was a stormy one. She advocated the necessity for population control beyond the traditional corporate sphere of basic service provision. Apparently, the unseen and unknown godhead operating in the shadow of the public image of the U.N. viewed public dissent as an impediment to efficient profit taking. She argued to Forrester that increasing law enforcement expenditures would degrade the quality of life for all. She called her latest corporate epiphany a 'fascism of the plurality.' Forrester viewed her theory as vigilantism, pure and simple.

Angelica advocated an elegantly simple and extremely brutal solution to the problem of dissent. All civil disobedience would be defined as terrorism. The authorities would use distillation to justify draconian measures against all those involved in or associated by geography with conduct in each subsector of origin at odds with corporate interests in the sector in which they resided. The authorities would punish all actions deemed subversive to corporate interests by subsector. If anti-corporate acts were reported in a particular subsector, all services (power, food, water) to that area of habitation would be severed until the perpetrators were delivered up to the corporate defense force authorities.

Subsectors would be instantly isolated by an electronic fence at the first sign of disruption. In theory, this ensured that the perpetrators were trapped at the scene. Vigilante action was not only encouraged, but essential to the survival of all within the sub-sector. Once the community identified the perpetrators, they would be delivered up to the authorities in exchange for the reinstatement of essential services. Naturally, the alleged terrorists would be found guilty after receiving a fair trial. Inasmuch as their peers had already designated them as guilty, there was little need for lengthy presentations of proof and rebuttal. Whatever the system lacked in the traditional trappings of justice, it made up for in efficiency.

Forrester sat in silence as Angelica finished her presentation. Nothing had been said, Forrester knew she could read the thinly masked disapproval of his silence. Overwhelmed by her brilliance, Forrester had risked teaching her what his research into brain-behavior relationships had revealed. She represented one of his principal delusions, namely, that great ability was intrinsically humanitarian and benign. 'Humanitarian and benign', as he heard these words echo through his head, he recognized the unraveling Gordian knot tying them to great ability. Angelica, now constitutionally fortified with great ability and made astute in manipulating others through Forrester's research, was fully engaged in servicing the authoritarian agenda of the powers that be. Forrester experienced disappointment of epic proportions, even more so with himself than with the astute young woman sitting before him.

She looked long and hard into his face, perhaps recognizing that this would be their last face to face meeting, and continued her exposition of the Natcorps' plans for the Earth's teeming populations. Elections would still be held for a wide variety of civil-corporate offices. Votes would be tied to each member of the population's shareholder status. At birth, every individual received one share in the Natcorp that governed his or her sector. Additional shares could be purchased over an individual's life time or awarded for services above and beyond the call of duty to the corporation. Each share owned could be applied as a vote for a particular candidate. This system replaced the old 'one man one vote' model. It was generally well received by a population who, by earning additional shares in their Natcorp not only increased their buying power, but also achieved, through their shares/votes, a greater sense of personal control over their destiny. Shares were owned for the life span of the individual, their validity expiring only with the demise of the original shareholder.

✄❖✄

Shares in one of the four Natcorp corporations counted as votes in any given election. However, at no time, did any corporation allow the total number of shares held by the general populace in a sector to exceed the total number held by upper level management of that corporation. In this fashion, the system maintained the facade of democracy because no one outside the 'boardroom' could discover the total number of shares issued. To preclude any rumblings from the mob about elections results that reflected little more than boardroom decisions, vote tabulations were reported exclusively in percentages. Although corporate control was in this sense authoritarian, procedural formalities successfully maintained the facade of individual choice.

Supplanting the press, a Natcorp consortium of public information replaced the free press and controlled the media in a planet-wide platform. Geared to attract the best and brightest of the upwardly mobile young who didn't have the technical gifts to pursue science or medicine, this consortium was, in fact, a perfectly homogenized amalgam of marketing and journalism. Rather than reflecting the tactics of some heavy handed propaganda arm of a fascist regime, it was an exquisitely tuned mechanism for providing the who, what, where, when, and how of daily events with a subtle consumer oriented spin that ultimately benefitted its Natcorp sponsors.

Forrester's horror grew as he listened to how Angelica purposed to incorporate and integrate not only life's necessities, the facade of decision making, and the flow of information, but also, the duration of each and every individual's life span into a grand corporate scheme of absolute dominion. As Angelica extrapolated her model for what she sincerely believed represented 'benign' social control, Forrester remembered an axiom that he had obviously been more successful at teaching to his students than he had been in learning himself. "The prey are those who believe that the game is played by rules that are, in fact, promulgated by, and intended to benefit, predators within the human species. The human race was divided into rule makers and rule followers.

Medical science could prolong a vigorous life into a fifth century for those who could afford it, which amounted to less than one half of one percent of the population. This meant that the general population might know the same exorbitantly wealthy individual as president of a Natcorp for eighteen to twenty generations of their family's history.

Persons not in the inner circles of power, but with talents particularly serviceable to a Natcorp might live as much as one hundred years longer than the general population. Every ambitious individual hoped to become useful, and more importantly, to remain useful, to their employer. Service to a Natcorp could become a ticket to longevity, but only if those in power perceived the service as profitable. The policy represented neither compassion nor beneficence. It was simply sound and straightforward venture capital investment.

The exposition of her model completed, Angelica leaned back in her chair and stared unblinkingly at her old mentor. Forrester returned Angelica's gaze feeling very much like the Baron von Frankenstein of fictional fame whose monster, in this scenario, had become both an amiable and incredibly successful force of nature. Saying nothing, Forrester rose from his seat, walked to and opened the door. Angelica, looked momentarily stunned, and then rising, walked to Forrester's side and kissed him gently on the cheek. As Forrester watched, her pace quickened as she walked down the hall and out of the building. He knew he would never see her again.

During the next five years, Forrester witnessed the gradual transformation of society along the lines Angelica had so systematically articulated. It became painfully clear to him that he had taught his best student well. Knowledge of what he had done ground mercilessly on his soul. Given the future orientation endemic to left brain thinkers, Forrester was not known for his ability to retrieve the events of the past. However, recalled with startling clarity his last conversation with Angelica.

It was early morning and Forrester was well into his third cup of coffee. His brain had sufficiently warmed to mange making the fourth cup without spilling it on the disarray on his desk. He enjoyed coming to his office on campus well before the start of classes. Early in the term, he used the time to fine tune his classes. On that one morning he was transferring a few left brain thinkers out of classes that were populated by right brainers, better for them, and from an instructional perspective, simpler for him.

Forrester had elected to bury himself in a small college town in what used to be western Canada. He taught a course in archeology with a neuropsychological spin and always had more student registrations than his classes could hold. He carefully avoided publishing anything that would draw attention to himself or his work. The head of the department growled at him periodically, but since everyone knew Forrester didn't need the job to pay his bills, the growls were muffled. There was enough money left over from the rights to the figures he and Arthur had found to live comfortably for decades to come. Arthur was there, of course, still working the cocktail circuit trying to smooze some Natcorp-PP executive's wife into a grant.

The vidscreen was reporting a subsector shutdown in response to some unspecified anti-corporate action by the residents of what was once known as Sicily when the unit's chime signaled an incoming call. The screen identifier scrolled out a very short sequence of amber numbers indicating that the caller was a highly placed Natcorp functionary. He hit the receive button and watched in amazement as Angelica's face appeared.

"Good morning, Doctor Forrester," She announced, her voice characteristically clear and upbeat, unchanged by the years.

"Angelica," His surprise made this one word response all he could muster.

Her face still revealed the finely carved marblesque features that had always singled her out as a beautiful woman, but about her eyes, Forrester saw lines tracing out a history of carefully contrived interactions.

"I wanted to talk to someone I could trust … someone who wasn't a player," Angelica's voice betrayed an uncharacteristically hesitant quality as she spoke.

"What the matter, Angelica?" Forrester responded.

Forrester's eyes strayed discreetly to two lights on the monitor console. One was emitting a steady blue indicating that this was a secure transmission. The second blinking a lavender hue, meant the transmission originated from off world.

Angelica continued, "I wanted you to know that your research is dead on. I've used everything you taught me to achieve my objectives. I remember exactly what you said, 'Convey your agenda in the neurological voice of the listener.' But …"

"But what?" Forrester responded, recognizing in Angelica's moment of hesitation the presence of some lurking and painful realization.

"Now that it's done … I'm not sure, it was the right thing," She replied, her voice laced again with the uncharacteristic hesitation Forrester had noted earlier.

"Vision and implementation not the same?" Forrester asked, his tone compassionate, almost to the point of consolation.

Here it was, Forrester mused, the Achilles' heel of the gifted. Another brilliant young mind who couldn't foresee the rift between her vision of the world and its nuts and bolts application. The gift of vision and a feel for power seldom arose in the same individual. When those who possessed the former fell into the hands of those who possessed the latter, someone usually got burned at the stake. It was never the one who understood the mechanics of control.

"I never imagined, they'd do everything I suggested," She responded.

"I know," Forrester replied.

He instantly recognized that his error had preceded and made hers possible. At its root it was the same error, the insane belief that great ideas would evoke noble intentions.

"Everyone has the basics now, decent air to breathe, food, clean water, adequate medical care and opportunities for education," Angelica announced in a tone that suggested she was interrupting an ongoing conversation in her head.

"All true, Angelica," Forrester responded.

For a long moment, he simply stared at her image on the monitor's screen. As he studied her face, he recognized that great ability and a thorough understanding of the human mind was insufficient to assure a positive outcome for the species. Something beyond man's feeble talents was required to achieve a millennium in which the needs of the individual and the group were equally served. Years of people watching caused him to immediately notice Angelica looking down and to the right. His research told him to expect left brain self-recriminations from Angelica.

"I should have been a teacher … I wouldn't have done as much damage," Her response was slow and deliberate, mirroring her gathering despondency.

"And, as your teacher, do you believe I am excused all responsibility?" Forrester quickly replied.

Forrester made a conscious attempt to point out the obvious without allowing his own feelings of guilt to detract from Angelica's attempt to reconcile her intentions and their bitter fruits.

"I loved it … God help me … I'd watch their faces and then play them like a well tuned piano. Just like you said, never raise a question that could make the answer an obstacle to your goal," Angelica said, her tone mixing equal measures of guilt and pride in her skill.

"And you succeeded …" Forrester began.

"Oh, yeah, I succeeded … succeeded in taking what you created to help people realize every scrap of their potential and put it into the hands of power addicts who will outlive everyone in the population," Angelica stammered, her eyes dancing backing and forth as anxiety called the tune.

Recognizing that his whole body was taut as Forrester stretched himself toward the monitor, he relaxed and leaned back in his chair. Angelica had nearly reached her breaking point, but he suspected something, as yet unmentioned, drove her mounting anxiety. Like all those who shared her neuropsychological configuration, Angelica never counted the consequences if she was having fun, unless she'd hit a wall that she couldn't go under, over, or through. He suspected that she was standing in front of just such a wall now.

"Turn around," Forrester gently intoned .

He knew that she'd understand exactly what that phrase meant. Like all of his students, Angelica had heard him come back to that simple principle over and over again in his lectures. Every individual's greatest strengths are also their greatest weaknesses, becoming so through reflexive and excessive application. "Our strengths, not our weaknesses, drive us into life's corners", the thought flowed through his head at fast forward speed. The decision to stand in the corner was founded in the fear of grappling with life from a stance of perceived personal weakness.

"It's only partly the corner," Angelica responded in tones so soft that her words were barely audible.

"And the something else?" Forrester asked gently.

Angelica looked down so that Forrester could see only the crown of her head on the monitor.

"I've outlived my usefulness," Her tone was that of a youngster confessing that she had just wrecked her father's car. She slowly raised her head.

Forrester said nothing as he continued to stare at Angelica's image on the screen.

"I know these men better than they know themselves. I have nothing more to offer now that they've gotten what they wanted. I saw it happen in their eyes. They moved me from the asset to the liability column in a heartbeat. I know too much, and I can never be part of the little circle of mutual vested interest that allows them to halfway trust one another," Angelica said. Her tone now shook with horror.

"You need to get away," Forrester replied, his anxiety rising.

"There's no place to go that they don't control … besides it's already too late," Angelica replied, as a strange calm settled over her.

"Too late?" Forrester asked as he felt his muscles tensing again.

"There was a party last night after our last meeting. Sometime in the course of the evening, I was poisoned. I'll die within the next two hours. The cause of death will look like a massive stroke. Their doctors will certify the cause. There'll be no autopsy or investigation. See …" Angelica said as she held up the back of her hand.

Forrester hit the magnification control on the monitor and immediately saw a small black dot on Angelica's hand.

"Someone just brushed up against my hand at the party … and … and I'm dead," Angelica said, her control disintegrating.

"There must be an antidote," Forrester said, snapping forward in his chair.

"This is a closed shop. Any physician who could recognize the poison would know that, unless he or she wanted to suffer the same fate, they'd better pretend it isn't there. No … it's …" Angelica stammered.

"I have some physician friends, who …" Forrester interjected.

"I couldn't get there in time," Angelica interrupted. "Besides this call is really about creating a drop of redemption in an ocean of naive, personal villainy."

"I don't follow," Forrester replied.

"Do you remember a student by the name of Robert in my graduating class?" She queried.

"Robert was sorta hard to forget, more of a merchant than a scientist or clinician," Forrester responded.

"As short-sighted as I've been, I never taught anyone what you gave to me. One of my contacts let it slip that Robert has put your neuropsychological assessment system on the market to the highest bidder."

"How?" Forrester's shock allowed only a one word response.

"As to the how, I'm not sure , but somehow he's gotten hold of one of your old computer hard drives and is ready to make a sale."

"Damn!" Forrester exploded.

"Exactly. I wanted you to know. In my case, there's no place to hide from death, but you may have time to disappear. If you know the way I think, then as a student of your research, I know you. Everything that Robert needs to offer up a system that he only superficially understands isn't on that hard drive. Sooner or later they'll come looking for you."

"You know me pretty well," Forrester replied. "I keep the pivotal concepts and equations in my head, more because they are obvious to me than out of any paranoid tendencies."

"Hide!" Angelica exclaimed. "God help me, I designed the snares and dead ends in the system to trap those that run afoul of the Natcorps autocrats. If they can find you … you'll belong to them forever."

"Angelica …" Forrester began.

"What I know about your research dies with me," she interrupted. "Robert will give them everything but the central insights that are in your head. If they extract those pivotal pieces from you, and they will, it will mean the regimentation of all humankind … it will mean the …"

Forrester watched in horror as Angelica's face began to twitch. Then the muscles on the left side of her face went slack, her left arm dropping uselessly to her side. Reflexively, he moved closer to the monitor as the left side of her face sagged.

"Angelica!" His words escalated to a shout as he saw her feebly raise a trembling right hand.

"Soorry," the word, drawn out and slurred, was the last to emerge from her twisted mouth.

He sat before the monitor's image of Angelica's body as every muscle in it lost tone, her head tilting back and eyes glazing over. Like a mound of soft soil saturated by the rain, her form slid from the chair and disappeared from the camera's view. He was still sitting in front of the monitor's image of an empty chair when Arthur came through the office door. He looked at Forrester, then at the monitor.

"Some avant-garde program?" Arthur said with teasing sarcasm.

"Angelica's dead," Forrester responded.

"Dead?" Arthur said, quickly shifting to a serious mood.

"Murdered by Natcorp's inner circle," Forrester replied.

"Why?" Arthur asked.

"Used her up, but couldn't risk just throwing her away."

Forrester's response was laden with a generous portion of world weary disappointment. Like an old injury, he felt its twinges whenever his frustration with his own species awakened.

"Hell of a gal. What a waste," Arthur said, his tone mixed with despair and anger.

"It goes from bad to worse," Forrester added. "you remember my student Robert?"

"Yeah, I remember that conniving little weasel," Arthur said through clenched teeth.

"He's either already sold, or is in the processing of selling, my research to the same bunch who killed Angelica."

"How in the hell ..." Arthur asked, his hand trembling as he set down his coffee cup.

"The how isn't important. I know he doesn't have enough information in hand to make it work. That means they'll be looking for me," Forrester replied as he came to his feet and shut down the monitor.

"You need to get out of here, and I mean now. I have a friend in western Canada who has a little cabin in the middle of the woods where you can hide out. I'll handle everything with the Dean. Go ... now!" Arthur snapped.

In a matter of minutes, Forrester was in Arthur's old hopper, that had been programmed with coordinates that would take Forrester into the wilds. The ride was a long one leaving Forrester with nothing to do but ruminate over his failures. He had tried to emulate his mentor's example a brilliant scientist, who, horrified by the prospect of its indiscriminate application, had suppressed his brain-age quotient analysis. He had trusted Forrester only with the calculations that specified the difference between an individual's chronological and brain age. Forrester had not enjoyed his teacher's success at keeping secrets. It wasn't that Forrester trusted the wrong people. It was that he trusted everyone until they proved to be untrustworthy. Clearly an impractical approach to life. Now, he was left with only the bitter aftermath of that component of his makeup.

Unshaven and unkempt, Forrester had been at the cabin for two weeks. Wandering through the woods, Forrester attempted to drown himself in nature as a means of blocking out the real time horror of his predicament. Fatigue of the body and the soul forced him back into the refuge of the tiny sylvan hut. Upon his return, Arthur's message on the monitor was simple and to the point.

"Robert made his deal, but he couldn't deliver the whole package. They know where you are. Get out."

Apparently the cabin's owner had sleep problems. There was more than an ample supply of barbiturates on hand, as well as, a goodly store of Jack Daniel's. Gathering up a sufficient quantity of both, Forrester ventured off into the woods for a nap among the ferns from which he sincerely hoped never to awaken. Swallowing a generous amount of bourbon and barbiturates, Forrester closed his eyes. Despite the lethargy induced by his medication and alcohol picnic, he thought that he heard the hum of hoppers circling the area as the lights went out.

Forrester awakened not to a bed of ferns and the smell of pine, but to the antiseptic atmosphere of a sick bay on a PP Natcorp station in orbit around Mars. Once he had recovered sufficiently to process human speech, operatives of PP Natcorp genetics division gave him one day to supply the parts of the puzzle that Robert lacked. Forrester clearly recalled telling them to go fuck themselves. They simply smiled and left . An hour later they returned proposing an exchange of Arthur's life for the information only Forrester could supply. It was an offer he couldn't refuse.

For someone with Forrester's left brain bent remembering was hard work. He leaned back into the cushion backrest of the corridor bench and let out a sigh. The present charged back into focus. What was it that the old German philosopher Wittgenstein had said, 'an outward sign of an inward process.'

Forrester tried his best to let go of a past for which no remedy existed. Perhaps that was why left brainers had no interest or veridical access to the past, nothing could be done about it. A tendency to ignore history in favor of hopeful visions of the future might account for the left hemispheric processors' ongoing naiveté in the arena of interpersonal relationships.

Forrester felt the cushions of the bench shift under his weight. The act of retrieving memories from those desperate times caught in its train a scroll entry that appeared before his eyes like a pillar of light that dispersed all forgetful shadows.

SLAVE AND MASTER ARE YOKED
TOGETHER, EACH KNOWING HIMSELF
THROUGH THE OTHER. DEATH DRIVES
THIS UNEQUAL SPAN OVER ROCKY
GROUND INTO A PIT DARKENED BY
THEIR LOATHING ONE OF ANOTHER.

THE FRUITS OF THIS CULTIVATION
ARE BITTER TO BOTH. ITS INCREASE
A CONFLAGRATION THAT CONSUMES
BOTH OWNER AND OWNED.

Needlessly to say PP Natcorp got the information they demanded from Forrester. Key in hand to unlock the central features of Forrester's data set, the science division set immediately to the task of converting this new system of neuropsychological genetics into a PP Natcorp profit center. Exercising considerable ingenuity, they enlisted electronics experts to transpose the neuropsychological actuarials onto an electronic program that was compatible with the standard medical scanners. One quick sweep provided a picture of the psychological proclivities of any individual based on actuarials that Forrester had discovered and codified over the course of twenty five years . Problem-solving ability, sensory-perceptual biases, personality dynamics, likely reinforcers, right down to probable candidates in the individual's selection of a mate, were all instantly available.

Once they married Forrester's stuff to their genetic protocols, it was all over. They immediately began selecting and, in some cases, producing people with the 'right' neurological configurations, in the 'right' proportions from the general population. Having chosen the individuals they wanted, they sorted them into the 'right' working teams to produce the 'right' corporate outcomes in any given situation.

All very neat to be sure. The process represented a more complete realization of Forrester's worst nightmares than even his own prodigious imagination could have conjured. He had attempted, in vain, to convince them that putting a certain kind of neurological configuration in a niche where it didn't actuarially 'fit' was often a recipe for engendering startlingly creative outcomes. The genetic's gurus responded with paternalistic smiles, then, went about their business of creating personnel who suited the company's needs.

Over the course of several years , Forrester discovered a reality behind that arrogant facade of genetic omnipotence that differed dramatically from that portrayed by the Natcorp. Their geneticists learned, to their dismay, that as they tried to move the human population in a direction more consistent with corporate needs and goals, mother nature seemed to pull ever more strenuously in the opposite direction. They explained their failures to upper level management with the old metaphor about nature being a big ship that turned slowly and ate up a lot of ocean in the process. It was a bad metaphor and Forrester knew why. This big ship had been traveling for at least four billion years and its captain had a mind of her own. He had entertained the notion of a unseen force directing the course of evolution long before his discovery of the scrolls. Interrupting his stream of consciousness, a diary entry intruded in seeming response. It appeared to add support and credence to his mystical imaginings.

> THROUGH AN EYE OF CLAY, THE SOUL'S
> VISION IS MUDDIED, IT'S EAR SOUNDING
> ONLY TO BLUNT BLOWS MADE UPON
> UNSTRETCHED SKINS. BRIEF FLESH IS
> SWADDLED IN MUFFLED SHADOWS.
>
> THE STRIVING OF ALL LIFE SEEMS BLIND
> ONLY TO HIM WHOSE SPAN IS BUT A
> SINGLE DROP IN THE OCEAN OF TIME.
>
> THE HERB'S FULL FLOWER CANNOT BE
> SEEN IN THE KERNEL FROM WHICH IT
> SPROUTS, NOR CAN IT BE SAVORED IN
> THE WATERS THAT NOURISH THE DARK
> SOIL FROM WHICH IT SPRINGS.

OF ONE WEAVE, EACH THREAD OF LIFE
TWISTS WOOF AND WARP AMONG ITS
FELLOWS TO FIND THE PLACE CHOSEN
FOR IT IN THE TAPESTRY THAT IS THE
UNIVERSE. NEITHER THE THREADS
LOOSED UPON THE FLOOR, NOR THE
FRAMEWORK OF THE LOOM, REVEAL
THE MIND OF CREATION'S WEAVER.

Even with his rickety excuse for a right hemisphere, Forrester had no trouble understanding that parts laid out in a righteous order of assembly were not a certain road map to a vision of the final product. Perhaps that was all the diarist was saying. If you don't know what you're supposed to end up with, how can you know whether something is being put together rightly or wrongly. At a personal level, it didn't make any difference how Forrester's life got assembled. He no longer had any control over his destiny.

Natcorp-PP decided Forrester was too valuable a commodity to languish in some schlock teaching job, especially in an area that concerned itself with the past rather than the present or the future. Forrester, for his part, was all too aware, as this horrific melodrama played out, that they couldn't just cut him loose. It would be too easy for him to teach people to dissemble their presentations to the scanners. The genetics division could have simply made him disappear, but that would have amounted to destroying an asset. Such actions were not only considered bad accounting practice, but, more importantly, qualified as the new 'original sin' of Natcorp dogma. Such sinners were routinely cast out of the garden of corporate advancement, their hopes of outliving their peers summarily quashed.

Orders written on tablets that came down from the heights of PP Natcorp Sinai, indicated that retraining was to be Forrester's fate. Application of PP's new proprietary management tool to Forrester's configuration suggested he'd be a good researcher - surprise. However, the prospect of cutting Forrester loose to do personnel research struck PP Natcorp as a little too risky even, under supervision in their own labs. Instead a new word came down, physician. That calling would draw on what Forrester's actuarial characterized as an inexhaustible reservoir of service orientation. Naturally, Arthur would be trained right along side him. Arthur had to be kept nearby for reasons that were painfully apparent to Forrester.

Arthur perceived this chain of events as an enormous stroke of good luck. He'd get to work with his 'good bud,' live in great digs on a space station, and deal only with corporate patients who were already in good health. Arthur didn't grasp that he was living in a very luxurious prison and Forrester was not about to tell him. Knowing Arthur, Forrester realized that if he told Arthur that his life hung on the thread of Forrester's cooperation, Arthur would get monumentally pissed. For Arthur, as for all those generously endowed with right hemispheric strengths, such righteous indignation meant frontal lobe shutdown and he'd probably end up in a cell. Natcorps wouldn't liquidate Arthur. He was their leverage on Forrester, but they could make life miserable for both men.

Thinking back over their time together, Forrester recalled that bouts of strong emotion invigorated Arthur. Sometimes he purposefully sought them out for just that reason. Such affective marathons left Forrester, like all other members of his purely left hemispheric tribe, exhausted. Rights possessed a broad old brain-right hemispheric channel through which surging feelings could flow unobstructed into an ocean of actions. Their alliance with strong emotion empowered their actions and exhilarated their lives. Slowed and stilled, the left-brained minority's experience of such surging waves of intense emotion was calmed. An endless series of dams, recirculating back channels, locks and settling pools quietened such swells. Nature had carefully construct-ed levees between the left brain and the surging limbic vortex over the eons so that the left brain might more successfully cope with the right brain's irrational energy. Even with the benefit of all of these cerebral shock absorbers, left brain processors found the emotional energy of their right hemispheric brethren overwhelming. Next to their right hemispheric siblings, all left brainers felt bland and inconsequential. Lefts might do the right thing, but they almost never felt justified in doing so. In contrast, Rights felt warranted by virtue of whatever emotion propelled them through life.

For Forrester, it was the dilemma of the scrolls all over again. Was he act-ing out of cowardice or good sense? It made no difference whether he held the scrolls or Arthur's life in his hands. He would act out of 'good sense' and forever consider himself a coward. Then, without any warning, a passage from the scrolls interrupted the flow of his thoughts, seemingly mocking his despair with the timelessness of the question. The words provided only small solace in declaring that the quandary was not his alone.

> THE DARK HUB OF ALL DESPAIR IS
> BUT MEMORY LOST OF WHENCE WE
> HAVE COME AND TO WHITHER WE
> SHALL RETURN. UPON THIS AXIS

TURNS THE WHEEL OF DOUBT,
CHURNING UP DUSTY SPECTERS OF
FLESH'S PERIL AND SUMMONING
DEFENSE.

DOES DOMINION GOAD FEAR OR FEAR
DOMINION? IS A WHEEL ITS RIM OR
SPOKES? DOES NOT THE WHEEL OF
STRIFE, RIM AND SPOKES, GOUGE AN
EVER DEEPENING FURROW INTO THE
HEART OF MAN.

ONCE CUT, THE FURROW BECKONS
TO ALL WHOSE WILL FOLLOWS THE
ANGLE IN WHICH THE GROOVE IS
WENDING. THE COLUMN OF MAN,
THROUGH THE HILLS OF TIME
TRAVERSING, BRINGS WITH IT THE
FEET OF SONS TREADING IN THEIR
FATHERS' STEPS. THE FURROW
THEY GOUGE DEEPENING CREATES
A CHASM FROM WHICH NONE
ESCAPES.

The picture of fated history, clearly portrayed in this entry, suggested to Forrester that little fundamental progress in disentangling the human dilemma had been achieved with the passage of three millennia. The quest for dominance was the flight from fear, with this dynamic functioning in the human character like a zero in a multiplication operation. No matter what other human attribute you factored into the equation, once you multiplied it by the zero of dominance/fear, it always produced zero. In human transactions, the quest for dominion always engendered fear. Fear, in turn, spurred greater need for dominion. In the parlance of Forrester's time, all defensive weapons had offensive applications.

Looking up from his extended reminiscence, Forrester noticed a bead of sweat shed from his nose float upwards momentarily. They're recircuiting the antigrav generators again, he thought to himself. The saltwater droplet danced in the air briefly and fell to the floor. When he was living through the events he was now only recalling, he didn't sweat. He just managed them as best he could. Recalling what he had experienced generated anxiety. Odd. Perhaps anxiety was kindled because the compressed presentation of those bits of history so poignantly illustrated the self-destructive consequences of his high-minded principles.

Relative to the bulk of living systems that occupied Earth, the working dynamics of the left hemisphere stood as a noteworthy exception. For left hemispheric processors, concepts and symbols were the reality. While for the balance of sentient living systems, they remained tokens. Given the degree of separation between left hemisphere thinkers and the dangers lurking in the real world outside of their brain cases, it was a miracle that they were still represented in the gene pool. Indeed, the Darwinian dictum specifying the survival of the fittest suggested that Forrester and left brained individuals like him shouldn't be here at all. Curious, he thought to himself. He suddenly recalled that Arthur would be along soon. He always came to collect Forrester at shift's end.

Good old Arthur accomplished reflexively what Forrester had to work at with compulsive fervor. Arthur just didn't concern himself with things about which he could do nothing. Forrester admired the outcome, but not the means. For Forrester, that sort of dismissive slight of hand was unacceptable. A thorough and dispassionate analysis was required, before issues could be set aside Every outcome scenario had to be carefully scrutinized. Each inference had to be evaluated for logical consistency and most importantly for evidence of an irrational, self-serving, emotional bias. The process amounted to nothing less than a conscious mobilization of an obsessive defense against error and the encroachment of insidious narcissism.

For Arthur, such dilemmas were swept away instantaneously through the miraculous, albeit primitive, action of repression and denial. Arthur was fully immersed in the human tribe and everything inherent to mankind's nature found a comfortable home in his psyche. People and situations were what they were. Any rational right brainer accepted that fact with good humor and worked with what the situation offered. The left brain elements in the population were destined to be relegated to the side lines by the inertial juggernaut of millions of years of right hemispherically driven simian-human temperament.

What Forrester saw as a primitive form of perception based in denial and implicit arrogance, was for Arthur, the simple unvarnished reality of living. From the perspective of Forrester's own research, the realities of left brain-right brain differences were really pretty simple. The right brain majority of the race just did whatever the tribe let them get away with, while the Lefts wrestled with themselves to bring the world in line with standards engraved on stone tablets in their heads. Lefts understood that goodness and service weren't rewarded. They just had trouble believing it.

That feeling of world weary disappointment was peeking around a corner in his head again. Absent any conscious intention to do so, the scanner had come to hand and he had automatically thumbed to an entry, read a hundred times before.

EVER A YOUNG AND TENDER FLOWER,
GOODNESS IS SOON WILTED BY FEAR,
WHICH LIKE THE RAYS OF THE
NOONDAY SUN, LEAVE NO SHADE
OF FAITH IN WHICH IT MAY PROSPER.
EVEN SO, SERVICE IS A REED SET
AGAINST THE STAFF OF DOMINION,
THE OUTCOME IS CERTAIN.

It was the old 'why do the evil prosper?' schtick. Forrester knew the answer to this quandary, but he didn't like it. The word 'living' could be justifiably substituted for 'evil' in this ancient question. Why do the living prosper? Answer, because if they didn't, they were the dead. Living systems are programmed to defend and propagate themselves. When limited resources and space are thrown into the equation, well, the rest was obvious. Service wasn't part of the plan. Forrester could recite verbatim what Arthur would say about this conundrum having heard the sonorous phrase so many times before. 'Service is only service if it also serves the server.' Forrester genuinely cared for Arthur, but could no more think like him than Arthur could grasp Forrester's endless ruminations.

Recognizing the cadence of Arthur's footsteps along the passageway, Forrester looked up in time to see Arthur running his hand along passageway walls that could not be smudged. Arthur liked the fact that he couldn't trash the place with what Forrester considered to be unnecessary and careless personal habits.

"Hey Nate, how about some of that good corporate juice?" Arthur's question reverberated along the corridor.

Arthur was referring to the fact that only the Natcorps could afford tracts of land for vineyards. The general population had to be satisfied with transubstantiated synthetics.

Forrester tried to casually slip the scanner back into his smock, but missing the pocket, he heard it crash to the floor. Of all people, Forrester should have known better. The best left hemisphere in the universe couldn't get a visual-motor deception by even the most decrepit right hemisphere ever to burn glucose. Left brainers were adept at moving words and ideas around in their craniums, not making their hands and feet work.

"Yeah, Nate, I've got one of those too," Arthur said, his tone was neither competitive, nor condemning.

The notion of saying 'what do you mean?' passed through Forrester's mind, but he dismissed it. He had more respect for Arthur than that.

"I promised myself … that if I saw you looking at that thing one more time, I'd come clean. It's more for your benefit than for mine. I know how you chew on this stuff. It's like watching some damn rat bar press for guilt reinforcement. Enough is enough!" Arthur said, straightening himself to his full height.

Speechless, Forrester simply stared at him. Arthur hardly ever put this many words together in a row unless he was pitching for gossip, money or sex.

"You're untouchable when it comes to analyzing complex stuff, but you get a 'F' in deception 101," Arthur said, obviously enjoying his little speech.

It was always recognizable when Arthur hit his stride. Everything rolled out like a prepared speech, except it wasn't.

"Twenty five years ago back at the dig, I saw right away that your secure case was locked. You never do that unless there's something in it. I guess that people like me watch smart people like you so we can get smarter. That oval was too nice and too big to house those four lousy wooden figures. Come on Nate, I wasn't born yesterday! The rest was easy. You never could hold your liquor, so, when you finished puking and finally fell asleep, I pulled the scrolls out of the secure case and made my own scanner record. Before you ask, secure cases aren't infallible. After all the damn case doesn't know whether your hand is awake or asleep."

Forrester was stunned. Twenty five years of living as some kind of half-assed suffering servant, racked with guilt, alternately feeling like the savior of transcendence or an abject coward, and Arthur had known all along. In that instant, Forrester reassured that his resolution never to play poker with Arthur had been a rare example of intuitive insight on his part. Characteristic of those with his neuropsychological makeup, Forrester never trusted his intuitions until the progression of events validated their accuracy. It was a left brain thing. He just didn't trust his judgment when it was based on a momentary feeling. For Forrester, certainty required years of watching ideas swirl, transfigure and eventually refine themselves in his head before he took action.

Watching his friend closely now, Arthur said nothing. Instead, following tried and true right brain protocols, he took action. Producing a scanner from his pocket, he called up an entry and unceremoniously shoved the unit into Forrester's hand.

Forrester carefully read the verse that Arthur felt was so significant.

> THE COURSE OF A SINGLE LIFE
> MIRRORS THE WANDERINGS OF
> MAN ACROSS THE AGES. EACH
> IS ALL, AND ALL ON PILGRIMAGE
> THROUGH TIME'S WILDERNESS
> SEEK THEY KNOW NOT WHAT.
>
> A DROP OF WATER MAY NOURISH
> A SINGLE SEED, OR JOINING A
> FLOOD, BRING LIFE TO THE FIELDS
> AND DEATH TO MANY IN THE
> DELUGE.

"Well, Nate, you *ain't* no single seed," Arthur said, driving the point home with a reprimanding gesture.

Hitting that 'ain't' real hard was something Arthur did because he knew it would aggravate Forrester. It was Arthur's way of saying there 'ain't' no transcendence, just another day of the same old, same old.

"You kept it secret because you were afraid it would make some big difference in the way people lived their panting, grasping little lives if it were published. I never said anything because I knew it wouldn't. Besides, we raked in more than enough from those wooden dollies," Arthur said, as he put his foot on the bench.

Forrester had never experienced real psychological shock until this very moment. He had always cautioned his students against precipitating it in their patients. Never take away the pivotal foundations of a person's world view, regardless of how compelling the therapeutic need, unless you're certain you can replace it with something bigger and better. Now, he knew why he had been right for all those years. This 'felt' awful!

'Felt' was not a word Forrester often used when referring to his own experience. He didn't like to think of himself as someone easily swayed by feeling. However, at this moment, panic and confusion directed the score in the symphony hall of his head. Although named on the program as the conductor of the piece, he knew that he had been relegated to the audience as the orchestra played on. The tune, a continuous flurry of anxious crescendos pushed his sense of self all over the cognitive map and hinted at no coda.

"Hey, Nate. You still in there?" Arthur asked, leaning into Forrester's face.

The sound of Arthur's voice sounded as though from a great distance, but it was getting closer.

"Come on buddy. It was just some guy writing in his diary three thousand years ago. We're not talking about the end of the world. Hey, sick people, the war, blood and guts, real time action," Arthur's intoned, his volume rising.

The station's surroundings, as well as Arthur's voice, were closer now. He looked down at the scanner, which he had replaced half in and half out of his pocket. It appeared smaller now, but he knew it wasn't. He had a flash of burying the secure case in one small plot of mountain top land he owned in western Canada and felt foolish.

"You back in the land of the living?" Arthur asked, his tone betraying a soupcon of compassion.

"So, you don't think it was anything special?" Forrester asked as he looked up.

"What do I know? Fact, we found this old journal. Fact, the guy who wrote it didn't have the balls to let anyone see it. Fact, in hiding it, we didn't do anything he hadn't done already, and a long time ago. End of story. Everything else is just speculation," Arthur said, ending his speech with his characteristic gesture of finality.

A smile signaled its furtive beginnings on Forrester's face. He had seen Arthur do this a hundred times before. Arthur was the kind of guy who could look at gas pillars in the Eagle Nebula, where new suns were being born that might well shine on life more able than ourselves billions of years hence, and see it as a lot of hot air and dust. What a guy. For a moment Forrester doubted his own appraisal of the importance of the scrolls, but Arthur had not seen the oval glow, the moving shadows, or the every point illumination in the hut. Hell, even if he had, Arthur would have come up with some way to write it off or use virtual reality recreations of the phenomena as part of a merchandizing campaign for the scrolls.

From force of habit alone, Forrester chanted to himself what he had taught uncounted students over the years. "If everyone were a blank slate at birth, chaos would reign with each new generation. Individuals differed, but man remained the same. Self determination was an illusion. Nature's relentless sea surged behind 70% of personal destiny's tidal course. Nurture, benign or savage, was only a tributary furnishing but 30% to the wending of an individual's fate. The brain's hardwiring molds perception, perception is individual fact, and perceptions shared become socially actionable reality."

"Too much heady shit … time to fuck up our body chemistry. I'm buying,"

Arthur proclaimed.

Forrester looked up at his friend with eyes devoid of evidence that anyone was at home within.

"Do I have to carry your existential ass to the bar, or can you relate to real tissue enough to walk?" Arthur asked with a smile in his eyes.

Broadening to a grin, the smile on Forrester's face disappeared into a mass of well lined tissue. Arthur's concrete warmth was what made him Forrester's best friend. Such simple segways represented the phenomenal degree of acceptance that bridged, no ignored, the differences between them.

"Thanks, Arthur. And by the way, fuck you," Forrester said as he stood up and grasped Arthur's shoulder.

Returning Forrester's smile, Arthur led the way to the bar in quick time.

It was shift change, and, as usual, the bar was crowded with personnel representing every work sector on the station. Oddly, no music played in the background. Instead, everyone's attention was fixed on large vidscreens drifting around the room. The news wasn't good, and the commentator seemed bereft of his usual calm detachment. The all is well vocal tone, rigorously trained into all corporate broadcasters, was notably absent.

"Despite a second week of devastating losses sustained across several Natcorp defense units, talks have failed to produce a consensus that would effectively unify corporate defense forces."

"Fools!" Forrester said aloud as he killed the rest of the wine in his glass.

"That's you all over, Nate, no patience. This is the way people get together. Don't be such an asshole. Trust has to become a life and death necessity before anyone is going to take the risk. The conceptual reality of the threat has nothing to do with it. Actions, Nate, actions," Arthur remarked, looking him dead in the eye.

All news was war news these days. Natcorp commercials, replete with adoring females surrounding uniformed men, were extolling the macho rep of becoming a pilot or gunner for their fleets. The commercial spots absolutely oozed with promises of the good life on stations whose available space, at least according to the marketing arm, was equally divided between training and entertainment. There was no mention that less than half of the strike ships that flew off into combat ever returned to base.

The war began as what everyone thought was just another one of the many 'wars.' Everyone understood that the plural pointed to the continuing conflicts between one or another of the Natcorps. This war began with a raid on a remote Martian mining installation under MM Natcorp protection. The station's defensive squadron was completely wiped out and the domes leveled. There were no survivors. No last minute calls for help. Even the automatic recording cameras were incinerated.

Everyone immediately blamed PP Natcorp. It was a good bet. PP Natcorp was a conglomerate formed out of the old oil cartels. It included the most successful German engineering and technology consortiums. PP was responsible for every scrap of new 'defensive' technology, supplying all other Natcorp security units with armaments. Even the man in the street believed that PP always held a little something back for their own defensive arm should push come to shove. It wouldn't have been the first time PP Natcorp had done a live action test of new firepower. However, the complete obliteration of a capital investment installation directly violated every intercorporate protocol. If PP Natcorp's forces could be implicated, there would be repercussions and fines handed down by the United Nations.

MM Natcorp retaliated, of course, and lost half of another squadron to the PP Natcorp forces' improved shielding the corporation had not included in its latest armaments' sales brochure. The U.N. security board intervened activating a stop loss mandate. All corporate heads were ordered to a face-to-face at the U.N.

In the midst of PP's denials and the process of haggling out the issue of fines and loss defrayment, a second attack took place. This time, the target was a CC Natcorp provisioning station in extreme Martian orbit. Remote docking cameras recorded and transmitted the attack upon, and rapid destruction of, both the station, and all but a few of the strike craft guarding it.

Three glasses of wine over what he knew was his limbic limit, Forrester looked around a bar suddenly suffocated by silence that would have made a Quaker meeting seem raucous. Every eye was glued to the chronicle of the devastation. This was the first showing of the recordings to corporate employees below full administrative rank. The general population on the Earth below would not see this horror until the U.N. security board deemed it advisable.

Automatically orienting to any craft approaching the station at excessive speed, the CC station's docking cameras faithfully detailed the devastation. The only audio accompaniment to the video was the automated warning beacon, repeating its message over and over, "Reduce velocity, your speed is in excess of approach limits." All the vidscreens showed a six way split image, with each docking camera providing its own perspective on the carnage.

Transfixed by the images, Forrester didn't touch the brimming glass of Black Tower before him.

Grunting, Arthur tossed down another shot of Glenlivet without looking away from the screen.

Larger by half than the silver strike craft that rose from the station to meet them, the attacking ships were bloody orange in color and considerably less maneuverable than the defenders. The six way image of the battle included a lot of overlap, making it difficult to estimate strength, but it looked like equal numbers of craft on both sides. The attacking force seemed to wallow in space when compared to the quick moves of the silver strike craft. The invaders bristled with firepower. Broad blue white laser lines flashed from nearly every point on attackers' hulls except the aft engine exhaust ports.

It was clear that the strike craft shields were useless. If a CC Natcorp strike craft was hit, it was vaporized. As Forrester watched CC's fighter craft wink out of existence, like so many fireflies swallowed by the night, he remembered a physicist friend's discussion of the theoretical possibility of a propagating laser that could initiate a fusion reaction in anything it struck.

A gutsy bunch, the CC strike craft pilots targeted the attacking squadron from every conceivable angle. The little silver strike craft came in, lasers set on automatic continuous fire setting, pulling up only when the laser generators went into thermal shutdown. Their direct hits remained completely ineffectual. The big orange invaders absorbed their laser stikes without so much as a shimmering of their shielding. Forrester could not be sure, but he saw only four CC strike craft left as the big orange ships turned toward the station, opening fire as they came.

Glancing quickly over at Arthur, Forrester took note as his old friend held up four fingers without taking his eyes off the screen.

Pursuing the orange swarm of alien ships attacking the station, the strike craft looked like so many gnats nipping at a herd of water buffaloes. One pass over the station by the invaders and it was gone, and with it, another of the strike craft. The big orange ships completed a figure eight maneuver departing an orbit that once housed a bustling complex of over one thousand souls and set a heading that would carry them beyond the confines of the solar system.

Suspended in close proximity to the docking cameras, only two strike craft were clearly visible on the vidscreen. The third was just a point of light tailing the orange attack fleet. The sole pursuing craft zeroed in on the afterburner of one of the big orange ships, lasers firing continuously. The alien craft seemed to swell under the attack, exploding with such force that one of its sister ships was pushed out of formation and clearly damaged. The strike craft and her pilot, enveloped in the detonation of the enemy ship, evaporated in a solitary flash of energy that quickly dissipated in the deep darkness of space.

The two surviving silver strike craft hung in the cold black plane of space for an interminable moment before wheeling about the docking cameras. The screen was empty now except for pinpoints of light, propelling the attackers into the big empty beyond the solar system. Then, the vidscreens went blank.

A deadly silence hung over the bar for what seemed like forever. Then the bartender broke the lull by switching the vidscreens back to preprogrammed music videos. The blaring mindless fare on the vidscreens shocked Forrester out of his trance. He clutched his wine glass and downed the contents with uncharacteristic speed.

"Taste not that important anymore?" Arthur remarked, his expression one of feigned shock.

Forrester didn't answer. If he had been entranced before his mind was racing now.

"You're not gonna pick up your cross again are you?" Arthur asked as he noticed guilt lines deepening on Forrester's face.

In a strange sort of way, Arthur's snide comment helped. Nevertheless, Forrester noticed his hand had produced the scanner from his pocket without any conscious intention on his part to do so. He had spent many years teaching hypnosis to clients and students, so he doubted that only his hand was engulfed in some dissociative fugue state.

"Oh hell! Here comes that combination rosary and fortune cookie dispenser!" Arthur's voice was loud enough to momentarily carry over the vid music.

Forrester ignored the gibe, reasoning that if he could be in the midst of an alcohol induced lobotomy, so could Arthur. As Forrester had told his students on many occasions, drink if you can be the same person drunk or sober. For Arthur, as for so many right hemispheric, fight-flight driven individuals, alcohol dissolved the bulwarks of denial and a lot of unfinished business spilled out. For parasympathetic left brainers, like Forrester alcohol just made them silly, precipitated throwing up and falling asleep. Like so many things that Arthur said when he was drunk, there was a passionately precise point to his inebriated condemnation.

Fixing his gaze on the scanner, Forrester wondered if the diary entries were personal cram notes for living, some sophomoric version of the Delphic oracle, or just a very, very old diary. Dredging up the few vestiges of empiricism that remained unravaged by that excellent German white wine, he punched a random selection on the scanner. An outstanding application of the experimental method for a drunk, he thought.

"Let's see what it coughs up," he muttered to himself just loud enough for Arthur to hear.

The reader momentarily blurry. Then, it stopped and centered an entry.

DEATH IS A MOTHER WITH TWO FIERCE
SONS, FEAR AND DOMINION. A FAMILY
OF DARK VESTMENT, THEY ARE THE
CONSTANT COMPANIONS OF MAN'S
TRAVELS THROUGH TIME AND THE
BLOODLETTING THAT IS HIS HISTORY.

WAR IS ALL THAT IS UNCLEAN, MOTHER
DEATH JOINED IN INCEST WITH FEAR
AND DOMINION. TOGETHER THEY LAY
WASTE TO THE EARTH, HERALDING ITS
CLOSE.

Unable to resist, Arthur leaned over, drink still in hand, to read the entry over Forrester's shoulder.

Jerking back in his seat with such force that he spilled some of his drink, Arthur's glare suggested that something about the entry had deflated the comfortable cushion of denial upon which he rested.

"Shit! Aramaic magical, mystical, fortune telling, fucking, bullshit!" Arthur exploded, glaring at Forrester.

It was seldom that Arthur lost his cool to the point of excessive scatological references. The distilled mists of Scotland, notwithstanding, the entry had gotten to him. Nevertheless, Arthur appeared considerably more composed after his outburst. An outpouring of emotional energy seemed to help right hemispherically endowed individuals to close the door of denial on issues, or at minimum, it served to distance everyone who was audience to the affective explosion. This was evolution's right hemispheric answer to the problem of emotional loose ends. Denial sheared off the trailing threads of uncomfortable feelings, an act that was instantly reinforced by the comfort attending limbic closure. Uncluttered forward motion through life, facilitated by selective exclusion of troublesome thoughts or feelings, it was the height of psychic efficiency in the right hemisphere.

Such explosive episodes, on the exceedingly rare occasions when he experienced them, always left Forrester with a sort of open-ended feeling of agitated fatigue that would not abate until a dreamless sleep smoldered his limbic fires sufficiently to provide space for coherent thought.

Staring down at the entry on the scanner, Forrester noticed what he had come to call the invigorating 'scroll sensation,' forming as a 'Y' in his head. A sensation of well-being spread throughout his body as he mustered the last remnants of his empiricism.

"A conditioned response, based on hopeful memory, fueled by booze," He muttered under his breath.

Having a complete knowledge of the characteristics of his own group's neuropsychological configuration proved helpful in times like this. We have no mechanism that supplies self-verifying conviction when it comes to our internal experience, he thought to himself. Neither the most rigorously refined cognitions, nor certainly, the most compelling emotion carried the imprimatur of actionable truth. Everything was suspect. Arthur was fortunate in this regard. If it sprang to mind for him, thought or feeling, it must be universal law. Forrester and all those like him lacked this ability. They were deficient in the neurological structures that simultaneously informed fear-aggression, unabashed vying for dominance, and the incontestable confidence flowing from the momentum of the tribe being fully vested in each of its individual members.

Rummaging through his pockets, Forrester finally located a detox patch. Marvelous little medical innovation, he thought to himself. Slap it on, and within moments, brain cells awaken from their ethanol stupor and do their best to fire along pathways consistent with our just-out-of-the-muck level of evolutionary ascension. He sat back and waited for the welcome and familiar snap into focus that meant the patch had done its job. When it came, he immediately looked at the entry on the scanner and was hit by the 'scroll sensation' in spades. Fascinating, he thought to himself as his internal monologue rolled on, alcohol just gets in the way.

Three words in the entry glowed in relief on the screen, "heralding its close." Weaving itself into the scroll sensation, the verbal triplet circuited through his frame, returning to sit at the juncture point of the 'Y' in his head. Like some endless auditory loop in a cosmic echo chamber, it repeated itself over and over in tones reminiscent of a one line Gregorian chant.

Without any conscious intention, he reached for his wine glass, but found it empty. The promise of another dose of velvet lined escape, courtesy of the north German vineyards, was gone. For a split second, he regretted applying the detox patch. What the hell was this about? Had his psyche bridged over into the valley of the shadow of obsessive-compulsive crisis or were the verses served up by his scanner roulette, now insistently tolling in his head the word of God incarnate in an emergent psychosis?

Panic was not an experience that came easily or frequently to Forrester. Indeed, when angst shrieked at him, its howls were not usually prompted by things that drove others to distraction. Panic was his personal reaction to an avalanche of emotion formed by the perfect conviction of inevitability. An anxiety experience of this magnitude was all the more terrifying when it presented itself naked and detached from any empirically testable framework.

In contrast, Arthur experienced the conviction of inevitability as affirming. He was buoyed up in its swell and surfed with ease upon its curls. The tide of emotional conviction made him feel at one with the larger human tribe of which he was a member. To be convinced without evidence other than one's feelings was at the core of what it was to be a right hemispheric human.

For Forrester, such tidal surges of feeling were tsunamis that inundated the dry land of reason and laid waste all the delicate edifices of thought he had carefully erected during hours of rigorous empirical meditation. He saw holistic, nonlinear conviction as disassembling. Forrester feared that, torn to pieces by its momentum, the fragile center from which he thought and spoke would be scattered by its remorseless currents.

Chapter 3

If the contemporary social order honored a warrior caste, Sydes would be its poster child. In his middle twenties, he demonstrated the quiet intensity of a professional truly at ease only when his energies were realized in actions. Recruited as a child, and flying since he was eleven, Sydes led PP Natcorp's pilots. He had long since lost count of the number of intercorporate battles in which he had fought. He did, however, retain a clear memory of the comrades lost in those skirmishes. Like his American Indian ancestors, Sydes preferred to count coup against the enemy by disabling rather than destroying, their craft. Nonetheless, he had more kills than he cared to recall. For his adversaries, Sydes was death in the void. A lone bird of prey, his strike craft was an unwelcome specter in any opponent's viewer.

Vested not only with an unmatched 'feel' for the craft he flew, Sydes also had a complete working knowledge of its every component. Had he been a horse soldier in Earth's past, Sydes would have dissected the animal at some point in his career. It was not uncommon for the PP engineers, fists full of design schematics, to comb the station's many bars seeking the experiential input only his flight expertise could provide. Rumors even hinted that Sydes' tactical successes in penetrating the first generation shields of opposing craft in battle motivated the new envelope design of PP Natcorp's shielding.

Preferring bars that featured the best 'corporate ladies,' Sydes rarely lacked a companion. Drinks cost more in these full service bars, but Sydes wasn't saving up for anything. Every inch the fighter pilot, Sydes evaluated his consorts on both their lines and performance characteristics. Attraction inspired the transaction, but credits sealed the bargain. He was in the process of acquiring his next target when the alarm klaxon rang.

Sydes had suited up and climbed into his strike craft long before any of the other pilots entered the bay. The high sheen black skin of his craft made it easy to spot among the silver fighters on the flight deck. The PP engineering division arranged this color change to honor their premier ace. Sydes extended only passing attention to this change. His focus was singularly devoted to the realities of battle, not its decorative aspects. A well myelinated circuit dedicated to action, he was his fighter craft's central processing unit. Sydes never noticed what he was doing. He just did it giving only passing consideration to the aftermath. Recently, one of his admirers had etched a bold red "Solo" on the black fuselage of his strike craft, just below the cockpit. Sydes wasn't concerned with the logo. It wasn't relevant. He did object to the rows of kill hash marks engraved next to the deep red name, and heat erased them. For Sydes, the numbers weren't important. Two men met in space, one came back, that was all that mattered.

Checklist complete, he ignited the strike craft's thrusters as the huge metal doors of the bay had just begun to slide open. With the fighter's engines at half throttle, he brought his craft to the flight line long before the word to launch came down from the command cubicle. The shields had only begun their breaching cycle as Sydes, accelerating the Solo to full throttle, sped toward the launch lip. Streaking out of the bay with just enough clearance between the shield boundaries to accommodate the body of his sleek black craft, he spiraled into his hunting ground. His focus every bit as intense as his Plain's Indian ancestors must have been millennia ago, he knew the form of his quarry. Sydes always did his homework. In this case, that meant spending hours studying the tapes from the mining installation attack frame by frame. While the other pilots had lounged in the station's many bars, Sydes had prepared for the hunt by calibrating his sensors to the bloody orange ship's energy signatures.

Although not visible to the eye, Sydes knew the location of each of the invading ships. His console clearly revealed their energy emissions. The position and speed of the invaders indicated an attack vector to his home station.

"You do not hunt on my ground," Sydes muttered as he began sizing up the targets.

Chatter on the comm-link from the PP station's bridge remained in the background of his awareness as he focused on the invaders. Then, he heard the station's sensors confirm the invader's approach. Almost immediately, he recognized the station Commander's voice as he frantically ordered that the shield envelope around the station be sealed.

Activating the comm-link, Sydes transmitted a single word, 'No,' already aware that his warning would come too late.

Pivoting his craft at hyperburn, he watched helplessly as the balance of his squadron, exiting the bay at full thrust, crashed into the shield wall activated by the panicked station Commander. In a cascade of explosions, first the strike craft, then the bays detonated. Contained by the shields surrounding the station, the fireball took out each section of the PP orbiting complex, blasts following one another like firecrackers on a circular fuse.

For a long sad moment, the mass of spinning debris churning in the dark void of space that had once been illuminated by the station's many portholes of light held his attention. Then, unzipping a portion of his flight suit, he produced a small, heavily beaded leather pouch. Opening it, he poured a portion of finely flaked tobacco into his hand and brushed the flakes into the cockpit ejector port. The thrusters roared to life as he moved the craft over the small enclave of space that had once housed his comrades and their strike craft. He pushed the evacuation switch and watched as the running lights illuminated the particles of tobacco as they mingled with the molecules of his fellow warriors.

"Good hunting," he said softly.

Activating the thrusters, Sydes turned his fighter toward the now visible brilliant red orange shapes hurtling toward him.

⚜

The Arab Commander of the CC station closest to the spinning debris that once represented the rival PP installation, stared coldly at the viewscreen. He centered his viewer on Sydes' strike craft knowing what would happen next. He watched solemnly as the lone fighter kicked into full burn, moving off in the direction of the growing bloody orange spots of light in the distance. Ten years as Commander of the CC Natcorp flagship control station directing sorties in the corporate wars informed a certainty in his perception. The strike craft pilot was a brave man going to his death. A half hidden smile crossed his face. He wouldn't want to be one of those orange points of light moving through the darkness. There would be losses for the commander of that squadron as well.

Unmistakable by its signature black hull and the way it maneuvered, he knew both the craft and her pilot. His CC squadron called the ship A.A.S., 'ass.' The fighter was stripped down to attack essentials: **A**rmaments, **A**fterburners and **S**hields. It was the Solo. Neither he, nor any of his current staff had ever met this warrior in battle. Yet, they all knew him, if only through his thinning of their ranks in innumerable corporate conflicts.

Turning to his number two, Lieutenant Sadad, Commander Tutunji ordered up the station's fighter squadron.

"Sir, that was a PP Natcorp station, and that's a PP fighter out there, Solo, the worst of the bunch," Lieutenant Sadad sputtered.

"You mean the best of the bunch, don't you?" Commander Tutunji retorted. His tone had an edge.

"That pilot killed three of my friends and your nephew!" Sadad exclaimed.

Thumbing through his worry beads with increasing speed, Commander Tutunji suddenly grabbed Sadad by the arm and pushed him toward the viewscreen until his nose nearly touched its surface.

"Do those orange dots look like MM, PP, FF or our own CC fighters coming this way? Do you think that whoever or whatever they are, they give a damn about our corporate insignia?"

Wise enough not to struggle against the Commander's iron grip, Sadad stood perfectly still. Although forty years his senior, Sadad had witnessed Commander Tutunji break a rapist's neck in one motion after he caught the man in the act. Using his free arm, Sadad sounded the klaxon.

"Flash charge the auxiliary fuel cells. I want all strike craft at hyperburn until you catch up with that fighter." Commander Tutunji ordered as he activated the fighter bay comm-link.

Closing the link, Tutunji loosened his grip on Sadad and focused on the main viewer.

"I don't want Sydes defending our honor, while we huddle like frightened women in our tents," Tutunji said evenly.

"Shouldn't we hold back a reserve?" Sadad asked in a startled tone.

"A few ships are going to do what the squadron's full complement can't accomplish?" Tutunji paused for a long moment. "We're sending them all."

For a few seconds, the station's viewer lit up like the noonday sun as the entire squadron went to hyperburn. Fighters quickly dwindled to pinpoints of light as they rapidly closed on the attacking ships and Sydes' lone strike craft.

⚔✦⚔

Now clearly visible to the naked eye, Sydes could see the configuration of the attacking ships. They were almost perfect ovals and three times the size of his strike craft. His eyes and the sensors agreed, the bloody-orange glow, which cast the ships in relief against the darkness, was their shielding. Recordings from the docking cameras activated during the attack on the Martian installations told him that the old strike craft shielding wouldn't hold against the enemies' armaments. His only hope now was that the new power grid and shielding envelope in his strike craft would allow him a pass or two. Although Sydes thought in neither words, nor pictures, he knew exactly what he was going to do.

Slowing as he approached the enemy force, Sydes pulled the Solo into a steep climb, an attitude that would completely overfly the oncoming ships. As he had anticipated, two of the big bloody ships broke formation to engage him. He corrected his course to fly precisely between them, and kicked the fighter into hyperburn. The alien vessels grew larger by the second as Sydes watched his range indicator. They opened fire at five thousand kilometers, a useful thing to know should chance favor his living through the engagement. The new shielding held the first laser strikes without flinching, but as he closed to within a few hundred kilometers, it began to fluctuate and overheat. Using one of his jury-rigged gadgets, he recircuited laser power to the shields and they settled down. For what he had in mind, he wouldn't need the lasers anyway.

Laser fire from the two alien vessels against the Solo ceased as he flew through the perilously narrow corridor between them. Well, they reason like us, he thought to himself, at least to the extent that they're not going to risk hitting their own ships at point blank range.

Sydes quickly shifted his viewer to an aft perspective and activated the tactical grid as soon as the thrusters of the alien vessels became visible. Reaching down, he hit the emergency reverse control on the Solo's thrusters. The small craft shuddered and pitched as the thrusters brought it to an abrupt static firing halt. Allowing the residual momentum of the maneuver to roll the fighter through a complete full nose over rotation, he brought the missile tubes to bear. The big alien ships desperately tried to execute a turn as his targeting computer locked onto their thrusters. The instant the targeting computer confirmed acquisition, Sydes dispatched two one hundred megaton fusion missiles set for short run maximum burn. The missiles lanced toward the fiery tails of the enemy ships at incredible speed. The missiles were within seconds of achieving their targets when he felt the Solo's huge thruster engines cough, shudder and die.

Repeatedly thumbing the emergency engine restart button produced no response. Well no surprise, he thought. Two ships for one, not a bad exchange. For a millisecond, the blinding light of nuclear fusion freed from its prison supplanted the blackness of space as his missiles struck the thruster arrays of the attackers and the bloody orange ships were gone.

Suddenly relegated to the status of a spectator, a role he equated with what it must be like to be dead, but somehow still wandering among the living, he stared blankly at a battle in which he could no longer participate.

Their auxiliary fuel cells jettisoned on approach, the full CC squadron plus reserves, entered the fray. They assumed a high frontal attack vector at full burn, and dove to meet the alien vessels. Sydes' range finder informed him that the incoming strike craft were well within their laser turrets' effective range. However, no flashes from the CC strike craft indicated tactical targeting strikes. In that instant, he grasped what they had in mind. Switching his helmet visor to extreme opacity, he transferred battery power to the Solo's forward shields.

As the CC squadron came into the enemy's laser range, the strike craft kicked into hyperburn, leaping forward toward the bloody orange cluster of ships. Enemy lasers lanced out, vaporizing first two, then six of the strike craft. Each of the remaining ships launched its two multimegaton missiles at the alien vessels which had taken on the appearance of psychedelic porcupines of continuous laser fire. Two more strike craft were destroyed before their missiles reached the target.

Five more CC strike craft were vaporized by the detonation of their own fusion missiles among the ships of the enemy squadron as the enormous bloom of nuclear fire reached out and enveloped some of its creators. The attendant shock wave shoved Sydes' fighter clear of the battle, vaporizing all but the cockpit of the Solo, which was preserved by its isolated emergency power grid and dedicated shielding.

⚜

On the CC station's main viewer, it appeared as though the Sol system had become the site appointed by the universe for a holocaust variety collision of comets. Commander Tutunji watched the fiery plume of devastation, knowing what would come next. The obliterating wave of nuclear energy now coursing towards the station was the reason fusion missiles were verboten in corporate conflicts.

"Divert all power to the shield grid," Commander Tutunji shouted into the comm-link.

Then, he sat down with the sort of resignation reserved for a man whose job description required only one action once he had taken it. The Commander suddenly felt useless. Like Sydes, Tutunji was now a spectator, and he liked it no less than that hapless ace. All he could do now was watch as the fusion shock waves overtook and destroyed what remained of his fighter squadron before it rolled on, its energy unabated, towards the station.

At least there will be record, the Commander thought as he hit a switch propelling the docking cameras to extreme range.

Like a supercell storm bloated with lightning and looking for a ground, the shock wave struck the station. The blast instantly destroyed fifty of the one hundred compartments. Many more were severely damaged and only ten retained airtight integrity. From the Commander's viewpoint, it was a singular dishonor that the command bridge on which he stood remained intact.

The green glow that indicated subsection integrity in an electronic schematic of the station shone for just ten compartments scattered through the superstructure. The reactor enclave and one of the shuttle docking bays remained intact as was the maintenance unit. The central transubstantiator signal bunker was uncompromised. No surprise, the dedicated shield power it drew equalled that allotted to the entire station. He didn't have to look at the green-house-park subsection indicator. Several small trees were among the bits of twisted metal floating past the viewer. Then there were the bodies, so many, like some macabre parade passing before the viewer.

Fingers flying, the Commander thumbed first one then another switch redirecting power flow to the subsections that remained intact. Looking up at the main viewer, he saw a little girl dressed, perhaps for a birthday party, drift by, her hand frozen in her mother's grasp. Damn the corporation and their policy of keeping family units together on stations that could come under fire.

Unable to shift his gaze from the mother and child as they danced among the swirling debris, a feeling of undirected anger overcame the Commander. If God has a hand in this, he had a lot to answer for. Not a religious man, the Commander couldn't shake the feeling that if there was an afterlife, it had better be good to make up for this kind of slaughter.

"God knows," he muttered to himself. "We're good enough at butchering each other without outside help."

"Sir …" Lieutenant Sadad's voice broke through the Commander's carnage inspired rumination. "Sir, the infirmary is gone along with the staff. We have injured everywhere."

Commander Tutunji slowly turned away from the viewer to look at Sadad. Sadad's uniform was splattered with blood. His face, also flecked with blood, was a mask of anxiety and helplessness. Lieutenant Sadad was a good executive officer, but he would have made a better medic. His temperament was more in line with saving people than ordering them into harm's way.

"Call the PP Natcorp command control station. It's the closest to us," Tutunji's tone was steady, but coiled for Sadad's response.

"But sir, they're PP Natcorp. They aren't going to help a CC station," Sadad replied.

"They have viewers, number one. They can see this isn't some kind of corporate scrap," Tutunji retorted.

Then, the Commander's manner and tone softened as he looked Sadad squarely in the eye.

"It's not us versus them anymore, Jenab. This enemy is a 'them' for all of us."

Lieutenant Sadad's posture relaxed a bit from its taut presentation. Reassured by the use of his first name, Sadad was even more heartened by the look of fatherly concern in the Commander's eyes.

"Yes, sir," Sadad replied.

Then, the shaken executive officer quickly turned away to conceal the beginning of tears in his eyes. Suddenly, all he could think of was his own father

... a man killed by his own kindness. His father had fallen to an extremist's bullet, while attempting to aid a badly wounded member of a force that had attacked their subsector. Sadad pushed the feeling away, the Commander was not his father. Busying himself with the horrors of the present would distance him from past sorrows. Gritting his teeth, he punched up the comm-link to the PP station.

Initiating the firing of the few remaining stabilizing jets, the Commander attempted to establish what was left of his station in the new orbit the blast had created for it. As the broken wheel of his command creaked and groaned into its new place in the heavens, he watched as debris and bodies moved on a trajectory that would eventually carry them into the sun.

"Returning to the maker," the Commander said in tones so reverent they might have been a prayer.

Now clear of the debris field created by the destruction of most of his station, the view of automatic docking cameras was unobstructed. He refocused the cameras at extreme range on the scene of the battle, where Tutunji saw a tiny object swimming in the blackness. The object, now identifiable as a cockpit capsule, was framed by the propulsion flickers of the attacking enemy squadron as it exited the solar system. Tutunji counted the tongues of thruster exhaust and estimated that the enemy had lost one third of its force. His losses had been total. He knew that the small cockpit capsule could not belong to his CC strike force group, their shields could not have withstood all the megatonnage they had unleashed. It could only be the Solo.

Activating the link to the shuttle bay, the Commander could hear the panic in the bay Chief's voice as he responded.

"Yes sir," The bay Chief responded.

"What's left?" The Commander asked.

"Only two personnel carriers and ... and two cargo haulers, Sir ..." the Chief replied, his voice shaking. "the other three cargo haulers were off station, and we can't raise them."

"I'm feeding some coordinates to your navigational unit," the Commander replied after a moment's pause. " I want you to send a hauler out there and pick up a pilot."

"One of our boys make it, Sir?" The Chief asked expectantly.

"He's one of our boys now, whether he knows it or not. Bring him home Chief."

An expression of startled confusion on his face, Sadad approached his commander as Tutunji closed the link to the shuttle bay.

"The PP command station is sending a medical ship and a couple of cargo haulers with technicians and supplies. They'll also be sending some personnel carriers to evacuate our injured. And … and they're mustering half their strike craft wing to provide station security. No questions asked."

The Commander fell into the command chair as if he were being carried down by a great sheet of sliding sand. Then, he looked up at his exec's face through eyes wearied by years of experience. Sadad still retained some elements of a surprised expression.

"What did you expect them to do, number one?" The Commander asked.

"I don't know sir, but not this," Sadad replied.

"The little fish fight each other over every morsel …" the Commander said as he leaned back in the command chair. "until the big fish rolls in. Nothing has changed, number one, we're still just a bunch of little fish, but now we have a bigger problem than each other."

❦

The bay Chief elected to pilot the cargo hauler himself, and shortly sighted the remnants of the Solo. The chief viewed this mission as important because it had come as a direct order from Commander Tutunji. The Chief didn't want any slip ups, so it never occurred to him to relinquish command of the mission to any of his staff. The strike craft's emergency beacon led him directly to the cockpit, which was all that remained of the lone fighter adrift in space. Activating the handler beams, he gently drew the scarred cockpit into the hold. As soon as the atmosphere in the hold was established, he ordered the cockpit lased open.

So this was Sydes. Everyone knew of him, but no one on the Chief's side of the Natcorp line had ever met him face to face and come back alive. He passed the first aid scanner over the unconscious pilot. The readings indicated a skull fracture and compression injuries to the chest. This would take a medico. Pulling a life support unit out of its pack, the Chief attached it to Sydes right thigh and coupled the leads back to the power unit in the pack.

"That will keep him alive until we can get him to a medic," the Chief said.

As he came to his feet, the Chief took one more look at the fighter ace who, until this very moment, had been only a name whispered with fear and respect. Now, the Chief saw just another man who hovered with each breath between this life and the next. Quickly climbing the ladder back to the command deck, the Chief ordered the shuttle back to the station.

❦

The door to the command bridge had jammed open during the blast. Commander Tutunji noticed that every cry of pain wafting down the passageway captured Sadad's attention. Carefully observing his executive officer, he waited for the right moment to catch Sadad's eye.

"Go on, I can handle this," the Commander said.

"Yes Sir," Sadad replied instantly.

A slight smile on his face, Sadad snatched the first aid pack off the wall and disappeared down the passageway.

The Commander slowly rotated his chair to face the viewer. There in the void, he could just make out the cargo shuttle returning with what remained of Sydes and his ship. Sydes and Sadad, a study in contrast, he thought to himself. Both young, both military, representing two very different poles in the fight to preserve humanity.

Sydes represented the hunter whose purpose was fulfilled in saving the species, while Sadad embodied the nurturer who was intent on rescuing the individual. A single species with a division of labor that generated conflict among its members, yet served the survival of the whole of the race. Given the uncompromising nature of this attack, it was clear that these aliens from beyond Sol's circle of children were intent upon generating work for both of these young men.

Chapter 4

The raucously blaring klaxon brought the whole PP station to life and sent personnel scurrying off in every direction. Forrester and Arthur looked at one another, then, came to their feet as the station's comm ordered all front line medical personnel to the shuttle bay.

Most off duty station personnel had already seen the recorded feed from the CC station's docking cameras. A PP station and squadron had been annihilated and a CC station was barely hanging on. Hurrying to the medical shuttle, Forrester's steps faltered as the vid-images of bodies adrift in space distracted his attention from the simple act of walking. So many bodies. So many women and children. More than seventeen hundred souls, cold and cast away. He said nothing to Arthur as they made their way along the corridor, but the scroll was calling. An entry unfurled in his head, superimposing itself on the macabre panorama of bodies drifting in space.

> IN ALL BEGINNINGS ARE THEIR ENDINGS CONTAINED. EACH OF LIFE'S DANCERS ARE NOW AND FOREVER JOINED TO THE OTHER IN A WHIRL OF COMINGS AND GOINGS.
>
> DEATH IS IN THE FLOWER OF THE WHEAT THAT MAKES OUR BREAD AND IN THE BABE OF THE EWE IS THAT WHICH NOURISHES OUR CHILDREN. GRIEVING THE DEATH OF OUR OWN, WE SLAY TO LIVE.
>
> HOLDING OUR OWN LIVES DEAR, WE KNOW NOT THAT WHICH CAME BEFORE OR THAT WHICH ARISES AFTER OUR BRIEF MOMENT OF EATING, DRINKING, JOY AND PAIN.

WE AWAKEN IN A STREAM NOT KNOWING
IT HAS FLOWED BEFORE WE ROUSED. AS
OUR PASSAGE ENDS, CLUTCHING THE HOPE
THAT THE TORRENT OF LIVES WILL ENDURE,
WE SINK BENEATH THE SURFACE.

Confronted with the horror of so many lost lives, it was not the individual deaths that troubled Forrester. In truth, he had companioned the ending of life with so many, often secretly envying their stealing away from pain, that he was inured. Without ever so intending, his concerns were now cosmic. For the first time, Forrester seriously considered whether the 'torrent of lives will endure.' His master motive at that moment was to escape this thought that enveloped him like a shroud. He would throw himself into saving individual lives and dispel the wraith of absolute endings that haunted him.

Unencumbered by apocalyptic concerns, Arthur had gotten a few paces ahead of Forrester. As Forrester entered the shuttle bay, Arthur was already busy loading life support units into the shuttle's hold. The station's comm droned on about the need to protect PP's interests by supporting CC's command control station. It was the old 'you can't eat power speech.' CC supplied technical support for the transubstantiators. PP's life and death stranglehold on the economy, however, came in the form of a continuously scrabbled signal transmitted through well defended relay stations without which the transubstantiators wouldn't function. If that signal was interrupted no one would eat.

Forrester shoved a carton of universal blood substitute units into the shuttle's hold. This stuff was a marvel of science. Each bag contained a limited use transubstantiator chip in a saline organic soup solution. A drop of the patient's blood in the receiver compartment activated the chip, and in a matter of seconds, you had a unit of DNA compatible blood ready for immediate use by the patient.

In the midst of this life threatening crisis, technicians and supply personnel around Forrester carped about the inequities of the system. Snatches of conversation revealed that the inter-corporate propaganda departments had earned their salt.

"The goddamn, blood sucking CC's got what they deserved," one burly man said as he shouldered a pack.

"Yeah, and now we're supposed to save their ass. You think they'll cut the transubstantiator charges when we bail them out?" a middle age woman added as she stacked dialysis units.

"Right, and tomorrow it'll rain beer," added a young man, smiling wryly.

It was population control at its best, divide and conquer. The system generated a carefully orchestrated tension among the consumers in which first one, then another Natcorp played the 'bad guy.' Eventually, the 'bad guy' became the 'fall guy' for any frustrations the consumer base was experienced. It was the ultimate refinement and application of the melodramatic dynamics of professional wrestling to the political arena. The black hood of the 'bad guy' passed from one corporation to another under the direction of the U.N. security directorate. William of Ockham had been right over sixteen hundred years ago - *all things being equal, the simplest approach is the best.*

Fully loaded, the medical shuttle silently rose, exited the bay and glided effortlessly through space toward the remains of the CC command station. Inertial dampers suppressed almost all sense of motion as the craft nosed its way through the darkness. No matter how many times Forrester traveled through space, he felt the efficiency of the craft's functioning somehow gutted the event of its significance.

A cloud of drifting debris, the remnants of the PP station's destruction, was suspended between the shuttle and the CC station. Inasmuch as speed was important if the medical aid was to be of any use to those who had survived, the shuttle pilot speedily, but carefully threaded her way through the spinning wreckage. She skillfully avoided the tumbling bulkhead fragments, but occasionally Forrester felt a vibration as a drifting cadaver struck the hull. Through the porthole, he saw crowds of corpses, faces frozen in endless variations of fear, drifting in the void. Congregations of bodies contorted in stances unbecoming to their gracefully swirling movements waltzed to the momentum of the blast that had ended their dreams, loves and hates. Immersed in the dance macabre, Forrester suddenly saw the diarist's words, scrolling themselves out upon the dark ballroom of space.

> THE DUST RISES AND DEATH IS
> CARRIED ON THE WIND. A GUST
> FILLING EVERY LIFE'S SAIL
> THRUSTS EACH INTO THE DARK
> DOLDRUMS OF THE GRAVE.
> ENTERING UPON THIS MOMENT
> OF COMPLETE STILLNESS, ALL
> HOPE TO BRIDGE THAT INSTANT
> OF ENDING, STRIVING TO A
> BRIGHTNESS OF HOPE PRESERVING
> THE BEST STRENGTHS OF APPETITE,

HEART, AND MIND BEYOND THE
CHAINS OF TIME, THE COLD
DARKNESS FOLDS SOFTLY OVER
THEM.

ALL THAT THE EYE BEHOLDS OF
MAN IS BUT A DRIFTING HAZE UPON
THE FORGETFUL WINDS OF FOREVER.
WITHIN THAT UNSEEN GAIL, OUR
RUDDER IS FAITH, AND OUR PILOT
THE SOUL. THE PILOT'S INVISIBLE
MATE, HOPE REMAINS HIS
ONLY STEADFAST COMPANION.

Commander Tutunji came to attention and offered a salute as a tiny armada of PP shuttles landed in the CC station's receiving bay. He wanted to be there at their arrival to 'make it right' for his people as the PP personnel invaded their territory. Watching as the medicos disembarked, he noticed Forrester immediately. Moving forward for a closer look, he focused in on Forrester's medical insignia that simultaneously indicated his years of experience and his degree of case by case proven competence. The splash of colors and symbols in the emblem indicated not only extensive experience, but a strong record of successful medical interventions.

"Doc," Tutunji called to Forrester.

Forrester turned reflexively in the direction of the sound and found Commander Tutunji confronting him.

"Doc, I've got a genuine PP hero for you to patch up," Tutunji said as he beckoned for Forrester to follow.

Tutunji turned and hurried from the receiving bay with Forrester in tow. Enroute to the Commander's quarters, the two men threaded their way through the wounded who, leaning against the walls and lying on the floor, crowded the passageway.

As they entered the Commander's billet, Forrester saw a man in a PP flight suit on the bunk. He was hooked to a first aid life support unit. The Commander stepped back as Forrester activated his medical diagnostic scanner and completed a full body pass over the unconscious pilot. The readings unequivocally reported, no tissue damage from ionizing radiation, two non-penetrating skull fractures without notable compression, no cerebral edema, thoracic compression due to multiple rib fractures without splintering, moderate difficulty breathing, and minor vascular damage in the chest cavity. Internal bleeding was not a significant factor, but Forrester drew a blood sample from the pilot's life support pack and started a unit just in case something unanticipated cropped up.

Being useful again, Forrester thought to himself, that's the ticket. During these times of active service, he was least likely to be plagued by apocalyptic thoughts.

Forrester visualized the chest cavity initiating the diagnostic scanner to hover over the thoracic field. As he applied the gravity suspensor forceps to the exterior of the patient's chest, he mused at how, in times past, the bodies of patients had to be opened to make repairs. When the indicators flashed that the ribs had been appropriately positioned, he applied the bone knitter. With the pressure alleviated, the chest bleeders declared themselves. Out of the corner of his eye, he noticed that the blood unit had activated. It responded to volume changes and its activation was a clear indication that vascular intervention was required. Reaching back to his pack for the vascular stitcher, Forrester suddenly found the Commander had placed it in is hand. This guy was more than a simple military administrator, Forrester mused. He focused the stitcher over the areas indicated by the scanner and the blood supply unit ceased its pressure feed.

Reading the diagnostic scanner, Forrester noted the global vital signs indicator was bridging over into the stable range. He could now safely turn his attention to the skull fractures. Retrieving the ultra-fine suspensor forceps unit from his pack, he gently lifted the skull plates into correct alignment. This would be an interesting case as the fractures followed the natural suture lines in the skull. Forrester was more accustomed to dealing with patients over the age of thirty in whom these suture lines were completely calcified. Readjusting the bone knitter to a gel setting was required to work along the suture lines as the readings indicated the patient was under the age of twenty-eight.

The body presented such a marvelously level playing field. Once you understood the players and the rules, the game was always played fairly. The lungs didn't conspire with the kidneys to operate outside the game's parameters in order to gain ascendancy over the cardiovascular system. The pancreas didn't make a clandestine stock deal with the thymus to oust the frontal lobes from their position of executive decision making. The body worked as a unit, one system attempting to make up for deficiencies in another, and presenting a united front, particularly when a foreign invader or injury was at hand. The human body was one vehicle that was smarter than its occupant.

Restoring the fractures along the suture lines took a bit longer than usual as they had to gel at an appropriate level of elasticity. In moments, the diagnostic scanner array registered that the knit was complete. It indicated that there were no mini-bleeders or contrecoup bruise bleeds in the brain. Having your skull fractured sounded awful, but the shock had been absorbed by the bone fracturing, not the brain being squashed. A fringe benefit, if you could call it that, Forrester thought to himself.

"This guy has a hell of a constitution," Forrester muttered to himself.

Glancing at the global vital signs indicator, he noted that it was beginning to register in the optimal range.

"He'll be OK. We just need to wait for his mind to wake up," Forrester said as he turned to the Commander.

"How long?" The Commander asked.

"What were the circumstances at the time of his injury?" Forrester queried as he reached into this medical kit.

Before the Commander could answer, Forrester produced a small set of headphones attached to a little black box. Activating some controls on the small unit, he held it up to the Commander's mouth.

"Please go ahead, describe the chain of events that led up to this man's coma," Forrester said looking at the Commander with an encouraging expression.

A quizzical look passed over the Commander face. Then, he related how the fusion blast's first shock wave had flung Sydes' strike craft clear of the fireball and how he had been brought to the station.

Looking up at Forrester, the Commander nodded, indicating that he had provided a complete explanation of the sequence of events. Forrester responded by holding up his hand signaling silence and then spoke into the little black box.

"You were injured and fell unconscious. Your injuries have been repaired. You are in a safe place with all your parts intact. You may wake up in a fully functional body whenever you wish. You are needed."

A quizzical expression crossed the Commander face as he looked at Forrester. Despite the medico's success up to this point, Tutunji wondered if he was, in fact, dealing with a practitioner of the mystical arts.

Noting the Commander's discomfort, Forrester instantly knew what it meant.

"This is just something a colleague of mine and I cobbled together," Forrester explained as he placed the head phones on the unconscious pilot.

"It's sort of a coma wake up call. The feed from the medical scanner will give the patient as much information as he requires with respect to his injuries and their repair." Forrester continued as he attached a lead from the diagnostic medical scanner to the little black box and pressed feed.

"Most importantly, it will gently but firmly convince him that he isn't going to wake up maimed or dead, " Forrester said as he turned to the Commander.

One of the best imitations of a buddhistic smile of enlightenment that Forrester had ever seen crossed the Commander's face. Given this kind of encouragement, Forrester couldn't resist going on about the little gadget that he and Arthur had pieced together more out of clinical experience than technological know how.

"The unit will speak to him in his own internal voice that is, the way he hears himself in his own head. It will provide him reassurance in a manner that conforms to his particular neuropsychological configuration. The net effect is that it will be factually convincing and what we call egosyntonic, that is, feel right."

Nodding, the Commander appeared to be following everything Forrester was saying.

"When he wakes up and takes it off, the guts of the unit will self-destruct." Forrester was tempted to explain the 'why' of the self-destruct feature, but he could see from the Commander's expression that this was unnecessary.

Closure on a job well done was one of Forrester's principal pleasures in life. Without immediately realizing it, he smiled at the Commander. That was rather remarkable as Forrester hadn't smiled at anyone except Arthur for a very long time. There was just something genuine and compelling in the Commander's manner. Picking up his medical pack, Forrester glanced over his shoulder as he started out of the door. He saw the Commander tucking a blanket up around Sydes' shoulders with nearly parental care. Then, turning about, the Commander followed Forrester out of the compartment.

Injured and dying humanity immediately confronted Forrester as he stepped from the Commander's quarters. The bodies of those who had survived the devastation of the station, filled the passageway. It was even more crowded with their cries of pain. For a moment it was as if the agony of the universe had been crammed into this tiny space. Forrester's gaze, threaded its way through the crowd. He spotted Arthur desperately working on a woman who had sustained freeze dry injuries over half of her body. Forrester guessed she had been subjected to space exposure when a bulkhead blew out during the nuclear holocaust.

Moving quickly to Arthur's side, Forrester immediately noted that the patient was on full life support. The diagnostic scanner dispassionately revealed massive rupturing of her internal organs on the left side of the body induced by the vacuum of space. Forrester pitched in, but despite their joint efforts, she simply stopped. Even if a full cloning lab were at their disposal it would have been difficult to sustain her life.

His face cast in lines of grim resignation, Arthur looked up from the patient, his focus coming to rest on a slight figure in the crowd.

Forrester followed his friend's gaze to a teenage girl whose features clearly indicated her relationship to her mother. He immediately saw the anger and grief welling up in her face.

"You fucking PP bastard!" She screamed.

Instantly on her feet, the slender young woman lunged at Arthur. She was incredibly quick. With one hand on Arthur's throat she was still screaming.

"Your pilots kill us by the hundreds and then you fuckers show up to finish the job."

In the midst of her flailing about, Forrester saw the glint of a shard of jagged metal in her other hand. Arthur desperately tried to restrain her wiry form without harming her, unaware of what she carried in her free hand.

Lunging forward in an attempt to help restrain her, Forrester heard a sizzling pop echo from behind and saw the girl drop limply to the deck.

Medical scanner in hand, Arthur knelt at her side and assessed her condition as Forrester turned to see the Commander holstering his sidearm.

Worry beads coming to hand, the Commander tracked Forrester's gaze down to the endless loop Tutunji held in his hand. Somewhat self-consciously, the Commander replaced it in his pocket.

"She has the heart of a warrior …" Tutunji said in carefully measured tones, "but her passion lacks the discipline of her head. Her father and brother were good pilots. They were killed in two separate skirmishes with PP flight wings over the past three years. Her mother was all she had left."

"She's only stunned … she'll come out of it in a few minutes," Arthur said as he stepped away from young girl's crumpled body.

The Commander stepped forward and scooped the slender young girl's form into his arms. He looked momentarily at Forrester and then carried the body of yet another orphaned child down the passageway and out of sight.

Long after the Commander had disappeared from sight, Forrester stared down the passageway. The passageway seemed somehow darker now, its flickering light dimmed by yet another emotional casualty. The young girl's sense of loss had been wholly focused on those attempting to prevent it. How human Forrester mused. One of the darkest entries from the scrolls whispered to Forrester mirroring the despair that like fog clouded the corridor.

WE ARE, EACH TO ONE ANOTHER, THE
MEAT THAT CANNOT BE EATEN. IN VAIN
STRIVING TO REPLENISH A PART TORN
FROM OURSELVES, WE SLASH AT OUR
BRETHREN IN RAGEFUL HOPE OF
RECOVERING A LOST PORTION OF THE
COMMON FLESH IN WHICH WE ARE
ALL ARRAYED.

THE DARKNESS THAT REIGNED BEFORE
THERE WAS LIGHT, IN SECRET CHAMBERS
OF THE HUMAN HEART DWELLS THERE
STILL. SOUNDLY NOURISHED, IT DINES
UPON THE MEAT OF HATE AND DRUNK
WITH THE BITTER WINE OF VENGEANCE,
IT PROSPERS. TAKING UP RESIDENCE
IN THIS ABODE FROM BEFORE THE STARS
WERE A SOURCE OF WONDER, IT PLOTS
AND SCHEMES TO UNDO THE LIGHT OF
CREATION.

EVERY MAN PROWLS THE WORLD, HIS
OWN SCALE OF JUSTICE IN HAND. FOR
EACH, THE RAGE AND GUILT OF HIS
FELLOWS WEIGHS MORE HEAVILY THAN
HIS OWN AND CRIES FOR REQUITAL. THE
KILLING ENDS ONLY AS THE LAST OF THE
SLAYERS PASSES BACK TO THE DUST
FROM WHICH ALL MEN SPRANG.

No loss can ever be recovered by quelling the spark of life in another. A timeless injunction, seamlessly rational, and yet universally ignored, Forrester thought as his mind spiraled into a morass of hopelessness.

A dark thought for dark times, he thought. The apparition was quickly dispelled by the encroaching onslaught of pain encircling him. Picking up his medical pack, Forrester moved quickly to the next victim. Tending to a small child, who, battered by the momentum of the blast, would never rise to play again, he wondered how this kind of suffering could ever be reconciled with the quest for dominion. He instantly went about the business of making the passing of this tiny life as painless as medically possible. Forrester felt ashamed as he saw a smile of relief pass over the little girl's face. In moments, he knew that she would fall into a nap from which she would never awaken. In seeming response to his despair, another entry from the scrolls forced its way into his consciousness.

ONLY WHEN ONE MAN'S PAIN BECOMES
THE AGONY OF ALL WILL THEY CEASE TO
INJURE ONE ANOTHER. LIFE, TO WHICH
END THE WHOLE TAPESTRY OF CREATION IS
WOVEN, CANNOT IN PART BE INJURED SAVE
THE WHOLE ANGUISHES AND BLEEDS. THE
MAKER KNOWETH THAT THE RIVING OF
BUT A SINGLE STRAND WEAKENS THE
WEAVE UNTIL THE WHOLE FABRIC IS RENT.

BORN SOLITARY OF HEART AND MIND,
MAN SEES NOT THE MANNER IN WHICH
HE IS BOUND TO ALL THAT LIVES. IN THIS
BLINDNESS IS COMPASSION'S WANT.

Although he had removed the pain from the little girl's face, Forrester was unable to reawaken the brilliance of youth as the light slowly faded from her eyes.

"Another tear in the common cloth of our existence," he muttered to himself as he reached down and closed her eyes.

⚜

Sydes was awake. A quick glance around the room and he knew, not only where he was, but how he had gotten there. He found his lack of confusion about all these facts disturbing. Then, he noticed the earphones and the little black box. He threw both to the floor. The wisp of smoke curling out of the box held his attention for only a few seconds.

"Some kind of damn mind control gadget," he muttered to himself.

Mind control was not something that Sydes could tolerate. Information and thought control was OK. He appreciated the facts the head radio had provided. What really pissed him off was that he felt good about it.

Not built to pay much attention to what he thought, in words or pictures, Sydes was primarily concerned with what he felt, and how those feelings drove his actions. For Sydes, feelings, thoughts and actions were, in truth, indistinguishable. To think was to feel and to feel was to do. This homogenization of emotion, thought and action lay at the foundation of his incredible reaction time and skill as a pilot. An archetypal warrior, Sydes was his passions.

Sydes decided he'd really like to find the son of a bitch who built that thing, and, depending on what he saw in the guy, either wring his neck or recommend some changes. It was more likely to be the former than the latter. Of course, it was nice to be alive, but that just amounted to the Doc doing his job, just like Sydes' job was killing the enemy, any enemy.

He slowly got to his feet and looked the room over more carefully. It was a CC installation and a commander's quarters at that. Book and music discs were racked everywhere. It was mostly old stuff, Da Vinci, Shakespeare, Kant, Mozart and Beethoven, an odd collection for a military commander. He considered this observation only briefly. It was time to get out of there and back up to speed on the here and now.

Walking toward the compartment door, every muscle tensed as it slid open, Sydes felt his body preparing for action. Flickering light framed the doorway as agonizing moans rushed with the gush of air through the portals. He instantly recognized a CC uniform surrounding the form of a large man. Sydes reflexively drew his sidearm.

Slowly raising his open palms, the Commander stared at the ace pilot, but said nothing as the compartment door automatically closed behind him.

Weapon in hand, Sydes' attention was focused on the Commander's holstered sidearm.

Tapping his index finger and thumb together, the Commander gingerly used this grasp to pull his sidearm from the holster and drop it to the floor. Without taking his gaze from Sydes', Tutunji kicked the pistol along the floor toward the newly awakened pilot.

Sydes slowly replaced his weapon in its holster and then stared at the Commander for a long moment.

"So, how did it come out?" Sydes asked.

"I engaged the enemy and lost my entire squadron, plus the reserves. We used nukes, just as you did, but we couldn't get a stern on advantage. I'd estimate we took out about one third of their ships," the Commander responded.

Studying Sydes as he completed his report, the Commander realized that the fighter ace, alive and awake, was exactly as he had imagined him lean, intense and with the cold steady look of a hunter in his eyes.

The Commander glanced down at his sidearm that still lay at Sydes' feet before allowing his gaze to return to Sydes' face.

Without taking his eyes off the Commander, Sydes reached down and returned the weapon to its owner.

From the expression on Sydes' face, he clearly heard the furor in the passageway. The Commander knew the recovering pilot would want to know the why's and wherefore's.

"The shock wave from the nukes took out ninety percent of my station. The PP auxiliary station sent over medics, techs, supplies and half a strike wing," the Commander said with matter of fact finality.

"I didn't think the suits could think beyond their profit margins," Sydes said wryly.

Sydes resumed his quiet stance. The lack of any movement in his eyes told the Commander the fighter ace had said all that he was going to for now.

"As soon as I can find the PP strike wing leader, I'll let him know that you're awake. I'll also arrange for an identity card so you can access the station's transubstantiator units ... and find your way around the bar," the Commander said as he started for the compartment door.

"By the way, thanks ... I know you had more to do than save my ass," Sydes said as the door to the compartment slid open.

"Make yourself at home here until you get your bearings," the Commander replied and disappeared into the passageway.

Staring for a moment at the closed compartment door, Sydes moved deliberately to the Commander's cabin viewscreen. Under his touch, it sprang to life. A few key strokes summoned the coordinates he knew would have been programmed into the unit. The touch pad brought the screen to bear on an empty frame of space marked now only by bits of wreckage where once his home station had maintained its orbit.

In his eyes, that emptiness was once again filled with hundreds of welcoming porthole lights, the sound of laughter, the sting of good whiskey, and the liquid grace of beautiful women. There, upon the black screen of space, were the open faces of comrades whose battles now raged beyond this time and place waving him over to a table. Among the debris floated hundreds of stories, good-natured rivalries, and deep wells of trust. Now, all those people and the memories they had created were scattered into insensate atoms wandering cold and alone in the darkness.

He had never experienced loss of this magnitude, nor had he anticipated that it would bring with it a pain that cut so cleanly through his tough exterior. He had lost friends before. He had sent many men to their deaths in battle, but that was the price of his profession. Everything, and more importantly everyone who had made up a universe in which he could feel pride in his ship's name, 'Solo', was gone. 'Solo' no longer carried with it the deep pride of being the best for his comrades. Now, for the first time, the word simply meant what it said, alone.

Having earned the title 'lone wolf' early in life, Sydes had never realized that the term had no meaning unless there was a pack to which that detached animal was somehow related. Now, the pack he had run with for the past fifteen years was gone. Dropped into another predator's territory, he was on unfamiliar hunting grounds. He let the screen go blank, realizing in that moment he had become what he had always secretly feared, but never admitted to himself, a solitary hunter thrust into a tribe with which he had no history. The lone wolf was truly alone, an outsider.

Chapter 5

Rumor had it that Nicholas Cabot was over six hundred years old. Not even his physicians knew his age with any certainty as he had destroyed all evidence of his birth. Tall and lean with just a bit of gray at the temples, he looked to be in his early forties. One of his closest associates, a trusted personal physician knew Cabot was over five hundred. However, even the best medical scanner couldn't read beyond that marker for lack of a cohort of individuals older than four hundred years. Cabot was the oldest human being the planet had ever housed, certain biblically referenced characters notwithstanding.

A solitary man whose destiny was directed by a vision of absolute personal dominion, Cabot had never maintained any romantic affiliations beyond a few months or spawned any heirs over the centuries. It was said of him that he could be leveraged by neither passion, nor progeny. An only child, he would be the last in line of one of the oldest and wealthiest families in the American continent's political-oligarchical dynastic constellation.

Cabot's longevity stemmed in no small proportion from his enormous wealth and political power. At twenty-four he became sole heir to his family's enormous fortune following the death of both of his parents in a hopper crash. Whisperings suggested that the crash occurred under suspicious circumstances, but no formal charges were ever lodged.

After his parents demise, he used the family resources to purchase influence in the halls of power of several governments and multinational corporations. He showed a particular interest in human physiology and acquired a controlling interest in a variety of medical research companies. However, his rise as the single preeminent power in the world economy during the decades following his parents' death principally derived from the tendency of those who opposed him to die of 'natural causes.'

Cabot had rapidly ascended to the post of chairman of the U.N. security directorate. He held that position for the next three hundred years. In that same time, he survived over one hundred well executed assassination attempts. This invulnerability alone had earned him the title 'the ole Nick.' A title, no one understandably ever used to his face. Enormous stock holdings in each and every Natcorps, coupled with strategic liaisons with several members of boards of directors, placed him at liberty to unilaterally exercise his will at any time. Perhaps of greater importance, the compendium of misdemeanors he had assembled on every significant player in the world market allowed him to convince his opponents, with a well placed word or the contents of a compromising videodisk, to back down. Cabot viewed his huge spy networks, that supplied these leverage commodities as a venture capital investment that paid dividends on a daily basis.

A man of legendary privacy, Cabot appeared before the general public only during the yearly videocast of the final match of the three dimensional chess tournament he underwrote. He had revived and refined the mid-twentieth century game and always played the winner of the world wide competitions he sponsored. In over three hundred matches, he had never been bested. As secretive and conniving as he was reputed to be, his closest associates knew that the matches were fair. He was quite simply the game's master. As a consolation prize the remaining finalist was admitted to Cabot's personal strategic planning division. Needless to say, the competition to lose to the master was fierce.

Three dimensional chess represented more than a competitive entertainment for Cabot. It's multiple levels, complex strategies and vertical action stacking, suggested a food chain presenting opportunities for predation from both above and below. For Cabot, the game embodied the Darwinian tenet that the strong prey on the weak. Assigning this belief no moral significance, he simply accepted it as a foundational fact of living systems. Cabot, perhaps more than any other human being who had come before him, was the incarnation of survival of the fittest. He assured his personal survival, often at the expense of others, by becoming a corporation unto himself. He maintained his own cohort of the best scientific minds, a vast army of strategic planners, and most importantly a truly formidable security force.

Inasmuch as the value of his person greatly exceeded the value of his holdings, Cabot took extraordinary steps to ensure his individual safety. The armaments division of PP Natcorp, which ranked as the most technologically sophisticated collection of corporate brain power on the planet, suspected that Cabot's people had engineered an individual shielding grid for his personal use. 'The Ole Nick' possessed, what for centuries had eluded the best minds of the species, a personal velocity-modulated-snap-field. It constantly enveloped the wearer with an impenetrable force field that created no interference with physical functioning at the cellular level. The intensity of the field changed instantly relative to the velocity and magnitude of any attempt to penetrate it. In a word, it made Cabot invulnerable.

Cabot fully appreciated that a constant flow of information about every aspect of the world in which he lived was the most reliable form of life insurance. He paid the premiums on that policy by maintaining and expanding the flow of information that assured it. No more colossal understatement could be imagined than to note that Nicholas Cabot had an information addiction. He continually upgraded his computer complex, located deep within the Ural mountains to that end. His strategic planning division provided a steady stream of new cognitive models for the computer, while his engineering division regularly supplied cutting edge hardware technologies to this information processing complex. A continuous flow of intelligence supplied by a covert electronic surveillance network that ignored corporate and personal boundaries, kept Cabot apprised of everything worth knowing.

Cabot maintained constant contact with the data cruncher buried deep in the Ural mountains through a mastoid transceiver implant. The transceiver allowed him to move freely between his thoughts and the computer's analytic modes and boundless data storage capacity. Nearly two centuries ago, he had genetically enhanced his immediate memory via a processes called 'catch categorization.' A relatively small change in tissue allowed him to interface with the multiple engram driven computer complex at any level.

The computer complex functioned more like a living organism than the term 'computer' suggested. Fashioned from the electronic analogues of brain patterns and structures, it could easily interface with Cabot's cerebral cortex. The engrams and cerebral structures that served the computer complex had been tissue donations from some of the most brilliant minds ever to have graced the planet over the last three centuries. Donations had been inadvertent, with tissues collected from the cerebral giants postmortem by Cabot's agents. Translated from physiologic structures to electronic algorithms, the thinking styles of these Titans of intellectual accomplishment had become permanent fixtures in Cabot's thinking machine, sequestered, in its own cavern below tons of granite. Any momentary insight experienced by Cabot instantly brought the enormous resources of the computer on line. The complex provided him with a stream of carefully analyzed permutations and instantaneously derived insights flowing from historical and contemporary analogues. Cabot had the closest thing to a global awareness of people and events as technologically possible.

Control was Cabot's watchword. He craved control over the lives of others. He also coveted territory. He was the largest single land holder on the planet. His well defined and impenetrably shielded reserves scattered all over the globe, represented almost every ecological niche the planet had to offer. Carefully selected 'native' populations lived within heavily shielded domains.

Here, Cabot conducted 'sociological experiments' focused on new forms of political control that circumvented the individual's dissatisfaction with being dominated. These reserves also served as large paleontological- genetic laboratories wherein extinct species of flora and fauna were cloned into existence and evaluated for their possible 'usefulness' relative to his current and future corporate goals.

Regardless of his enormous power, practical immortality and invulnerability, fear drove Cabot's daily ruminations. If 'the Ole Nick' was the personification of the strong preying on the weak, then he also embodied 'savvy' or what he preferred to call 'equal and opposite biological reasoning competence.' His incredibly long life, supplemented by the sum of human knowledge resident in his auxiliary brain in the Urals, allowed him to clearly see that for every Ying there was a Yang. He realized that on a planetary scale, if not a cosmic one, every living organism, by simple virtue of its existence, summoned into being a living counter force. This fundamental realization accentuated his fear.

Rightly casting himself as the avatar of predation, then, according to his own equal and opposite law of living systems, those upon whom he preyed must have some competence, equal to his own, that he didn't possess. This meant quite simply that he was vulnerable in some unknown manner. Cabot became obsessed with these human prey whom he named the 'meek.' True to his dictum of equal and opposite biological competence, he was intent upon discovering the power or capacity of the meek that was comparable to his own, and therefore, dangerous. When Forrester's research first came to Cabot's attention, it's basic framework appeared to provide a way of further elucidating the predator-prey relationship among human beings.

Cabot was renowned for never accepting anything as axiomatic, with the possible exception of his own edicts. His centuries of living had taught him that first principles and governing dynamics, as useful as they were as beginning points, could transfigure over time into sisyphean obstacles that thwarted creative insights. In this acknowledgment rested his principle fear, namely, that his obvious and sustained success in living out the predacious dictum blinded him to a more inclusive, and therefore more powerful, paradigm at the center of which stood the prey. The possibility of an as yet unknown competence intrinsic to the 'meek,' made them something more than the pejorative term 'prey' suggested. That idea had haunted Cabot for more than a century.

Like most men who had wrested the power of the many unto himself and possessed the grim determination to keep it, Cabot had never before experienced fear of this magnitude. This new terror resisted instant translation into an angry resolution to remove whatever impediment stood in the way of his desires' realization. For a long time now, the impatient angst instilled by the meek had been astride his shoulders. He couldn't buck it off. He had to know if the prey were powerful in some way he could not foresee, and, therefore, could not prepare to effectively counter and eventually subdue.

Hence, Forrester's research spurred Cabot's interest. The neuropsychologist's longitudinal study revealed a way to find the meek in the human population using a straightforward scanning procedure. The 'Ole Nick' had knowingly allowed PP genetics' division to do his foot work for him. Then, he had covertly appropriated Forrester's original research findings. Commissioning his scientific arm to produce neuropsychological scanners of the highest quality in accordance with Forrester's actuarials, Cabot laid the groundwork to finally set his fears to rest.

Feigning an expression of surprise and excitement when the PP board member presented Forrester's configuration sorting scanner for sale to the United Nation's board at large, Cabot said nothing. He would not be among the buyers. He had an unerring eye for when the information already in his hands was worth more than the dollars it could pull away from PP Natcorp into his own coffers.

The intelligence arm of Cabot's vast corporate empire had been busy for a long time gathering everything Forrester had written, whether or not it was germane to his neuropsychological research. Cabot knew Forrester's configuration. He was probably more aware of the life vector formed by Forrester's habits and quirks than Forrester's own rigorous introspection could conjure. He knew that Forrester had revealed the key to his research paradigm to save a friend's life. Apart from this single instance, Forrester had made no reference to his research for twenty five years. Cabot didn't know 'why.' A piece of the Forrester puzzle was missing, and Cabot knew it.

With Cabot's computer driven access to the information and near methuselahian life span, he had a perspective on Forrester's research which was broader and more detailed than Forrester could have mustered at any given point in his comparatively brief sojourn on the planet. Cabot had succeeded in replicating Forrester's research, with a wide variety of carefully selected samples, several times over the decades since he had appropriated it. His initial interest centered on discovering if the ratio of predators to prey in the human population had remained the same since Forrester completed his inaugural research effort.

A half century ago, in his original research cohort, Forrester noted fifty one percent of the human population exercised predator-like dominion over their fellows at a genetic level. Cabot's commissioning of a complete replication of Forrester's research once every ten years for the past half century demonstrated Cabot's investment in having his questions answered. Data analysis repeatedly showed a dramatically progressive increase in the proportion of the population that fell in the genetically driven need for dominance range.

The most recent figures, now almost five years old, revealed a rise in the predaciously driven component of the population from fifty-one to seventy three percent. Cabot's band of competitively selected genetic neuropsychologists joked that it was a simple racial purging of the timid and sedentary neanderthal strands nascent in the gene pool. Others among them of a more classical bent cited the findings as evidence of nature's final liquidation of the 'hobbits.'

Rather than amusing, Cabot found the genetic-behavioral vector frightening. The proportion of individuals in the population with the predatory instincts, namely those drives Cabot had refined to their ultimate perfection over centuries, was increasing. It reflected an unacceptably irresistible and covert tidal force in the human genome, that was neither in his ken nor control.

Utilizing a series of untraceable dummy corporations, he bought up a sizable chunk of western Canada, displacing innumerable local populations in the process. This land mass represented his largest single territorial reserve. Applying his considerable corporate resources, he restored the region to its pristine character. His many tentacled corporate entities purified the lakes, reforested the mountains and removed every shred of evidence that human beings had ever dwelt there. Cabot systematically prepared to investigate the vanishing prey component of the human population. To the tiniest detail, he want to know whether his suspicions regarding a hidden strength intrinsic to the meek could be confirmed. Once he knew the presumed strengths of the meek, he planned to eviscerate both their strengths and his own fears.

In the largest single covert operation his corporate conglomerate had ever mounted, hundreds of neuropsychological technicians fanned out across the globe. 'Forrester scanners' in hand. He commissioned them to find the prey in the human species. Turning the planet upside down looking for the meek, or 'dominance deficient' as Forrester had labeled them, they successfully located the objects of Cabot's obsession. They found seven hundred and fifty million of the best and brightest of the meek among a world population totaling more than nine billion human beings.

With all preparations duly made, Cabot prepared to begin the most significant and far-reaching enterprise of a career that had stretched over half a millennium. At the heart of this research effort rested Cabot's hope that he could find answers that would make his dominion over his fellows absolute.

꧁❖꧂

Sitting at the head of a large table shaped rather like an upside down question mark, his chair at the dot, Cabot manifested an imperial presence. Gathered around the half circle of the question mark were the men and women representing his inner circle of senior neuropsychologists, mathematical modelers and geneticists. A hologram illustrating the findings from the survey of the meek by global region rotated in suspension above them. At the apex of the hologram, a continuous read-out cycled through analyses of the data based on a variety of mathematical models.

Unlike the matter of fact mask he usually displayed, Cabot wore a concerned expression as he surveyed the holographic representation of his data gathering enterprise. Then, with a look that functioned like a gun muzzle targeting their heads, he directed his attention to each member of his assembled scientific team in turn. His aim came to rest on his chief neuropsychologist, Doctor Philip Lawless, who also doubled as a behavioral geneticist.

"We're sure of the genetics on this?" Cabot asked.

"Yes sir. These numbers represent a survey completed just last week. We used the latest generation of cloning grade medical scanners with built in continuous self-diagnostic programs to avoid any misreads," Doctor Lawless replied.

"So ..." Cabot said, directing his attention to the rotating hologram. "I'm to believe that in the last five years the dominance deficient gene pool in the world's population has dropped from twenty-seven to about thirteen percent?"

No one with the intellectual resources and political sagacity to have achieved a seat at this table would respond to what was in all likelihood a rhetorical question. A silence rivaling that of an ancient tomb shrouded the room. Cabot, lost in thought, continued to stare at the hologram while his staff practiced the prudence that guaranteed their executive status.

"OK, Phil, give us a background briefing on Forrester's assortative mating findings," Cabot said and turned to Doctor Lawless.

"Forrester found in his original survey of the general population that partners in eighty percent of the first matings showed a significant dominance need discrepancy. This was principally evident in a consistent tendency among the dominance driven to marry the dominance deficient, the meek. This finding held true whether the males or females had the higher dominance ranking, although in most cases the female demonstrated an intrinsically higher dominance rank. In any mated couple selected at random, the dominance need deficient individual typically selected a mate with stronger dominance needs.

The current sample, taken exclusively from among mated pairs in the dominance deficient population, shows the dominance deficient wed one another. In short, Sir, the meek marry the meek. This development appears wholly at odds with Doctor Forrester's assortative mating model," Dr. Lawless paused before continuing.

An almost imperceptible shift in Cabot's posture caught Doctor Lawless' attention. He immediately terminated his presentation.

"So you're saying that the meek are mating with each other?" Cabot's asked, his tone's had an edge to it.

Leaning back in his chair, Cabot seemed lost in thought for a moment. In a process no one could see, Cabot, through his mastoid implant, consulted his computer juggernaut thousands of miles away, deep within the Ural range.

"Forrester predicts the dominance deficient mating with each other, only at a level of twenty percent, or less in first marriages. These figures suggest that meek to meek matings are occurring more than eighty percent of the time, which is twice the rate even for second marriages," Cabot said, raising his eyes to Phil.

"Yes, sir. The scattergram analysis shows that members of the meek group travel great distances to locate their prospective mates. These excursions have no other work or recreational purpose. Such trips seem directed solely to purpose of finding a spouse. Once they have located a mate and married, these couples tend to take up residence together in communities that are exclusively populated by other dominance deficient mated pairs. This finding represents a significant change in the meeks' behavior. It is altogether without precedent in Forrester's original research," Phil replied.

Doctor Lawless or as Cabot called him, 'Phil' read nonverbal behavior well enough to recognize that despite Cabot's level of control over his facial expression, he was not pleased.

Interlacing his fingers, Cabot leaned back in his chair. His demeanor and extended silence indicated an episode of intense contemplation.

"It follows, then, from these findings that the dominance driven majority in the population have to be mating almost exclusively with one another, yes?" Cabot asked, turning to Phil.

"Yes, sir, just as the Forrester model predicts. Among the population of individuals who have overwhelming needs for dominance, those with comparatively lower dominance needs mate with those whose needs for dominion are slightly stronger. Among the dominance driven, a female with a rank of one hundred will typically be attracted to a male with a rank of ninety," Phil concurred.

"And the meek?" Cabot asked.

"The Forrester model is just as descriptive of matings among the meek, whose needs for dominance are negligible. For example, if a female among the meek has a dominance need ranking of two, she is likely to be attracted to a male with a dominance need rank of one. It's the same mating dynamic among the meek, just racheted down to the lowest conceivable level of dominance drive in the human population, " Phil replied.

"Just how long, will it take before we have two entirely different species of homo sapiens on this planet?" Cabot snapped as he leaned forward in his chair.

Jerry, the genetic modeler who was known more for his surpassing brilliance than his political acumen spoke without being called on.

"If the dominance deficient group remains part of the general population, then, at most ten generations."

"And if we separate them out?" Cabot asked, pointedly.

No one at the table, save Cabot, had considered this contingency. Expressions on the faces of the staff as they conferred with one another clearly indicated that they now fully appreciated the magnitude of what Cabot had in mind. Hand held multiplex computers came out of pockets everywhere. In a few moments some agreement seemed to have been reached among them.

"Sir …" Jerry began. "we can't be entirely sure, but Phil and I believe that a range of certainty between one and three generations would capture the emergence among the dominance deficient of a species very different from what we have defined as homo sapiens in the past. This projection is based on the total isolation of the dominance deficient, the meek, from the general population, thereby assuring only matings within their ranks."

To someone with acutely sensitive hearing, the room would have seemed quieter. Only Cabot was breathing. Leaning back in his chair, he was clearly thinking something through, but he was also enjoying the developing anoxia of his executive staff.

"Well … that works for me," Cabot said as he came to his feet.

An imperceptible joint exhalation among the staff greeted Cabot's pronouncement. Suddenly, they felt free to move in their seats for the first time since Cabot posed his question.

"Thank you gentlemen," Cabot remarked.

Then, the aged corporate monarch exited the staffing room, his personal shield flickering momentarily as he stepped through what appeared to be a solid wall near the head of the table.

Immediate to their boss' departure, the staff surged to its feet feverishly exchanging views. Someone punched up the minibar. Every member of

Cabot's brain trust tossed down a shot of whatever came to hand.

Jerry , his characteristic hyperkinetic demeanor released with Cabot's disappearance, first raised the obvious question.

"Holy mother of God, what the hell do you think he's got in mind?"

Phil, whose seniority derived not only from the fact that he was two hundred years older than everyone else, but also from his status as the only three dimensional chess championship finalist in the group, was the first to respond to Jerry's frenetic outburst.

"It's a two and two make four thing, Jerry. Nick bought up most of western Canada years ago. Guess who's gonna live there?"

"Ah hell, not the whole meek cohort!" Jerry responded with his usual 'scientific detachment.'

"No, my bet would be only about two hundred and fifty thousand of the best and brightest couples we've found. Using only a portion of the meek we've located would insure a sparsely populated region with lots of unspoiled and uninhabited natural areas. The demographics and attitudinal surveys of the dominance deficient sample suggest they like that," Phil replied.

Josh, the population control guru finished his vodka before chiming in.

"I'll go along with Phil on that. Using only use the brightest couples with the best genetics gives us the best shot at a second generation that breeds true. If I know Cabot, the Canadian reserve will have a hard shield grid, no one in and no one out to ensure a closed breeding sample."

Phil smiled and nodded.

The only bench trained geneticist in the group, Chandra, who had been quietly listening to the exchanges among her colleagues, finally spoke.

"There are bound to be some recessive manifestations of predatory dominance need among the meeks' first generation offspring, maybe even more in the second generation. I don't see how this whole thing will work. The predatory momentum of the human species represents an irresistible force of billions of years of genetic inertia."

Taking one step back from the group, something everyone noticed, Phil's silence seemed to pervade the room. Like Cabot, he appeared to be perpetually in his early forties. Now, quite suddenly, he appeared weighed down by centuries of grim reality. As he lifted his gaze from the floor, all eyes turned to Phil.

"I've been through this with Nick before when he was trying to breed perfect corporate assassins. Among the children of the meek, there'll be, well, accidents, diseases, terminal conditions, still births, God knows. No child will reach puberty with anything beyond minimal dominance needs in any generation, first, second or third. Nick is nothing, if not thorough ... very thorough ..." Phil said his words trailing away.

No one, not even Jerry, had anything more to say. Almost simultaneously, they set down their glasses and filed out of the dark silence that suddenly pervaded the conference room.

⚔❖⚔

Phil looked eastward. The early morning light swept away the last patches of darkness from the eastern Colorado plains. Phil always rose with the sun. He derived a nearly spiritual satisfaction from watching the light dispel the darkness despite his knowledge of the astrophysics of the event. Morning was his memory time. Phil wasn't much for reminiscence, except in this brief interval immediately after he awoke. He understood the hypnopompic mechanisms that governed this transition from sleep to complete wakefulness and used these moments to look back. As a full left hemispheric processor, he knew the interval of recall wouldn't last long. In less than twenty minutes, his dominant left hemisphere would snap him face front into the future until he fell once again into the stupor of sleep that night.

He must have dreamed about that fateful meeting with Cabot and his inner circle four years ago. He awakened with it still stuck in the revolving door of his brain. Cabot had done exactly what Phil had predicted, but with a speed that defied belief. In less than a month, he had moved two hundred and fifty thousand couples representing the 'best and brightest' among the dominance deficient population into his western Canadian reserve. Each couple received a parcel of one thousand acres and a wholly self-contained home built to their specifications. Small towns or service centers as Cabot preferred to call them, were already in place. Antigrav hoppers with homing programs made roads unnecessary as any individual could connect with any other in minutes.

The reserve was beautiful, filled with crystal clear rock bound lakes, verdant meadows and seemingly endless expanses of evergreen forest. Phil liked it there, but then he should have; after all, the area had been selected to appeal to the left hemispherically predisposed. Crafted to Forrester's descriptive specifications and tailored for those with little to no drive for dominance, it was tinted in cool, tranquil hues of green and blue.

Phil's own property in Colorado, at nearly nine thousand feet, afforded him a panoramic view of the expanse of the Rocky mountains. In particular Long's peak. Evergreens and deciduous forest covered the foothills. Occasionally residential communities, punctuated the plain; Colorado had been transformed into a Grimm fairy tale version of the black forest with the development of the satellite based water witcher and the tunneling laser well driller.

Like one of the left brained 'meek' he monitored, Phil had created his own reserve here in the mountains long before he knew of Forrester's research. Left hemispheric processors, like Phil, retained the tastes of their tree dwelling simian progenitors. As denizens of the high canopy, Lefts enjoy the high vistas afford by the trees, as well as, the protection provided by being enclosed within a living community of plants. Hiding in the trees, with lots of opportunities to foresee, withdraw from, or escape danger, made cautious vigilance an asset. Information, more often gathered by listening rather than looking, coupled with planning and hiding as means of staying out of trouble, characterized the dominance deficient.

In sharp contrast, dominance driven right brainers liked the wide open spaces. Just as left brain meek represented the forest canopy tributary of the human family, so the right brain predators exemplified the characteristics of the savannah roaming branch of the human evolutionary line. On the open plains, visual attentiveness and judgment, dominance , aggression, and tribal solidarity became essential genetic features for the clan's survival to be assured. Right brained progenitors are about confrontation to the same degree that Lefts are about planful avoidance of conflict.

For Phil, his left hemispheric Eden provided a sanctuary wherein he pretended to hide from Cabot's right hemispheric horrors. A pretense of seclusion was ineffective as Phil could not escape the realization that he had been entirely and knowingly complicit in all of those abominations. To be left hemispheric in perception and processing was to know that all justifications were hollow and all rationalizations were lies. Without the right hemispheric drive to dominance to fuel them, all of these species of self-deception were transparent intellectualizations. Yet, intellectualization provided Phil's only ego supportive buoy in this troubling sea of reality. True to his neuropsychological configuration, he applied that defense mechanism now. Somehow, Cabot's great experiment would benefit mankind, Phil mused. This intellectual deceit crumbled before his certain knowledge that Cabot's singular motivation was maintaining and acquiring more dominion over his fellow creatures. Perhaps the momentum inherent in a billion years of evolution would prove more powerful than Cabot's feeble machinations. Phil hoped that, regardless of Cabot's motives, nature might just spit in his eye. Like all intellectualizations, these passionless ideas were covert internal events that counted for little next to the the right brain juggernaut of definitive action in the real world.

His thoughts mixing amusement with disappointment, Phil considered this as elegant an artifice of intellectualization as ever he had witnessed pass through his cranium. However, this moment of shallow self-assurance, purchased at the cost of emotional misdirection, died a quick death. In its place, crowding out all of Phil's idle and self-serving internal chatter, came a real time vision of the ongoing slaughter of the reserve's innocents.

Chandra had developed an algorithm for the medical scanners that supplied genetic cutting scores for dominance deficiency. Each newborn was scanned before being bundled for presentation to the happy parents. If a hapless infant registered above the 'meek cutting score,' as it had come to be called, he or she would not see his or her first birthday.

Carefully distributed, the causes of these infanticides were spread across the population according to a computer model that Jerry had fashioned. The model took into account the perception of the parents, the incidence of various causes of infant mortality, the time of year, the constitutional history of the extended families and factored in the general character of current events as they were portrayed in the news media. All these facts were derived from hundreds of years of Cabot's 'sociological experiments' in his diverse reserves scattered across the globe.

Cabot applied the euphemism, 'enlightened prompting of evolutionary change' to this human culling operation, but Phil knew that it was wholesale murder. Four out of every ten perfectly healthy infants were butchered by a variety of so-called painless and compassionate means. Viral infections, still births, and constitutional anomalies were some of the most popular explanations. A few carefully engineered accidents were incorporate in order to satisfy the computer model's requirements. As Forrester's work had predicted, the incidence of dominance needs above acceptable levels was greater among female than male births. Accordingly losses to that gender were significantly greater. Regardless of the particulars, Phil knew that the daily murders proceeded with every revolution of the planet.

Having read Forrester's personality profile many times in the past, Phil knew that this meticulous neuropsychological researcher had a tendency to appropriate guilt for his own actions and the ramifications of his research that surpassed all rational criteria. Forrester was blessed in his blindness to the great darkness cast by Cabot's actions. Whoever said ignorance was bliss had a firm grasp on the truth! If Cabot was guaranteed a position of prominence in the eugenics murder's hall of fame, then Forrester's unwillingness to utterly destroy his work, or his lack of confidence in its power, would land him in a Nuremburgesque prisoner's dock along with Phil.

Now, according to the daily broadcasts, someone else had joined Cabot in the task of culling the human race. Pictures of the bloody orange ships displacing humanity in favor of their own kind filled the news media. Neither Phil nor anyone else, had ever seen the pilots of these harbingers of death. However, Phil knew that they had a lot in common with the species they killed. They simply cleared the way for an expansion of their race --- 'lebensraum.'

With the supreme assurance supplied by the only source in the universe powerful enough to fuel it, the manifest destiny of dominance, the alien invaders destroyed all in their path. They had losses to be sure. Often as much as a third of their forces were destroyed, but that was nothing compared to the ninety five percent casualites sustained by the corporate strike craft dispatched to oppose them.

If the mathematics of the invasion were evident to Phil, their clarity was actionably compelling for Cabot. Nick had precipitously transferred immediate supervision of the meek reserve to Phil before dropping out of sight.

Phil derived enormous personal satisfaction from the fact that he gathered as much intelligence by being trustworthy as Cabot did by using his complex network of spies and portfolio of leveraged threats . Phil knew exactly where Cabot was, what he was doing, and, more to the point, why he was doing it.

Phil knew that a small portion of humanity derived some intrinsic and irreducible fulfillment from trusting and being trusted. He also knew he was one of these, as were his informants. Indeed, individuals of this curious ilk wholly accounted for cohort of the meek. Quite simply, a dense population of men and women who felt that being trusted carried with it the obligation to be trustworthy populated the reserve. This simple, immutable characteristic of 'hopeful belief,' more than any other aspect of human behavior, consistently eluded the Ole Nick. For Cabot, trust was not a foundational quality of the human character. It simply greased the course of naive human interactions. This fact was pleasing to the pantheon of the gods of self service, whose chief deity was Cabot. For the Ole Nick, all those who trusted were but grist for his personal mills of profit and power.

Based on intelligence supplied by his informants, Phil knew Cabot was personally supervising the construction of an enormous vessel on the dark side of the moon. He had committed more than ninety percent of his incalculable fortune to its completion. The vessel would house upwards of a half a million people and sustain them for centuries. Cabot planned to get out. The size of the ship provided an unconscious testament to his dependency needs. Cabot required people to dominate. He needed to subjugate others to keep his own demons at bay.

Quite unexpectedly, Phil experienced a mini-epiphany. He didn't feel blessed. Instead, he felt stupid that he had not grasped the obvious earlier.

In the marginal notes accompanying his original research, Forrester indicated quite expressly that the fifty-one percent of the population committed to dominance and competition had a 'death wish' from which they were endlessly retreating along a long unbroken line,. Their need for distraction from this internal ogre was uncompromising. Holding this insatiable beast at bay required its keeper to constantly compete with others and emerge victorious. In its most extreme scenario facilitating the death of another verified the right of the victor to live.

An academic belief, fully supported by the business community, held that competitive interactions functioned as a bulwark against any individual's narcissistic self-deception. In short, most people felt they could do anything. Competition insured that only those who performance met the criterion would get the job. Forrester retorted that if this dynamic were treated as a demonstrated fact of human behavior, the mechanism clearly didn't work. Individuals who lost in any given competitive endeavor, the vast majority of persons in any such contest, inevitably found reasons outside of themselves for their failures. Even in the outrageously unlikely event that such contests were 'fair,' the inevitable outcome created one winner who felt overwhelmingly endorsed and ninety-nine losers who felt cheated.

Addressing the Darwinian argument that winners in such competitions represented the 'fittest,' Forrester noted simply that the fittest, whether individuals or cooperative teams, were no more or less than those with the most surpassing dominance drives. Turning on the axle of dominance precluded a species from accomplishing anything beyond the elevation of its most domineering members to the top of the pecking order. Although humanity regularly bewailed the psychopathic character of its leaders, mankind routinely elevated to absolute power those, so enthralled with conquest, they would dominate at any cost.

Among the dominance driven, striving was singularly directed to a daily verification of their right to live. However, an individual could realize this certification of entitlement to life only in the moment of triumph over their fellows. The reward came in the form of a cascade of the hormones of victory that provided unassailable proof of their right to live in the face of internal mechanisms naysaying that claim. Winning, a biochemically driven, ego enhancing, experience was reserved by definition, for an infinitesimally small proportion of the population. Forrester interpreted this state of affairs as suggesting that the bulk of the dominance driven individuals who now constituted the overwhelming majority of the human race survived only on the hope of besting their fellows. Cabot, the uncontested winner in this global contest, personified this dynamic, and Phil worked for him.

Phil's growing tension within was a familiar but foreboding feeling. It represented a unique vexation that always heralded an epiphany of a dark sort. In his mental foreground loomed the ship, built to carry more than half a million people in a centuries' long quest for a new world. The meek reserve, upwards of a quarter million couples with negligible dominance drives, all serving at Cabot's whim forever and ever formed the vision's background. Phil sat lost in thought for a long moment until the pressure in his head reminded him to take a breath.

Cabot was embarked on an undertaking that amounted to no less than the founding of a new civilization. His invulnerability assured by technology and his immortality vouched safe by medical science, he would become a dynasty of one ruling over people engineered by nature to submit and serve.

Looking over the peaks and deep ravines of the Rockies stretching out before him, Phil attempted to wrap his mind around the enormity of what he was helping Cabot accomplish. Even the everlasting hills couldn't hide him from the horror growing in his head. He had helped Nick establish a Fascist dynasty that would make all dictatorships in the historical record look like egalitarian communes. Phil felt the coils of this horror snuffing out the light in his intellectual sanctuary. Action was the only remedy.

Chapter 6

Sydes wasn't accustomed to this kind of attention. He had no sooner grabbed some mess, than he got word that the PP Natcorps' armaments engineers and strategic planners wanted him. The gradually fading voice of the 'mind radio' in his head had caught up with current events. He was needed. Sydes didn't like being needed, but there it was. As the only pilot to have survived a head on fire fight with the blood ships, as the denizens of the bars called them, he was the focal point. For the past ten years, indeed, since the age of fifteen when he was first honored as a premier pilot, PP Natcorp had promoted twice a year. They wanted him as supervising pilot for their fleet. They wanted him as commandant for their flight school. In short, they wanted him for administration. Sydes turned down every advancement without comment. For Sydes, there was no honor in ordering other men to their deaths. Administration was a job for old men whose days as warriors were frayed memories worn about the edges by reminiscence of past battles.

Threading his way through the throng in the bar, Commander Tutunji spotted Sydes, grabbed two Jack Daniel's doubles, walked to the fighter ace's table and sat down next to him. The Commander pushed one drink in Sydes' direction.

"Here they come … you ready for this?" Tutunji said, nodding toward the approaching suits.

"Nope," Sydes responded and killed the Jack in one gulp.

Reaching under the table, the Commander hauled up a burnt piece of metal emblazoned with the word 'Solo' and set it on the table.

"Just something my boys snagged when they picked you up. Thought you might like a reminder of who you are before the corporate crowd start working on your case," Tutunji said as he glanced off to his left.

Sydes glanced in the direction the Commander had indicated. A knot of well dressed corporate types picked their way through the pilots and working girls who packed the bar. He didn't have to ask. It was the PP Natcorp brain trust of engineers and strategic planners attempting to maintain decorum and group solidarity in the jostling crowd. One among them spied him. A moment later, and they arrived at the table.

A short, chunky member of the group with a heavy German accent spoke first.

"Kapitaen Sydes?" The little man asked.

The warrior ace looked the intruder up and down as though he were a prospective wrestling opponent.

"Yeah," Sydes responded.

"Doktor Eric Von Strohheim, head of the aerospace armaments group. We very much wish to speak with you," the diminutive doctor said.

Von Strohheim made a smart half bow that lacked only the sound of his heels clicking together to complete the Prussian stereotype. He had a goal oriented, factual linearity to his tone that seemed wholly consistent with both his profession and his surname.

Von Strohheim's entire entourage clustered about the table like a flock of pointy headed vultures waiting for the alpha bird to take the first bite out of the carcass.

"May we sit down, yes?" Von Stohheim asked.

The doctor's manner was exceedingly polite. but his nonverbal insistence made it clear that he was not prepared to take no for an answer.

Glancing over at the Commander, Sydes noticed that the old warrior was smiling again. Sydes shot him a frown.

"Yeah, sit already," Sydes responded.

Selecting a large table for mess had been one of Sydes' lucky choices. Even so, Von Strohheim's group hauled chairs from all over to find a seat at what was beginning to look like a student cram session at a beer hall in Heidelberg.

One lean young man attempted to brush the fragment of metal imprinted with 'Solo' from the table. The Commander's hand instantly clamped on top of the burnt shard.

Suddenly, all eyes focused on the Commander whose uniform clearly marked him as the only CC Natcorp presence at the table. The Commander's gaze remained unwaveringly focused on the brusque young member of Von Strohheim's entourage.

"It stays ,' Sydes said viewing the shard, and then added in a hard and un-yielding tone, "He stays" Casting his gaze on the Natcorp Commander," Sydes' adamantine gaze returned in its fixation on Von Strohheim.

"Yes, of course, Captain Sydes," Von Strohheim replied, nodding deferentially.

Sydes took note of the unwavering return of Von Stohheim's gaze. He thought that he might just like this little German scientist. There was no PP versus CC crap, just business. He respected that.

"I have long admired your skill, Kapitaen," Von Strohheim said, unrolling a glowing computer flatscreen.

Sydes made no response but continued to stare at the little Doctor.

Tutunji looked down at his own empty glass. Making a quick visual survey of the table, he waved a waitress over and ordered an assortment of bottles and glasses.

Sydes knew Von Strohheim only by reputation. In the past, the little wizard had cobbled together some gadgets for the 'Solo' to Sydes specifications. PP Natcorp considered Von Strohheim a genius and gave him a budget to match his reputation. It was generally known he had about as many scientific degrees as letters in his last name, but, as far as Sydes was concerned, all that mattered was Von Strohheim's gadgets worked.

"Kapitaen Sydes, we have a problem …" Von Stohheim said, briefly glancing at his antique pocket watch chain. "Our group has gone over the recordings from the long range docking cameras and even our best shields don't seem to retain integrity very long against the enemy's lasers within their effective range."

"Tell me about it," Sydes responded as he leaned back in his chair.

Appearing initially a bit perplexed, Von Strohheim's expression suddenly brightened.

"Nein, no, please, you will tell me," Von Strohheim replied.

Casting a sidewise glance at Sydes, the Commander recognized signs of fatigue in the wounded pilot.

"I think they have fusion propagating lasers. The kicker is I'm convinced that their shields won't hold against their own weapons," Sydes said as he shot down the rest of his drink.

Von Strohheim's face lit up like a kid who had found a friend on the block with the same chemistry set.

"Jah, this was my feeling too. We have many examples in our own history of weapons whose development surpassed our ability to defend against the destructive potential we had created. Perhaps, they are confronted with the same problem," Von Strohheim replied and downed a shot of apfel schnapps.

Leaning back in his chair, the Commander allowed just a trace of nearly paternal pride to cross his expression as he watched Sydes manage the scientific brass.

"I passed between two of their cruisers. Despite being an easy shot for alien gunners with their targeting precision, I didn't even draw a sputter from their laser turrets," Sydes continued.

"Jah, we see this too. Attacking their propulsion units, this was, jah, brilliant!" The little maestro said, his eyes riveted on Sydes.

"The fusion missiles were the only thing that gave them a bloody nose," Sydes said, a cold determination growing in his eyes.

Pouring another shot of Jack Daniel's, Sydes put it away and stared into the empty shot glass. For a moment, he saw the starry emptiness in the glass receptacle, the bodies of his brother pilots and drifting within it.

"I just got lucky ..." Sydes continued and turned to the the Commander. "This is the guy who did most of the work."

Startled by the sudden turn in the conversation, Commander Tutunji looked at Sydes with displeasure. He had expected to sit this one out. Damn that Sydes.

Von Strohheim quickly turned his attention to the Commander, anxiously awaiting a response.

It was the Commander's turn to kill his drink. Doing so, he pushed his glass aside and glowered at Sydes "We didn't have a lot of choice. Their first attack proved our lasers didn't work. After Sydes had a go at them I knew the alien ships wouldn't let us get in behind them twice," Tutunji said.

Retrieving his glass, the Commander filled it to the brim. He drank it down, and stared past Von Stohheim to a scene no one else at the table could see.

"My boys, damn ..., just kids, emptied their missile tubes into the alien formation. You know the rest. They took out about a third of those bloody ships, but I spent all their lives ... all their futures, to do it," Tutunji said and fell silent.

No one spoke for what seemed an eternity. Everyone's eyes remained on the Commander, who was now staring at the table as though reverently pausing at a grave.

"Well, now that we're all up to speed," It was the voice of one of the fast track suits from strategic planning.

All heads turned toward him, each face wearing an expression of disdain usually reserved for someone who had just defecated on the dinner table.

"This is a wholly unacceptable and entirely regrettable loss of men and ... and material," Von Stohheim said, jumping into the tense silence .

Shooting a reprimanding glance at the young strategic planner, Von Strohheim's voice supplied the muted and conciliatory tones that should have come from the insensitive young turk.

"Kapitaen Sydes. Commander. I want you to see this."

Von Strohheim pointed to the lighted display of his computer flatscreen rolled out on the table, touched a few icons and the screen sprang to life. Amidst finely drawn lines and color coding, there appeared a carefully executed schematic illustrating a huge spherical vessel with an immense hold.

"We have been building this ship for some time now. It is almost ready to launch. The bay can hold thirty strike craft. Will this be useful?" Von Strohheim asked, moving the screen closer to Sydes and the Commander.

Reaching out together, Sydes and the Commander pulled the screen closer and examined it in silence. The Commander looked at Sydes and nodded as though they had just completed a lengthy conversation and were in complete agreement.

"This was built to be a carrier ship?" Sydes asked.

Von Strohheim nodded with a measure of pride. However, as he examined the faces of Sydes and the Commander, his enthusiasm faded.

"Strike craft are useless against these bastards ..." Sydes continued. "... unless you're looking for cannon fodder."

Nodding in agreement, the Commander's memory was still awash with images of his lost fighter squadron.

"Tear out these receiving bay mounts. Then, fill the hold with screen generators, fusion missile stores and automated delivery chutes," Sydes said, his finger moving over the schematic.

"It needs fore and aft missile launchers ... and drop the laser arrays," the Commander chimed in.

Sydes leaned back, a look of satisfaction on his face, and nodded. He and the Commander had agreed without exchanging a word.

"The ship is nearly complete, we can't refit it just because you say so," the strategic planner opened his mouth again.

Displaying the commanding presence characteristic of the eighteenth century head of a Prussian household, Von Strohheim impaled the young man with a penetrating stare.

"Heinrich, you are excused. Geh!" Von Stohheim ordered.

The young man paused for a moment, looking as though he had been struck by a laser on stun.

"Geh, jetzt!" Von Strohheim demanded as he rose from his seat.

The young man sprang to his feet, and appearing somewhat unsteady in his gait, retreated from the table and headed toward the bar.

Tracking the young strategic planner with mechanical precision, Von Strohheim watched the corporate striver disappear into the noisy throng congregated at the bar.

"I hope you gentlemen will excuse this. He's very able but young and lacks a sense of time and place," Von Strohheim remarked as he fumbled with the Phi Beta Kappa key on his antique watch chain.

"Please continue," Von Strohheim said in pleading tones as he sat down.

The Commander placed his hand lightly on the fighter pilot's shoulder. Reluctantly, Sydes released the targeting focus of his gaze from the suit at the bar.

"Well Doc, I think you need to line that bay with independently functioning shield grid generators. You know, generators that produce completely autonomous, non-interlocking fields of force," Sydes remarked as he downed another shot.

Appearing a bit puzzled, Von Strohheim glanced down at the computer schematic of his baby. Then, wearing the same quizzical expression, back at Sydes.

"Like an onion, Doc, several layers of shields with the ship at the center," the Commander added.

A confused expression dissipating, Von Strohheim's face suddenly lit up like a mirror reflecting the sun.

"Ausgezeichnet. Brilliant. Yes, this can be done! We can drop in two more fusion reactors and triple the power output," Von Strohheim replied.

Now completely oblivious to his surroundings, Von Strohheim feverishly began making changes on the flat screen. His electronic stylus fairly flew over the glowing sheet, muted beeps sounding each time he applied the stylus to the schematic.

"Jah. We can automate alles. Everything but the weapons and flight control these will have to be separate, yes," Von Strohheim said and paused.

Looking up from his schematic, Von Strohheim's gaze encompassed the last fragment of Sydes ship resting on the table and its logo. The Doctor paused as he studied the word 'Solo' on the shard of burnt metal.

"Piloting the vessel … this will require two men," Von Strohheim added in a cautious tone. .

Sydes didn't like the little wizard's conclusion, but he knew the Doc was right. Every man Sydes had even half way trusted was dead, murdered by that idiot PP station Commander. He knew he was the only man who could fly this monstrosity. For that matter, he was only one crazy enough to go out in a ship that was a cross between a reactor facility and a missile launch pad. If the shield layers were compromised just once, well, there'd be a second sun in the solar system, at least, for an instant.

Sydes sat in stony silence for a moment, staring straight ahead, and not moving a muscle. He wanted to look at the Commander, but he didn't want anything in his expression to betray an implicit request for aid. He'd never asked a living soul for help, and he wasn't about to start now.

Returning to his flatscreen, Von Strohheim was again wholly immersed in the task before him. Oblivious to both the sights and sounds of the noisy bar, he scribbled and corrected entries on the schematic.

After what seemed like an eternity to Sydes, the Commander picked up the last burnt vestige of Sydes' fighter. Slowly withdrawing his belt dagger, Tutunji scratched 'Duo' above the scorched 'Solo' emblem.

Sydes felt himself exhale. Without looking at the Commander, Sydes cracked his shot glass on the table. Grasping a sizable shard of the broken glass, he scratched a crude 'X' over the 'Solo.'

The grating sound of glass on metal caused the little wizard to look up. The flicker of a smile hurried across his face as he took note of the change in logo. Then, almost immediately, Von Strohheim returned to his narrow world of technological miracles, rolled up the computer screen and downed one more schnapps. Rising quickly from the table, he appeared to have more than two hands as he gathered together stylus, computer screen and the scraps of his thoughts. In truth, Von Strohheim was, in that moment, a one man violation of Newtonian physics. While he was physically there at the table, most of him was already back at his ship.

Von Strohheim stepped away from the table. Pausing, he turned and grasping first Sydes and then the Commander's hand, he shook each vigorously.

"Mutiger kerle, tapfer, three days, es ist jah moglich."

Launching himself into the mass of patrons in the bar, his disciples in hot pursuit, the little maestro merged with the milling horde. Fragments of a lively conversation in German, barely audible above the establishment's hum of voices, was the only evidence of his passing through the crowd.

Sydes grabbed a bottle off the table. Glancing quickly after the Doctor and his entourage, he poured a generous portion of whiskey for the Commander and himself .

"So what the hell did he say?" Sydes asked as he raised his glass.

"I'm not entirely sure. Something like brave boys," the Commander responded with a smile.

"Yeah or suicidal idiots," Sydes replied chuckling.

Laughter was not something that Sydes had allowed himself since the death of his father nearly five years ago. It felt right somehow. Safe to do so. Almost like the old man sat across from him ready to go to the wall for his boy.

Sydes finished his drink and stared at the bar viewer, which was tuned to the black void of space that surrounded them. Von Strohheim had given himself only three days to refit the carrier. As far as Sydes could tell that was damn near impossible but if anyone could do it, that stumpy little Einstein would make it happen. As he looked at the Commander, Sydes could see it in the older man's face. A lot could happen in three days.

Commander Tutunji tapped his ear piece, listened for a moment, and came quickly to his feet.

"Understood,"Tutunji responded.

Turning to Sydes, the Commander nodded and the two men left the bar together.

⚶⬦⚶

The injured crowded the passageway, but Forrester and Arthur were making headway in treating those who had survived the holocaust. His ear caught by the cadence of a military gait, Forrester looked up and caught Sydes' eye as the fighter ace and Commander hurried by.

Glancing curiously at Forrester, Sydes watched as the medic turned back to an injured child. Pausing for only a moment, Sydes caught up with the Commander in quick time.

"Who was that?" Sydes asked the Commander.

"The guy who pieced you back together," the Commander replied without breaking stride.

Upon arriving at the receiving bay, managing the destruction that greeted them completely engrossed the Commander. Speaking rapidly into his headset, he fumbled with his worry beads with one hand and gestured emphatically with the other.

Swallowed in a view of what remained of the strike craft bay, Sydes came to a greater appreciation of the destruction the station had sustained. All around, shield grids created airtight, transparent walls where receiving bay bulkheads had once enclosed the station's defensive force. A convoy of large tractor shuttles gathered outside the transparent shield grids eased prefabricated bulkheads into place, forming walls to expand and repair the bay. The bay was not only being rebuilt, it was being enlarged. However, the prior destruction of the station made expansion a relatively easy task. Sydes couldn't be sure, but it looked like the augmented bay would house at least three times as many fighters as the station's usual complement. Suddenly, the Commander's voice interrupted Sydes' analysis of the furious construction effort.

"This is what I brought you here to see," the Commander said as he gestured toward the void.

There in the window of space beyond the lights and the tractor shuttles, Sydes saw first one, and then another, strike craft squadron easing into formation in front of the incomplete bay. There were at least one hundred ships. Floating side by side were corporate insignia never seen in the same mix except in battle. Here, PP strike craft lay next to CC, while MM and FF colors

❧ 107 ❧

were berthed peacefully together in space. A common threat now united so many old enemies.

"I thought you'd like to see your new fleet, Chief," the Commander said as he attempted to maintain a deadpan expression.

"What's this 'Chief' crap?" Sydes asked as he came nose to nose with the Commander.

His deadpan expression eroded by a convulsion of laughter, Commander Tutunji's dropped his worry beads to the deck.

"What the hell is so funny?" Sydes blurted out.

The Commander had difficulty regaining his composure.

"The U.N. board of directors … they've made you … chief pilot of … of the combined Natcorps' fleet," the Commander choked out.

"This is a joke, right?" Sydes asked, his face preparing a smile .

"No, no … that's what makes it so … funny," the Commander gasped.

Suddenly, Sydes got the point. The U.N., sons of bitches, had accomplished what PP Natcorp hadn't been able to shove down his throat for a decade. They'd made him a fucking administrator. Feeling as useless as the newest ad-mission to the old soldier's home, Sydes slowly reached down and retrieved Tutunji's worry beads from the deck.

The Commander wiped away some tears that had flowed during his con-vulsions of mirth and accepted the return of his worry beads.

"You were the only guy the security council could agree on to run this op-eration …" Then, drawing a deep breath, Tutunji added, "Don't worry, they're not going to put you behind a desk."

Sydes wasn't sure he believed that. The specter of unspecified responsi-bilities already haunted him filling his head with a dense fog that obscured the simple targeting alignments that made him a warrior. He had always been an individual player. Any 'leading' he did was only by reckless example. He couldn't do this.

"Hey, relax…it's a show and tell thing. They just want you to come up with some field strategies and help these pilots get a handle on how the enemy works their battle plan," the Commander said, his tone reassuring.

"Yeah, relax," Sydes muttered.

"They're all here to be refitted. Every fighter will get the new PP shield generators and auxiliary missile tubes," the Commander continued, pointing to the formation of strike craft.

"Right," Sydes replied.

Sydes still felt a little dazed. The situation was moving way too fast. He had grown up on a corporate chess board with the white and black pieces regularly shooting at one another. Now, all of a sudden, there were no more white and black pieces, just gray pieces of humanity arrayed against a red enemy on a board he had never seen before.

"Come on … there's a whole bunch of squadron flight leaders who want to meet you," the Commander said as he grabbed Sydes by the arm.

⋰⋰❖⋱⋱

Even with all the med-techs at their disposal, an endless stream of patients, and the hours of horror had drained Forrester's energy. The idea of working two or three consecutive shifts didn't make any logical sense, but the injured drove the schedule. As if by design, the medical supplies, the crowds of the harmed and the energies of the caretakers ran out simultaneously. All of the most serious cases had been stabilized. Those whose injuries surpassed the scope of medical science were free of pain. There was nothing more to do and rest sounded good. Like a period at the end of a some torturous sentence, word came down from PP Natcorp central that Forrester and Arthur were to be permanently stationed on what was left of the CC command base. The decision didn't make a lot of sense to Forrester and he said so.

"You ought to look out of a porthole every now and then," Arthur said, his tone chastising.

Hungry, and tired Forrester not up for one of Arthur's lectures extolling the merits of paying attention to the outside world from a holistic perspective.

"Yeah, so what's going on?" Forrester snapped.

"They're rebuilding the place, take a look," Arthur said as he pulled Forrester to a corridor porthole.

Illuminated by beacons floating in space, tractor shuttles aligned prefabricated living compartments along the ravaged skeleton of the CC station.

With a smirk Arthur, produced a compartment code card from his pocket.

"You must have friends in high places," Arthur remarked.

"Friends…" Forrester mumbled.

"This unit is hooked up and ready to go, let's take a look." Arthur said nudging Forrester. The two were off down the passageway.

Shuffling along, Forrester mustered just enough energy to notice hastily repaired scarring on the walls of the passageway. He could see where new construction met the remnants of the old, clearly evidenced by shiny, nondescript bulkheads with compartment accesses.

Arthur inspected compartment numbers as they went. Then, he stopped, checked the number on one particular door against the code card in his hand and inserted it. The door slid open to a warm, well lit executive suite with a immense space side viewer.

"Friends in high places, my ass. This is a division president's suite. I've seen them before," Arthur said, his eyes shining as he spotted a large well stocked wall bar next to a transubstantiator.

Forrester's eyes played over the compartment. He did not find such amenities particularly impressive. He liked the extra space, but the compartment's most endearing feature was the fact that it provided a secure sanctuary against the craziness of the outside world.

"Hey, maybe there's a cutie in the closet …" Arthur said as he walked to a side wall and slid back a door. "…nope, just a head. What a lay out. This is first class treatment. Hey, you're not one of Cabot's nancy boys are you Nate?"

Shrugging off the comment, Forrester made for and climbed into the sonic shower. Immediately setting the activator for attire, he felt a slight stirring of the air in the chamber as the sonic projectors activated. In moments, his uniform was clean. He peeled it off and enjoyed the body cycle that included a shave. Sometimes he missed the gurgle and splash of a water shower and the feel of the warm liquid on his skin, but this would do. The clean uniform felt good against his skin as he pulled it over his frame. He was hungry.

Busily sampling a little of every bottle of the 'good stuff' in the bar, Arthur would be engaged for some time.

Forrester retrieved a personal menu card from his pack as he prepared to withdraw from the horrors he had just witnessed by engaging in some gustatory nostalgia.

Spying the menu card, the entirety of Arthur's attention immediately riveted on Forrester. Arthur's gaze remained firmly fixed on his partner as Forrester inserted the card into the transubstantiator and made selections from the readout on the computer screen.

"Oh, hell, Nate, you're not gonna smell up the place with that Pennsylvania Dutch farm crap, are you?" He exclaimed, holding his nose in a mocking posture.

The answer to Arthur's question appeared on the transubstantiator vending tray; a steaming plate of hogmaw, red beet eggs and a slice of shoo-fly pie. A treasure trove of comfort food. I must be both exhausted and depressed to require this kind of regressive mini-vacation, Forrester thought to himself.

Staring at him aghast, Arthur's expression suggested someone observing a cannibalistic version of a church supper. He seemed momentarily stunned.

"Shit, I can see I'm gonna have to drink a lot more," Arthur uttered in disgust.

Arthur quickly hauled down two more bottles and a glass and turned to leave the compartment, which he considered irredeemably contaminated by the vile vapors of Forrester's repast.

"I'll be back when the air purifiers clean up this toxic fog," Arthur cast over his shoulder as the compartment door closed behind him.

That was OK with Forrester. He planned to enjoy his little sojourn into an agrarian childhood, cold fall evenings, the damp odor of newly fallen leaves and a steaming plate of hogmaw that he couldn't finish. I guess my eyes got fixated in childhood while my appetite aged, he mused.

Depositing the tray and its contents into the assimilator chute, he sat down with a snifter of Grand Mariner. Now, he was ready to open the door to the horrors of the day's events.

Many maimed and dying children had been among those requiring help. Station designers had allotted additional shielding to the school section but not enough. Most of students' parents were presumed dead. Although no one appeared willing to tell the kids that their moms and dads wouldn't be picking them up, they all seemed to know. Little people with missing arms and legs littered the classroom complex. Appendages had been mercilessly cut away by the shearing force of the shock wave and lost to the freezing vacuum of space. So many arms and legs were now drifting in the void that could have been reattached with the tissue knitters, if only the tiny limbs could be found.

Constitutionally afflicted with survivor's guilt, Forrester reviewed his own medical history. He had been run down by a hopper, nearly died from a rare form of diphtheria, almost bleed out after a run in with broken glass, and had an arm torn off and reattached. Yet, here he was. He had witnessed the deaths of so many classmates in high school and college, boys and girls so much more able and charming than himself, all gone to dust. Accidents, diseases, war casualties, and death by their own hands, took their toll on those around him. Yet, for reasons he could not fathom, the angel of death inexplicably passed over his life.

All the station's children were alive in his mind in vivid detail. Their presence scattered in pieces all over the nursery and classroom floors waiting for the magic of medicine to turn back the clock of tragedy. To be sure, he and Arthur had saved some, but so many more could only be made comfortable as they slipped into a nap from which they would never awaken.

Dragging himself out of his chair, Forrester walked to the bar, refilled his snifter and sat down in front of the wide expanse of the viewer. Immense stars shining as mere pin points at unimaginable distances provided the only lights in the black expanse. For Forrester a scene such as this, uncluttered by the organic striving for survival, empty of want and desire, and unencumbered by the chimera of dominion was somehow clean. He knew what Arthur's response to this line of thinking would be, "In life some struggle is involved", he would intone with matter of fact finality. Forrester's part in this internal conversation was inelegantly simple. Bullshit! Life is struggle, period.

He dipped into his pocket with the fumbling desperation of a man grasping for a life preserver and extracted his scanner. He wanted to be certain he correctly remembered two entries toward the end of the document. Thumbing the scanner, he recalled the many times he had studied these entries. Like a poor student of Zen, he had yet to achieve enlightenment. In moments, the entries filled the screen. They were just as he recalled them, a continuing enigmatic indictment of his inability to see the forest for the trees.

> WORDS ARISE IN THE MIND OF MAN ONLY
> IN THE TWILIGHT OF THE DAY WHEREIN
> EDEN IS MORNING'S FIRST LIGHT. TO SWAY
> THE SOUL, THEY MAY HAVE POWER, BUT
> TOUCHING NOT THE BODY, THEY REMAIN
> UNREVEALED BY THE ACTIONS OF THE SOUL
> THAT DWELLS WITHIN.
>
> IT IS ONLY IN THE HEART OF THE HEARER
> THAT WORDS ARE QUICKENED TO ACTS.
> THE MESSAGE CALLS TO THE SPIRIT OF
> HE WHO HARKENS AND NONE ELSE.
>
> IN THE MORNING OF LIFE, FROM ONE
> COME MANY. IN THE NOONDAY, MANY
> BECOME ONE. AS THE DARKNESS OF DAY'S
> END GATHERS, ONE BECOMES TWO. FROM
> THIS BRANCHING SPRINGS A BOUGH OF
> THE SPIRIT, AND A LIMB OF THE FLESH. OF
> COMMON ROOT AND FLOWERING UNTO THE
> LIGHT, THEY GROW BY SEPARATE PATHS,
> BENDING FINALLY BACK UPON THEIR
> BEGINNINGS.

He felt like one of the Philistines confounded by a vexingly important riddle. However, this age supplied no Samson to unravel the sage saying. Even so, he'd sleep now, disappearing into the oblivion of that little snatch of death.

Sydes found himself seated next to the Commander at a large table in a brand new briefing room module. He counted eight flight leaders, two from each of the four Natcorps squadrons. All wore different uniforms. Sworn corporate enemies were now engaging in some surprisingly good-natured banter. Judging by the number of flight leaders at the table, the number of strike craft parked around the station must have risen to over two hundred.

Lost in his own personal analysis of the situation, Sydes tried to figure out the warning signs he had missed that landed him in this mess when the Commander nudged him.

"I'm gonna get this thing started ..." the Commander announced as he came to his feet. "... gentlemen, you all know Captain Sydes,"

Moving about restlessly in his seat, Sydes' only discernible response was some embarrassment he desperately tried to conceal.

"I'm Commander Tutunji. Welcome. We all know why we're here. We're taking a brief break from killing each other to blow the hell out of whoever is trying to wipe us off the face of the universe."

Sydes immediately appreciated what the Commander did. He talked straight and got people's attention. Maybe he could sit back and the Commander would handle the whole damn thing. Just then, he noticed the senior FF flight leader coming to his feet.

"Our brain boys have wrung out the flight paths of these bloody bastards. The analysis suggests they always come in on the same trajectory."

Activating a holographic projector in the center of the table, a tactical plot appeared depicting the mean flight path of the invaders as they entered the solar system.

"So maybe their fleet is out there along an extension of that line, or at least a couple of carriers for their fighters," the senior flight leader from CC chimed in.

Sydes began to feel good about this exchange. It sounded like a bunch of big burner jockeys trying to hassle something out. He decided to test the waters.

"It looks like a pretty narrow flight path," Sydes interjected.

All chatter stopped. As one, the group turned in Sydes direction. Maybe this was what the Commander called respect, Sydes thought to himself.

"It would be nice if we could put something along that line to help us out," Sydes muttered.

Sydes didn't say it straight up, but everyone knew what he meant and who had the gear to make it happen.

"I bet you guys are thinking about the space mines we used a while back that got outlawed. The U. N. said we had to destroy them, but I might know where all the pieces are … and they might find their way here in about four hours," the senior MM flight leader remarked, a crooked smile plastered on his face.

It began as a knowing grin on the face of every man there and spread to a back slapping laugh fest. The Commander said something into his headset and armloadsof bottles and glasses were carried into the room.

After everyone was finished harassing one another about how they could drink that wimpy shit, the noise level settled down to tolerable levels.

"You know outlawed mines aren't the only things just lying about. We sorta tinkered together some stealth technology that the U.N. didn't like. If we add our stealth cloaks to those little cherry bombs, they won't show up on the red ships' sensors. It'll probably only work once. Then they'll get the signature, but hell, something's better than nothing," the MM flight leader said sweetening the pot.

"We could up the megatonnage yield on the mines with a little help from PP," the senior MM flight leader said.

"Shit … we have enough megatonnage floating around up here to stuff those mines to overflowing," the PP flight leader replied as he finished his drink.

The FF senior flight leader, a woman who carried the scars of an encounter with Sydes years before, leaned forward on the table and fixed Sydes with a predatory stare. She ran her finger slowly down the scar on her cheek that served as a reminder of her encounter with the Solo. Looking into Sydes' eyes, she realized for the first time that he could have finished her instead of just disabling her ship. Her expression softened as she leaned back in her chair and sipped her brandy.

"I've got ten shuttle pilots sitting out there picking their noses, who can lay those mines for you," she said hoisting her snifter in salute to Sydes.

Returning her salute with his shot glass, Sydes managed a slight smile.

The Commander sat back and watched Sydes being pulled to his feet by the flight leaders, try to do his best to tolerate the close quarters of so many former enemies. They were all shaking his hand and clapping him on the back while Sydes tried to accommodate all the amicable attention with good humor. The Commander felt satisfied at the outcome. He knew Sydes was considerably more pleased than his face revealed.

Chapter 7

Chen, a slender young man whose name bespoke his Asian ancestry, was Phil's man on the ground at the reserve. Chen had hands on management responsibility for getting the dominance deficient to western Canada and settling them into their new digs.

A life time of research founded on Doctor Forrester's work motivated his pilgrimage to this post of scientific and administrative significance. Principal among his skill assets was Chen's absolute mastery of the face to face neuropsychological assessment techniques that lay at the foundation of Forrester's research.

Carrying the greatest weight, Chen had been Cabot's candidate for the position. This was one of the few occasions when Cabot's scientific staff had ever opposed him. Yet, they all agreed that Chen was a brilliant population geneticist and neuropsychologist, but the staid academic establishment saw him as a maverick.

His published works included a monograph in which he clearly delineated an increasing incidence of the birth of children subsequently diagnosed as exhibiting either autism or Asperger's syndrome.

Autistic children typically withdraw and show an obsessive desire to keep things from changing. Asperger's kids seem all intellect, lacking interest in and facility with social interactions. Chen also discovered that the incidence of these two diagnoses increased on a par with each other, almost as if they were somehow yoked. His analysis, derivative of Forrester's research, revealed that exclusive right hemispheric perceptual and processing dominance characteristically marked, autism, while Asperger's syndrome showed the same level of exclusivity with respect to left hemispheric dominance. Mother nature appeared to be pumping out two streams of single brain kids; autistic, right brainers and Asperger's, left brainers. Although university medical faculties considered his analysis flawless, the conclusions drawn from these findings were labeled as speculative at best, and mystical fantasizing at worst.

The medical and scientific community saw the dramatic increase in these two conditions as related to some, as yet unspecified environmental or disease factor. Chen theorized that the tenfold yoked increase in the incidence of autism and Asperger's syndrome suggested a long wave genetic alteration in the human species. He reasoned, that despite a long history of seeing these two syndromes as pathological in character, nature was, in fact, taking the first stumbling steps towards evolving something new in the human race. His reasoning was informed, in part, by the notion that once populations reached a certain density, genetic mutations were compulsory and these changes often demonstrated themselves with dramatic velocity.

Up to this point in his argument he retained considerable support in the scientific community. His next argumental inference caused wholesale defections among the academics. Chen proposed that nature was splitting the human race into two separate species. On the one hand, he suggested the mounting incidence of Asperger's syndrome represented kids living solely out of the left hemisphere. On the other hand, autistic children managed reality using only the right hemisphere of the brain represented the leading edge of that change.

Drawing heavily on Forrester's early work, Chen theorized that the vigilant competence of the right cerebral hemisphere had been the key to the race's primeval survival. He further reasoned that the species had experienced a technological coming of age mediated by the joint action of the left and right halves of the brain. The next step in evolution, as he proposed it however, would proceed along two separate and exclusive tracks, one for those whose strengths were resident in the left hemisphere and one for those whose right hemispheres ran the show. Nature, as Chen perceived her actions, was dividing the human race into vigilant visual-spatial right hemispheric actors and abstract conceptual left hemispheric meditators.

This latter notion caused Chen's expulsion from the halls of legitimate scientific inquiry. Perhaps more importantly, he was unceremoniously expelled from under the sanctifying umbrella of academic discourse and relegated to the damp and seamy environs of lunatic fringe speculation. It was also this notion that brought Chen to Cabot's attention, and Cabot generally got what caught his eye.

Investment in the ethereal regions of scientific and academic discourse had never schooled Chen in the churnings of commerce and the brokering of power that were Cabot's daily fare. However, Cabot knew all there was to know about Chen, particularly, his theories about the division of the race. That's was the way it was for everyone whom Cabot took under his wing.

Chen knew only that the single most powerful man in the world had scooped him out of the abyss of poverty and public infamy and given him a job that represented a population geneticist's fantasy. Cabot provided him with nearly unlimited funds, aid from personnel of his own choosing and time to monitor and analyze Cabot's great experiment in the most fully controlled setting a researcher could ever have imagined.

Chen's respect for Cabot derived in large part from the simple fact that this eminently influential man supported Chen's theories. This kind of backing contrasted sharply with everyone who saw Chen's notions as examples of science fantasy rather than well reasoned empirical speculation from the intelligentsia to the man on the street.

Without Chen ever personally applying to Cabot's scientific foundation for a grant to test his theory, Cabot had identified and collected examples of the very splitting of the species Chen had predicted. Here was a tailor made test of his notions already in progress. The experiment Chen envisioned could only be undertaken over many generations of genetic approximation, but Cabot's resources had made it an immediate reality.

Chen saw the autism and Asperger's indices in the population as the first halting and understandably pathological 'misses' in a linear progression leading eventually to the development of two species. Cabot's assemblage of a large dominance deficient population provided a wake up call to Chen's linear thinking style. Here Chen found half of the phenomenon he had only conjectured would appear already on the scene. Cabot had located left hemispheric processors, namely the dominance deficient, and gathered them together in one place effectively cutting them off from the balance of the gene pool. Chen had never imagined so many full left hemispheric processors existed in the world. Of greater significance, none of these left brainers demonstrated even a hint of Asperger's symptomatology.

Chen knew that if he were going to think in straight lines from now on, he needed to draw more than one line and to believe his own projections about how fast evolutionary changes could occur. Chen knew that nature almost always moved along multiple fronts simultaneously; his own theory suggested she would. The problem lay in the strength of his own linear-sequential reasoning that predisposed him to just one line of inquiry to begin with. Mired in the intricacies of the Asperger's-autism model, his own thinking style had prevented him from looking beyond it.

Predictably, autistic and Asperger's kids were evolutionary dead ends. Cabot's 'meek' represented a stable genetic cohort pointing toward the future. However, the meek represented only the left hemispheric vector, the one on the Asperger's side of the split. Where was the autistic group, the stable right hemispheric vector? Chen knew of only one paradigmatic example for certain, and that was Cabot himself. He seemed the singular and most comprehensive expression of vigilant right hemispheric striving for dominance ever fully manifest in tissue. Chen confirmed this conclusion during his one and only meeting with Cabot which occurred as a footnote to his appointment as working head of the reserve. The fact that Chen was the only person he knew who had fully mastered Forrester's face to face neuropsychological assessment technique gave him confidence to the point of scientific certainty in his appraisal of Cabot.

⚜

Four years into Cabot's great experiment left Chen considerably less enamored with his post. What had begun as a love affair with the perfect experiment had become a soul wrenching exercise in endurance. Despite his enormous intellectual reach, Chen never imagined to the lengths to which Cabot would go to force the hand of evolution. A mere ten months after settling the meek in the reserve, Chen recognized why Cabot had specified that the couples selected for inclusion in the great genetic venture must be childless. Chen was unceremoniously confronted with what he could not, or refused to, foresee. Cabot's handpicked medical technicians euthanized infants born to these couples, whose dominance quotients ranged above the meek cutting score.

Chandra, an extremely competent geneticist who had been assigned from Cabot's executive staff to assist him, joined Chen at the reserve nine months after he took over the reserve. What had begun as a successful scientific collaboration for Chen and Chandra became an intimate relationship over the years. Together, they visited one or another cemetery at night, almost craving the inoculation of reality provided by the rows of tiny graves. They would drink, talk, and end up weeping in each others arms under a moon meant for lovers, not conjugal despair.

They discussed endless remedies for their guilty complicity in Cabot's 'scientific culling' operation. They entertained every abrogation of personal responsibility. They would conceal the infants, run away, they would die in a joint suicide pact, or they would tell the media what was going on. However, they both recognized that Cabot, directly and indirectly, controlled the media. They had personally tried to save some of the infants. Unfortunately, Cabot's medical technicians had been pre-selected for their compulsive traits. The children were always found.

The reserve's parents in waiting, aggrieved by the loss of their children nevertheless muddled through. Chandra considered telling them what was going on, but Chen dissuaded her knowing the lengths to which Cabot would go to set things right again. The draconian remedies applied to the infants would doubtless be applied to them and anyone they enlightened about the true nature of the children's' deaths.

When he and Chandra had plumbed the depths of their despair, Chen would remind her that the inhabitants of the reserve experienced a richer living environment than anyone in the history of the species had ever enjoyed. This rationalization satisfied neither party. Yet, careful observation of the reserve's inhabitants revealed a degree of satisfaction in the daily acts of living that was difficult to dismiss.

Although all the residents knew that the reserve represented captivity, they seemed content with the opportunity to pursue scientific and artistic interests within the pristine setting rather than decrying their status as prisoners. No one longed for the shining sands of an ocean beach, or pined for the noisy bustle and excitement of a large metropolitan complex. Of even greater interest, no one voiced feelings of deprivation because they couldn't travel outside of the reserve. Focusing instead on the benefits of their isolation, they emphasized the fact that large throngs of tourists couldn't travel into the reserve.

Every member of this widely dispersed population had remarked at one time or another that it was a 'fantasy fit.' No one had been forced to live here. Cabot had quite simply made them offers and assurances that could not be had anywhere in the world. The land and homes were theirs free and clear in perpetuity. Transubstantiators were provided free of the CC scrambled signal and the expense of creating necessities. In-home fusion units supplied all the power they would ever require. A household maintenance robot in each residence kept everything tidy and in repair. Service centers only hopper minutes away from any residence supplied medical care, which they apparently required very little, and other needs of all imaginable sorts.

Holographic image transmitters connected each residence with each other, and the service centers. Cabot had read the book of Forrester thoroughly. He knew the meek and their left hemispheric inclinations well. He had made provision for continuing education opportunities such as the world had never seen. Replicating the files from his encyclopedic computer, each residence had access to the sum of human knowledge to the extent that Cabot had been able to gather it. The meek were both curious and industrious, and both needs would have to be served.

Ideas and tangible artifacts evidenced the productivity in the community. The flurry of work and thought engendered by their varied interests led to the formation of small groups that met on an as needed basis to exchange views or examine each others' work. Conflict often resulted from such exchanges, but difference resolution took conceptual rather than physical forms.

Despite their predilection toward isolation, the members of the reserve, or 'people of the trees'; as they called themselves, met with each other on a regular basis to resolve disputes or to discuss the news of the world outside of the reserve, which they received without censorship.

As Forrester had speculated, a group made up of entirely dominance need deficient, left hemispheric individuals showed insufficiencies in and required daily boosting of sympathetic (fight-flight) nervous system input. Before coming to the reserve, the meek living within the general population derived sympathetic stimulation from four principal sources. These included carefully self-titrated doses of central nervous system stimulants such as nicotine and caffeine, a diet rich in salt, a compulsive work style, and, perhaps most significantly and least productively, anxiety engendered by dealing with the the dominance driven majority of their fellow human beings.

Within the confines of the reserve, the first three sources of stimulation were readily available. The fourth, and perhaps the source that goaded the most pronounced fight-flight reaction was entirely absent, namely, the incitement induced by the implicit and explicit threat supplied by their dominance driven counterparts.

Inasmuch as the meek were paragons of parasympathetic (rest-digest) nervous system influence, they required sympathetic nervous system supplementation to make up for the loss of the energies of victimization supplied by the dominance driven. True to their parasympathetic governance, judicious energy conservation was the rule. Among the meek, with the exception of dynamic energy mobilized to feed curiosity fueled creativity and acts of service to others, energy was used sparingly. Without the apprehension fueled readiness supplied by living with the dominance driven, they could not maintain the level of physiological tone required to respond rapidly to physical emergencies.

The meek were not predisposed to excesses of physical risk taking. Nonetheless it became clear that long term parasympathetic energy conservation across an entire population would eventually result in individuals who could not respond efficiently to physical challenges. Although Cabot had done his level best to eradicate such challenges, they were bound to arise.

Sympathetic nervous system support was provided utilizing systems that had millions of years of tried and true reliability. For the next generation alterations were made at birth. For the adults, the change was implemented during routine inoculations. The alteration consisted of a nanochip with homing capacity, when injected found its way through the blood stream to lodge in the hypothalamus. From here, it bolstered the action of the hypothalamic-pituitary-adrenal axis providing emergency arousal only when absolutely required. Inasmuch as the meek experienced very little in the way of anxiety when their daily interactions excluded contact with their dominance driven brethren, the artificial booster became operative only in times of life threatening emergency.

The life style of the community of the meek was a source of continuing wonder for Chen. When seen as part of the larger planetary population where they were massively outnumbered by their dominance driven fellows, they appeared incompetent. The most gracious description of these misfits was they lacked social skills. Their interests were exclusively directed to the domains of science and art. They possessed no driving urge to impress anyone with what they knew or had accomplished. In short, living in their own world, they were endowed with none of the skills required to fit into the ever changing rituals and tribal practices that had characterized the sojourn of right hemispheric mankind for eons. The more specific kernel of truth inherent in their deviance was because they lacked dominance drives they could not acquire the social reflexes necessary to deal with those genetically predestined to dominance. They quite simply possessed absolutely no desire to dominate their fellows.

Living among those of their own genetic subset, and within the protected confines of the reserve, a picture more consistent with the meeks' fundamental nature emerged. When faced with conflict, they either talked out their differences or simply withdrew. During these periods of withdrawal, they contemplated the pro's and con's of the disputed matter and eventually came to compromises they could live with, or failing this outcome, no longer addressed the disputed issues with the other parties involved. Their geographic isolation facilitated this strategy of meditative withdrawal, but of greater moment, no individual's sense of personal value seemed to rise or fall based on another's solidarity with them. In short, no one attempted to persuade, mobilize or otherwise coerce others to a unifying community viewpoint.

Inherent to their amicable individuality was the ability to draw marvelously clear and simple lines in their lives between the essential and peripheral. Multiple viewpoints were enriching, not divisive. Conflict was to be embraced, persuasion eschewed, and, perhaps of greatest social utility, civility and commitment were not seen as polar opposites on passion's continuum. For the meek, the perception of beauty and its intrinsic order was the seat of creativity.

Central to their shared culture was a belief that past, present and future were foreordained in the space-time landscape of eternity, making them day hikers through life, not fatalists. At the core, they saw themselves as representatives of the need for the universe to know itself made manifest. Consistent with this view of their mission, they perceived learning about and contributing to creation as their daily duty, but understood in this commission no mandate to dominate the environment of which they were a part. In their view of the cosmos, the universe needed knowing, not subduing. Lacking the need to prove anything to anyone about themselves, overt evidence of aggression disappeared. The meek lived within themselves and so eminently well with one another.

Early on, the meeks' spontaneous development of a series of practices for managing unexpressed internal dissatisfactions and disappointments captured Chandra's interest. What she observed transpiring among them was so counter intuitive to her experience that she invested considerable time and effort searching for historical examples of their way of relating. Her researches were finally rewarded when she ran across an ancient document describing the Senoi culture. Chen immediately referenced the data array available to the reserve and found no mention of this culture or its practices that the members of the community might have accessed. Despite Cabot's encyclopedic coverage of humankind's history, the Senoi's curious manner of relating had simply been overlooked.

"They came up with this all on their own!" Chandra said, her matter of fact tone dropping away.

"Yes, entirely on their own. They fell into this way of sorting out covert feelings and fantasies because they were neuropsychologically destined to do so," Chen replied, sharing her excitement.

A degree of insufferable satisfaction that Chandra seldom saw in her interactions with Chen suffused his remarks. She felt compelled to take him down a notch. Her counter argument was succinct and direct.

"Bullshit!"

"No, really … if you pull out the need for dominance in human interactions what's left?" Chen responded, somewhat shocked.

"Hell, I don't know …" Chandra said angrily and then paused, "just living, I guess."

Chandra knew what was coming and she hated it. Chen was about to recruit the sum total of human knowledge to prove his point.

"Just living. Just getting along with others. Just getting the jobs of living done. Just learning, just loving, and that's all. Look at what they're doing! They're not avoiding competitive and dominance directed interactions. If you go at it that way, you end up defining a living human interaction with a conceptual negative. Plato was right, you can't prove the negative. For these people, competition and dominance just aren't in their equation for living, period!" Chen announced, beaming.

"OK, let's look at an example of what they do," Chandra replied, recouping.

"I love examples," Chen replied.

"Some guy goes to a service center and sees another guy's wife with a great figure in a tight dress. He goes home that night and dreams about making love to her," Chandra said.

"Yeah, I'm with you," Chen responded, as he perched on the edge of his chair.

Beginning to feel the sort of edginess that arises when a chess opponent smiles as you make a move, she continued, but at a much slower pace.

"So, this ideational Lothario gets up the next morning, tells his wife about the dream and provides her with both an apology and a gift that he made himself," Chandra continued her description.

"Yes, yes, that's important," Chen said, fairly vibrating in his chair.

"Then the fantasizing rake climbs in his hopper and sets off to visit the guy whose wife he ogled," Chandra said.

She was carefully spelling out what she had personally witnessed. However, as she proceeded she couldn't escape the feeling that behind Chen's enthusiastic agreement lay a trap.

"Right," Chen said, nodding and smiling.

"So the guy with the wet dream, confesses his fantasy to the husband and the paramour of his dream. Then, he apologizes and gives them both a handcrafted gift," Chandra said with a note of finality.

As she listened to herself report what she had, in one form or another, seen transpire among the meek on many occasions, she heard herself say it, but even though wasn't sure she believed what she was saying.

"The dominance deficient just don't have the equipment to produce continuous repression and denial. That's reserved for those with strong dominance needs. The stronger the need for dominance, the greater the need for denial and repression," Chen said, his tone matter of fact.

"Give me a fucking break. If they're alive then they're subject to repression and denial!" Chandra exclaimed.

"Have you ever tried to get them to keep secrets from one another?" Chen asked, his gaze narrowing.

"Once. It was about a surprise party," she replied.

"Well, what did they say?" Chen asked, a smile tugging at the corners of his mouth.

"They said they couldn't," Chandra responded.

Suddenly, she felt like someone who was being invited to walk over a bit of particularly well groomed jungle floor knowing a tiger trap had been dug in the vicinity.

"Right, not wouldn't, but couldn't. They use language precisely. I've had long conversations with Esther and her husband about this," he said gleefully.

Chandra knew Esther, a beautiful woman, but more importantly someone under the age of two hundred to whom the word 'wise' could be unabashedly applied.

"Esther has said on more than one occasion that misrepresenting thoughts or feelings by either commission or omission is not a matter of honesty for the meek. The practice of 'honesty', well no, the trait of honesty is simply essential to good cognitive housekeeping for these people. Concealment from self or others amounts to the same thing, head clutter," Chen continued,

"Head clutter?" Chandra responded quizzically.

Without knowing exactly how, she recognized that the ground over the tiger trap was giving way. In point of fact, the discussion was over, only Chen wasn't aware that the clock had run out. She could see his devastating conclusion peaking over the horizon although she couldn't make out its form and character. He had a lower dominance quotient than she did and even if Chen didn't understand that fact, she did. Not being invested in conquest meant Chen wasn't really aware of when he'd won an argument. Maybe didn't care as long as he reasoned the issue through to its logical conclusion.

"For the dominance deficient, the value of clear and clean cognitions is paramount. To accomplish clear thinking, there can't be unfinished or pending business cluttering up head space. There are no mirrored closets to store deceptions in the mind of the meek. It's all open space devoted to conceptualizations pointing, like the arrow of space-time, toward the temporal topography of the universe labeled the future," Chen said, his smile mimicking a Buddhist benediction.

She would never admit it, but Chen's explanation had helped her to understand what Chandra had been watching these people do for over three years.

"So if you lie, you can't think! I think better than average and ... I'm not above lying, if the situation demands it," Chandra said, wearing a crooked smile.

"That's right, but you and I both have significantly higher dominance need coefficients than any of these people. We deceive because we understand that the dominance motivations of those with whom we interact require it. Telling the truth on a regular and indiscriminate basis would represent a masochistic operation, if not a death wish when you're surrounded by the dominance driven," he replied in a softer tone.

That single, unequivocal statement stunned both of them into what seemed like an endless silence. Having lived among the meek so long, they had begun to think of themselves as part of the group. Chen's simple and direct insight made it irrefutably clear that they were not, nor could they ever be.

Plainly visible on his face, at least for Chandra to see, were the signs that Chen was about to pontificate. But there was something different in his expression. It was softer somehow, not paternalistic, almost sorrowful.

"The need for dominance is not some wholly disconnected capacity roaming about with only itself for company in the human psyche. It's more like a nexus, and a sticky one at that. For every living system, dominance is the centerpiece of survival beginning with single celled organisms. Dominance need is not an entity, its a community of drives and traits, which includes competition, that is focused in the individual but serves the survival of the species. However, no natural built-in fail safes limit these drives. Even when the survival of the species or the individual is reasonably assured, dominance remains in action and on target," Chen said, leaning back a bit in his chair.

The horrific scope of Chen's vision became startlingly clear for her. He saw the drive to dominance as a integral part of the reflexive survival instinct built into every living system. Dominance was the master controller drive, almost older than time itself, and it didn't have an off switch.

"So the members of our species are fated to wage never ending war with one another?" She asked, her voice trembling.

"I think its worse than that … I believe dominance striving is the common denominator of living systems in the totality of the cosmos," Chen replied, his tone darkening.

She knew immediately he was referring to the invasion. Images of the bloody orange alien vessels indiscriminately destroying everything in their path that represented a life form other than their own filled the broadcasts.

"Whether it's us or a life form alien to us, it's the same drive. Each life form seeks to displace all others in favor of itself. The same dynamic functions within a species as the individual strives to supplant others' needs and genes in favor of his own," Chen continued, his gaze falling to the floor.

A light breaking through her resentment of Chen's clockwork reasoning, Chandra saw the flaw in his argument.

"Struggle against confining conditions in nature and in the behavior of those who would subjugate us is what drives scientific innovation and social progress. Curiosity may be the spark that ignites new and creative solutions to problems, but frustration with thwarting circumstances is the dry kindling that fuels the push to an eventual resolution of the challenge," she countered.

"I am in one hundred percent agreement with everything you've said," Chen responded as he looked up.

It was Chandra's turn to lean back and smile. She'd finally nailed him in his area of weakness. Chen always overlooked the forest by focusing too closely on the individual trees.

"Your reasoning within a system characterized by survival-oriented dominance striving is wholly consistent with the parameters of that model. Although I think you would grant me that this struggle of which you speak is often against our own arrogance and fear or these same motivations in others. That's what makes the meek so extraordinary," Chen replied, his voice unusually clear and steady.

She could see the rebuttal coming like a tornado on the horizon. Even more prophetic of the magnitude of the storm to come was Chen's calm and measured presentation, which suggested that the counter argument would be a devastating one.

"The meek are an evolutionary innovation, not a social invention," Chen said as he looked around as if searching for a blackboard.

Without realizing it, Chandra's eyes tracked his movements as if she was attempting to assist him in finding that for which he was searching.

"Struggle is not intrinsic to the meeks' physiology so the drive to dominance is absent as well. There's no war in their brain. No interminable conflict between their frontal lobes and their limbic systems. The battle has been won and the victor is the seat of imagination and curiosity, the frontal and prefrontal cortices. Indeed, if there is anything that's intrinsic to the meek, it is curiosity and imagination. The desire to know becomes the master motivator of behavior and operates for no reasons external to itself," he said, staring at the ceiling as if searching for inspiration there.

Chandra had watched Chen engage in this behavior many times in the past. His eyes would track a route across the ceiling as though following some rigorously sequenced line of reasoning written there in a script only he could see.

"And service … yes, service … the provision of knowledge and insight as a service to others is what the meek are about. They offer guidance freely without a hint of coercion or a trace of the need to persuade. The meek are nature's consultants, providing knowledge to any who request it and accepting remuneration only in the coinage of having rendered a service to others," Chen said as he lowered his gaze to her face.

"That's easy enough to do when everything is provided for you," Chandra replied, her tone resentful.

"I won't dispute that technological advances support the evolutionary success of the meek. However, history suggests that curiosity and service have not been the universal reactions of the idle rich to their station in life. Indeed, quite the opposite seems to have been the case," Chen replied, his tone conciliatory.

"Gimme a break … some of the rich have been workaholics," Chandra spat back.

"True, but usually just the niveau riche generation," Chen responded.

"Well … maybe," Chandra grudgingly replied.

"In the main, the ruling classes have been populated by those with the strongest dominance drives regardless of the name given to the form of government in which they rose to power. The history of the aristocracy of wealth and power suggests that these alphas have spent most of their time and energy in three categories of endeavor; questing for greater dominion, defending their power base, and amusing themselves at the expense of those they governed. No, the meek are something new. Something wonderful! 'Nature is saying, what if we pulled the struggle for dominance out of the equation? What would the human species look like? I give you the meek,' " Chen concluded as he folded his arms.

"I think that what you're forgetting is that uncertainty and scarcity have been effectively removed from the lives of these pampered people. Their lives are a perpetual Sunday school picnic. No uncertainty means no need for vigilance, no need for vigilance means no need for a strong right brain and the mechanisms that you lump under the heading of dominance," Chandra retorted.

"That's an excellent point. Would you agree that the meek are the most curious group you've ever run across?" Chen asked.

Chandra felt a shudder climb her spine as the feeling that yet another trap was just around the next bend in the verbal trail nagged at her.

"Well, yes, I guess ... I'd have to go along with that," she replied hesitantly.

"Curiosity arises out of uncertainty, does it not?" Chen asked.

"What's the point! Of course, if your certain about something you're no longer curious!" She replied, her patience waning.

"So to be endlessly curious is to be forever uncertain. Listen, I don't want to sound like a teacher here, but as far as I'm concerned, to be alive is to be uncertain. Uncertainty is a defining characteristic of living systems. It's not uncertainty that's at issue here, it's the individual's emotional reaction to the unresolved character of life that makes the difference," Chen replied.

"I don't get it!" She responded, anger replacing impatience.

"The uncertainty of the meek is neither fear, nor anxiety," he replied.

"Then they're fools ..." Chandra retorted. "... the world's a dangerous place!"

'That's true enough. But suppose you knew, beyond the shadow of a doubt, that the most important thing in life was not survival?" He replied.

"You can't ... every cell in the body is geared to survive at any cost!" Chandra responded emphatically.

"Our bodies, to be sure. However, I'm not sure that's the case for the meek. I have come to believe that evolution has endowed them with new cellular mandates that read, learn and serve. As you'd said, in order for life to begin and survive the long climb toward sentience, the fundamental program for life had to be to exploit and subdue everything outside of the cellular membrane. It's almost like when nature made the meek, she said, 'OK, we've arrived, now its time for something more constructive,' " Chen replied.

"If you're right, then without the protection of Cabot's little Eden, the meek would go under," she retorted.

"That may still happen. But once again, to be alive is to be uncertain and vulnerable. The evolutionary experiments of nature have included both successes and failures. Many species on our planet have risen to prominence and dwindled into the dust because of environmental changes," Chen responded.

"So what you're saying is that Cabot *created* this 'new species' of humankind," Chandra said pointedly.

"Not created, but he is most certainly sustaining them. The situation is almost paradoxical. Cabot is the paragon of right hemispheric vigilance and dominance striving. He fears the uncertainty of life and assuages his apprehensions through actions meant to achieve greater dominion over anything and anyone who might perturb his need for certainty. The meek arise at the other end of this continuum. Their response to uncertainty is trust in the future. That trust informs their lives in learning about, and living within the natural environment as they find it. They feel themselves gifted with life by nature and owe a debt of service to her in return. Hence, the name they have given themselves, the people of the trees," Chen replied and then took a deep breath.

"People of the trees ... I've always wondered how they came up with that moniker," Chandra mused.

"For Cabot, the environment exists to be exploited. Any impediment to his need for dominion is subdued or removed," Chen continued, his expression darkening.

"For all the good he's done for the meek, he's also exploited them to his own ends," Chandra added.

"In Cabot, evolution's plan for the right hemisphere achieves its ultimate expression. All of his internal deficiencies and uncertainties are perceived as external threats and vanquished as such. The mechanics of the right hemisphere are perfected in their simplicity through endless conquest of his perceived antagonists. It's an elegantly self-serving and eminently practical mechanism that distracts Cabot from the darkness and jumble within his own mind," Chen said and fell silent.

"So it comes down to fear or trust in the face of uncertainty. That's a pretty simple minded distinction. I could just as easily say that the meek are naive hysterics and that everyone else on the planet is a rabid paranoid. It's just a matter of words. What's the point?" Chandra asked.

"The point is head clutter. The dominance driven have it, and the meek don't," he replied.

"Oh, hell! Not the head clutter again," She spat back.

"Yes, the head clutter again. Think about it. The meek begin each day's thinking and feeling on a clean cognitive playing field. There's no unfinished business, no hall of mirrors in their heads and no litter of remorse to dodge as they address that day's demands. They carry nothing on their cognitive books for days or years that one half of their mind is trying to remember, while the other half is desperately attempting to forget. They have nothing to prove in the present based on events that occurred in the past. It's little wonder they can be both open to experience and fundamentally optimistic in their thought process," Chen responded, a smile growing on his face.

"And the dominance driven?" Chandra asked.

"The dominance driven have always represented the majority of our species so everything about them, about us, will seem familiar, and even at its worst, somehow appropriate. The mental landscape for those of us fated to dominance is clutter incarnate. We routinely hide things from ourselves and work to keep them hidden while we search for them. The energy drain is enormous, but since we've always done it that way, we don't notice the nonproductive loss of energy or its intrinsic futility. Of much greater significance, this process of hide and seek creates an additional source of uncertainty beyond that which comes as standard equipment for living systems. We experience a general uneasiness within, not knowing how to think in straight and unobstructed lines for fear that we'll run into something we don't want to find," Chen said, his brow furrowing.

"That doesn't make any sense. The most dominant individuals I've ever met are marked by incredible personal confidence and decisiveness," Chandra responded.

"On the contrary, it makes perfect sense. If the inside of your head is uncertain territory, you'd naturally want to live your life outside of it as much as possible. Life rapidly becomes a series of actions designed to bring closure, to create certainty and generate security in the world around you. In the course of making sure that you stay outside of the inside of your head, you're naturally going to appear stronger and more dominant than those around you," Chen remarked, a faint smile growing on his face.

"Don't you have that backwards ... I mean, dominance increases the likelihood of winning and winning is self-reinforcing?" Chandra asked.

"That's called begging the question. It's like saying that dominance is good because dominance is. The very existence of the meek in the human species suggests that dominance can't be the only way of doing business. What I'm saying is that dominance is an effect of internal uncertainty not a primary cause in human behavior," Chen remarked.

"So if people felt better inside of their heads, there wouldn't be any competition," Chandra replied.

"Exactly. The dominance driven are marked by their tendency to be constantly testing themselves against each other and challenges in the environment to prove their worth. Inasmuch as they can derive none from within, this process of continually testing themselves is the only way they achieve any feeling of confidence. In our species, the most profoundly dominance driven among us we call leaders," Chen said, a smirk forming.

"Give me a break. We're a tribal species and every tribe needs leaders," she responded.

"Each of us is stuck with reasoning from the known to the unknown. If we all need leaders as you suggest, then who leads the meek?" Chen asked, the smirk giving way to sadness.

Looking intently into Chen's face, Chandra didn't see someone who had won an argument. What she saw there was a mixture of near cosmic resignation coupled with an expression of quiet satisfaction at having understood the meek even if he could not participate in their reality.

"No one, really," she replied in a barely audible tone.

"Yes, no one," Chen replied in a equally quiet voice.

Directing his gaze toward the window, Chen stared off into space, apparently lost in his own thoughts.

In the blink of an eye Chandra grasped Chen's unconditional devotion to the reserve and the meek. He saw them as standing apart from life's universal need to dominate and devour in order to survive. A new evolutionary invention, permitted, or perhaps even produced by a universe working through individuals but completely indifferent to the petty motivations of those through whom it operated, the meek represented a new direction. The meek were a unique life form with goals such as the universe had never seen, but, for reasons of its own, now required.

More than ever she was convinced that Chen would never jeopardize Cabot's experiment, not even if the Ole Nick doubled the head count of slaughtered infants. Chen, although he could not see himself as one of the chosen in this birth of a new species, would jealously defend his position as one of its midwives.

Suddenly Chandra felt cold and alone. She and Chen had shared so much, their love of science, their commitment to the project, and a bed. A soul destroying hurt looming, she could feel herself frantically trying to create distance between herself and Chen. It would be easy to see him as psychiatrically disturbed, certainly a lot of other competent individuals would concur. But that was an easy shot, and she knew it. He was obsessed, but that psychobabble label could be plastered on the forehead of any scientist worth his salt.

All that she was certain of at this point was that she could not go down this road with Chen. She still loved him, but the deep intimacy that comes only from a sense of shared personal vision had vanished. Her realization was that much more horrific because she knew why their paths had diverged. More to the point, Chen knew the 'why' as well. Chandra had a much higher dominance need coefficient than Chen. Because he was more like the meek than her, Chen could more easily follow the meeks' path, even with the abominations that greeted him at every turn in the road.

As she looked over at Chen, who still appeared enrapt by whatever his imagination was painting on the scene outside the window, she knew that he could be wholly raptured by a vision of the meeks' future. His extrapolations stretching out across eons, he could envision the meek as a singularly significant piece in some great cosmic plan. He was perfectly willing to cast himself adrift on the unseen currents of the sea of the universe with only his faith to buoy him up. Then, she saw it, too clearly to deny. Chen simply had faith that evolution was bending toward some benign outcome. Indeed, his faith was more generally one in a space-time future that was burgeoning toward a cosmically benevolent culmination. She had no such faith.

Chandra forced herself to concede the accuracy of the canvas of humankind's diversity that Chen had painted. The mentation of the meek was different in kind from that of the dominance driven. No matter how she thought it through, she was still sorting ideas and feelings in terms of asserting herself, coming out a winner in competition with her peers, or rebelling against someone or something that was attempting to oppress her. In a single compelling moment of clashing, scratching agony, she recognized that despite her enormous intellectual resources, she was utterly and forever trapped by her own dominance driven neurophysiology.

Having completed his conceptual work on the greenery beyond the window, Chen stared at Chandra. He loved this woman, which in a life dominated by scientific crusading, was a first for him. He monitored the subtle movements on her face and knew they had come to a parting of the ways. Taking a page from the book that the people of the trees were writing through their actions, he would let it go. Living civilly with those to whom you are committed meant letting go of differences and accentuating similarities.

"I know we've reached an impasse, but an obstacle in the road is defined only by the traveler's insistence on moving along what he perceives to be the path. By the way, I still love you, that doesn't change," Chen remarked, breaking the silence.

Shifting restlessly in her chair, Chandra could feel the sickly yellow-brown glow of repression and denial creating a feeble hollow of light against the encroaching darkness within.

"I know you do," she offered.

"We have to go or we'll be late," Chen interjected as he gathered up his scanner.

"Of course, the meeting," Chandra replied as she shook her focus inside out.

Neither Chen, nor Chandra spoke enroute to the hopper or on the speedy flight to the large assembly hall at the nearest service center. This was the first time they had been invited to one of the project group meetings that the people of the trees held from time to time. Esther had made the invitation in person. The topic to be discussed was the invasion. She indicated there would be a significant number of people attending in person, and an even larger holographic audience of participants.

Upon entering the hall, they noted that most of the inhabitants of the eastern district of the reserve were in attendance.

Esther and her husband strode forward to meet them. Her warm and open expression spread over a face that showed none of the lines etched by years of concealing hidden agendas.

"It was so very kind of you to come," Esther said.

Focusing in on Esther's expression, Chen never ceased to be amazed at the appearance of a human face on which neither the right nor left halves betrayed camouflage control, or leaked years of stored fear and anger. Perhaps it was this unique quality of expression, shared by all the dominance deficient, that made him feel invigorated by the company of the meek.

"We are honored," Chen responded warmly.

Chandra said nothing. She felt different, at odds and almost embarrassed by the good will evident on the faces and in the demeanor of the 'people of the trees' clustering around them. Chen belonged among these trusting and benign people. Chandra knew she didn't.

Esther found them seats. Surveying the hall and seemingly reassured that all, including the holographic participants, were present, she walked to a modest podium to begin the meeting.

"There has been interest in sharing views on the part of the whole of the people of the trees. A fullness of uncertainty in the community prompts curiosity that needs to be shared and satisfied. We are all aware of what is happening in the solar space of which our world is a part. Of the battles and the deaths, we know little save that we grieve for both. The community is gathered together to share its vision," Esther said with a solemn cadence.

This was something that Chen had not seen before. These people were apparently gathered together to search for the commonalities in their individual projections of the future.

One of the holographic participants, a young man with soft brown eyes spoke first.

"We are all called to witness what the universe has decreed."

While the phrase, 'the universe has decreed,' vibrated with a transcendental tone for Chen and sounded like fatalistic cowardice to Chandra, it seemed to strike a chord with the participants. No one spoke for a long time as they digested and permutated the ramifications of the young man's statement.

After an extended interval of meditative silence, Esther rose. Her gaze slowly surveyed an audience of translucent holographic attendees and those physically present.

"It is sufficient?" Esther queried.

Not one among those present in the flesh nor those who were electronically projected spoke or moved.

"It is sufficient." Esther said as she smiled.

The meeting was over. Those in attendance bantered among themselves as holographic participants winked out of view. Chen and Chandra sat in befuddled silence.

As the hall began to empty, Chen approached Esther and her husband through the rapidly thinning crowd. He felt like some benighted savage trying to understand how a more enlightened tribe made fire. He wasn't entirely sure what questions to ask.

"So what just happened?" Chen asked.

Smiling with her whole body, something Chen knew only the meek could accomplish, Esther turned to him.

"The vision was shared," Esther said simply,

Chandra listened skeptically. As far as she was concerned, it was like having a conversation with a Zen master, or more likely a palm reader.

"This was a first for the community. A vision shared by all, exactly as each experienced it individually," Esther responded, her expression and tone kind beyond measure.

Suddenly, Chen noticed that he wasn't breathing. This was something that neither Forrester, Cabot, nor Chen had foreseen.

"So you all had the same vision of the future?" Chen asked as he began to breathe again.

Esther's expression was reminiscent of some great and forgiving earth mother as she held Chen's gaze.

"Experienced, thought or felt, these all mean the same when the community looks into what will be the future. A vision is but a momentary burst of light illuminating the temporal topography of space-time not yet under our feet. We see where we have not yet trod but know that we shall go by and by. Where obstacles arise along the way, then, that is not the path. The universe marks the way for those who would see and follow," Esther said.

Esther was a physicist and it showed in her choice of words. "Not yet under our feet." What the hell did that mean? The phrase reverberated like some giant unhinged bell gone berserk in Chen's head. The words suggested that every now and then the meek just sort of tiptoed into the future to make sure they were moving in the right direction. Did the meek really see the future or did they, in some inexplicable fashion, derive some of their life energy from that dimension of the space-time continuum?

In any event, the meek all seemed to be in agreement that there was a path and that the way was well marked, perhaps even to the point of being foreordained. Suddenly, Chen didn't feel so smart. If he had been, in fact, a midwife to the birth of this community, then his job was done. The more troubling question was had his efforts ever been required?

Perhaps Chen's inner turmoil showed on his face, or maybe there was something less conforming to Newtonian physics at work in the situation. At the very instant Chen completed his thought, Esther turned and stared intently into his eyes.

"For the community, walking the map of space-time is as sure-footed as treading the path when time has caught up with the vision of its arrival," Esther said and then walked away.

Recognizing that his mouth was ungraciously open, Chen closed it. He wasn't certain he understood Esther's words, much less the larger vision toward which they pointed. With all his carefully crafted and finely delineated conceptualizations of the meeks' abilities, he was now completely certain he had not even scratched the surface of their intrinsic capabilities. In the meek, nature had replaced the struggle for survival against unknown odds with a certain knowledge of creation's unfolding. Once again he was overwhelmed by an image of himself as some forlorn savage fumbling with sticks, stones and twine vainly attempting to conjure fire from these simple objects with no instruction manual. A Salieri to the meek's Mozart, he could appreciate the genius of their mastery of space-time but was blind to their cosmic vision.

Chapter 8

Perched in the operations chair, the Commander stared at the huge new viewer that had just been installed in the bridge. It incorporated the most sophisticated long range sensors, as well as, remote feed units scattered over several million miles of space. The huge screen revealed quite a show in the space around the station as Sydes led strike craft from all four Natcorp squadrons through a variety of high speed attack maneuvers. For the Commander, it was a bittersweet experience. Instead of killing each other, old corporate enemies flew flawlessly tight formations and performed dangerous squadron complement full burn braking spins. How completely human, he thought to himself, the best of the best, functioning as teammates rather than adversaries.

Not readily apparent in these spectacular displays was the single implicit, but essential component supporting these exercises, trust. Here were men and women executing high speed maneuvers that allowed no time to check and see if the other guys were doing their job. You just had to trust that they were going to get it right the first time.

Carefully watching Sydes demonstrate the dead duck stunt over and over again, the Commander marveled at the degree of respect the lone wolf now received from his erstwhile enemies. His new strike craft, on intermittent burn, tumbling and spinning to the flank, soon fell behind the aggressor squadron. At just the right moment, the ship suddenly righted and mock fired on the aggressor squadron's exhaust ports. Trust made all this possible, but trust was a rare coinage among the perpetually contentious members of the vast human community. It was minted only in times of great travail and distributed only to create solidarity against a common threat. It was a formula as old as the race, when the little fish are squabbling with each other, drop a big fish in the tank and the minnows will work together.

Motion alarms blinked on the viewer. The little flashes signaled the return of cargo shuttles from their mine seeding operation. The shuttles had positioned the supercharged explosive booby traps all along the front the alien ships had used to enter the solar system twice before. The Commander didn't have to count the number of returning vessels, he knew two were missing. He didn't like losses in battle, much less those incurred in the preparation for conflict. The sortie had set over nine hundred stealth mines, with the price being two shuttles and twenty personnel. Numbers were lifeless and unfeeling sentinels of human suffering. Good friends, brave men and women, reduced to ciphers, were noted, and then, forgotten.

As he looked up, he saw that Sydes leading the squadrons back to the station for refueling. The Commander decided to meet the fighter ace in the receiving bay.

As soon as the hiss of the big door closing indicated the bay was pressurized, the Commander activated the bay access and strode to meet Sydes.

"You cut the war games a little short today," Tutunji remarked as Sydes approached.

"Yeah, I don't like all those fighters out there with their fuel cells more than half empty," Sydes replied as he tucked his helmet under his arm.

The Commander nodded his affirmation, but his expression betrayed concern about something as yet unmentioned.

"Not all the shuttles came back?" Sydes asked as he looked into the Commander's face.

"A mine got loose, we lost Samis, Erica and eighteen others," the Commander replied solemnly.

It seemed now that every day Sydes was reminded that being a loner was different from being alone after losing everyone you knew.

"You know, if those bastards fly that same course again and detonate those mines, the radiation cloud from the explosions will make it impossible for us to navigate that space for a long, long time," the Commander said as he noticed the squadron pilots approaching.

Turning away for a moment, Sydes watched as his pilots, laughing and shoving each other, ambled down the passageway enroute to the bar.

"We can only hope it does the same for those bloody bastards," Sydes replied.

As if on cue, both men turned and followed the jostling pilots down the passageway toward the station's watering hole.

⚜

Scuttlebutt was Arthur's stock and trade. He felt a personal responsibility to keep Forrester up on everything that was happening. He knew about the mining operation and was aware of the gathering Natcorp armada through the considerable increase in routine physicals he did for pilots from all four Natcorp defensive groups. The station had become a staging area for the Earth's defense forces. Armaments and technical components were being shipped in on a daily basis and passageways once littered with the wounded were now overrun with weapons specialists.

Those injured in the conflagration that had swept over the station were on the mend. Some were back at their duty stations. A few who required long term treatment had been transferred back to Earth, leaving little for the medics to do. Temporarily unemployed, Arthur was free to pursue his preferred vocation of chatting up the pilots and the waitresses in the bars. Sharing Arthur's unemployed status, Forrester spent most of his time in their compartment. Often times, as now, he would just stare out the viewer. Occasionally, he accessed the station's mainframe, that provided panoramic external views, as well as, images of the station itself from scanners positioned in space.

Little recognizable was left of the old CC installation. It had lost most of its symmetrical contours and currently looked more like a cubist painting than a military space station. An endless train of huge cargo shuttles brought load after load of carbon fiber alloy girders to reinforce the burgeoning superstructure. Sometimes, the deck shuddered as an additional fusion reactor was wedged into place in the guts of the station to feed the hungry shield generators.

As Forrester watched, several large tractor shuttles eased a mobile missile launcher into position about one hundred kilometers off station. Perhaps this island in space was the best place to stand watch against the aliens. A shiver inched its way down Forrester's spine. All this preparation had the telltale earmarks of a last stand for humanity.

The Earth had no planetary defenses, which was hardly remarkable on a world focused more on controlling its inhabitants than defending against attacks from beyond. To be sure, there were lots of stations in Earth orbit, but their mission was to expedite commerce not protect the consumer base. The human race had spent itself in endless attempts to gain dominion over its own. Mankind simply wasn't prepared for the arrival of another species as committed to domination as itself. If the big red ships got past these outlying stations, goodbye mother Earth.

Lifting his personal scanner off the ledge by the viewer, Forrester, out of force of habit, looked over his shoulder to catch Arthur's reaction. Arthur would typically have made some crack about fortune cookies or tarot cards at this point, but Arthur wasn't there. Playing with the control buttons, Forrester was looking for a particular entry that seemed to call to him at this moment from dim memory. This passage had always troubled him. He had returned to it over and over again recognizing its importance, but not comprehending its content.

> THE BRIGHTER THE FLAME OF A THOUGHT'S
> BURNING, THE DEEPER THE SHADOW IT CASTS
> UPON THE SOUL'S FOUNDATION. LIGHT,
> THE FIRST CREATION, AND SHADOW, THE
> SECOND, EACH MARK THEIR OWN CIRCUIT
> UPON LIFE'S STRAINING REACH.
>
> IN THE BEGINNING IS LIFE, WHICH PASSING
> FROM THE LIGHT INTO DARKNESS AND TO
> THE BRIGHTNESS AGAIN, FULFILLS ITS ROUND.
>
> THE SPARKS AND SHADOWS OF THESE
> THOUGHTS, MADE PLAIN, JOINS THEM
> AND ME TO A DARK PATH AT WHOSE
> ENDING DWELLS THE LIVING LIGHT.

Soul wrenching studies of this entry in years past had always comforted Forrester in his decision not to publicize the scrolls. As the words stared at him now, framed all about by the horrors of the war, he felt the beginnings of a dark realization growing within. Perhaps he had wholly misconstrued the phrase, 'made plain.' Suppose 'made plain' was intended not to point to a single reader, but to the millions who might have read these words had they been published? Like he needed the additional guilt that came in the wake of such an interpretation. Had he stuck himself and humankind at midpoint on the 'dark path', or had his actions advanced them all toward the 'living light?'

He felt desperation growing. All that bright and shiny conceptual machinery in his head began churning out intellectualizations. Maybe it was a matter of timing? Perhaps someone was destined to find it sooner or later because it was supposed to be discovered? Could he have been destined to read it and do nothing? It was all rationalizing bullshit, and he knew it. Then quite unexpectedly, his eyes were drawn to the entries immediately following the one that incited all his angst. He liked these ominous entries even less than their predecessors.

> THE TEARS OF SUFFERING EONS, A CLOUD
> OF DESPAIR CREATE THAT FILLED TO
> OVERFLOWING, POURS OUT IN A RAIN
> OF TORMENT UPON THE LAST GENERATION.
> THE WATERS OF AFFLICTION DESCENDING

UPON A WEARY EARTH BECOME GREAT
RIVERS OF PAIN, FLOWING INTO A SEA OF
SORROW.

THE SORROWFUL SEA, KINDLED AND
OR'FLOWING ITS BRIM, STREAMS OUT
IN FIRE CONSUMING THE WHOLE
WORLD, PREPARING THE WAY FOR NEW
HEAVENS AND A NEW EARTH.

Suddenly he felt it. Not the comforting 'Y-shaped' invigoration, but a bone rattling vibration that seemed to begin at the bottom of his spine. The shudder began as he finished reading the entry, but before the throbbing could complete its circuit through his body, he was startled to his feet by the station's klaxon. Relief replaced the brooding horror within. Now, he could busy himself with saving lives instead of dwelling on the vision of himself as some half assed mute prophet whose oracular cowardice provoked the apocalypse.

⁂

The first gong of the klaxon brought the whole bar to their feet. Pilots dropped their banter and their drinks and started at a dead run out of the bar enroute to the strike craft bays.

Sydes instantly recognized the Commander's voice on the comm.

"Long range sensors have incoming right down the middle of mine alley. Scramble all squadrons."

Grabbing his helmet, Sydes became part of the pack of pilots speeding down the passageway to the fighter bay. Then, In his headset, Sydes heard a familiar voice.

"Don't be one bit more reckless than is required ... to come back alive." the Commander said.

Sydes made no response. None was necessary.

Not first out of the bay, Sydes was, nevertheless, in the first flight to light the darkness with their afterburners. The strike craft climbed into formation, nearly two hundred strong. Full burn brought them to the terminator boundary quickly. Von Strohheim and his crew had calculated the minimum safe distance for the fighter fleet should the bloody ships trigger the mines as planned. The strike craft held their position at this boundary. The sensors on the fighters had been stripped down to provide more shield capacity, and so, were not up to the long range scanning necessary to see the enemy at this distance. The station's remote sensors would provide visuals from its drone cameras to the fleet by relay feed to each fighter console.

✦

Never taking his eyes from the viewer's multiple visual feeds and scrolling readouts, the Commander could not avoid the thought that he'd rather be in a strike craft flying wing man to Sydes than watching the show from the bridge. Like Sydes, he didn't like the role of spectator, especially when his job description consisted solely of witnessing brave men and women die.

Then, the Commander's eye caught what he hoped he would not see. The long range scanners registered fifty red tinged blips coming in along the same vector they had flown in the past. Hopefully, the mines would do their job. Secretly, he doubted that the wall of fusion fire would hold off the invaders. He wanted to believe all the same.

For reasons the Commander could not explain to himself, Sydes felt like the son the Commander had never had. This unexpected sense of kinship caused the Commander to order a dedicated frequency installed in Sydes strike craft.

"They're in the alley, get ready," Tutunji said as he opened that frequency.

Suddenly, the entire viewscreen was blanked white. The Commander watched the console as one, two, then three, remote cameras went off line. In a flickering confusion of lines and colors, the main viewscreen slowly came back to life. Mine alley was a boiling froth of debris and lancinating bolts of energy. The radiation readings indicated the cloud of asteroid fragments and swirling energy was a man made nebula of white hot death.

Views from a laterally positioned camera showed that the strike craft armada holding beyond the terminator line was unperturbed by the blast. Good for Von Strohheim and his number crunchers, the Commander mused. Tutunji had been staring at the viewer so intently and for so long he could feel his eyes aching. He was looking for what he hoped he would not see, bloody orange ships that had made it through the holocaust. He knew Sydes would not have such internally contradictory thoughts running through his head. Like the archetypal hunter, Sydes was just sitting there waiting for the game to appear.

✦

Sydes' eyes were firmly fixed on the cockpit scanner. His strike craft's internal sensors were adequate for the degree of range finding required to determine whether any of the enemy had survived the mines' detonation. He knew exactly what he was looking for in the fusion fog, any hint of a red-or-ange tinge emerging from the holocaust. He was not disappointed. First, there was one, now four, then eight of the bloody red ships. Hitting the call button, one hundred strike craft leapt forward with him at full burn. The balance of the fleet would support this first sortie.

Damn, the alien ships appeared even larger than those he had fought be-fore. These were at least destroyer or cruiser class. As he activated his missile launchers, he wondered if the alien's fighter craft had been destroyed or maybe they just hadn't sent any this time.

The laser turrets on the enemy ships, all firing continuously, lit up the night of space. Sydes took the lead as he and ten hand picked pilots climbed above the alien formation. In the aft viewer, he watched as enemy fire vapor-ized twenty strike craft of the frontal assault group.

As planned, when his attack group reached the apex of their climb above the bloody ships' formation, Sydes' position functioned as a signal for the remainder of the frontal assault group to release their fusion volleys. The mo-ment the missiles detonated, the sensors of the lead ships in the alien formation were blinded. Sydes' sortie, its sensors specially shielded, now spiraled down toward the huge cloud of energy released by the missile barrage. Sydes knew from the planning sessions that visuals would be useless at this point. However, the magnetic sensors would guide them to their firing positions. The missiles of his sortie had been specifically programmed to home in on actively firing sources of energy emission to avoid going astray in the fusion devastation that spent itself all around them. The missiles' targets were the thrusters of the bloody ships maneuvering within the cloud of devastation. His sortie, reaching its optimal trajectory behind the alien fleet, released the heavily shielded mis-siles into the churning nuclear vortex that formed a wall before them.

Marking the time when the missiles entered the wall of bristling energy, Sydes counted quietly to himself. Reaching the count of six, he saw the cloud expand and felt his craft pushed backwards by the wall of force generated by the detonations. Half of his sortie now climbed above the presumed position of the alien fleet and half below. Now they would wait for any surviving ships to emerge. There was no point in trying to establish communications with the other fighters or the station, the fusion cloud scrambled everything. He would hang there as one among many spiders on the black curtain of space, waiting for anything that escaped the web of indiscriminate devastation they had spun.

The vigil seemed a long one. Then, as no surprise, at least to him, one of the blood ships, as his pilots had labeled the alien vessels, emerged from the cloud. He had to admire the alien vessel's targeting capacity even as its lasers took out six of his flight group. Then, the sole surviving alien vessel turned and accelerated toward the rocky profusion of the asteroid belt.

Sydes and the remaining three strike craft dispatched the last of their missiles after the fleeing cruiser. The missiles fell short of the alien ship. As it fled, the blood vessel ceased firing. The alien cruiser's increased acceleration suggested that the craft was devoting all its energy to just getting the hell out of there.

⚜

Of all the loathsome aspects of his job description, the Commander hated body counts the most. Mathematics was the necromancer's tool that accomplished almost all technological progress, but, like any tool, it was heavy and cold to the touch. Two hundred strike craft had gone out and he had watched twenty vaporized before a single missile was released. Fifty more went up in plasma bursts before the missiles they had released detonated among the remains of the alien armada. Twenty five more brave pilots died as they dove to release their missiles against the shields of the eight remaining enemy cruisers. That was half of the force they had marshaled, and of Sydes and his flight group, the Commander knew nothing.

It was almost inconceivable that any of the enemy ships had come through what amounted to a man made supernova, but they had. Whatever they wanted, they wanted it badly. They'd be back. He knew they would. As he heard these words echoing in his mind, he could feel a confirming chill running its course over his body.

Slumping down in the command chair, he knew there was nothing to do now but alert the medicos and wait. The comm-link sprang to life, crackling and sputtering. It was Sydes dedicated frequency.

"You son of a bitch," the Commander said happily as he activated the link.

"One of them got away, lost six ships, heading home," Sydes' responded.

Pointing to the viewer, Lieutenant Sadad caught the Commander's eye as he closed the link to Sydes.

As Tutunji looked up at the viewer, he could see a small group of returning strike craft. Many were badly damaged, but, intact or in pieces, they were all lining up at the receiving bay. There would be a lot of empty berths in the station tonight.

⚜

Arthur waited with a crowd of medical technicians as the receiving bay pressurized. Forrester knew that many of the dead would climb out of their fighters with all their parts intact. He had instructed the technicians to bring along all the kidney dialysis units they could find. Even with the most heroic of measures, radiation exposure would claim the lives of many pilots who had escaped death at the hands of the alien invaders.

The entire medical team hurried into the bay as soon as the pressure doors opened. Every member of the team was helping pilots out of their strike craft to begin immediate treatment on the bay floor. The patients' kidneys were placed on artificial shutdown as dialysis units were pressed into service. Massive quantities of the drugs necessary to trap irradiated tissue in solution were injected, while the dialysis units screened them out of the blood stream. This heroic approach would save many, but not all.

Forrester knelt down beside an semiconscious young pilot, a beautiful woman no more than twenty. He took her kidneys off line and attached a dialysis unit. It was an intervention undertaken only because he was dialyzing everyone around her. His radiation counter was coldly accurate. She must have flown directly into the front line of the battle during the fusion detonations. Despite the strike craft's shielding, her exposure was such that he could do nothing for her.

He reached into his pack, and holding the unit so that she could not see it, he placed a central nervous system isolator on the nape of her neck. The unit would sequester her from all discomfort. Her conscious experience of herself and her surroundings would be preserved to the point of death, sacrificing all else.

"How am I doing Doc?" She asked as her eyes opened.

Ignoring the confusion around her, she looked directly at Forrester. Her lucidity instantly alerted him to the fact that the isolator unit had done its job. Forrester paused, and in that moment of hesitation she spoke again.

"Its OK, I rolled the dice. How did we do?"

Even the few minutes he had been in the bay allowed him to catch snatches of the brief exchanges among the pilots. He knew one of the alien ships had made good its escape. He lied all the same.

"You got 'em all," Forrester replied, mustering a sense of pride in her sacrifice.

Out of the corner of his eye, Forrester watched helplessly as the global life signs indicator began to fade.

"It's OK, Doc ... it was a good lie," she said as she slipped away.

Feeling the emptiness he always experienced as a life slipped through his fingers, Forrester closed her eyes and knelt by the young pilot for a few seconds. A technician pulling at his arm jolted him from his dark downward spiral of emotion.

"Doc, Doc," the technician said anxiously.

It was a green kid fresh from an Earth side training school and Forrester could see that he was panicking.

"Doc, I don't think there's anything we can do for this guy. His radiation counts are off the scale."

Standing in one clean movement, Forrester grabbed the tech by the shoulders and spun him around to face his patient.

"That's a spark from God's fire. You keep it glowing and out of pain as long as you can!" Forrester snapped.

The tech looked startled, but Forrester's statement had galvanized him into action and he moved quickly to the dying pilot's side.

"Right, right, Doc," he cast over his shoulder.

As he knelt by his dying patient's side, the young technician adjusted the dialysis unit and set the isolator in place.

Turning to the next patient, Forrester felt a little better. There was something he could do for this guy. He attached the dialysis unit, administered the drugs that would leech the irradiated material into the blood stream and started the pump. Neural pain blockers were in order, but no isolator for this guy. He was going to make it.

He pulled the soft tissue knitter and stereotaxic antigrav positioner from his pack to deal with the pilot's dislocated shoulder. It was great to have something simple and straightforward to 'fix' for a change.

The joint action of the dialysis unit and the neural pain blockers began to make a difference for the pilot and his consciousness was clearing.

"Great line, Doc," he said feebly.

Startled, Forrester hadn't realized that the pilot was with it enough to have heard anything.

"What line?" Forrester asked.

"You know the one about the sparks from God's fire. Great line ...," the pilot said and then drifted into a twilight state.

Yeah, a great line Forrester thought to himself as he stood up. The words should be. They came from a great writer, but not him. He could hear the whole entry from the scroll spelling itself out in his head as he surveyed the bay filled with suffering humanity.

NEVER WAS DARKNESS THE SOLITARY
LORD OF ALL THAT IS. IN THE MIDST
OF ALL BEGINNINGS' GLOOM, EVEN

SO, THERE WAS LIFE'S TWINKLING,
WHOSE VOICE, STILL AND SMALL,
SAID, LET THERE BE LIGHT.

THE BLAZE OF LIFE HAS BURNED FROM
BEFORE THE UNIVERSE DONNED HER
ROBES OF LIGHT AND TO THE STARS
GAVE BIRTH. TO LIFE'S PURPOSE IS
THE WHOLE OF CREATION SET IN
EVER RENEWING MOTION.

EACH SOUL A SPARK FROM GOD'S
ETERNAL FIRE, A DYING EMBER UPON
THE HEARTH OF LIFE'S TRAVAILS MUST
BECOME. NO EMBER SPEWED FROM
THE BLAZE OF ALL BEGINNINGS CAN
LONG SURVIVE APART.

I wonder, Forrester thought to himself, if the diarist of the scrolls would be able to write so poetically about death if he could see the slaughter house floor that Forrester was surveying. The more frightening thought that intruded on his musing was that perhaps, in some way Forrester couldn't or wouldn't entertain, that ancient writer had and continued to behold just this sort of carnage. The ancient writer's perspective on such butchery, however, may have played out on a stage that encompassed the whole of the cosmos.

Walking among the dying, irradiated warriors looking for any who were not receiving care, he felt overwhelmed by the cost continuously paid to maintain and justify human existence. Without these bloody struggles, history clearly indicated the majority of the human race turned in upon itself in endless diversions of self-gratification. Poverty, disease, disaster and the routine bloodletting of war kept the race focused on the lowest common denominator of shared value; namely, life and death. For both individual and the species, survival was a cycle consuming its sons and daughters to create and continually shore up its value. The wheel of life, to which the ancients had so often referred, turned on the spindle of death, not life. Without the axle of mortality, the wheel's rotation became eccentric, slowed, and stopped. Forrester's mind's eye falling on the next entry, the magnitude of the diarist's more encompassing perspective was revealed.

THE LIGHT OF THE UNIVERSE, A CIRCLE
UNBROKEN BY TIME'S ILLUSION, TURNS
UPON EACH LIFE, LARGE AND SMALL. FOR
LIFE'S PURPOSE AND IT ALONE ARE THE
ENDLESS STARS OF HEAVEN SET TO DEATH
AND REBIRTH. IN EACH SPECK OF DUST,
SWEPT UP IN STARRY PASSAGE, IS ALL THAT
IS, PART AND WHOLE, COMPREHENDED.
EVERY MOTE, A LONELY SOJOURNER IN THE
VOID HAVING FINALLY OF LIFE TASTED,
CREATION SHALL AS ONE DRAW ITS FIRST
BREATH IN JOY

IN ONE LIFE IS ALL THAT LIVES CONTAINED.
YET, NO ONE SPARK'S SOLITARY GLOWING
CAN SHOW FORTH THE GLORY OF CREATION'S
FIRES.

In the words of the diarist, the whole of life was somehow manifest in each of its parts. That was the key, one life. His eye fell on a lone unattended pilot lying in a corner of the bay. His vision broke through the horror of the slaughter house floor the bay had become. Here was an opportunity to make a difference in one life, even if nothing could be done to confront the dread of the cycle in which his perception had trapped him. He hurried to the young man's side with a speed he hoped would leave the clinging shadows of his dark thoughts behind.

Chapter 9

The Atlantis project brought Chauvez to Cabot's attention. A world wide competition to design a habitat in the middle of the Atlantic ocean left Chauvez as its walkaway winner. Natcorp foundation funds administered by the United Nations security board of directors funded the project and Chauvez was selected to supervise the construction of his spherical design. The habitat was a marvel of sustained antigravity construction capable of descending to the ocean's depths, riding just above the waves, or ascending to heights of over two thousand meters above the bounding main.

The population at large believed that the huge airtight sphere would serve as a center for oceanic studies. However, Atlantis was in truth a recreational area for upper echelon administrators from all four Natcorps. The installation served as a sanctuary for all four Natcorps and no corporate assassinations were tolerated within its confines. Functioning as a free zone in which deal making was the principal activity, all forms of retribution for past slights were forbidden.

With the completion of Atlantis, Cabot's recruiters snapped up Chauvez and later appointed him chief aerospace engineer. Over many years and an equal number of projects, Chauvez had become accustomed to being handed impossible tasks, but this one was the mother of all nightmares. Chauvez was commissioned to build a huge space vessel in orbit around the moon. The specifications required that the ship be capable of sustaining the lives of over one-half million people for a voyage of indefinite length. Cabot made an outright purchase of an immense MM Natcorp installation on the dark side of Earth's moon to serve as his base of operations. This complex now teamed with thousands of personnel, all working in one or another capacity on Cabot's 'ark', as everyone on site had come to call it.

The twenty-four hour work day was divided into two shifts, with thousands of men and women putting in their twelve hour stints. Cabot paid triple wages and new hires always packed the shuttles from Earth. As a math and materials man, Chauvez marveled at how well Cabot's human resources people managed this growing population of workers. The moon's surface housed decent living quarters and recreational facilities with lots of bars and an endless supply of free alcohol detox patches handed out to workers coming on at shift change.

Chauvez supervised this monumental undertaking from a command center in stationary orbit above the surface of the busy moon complex. His base of operationswould eventually become the bridge of Cabot's enormous vessel. Its huge carbon fiber steel hull plates sealing the bubble of atmosphere within, the bridge complex was a self-contained environment. Plating of the same sort would eventually cover the whole sphere and contain its breathable atmosphere.

From his operations center on the bridge, Chauvez directed tractor shuttles as they ferried and positioned huge carbon fiber alloy girders to form the exterior supports for the outer skin of the ark. In the center of this spherical skeleton of girders, huge fusion reactors and equally large shield grid generators floated on stabilizing propulsion platforms. The shielding units were already on line and would be energized as soon as the skeletal girder structure was coupled together with the shield generators. The activation of the shield generators would create an impermeable seal around the vessel's exoskeleton by projecting lines of force following receivers and relays set into the girders.

Cabot's schedule was as tyrannical as its maker. In order to meet the demands of both, Chauvez had sections of girders forming whole segments of the sphere assembled on the moon's surface and brought up as a unit. He watched attentively as one huge segment rose from the lunar surface on its own antigrav units propelled and guided by fifty tractor shuttles. As the tractor shuttles eased this latest section into coupling position in the skeleton of the ship, he immediately knew what was going to happen.

"Tractor nine, pull back, pull back now," he shouted, mashing the commlink control button.

It was too late and he knew it. Propelled by the other tractor shuttles, the huge section had just enough momentum to lock into the couplings of the larger structure. It would occupy the same space as tractor nine and nothing was going to stop it. Chauvez watched helplessly as the tractor, trying desperately to pull away, was cut in half by the girder assembly. As the beam's couplings locked precisely into place in the sphere's steel skeleton, several of the tractor shuttles sped toward the two halves of their distressed sister ship with grappler arms extended. Vainly searching in the darkness, the tractors found no one left alive in the freezing void to draw into the safety of their holds.

At the outset of the project, Chauvez had mandated that all tractor shuttle crews wear space tight gear, but he couldn't blame them for not doing so. The suits were cumbersome and made working in the close confines of the shuttles difficult. The shuttles coming to the aid of their fallen sister ship could only scoop up the lifeless unsuited bodies spinning about in the wreckage. Cabot had a large accidental death benefit as part of his recruitment package, but somehow, the dollars promised on the front end didn't seem to measure up to the loss Chauvez witnessed on the back end of these contracts.

The hiss of the air lock exhaust pulled Chauvez's attention away from the devastation below. Piatra, Chauvez's number two on the ark project, having docked her shuttle to the command bridge, was standing by the airlock removing her helmet. Piatra was a disturbingly attractive young black woman and an engineer of the first water. She was absolutely indispensable to Chauvez in managing the enormous challenges building the ark presented. This fact made her physical beauty all the more distracting. Piatra had more than scientific smarts. That was obvious as she placed the helmet from her space tight gear within arm's reach. She knew just how dangerous their work environment could be.

"Five people gone and for no good reason!" Piatra spat out.

Piatra's fiery and wholly characteristic anger was easily kindled and became particularly intense when lives were lost. Her medium of emotional expression was rarely demonstrated in the soft pastels of sadness or anguish, more often, the bold primary colors of anger and retribution colored her feeling palette.

Clad in his pressure suit, Chauvez moved a little closer to his helmet. He knew Piatra well enough that he didn't want to summon the lighting of her anger.

"We can't force them to wear the gear, Piatra," Chauvez said as quietly as he could manage.

This was one of Chauvez's technically correct, but wholly inappropriate comments. He knew it almost as soon as the words fell from his lips. It drew the expected response.

"We should. There ought to be security at every shuttle bay. No suitie, no getti on shuttle," Piatra said, still fuming.

Chauvez had one of his rare kill two birds with one stone ideas. Punching the comm-link to the surface, he ordered security to implement Piatra's mandate. Then, looking up at her with his best 'how's that' expression, he fumbled with controls on the console.

Piatra seemed somehow satisfied. At least, she didn't look mad as hell anymore. After a few seconds of silence, she finally spoke.

"You know it isn't just the money that gets these people to take risks like that."

Sorting desperately through a number of possible responses before he began, Chauvez hoped not to trip Piatra's detonator.

"Yes, they all have hopes," he said carefully.

"Hopes, my ass ! These poor assholes actually think that Cabot is gonna take them along when he pulls out of this parking space to parts unknown," Piatra shot back.

Piatra was right of course and Chauvez knew it. Cabot was not building his ark to haul space dock workers around the galaxy. Everyone knew Cabot had something else in mind, but no one was sure what. Chauvez didn't know what to say, but he was certain that he didn't want to volunteer to be Piatra's lightening rod.

"You know Ole Nick is betting against the human race. He's planning on saving his own ass because he's sure we're gonna lose the war," she continued.

Piatra's tone rang with a finality heard only in ancient Papal pronouncements. Then, she stepped to the viewer and looked for several moments at the crews working on the structure below.

"For sure, he's taking a whole bunch of somebodies with him, but none of these poor saps," she said pensively.

Quite unexpectedly, Chauvez felt like some ancient, itinerant Egyptian construction foreman building a pyramid for a modern day pharaoh in the person of Cabot, just another god/monarch who wasn't about to be buried with stone cutters, sand carters or construction foremen for that matter.

"Look at the math ..." Piatra began as she spun around. "... maybe you need seventy-five to one hundred thousand technical people to keep this big beast running, but that leaves a hell of a lot of space inside and that son of a bitch Cabot is automating everything he can."

"Yes I know that leaves us about a half a million occupants short," Chauvez said, gingerly opting into the fray.

"Damn straight!" Piatra replied.

Piatra moved to the console and called up the schematics of the ark on the main screen.

"Look at these conduit diagrams for the internal structure of the ship. Ole Nick built surveillance and counterstrike options into every common space and compartment. The bastard looks like he's anticipating rebellion. Hell, he's got more countermeasures to ward off aggression from inside the ark than attacks from the outside," Piatra said as she ran her finger across the screen.

Taking note of an indicator light on the console, Chauvez hit a switch confirming the requested release of another major girder section from the surface. It would be floating up for coupling in the next fifteen minutes or so.

"So you think Cabot's anticipating a captive population of fellow travelers?"

Chauvez remarked as he turned toward Piatra.

"I don't know, but I'd be willing to bet that whoever is going to fill out this passenger list doesn't know it yet," Piatra replied.

Nodding his agreement, Chauvez turned his attention to what would become the next to last major section of the ship's skeleton rising to meet him. As he watched the tractor shuttles tow the huge section toward its place in the skeleton's puzzle, Piatra's observation occupied a good chunk of his attention. He had studied the ark's schematics hundreds of times, but he had never really noticed how many internal security measures were incorporated within the design. Could Piatra be right? Were Cabot's guests to be pressed into service rather than coming as willing volunteers on his galactic junket?

❧✦❦

Somewhat apprehensive, Phil wasn't sure why he had been summoned to the lunar installation that served as a staging area for the construction of Cabot's big ship. Almost as soon as he arrived, Cabot's security people hustled him onto a shuttle that gradually rose from the moon's surface and carried him swiftly to Nick's yacht positioned a few hundred kilometers off the site of the ark's construction. With the shuttle's arrival, the yacht's chief of security ushered Phil into the holy of holy's, Cabot's private apartments.

Sitting behind an imposing desk, Nick poured over schematics, made changes and gave orders to aides. As Phil entered, Cabot rose and his minions discreetly disappeared.

"Awfully nice of you to come, Phil," Cabot said.

"Thank you for inviting me," Phil said politely.

Phil knew he really didn't have much choice about accepting Cabot's invitation. However, his primary concern was Cabot's genial facial expression, casual demeanor and smiling politeness, all of which made Phil very uneasy. This was not the hard driving, no nonsense Nick Cabot Phil had known for over two centuries.

"Like some coffee, Phil? I just had this brought up from the Colombian reserve," Cabot asked as he picked up a cup.

Phil accepted the offer and poured himself a cup, but even Nick's cordiality and the aromatic brew did not dispel Phil's uneasy feeling.

Armed with cups of the steaming beverage, both men stood for a moment in what was an awful silence for Phil. He knew that Cabot never whiled away the time with anyone. He always had an agenda.

"You know Phil, I've always liked you," Cabot began.

That was a lie and Phil knew it. Cabot didn't 'like' anyone. For Nick, other human beings fell into two categories, instrumental in achieving his ends or functioning as obstacles in his way.

"I knew I had to have you on my team ..." Cabot continued, "... since our 3-D chess match more than two hundred years ago. You came the closest to beating me of anyone I've played before or since. That last platform move caught me by surprise. I never figured you for someone whose willingness to sacrifice men rivaled my own."

"That's kind of you to say," Phil remarked.

Phil's thoughts drifted back to that game and the decisions made by a much younger man so long ago. Years spent buried in the video archives, he had studied every final round of Cabot's tournaments that had been broadcast. In preparation for the final's match, he had formulated a strategy to beat Nick, but of surpassingly greater importance, he created a game plan to lose to the master in a way that would inspire respect. That hard fought loss was the most difficult bit of strategy he had ever engineered. Even as a young man, Phil realized that beating 'the Ole Nick' was a one way ticket to nowhere. As the elderly philosophy professor who had taught him 3-D chess as a child was want to say, 'winning is a matter of how big you believe the board to be.' As Phil looked up, he saw Cabot walking back to his desk.

"I want you to see something," Cabot said.

Setting down his coffee cup, Cabot picked up a holographic controller and touched an icon. At once, a huge holograph that nearly filled the open space in the center of Cabot's office appeared. It showed a big ship, a huge sphere rendered to scale floating there in mid air with each section fully illustrated.

Immense fusion reactors, antigravity propagators, shield generators and the guts of the propulsion units filled the center of the sphere. The level surrounding this one was devoted to automated control units with conduits leading to a bridge located in the outer circumference level. Beyond the power generation level was one labeled crew's quarters with compartments and recreational areas indicated.

The next level, which accounted for more space relative to the total volume of the sphere than all the other sections summed together, was divided into huge segments labeled eco-sectors. Enormous reservoirs of water with each connected to purifiers and recirculating elements that Phil was certain could reproduce clouds and rain were prominently displayed.

In the level supporting the outer circumference of the sphere, were shuttle bays, huge laser generators, fusion missile tubes, maintenance areas, and supply units for the outer defenses. Scavenger ports too numerous to count surrounded the bridge. These were designed to scoop up the gases and particulates of deep space to feed the transubstantiator units spotted throughout the sphere.

"The workers call it the 'Ark.' It sort of fits. What do you think Phil?" Cabot said as his eyes lit with pride.

"It incredible. The complexity and size of the vessel is breathtaking. It looks like it will take years to complete," Phil replied, his tone tinged with awe.

"I grant you it has the appearance of an enormous undertaking, but only if you look at it linearly," Cabot said and smiled.

All at once, Phil got the point. Nick was assembling all the parts of the ship simultaneously. The actual construction of the ark, visible in the huge viewscreen set in one whole wall of Cabot's apartment, was just the point of synthesis for this herculean project.

"That's right, Phil, every part of the ark is just about complete. Now all that remains is to fit the pieces of the puzzle together," Cabot said as he read the epiphany on Phil's face.

Grasping Cabot's vision clearly now, Phil was even more impressed. On the viewscreen, he saw the huge spherical skeleton of girders emanating a faint blue aura indicating the presence of an impermeable shield enclosing the structure. Near the fusion reactors, suspended at the sphere's center, he saw atmospheric generators beginning their task of creating breathable gases within the sphere so that the construction workers could do their job without space gear.

"All those reserves, Phil, each one representing a major ecosystem on the planet, will be transplanted into the ark. A portion of the land surface of each reserve will be physically isolated and then fitted with shield generators and antigravity units. One by one, they'll all be transported here and positioned in their apportioned eco-sector. A sampler of the whole planet, as it were, preserved here in the ark. It's all coming, even as we speak," Cabot said, and then was lost to his vision.

Overwhelmed by the undeniable reality of what Cabot had wrought, Phil was momentarily speechless. However, a darker apparition now replaced the bright vision he had shared for a moment with Cabot. Nick planned to rape the Earth to outfit his little planetoid, but why? He was already, for all intents and purposes, emperor of the planet save only the title. Nick must be certain that the Earth would no longer be there for him to play with if he was willing to go to these lengths. He was pillaging his birth place to create a home away from home. However, the most immediate question didn't have a thing to do with any of that, Phil thought to himself. The most pressing question was why is he telling me all this?

Staring intently at Phil, Cabot waited for his ancient colleague to complete his internal analysis of what he had seen and heard.

"Phil, there are berths for you and your family on the ark. This whole project represents a reaction to events I couldn't anticipate. You know I don't like that. I prefer to be out beyond the cutting edge of change, but the invasion is forcing the plays in this game," Cabot said solemnly.

"All of this looks like your certain that the human race is going down in this one," Phil's said carefully.

"I don't know for certain, Phil, but I have the feeling that our block in the solar system is going to suffer a cosmic form of inner city blight. We already have nuclear fusion clouds from the most recent fire fight being relocated by solar gravitational forces and may well end up in the atmospheres of Mars, as well as, our home stomping grounds. Even if there are no more fire fights, which I doubt, it looks like we could all get fusion fried by our own home made nebulae over the next ten years or so," Cabot replied, his tone was somber now.

Even though Phil was no physicist, Cabot's argument sounded solid. However, he couldn't help but wonder what difference Cabot's resources might have made, had he committed them to the war and to solving the radiation problem. But, all that was iffy, and Nick didn't bet on iffy, he always went for the sure thing. For Cabot, a sure thing required something he personally controlled from inception to completion. By definition, helping the race resist an invasion needed a cooperative effort, resulting in no particular personal advantage for the Ole Nick.

From his own narcissistic perspective, Cabot was in a tough spot. In the past, he had played exclusively with the political chess pieces of his own species. After more than four hundred years, he knew all the pieces, all the plays and most of the players. The invaders represented new pieces, maybe new plays, or worse yet, an altogether different game. It was pretty simple really, if Cabot couldn't be master of the game, he was going to take his ball, well a sphere actually, and go away. Suddenly, Phil could feel Cabot's eyes on him and he looked up from his reveries.

"Phil, I want you to be my number two on this project, especially as respects the installation of the ecosectors. I don't need another specialist, I've got them coming out of my ears. I need a life sciences generalist, and perhaps more importantly, someone with a different thinking style than mine. This project requires a zero tolerance for error mind set. The first solution has to be the right one. There are no second chances," Cabot said, his imperious tone returning.

The inside of Phil's head was whirling round and round and his stomach kept time with the motion. He knew there could be only one answer to Nick's request. He was all the more certain of what that answer had to be as he had seen a sheet of paper on Nick's desk with six names on it. He recognized all six. They were the names of Phil's six most trusted informants in Cabot's organization. The list had been set where Phil could see it for a purpose. Cabot wanted Phil to know that his moles had been unearthed. If Phil refused Nick's commission, there would be at least six accidents in retribution for that refusal and Phil knew it. Cabot never made an offer if he didn't have leverage on the offeree. The answer to Nick's question was a foregone conclusion.

"Of course, Mister …," Phil began.

"*Nick*, after two hundred years, its about time you call me Nick, don't you think?" Cabot interjected.

"Of course …Nick, I'll do whatever I can," Phil replied.

"Good, I've got some bits and pieces to tidy up now. If you'd see Rachel on your way out, she'll fill you in on where I'd like you to get started," Cabot said, smiling.

Years of interaction with Cabot made Phil immediately aware he had been dismissed. Turning on his heel, he left the office. Walking down the hall to Rachel's office, he pondered how simple, cut and dried it had all been. He could have said 'no' of course, but then six good friends, his entire family and he would be dead. Without skipping a beat, Cabot would move on to the next name on his list of potential number two's. In the end, Nick was just filling administrative slots with bodies. If you willingly, indeed, eagerly, climbed into a slot, you were one of the quick. If not you were one of the dead.

Possessed of both the power and the will to actualize his visions, Nick always had his way. In Cabot's game plan, which by the way included the whole world, you were either predator or prey. There were no bystanders.

Following a classical bent in his musing, Phil could imagine a resurrected Dante desperately struggling to pen some new echelon in hell where Phil would pay for the slaughter of innocents and the rape of the Earth. Cabot would doubtless be exonerated from such endless torment. He was, after all, just doing what, as a perfect predator, he was engineered to do, namely, prey on the weak.

Phil was not a predator and he knew it. Phil fell into that group of people who allowed themselves to be leveraged into evil by their own good conscience and concern for the welfare of their fellow creatures. Phil never could buy into the notion that the ends justified the means, and so, became the tool of someone like Cabot, who saw that dictum as an indisputable fact of nature. Phil was a toady, an accomplice to a bully who was in the process of ravaging the whole Earth. Each obediently rebellious step that Phil took down the garden path confirmed his complicity in Cabot's monstrous plan.

Chapter 10

A leisurely tour around the station was now an integral part of the Commander Tutunji's day. Before coming on duty, he fired up the command shuttle and made a circuit of what was, at one time, his quite ordinary CC Natcorp station. Given the ongoing construction efforts, evidence of the damage caused by the shock wave had been all but erased. Where once his simple station hung upon the black sheet of space, now, a constantly growing assemblage of living units, strike craft bays, laser turrets, and fusion missile launchers had grown doubling the total mass of the installation. Shield generators were moored in space around the growing assembly of modules, providing six levels of overlapping coverage. Were it not for the blue aura that marked the limits of their extension, it would have been easy to fly dead on into one or another of these walls of energy.

Sydes required the shield coverage around the strike craft bays be fitted with internal motion detector fail safes. Despite his trust in Commander Tutunji, Sydes was not about to risk the sort of fiasco that had killed his comrades on the PP station. If a ship was leaving the bay, the shields could not be activated. The engineers thought it an odd request, but then again, none of them had witnessed the loss of a whole squadron.

Having witnessed the destruction of Sydes comrades, Commander Tutunji took no personal offense at Sydes' request. Tutunji felt a small measure of satisfaction as he remembered how surprised Sydes was when the joint Natcorp engineering staff automatically complied with his demands. It would take a long time, if ever, for Sydes to get used to his status in the new order of things.

Directing the viewer out and away from the station, the Commander took stock of his surveillance capacity. The console registered the presence of remote scanners scattered across millions of kilometers of space, but they couldn't be activated from the shuttle. The controls that accessed that feed were confined to the station's bridge. Instead, he mobilized the shuttle's viewer to focus on the huge belt of radiation that was the only memorial to the men and women who had driven off the blood ships at the cost of their personal futures. The belt was there, but suddenly, appearing in the foreground of the viewer, an enormous formation of tractor shuttles appeared, traveling toward the station.

The appearance of the returning shuttle flotilla awakened him to the reading on the chronometer glaring at him from the console. As he activated the controls turning the shuttle toward the receiving bay, the comm-link crackled to life.

"If you're coming along on this ride, it's time to get onboard," Sydes announced.

"Copy that, on my way in," the Commander replied.

Securing the shuttle in its berth, the Commander reached his greatly expanded bridge in record time. Sydes was waiting for him.

"Trying to get a little radiation tan?" Sydes said wryly.

Smiling as he moved to the viewer, the Commander could see Sydes was recovering a sense of humor despite the personnel losses he had witnessed. Just then, the comm-link came to life.

"All craft secure," the bay crew Chief said.

Sydes quickly activated the computer and called up the ships' registry program. The precisely engineered computer protocol was one of his special 'gadgets.' Sensors in the several receiving bays of the station registered the comings and goings of vessels by detecting a number code electronically imprinted on their hulls. The ships' registry instantly told him which vessels were in the bays and, hence, behind the shield grid. His expression clearly indicated that he didn't like what he saw as he torqued the comm-link switch.

"Chief, my count shows one shuttle still out there," Sydes said, his tone pressured.

"Sorry Captain, we didn't have time to enter the loss. Garland's shuttle lost guidance control. They got caught between two of the asteroids and the shuttle exploded. We couldn't even recover the bodies," the Chief reported in an apologetic tone.

"Thank you, Chief," Sydes responded and closed the comm-link.

Sydes looked up and stared at the viewscreen for a long moment. Garland was a good man, he would be missed. Never turning to look at the Commander, Sydes busied himself making the necessary corrections in the registry.

Losses hit Sydes hard, particularly when he wasn't part of the action in which they were sustained. The Commander knew that feeling all too well and recognized that the ace pilot wasn't about to make small talk. Looking down at the console, the Commander noted that the readouts indicated that phase one of the operation was ready for implementation.

Von Strohheim's strategic planners had come up with the idea to use tractor shuttles to move additional small asteroids into the radiation belt. Each lifeless rock was mounted with a fusion charge and a laser bore. Once the asteroids had been propelled into the radiation belt by the tractor shuttles, the laser bores would be activated, carrying the fusion charges deep into the rock where they would be detonated. It was a simple idea really, namely, create radioactive dust, and lots of it, to scramble the enemy's sensors. Sydes had provided refinements to what he called phase two of the operation. Once the charges in the asteroids had been detonated, the shuttles would stand off at a safe distance and propel mines into the cloud of irradiated particles, seeding it with death.

The idea was simplicity born of necessity. The strategic planners had, after hours of computer simulations, made their best guess as to the location of the enemy task force, which was believed to be far outside of the station's scanner range. Based on this model, they had designated the three best tactical routes into the solar system for a force attacking from deep space.

Everyone knew that there weren't enough ships to cover all three fronts, so a decision had been made to cancel out one of the three. The route the aliens had initially taken, which was assumed to be the one most tactically advantageous to them, would be flooded with radioactive dust to blind their scanners and subsequently mined. At Sydes suggestion, the energy signatures of the mines would remain unchanged. He reasoned that if aliens could detect the mines, that route would be all the more unattractive. If aliens couldn't see them, they would sustain losses comparable to the last go around.

Nobody liked standing on this shaky pile of assumptions, but war was the real time translation of assumptions into definitive action. Action had always been the furnace used to refine assumptions into brilliant strokes or reduce them to slag.

Looking at the chronometer and, then, at Sydes, the Commander knew it was time to jump into the furnace.

"Are you ready for the real craziness?" Sydes asked.

There was no need to respond, the Commander knew what the real craziness was. The station needed to be moved to a better tactical position to support action against the blood ships coming through the two remaining invasion avenues. Towing the station to its new position would take a lot of time and tie up all the tractor shuttles. That was unacceptable when so much had to be done to fortify the two avenues the planners hoped the aliens would use in their next attack.

Enter the Commander's crazy idea straight out of the ether. They would sail the station to its new position using the shields as canvas and the station keeping propulsion units as a rudder. The wind would be supplied by the tidal force of the explosion in the asteroid belt they were about to detonate. There wasn't time to evacuate the station so everyone, like it or not, was coming along for the ride.

Like a good sailor fastening the rigging on an antique sailing ship before setting sail, Sydes checked and rechecked every shield generator.

"We'll have about ten seconds before the shock wave hits us," Sydes remarked.

Sydes' matter of fact manner seemed more consistent with a comment about the sighing advent of a balmy breeze than the arrival of the hurricane holocaust they were about to create.

"Secure shield moorings and bring station shields to maximum," the Commander shouted into the comm-link.

The fusion reactor lights of the console indicated full capacity output. We'll need it, Tutunji thought to himself. Several layers of shielding would have to do double duty, roughly half of them protecting the station and half serving as sails against the blast.

"Propulsion units on line," Sydes said as he looked across at the Commander.

The Commander looked up and acknowledged Sydes with a nod.

"I guess we're ready for the fireworks," Sydes said, his tone laced with excitement.

"All hands, grab onto something we're about to start this ride," the Commander announced over the station wide comm-link.

Looking over at Sydes, the Commander realized that there was nothing more to say. Sydes would control the shield planes that functioned as sails against the shock wave and the Commander would manage the propulsion units that would hopefully serve as their rudder. His gaze sweeping the console one last time, the Commander hit the remote detonation switch that controlled the asteroid fusion charges.

An explosion of stupefying dimensions filled the viewscreen. The area of detonation expanded like a ball of bread dough rising on fast forward. It was, of course, a silent blast, but the Commander could hear a roaring and booming in his head. Funny how reluctant the brain is to give up conventionally paired experiences, he thought to himself. As the booming in his head subsided, he heared Sydes counting.

"Seven, eight, nine ...," Sydes muttered as his fingers played over the shield controls.

Jamming the activators of the beefed up station keeping propulsion units to full, the Commander watched as Sydes played the shield grid planes as though he were a virtuoso organist rendering a Bach fugue. The shock wave struck the station like a manic tsunami. Instead of shattering, the station lifted, amidst groans of straining metal, and moved out and away from the wall of force. Everything not nailed down on the bridge went airborne, including a young second lieutenant, who thrown into a corner, suffered more from fractured dignity than any real injury.

The Commander could see it clearly all over the fighter ace's face. Sydes was having fun. He corrected each clockwise tendency to spin by a flaring the shield planes on the opposite side of the station. The leading edge of the blast had passed them now and Sydes activated the shield planes to full extension to catch the force of the after ripples.

"Well, we're through the rapids. Now its just a tourist cruise from here to our new perch," Sydes remarked as he leaned back from the console.

The Commander saw the disappointment on Sydes' face. His expression mirrored that of a cadet whose hyperthruster had cut out during his first flight.

As the ride smoothed out, the Commander gradually adjusted the propulsion units, refining the heading that would bring them to their new position, or perch as Sydes had jokingly named it. Switching to one of the remote long range scanners, the Commander summoned a view of the station speeding through space. The dark bulk of the station in flight was punctured by porthole lights and bedecked all around with the shimmering blue of fully extended shields. Seen from this angle, the station looked like some hastily assembled Christmas tree hurtling through the cold night of the solar system.

Looking up from the console, a satisfied expression on his face, Sydes was in his element. All action-reaction, he milked the last bit of propulsion from the remaining eddies of force, as his hands effected subtle changes in the angles of the shield planes.

"The readout says that the asteroids went up, and the mines are still intact where we buoyed them out of harm's way. As soon as the cloud stops boiling, we can order in the tractor shuttles to fire our mines into the dust cloud," Sydes said as he looked up from the console.

As the momentum of the station slowly dissipated, the Commander activated the navigational range finder. Scrutinizing the reading, he looked over at Sydes.

"We should come to within eight hundred kilometers of the target area."

The Commander was unable to completely conceal a feeling of pride in the fulfillment of his crazy idea.

"I was hoping for more like five hundred, but I'll take eight hundred. It shouldn't take more than an hour and a half for the tractors to tow us to the final position," Sydes replied, a feigned frown crinkling around his eyes.

Although his face bespoke the contrary, Tutunji could see that Sydes was pleased with how the Commander's craziness had turned out.

"Nice shot," Sydes said as he gripped the Commander by the shoulder.

This show of respect and affection took the Commander completely off guard. Sydes' words were a code phrase that pilots used with each other, parsimonious in word count, but rich in regard and admiration.

"Yes, well … we did it … joint effort …" the Commander replied, fumbling a bit.

Traces of a grin fleeting over his face, Sydes turned back to the console. There was still a little bit of flying to enjoy.

✦

As soon as Forrester got the word of the station's maiden voyage, he and Arthur organized the medical techs into a child care unit. They rounded up all kids who had lost their parents but had not yet been evacuated back to Earth. The orphans were clustered into small groups on the nursery floor when the 'big bump' happened. Arthur wisely suggested lots of cookies and candy, but no milk. Forrester found that curious for a man like Arthur who wasn't distressed by disorder, but perhaps it was only his own carelessness that wasn't troublesome to him.

By and large, the kids seemed to find the rolling and pitching fun, particularly because there were adults around to hang onto. As the ride smoothed out, the children got up to look out of the portholes and watched the stars slipped by. As soon as the general excitement was over, Arthur and Forrester excused themselves to check for injured in the station at large.

It was Arthur's idea to check the bars first. Arthur always had a better grasp of the mean common denominator of human behavior than Forrester. There were lots of head and back injuries among the patrons. Sitting on a bar stool, drink in hand, was not the best way to experience a nuclear explosion, especially if you survived the blast.

Busy solidifying small fractures, Forrester was also in demand reinflating and sealing lumbar discs. From the look of this lot of patients, these would be the only skills he'd need. Interventions of this kind never struck Forrester as the practice of medicine.

These sorts of jury-rigs were more like the body work a minimally trained mechanic might do. He slapped transdermal pain patches on everyone, whether they complained or not. The patches contained a mild tranquilizer that might be more useful than the primary analgesic. The strike craft pilots were the most trouble. They didn't complain about the pain, they only wanted to be reassured that their injuries wouldn't take them off the flight roster.

After checking with the medical call-in register, Arthur announced he and Forrester were finished and ambled over to the bar to order a drink. Arthur muttered something about staying in the bar to do some post-traumatic psychotherapy with the injured and downed his drink.

Not engineered by nature to be convivial in company, Forrester returned to their compartment. He felt a sense of relief as he heard the automatic door slide shut behind him. Alone represented Forrester's idea of the most congenial sphere of interpersonal space. However, isolation often conjured the worst in internal strife. Nevertheless, in solitary company, he could bring up the lights inside his head without being concerned about the reaction of others. He could feel it beginning, the head journal in his socially segregated brain case had opened. Head journaling was a habit, no, a character trait, the inception of which predated even his earliest childhood memory. It was not an intracranial monologue, it was a dialogue between him and him without the benefit of a schizophrenic diagnosis to justify its existence.

⚜

Recently, Forrester found his cognitive inner sanctum repeatedly invaded by thoughts about the personal life of the scroll's diarist. Perhaps these thoughts were inspired by the war and all the human sacrifices he had seen laid upon that altar. Whether it was conflict with an enemy, unrevealed except through its aggression, or some indescribable process driven by the content of the scrolls, he could not discern. Regardless of what prompted them, he found his thoughts directed to the imminence of some awful consummation. A looming and palpable sense of urgency attached itself to that ancient author's need to reveal himself. The feeling was so compelling that Forrester wasn't sure whether he wanted to know more about the diarist, or the diarist's desire to more completely reveal his personal thoughts and feelings was at work.

Being transfixed by a belief that the scroll's author wished to declare himself was not a new experience. On one previous occasion when this feeling had struck him, Forrester had catalogued a collection of scroll entries that seemed to exemplify the author's need for personal disclosure. These entries contained revelations of inner pain, but were devoid of self-pity. A menu of private anguish illustrated within these entries called to and dogged Forrester's soul.

Anguish that was alive in Forrester as much as in the diarist's experience, vividly revealed itself as he read the words. Forrester and the scroll's scribe seemed to share a profound sense of impotence when confronted by the essential self-destructive inertia of the human condition. This sense of helplessness, more than anything else, tied them together in a bond of despair across three millennia. Faced with his own version of a strife filled reality fashioned and maintained by his own species, Forrester could understand the diarist's sense of isolation. Referenced in his personal scanner under the phrase, 'I am alone,' this catalogue of entries was so named as each entry concluded with that coda.

> IN THE HEAT OF THE WORKSHOP, DUST
> DANCES IN THE AIR LIKE GUESTS AT A
> WEDDING FEAST. THE WINE OF SWEAT
> STAINING THE WOOD TO A DEPTH ONLY
> THE PLANE CAN REMOVE, ADDS TOIL TO
> THE DAY'S LABORS. THE HANDS MOVE
> ACROSS THE FACE OF THE BOARD GUIDED
> BY YEARS OF WATCHING, FAILING AND
> FINALLY CRAFTING, WHILE WORDS THAT
> PENETRATE THE HEART OF MAN WITH NO
> LESS BITE THAN THE AWL UPON THE JOINT,
> FILL MY HEAD.
>
> LIKE AN IMAGE IN THE MIND THAT
> RESISTS THE CARVER'S SKILL TO FIND ITS
> FORM IN THE CURVES OF THE WOOD, MY
> WORDS SHAPE NO BEAUTY IN THE TIMBER
> OF THIS WORLD. NO MATTER THE ANGLE
> OF THE BLADE OR THE CARE GIVEN TO THE
> STRIKING OF THE MALLET, THIS WOOD
> SPLITS ONLY ALONG THE GRAIN OF POWER.
> I AM ALONE.

Forrester found the metaphor compelling. Especially intrigued by the phrase 'splits only along the grain of power,' he dwelt for a moment on the confluence of survival drives that had brought his species to their dubious pinnacle of mastery over their birth place. There was little doubt that this same unchecked and endlessly ramifying survival need lay at the root of all the infamies perpetrated in his species' quest for power.

It was a simple formula really. A burgeoning force sufficient to enliven the inorganic entailed the vigor to destroy the organic. He imagined that Arthur, when he read the scrolls, had found the premise equally compelling. However, Arthur would very likely restate this sentiment much more simply, 'people are what they are.' The author of the scrolls would agree, but unlike Arthur, the diarist anguished over this central feature of the human character. The unimpeachable fact that humanity was motivated by fear and a quest for sufficient power to quell that fear inspired in this ancient scribe a feeling of overwhelming despair. Forrester's reading of the text suggested to him that the diarist felt he had a job to do, but try as he might, he couldn't finish it. The next entry in the catalogue seemed to support this belief.

> THE MIGHT OF ROME SHUFFLES WEARILY
> THROUGH THE COOL OF EVENTIDE, PAST THE
> OPEN WORKSHOP DOOR. CLAD IN DUSTY
> RED WITH SHARP METAL HUNG ABOUT
> THEIR LOINS, THESE MASTERS OF THE WORLD
> ARE BUT THIS DAY'S EMBLEM OF DREAD'S
> VICTORY OVER FAITH.
>
> SACRIFICE IS KNOWN TO THOSE AMONG WHOM
> I WANDER ONLY IN DEFENSE OF SEED, TRIBE
> OR TERRITORY. WHERE NO TERRORS LOOM,
> THEY FALL UPON ONE ANOTHER SPURRED BY
> GREED, AGGRIEVED BY OFFENSES OF THE
> HEART, AND IN ENDLESS QUEST FOR BADGES
> OF OFFICE.
>
> ONLY TERROR AND REWARD SPEAK TO THE
> BLOOD AND BONE OF THOSE RISEN FROM
> THIS DUST. UNGOADED BY THE THREAT
> OF LOSS OR THE PROMISE OF POWER, THEY
> ARE UNMOVED. I AM ALONE.

To 'move' mankind toward motivations other than the pursuit of dominion and the flight from fear was the perceived mission of the scrolls' author. The diarist's lament was plain. No matter what avenue he pursued, no path would long feel the weight of human feet unless it was paved with fear and wended its way toward the promise of dominion. Whatever message he hoped to impart, whatever motivations he hoped to call upon in the mass of slowly evolving tissue around him, was clearly lost on the audience.

Completely alone in a sea of motivations alien to him, the diary's scribe did not rail against his solitude, nor did he arrogantly embrace it. He was called to preach the doctrine of the third dimension to those who could grasp only length and width. As the next entry indicated, he clearly had four or more dimensions to reveal, but was thwarted in his mission by limitations inherent to the fundamental constitution of his listeners.

I FIND NO PLACE TO BEGIN. THE DYER OF RAIMENT, WHOSE VATS STAND BEYOND MY WORKSHOP DOOR, CANNOT HEAR EVEN THE VOICE HIS CHILDREN GIVE TO THEIR SUFFERING, HIS EARS BEING STOPPED. A FRIEND OF MANY YEARS, WITHOUT WORD OR MOTION, HEAL I HIM AND HIS SEED. YET, STILL HE HARKENS NOT AS I SPEAK OF THE LIFE AND LIGHT FROM THE BEGINNING. HIS EARS OPEN AND EYES BRIGHTEN ONLY WHEN I PRATTLE OF GOODS AND TAXES. MADE WHOLE, THE BODY'S ROUGH HUSK STILL ARMORS THE SOUL AGAINST THE TRUTH.

IMPRISONED IN THE BODY'S DARK CELLAR, THE SOUL GLIMPSES POORLY AND SELDOM THROUGH THE LATTICE OF THE FLESH, GRASPING BUT FEW SHAFTS OF THE LIGHT FROM WHICH IT SPRANG. WHEN WORDS ARE LENT TO THIS VISION OF ALL BEGINNINGS, THE REVELATION IS OFT SEEN AS MADNESS. THE MEMORY OF ALL BEGINNINGS IS LOST TO TIME, TRAVELING IN BLOOD AND BONE. STILL FRESH AT BIRTH, IT WANES IN MANHOOD, ACHIEVING BRILLIANCE AGAIN ONLY IN THE MOMENTS BEFORE DEATH AS THE SOUL IS SET UPON ITS JOURNEY HOME.

THE CHILDREN OF THE VILLAGE AND THOSE WEIGHED DOWN BY YEARS ARE MY GREATEST COMFORT. FRAIL FLESH'S BEGINNINGS AND ENDINGS ARE CLOSER TO THE LIGHT, WHEREIN LIES MY SOUL'S LONGING AND RELEASE.

WHEN I AM BECOME BUT A CHANNEL
FOR THAT WHICH ENLIVENS THE WHOLE
OF CREATION, THEY LOOK NOT TO THE
SOURCE OF THAT QUICKENING FIRE, BUT
ARE FIXED ON THE FEW SPARKS THAT
TOUCH THEIR LIVES. WERE I TO OPEN
THE VISTA OF ALL CREATION, YET I FEAR
THEY WOULD REMAIN UNMOVED. I AM
ALONE.

Forrester had read this entry many times before, focusing on the scribe's sense of frustration, but this was the first time its broader meaning sunk in.

Nested within the text was the author's belief that he somehow tapped into whatever it was that made the universe run. Forrester read the entry several times, studying each word intently as though trying to wring every drop of meaning from the characters huddled together to form it. Although a black and white scrutiny of the entry's symbols occupied the foreground of Forrester's mental activity, the contrasting background was a full color memory of the aura emanating from the oval that contained the scrolls, the moving shadows on the wall, and the every point illumination of the hut. Then, there was his personal experience of the 'Y' shaped invigoration felt on so many occasions since his discovery of the scrolls. That uplifting sensation was impossible to dismiss.

He wondered whether these few personal experiences with the scrolls amounted to what their author called 'that quickening fire.' Certainly none of these experiences taken individually, or for that matter, all of them lumped together amounted to a parting of the Red Sea or a burning bush.

Jerked to attention as though someone had struck the primeval funny bone wired to his entire body, Forrester sat bolt upright. There it was, precisely what the diarist had attempted to describe in so many different ways, the allure of power. Like all those who had gone before, Forrester sought confirmation of the diarist's words in the big and dramatic in life. The ancient writer had laid no trap for him. Forrester could not escape the realization that he leapt eagerly over the precipice, like some human lemming, driven by the functioning of every unrepentantly primitive cell in his body. He yearned for the conviction that some compelling event could provide.

No wonder, this lonely writer from so long ago felt isolated. Three thousand years of technological progress, with a smidgen of evolution thrown in, hadn't helped Forrester one little bit. He had personally witnessed some truly exceptional events, had been individually touched by 'that quickening fire,' and yet, he was still searching for some holographically compelling, space age equivalent of the burning bush. Then, as now, the diarist's words and witness were but a straw before the hurricane of the human genome.

What a waste! Forrester had always seen himself as different from his fellows in his quest for the transcendent in life and his openness to its manifestation. However, at the level where it counted, hearing the words and seeing beyond 'the few sparks that touched his life' to the 'source of the quickening fire,' he had accomplished no more than those who, now dust these three thousand years, had seen and heard the diarist. He was just one more among the throngs who listened, but did not hear. Certainly words, like faith and conviction were meaningful, but they referenced feelings that were notoriously fickle biochemical events. The diarist sought to instill perfect knowledge in his listeners, but the larger realities his words portrayed were lost in the ebb and flow of sea water from which his audience's emotional states arose. The next entry on the menu seemed to confirm the diarist's appreciation of the universal nature of the human experience that Forrester had just despairingly encountered in himself. There was no avoiding the conclusion, Forrester was just one more emotionally jostled bag of biochemical soup among billions.

IN A MOMENT OF REST, I WATCH AS THE DYER
OF RAIMENT EMPTIES HIS VATS. STREAMS OF
COLOR SINKING INTO THE DUST ARE CARRIED
AWAY ON THE SANDALS OF THOSE WHO PASS
THIS WAY. TROD UNDERFOOT, BOTH BEAUTY
AND THE TRUTH IT REFLECTS ARE FOREVER LOST.

LIKE THE DYE THAT FASTENING NOT TO THE
STRANDS OF THESE LIVES IS WASHED AWAY
IN THE WATERS OF DAILY USE, SO MY WORDS
ARE BLANCHED BY TIME TO THE COMMON
COLORS OF THIS CLAY. SURVIVING THE DUST
OF CENTURIES, WHAT WAS SAID ABIDES,
WHILE WHAT IS MEANT PERISHES. I AM
ALONE.

The immediacy of his own existential failings represented a soul destroying realization for Forrester. The bulk of humanity courtesy a million years worth of time tested emotional defenses designed to sweep away uncomfortable thoughts and feelings readily dimissed the pain of such epiphanies. However, if in no other way, Forrester differed from his fellows in that he was racked by the condemnation inherent to the unavoidable realization of his own abysmal fallibility. His desire to embrace transcendence was buried under the muck of an evolutionary heritage oozing, as it were, out of every nook and cranny in his feeble, simian derived brain. He was sinking in the same mire that all members of his species settled into. Unable to shed what they were, humanity was forever dragged down by the very tissue that informed their vision of what they could not become.

Then, as catastrophically as it had begun, it was over. Forrester sensed a calming presence replacing his feeling of soul destroying futility. At once alive in his mind, it was the stillness that had attended the light, a perfect memory of a desert night so long ago made real within his mind. Forrester knew nothing he thought or did had created this still light, unless he counted giving up on himself.

In a way, he could not adequately describe to himself, he imagined that somehow he had glimpsed 'that which enlivens all of creation.' He had been forced, or perhaps simply allowed, to grasp a portion of the diarist's mission. For the briefest moment, he saw beyond the 'few sparks that touched his life' to the 'quickening fire.'

Epiphany was too small a word to describe this experience, but he could conjure no other. Whatever had occurred, and seemed somehow to continue in his inner experience of himself, directed him to the last entry in the 'I am alone' catalogue. Mentally and emotionally animated by the stillness of the light within, he felt he might finally grasp the meaning of an entry that had long eluded him.

> FEVERED BY DREAMS AND VISIONS, I GO
> ALONE TO THE WORKSHOP THERE TO DRINK
> IN THE STILLNESS OF A NIGHT IN WHICH
> EVEN THE ANIMALS QUIETEN THEIR CRIES.
> THROUGH THE LATTICE I SEE THE STARS
> THAT SEEM MORE A HOME THAN THIS
> DARK AND DUSTY ABODE IN WHICH MY
> FEET ARE PLANTED. MY MIND GRASPS
> LIVING LINES BINDING THEIR FIERY
> BODIES TOGETHER THAT ARE BY THE
> EYE UNSEEN, YET ENTWINE ALL PARTS
> INTO A LIVING WHOLE. IN THOSE TRACINGS,

THE MAP OF ALL CREATION, SUSTAINED BY
AND FOR LIFE, IS SEEN.

DRAWN UP INTO THE WEB OF THE
FIRMAMENT'S LIVING BODY, I AM
QUICKENED IN THE SPIRIT, OR MADE
MAD BY THE WINE OF ITS GRANDEUR.
FROM THE ARC THAT BEGINS THE
THE CIRCLE, I HAVE, AM NOW, AND
WILL EVER AGAIN TURN UPON THIS
WHEEL UNDER SUNS WITHOUT
NUMBER IN FORMS MANY AND
VARIED.

I SPEAK AND GO UNHEARD, UNVEILED
AND GO UNSEEN, TRANSFORMED AND
AM UNCHANGED. ON WORLDS
WITHOUT END, I AM THE WAYFARER
OF THE LIGHT, TILL THE DARKNESS
SHALL PASS INTO THE LIGHT OF ALL
GENERATION. I AM FOREVER THE
STRANGER IN A STRANGE LAND. I AM
ALONE.

Forrester read the entry only once. He understood and knew that he understood. The stillness in the light came only when he wasn't home. The moment his attempts to wrest his own intent from the scroll's entries failed, the diarist could voice their meaning across the millennia. It was a simple lesson, but under its tutelage he recognized that he was a simple man who had to learn in small and painful increments. It was sufficient.

Chapter 11

Esther had taken Chen and Chandra under her wing and included them in community events as though they were members of the people of the trees. The opportunity to learn so much more than he could have as an outside monitor of the group pleased Chen. In particular, he was excited by the prospect of watching Esther and Jacob's little girl, Crystal, grow up. Chandra came along, but more to be with Chen than to fulfill any scientifically driven need. If she could not compete directly with Chen's infatuation with the meek, she would at least make appearances that suggested she shared his interest.

Visiting with families in the community, Chandra seldom called at Esther and Jacob's home by herself. In contrast to her individual visits, Calls made in Chen's company seemed greeted by a warmer reception by Crystal's family. Nevertheless, the position Chandra shared with Chen as a monitor of the meek required her to observe their social interactions and Chen was not always available. Such visits had particular importance to the project as Crystal was the first child born to the community.

Chandra's level of felt discomfort among the meek may well have been related to the fact that her dominance need coefficient was significantly higher than Chen's, and miles beyond that which the meek experienced. Chandra spent a lot of time and energy trying to dismiss this observation of Chen's as academic claptrap, but at the same time, the notion burned in the back of her mind like a flame that could not be quenched. The idea that, implicit to her interactions with others, was a need to dominate them was attended by an anger that was equal in magnitude to the irrational ire she experienced when she dealt with the people of the trees.

An insufferable lack of overt expressions of passion among the meek when confronted with the vicissitudes and frustrations of daily living lay at the root of Chandra's fuming resentment of them. Chandra's anxiety ridden, but primal, belief was that the meek must function exactly as she did. Just like her, she thought, they must boil over with emotion every time they felt thwarted, but somehow exercise a measure of control over their raging inner cauldron to a degree that she could never hope to approximate.

If she were correct in her belief that the meek shared her turbulent passions, but were vested by nature with superior control over the expression thereof, then, she felt left by evolution's wayside. If Chen was correct in his observation about her exaggerated need for dominance, she was still relegated to a bus stop abandoned by a genetic line that had taken a new route into the future. Regardless of the belief she embraced, the personal outcome was a feeling of angry shame. She felt discarded by mother nature.

Mastering her own passions as a woman was only part of Chandra's dilemma. As a geneticist, she knew nature did not backtrack along old routes once forward motion had been established in a new direction. In the company of the majority of the dominance dedicated human race, she saw herself on a path that was a genetic dead end. She tried desperately to control the pain and resentment attending this realization whenever she met with the meek.

Her emotional baggage in hand but firmly under control, Chandra visited Esther and Jacob's home. Over the course of several visits, she observed Crystal always seemed to know when her parents wanted to hear from her. On more than one occasion while Chandra was visiting the family, Esther or Jacob would, in conversation, wonder where Crystal was and what she was doing. Within moments, the comm-link would chime and Crystal would report in.

Several examples of this more than coincidental event prompted Chandra to question Esther and Jacob about what appeared to be more than serendipitous clairvoyance. Their only response was to smile and say 'she knows.' Chandra found this answer wholly unsatisfactory. Her face masked in the best blank screen she could muster, she tried very hard not to let her infuriation intone in her voice. As far as she was concerned, the response of Crystal's parents was an evasion meant to conceal, not a direct answer to a direct question. Her sense of fury at being patronized in this way boiled within her when, upon her return to the service center, she ran into Chen.

"I'm really sick of these faux Zen responses," Chandra said as she related the events of her visit.

Chen listened attentively and without comment.

"I ask a straight up question and get a fortune cookie answer and pat on the head!" Chandra snapped.

She was in the full bloom of her rage now. Hers was an outpouring of previously unexpressed adolescent resentment sufficient to sweep away everyone over the age of fifteen.

Listening patiently to what represented a primal cache of chaotically churning emotions, Chen pondered what sort of reply would be helpful to her. He focused equally on fashioning a response that would not place him at ground zero for an explosion of feeling that would level the hills and fill the

EDWARD E. STAMBAUGH II, PH.D. AND J. CONRAD STAMBAUGH

valleys of their common experience.

"Hypothetically speaking, how do you know when you're sexually attracted to someone?" He asked in a hushed tone.

"What kind of asinine question is that? Are you trying to pick up where Esther and Jacob left ... left off ... with your own brand of quasi Zen, double spun, professorial, socratic bullshit," she sputtered angrily.

It was Chen's turn. He elected a different approach. He used what he knew about her need for dominance rather than drawing on his own reflexive need to pacify the situation. He found the tactic distasteful, but he sought to inspire fear to counter her overweening self-endorsement. He went nose to nose with Chandra and raised the volume of his voice to nearly a shout.

"You're pissed because you didn't get a scientific answer to a scientific question, right!" He exclaimed, holding her gaze.

"Right!" Chandra responded, calming down just a bit.

"So, I'm asking a scientific question and all you're doing is screaming and jerking me around. What's the difference?" Chen said without flinching.

"I just know ... if I'm attracted to someone," Chandra replied backing away from Chen.

"And what happens if this other hypothetical party isn't attracted to you? Do you still, *just know*, you're attracted to him?" Chen asked, his tone edgy.

"OK, OK, I get it. Intuitive apperception, gut level stuff," Chandra replied, her indignation softening.

He had a lot more to say, but Chen had grown wise enough not to say it aloud. Recognizing that Chandra's rage was that of a rejected child, he could appreciate that she felt left out. He knew she watched enviously as his daily interactions with the meek seemed to gain him more and more acceptance among them. He was also aware she felt she had been set aside in favor of the meek, or perhaps, more precisely left behind in Chen's pursuit of a more complete understanding of the evolutionary leap the meek represented. He would verbalize none of these observations given her current, excellent imitation of an emotional cement mixer.

Staring at Chandra for a long time while she studied the floor, he wondered how he might strike a compromise between her bottomless needs and his interest in the meek. Then, looking at his watch, Chen shot to his feet.

"Gotta go, I promised Crystal, I'd go along on one of her excursions. I'll see you around supper time."

Out of the door of his office, Chen moved at a pace just short of a run. He had to get out of there and away from Chandra's feelings of rage and resentment that seemed to hang like an oppressive cloud in the room. He knew his frantic exit would only confirm her belief that the meek occupied a higher rank on his reinforcement menu than she did, but, at that moment, he only knew he wanted out.

$$\star\!\!\diamond\!\!\star$$

In a hurry to exit the service center, Chen paused at the glass doors as he saw Crystal seated at the pilot's console of a hopper. She waved Chen over to the craft as he left the service center in full flight from Chandra's scorning wrath. Crystal had her mother's ability to smile with her whole body without any pronounced grin showing on her face. It was a wonderfully curious ability that Chen had attempted to analyze on more than one occasion. As he looked at her now, this total body smile seemed to have something to do with the absence of any evidence of tension in her body, save that necessary to work her limbs and maintain her posture. In short, she appeared at ease with and open to the world around her.

Crystal held a special status for Chen as she was the first recorded, unslaughtered birth in the entire reserve. Now, almost four years old, her ability and stature more closely resembled that of the average eight year old. Her hair was the platinum blond color so often seen in very young children and her eyes were such a light blue that they appeared almost white. Despite her precocious ability and exceptional height, her face held the features of innocence associated with the very young. She possessed her mother's kindness and serenity and her father's sense of adventure. She had learned to fly a hopper shortly before her fourth birthday and spent hours everyday exploring the enormous reserve.

The craft, under Crystal's able control, climbed smoothly over the tree tops and headed straight toward a mountain range about three hundred miles away. This was not going to be some meandering outing, Chen thought to himself. Crystal had planned this trip with a specific destination in mind.

In less then fifteen minutes, the hopper landed so gently near the crest of the mountain that he hardly felt the touch down. Crystal stepped out of the craft and walked directly to a cluster of large rocks and knelt down by a small hollow in the earth.

Coming to her feet, she turned and looked at Chen. Somehow, Chen knew what she required and, finding a small shovel in the hopper, joined her at the site she had chosen.

Applying the shovel to the hollow she indicated, he excavated a hole just shy of two meters in depth. Chen sweated, something his job description didn't often require of him. Just as he was about to take a breather, the shovel struck something solid. Crystal watched attentively as he cleared away the loose dirt and, then, tossed the securecase out of the hole.

Out of breath and hauling himself from the hole, Chen's words came between pants.

"Crystal, this case … can only … be opened … by the person … who sealed it."

Her reaction to Chen's statement could in no way be described as disappointment. Kneeling down beside him, she helped to brush away the last bits of soil atop the securecase. As the cleaning process revealed the hand print receptor, she examined it curiously for a moment and placed her tiny hand into the receptor.

Despite the marvels he had observed among the meek, Chen continued to be startled by the little bits of wizardry they performed with such nonchalance. This time, his astonishment manifested itself in a poorly muffled gasp as the securecase lid popped open with a resounding snap. With the lid's rising, Chen thought he saw a glowing white light within the dark confines of the case. The experience was a momentary one that he quickly dismissed as the sun's light reflecting off the polished metal interior. Peering into the case, he saw carefully arranged rows of cylindrically shaped leather sheaths.

Smiling simply, as though the opening of the case was just what she expected would happen, Crystal watched patiently as Chen picked up the securecase. Crystal dragging the shovel and Chen cradling the case in his arms, the two made their way back to the hopper in silence.

As he pondered the artifacts resting within the case in his lap, Chen imagined their conversation on the hopper ride back to Crystal's home would be as intriguing as the discovery of the leather quivers.

"Crystal, did you know there was something hidden in the mountain?" He asked.

"Yes," she responded, as she prepared for lift off.

Chiding himself internally, Chen knew better than to ask a question like that. The meek expressed and comprehended language with a precision that worked for them, but often left those outside of the community with the feeling that the implicit content of a question was being evaded. Although he didn't experience an emotional reaction of the kind or magnitude that Chandra had expressed earlier, Chen understood the feeling of frustration.

"How did you know something was there in the ground?" He asked, attempting to be more specific.

As the hopper rose into the air, she reached down to the instrument panel and punched her home address into the automatic pilot program. A gentle smile coming to her face, she leaned back from the console.

"It said it was there the first time I flew over the mountain. Then, every time I flew near there, it said it was there, only a little louder," she replied looking at him curiously.

"So, you heard it calling to you?" He asked, trying to contain his excitement.

"Not with my ears, inside my head," she replied, suppressing a giggle.

Veins and arteries filling to the brim, Chen knew he was on to something. In an attempt to formulate another question, he chanted to himself, it has to be simple but precise. He posed his question only after carefully sifting through the universe of possible word choices in his head.

"Do other things call to you in your head?" He asked.

Perhaps in a reflexive reaction to Chen's question, Crystal's incredulous expression seemed to wipe away her characteristic open and pensive mien. She paused a moment, then, her mother's kindness returned to her face.

"Everything that is, was, or will be alive has a voice. Things that are alive in the now just make a louder sound. Things that are alive in the not-now have a softer voice. You have to be very quiet inside to hear them. If you go into the not-now, you can hear them much better," Crystal said, her tone instructive without a hint of condescension.

He stared at her incredulously for a moment, and then, reminded himself to breathe. He wasn't entirely certain, but it sounded as though this little girl was talking about the space-time continuum. Her tone suggest that this domain was a familiar as the backyard in which she pursued the diversions of childhood. Chen tried to be a good student, but he was having trouble with the 'now' and the 'not-now.'

"Crystal, I don't hear the voices," he said.

Instantly, her face betrayed the sort of sadness one might see in a youngster who had just learned that a deaf playmate couldn't play Simon Says.

"Could you tell me about the now and the not-now?" Chen asked.

Traces of sadness in her expression gradually dissipating, Crystal now looked a bit puzzled. Then, her countenance brightening. It became clear that she had found a way to extricate poor Chen from the sticky mire of his confusion. She disengaged the automatic pilot and brought the hopper to a hovering halt at one end of a beautiful alpine meadow that had appeared in the midst of the heavily forested hills.

Turning in her console chair, she looked directly at him, drew a deep breath, and pointed to the meadow below.

"This is the now," she said simply.

Then, activating the controls, she brought the hopper to the middle of the heavily flowered pastoral expanse.

"This is the now and where we were before is the not-now," she remarked as she pointed to the grassland below.

Activating the hopper again, she guided the craft to the point where the meadow ended and the forrest began.

"This is our now and the places where we were before are both the not-now," Crystal announced as she pointed to a small pond at the edge of the pines.

Like a kid in kindergarten who had not yet grasped the concept of '1', Chen suddenly felt like he was being required to deal with calculations involving negative numbers.

Hands once again on the hopper's controls, Crystal brought the craft to an altitude from which the whole expanse of the meadow could be easily seen. Gazing at the meadow almost lovingly, Crystal pointed once again to the scene laid out in verdant splendor below them.

"All the nows and the not-nows are the now for us," she said, pointing to the broad expanse of the meadow.

Growing within him was a sense of wonder. However, it was not a captivation informed by Crystal's precocious explanation of the space-time continuum. Rather, it was a fascination with her nonverbal behavior that suggested this dimension of experience was as familiar to her as walking up steps was to him.

"Crystal, do you always see and hear all the nows and not-nows from this ... this altitude?" Chen asked, after taking a deep breath.

"Yes ... but only if I'm very, very quiet inside, and then, the light comes. When the light appears, I can see and hear the whole meadow and its all the now," Crystal replied after a long pause.

Chen's personal pillars of perception crumbled and the foundational concepts they supported went with them. Standing in the rubble of his previously undisputed sense of personal reality, the inside of his head was reeling and he loved it. Chen was raptured, by what he knew beyond any doubt was a new direction for his species inherent to the people of the trees. It was an transcendental personal transformation he had never hoped to see in his life time. In a moment of time, Chen knew that all of his speculative assumptions regarding the nature of the cosmos were peanut butter and jelly sandwiches for Crystal. The universe had folded this little girl into its bosom. Despite, or perhaps because of, his newly found sense of incompetence, he felt compelled to ask just one more question.

"Crystal, please tell me about the light?" Chen asked eagerly.

If her expression as one of the illuminati marveling at the ignorance of an underachieving savage had been disdainful, he would have understood. Instead, her face was that of a kindly teacher who struggled with her own difficulty in making the lesson plain.

"The light comes only when the 'you' isn't there. First, it's like the sun behind the mountains, then, it's the light of midday. The less 'you', the more light. If you can keep still long enough, the light becomes you and you become the light. Then, you can see and hear everything and its all right," she said, as her eyes closed.

A history of beliefs and rational operations ground into finely dispersed dust, Chen felt adrift in the void. He reflexively grabbed at empty space, searching for something solid to hang on to, but finding nothing.

By force of will alone, Chen gathered himself to frame one more question.

"Of all the voices you hear in the now, how did you pick the one we excavated on the mountain?"

As Chen studied her face, he imagined he saw a small trace of respect creep across her features. Perhaps he had finally asked a worthy question.

Summoning up the full extent of her four year old stature, Crystal opened her eyes and, after a few moments of reflection, responded.

"The voice in the mountain was the Now voice. That voice could see the whole meadow, and all meadows everywhere. It was one of the people of the trees, but not one of the people of this now. This voice existed from before the now above the meadow. It was the first voice of the meek, the word at the beginning of the circle."

Among the people of the trees, Chen had seldom seen the frustration now written on Crystal's face. She stared off into the sky, fumbled with her hands awkwardly, turned, looked directly into his eyes and reaching out touched his hand.

In a moment of blinding clarity, Chen saw what was everyday fare for Crystal. He could neither describe, nor explain, what he saw and heard, but he knew with greater certainty than her words could impart that what she had been trying to explain was real. The knowing lasted but a moment, and then his vision encompassed only the hopper and the meadow. As Chen glanced over at Crystal, he saw she had activated the automatic pilot. Soon, the craft would land with computerized efficiency on the pad at her parent's home.

No further conversation passed between them as the hopper moved swiftly through the lengthening shadows towards Crystal's home. Alighting like a small bird, the little craft silently touched down. Esther and Jacob waited at the pad to greet them. Their expressions suggested a measure of anticipation as to the contents of the craft even before the hopper doors slid open. Chen handed the case containing the leather quivers to Crystal, who proudly presented it to her parents.

Standing back from the little family's reunion, Chen wasn't sure whether fatigue, a trick of the gathering twilight, or something else he would rather not consider, made Crystal look different. He looked away, rubbed his eyes and, then, stared once again at the family. There was no doubt, he saw a bluish white aura surrounding Crystal's body.

As Esther and Jacob received the case from their daughter, the aura passed to them without in any way diminishing the hue or intensity of that which surrounded Crystal. In the gathering gloom, the little family joined one another in an embrace. Their joining caused the aura of blue white light to expand and grow in intensity. Now, a sphere of energy formed a shimmering bubble around Crystal and her parents that seemed to envelop them entirely. Within moments, the tiny cluster of humanity, companioned by the light and a soft stillness that attended their aura, disappeared into the house.

It had been a long day, Chen thought to himself. He would not have been surprised if he had imagined the shade of Caesar, bloodied by Brutus' dagger strokes, having a beer with his assassin on the patio. Pulling himself together, he walked toward a nearby utility hopper that would carry him to his apartments at the service center some miles away.

Chen had no idea what the leather quivers contained. He wasn't sure he wanted to know at that moment. Whatever the leather cylinders contained, its included the voice at the beginning of the circle according to Crystal. That voice was heard by the meek and in the hearing they were somehow transformed. How they changed and what that change meant were matters he didn't trust himself to analyze at this moment. There had been a moment in the hopper as it hung over the meadow when Crystal had touched his hand and he had understood. Chen remembered clearly that he had grasped the meeks' vision, but he could no longer retrieve the content of what he had seen. Whatever made the meek different from their human brothers and sisters allowed them not only to see the not-now, but to continue in its presence. With Crystal's assistance, Chen's feeble neurons had momentarily glimpsed the whole of reality. Now, with only disjointed fragments of the experience remaining, he felt like there just wasn't enough room between his ears to contain and retain the expanse of that panorama.

That simple hopper flight over a meadow had generated the tangible realization of what years of research had only hinted. He had fumbled for decades to understand how the evolutionary arrangement of genetic building blocks was being resorted to produce something new. Well, here it was, and it in no way resembled what he had anticipated. In the meek, nature had not produced a permutation of existing human abilities, she had created a whole new way of perceiving the universe that ignored, no, superseded, the sensory illusions of space and time.

Quite unexpectedly Chen was hit by a feeling of overwhelming exhaustion. This was no ordinary fatigue. It seemed to reach down to and cause whatever small flame kept him alive from moment to moment to flicker. Even though his exposure had been only momentary, whatever enlivened Crystal and her family had drained him.

The simplest explanation was the meek represented suitable receptacles for what the voice from before the now above the meadow had to say, and he was not. He had felt the presence emanating from those leather quivers only as the experience was mediated by Crystal's touch.

The realization brought a stark, cold emptiness from which he desperately yearned to escape. The discrepancy between his experience of the universe and that in which the meek participated, was even greater than the gulf that separated him and Chandra. He could bear witness to the incarnation of light, but he could not count himself as one of the chosen. Activating the hopper to return to the service center, he yearned only for the oblivion of sleep, and, hopefully, a dreamless stupor at that.

Chapter 12

Sailing buoyantly on the force of the tidal shock wave produced by explosions in the asteroid belt, the station made it to within four hundred and fifty kilometers of the target area. Nearly half of the tractor shuttles available to the Commander were harnessed to tow the station the remaining distance to its designated position. Here it would hang, squarely between two avenues the computer model suggested represented the most likely alien attack vectors. The balance of the tractor shuttles remained in a sheltered area near the radiation belt. The force of the asteroid detonations now dissipated, tractor shuttles would be approaching the cloud to propel the mines into its shrouded confines.

Seated comfortably at the bridge console, the Commander watched closely as a swarm of shuttles, cables taut, towed his station slowly toward their goal. Soon, they would deposit their burden at an imaginary spot in space where it would become the base of operations for the Earth's defensive forces. Without shifting his attention from the viewscreen, the Commander felt a broad smile forming on his face as he recognized Sydes' footfalls behind him.

"What the hell is this?" Sydes said gruffly.

His smile now accompanied by chuckling, the Commander looked up from the console chair to face Sydes who was flourishing a large wad of currency in the Commander's face.

"Thought you might …" the Commander replied through his chuckles. "… enjoy throwing around a little … cash."

"A little cash! There must be nearly three thousand credits here," Sydes said, shaking the huge bundle of bills.

"I entered your estimate of the station's final position in the pool. Guess what? You won," the Commander said, enjoying his own good humor.

"No kidding," Sydes replied.

The Commander, despite his obvious attempts to contain himself, was laughing again. His mood was infectious and soon the whole bridge crew joined in.

"Sydes, you're not only a man in authority, you're rich too. Ought to change your name to … to Cabot," the Commander said between chuckles.

In the midst of this circus of mirth, Sydes wavered momentarily, not knowing what to do. Then, it struck him, these people were not laughing at him. This was well intended humor at his consternation. Grimacing, he finally chuckled a bit. Then, summoning up his best imitation of the sort of expression that crossed his face when he activated his lasers against a rival in one to one combat, he braced himself to speak.

"I'll get you all back, right down to your livers," he said in threatening tones.

Having produced a better imitation than he imagined, Sydes looked around as the entire bridge crew suddenly fell silent. The Commander, however, was not impressed as the knowing expression on his face and low chuckle indicated.

"I'm gonna put this on account at the paradise bar and you'll have to drink it up," Sydes said as his gaze tracked those on the bridge.

Gradually expressions of recognition began to flicker across the faces of the command crew.

"Well, I don't know about anyone else, but I'm prepared to sacrifice my liver," the armaments Chief offered.

"Chief, that's not much of a sacrifice," the scanner Exec retorted.

Soon a small knot of people formed around Sydes, each member of the bridge crew taking their turn slapping Sydes on the back and exchanging small talk.

Working intently at the console as he adjusted the long range scanners, the Commander did not join the group. Soon, the cluster of well wishers scattered back to their stations and he motioned Sydes over to the viewer. The Commander enhanced the magnification on the long range scanners to maximum and an image of Von Strohheim's ship, the Duo, filled the screen.

"I thought you might like to see your baby come in," the Commander said.

Lieutenant Sadad joined them to watch Von Strohheim's refitted carrier on approach to the station.

"It's so much bigger than I imagined," Sadad interjected.

Never taking his eyes from the screen as the approaching vessel grew larger by the moment, the Commander remembered that Von Strohheim said he had been building a carrier that could house thirty strike craft. The vessel that filled the screen was certainly every inch the size to accommodate that many ships and more.

Departing radically from the configurations of both shuttle and strike craft designs the Commander was accustomed to seeing, the Duo was essentially a sphere that jutted out into smoothed towers at six equidistant points on its surface. In a curious way it looked like one of the old style marine mines that had been used on Earth during oceanic warfare. Her hull was an absorbent black with no evidence of portholes and only a single set of red running lights that focused on her name, 'Duo.'

As the ship closed on the station, Sydes focused the main viewer at full magnification on the base of first one, and then another, of the towers.

"Those are propulsion units clustered around the base of each tower. If those units have independent burn capacity and can be linked, the damn thing could spin like a top," Sydes said, excitement in his voice.

"I'll wager those towers house the missile launchers, and ...." the Commander added.

A transmission from the huge vessel whose logo 'Duo' was now in central focus on the viewer interrupted the Commander's conjecture.

"This is the Duo requesting permission to take up parking orbit."

The voice was a familiar one. It was Doctor Von Strohheim.

"Permission granted Duo, and welcome," the Commander responded.

"She's a beauty, Doc. May we come aboard?" Sydes interjected.

The fighter ace's voice intoned the qualities of a child tugging anxiously at sleepy parents on Christmas morning.

"Of course Captain Sydes. We await your inspection of the vessel," Von Strohheim's responded.

Looking over at the Commander, an expectant excitement spread across Sydes' face. He was clearly ready to board the Duo.

As he rose from the console, the Commander motioned to two of his aides who joined him there.

"Mister Sadad,"Tutunji said, addressing his executive officer.

"Yes sir," Lieutenant Sadad replied as he came to attention.

"Mister, you are, from this moment, acting Commander of this station," Tutunji announced.

Then, Tutunji took a small emblem of rank from one of his aides and pinned it on his Exec's tunic.

"Thank you, Sir," Sadad uttered and hesitantly saluted.

Gripping his still mildly confused Exec by the shoulder, Tutunji turned Sadad around to receive his first salute from the bridge complement. Then, the entire bridge crew came forward to offer their congratulations and shake the new Commander's hand.

Already on his way toward the security door of the bridge, Sydes glanced back at Tutunji, who started after him, pausing only a moment as he passed Sadad. Tutunji's expression indicated earnest confidence as he shook Sadad's hand.

"Your station is at the defensive heart of all we'll do from this point forward. Keep her well and soundly," Tutunji said and followed Sydes from the bridge.

Tutunji and Sydes made record time to the receiving bay. With the fighter ace at the shuttle controls, they were soon circling the Duo. The size of the enormous vessel was even more apparent when seen in contrast to the shuttle that Sydes piloted into the small receiving bay of Von Strohheim's creation.

As they disembarked from their shuttle craft, Von Stohheim and his entire entourage moved forward to greet them.

"Captain Sydes, Commander, welcome aboard. I am sorry that completing the ship took longer than I promised, but I wanted it to be the best we could make it. We should begin the inspection, yes?" Von Strohheim said, his tone apologetic.

Nodding their affirmation almost in unison, Sydes and Tutunji moved to join Von Strohheim's tour.

Ushering them out of the small receiving bay into the guts of the sphere, Von Strohheim excitedly took the lead. Narrow catwalks carried through a maze of fusion reactors, shield generators, missile storage racks and delivery chutes stretching out in every direction toward the hull and the sphere's towers beyond. The interior of the ship built to house thirty strike craft, maintenance equipment, and crew, had been transformed into a tightly packed labyrinth of power generation and armament, with only minor concessions made for the narrow catwalks. Von Strohheim paused as the walkway brought them close to the plating that formed the outer skin of the ship.

"This is something new. The ship's hull is made up of six separate layers of plating and every layer of carbon fiber alloy plating is polarized. Each layer is set at an angle to the one before it so that the polarized lines of the alloy never match from one layer of plating to the next. If the shields fail, it will take six times the force of a 100 megaton fusion missile strike to make any section of the hull buckle," Von Stohheim said as he looked expectantly at Sydes.

Sydes admiringly ran his hand across the hard, polished finish of the inner hull and turned to Von Strohheim.

"Outstanding, Doc."

"The shield design is also a radical departure from all previous models. We thought long and hard about your onion idea, Commander, and refined it a bit. Now, its an onion that gets bigger with every bite you take out of it," Von Strohheim's said, his eyes twinkling.

"Bigger?" Tutunji interjected.

"Vell, if not bigger than tougher. The shields conduct the energy of an attack rather than deflecting it. The energy of a laser or missile strike at any particular point on the shield's surface is spread over the entire spherical expanse at that level of shielding. Any excess is then absorbed by the shielding layer below it. There are four levels of shielding with capacitors linked through modulators to the inner three layers of shielding. These capacitors will store any energy not fully dissipated by the four levels of shielding. In this way ..."

"So the more times you're hit the more energy your have?" Tutunji interrupted.

"Yes, Jah, exactly! And when the capacitors are fully charged, they feed back to the reactors, reducing their fusion output or adding to it if the ship's demand overwhelms the total output yield of the reactors. This provides ..." Von Strohheim said, forging on.

"So we can use some of the energy of the enemy's attack to strike back. Hell, that's great Doc. That means the more they try and kill us, the more of them we can kill," Sydes said, jumping into the conversation.

"Jah, precisely. Strike back, yes, of course ..." Von Strohheim responded and paused.

Von Strohheim had lost his place on the long checklist in his head. Looking about, he assembled his thoughts and pointed to the mass of machinery surrounding them.

"Three thousand, one hundred megaton fusion missiles are here. Five hundred are stored in each of the automatic loaders that individually serve the six firing towers," Von Strohheim said and looked down.

His gaze rising, Von Strohheim's expression looked a trifle sheepish as he addressed Sydes directly.

"Also ... I hope you will excuse me Captain Sydes, but against your advice we have installed one broad beam laser. I know you have said that our lasers don't work against this enemy, however, this is something new. We engineered this one to function as a drilling tool. When you target an enemy ship, a sensor beam incorporated into the laser projector will maintain continuous fire and keep its focus locked on the ship, no matter how the vessel maneuvers, until the range of the weapon is exceeded."

"So if I target their engines, it would be sorta like a cross between hooking a fish and drilling a tooth?" Sydes said, struggling to contain his excitement.

"Yes ... a fish and a tooth ... yes ... vell, we go to the bridge now," Von Strohheim muttered, clearly mystified by the metaphor.

Chuckling quietly, the Commander noted the fleeting trace of a smile Sydes allowed to pass over his face.

"Fish, tooth, Ich weiss nichts," Von Strohheim muttered.

The teutonic wizard rubbed his head and led the way to the tube that would carry them to the vessel's bridge.

Design specifications for the transport tube clearly called for only two people, but somehow Sydes, the Commander, and Von Strohheim wedged themselves into it. The cramped conveyance carried them to the north polar area of the sphere.

"This bridge is very different from what you might be accustomed to, but I'm sure you will learn it quickly," Von Strohheim said as the lift rose.

The tube door opened silently and the trio was greeted by a circular cat-walk surrounding what initially appeared to be a large open space in the upper cap of the sphere. Squirming out of the tube, they spread themselves out along the narrow catwalk. In the largely unoccupied space below, two nearly skeletal chairs with consoles attached were suspended on antigravity units one above the other.

Opening a compartment in the wall, Von Strohheim reached in and produced two antigravity belts, handing one to Sydes and one to the Commander.

"With these, you will reach the consoles. Captain Sydes, you are above in flight control, and the Commander is below at the armaments' control console," Von Strohheim said, pointing to the chairs.

"Well that's great Doc, but how do we see where we're going when we're flying this lady?" Sydes asked.

The fighter ace looked at the belt Von Strohheim had handed him and then down at the console chairs suspended in the dark void below.

"You will see … Captain Sydes, Commander, bitte," Von Strohheim said as he smiled knowingly.

Strapping on their belts and activating the antigravity units, Captain Sydes and the Commander floated down into the dark interior of the bridge until they were both seated in their designated console chairs.

"Ok Doc, now what?" Sydes asked and glanced up at Von Strohheim.

"There is a black power switch at the top of the console. You will press this and your question, it will be answered," Von Strohheim said as a smile formed on his face.

The little wizard's glad expression gradually broaden to one reminiscent of a parent watching in happy anticipation as his children opened Christmas gifts they hadn't expected to receive.

Depressing the power switch, Sydes found himself instantly surrounded by projected viewscreen images of the space around the entire ship. He was in the imaginary center of the spherical ship with views in every direction. The quality of the images was extraordinary. He felt as though he could almost reach out and touch a passing shuttle.

As he leaned forward in the console chair, which was little more than a spine support, to get a better view of the images below him, he discovered the chair and console moved with him. In the midst of spinning about enjoying all the right side up and upside down views, Sydes discovered the tactical displays. With the activation of a single icon, he found he could superimpose grids and firing vectors on any object outside the ship.

"It's like being inside a big glass ball. We can see out, but no one can see in ... outstanding!" Sydes said excitedly.

Sydes superimposed the targeting grid on another shuttle. Almost at once, a green curvilinear line traced its way from the center of the amber grid to the shuttle. As soon as the line touched the shuttle's image , it split into two lines, one red and one blue, both of which began to blink.

"The ship has found a firing solution and locked on the target. Red means within the range of the tunneling laser and blue within the missiles reach," Von Strohheim announced.

"Looks like we could go with either weapons system," Tutunji interjected.

"Exactly," Von Strohheim responded.

"This is great! How does she maneuver?" Sydes exclaimed.

"The ship, she is very quick and responsive despite her size. The thrust to mass ratio is about the same as your strike craft. Each tower is completely surrounded by propulsion units that are individually directional or can be fired in any sequence you select. The tower units can also be linked in any combination you chose."

"Motion along the infinite radii of space," Tutunji murmured.

"Ninety-nine percent of the ship's volume is power generation, shielding support, and armament. You like it, yes?" Von Strohheim said, his excitement peaking.

"Like it. Hell, I love it, Doc! It's much more ... more than I expected," Sydes replied, bringing his spinning chair to a stop.

Having expressed his appreciation to Von Strohheim, Sydes' fingers once again danced over the console. In an instant, he was spinning and tumbling as he superimposed tactical displays on views of the space exterior to the sphere.

"Doc, if I read this right, all the missiles can be fired simultaneously?" Tutunji asked.

"Precisely correct, Commander. The ship can be maneuvered into the center of an enemy formation and missiles fired simultaneously from all six towers at a rate of one every five seconds from each tower," Von Strohheim responded crisply.

Momentarily stunned into silence, Tutunji tried to visualize the devastating omnidirectional firepower produced by the Duo, which the good Doctor had so matter of factly described.

"Unbelievable," Tutunji muttered.

"Captain Sydes, there is only one armament control on your console, the tunneling laser. It is under your control because you will have to maneuver the ship to keep the enemy in range once you have activated the laser mount," Von Strohheim called out.

"Oh, I get it Doc. It's like playing a fish once you've hooked him," Sydes said gleefully.

"Playing a fish. Playing a fish? Ah, jah, playing the fish. Jah this is correct! Ha, playing the fish, drilling the tooth, jah, I see …" the Doctor said, his words trailing off into a low chuckle.

"Doc, there's a symbol here that's marked technical information. What's that?" Tutunji asked as he stared at his console.

"This activates a menu of the technical schematics of the ship. It begins with very broad descriptions and becomes more detailed as you pursue specifics. It will provide you with everything there is to know about the Duo's functioning and construction," Von Strohheim said, his tone betraying profound engineering satisfaction.

"This is great Doc. I can hardly wait to wring this beautiful lady out!" Sydes exclaimed.

Leaning back against the hull supports, Von Strohheim responded with a comment neither Sydes nor the Commander had anticipated.

"Jah, this is necessary. In the beginning, the ship's computer will help you learn about the Duo's capabilities. However, the more you fly her and use the weaponry, the more she will learn about you. She will, wie heisst es? Jah, she will conform to your style. Yes, you wring it out. We will go now, so that you can get started. We will take your shuttle, yes?"

"It's all yours Doc, and thanks," Sydes said.

Then, the fighter pilot turned his attention to a search for the main ignition switch for the engines.

"Where is the damn thing?" He muttered in low tones.

"It is three centimeters above your left index finger, Captain Sydes. Ah, yes, I almost forget … the thrust to mass ratio is actually 1.5 times better than the strike craft you are used to flying. She will respond very quickly," Von Strohheim remarked as he entered the tube.

"Shit, that's unbelievable!" Sydes muttered.

Clambering into the shuttle through the tiny receiving bay, Von Stohheim and his party barely had time to clear the closing bay doors before Duo's engines sprang to life and the big ship began to ease out of her orbit around the station.

One of the junior design engineers in Von Strohheim's group watched in horror from the shuttle as the Duo, her shields glowing, spun first on one axis and then another as she accelerated away from the station.

"Mein Gott, Herr Doktor," he said apprehensively .

"Nein, this is exactly correct. First, the ship will teach and the pilot will learn, then, the pilot will teach and the ship will learn. This is just as it should be," Von Strohheim responded, his face glowing with pride.

⚜

Newly instated, Commander Sadad, his gaze fixed on the station's main viewer, watched as the Duo spinning and tumbling, gradually increased her velocity and distance from the station.

Wholly engrossed in the ship's gyrations, the weapons Chief by Commander Sadad's side used the main viewer's programming to overlay angular templates on the Duo's motion as she sped away.

"The damn thing can move at right angles to its own trajectory," he exclaimed.

"A good ship and two good men. If we had ten more like the Duo, I'd feel better about our chances of surviving this conflict," Commander Sadad responded, never taking his eyes from the viewer.

Standing in almost reverent silence, the two men watched as the Duo passed out of the range of the close proximity scanners. On her maiden voyage, she was accelerated at better than strike craft velocity along a vector that would take the huge spherical vessel into an intact and uncontaminated area of the asteroid belt.

Chapter 13

Even though Chauvez's training allowed him to understand the component parts as well as the overall construction of, Cabot's ark, he woke up at the beginning of each shift with a growing appreciation of the grandeur of the project. The girder exoskeleton of the ark was complete and a good deal of the plating had been applied around the upper hemisphere of the ship. The entire interior structure was now air tight as shield generators and relays on the girders provided a continuous seal around the exoskeleton. All of the interior supports for the decks within the sphere were in place. This allowed the construction personnel to work more quickly as isolated gravity generators made each level a microcosm approximating Earth's gravity.

Huge reservoir tanks holding millions of gallons of fresh water, complemented by purifiers and recirculating units, already supplied the living environments of the ark. Enormous platforms had been constructed to receive the amputated portions of the Earth's surface from Cabot's reserves. Each ecosector representing a reserve was isolated from every other, allowing for the creation of truly independent environments representative of a sampling of the variety of flora and fauna mother Earth had produced over eons. One particularly large bowl shaped ecosector would receive millions of decaliters of sea water to which would be added a sampling of the plants and animals from Earth's oceans. The one half million mystery occupants of these diverse environments could enjoy almost every major ecological system the Earth had to offer.

Already visible in the long range viewer, Chauvez saw long ribbons of light climbing out of Earth's orbit headed toward the ark. Each ribbon represented a specifically selected portion of land mass from one of Cabot's reserves on Earth. Twenty kilometer squares of the Earth's surface each thirty meters deep were carved out, shielded and fitted with illuminators that mimicked a day and night cycle, and sent for installation within the ark. What Cabot was doing in creating the ark made building the pyramids look like an afternoon's diversion.

Turning away from the viewer, Chauvez surveyed the ark's operations center on the bridge which, at a glance, seemed somehow empty. To be sure, there was a large crew supervising thousands of construction workers, but Piatra wasn't there. Her presence seemed to fill up a compartment regardless of who else might be around. Chauvez hadn't seen her since they got the word that the ecosections of the reserves would be coming up. Her reaction to this news was an angry, bitter and public one.

At first, she had spoken openly and passionately about the rape of the Earth, her persuasive rhetoric coalescing the brooding suspicion and resentment that lay just beneath the surface for many who worked on the ark. Piatra's vocal opposition quite naturally drew the attention of Cabot's intelligence and security division, who began to monitor her statements and movements closely. Piatra was passionate, but she was not unaware that her campaign had made her a principal focus of Cabot's surveillance. At this point, she dropped out of sight.

Expending no small amount of effort, Chauvez desperately tried to locate her, fearing the worst because of the interest of Cabot's security forces in her activities. His efforts were to no avail. His attempts to persuade her to contact him were equally fruitless. He had approached many of the construction workers who had initially supported her protest, but no one was talking. The rumor mill had it that Piatra was trying to generate support for a plan to commandeer the ark and pilot it to join the combined Natcorp fleet.

Confidants among those who worked with Chauvez passed along information that suggested some support for Piatra's campaign to coopt the ark for the war effort, particularly among the construction workers. However, the majority of the work crews and their supervisors just wanted to do their job and collect their vastly inflated wages.

One of the principal forces acting against Piatra's efforts to foment rebellion on a larger scale was that every worker laboring on the project harbored the secret hope that they would be among those chosen to enter two by two into Cabot's ark. It was a natural oversight on Piatra's part. Her internal makeup simply buckled at the prospect that her own adolescent concept of freedom did not occupy the foremost rank on everyone's motivational menu.

After all of Chauvez's searching, Piatra simply appeared in his compartment late one night. Her ardor had not cooled over time. She was just as committed to disrupting Cabot's plans as she had ever been, but now she was working behind the scenes. Chauvez tried to dissuade her from the campaign against Cabot without success. She stomped out of his compartment, calling him a puppet scientist and a coward. That had been several weeks ago. He had not seen or heard from her since that midnight confrontation.

In his dark moments of self-reflection, Chauvez realized some of what Piatra said was true, but in the bright light of his professional role, he thought of himself as a realist. He knew she intended an assassination attempt on Cabot.

Her words, "cut off the snake's head," although metaphorical, could mean only one thing. There had been literally hundreds of such attempts on Cabot's life over the centuries. All ended with the death of the would be assassins and, often, their families. Chauvez knew he couldn't stop her, and to divulge the plot to Cabot would only result in her death before any definitive act of rebellion.

The chime of his comm-link interrupted these dark musings. He recognized Piatra's voice immediately.

"Go to the secure line in your compartment," she said and quickly terminated the transmission.

Quickly exiting the bridge, he barely got the door to his compartment open as the comm-link on his desk began to sound.

"Where have you been?" He began as he opened the link.

"I wanted to give your yellow ass one more chance to get on board," Piatra said, her tone confrontational.

"Don't do this babe. It's suicide. You know that everyone who has tried has died," Chauvez implored.

"You're living in a dream world. You'll put up with anything as long as that bastard lets you play with his big ball. We're gonna put him out of business for good. Are you with us or not?" she demanded.

Beginning to panic, he recognized that this moment was a hurricane of real time disaster with Piatra at the center of the whirlwind.

"Babe, don't do this, not after all we've, well, been to each other," he pleaded.

A long silence fell over the line, and for a moment, he imagined his appeal to their long term relationship might have had an impact.

"Some things are more important than what two people share. Sometimes you have to know who you're sharing it with. This is one of those times. I've got to respect the man I'm making love to. I've got to know that he feels like me, not just for me," Piatra replied, her tone carrying equal measures of affection and firm resolve.

"Now you sound like Cabot. Fuck the individual in favor of the larger issue, but the larger issue always just happens to reflect what he wants. You're every bit as arrogant as he is. Both of you are forever deciding what amounts to the greater good for everyone. You stupid bitch. You and Cabot are cut from the same cloth. Everyone who doesn't share your feelings and your agenda for life has to be moved out of the way," Chauvez said, his words a flight of angry hornets.

Suddenly, it was deadly silent. He'd heard that stream of long suppressed feeling coming out of his mouth, but he still couldn't believe he'd said it.

"He's a tyrant and we're freedom fighters. That's the way it's always been. Where there are tyrants, sooner or later, someone comes along who's willing to stand up to them," Piatra responded after a moment's reflection.

Now that he was fighting for the life of his woman, all the carefully considered and skillfully worded phrases dropped by the wayside as he ranted.

"What kind of adolescently fixated bullshit is that? Tyrant and freedom fighter are labels put on individuals by historians paid by whoever wins. Hell, where have you been woman?"

Piatra's response was quick and decisive.

"Yeah, and if I listened to you, no one but the most psychopathic bastards the race has ever spawned would continue to run things. I'll see you after we've gotten rid of this prick."

Piatra provided a quick and decisive response over the comm-link, leaving only a silence that draped itself over him like a shroud.

It was an ending. Even if his mind wasn't ready to accept it, his body knew as it collapsed into a slouch. He had never felt so impotent or so alone. Piatra was like a wave rushing toward the shore. Riding the crest of a surge of passion, she became a tsunami of action. All attempts to stand before the watery juggernaut of her resolve represented wasted motion. In the back of his mind, he had always known the lengths to which Piatra was willing to go to satisfy her emotional needs. His relationship with her over the years had evolved out of his own personal delusional system. He saw himself as the consummately rational man who admired a wild animal for her reflexive instincts, untamed passions, and unconscious grace. This much of the picture was true on its face. The delusion surfaced in his belief that he could tame Piatra to respond to his needs, while otherwise preserving the allure of her primitively passionate reflexes. Among male engineers, a mate like Piatra represented an archetypal fantasy. All the irrational impulses that any self respecting engineer suppressed could be vicariously experienced through a fount of passion like Piatra. Now, the fantasy disintegrated.

Whatever Piatra planned to do, she would do immediately, that much he knew. Switching on his compartment viewer, he noticed three shuttles moving away from the construction area of the ark toward Cabot's private yacht. One of the shuttles bore the insignia of Piatra's engineering division, it was her pet conveyance. Like a teddy bear, she took that vessel with her everywhere. Chauvez knew that this time Piatra's teddy bear would provide no solace against the horrors Ole Nick had doubtless prepared for her.

Phil grew accustomed to his daily visits with Cabot in the big conference room on his yacht. Cabot was very particular about the transfer of the ecosystems from his reserves on Earth to the ark. The only easy part of Phil's job had been arranging the necessary ingredients for the oceanic ecosector. Sea water didn't have an opinion and fish and seaweed didn't lodge complaints. The job got dicey when Cabot required Phil to move native populations out of the way and to concoct stories to explain why huge chunks of their land floated up into the sky. The stories about toxic residues, old radioactive materials dump sites and latent viral reservoirs got old. Phil had difficulty convincing the people he was displacing because the devastation he was wreaking had eroded his own belief in the project. The residents of the reserves just weren't buying the bullshit about square kilometers of their living space having to be jettisoned into the sun to save their families from some awful catastrophe.

The western Canadian home of the meek provided the only exception to the growing dissatisfaction among the populations of Cabot's many reserves whose homes were flying away. Here, Cabot had carved out one hundred times the land area of any of his other reserves and the meek simply smiled and said nothing. Phil found it doubly remarkable that 'the people of the trees,' as they had named themselves, seemed quite indifferent to huge chunks of their verdant forest disappearing into the clouds.

Mystifying was the only word that adequately described the smiles the meek seemed able to conjure. These were not the vacant smiles of children who didn't comprehend the seriousness of the events transpiring around them, nor were they the deceitful smiles of poker players with aces up their sleeves, theirs was a knowing and benign countenance.

Dealing with Chen had been a different problem altogether. Chen became protective of the meek and expressed outrage at the desecration of their home far beyond anything Phil had anticipated. Chen was also very bright and so, at an unspoken level, he understood that Cabot had ordered the ecological stripping operation. Chen allowed himself a brief rant at Phil's expense before accepting Cabot's will.

Planted at the conference table where he waited for Nick's return, Phil watched as Cabot conducted some business. On the far side of the room, Nick conversed intently with a distinguished looking man, who, after a moment, Phil recognized as Doctor Wilhelm Dvorak. A distant relation to the ancient composer of the same name, Doctor Dvorak was also the most brilliant automation design engineer of this, or any other, era.

In the past, Doctor Dvorak had refused to work for Cabot on principle. Dvorak's opinion that Cabot already had too much power was a matter of public record. The outspoken engineer wasn't about to lend his considerable talents to Cabot's striving for still more personal control. Apparently, Nick had found Dvorak's price or, more likely, some chink in the brilliant automation designer's emotional armor.

Even at this distance, it was clear Nick was pressing a point with Dvorak. Dvorak either didn't understand what Nick wanted or didn't want to understand. Nick gestured repeatedly to some schematics on his desk and, then, in apparent frustration cued up the hologram of the ship. Using a laser pen, Nick pointed first to the control section and, then, the technical crew's living quarters while Dvorak shook his head no.

From Phil's vantage point, the two men seemed to be at loggerheads. Nick paused for a moment in his explanation and, then, leaning close to Dvorak's ear, whispered something. The Doctor paused for a moment. His expression took on an aspect of somber resignation and he nodded affirmatively. Clearly, Nick had made another one of his arrangements to get what he wanted.

Bundling up some schematics from Nick's desk, Doctor Dvorak, head now slightly bowed, left the room.

All smiles, Nick strode at a brisk pace to the conference table where Phil waited.

"Well Phil, how are we doing?" Cabot asked, as he shook Phil's hand.

Phil never liked shaking hands with Cabot. There was no skin to skin contact, just Phil's hand against the hard and slippery surface of Cabot's personal shield.

"The ecosections are coming up as planned. I leased a whole fleet of commercial shuttles from FF Natcorp to tractor them up here. The sections should arrive within ten hours of each other, as you specified. The first one will be received by the ark's loading crew in the next two hours," Phil said as he recited his checklist.

Smiling and nodding as Phil completed his report, quite suddenly, a detached expression appeared on Nick's face.

Years of working with Nick allowed Phil to recognize that Cabot's momentarily blank expression indicated that he was receiving some feed through his mastoid implant.

"Sorry Phil, just a little something to take care of. Please excuse me," Nick said mechanically.

Standing up abruptly, Nick walked away from the conference table toward the large viewer occupying one whole wall of his office.

Phil rose cautiously from his seat and followed Nick at a respectful interval. He closed just enough distance between himself and Nick to catch sight of the viewer and to hear Nick speaking at a very low volume. Nick was obviously conversing with someone through the bone conduction microphone that was wired to his mastoid implant. Phil's own actions surprised him. Normally, he would have sat at the table and patiently awaited Nick's return, but something about Nick's expression and posture suggested a dramatic event was in the offing. Phil was close enough to hear Nick's half of the conversation.

"Yes, yes, I see the shuttles .... We're sure about this .... I see ... That's a lot of valuable talent to lose ... Of course I agree ... Well, let's get to it before they get any closer, I don't want any collateral damage to the yacht," Nick said.

His eyes remaining fixed on the viewer, Nick had nothing more to say.

On the huge screen, Phil saw three shuttles approaching the yacht. From the far side of the yacht, a large tractor shuttle emerged with a huge bundle of girders in its manipulator arms. The tractor's flight path took the craft between the yacht and the three approaching shuttles. As the tractor shuttle crossed in front of the three approaching craft, the manipulator arms torqued and released the bundle of untethered girders. Spinning wildly out of control, the girders careened into the approaching shuttles. One girder impaled the center shuttle, while the other two shuttles were struck nose on by several of the whirling beams. Out of control in the tangle of metal, the shuttles collided with one another. Finally, a series of billowing explosions in their propulsion units brought the incident to a fiery conclusion.

Increasing the viewer magnification to get a closer look, Nick watched as the large tractor shuttle moved cautiously among the debris left by the destruction of the three shuttles. Nothing remained that resembled a complete human form in the devastation. Fragmented parts of a torso floated around what was left of a bay door. Near one of the propulsion units, a disembodied arm seemed to embrace what was left of a helmet.

Turning around quickly, as if he had just become aware of Phil's presence, Nick captured Phil's gaze with a raptor's stare.

"Terrible accident ... I'm not sure what those three shuttles were doing up here. My people tell me they didn't have clearance to approach the yacht. I don't like losses, especially at this stage of the game," Cabot said in a carefully measured tone.

His attention caught by the movement, Phil reflexively looked down at Nick's hands. He fumbled with a small emblem he had produced from his pocket. This in and of itself was remarkable as Nick never allowed his hands to toy with anything. The artifact in his hand was the old Egyptian symbol for life, which had been coopted in the past as a talisman of peace. Welded at a left to right angle across its face was the distinctive shape of a gladius or Roman short sword.

Following Phil's gaze to his hands, Nick quickly replaced the well worn emblem in his pocket.

"Anything else Phil?" He asked, dropping his hands to his side.

"No Nick, I think that about finishes it," Phil replied.

An analytic scrutiny burning in his eyes, Cabot fixed on Phil's expression, held his gaze for a few seconds and turned and walked back to the desk. Deactivating the viewer as he sat down, Nick turned on the desk monitor. Phil knew this was Cabot's signal for Phil to exit.

Taking his cue, Phil hurried from the room at a pace that suggested a man fleeing from the horrors resident in the gathering gloom of nightfall. However, he knew even as he heard the door to Nick's inner sanctum close behind him that a great deal of the darkness within that chamber clung to his own shoulders like some parasitic cloak.

⚘

Intellectually, Chauvez knew he could do little more than watch the devastation playing out on his compartment viewer. This knowledge provided no bulwark against the limbically propelled wave of grief that poured over him as he watched Piatra's shuttle being impaled by a girder. He witnessed her little craft careen out of control, collide with one of its sister ships and finally explode. He adjusted his viewer to full magnification, but could see nothing in the swirling mass of debris that approximated the size and shape of a human form.

For the first time since Piatra announced her assassination plot against Cabot, Chauvez felt the tangible reality of his loss. She was now and forever gone. Never again would that dynamo of passionate rebellion fill the bridge with her presence, or, by touching him, generate a feeling of timeless pleasure in the moment of embrace. Everything that made up Piatra was now reduced to wandering molecules that might wait millions of years, if ever, to be reassembled into another example of the striving, burgeoning edge of life she represented.

In a moment of utter clarity, Chauvez realized that he would complete Cabot's ship for him. The ark represented a chance for mankind to survive in the face of the real possibility of complete annihilation by the invading alien force. With the same perfected conviction, he knew that, whatever it took, he would make certain Cabot never sailed off into some kind of galactic sunset at the ark's helm. He owed Piatra Cabot's death. The quiet fury building within him was driven by more than the need for simple revenge. He wanted to see the value Piatra set on self-determination triumph over the tyranny of money and power that Cabot personified. More to the point, he owed himself a categorical ending to the story that began with her death. He would honor a greater self that Piatra, in her death, but even more so in her life, had created in him.

Activating the comm-link to the bridge, Chauvez recognized the voice of his supervising construction engineer.

"Yeah, Chief," Boris answered.

"Boris, I wonder if you could take over loading the first of the ecosectors coming up," Chauvez said.

Chauvez spoke slowly in an attempt to conceal the emotion in his voice.

"Sure Chief …. look Chief, we're all sorry. We saw Piatra's shuttle go up. Damn shame, a good engineer, a good lady. You know anything we can do … I don't know, but …" Boris said, haltingly.

"Thanks Boris, I appreciate it," Chauvez replied.

Putting the poor man out of his well intended verbal misery, Chauvez closed the comm-link, hit the automatic lock on the compartment door and poured himself a large shot of tequila. He would drink to Piatra's ghost and summon her spirit from memory. When he had drunk his fill, he would meld her passion with his own meticulous attention to detail and plan a chess strategy directed solely to encompassing Cabot's doom.

Like so many of Cabot's top administrative strata, Chauvez had been a 3-D chess finalist in one of Cabot's tournaments. He had lost, and fairly, to the master, but in a moment of youthful rebellion he had turned down the offer to join Cabot's stable of talent. Only years later, a considerably wiser Chauvez accepted Cabot's offer to join his brain trust at the completion of the Atlantis project. He would play chess with the master again, but he would plan this game much more carefully. First, he would assemble all his pieces off the playing surface and, then, present his attack full blown on the board only when he was prepared to act.

In this moment of resolution, he recognized, perhaps for the first time, that the game of life bore no resemblance to chess. The illusion inherent in the chess game's pieces and the rules that governed their movements was that these miniature representatives of manorial society were required to operate within the confines of their designated roles.

Piatra's confrontation with Cabot presented a much simpler and more disassembling lesson. Kings could become knights and knights assassins when their wants and the circumstances demanded it. The point of competition was to win. The roles and rules didn't matter. The powerful remained so because their loyalty extended only to the expediency of opportunity and to no other idol. Life's game honored only winning, and winning meant surviving to tell the tale. In the singularity of that sorrowful and angry moment, Chauvez resolved to become the narrator of Cabot's demise.

Chapter 14

O bviously excited as he rushed into their compartment, Arthur paused and looked at Forrester, who was in the midst of polishing off some breakfast funnelkucken. Hurrying over to their viewer, Arthur redirected it so Forrester could catch a glimpse of the Duo leaving the station's orbit.

"She's a beauty, what do you think, Nate?"

Long ago, Forrester had vowed never to answer Arthur's questions unless they pertained to matters of fact. Like most people's utterances, Arthur's statements amounted to little more than a vocalization of his stream of consciousness.

"Man look at her go. Every possible direction. Turns at right angles. What speed. She moves like an oversized strike craft. Come on Nate. Get a little excited. We're looking at the salvation of the human race," he said excitedly.

Arthur's vocal intensity was part of a larger reaction that included slight movements all over his body reflective of those of a symphony orchestra responding to its conductor's direction.

Staring at the viewer with different eyes, Forrester could not share in his partner's excitement. All he saw was a ship of war, every inch devoted to the destruction of life. To be sure, it was intended to defend his native species against an aggressor with whom humankind had no known quarrel, but it was nevertheless a machine built for one and only one purpose, killing.

⛬

Killing to expand territory, killing to defend territory, these two slogans constituted a fair précis of human history. He felt the change more than he thought it, his head journal opened again. Since childhood, the covers of that ruminative log had gaped whenever he was confronted with the immutable motivations that represented the lowest common denominator of his species' behavior.

Quite unexpectedly, Forrester was struck by an existentially more terrifying prospect. Perhaps the whole universe was as adolescently fixated as mankind. That premise would certainly subsume the unknown aliens who seemed so bent upon humanity's destruction. The thought chilled him. Maybe the cosmos teemed with sentient life forms, all bent upon massaging egos so twisted that only the destruction of others would momentarily satisfy their need for dominance. It was an apparition so encompassing it could only have its origins in the aspirations of the fallen angel of light.

Certainly, these invaders seemed to share man's central premise of existence, that life was not about living, but devoted rather to conquering and controlling territory.

As if mirroring the dark specter of an impetus to destruction universal to all sentient life, a passage from the diarist's journal presented itself. For a moment, Forrester entertained the notion that his black moods might be prompted by unconscious recall of these entries, now so much a part of his memory. It was a convenient rationalization, but a lie all the same. Long before his discovery of the scrolls, he had often been swept away by a tide of cosmic despair when confronted by the irrational hostility of his own, presumably sentient, species.

> TWILIGHT STEALING INTO THE GARDEN,
> THE QUARRELING VOICES OF NEIGHBORS
> RISE ABOVE THE WALL AS THE SINKING SUN
> YIELDS TO THE NIGHT. THE COOL OF DAY'S
> LAST LIGHT, HEATED BY SUCH STRIFE, WILL
> FAN THE EMBER OF THEIR RAGE UNTO THE
> MORROW'S LIGHT.

> ALL LIFE AND LIGHT EMERGES INTO
> AND IS EMBEDDED IN, DARKNESS.
> THE BRIGHTER THE LIGHT OF
> DISCERNMENT, THE MORE THE
> DARKNESS, IN ENVY, ENCROACHES
> UPON AND SEEKS TO EXTINGUISH IT.

> THE GREATER LIFE'S ILLUMINATION,
> THE MORE DARKNESS IT DISPELS.
> THE DOMINION OF DARKNESS SO
> CHALLENGED, RISES, IN ITS IRE, TO
> WHOLLY QUENCH THE OFFENDING
> FIRE.

While possessed of cosmic complexity, the sentiments expressed in the diarist's journal seemed at once simple and clarifying. Unfortunately for Forrester, the foreground of his thinking was overwhelmed by the complexity he saw oozing out of every syllable in the entry. Surely, for most of humanity, these statements were more readily grasped.

A perfect memory of Sydes lying there on the Commander's bunk sprang to Forrester's mind. Sydes, probably the only man who could have piloted that immense spherical craft, would grasp the essential nature of the battles to come with a perfection of apprehension Forrester could not mirror. Drawing on his American Indian heritage, Sydes would intuitively grasp this was a struggle to the death over hunting ground, and nothing more.

⇜⟡⇝

The rumbling basso that was Arthur's voice unceremoniously roused Forrester from his internal monologue.

"Wake up, Nate. Real time. Real life. Shit, she's out of range now. Hell Nate, you're in history. Why not become a participant or, at least a more active spectator?" Arthur said as he twisted the magnification controls on the viewer.

Good-natured anger suffused Arthur's voice. He recognized their differences in thinking and feeling were unalterable, accepted that, and immediately tried to make changes. What a marvelously human contradiction, Forrester thought to himself.

"A brave man that Sydes, if anyone can save our unredeemed asses, it'll be him," Forrester remarked as he turned to Arthur.

"You've met him?" Arthur said, his tone fraught with incredulity.

This was the sort of situation that Forrester savored. Nothing appealed more to his ego than shooting holes in other people's perceptions of him.

"Yes, we had a drink together. We talked about warriors and shamen. He's an able man and, like all warriors, a poet with an appetite for mystery. His thinks warriors and shamen make each other possible. The warrior fights for life, the shaman tells him why the battle is redeeming. He believes a universe without both is impossible."

"And I suppose you're the shaman," Arthur retorted.

One eyebrow rising in a skeptical arch, a small measure of poorly concealed scorn tinged Arthur's tone.

"In his view, I suppose. I have trouble seeing myself in that role," Forrester said pensively.

Then, looking carefully into Arthur's face, Forrester saw something in their conversation had punched a hole in Arthur's characteristic shine it all on demeanor.

"So, if you're the shaman, what does that make me, the sorcerer's apprentice? That's bullshit. I'll tell you how it really is. You're not some damn shaman. You're the guy who opened pandora's box ... you ... you stupid bastard," Arthur stuttered in his agitation.

Having known Arthur for what seemed like most of his life, Forrester was startled by this response. In all that time, he had never seen Arthur so angry or so hurt. It reminded him of something he had taught his students many years ago. The greater the intensity of feeling, the more limited the repertoire of its behavioral expression. Direct but facile, Arthur usually got his point across with only minimal recourse to expletives. Not this time. Something of more than a momentary or circumstantial nature drove this outpouring of anger and pain. He attacked Forrester with a vigor that had no correlate in their past experience. This flood of feeling had built up behind a dam that Arthur had carefully constructed and maintained over decades. True to his own neuropsychological makeup, Forrester tried to smooth things over. He knew, before the words left his mouth, his own behavior was more a matter of neurological reflex than a studied and rational plan to defuse the affectively explosive situation.

"Hey, Arthur. It was just a conversation over drinks, just ideas, alcoholic patter, nothing more," Forrester said, his tone placative.

"Look you dumb son of a bitch. You've had your head up your academic, mystical ass so long you don't have the first idea what's going on. Cabot took everything, every bit of the research you did, and thought you had hidden away, and applied it to his little genetics experiment on Earth," Arthur said, his expression darkening.

Stepping back for a moment, Arthur seemed distressed by what had just spilled out of him. Pausing for a moment, he was apparently considering his next comment.

"Cabot's corralled a half a million people in his own version of a genetic concentration camp on good old Earth. He's putting your theories into practice, something that you never had the balls to do. And I hear he's killing off the kids who don't fit your projections."

'Stunned into silence' had never meant anything to Forrester until now. He knew Arthur when he was lying, he knew Arthur when he was exaggerating, and he knew Arthur when he was making a joke. Arthur's face fit none of those moods. Arthur was hurt, Arthur was angry, but he was telling the truth. Forrester wouldn't bother to ask how Arthur knew all these things. He had known Arthur too long and was aware of his facility for smoozing information out of people regardless of their station in life. Forrester suddenly became self-possessed enough to recognize he was staring at the floor. There, in the decking, he saw plainly an entry from the scrolls sent, or unconsciously summoned to, the occasion of the realization of his worst fears.

THE LABORS OF THE DAY ARE NOT BURDEN
ENOUGH TO SMOTHER ME INTO DREAMLESS
SLEEP. NOT AT REST, MY SPIRIT ARISES
AND WANDERS, TOWING A SHUFFLING
BODY IN ITS WAKE. BODY AND SOUL
RETRACE A PATH TO WHERE MEMORY OF
THE DAY'S TOIL COMPELS ITS COURSE.
IN THE COLD SHADOWS OF THE WORKSHOP,

WHILE THOSE I CALL KIN SLEEP, I AM ALONE
AWAKENED BY VISIONS THAT ROUT SLEEP.
ACROSS THE MARCH OF CENTURIES, I SEE
THAT CHRONICLE OF MY WORDS AND ACTS,
WHICH SURVIVING MY PASSING, PRESSED
MORE TO EVIL THAN TO GOOD. YET, SPEAK
I MUST, AND ACTIONS FOLLOW IN THE DAILY
COURSE OF LIVING. I CANNOT UNDO WHAT I
HAVE NOT YET DONE, NOR CAN I STEP ASIDE
FROM THE PATH APPORTIONED TO ME.

Studying the fading characters from an early entry in the scrolls so clearly portrayed in the plating upon which he stood, Forrester felt a sudden kinship with this ancient writer. What Forrester only feared might happen to his work, the diarist already knew was the fate of his own. Before the fact of anything he said or did, he clearly saw that his historical testament would be turned more to destructive than constructive ends. Just as he prepared to look up, he saw one more entry shimmering in the reflective metallic texture of the flooring.

SCRIBING THESE WORDS WHERE NO ONE
CAN SEE IS A TESTAMENT IN VAIN. YET,
WHAT CANNOT BE SAID FOR LACK OF EARS
IN THE MARKETPLACE TO HEAR, MUST
TAKE FORM, IF ONLY IN COMFORTLESS
MARKS UPON THESE FLATTENED REEDS.
THE SOUL GUIDES THE FLESH TO SEE
THAT WHICH IT KNOWS THROUGH HANDS
OF CLAY TO EYES OF MORTAL DUST.

SANDALED FOOT TREADING AMONG MY
FELLOWS, MY VOICE VAINLY SEEKS TO
WRITE IN THE CLAY OF LIFE FROM WHICH
WE ARE ALL ASSEMBLED, BUT IN THESE
ACTS OF LIVING, THERE IS NO SOLACE FOR
THE SOUL. SCRIBING IN BOTH WORD AND
DEED UPON THE VERY DUST IN WHICH
MAN HAS HIS LIFE, MAKES THIS A GOSPEL
OF MEAN CLAY THAT TURNS NOT TO MY
WORDS BUT EVER BACK UPON ITSELF. THE
FIERCE TIDINGS THAT TIME, UPON
BLOODIED SHOULDERS WILL BEAR ACROSS
THE CENTURIES YET TO COME WILL THE
EPISTLE OF MAN'S NATURE BE, AND NARY
THE MESSAGE OF MY WORDS.

Before the bulwark of man's constitution, the diarist saw his message shatter upon the mean common denominator of human behavior. Just as disappointment had crushed every thinker, before or since, who looked beyond human nature to a greater good, the diarist saw only too clearly the fallibility of creation's dust. If man was the medium of the message, regardless of the intrinsically transcendent nature of the tidings, man and man's motivations became the message.

Slowly looking up from the fading text below him, Forrester saw an Arthur he hardly recognized. The expression on his face didn't fit clearly into any known category. Forrester's best attempt at reading Arthur's face suggested the sort of expression that might sculpt the features of a man who had just mistakenly killed his best friend. Forrester's question, when he finally pulled himself together sufficiently to ask one, surprised him with its simplicity.

"How long?"

"Damn, Nate, I'm sorry. I've thought of a thousand ways to let you in on what's going on, but not one of them came out like this. I don't know, that little story about Sydes just set me off. Since I gave up on marketing, I've always felt like I didn't have a life. You know … just sort of following you around as you lived yours …." Arthur said, his voice drifting off.

Pausing for a moment, almost as though he was trying to stave off tears, Arthur turned abruptly to the bar and poured himself a drink. Two swallows later, and with a refilled glass in hand, he sat down next to Forrester.

"I think Sydes was right. You are some kind of damn shaman. Half the stuff you talk about, I don't even understand, but I can't get it out of my head."

"Hey, Arthur, its OK … I …" Forrester replied.

"No, Nate, its not OK! You've done some great things, and you've done your level best to be a responsible scientist, but, damn it, you just won't accept humanity for what it is. You probably understand how people work at an intellectual level better than anyone I've ever met, but you don't know shit at a gut level about the human condition."

Forrester watched as Arthur took another sip and paused to gather his thoughts. Forrester tried to remember the last time that Arthur's appraisal of Forrester's life had missed the mark. He couldn't. Arthur's special gift was an intuitive appreciation for who people were and what they were capable of that Forrester's scientific approach required hours of careful observation to approximate.

"Cabot took your life's work … and street fighter that he is, he made it work for him. You may have had the best of intentions with your neuropsychological configurations, hoping they would help people to get the most from their abilities with the least grief, but intentions don't count for shit," Arthur said and took another swallow.

"Arthur … look Arthur, what I did, is what I did. Maybe I should have burned the research, but I couldn't bring …"

"Yeah, I know you couldn't bring yourself to do it. Like you couldn't tell Natcorp genetics division to go fuck themselves because you didn't want to see them waste me," Arthur interrupted.

The look of shock on Forrester's face worked only a brief pause in Arthur's revelations.

"You didn't think I knew, did you? By the way, thanks. I don't think I'd like dead, no one to talk to. Look Nate, you may know a lot about people, but I find out what people know," Arthur said, his mood lifting just a tad.

"So how long Arthur?" Forrester asked.

"Oh, Cabot's experiment … I think he calls it the reserve, about three maybe four years now," Arthur replied, his characteristic mood reconstituting.

"And on the Natcorp genetics division thing?" Forrester asked, his eyes narrowing.

"Maybe a month, a month and a half at the outside," Arthur said and paused.

"So you've known all this time and said nothing," Forrester replied, more puzzled than angry.

Then, not wholly unexpectedly, Forrester saw Arthur's expression shift to its good natured 'Forrester you're a nerd' mode.

"Nate, for a guy who knows so much about how the brain works, you haven't spent much time looking at your own. Let's face it Nate, you could feel guilty about a supernova if you happened to see one go off. Hell, you gather in personal responsibility, like the winner at a poker table rakes in the chips. Besides, when all this was going down, there wasn't a damn thing you, I, or God almighty could have done about it!" Arthur said with liberal emphasis.

"But, now there is?" Forrester asked,

Looking for the kind of punch line payoff that Arthur, with all his connections, was in a position to provide, Forrester paused and waited patiently for a response from Arthur that was not forthcoming.

"You know ... I have to get to this reserve Cabot created," Forrester said, looking at Arthur earnestly.

"It might be possible. With the war and all, things are being handled kind of fast and loose. You could be killed in an accident, then, an empty coffin tube would be on its way into the sun and that would be that. It's getting you on a ship for Earth and to the reserve that's the real problem. Let me work on it," Arthur said, already on his way to the door of the compartment.

"Arthur, do you know where Cabot has this reserve?" Forrester called after him just as Arthur reached the door.

"As a matter of fact, I do. It's in western Canada, and from the description I got, I think it includes the area where you buried the scrolls," Arthur said, his old grin returning.

"Oh," Forrester replied.

Forrester's bland vocalization was the only response he could muster in light of yet another revelation of his inability to accomplish what he had set out to do. Arthur, intent upon his new mission, hurried out the door so quickly he may not even have heard it.

Forrrester stretched the muscles in his face using a variety of frightening grimaces. He attempted to relax his expressive musculature, that had become incredibly tense from repeatedly mirroring his startled mental state. He was looking for his bottle of Grand Mariner and a snifter when the door that had just closed, slid open.

"By the way, Cabot calls them the meek. He pulled the best and brightest he could find from among those your research specified as having the least dominance needs and planted them in the Canadian woods. See ya," Arthur said, the same grin plastered on his face.

For a moment, Forrester continued to stare at the door even after Arthur's face disappeared. Then, for fear that stupefaction would become his permanent mien, Forrester sat down by the compartment viewer, bottle in one hand, glass in the other. Now, he was intent on relaxing his entire voluntary musculature. As he poured the amber liquid into the snifter, he visualized the closely woven tapestry that was his life. He saw Arthur grasping one loose thread, while Cabot grabbed another. As they pulled, the carefully sewn pictures that made up his perception of himself and his work gradually unraveled until all that was left were snarled and inchoate masses of strands on the floor.

A Medusan horror growing within told him Cabot had control of everything that had ever been of value to Forrester. And now, whether Cabot knew it or not, he had control of the scrolls. If Cabot had transformed Forrester's research into some kind of eugenics experiment, what would he do with the ancient diarist's words? He drained the snifter.

✃✦✃

Its breaching accompanied by a resounding cerebral thud, Forrester could feel the weighty tome of his cranial journal opening. He poured another shot of liquid comfort and stared out into the void portrayed on the viewer. There was an animating force resident in both the scrolls, themselves, as well as, the words they carried. Forrester had no doubts regarding this fact as he had felt the ministrations of that force on more occasions than he could count. Suppose Cabot found some way to channel that energy to serve his need for control? Based on Arthur's revelations, there was no doubt Ole Nick had already completely corrupted the benign focus of Forrester's research. It was frightening to contemplate what Cabot could do with the work of a three thousand year old scribe whose perspective seemed to consolidate the past, present and future into one eternal moment. Cabot was a primal force, and primal forces had a way of carving new channels into the marrow of existence without asking for anyone's counsel or permission.

If he had no other mission in life, Forrester knew he had to get in the way of this particular primal force. If he could not undo Cabot's application of the research, then, the least Forrester could do was to thwart Cabot's project with the meek and prevent Ole Nick from obtaining the diarist's scrolls.

Gazing down into the abyss of the snifter of Grand Mariner, Forrester noted he had consumed more than half of what he had poured. Like the contents of the glass, less than half pretty much described the personal resources he could muster to lead the charge against the most powerful man on the planet. Of all the individuals he had known and evaluated over the decades, he considered himself the least likely candidate for the role of change agent. Possessed of neither the demons, nor the saints of a fully charged right cerebral hemisphere, he could hardly marshall the unquestioned and unqualified conviction to pursue such a course. The inside of his head was an ever changing kaleidoscope of abstracted realities and moral dilemmas, hardly an effective armory with which to wage war against an opponent such as Cabot.

What few brain cells he possessed not yet besotted with alcohol were firing along ancient tracks whose circuits accepted only fear. It was not a fear of death, or even a garden variety fear of failure. Instead a fear born of the perfect understanding of how evolution had fashioned the left and right cerebral hemispheres blossomed. He knew Cabot was nature's paragon of right hemispheric dominance, while Forrester represented the full expression of the ascendancy of the left. The equation was simple , Forrester's part of the bargain represented the short end of the stick. In any contest with Cabot, Forrester was the foreordained loser. Cabot had the resources of the whole world to marshall to achieve his ends. Forrester could muster only hope as his ally. It was an old conflict between the ethereal, indeed gossamer, light of the left and the darkly churning waters of the right brain. The left, new and hesitantly flickering in the winds of time, and the right, old and relentlessly striving to subdue all of creation, were uneasy co-inhabitants of the cranial vault. The clash between the left and right hemispheres was as old as the left brain's activation, and hardly new to this epoch or Forrester's circumstances.

It was not at all surprising that the diarist, writing during the first flowering of the left hemisphere's activation, was aware of this struggle. The pain of that ancient scribe, tormented by a truth Forrester's research had only lately revealed, seemed echoed in a passage from the scrolls that intruded on Forrester's own lamentations.

> ENTERING THE WORKSHOP, THEY WANT HERE
> A TABLE, THERE A CHAIR. FROM THE GLOOM
> WITHIN, EVERY MAN FRAMED BY THE DOOR
> AND LIT BY THE SUN IS REVEALED. IN THIS
> DISCERNMENT, I BEHOLD IN ALL WHO
> COME A DIVISION.
>
> IN EACH WHO COMES UPON THE THRESHOLD
> TO PURCHASE MY SKILLS ARE TWO PARTS
> EQUAL RESIDENTS. ONE OF THE SEA, THRICE
> REMOVED, AND ONE OF STARDUST, ONCE
> REMOVED FROM THE FIRES OF THE
> BEGINNING. FIRE AND WATER STRIVE
> WITHIN THIS HABITATION OF CLAY,
> YIELDING ONLY THE VAPORS OF DOUBT
> AND DISCONTENT.

THE TRIAL OF LIFE IS NOT BY FIRE BUT
BY WATER. BREAKING THE WATERS, WE
STRUGGLE UPON THEIR SURFACE AND
SUBMERGE AGAIN AT OUR VOYAGE'S
END. BORN IN THE FIRES OF CREATION
BEFORE THE FIRST WATERS OF MORTAL
LIFE FLOWED, WE EACH AND EVERY SOUL
LONG, WITHOUT RECALL, TO RETURN TO
THAT WARMTH AND LIGHT. EVER ABIDING
IN FAINT HOPE OF REUNION WITH THE
FIRST GENERATION'S RADIANCE, WE ARE
BECKONED HOME.

As he heard the passage pealing in his head, Forrester felt the conflict between fire and water within and saw its clear exposition in his proposed conflict with Cabot's agenda. If the scroll's entry was definitive, then, the war between fire and water was a perennial one played out within and between men from the beginning. However, the conflict between Cabot and Forrester contained, respectively, so much more water than fire.

Forrester's own research had uncovered a similar fire and water split in the brain. In this left-right division of the cortex, a variety of irreconcilable differences in perception and emotion were found.

Implicit to Forrester's left hemispheric driven feeling and thought was a belief, or at least a steadfast hope, that life wended its way toward some benignly consummating, perhaps fiery, synthesis. If this fulfillment failed to manifest itself in the microcosm of daily living, then, perhaps it would be revealed in the universal expanse of space-time. Despite moment by moment despair with himself, and the brief epoch of time that encompassed what he knew as his life, he was hopeful. That hope was the light at both the beginning and end of the tunnel.

A conscious attempt at honesty that consisted in an unswerving examination of his every thought, feeling or plan of action tempered his abstracted quality of hope. It was, Forrester believed, through this honest self-examination that he remained open to whatever avenues might eventually lead him along an unswerving heading toward that benign consummating synthesis. He was not so arrogant as to believe he could know the mind of God or the universe as the case might be. He aspired only to recognize that his steps remained on the path that tended toward that final culmination.

If the will was the master of war, then his opponent, Cabot, was already the victor in this struggle. Cabot was vested with a primordial right hemispheric advantage that guaranteed his triumph over the most efficient left hemisphere ever to pump plasma. The ancient and well tested right hemisphere was neither honest, nor dishonest in truth. These terms had no fundamental application to its functioning. As the oldest organ in the thinking brain. The right hemisphere was refined to the perfect simplicity of winning. Like water, with which the right brain was associated, it flowed to the lowest point and filled every available open niche, displacing everything and everyone in its path until it submerged the whole world.

The energy of the right hemisphere derived from a mandate inherent to all life since the advent of the first single celled organism, namely, functional expediency directed to personal survival. Inasmuch as personal survival can never be assured from moment to moment, the striving for security via dominance over the environment and one's fellows was a pivotal component of the imperative to survive. If to survive was good, assuring survival was the emergent morality.

Reasoning as he did in the ethereal realms of abstracted reality, Forrester recognized Cabot was not his enemy. His real adversary was that magnificently basic right hemisphere of which Cabot was the most immediately apparent and fully manifested incarnation. As the first thinker on the evolutionary trail, the right hemisphere would maintain its primacy at any cost. Yet, in a curious way, the right brain appeared to tolerate the left, sort of like an occasionally useful appendage. By the same token, the left brain was a limb the right would readily amputate if the left's endlessly diaphanous musings got in the way of securing water, food, shelter, a mate or ascendance over an enemy. The lesson of evolution became unabashedly clear, the right half of the brain could survive quite successfully without significant input from the left. Whether the left brain could make it in a hostile universe without the survival instincts imprinted in the right was highly questionable.

Resolving he would undertake the weaving of a new tapestry for his life, Forrester had to get to the reserve. He had to do something, anything, to help the people held captive there because of his research. He had not personally foisted a destiny upon these hapless victims, but insofar a his work was an extension of himself, he could not escape responsibility for its ramifications. No single life can disown the ripples it creates among its fellows. He didn't know where he had heard that sentiment, but he believed it. For now, all he could do was wait for Arthur to work his forager slight of hand. Of this much he was certain, if it could be done, Arthur would do it. Possessed of a facility in helping people to help him, Arthur's skills were without peer.

Amidst the crowd of considerations vying for attention in his consciousness, an entry from the scrolls appeared, gently nudging aside all other supplicants.

GRIEVING NOW THE DEATH OF HIM WHO
WAS FATHER TO ME, I SEE ONLY MY HANDS
UPON THE WOOD. TO THOSE WHO NOW COME
A TALENT TO PURCHASE, THEIR EYES FOLLOW
THE CRAFTING OF EVERY PIECE TO SEE IF THE
FATHER'S SKILL HAS COME DOWN TO THE NEXT
GENERATION.

THE WORTH OF THE APPRENTICE CANNOT
BE JUDGED WHILE THE MASTER YET LIVES.
PASSING THE CRAFT BEGINS IN THE HANDS,
JOURNEYS THROUGH THE HEAD, AND RESTS
IN THE HEART. THE LIGHT'S ARTISAN, I
CAN GUIDE THE HAND, AND REFLECT
WITHIN THE MIND'S EYE, BUT THE HEART
OF THE APPRENTICE MAY BE ILLUMINED
ONLY BY A FLAME FROM WITHIN.

Considering the magnitude of the task before him, Forrester knew his apprenticeship in the craft of the light had been all too brief. Without looking up at the bar, he secretly hoped that there was another bottle of that triple orange liqueur on the shelf. He was going to need it.

⚜

Swimming through space, clad only in the Duo, Sydes was in his element. The spinning black ball did everything he required of her and taught him things he never would have imagined a ship could do. The days of hard banking maneuvers and long looping reversals propelled by a single thruster system were over. Navigating the sphere was like a child's fantasy of flying in a dream. He could fly hell bent straight away, make a hard left, stop, and go straight up or down. It didn't take Sydes long to recognize Von Strohheim had done himself proud with the inertial dampers. Only his eyes told him that he was in motion. He experienced no feeling of being pushed about in the console chair as the ship accelerated, decelerated, turned or stopped. He could fly this thing forever without an ounce of seat fatigue.

With the execution of each maneuver, Sydes noticed the ship seemed to respond more quickly to his manipulation of the controls. To test what Von Strohheim had told him, he programmed a time lapse counter set to begin and terminate in concert with each maneuver. Then, executing the exact same maneuver three times in a row, he checked the counter. Just as the Doc had promised, the ship responded a second or two faster with each repetition. This was what Von Strohheim meant by the ship learning from me, he thought to himself. Every experience he had since igniting the thrusters, convinced him the Duo was a good teacher, but she was obviously a quick study as well.

Slowly but surely Commander Tutunji learned Sydes' moves. He knew this was the most crucial part of his job description if he were to take full advantage of every firing opportunity the ship's maneuvers afforded.

In the seat below, Commander Tutunji recognized that with each alteration in the ship's trajectory, the menu of potential objectives from the infinite radii of fire the sphere offered grew. His job became easier by the moment. Just pick the field of fire and select either laser, or missile strikes.

"Asteroid belt coming up. What's the plan, Captain?" Tutunji inquired over the comm-link.

"I'm gonna fly straight into that rock pile. You clear the way for me forward as we go and take out everything in range to starboard as well. Then, I'll pivot this lady and we'll fly a course right down the gravel road you've made to starboard. Got it?" Sydes replied.

"Got it," Tutunji responded.

Igniting the aft propulsion units, Sydes moved the ship forward, gathering speed with the passage of each fraction of a second. As soon as optimum launch range was achieved, the Commander released missiles forward and starboard in continuous five second volleys. The Duo literally flew through a nuclear firestorm of her own creation. Occasionally, unexploded fragments of rock struck her shields, and much to Sydes' surprise, a grouping of propulsion units fired on their own to maintain the course he had set. The absence of sound from the cascade of fusion detonations and the colliding chunks of fragmented asteroids served only to make the experience of flying through this man made hell all the more surreal. Emerging from the asteroid belt, the Duo pivoted and returned along a course marked by the rocky debris of the starboard missile detonations.

"Outstanding!" Sydes exclaimed.

Tutunji watched the progress of the ship on the viewer as it quickly cleared the debris field that was all that now remained of that portion of the asteroid belt in which they had been at play. Just then, a blinking indicator on the console caught his attention.

"Look at the ship's energy reservoir," the Commander observed.

Glancing down at the indicator, Sydes noted it registered a surplus in the capacitors of about one quarter of their containment quotient.

"What the hell is …." Sydes exclaimed.

"We soaked up a lot of the energy from the detonation of our own fusion missile launches. I imagine that all those rock fragments hitting us made their own contribution as well," Tutunji remarked.

Evaluating the ship's status with a quick glance at the console, Tutunji paused a moment as he surveyed the spherical view of space around them. Focusing, in particular, on the damage in the asteroid belt that only the Duo or a bevy of comets could have accomplished, he smiled as he looked up at Sydes.

"She's a good ship, Sydes. I hope we can perform up to her potential."

Sydes remained silent for what seemed to Tutunji a very long time. Then he spoke, not to his copilot, but to himself.

"A painted pony that runs like the wind, a good bow and lance."

"What was that, Sydes?" Tutunji asked after hesitating a moment.

"Just something my father said his grandfather had chanted to him. A charge passed from father to son over generations of warriors," Sydes said, his tone almost nostalgic.

"What does it mean, a pony, bow and lance?" Tutunji inquired.

"It's just an old American Indian saying. A warrior with a painted pony that runs like the wind, a good bow and lance must return with victory or only as a spirit whose passing stirs the tall grass."

Hanging there in space for a long time, neither of them said a word. Tutunji knew Sydes was pleased with the ship. Many more practice runs would be necessary to learn from the ship, to teach the ship, and for Sydes and his copilot to learn from one another.

Feeling the same weight of responsibility to defend the tribe of man that was woven into Sydes' heritage over generations, Tutunji said nothing more. Sydes had his painted pony that ran like the wind, and Tutunji had the good bow and lance in hand.

The outcome of the battles that must surely follow would be easier for Sydes to fold into his ongoing personal history. Sydes was a warrior. In battle, he would kill the enemy or the enemy would kill him. Sydes would accept no other outcome. Honor was the outcome of individual engagements for a warrior and honor was crafted in how one fought the battle. Self respect, the ultimate prize, could be claimed in either the heady moment of victory, or in a well fought defeat.

For Tutunji, his own honorable comportment in battle or death at the hands of the enemy, heroic or not, was not the point. Tutunji's standards were less forgiving than those which a warrior's honor required. For Tutunji, saving lives, maybe the whole of his species, was the only measure of his personal success or failure. No death would be an honorable one if he failed in this, his primary task. Honor meant nothing when thrown into the scales over and against billions of lives, the historic struggles, artistic accomplishments, and sheer determination that had vouched safe his species' survival over millennia.

Regardless of the divergence in their attitudes, these two men must each, and together, make good on the promise of the Duo and the genius Von Strohheim had crammed into her. They had to succeed, of that much Tutunji was certain.

Chapter 15

Awakening the next morning, Forrester felt profoundly relieved that he had slapped a detox patch on his arm before falling into bed. Blessed with the physiology of all those with his neuropsychological makeup, one sip beyond his limit caused him to react to alcohol like the poison it was.

A quick glance across at Arthur's bunk revealed that the bed had been slept in, but no Arthur. Forrester knew that, with the way his brain worked, he didn't really sleep, he fell into a coma on a nightly basis. However, this was ridiculous, Arthur had come and gone and Forrester was none the wiser.

Dragging himself out of the bunk, he punched up the transubstantiator unit, summoning from its guts the first of five or six cups of coffee he routinely consumed before noon. For those of his left hemispheric ilk, slow brain warming was the rule and lots of stimulants were required in the morning to rise from the dead. He recalled once, as a young man, foreswearing stimulants as an act of self-discipline. He also clearly remembered sitting at his desk in this stimulant free state staring at the same page in a technical text he was reading for over fifteen minutes without comprehending anything. Stimulants were definitely a necessary evil for those with a constitution governed by the left cerebral hemisphere.

Hypothalamic agitation revealed itself to him as hunger. To be hungry this early in the morning was odd for a man who seldom ate until he was almost ready to retire. Hauling out his personal menu card, he inserted it into the transubstantiator unit, which sprang instantly to life. He reeled through the menu's encoded contents until he came to Pennsylvania Dutch sourdough hardtacks topped by mustard and a spread with no trans-fatty acids. As bizarre as it might have appeared to an outside observer, it looked right to him. As with the majority of full left hemispheric processors, he craved salt, plant oils, vegetables and carefully titrated stimulants like caffeine and nicotine. Such specific hungers were messengers whose demands were familiar to individuals with left hemispheres starved for sympathetic input. Those with little right cerebral hemispheric activation required this sort of diet if they were to muster the most modest of fight-flight reactions to threat. In short, the left hemisphere's commitment to abstraction made it nearly defenseless in a world in which real threats arose unexpectedly.

Full right hemispheric processors were driven to dine on animal protein, sugar, and craved central nervous system depressants. The depressants were sought after to quell the abundance of emotional arousal supplied by the churnings of the ancient right brain. If theirs was a predator's fare, then certainly Forrester's dining pleasure was that of the prey. Blessed are the herbivores, the thought ran through his mind, but he couldn't recall the source of the phrase. He was munching down the last of his pretzels as Arthur burst through the door. Arthur was wholly reconstituted to his former glory as he snatched a Guinness from the bar and commenced to absorb it. The bottle of Guinness still firmly in his grasp, he flopped down in a chair next to Forrester.

"Damn, Nate, you aren't eating that poor farmer's feed again are you? Haven't you heard of bacon and eggs or donuts maybe?"

"I surprise even myself at times. I think I've got this worked out. Does it feel like a good day to die, Nate?" Arthur continued.

"Well I ...." Forrester began and instantly regretted it.

"No matter Nate, today's the day. This is what's gonna happen. In about four hours, we'll get an emergency call to respond to an airless section of the station where one of the construction guys is injured. I won't be available so you'll go in alone, but in a construction worker's environment suit. Once you get in there, there'll be a little explosion and I'll arrive to take you out. Everyone will think you're the construction worker. After the smoke clears, a crew will go in and find an environment suit with a medical logo on it full of nothing but unrecognizable goo. Everyone will assume that goo is you, and, of course, I'll certify the fact," Arthur said, his planning genius in full swing.

Marveling at his partner's creativity, Forrester simply stared at Arthur. Deception, regardless of its goal, good, bad, or indifferent, required the sort of arrogant, self-rationalizing confidence only the right hemisphere could muster. The left hemisphere could never get there. It would choke on every step in the sequence. Between endlessly permutating both the validity of the emotions and the greater good they were to serve at every point in the succession of actions and inferred reactions, there would be no forward motion. More to the point, among left hemispheric thinkers, all that internal rumination would demonstrate itself in nonverbal behaviors even a child could read as dissimulation.

Finishing his Guinness, Arthur seemed deep in thought as he went for another. Returning to Forrester's side, he popped the cap from the bottle and drew a deep breath.

"So how do I get to Earth?" Forrester asked.

"With you posing as a construction worker. I'll shepherd your care from start to finish. You'll go directly to the burn unit in sick bay, where I'll wrap you in duraplast like a mummy. Then, I'll certify that your injuries will require treatment in a cloning unit on Earth. Here's where we get lucky. One of the best burn cloning units on the planet is in western Canada, which is where I'll ship you. What do you think?" Arthur replied.

It was dumbfounded time again. Forrester shook his head as if to jostle all the parts of the plan into some kind of sequential order. Arthur had good simultaneous cognitive skills and provided all the particulars in one big lump. As a strong left hemispheric thinker, Forrester had to consider the pro's and con's of each step one at a time, but that was pointless, the escape was a fait accompli. Then, Forrester did one of the things he did best, which was to recognize when someone could do something better than himself.

"It's genius, Arthur, pure genius," Forrester responded.

"Damn right it is! And I'll tell you why. Besides you and me, there's only one other guy on the station involved. He's the one who'll smuggle the suit full of goo into the construction area. Think of that Nate, only one other guy and he owes me big time!" Arthur replied, beaming with pride.

Force of cognitive habit alone had Forrester still desperately trying to sort through the undifferentiated chunks of Arthur's plan in the hope of seeing the trees for the forest with which he had been presented. It was the old story of the preeminence of thinking reflexes in the human cognitive array over the circumstances and motivations to which they were applied. With a dissociated sense of helplessness, he watched himself dissect each piece of the Arthur's plan, positioning it in temporal sequential order in his head. The step-by-step cognitive coding built into his left hemispheric brain structures was completely irresistible, even in the face of what he knew to be a done deal.

In the midst of his cognitive parsing, Forrester raised the one question that seemed to represent a crucial tree in the woods of Arthur's plan. Behind this question also lay his belief that in all change some things remain the same, in this case, his partnership with Arthur.

"So Arthur, how do you get off the station?"

"I don't Nate," Arthur replied, a vacant stare in his eyes.

Forrester's shock, as was so often the case, derived strictly from assumptions he had made at a nonverbal level. That sudden skidding stop in his flow of mentation revealed itself in the cadence of his words.

"But Arthur, we're … a team, we've always … been …"

"Nate … I always thought of you as a guy with, well … a mission in life. I don't have the first fucking idea what it might be, but I'm convinced you have one," Arthur said solemnly.

Forrester experienced an unexpected and inexplicable feeling a wave of embarrassment sweep over him as he met Arthur's eyes.

"Arthur, I don't think …."

"Nate, just shut the fuck up!" Arthur said, his volume rising as he came to his feet.

More definitive than Forrester could ever recall having seen him, Arthur's gestures were consistent with his commanding posture. He was not about to allow sentiment to gain a foothold in this transaction.

"Everyone who's ever met you thinks you've got some kind of light burning inside. I know, I hear them talking. You're sorta like a smart kid, who knows enough to keep his mouth shut most of the time. Because you say so damn little, people tend to listen when you say something. It's because you're so fucking self-effacing that people pay attention to what you think. Everyone knows that you're not talking to run some half-assed competitive bullshit on them. I've hung around all these years, because I knew you had something special to do, but to do it you'd have to stay alive. That was my job," Arthur said emphatically.

"I never knew …, " Forrester began.

"You weren't supposed to know. That's the point! If you'd figured out that I was leading you around like some guide dog for the socially blind, you wouldn't have tolerated it," Arthur replied, his intensity increasing.

Forrester looked at Arthur with feelings of both embarrassment and gratitude vying for control within.

"You're a good friend, Arthur, Thank …."

"Ah shit Nate you're not going to thank me are you? Man, you just don't get it. I did what I'm suited to do, programmed to do according to your research. If your brain destines you to do something, than, mine fates my life. Hell, I used to hear you teaching this stuff to your students all the time. How did it go, a man's brain structure is seventy percent of his destiny?"

Painting a picture down to the last detail, Arthur's summation included all the years they had spent working together. Forrester got the feeling that his friend and partner wasn't finished. He was right.

"Nate, you're so fond of those fortune cookie entries in the scrolls we found, I know, I see you consulting that damn scanner every day," Arthur said, pulling out his scanner containing the scroll's contents.

Some kind of big finish was coming. Forrester could tell that from Arthur's tone of voice, and producing the scanner meant he intended to use the scrolls to cap off his argument.

"There's one entry I've never heard you talk about. It's the one I've read most often over the years. Here, take a look," Arthur said, as he shoved his scanner into Forrester's hand.

Looking down at the screen, Forrester instantly recognized the entry. He had seen it many times before and skipped over the passage to study others. Somehow Arthur knew Forrester would avoid this particular entry in the scrolls. Forrester marveled at how effortlessly and insightfully Arthur focused on the behavior of his fellows. Forrester's own means of discovering the intent of those around him was, by comparison, torturously complex. He had spent decades carefully observing the behavior of others, but always from the perspective of abstracting principles and governing dynamics that others saw as mundane fragments of behavior. Forrester didn't so much experience life as he watched himself and others live it. By way of contrast, Arthur wasn't systematically investigating the pillars supporting and informing human behavior, he just saw, understood, remembered and lived.

MY MINISTRY, BUT A BRIEF DAY AS
WITNESS TO THE LIGHT, IS UPON ME.
OPENLY I WILL PASS AMONG THOSE OF
THIS WORLD KNOWING THAT LITTLE OF
THAT WHICH HERE IS WRITTEN CAN I
UTTER. THE LIFE AROUND ME REMAINS
A DRAMA OF ENDLESS REPETITIONS, AS
ONLY PLACE AND PLAYERS CHANGE AND
ARE CHANGED AGAIN. THE BEST OF WHAT
I MAY SAY WILL NOT BE HEARD, AND SO,
MUST GO UNSPOKEN. IN TIME'S
RECKONING, THE SHADOW UPON THE
SUN'S DIAL IS PATIENCE AND IN THIS
STILLNESS OF PURPOSE IS WISDOM.

OF THOSE WHOSE EYES CAN SEE AND
EARS CAN HEAR THE WORDS HERE SET
DOWN, THIS GENERATION PRODUCES
TOO FEW. A RACE, YOUNG AND FULL OF
LIFE, THEY SEE NOT BEYOND THEMSELVES
TO THAT WHICH WAS LIFE BEFORE EVER
THEY GLIMPSED THE FEW STARS ARRAYED
ABOUT THIS TINY WORLD. UPON THESE

FEEBLE REEDS THEN, IN FUTURE'S HOPE,
I SET AND SEAL THIS SCRIPT OF MY SOUL.

JAMES, BROTHER AND FRIEND, BURY
THESE MY THOUGHTS UNTO MYSELF
DEEP AND WELL. LONG AFTER WHAT
YOU HAVE SEEN OF ME AND I OF THEE
IS CRUMBLED TO DUST, THEY WILL
SPEAK AGAIN. IN THE TIME THAT
IS TO COME, THE HAND THAT SWEEPS
THE DUST FROM THESE PAGES IS
ORDAINED SO TO DO.

Reading the entry word by word, Forrester understood why he had hurriedly passed over it on so many previous occasions. He didn't like how plainly it characterized his role in discovering the scrolls. In particular, he didn't like the word "ordained" in the passage. As he looked up from the scanner, Arthur stared at him.

"The ordained part sorta sticks in your throat, doesn't it?" He said.

Arthur's tone was not gloating. Instead, it demonstrated an uncharacteristically sober quality and became almost conciliatory as he continued.

"I still don't know if I believe half of this stuff. At the same time, I can't just dismiss it any more than you can say that a law of physics is just a collection of happenstances that hang together over and over again. The bottom line is there are just too many damn coincidences here to be ignored."

Forrester looked long and hard into his friend's face. Something changed in Arthur's eyes. His hard self-confidence and 'I told you so' squint was gone. In its place, there was a softness and acceptance that Forrester had never before seen in his long time partner. Arthur looked down momentarily and then began to speak as his gaze rose to Forrester's face.

"Nate, I know you got something more out of reading these entries than I did. I could see it in your face while you were reading. Something real, something transforming happened for you. For me, it was just reading words. So Nate, you're going back to Earth on your own. I'm as certain that I've finished my job for you as I am that from this point forward your life is going to take a different course. Cabot's reserve is where you're supposed to be, and by God that's where you're going."

Fixing Arthur's expression at this moment firmly in memory, Forrester knew that here before him, was the best friend he would ever have. He also knew, in a way he could not fully explain, that everything Arthur had told him was absolutely true. The silence between them appeared to be more uncomfortable for Arthur than for him.

"One more thing, Nate, try not to work out everything before hand. If you're foreordained to do something, you'll just do it. Hell, your own research tells you that. A man is what he is and can only do what he is. What's that bullshit you were always telling your students, a person only learns when he's required to do something he isn't prepared for? Look at it this way, whatever the hell you are supposed to do is who you are. You are the preparation, and if whatever you're supposed to do isn't coded into who you are, well, it'll be a great learning experience," Arthur said, doing his dutch uncle schtick.

"Of course, you're probably right Arthur ... and by the way, fuck you," Forrester muttered as he fixed Arthur with a feigned sneer.

"Well Nate, I've got some loose ends to tie up ... before I kill you off," Arthur said, doing his best impression of mafioso finality.

Turning in his chair, Forrester watched as Arthur hastened through the compartment door. He was off to do what Forrester knew Arthur most enjoyed, namely, working some intrigue that stuck it to the man.

The soft click of the compartment door sealing served as a coda on one of the most revealing conversations he and Arthur had ever had. He sat for a moment, lost in the silence of the compartment. The stillness seemed somehow different now. It no longer represented an opportunity to be alone with his thoughts secure from Arthur's interruptions. Soon, there would be no Arthur, no good friend, no right hemisphere to serve as a guide to the world outside of Forrester's head. He would have to mobilize his own feeble energies to attempt what had always been constitutionally difficult for him, dividing his attention between his inner life and the larger world in which he found himself.

Forrester's own right brain deficits, including difficulty with simultaneous information processing and finding his way from point A to point B in a constantly changing world, represented a very real threat to his survival. Arthur had always been there to deal with the flux that qualified as reality, and because he did, Forrester had the luxury of doing what he did best. His best amounted to enrapt study of one thing at a time, tracking the line created by that intensely narrow focus to a dispassionately logical conclusion. Without Arthur, Forrester would have to deal with life in its raw, jumbled and chaotically unprocessed native state. He wasn't certain, despite Arthur's assurances to the contrary, that he still could.

Sliding gracefully into orbit around the station, the Duo returned from her maiden voyage as a proven weapons system. As soon as a shuttle had transported them to the station, Sydes and Tutunji were summoned to the newly installed operations imaging room adjacent to the bridge. Von Strohheim and his crew had just completed their fine tuning of a viewer array very similar to the one on the Duo. The imaging room would correlate the input from thousands of long range scanners buoyed in space around the station and sprinkled at strategic positions along the projected alien attack routes. The room itself was remarkable by virtue of its simplicity and the claustrophobic feeling it engendered in those who entered it. The walls, floor and ceiling were covered in an absorbent black pigment and punctuating every surface at odd intervals were what appeared to be large projector lenses.

"Welcome gentlemen, please come in. I hope you will find this viewer useful. However, I must caution you that the initial effect may be somewhat disorienting," Von Strohheim said excitedly as he greeted Sydes, Tutunji and Commander Sadad.

Then, without any further warning, Von Strohheim produce a remote and activated the system.

Knees buckling slightly, Commander Sadad was most profoundly affected. Reflexively, he reached over and gripped Tutunji by the shoulder to steady himself. Sadad's mind told him he was but five steps from the familiar trappings of the station's bridge. His feet told him he was standing on a solid surface, but his eyes seemed to override all that input. The all encompassing visual array informed him he was suspended in the airless expanse of space. So convincing was the imager's impact on his senses that his respiratory rate increased to nearly a gasping rhythm in response to the illusion of space's vacuum. Up, down and all around as he turned were stars and the emptiness of space. Most disturbing of all was a view of his station in the distance, hanging, as if by invisible threads, in the blackness of the void. It suddenly occurred to him that Von Strohheim had activated the long range scanners at the frontiers of the solar system and focused these remote cameras back at the command station.

"This is extraordinary!" Sadad said, finally catching his breath.

"The lighting is such that you can see one another only by noticing that some portion of the view is obscured. The system is built to accommodate one or two viewers. It will reproduce two complete views if each person stands on the correct plate in the floor. For the purposes of this demonstration, I have bypassed this feature. Commander Sadad, the imager will allow you to stand in the midst of a battle and see the disposition of forces from any angle you choose," Von Strohheim said, his expression nearly gleeful.

"Doc, can this be used for simul ..." Sydes said as he turned to Von Strohheim.

"Simulations ... Jah ... simulations, like this,"Von Strohheim interrupted.

Touching the controller in his hand, a swarm of the blood ships suddenly filled one quadrant of the viewer.

Caught off guard by the three dimensional reality of the ships that appeared to be headed in his direction, Sydes felt his hands rise to a level that would have placed them on the Duo's console. He even felt his fingers move over the icon controlling the tunneling laser for just a moment until the reflexive action dissipated itself.

"Very impressive Doc. Can the Duo's performance characteristics interact with this display?" Sydes asked, never taking his eyes off of the approaching alien armada.

"Ah yes, Captain Sydes, you are so quick. I turn off the viewers now,"Von Strohheim replied.

With that, the void of space vanished and the four men found themselves back in the dimly lit black box.

Muttering something in German into his comm-link, Von Strohheim turned as the door to the imaging room opened. Two of his engineers brought in exact duplicates of the antigravity chairs and consoles from the Duo. They positioned them over the two plates in the floor that were marked with a series of concentric circles and activated the antigravity units built into the chair assemblies.

"Captain Sydes, Commander Tutunji ... the room, he will function like the bridge of the Duo in every respect. It is your flight simulator. The computer will extrapolate battle scenarios, based on our past experience with the alien force, and will record what the Duo teaches, and what the ship learns from your maneuvers in the simulator. All of this will be downloaded into the Duo at the end of each battle simulation."

The expression on Sydes' face was that of a child who had just received his first bow and lance from a favorite uncle as he reached out and shook Von Strohheim's hand.

"Thanks, Doc," Sydes, responded.

Von Strohheim seemed befuddled by Sydes' expression of warmth and his response was consistent with that state of mild confusion.

"Yes, gut ... we go now. The Duo's armament racks must be reloaded. I want to reduce missile firing intervals down to three seconds. Yes, vell ... the whole ship ... we must go over every part and ... and look for problems. Good day gentlemen."

His engineers in attendance, Von Strohheim bustled out the door and disappeared.

Both men watched as the little wizard hurried out of the compartment.

Sydes expression was still masked in approval when he glanced over at Tutunji, who nodded in response.

Having been there himself, Sydes knew what was happening for Von Strohheim. A picture of yourself painted by the respect received from others for your technical competence was one thing, being the object of sincere human warmth was quite another. The shift was a significant one, typically attended by some measure of emotional confusion. Sydes had made a few steps in that direction and he was sure Von Strohheim could do so as well.

✤

Glancing at his watch, Forrester knew it was about time for Arthur's version of the great escape to begin. Right on cue, his personal comm-link lit up. It was Arthur.

"OK buddy, it's show time. The medical alert will sound in about ten seconds. See you there," Arthur said and terminated the connection.

Allowing himself one last look at the vista of space provided by the viewscreen, Forrester came to his feet, prompted by the first chime of the station's medical alert comm. Exiting the compartment, he hurried along the passageway, arriving at the partially constructed bay in record time.

Quickly surveying the scene, Forrester's eye hit upon Arthur's inside man, who was there just as planned. He was a big burley fellow with a prominent black mustache. His grim expression suggested he was anxious to get his debt to Arthur off the books. Helping Forrester climb into a construction worker's environment suit, he shoved Forrester into the airless bay in a matter of minutes and disappeared. Forrester had just enough time to see a portion of a medical environment suit over in one corner of the bay when the 'little' explosion hit. The blast knocked him off his feet as bits and piece of debris crashed about in all directions. Arthur had failed to emphasize the magnitude of the explosion in this part of his little melodrama. Entering the room through a haze of smoke and fine particulate, Arthur hit the polarizer control on Forrester's helmet faceplate and loaded him on an antigrav litter. From his supine perspective, Forrester observed a small group of med techs hurrying into the bay to retrieve what would later be identified as his remains. Shooing several med techs away from Forrester's prostrate form, Arthur took charge of the antigrav litter and they were on their way to the burn unit.

Immediately upon their arrival in the burn bay, Arthur dismissed the technicians stationed there and sealed the door to the compartment. As he helped Forrester out of the environment suit, Arthur explained the chain of events that would land his partner back on Earth.

"OK Nate, I'm going to wrap you in this duraplast and put you in the burn isolation tube. I've adjusted the readings so that it shows you're severely burned, but in stable condition. I'll hook you into the fluid replacement module in the unit and pump a mild sedative into your bloodstream. It's a long trip to where you're going. Once you arrive on Earth, there'll be long hopper ride from the space port to Cabot's reserve in western Canada. The pilot is an old buddy of mine whose daughter I saved from being snatched up by a lecherous old FF executive. The pilot will see to it that your hospital receiving papers at the spaceport get permanently lost and then he'll drop you close to the reserve. You'll need to make you way to the reserve's shield portal on your own," Arthur said and paused.

Forrester looked at his friend through a thin veil of gauze, seeing only a flesh and bone incarnation of the principal argument against his own darkest visions of mankind's essential character.

"Now this is really important, Nate. When you get there, ask to see Doctor Chen. Speak only to him and let him know who you are. I hear he's one of the good guys and a real disciple of your research. My guess is he'll welcome you with open arms. On this end, I won't officially report your death until your coffin tube is well on its way into the sun."

Gifted with an extraordinary ability to talk while engaging in another activity, Arthur had already mummified Forrester in duraplast and tucked him into the burn tube by the time he had finished laying out the schedule of events.

"Thanks buddy, you're leaving a big hole in my life," Forrester mumbled through the duraplast.

"Hey Nate, don't get solemn on me. It was fun. Don't worry. Everything's gonna go OK and I've got this funny feeling that we'll meet up again," Arthur said as he reached over and activated the fluid module.

Almost instantly, the action of the mild sedative created a warm comfortable fog over Forrester's view of his surroundings.

"Nitey, night," Arthur said as he laid his hand on the lid of the tube.

Drifting upon the warm buoyancy of a narcotic induced sea, Forrester felt the gentle incursion of an entry from the scrolls attending his voyage into the death of the conscious mind.

> DEATH IS LIFE'S LEVEL. YET, THE
> LEVEL REVEALS ONLY THE WOOD'S
> OUTER SHELL, NOT ITS TRUE NATURE.

KNOWING WHEN AND HOW I MUST
SHED THIS MOMENTARY RAIMENT OF
CLAY GIVES LEASE TO THE NEEDS OF
THE FLESH. VISIONS OF WHAT
BRIGHTNESS AWAITS BEYOND THE
TRIAL MAKES THE FEAR AND PAIN NO
LESS REAL. HOW EASILY DOES THE
BODY'S FRAIL DESPERATION MASTER
THE SOUL.

DYING TO THE DESPERATE 'I' OF WANT
AND NEED EXTINGUISHES NOT THE GLINT
OF LIFE, RATHER, FREED FROM A LANTERN
OF CLAY, THE SPIRIT'S LIGHT MAY WANDER
AGAIN AMONG THE STARS FROM WHICH
IT SPRANG. IT'S WHOLENESS IN FREEDOM
FINALLY PERFECTED, LIFE'S LIGHT MAY
DELIGHT IN THE FULFILLMENT OF THE
SOUL ETERNAL'S QUIET YEARNING.

The diarist's words, slowly receding in the echoing halls of Forrester's now stuporous executive brain centers, had become music communicating beyond simple tokens of lexical meaning. Caught up in the symphonic vision they engendered, Forrester was well beyond any analysis of their meaning. All that remained, within circuits laid down before man walked upright, was a feeling of hopeful yearning. A fitting benediction, he thought to himself as he drifted into the darkness of a universe bereft of stars.

Chapter 16

Phil was not completely unknown to Chauvez. A common interest in 3-D chess had brought them together on three occasions previous to their assignment to the ark. At each meeting, they had played a game or two, with Phil winning each of the contests. The matches were very close and Chauvez knew he could eventually beat Phil, but it would take four or five more games to get a complete overview of his strategy.

Now, Phil worked with him on the bridge of the ark almost full time. Cabot wanted close order supervision of the loading of his ecosectors and Phil knew what he was doing. Chauvez had heard rumors that Phil had just about every degree the universities had to offer. As Phil maneuvered the immense ecosectors deftly into place in the girder web, Chauvez saw no reason to doubt the scuttlebutt.

There was something else about Phil that caught Chauvez's attention, a certain sadness in the eyes evident even when he smiled. Chauvez knew the deep grief that manifested itself most plainly in the windows of the soul, because he saw it in the mirror every morning when he shaved. It was this evidence of pain that first caused him to think that Phil might be an ally in his plan to remove Cabot as the Noah of this ark.

Compulsive attention to detail was the hallmark of Phil's working style. His meticulousness was clearly evident as he supervised the loading of the largest of the islands of landscape, namely, those coming up from western Canada. Phil had specified that he wanted the individual shields in each sector maintained even though the technicians had instituted an additional blanket shield over the entire ecosector array. These were living systems and Phil was taking no chances with their survival. Under Phil's direction, Chauvez supervised the completion of the water reservoir couplings and adjusted the humidity indices for each sector. It would rain in a number of the ecosectors before the next shift. Chauvez and Phil had been at it for eighteen hours straight, but Chauvez had enjoyed working with the individual widely regarded as Cabot's number one executive. Now, both men were tired, but each of them was too keyed up to sleep.

Seizing the opportunity of the closure provided by a job well done provided, Chauvez set down his schematics and looked over at Phil.

"Phil, there's nothing more to do here right now, how about a drink?"

Hesitating a moment, Phil looked down at the console. He was unaccustomed to anything but very formal relations with coworkers. He always imagined people didn't want to get too friendly with someone who was one of Cabot's closest confidants.

"Sure ... sure, sounds good," Phil replied.

"Well Phil, what's your pleasure? Do you want to shuttle down to the moon base or just have a drink up here in my compartment?" Chauvez asked.

"Up here sounds fine to me. Let me just tie up a few things here first," Phil responded.

Then, turning to his crew chiefs, he went over a list of orders to pass along to the next shift who would be completing the permanent power couplings from the ecosectors to the main grids. As he detailed the work orders with the crew, Phil weighed Chauvez's offer. One represented a public watering hole and one a very private venue. Phil had consciously opted for privacy. He sensed that Chauvez had something important to say and Phil wanted to give Chauvez the opportunity to say it.

"OK," Chauvez replied.

Chauvez successfully suppressed his relief. Phil had elected the option Chauvez hoped for. The meeting would offer an opportunity to find out a little bit more about the man who had been closer to Cabot for more years than Chauvez had been alive.

With Phil fully engaged in sorting out the upcoming tasks for his crew chiefs, Chauvez took the opportunity to stick a detox patch on his upper arm well above the sleeve line. He wanted to get to know Phil, but he wasn't sure how well he wanted Phil to know him, in particular, the ends to which Chauvez was committed. The rumor mill had it that Phil was a man to be trusted, but he was too close to Cabot to take any unnecessary risks.

Leading the way back to his compartment, Chauvez activated the door with his security code and voice print and the two men entered. Chauvez went immediately to the bar and poured himself a double shot of tequila and a triple orange vodka and lime for Phil. They exchanged a bit of small talk about the project before Chauvez decided to begin his gambit.

"So Phil ... do you think we'll bring this project in on time?" He began.

"I wish I could tell you. To give you any kind of idea, I'd have to have a completion date. All I get from Cabot is that everything has to be completed to spec and as quickly as possible," Phil replied.

Finishing his vodka, Phil got up and walked to the bar to mix himself another.

Caving into a growing dissatisfaction with this sort of small talk, Chauvez remembered he was not a particularly patient man when it came to social interactions.

Although he was capable of hours of unbroken concentration on matters mathematical, he didn't have what it took to engage in even a few minutes of diplomatic chatter. He excused himself to the bathroom and removed the detox patch and with it a considerable portion of his frontal lobe inhibition. Now, for better or worse, he would forge ahead leaving behind both his painstaking planning ability and his caution.

Returning to the living room firmly committed to driving the conversation to the issue of Phil's opinion of Cabot's actions, Chauvez poured himself another tequila, sat down and turned to Phil.

"So Phil, who do you think is going to ride this microcosm of Earth out into the wilds of the galaxy?"

Drawing a deep breath, Phil was taken off guard by Chauvez's direct question. Like himself, Chauvez was one of Cabot's 3-D chess bright boys, but the games Phil and Chauvez had played together suggested the chief engineer was a very cautious player. There was no way of knowing where Chauvez was heading with this question. More to the point, Phil didn't know how close Chauvez was to the seat of power. It was not improbable that Chauvez had some clandestine liaison with Cabot of which Phil was unaware.

Looking nonchalantly down at his wrist chronometer, Phil instantly ascertained the room was not under surveillance. The microscopic bug detector he had installed in his watch had cost him a fortune, but it had saved his ass more than once over the centuries. He carefully responded while trying not to appear suspicious.

"Well, I'm not altogether certain. You never can be with Nick. What I gather is that, whoever they are, there's a lot of them and there coming from one of Nick's reserves."

An impressive response, Phil's answer had the appearance of taking a risk in sharing insider information, which was, in reality, no more than a distillation of current gossip among the construction workers building the ark. Chauvez, visualizing a 3-D chessboard in his mind, decided to move one whole platform to see how Phil would respond.

"That certainly seems to be the common wisdom of the work crews," Chauvez replied, maintaining a matter of fact tone.

Startled, Phil shifted his weight restlessly in his chair. Chauvez was clearly a good chess player, but in contrast to his usual game strategy he was becoming increasingly decisive in his moves. He obviously wanted the game to move along at a faster pace. It was time for Phil to respond with some decisive risk taking of his own, or topple his king and retreat into a fog of evasive responses. Had he known about the relationship between Chauvez and Piatra, what he was about to say would not have loomed as so large a risk in his mind.

"I'm pretty sure that they'll all come from Cabot's reserve in western Canada. He's been conducting some eugenics experiments there," Phil said, watching Chauvez closely.

Suddenly, Chauvez felt darkness closing in around him. Piatra's anger had been well placed. She just hadn't realized how completely justified she was in her indignation. Not only were none of the construction workers who had slaved to build Cabot's big ship going along, but Ole Nick planned to import a bunch of genetic freaks to fill out the passenger manifest. Looking over at Phil, Chauvez saw traces of apprehension on the face of Cabot's confidant. However, overshadowing that anxiety was a depth of pain in the man's eyes that made plain his need to share some awful burden. Inspired by the familiar quality of that pain and the need it implied, Chauvez dove straight in.

"So, what's it all about Phil?" Chauvez asked pointedly.

Looking down into his half empty glass, Phil was not startled this time. He had anticipated another very direct question. Maybe it was the vodka, or maybe it was Chauvez's unvarnished style, which made him sound different from one of Nick's moles, that prompted Phil's response.

"The whole thing's a pile of shit, Chauvez. Nick's eugenics experiment in Canada is supposed to produce a race of completely docile people over whom he can reign forever and ever, Amen. He wants to fly off in his mini-earth as some kind of sun god, and, for all I know, establish himself as the absolute lord of whatever planet he runs across that will serve as a suitable domain."

Struck dumb by shock, Chauvez felt his gut turn over as his worst fears, fully metamorphosed into realities, crested the horizon of the future. He drew a deep breath and turned to Phil.

"I've believed, since I first saw the ark's schematics, that the ship would be a world unto itself. With so many reactors, a nearly inexhaustible fuel supply, transubstantiators everywhere, and so much medical support, it is completely self-sufficient in every respect. I never bought the idea that the ark was a big ship built to go from point A to point B. The ark has the capacity to function as an independent living environment for centuries," Chauvez said, holding Phil's gaze.

"The huge medical and biological research facilities are primarily in place to keep Nick alive and healthy. Some new research his people have done suggests that, with regular DNA cloning interventions, he can live forever," Phil replied.

Astounded, Phil hadn't recognized that he had so much to say. Reaching down, he hoisted and emptied his glass. Then he got up and poured himself another drink. As he returned to his chair, he felt centuries of resentment against Cabot's ruthless abuses of personal prerogative and power rising within him.

"His people have found a way to dedifferentiate Nick's DNA to fetal developmental levels, clone and introduce it nanoscopically. The fetal material selectively supplants strands that show signs of aging, and well, he remains forever young," Phil said in barely audible tones.

Sensing the tension around his forehead, Chauvez felt his eyes were open as wide as the constraints of anatomy allowed. Cabot was reputed to be over four hundred years old, but Phil was talking about virtual immortality.

"Absolute power over his own world and eternal life. That's a pretty good approximation to most historical conceptions of God," Chauvez responded.

"I've known Nick for more than two hundred years. He is essentially the same man as when I first met him. I have a colleague who runs the reserve from which Cabot will draw the worshippers to complete his court. He describes Nick as the most perfect predator the human race has ever produced. I've experienced nothing in my interaction with Nick over the centuries to call that description into question. And I've helped him ... helped him along every step of the way," Phil said in barely audible tones as he stared at the floor.

Flooding over him, Chauvez experienced a wave of undifferentiated positive feeling that he finally identified as feeling honored. Here was a man more than two hundred years his senior whose trust was more than amply demonstrated in the information he had shared. He looked at Phil, who now appeared much smaller slumped down in his chair, staring at the floor.

"We've all done what we've had to do," Chauvez said, his tone supportive.

"To be sure, but some of us have done more of it ... longer," Phil replied.

In Phil's statement rested the foundations of the trust that he inspired in those who knew him. Chauvez had offered Phil an unassailable, even axiomatic, way out. He would not have been less of a man had he agreed that people, including himself, had to do what circumstances forced upon them for at least a good chunk of their lives. However, Phil was the kind of man who could forgive the whole world for bowing to circumstances, and yet not allow himself the luxury of diving down that escape hatch himself. Chauvez drove home his agenda with new appreciation of the man who was seated across from him.

"If Cabot is the perfect predator, then, I guess that makes all of the rest of us prey."

There were ages worth of world weary resignation in Phil's voice as he replied.

"Yes, I suppose so. Lackey, or rebel at the barricades, sooner or later, we're all just meat to old Nick."

Chauvez saw his chance. Heart pounding, he jumped in with both feet. He could palpably feel Piatra at his back impatiently pushing him to call for a commitment from Phil.

"So Phil, what's to be done?"

Staring into a half empty glass, Phil allowed himself a moment of reverie. How much his life was like that glass, he pondered, not full of any one thing, always just half and half. It was a simple thought really, but he found it strangely energizing.

"I guess old Nick will have to go," Phil intoned as he stared directly into Chauvez's eyes.

No clash of cymbals in his head attended the accomplishment of Chauvez's goal. Rather, he experienced a sense of dark purpose that beginning now, would grow only larger and blacker as they plotted their sedition. He looked at Phil and saw in him an ally he could trust in fulfilling the mission that Piatra's death had created for his life.

Hauling himself out of his chair, Chauvez popped out a drawer in his desk. He rummaged through its contents until he came up with a couple of detox patches. He slapped one on his arm and handed the other to Phil.

"Would you like to look at this situation with a whole brain?"

"Got any coffee and some cleaner?" Phil asked as he applied the detox patch.

Chauvez ambled over to a small console next to his transubstantiator unit. He punched up a couple of large cups of espresso from the menu and produced two cleaner capsules from the console. Cleaner capsules, like the detox patches, were everyday medical miracles. The little capsules prompted a more generic detoxification of the body than the detox patches by speeding up waste product removal at a cellular level. They were perfectly safe when used only occasionally and often produced a sense of well being not unlike the best night's sleep imaginable.

Capsules swallowed, Phil and Chauvez both quietly sipped from the steaming cups of espresso, hoping to hasten their recovery from the alcoholic excesses of the evening.

"All of the assaults on Nick's life have failed because, in one way or another, they represented attempts to penetrate his security forces or his personal shield. Nick has had a half a millennium to permute all the strategies necessary to foil that kind of attack. Based on the fact he has survived at least two hundred such offensives on his person, I'd say he's untouchable if you come at him head on," Phil said between sips.

Chauvez looked directly at Phil and listened to his every word, but the big screen inside his head was wholly occupied with a playback of Piatra's shuttle being impaled by a girder and the craft exploding.

"Yes, I'm aware of that from a recent personal experience," Chauvez said, his voice heavy with sadness.

"You knew someone on those shuttles that Nick destroyed," Phil responded.

"My woman was the instigator of that attempt," Chauvez said as he pulled himself together.

Visualizing what he imagined was Chauvez's mental chessboard, Phil now appreciated the vulnerable position in which Chauvez had placed his queen on the playing surface. This was why Chauvez had approached Phil so directly. Only a motivation so compelling as the need to avenge the loss of a mate could have propelled Chauvez to gamble on such a frank exchange with Phil.

"I'm sorry for your loss," he said, looking at Chauvez with softer eyes.

Exercising considerable intellectual control, Chauvez was able to offset the image of Piatra's death to the periphery of his inner focus and fought back the mist forming in his eyes.

"How about poison, has that been tried?" Chauvez asked as his eyes cleared.

"Only once, a long time ago. Damn near killed old Nick, but his Docs pulled him through. It was a skin contact central nervous system toxin. As soon as Nick recovered, he had the guy's entire extended family murdered, as well as, all of his associates. After that, his whole scientific division set aside all of their other projects and worked full time until they came up with the personal shield grid he has worn from then to now as an unchanging accessory to his attire. At about that same time, he had a dedicated comm-link to the central computer installed in the mastoid process of the temporal bone of his skull. An array of molecular sensors built into that comm-link continuously samples the air relative to what he breathes, what he touches and puts in his mouth. That sensor array cost the equivalent of building ten space stations. The array taps into his main computer and assesses everything around Nick at a molecular level relative to its data banks. He's pretty much untouchable from the poison angle."

"A real keystone predator, he eats everyone and nothing eats him," Chauvez replied.

"Like I said, I don't think Nick can be gotten to from the outside in, but maybe we can deal with him from the inside out," Phil said as he leaned back in his chair.

Chauvez instantly grasped Phil's suggestion.

"You mean that mastoid implant, you mentioned."

"Right! If we can gain access to the dedicated frequency that connects the comm-link to the central computer, we might be able to fry his brain. Leads connect that comm-link directly to Nick's frontal lobes. The right amount of feedback along those lines could cook his cortex like an old style microwave oven heats up sweetbreads," Phil said, leaning forward.

"That sounds promising, but that level of technological skill is way beyond me," Chauvez said, allowing a hopeful tone into his voice.

"Me too … but, I think I know someone who could help us out on that end," Phil responded.

"Someone who can be trusted? "Chauvez asked.

"I don't know yet, but I think so. You might know him Doctor Wilhelm Dvorak," Phil said carefully.

"The automation guru … How does he figure into this?" Chauvez asked.

"I suspect Nick wants to do away with the seventy-five thousand technical support personnel he originally envisioned as necessary to operate and maintain the ark. Dvorak may be able to do that for him."

Restlessness overtook Phil again as he moved about in his chair. On speculative ground now, his demeanor betrayed some of the tentativeness he felt churning in his gut.

"I suppose Nick doesn't want anyone on the ship not genetically engineered to serve. In particular, he doesn't want anyone who might cause trouble because, in some small way, they mirror his degree of self-investment. Nick's gonna be the only shepherd and everyone else on board has to be sheep," Phil said nervously fiddling with his chronometer.

"You know Phil, I wondered why the two sections scheduled to be completed next, the automation couplings and the technical crew's quarters, were held up. It's been hell trying to work around those two divisions and get on with the construction of adjoining areas," Chauvez replied.

"I witnessed an interaction between Dvorak and Nick. Dvorak moved from a stance of absolute rejection of Nick's proposal to subjugated compliance in just a few seconds. That can mean only one thing. Nick made him an offer he couldn't refuse. Knowing Nick and Dvorak, it probably had something to do with a threat against the lives of Dvorak's family," Phil said, taking another sip of coffee.

Vivid images of Piatra's fiery demise and its impact on his life moved momentarily into central focus in Chauvez's mind. Chauvez found he had to remind himself to breathe. After a moment's pause, he focused once again on the task at hand and Phil.

"It's beginning to sound like Dvorak would make a good fellow co-conspirator, both by virtue of his computer competence, and his need to protect an emotional investment."

"We'll have to go slow with this. However, there may be plenty of opportunities to approach Dvorak if he is, as I suspect, charged with automating every system in the ark. If that's the case, I'll be meeting with Dvorak fairly regularly from now on," Phil said, nodding his agreement.

Suddenly, Chauvez felt very tired. He could see that Phil was ready for sleep as well. Funny how emotional closure allowed you to shift your attention to basic physical needs. It was also likely that the cleaner capsules had made some contribution to a feeling of well being for both of them. Perhaps more than the capsules and the beginnings of a plan, Chauvez's sense of well-being derived from something he hadn't felt in a long time, hope. If they could enlist Dvorak's commitment and expertise, this coup had a good chance of succeeding. He stood up, shook Phil's hand, and both men walked to the door of the compartment.

"It's a good beginning," Chauvez said as he paused on the compartment's threshold.

Nodding his agreement, Phil tried unsuccessfully to manage a smile through his worried expression. Placing his hand on Chauvez's shoulder, he gripped it slightly, turned and disappeared down the corridor.

As the compartment door slid silently closed, Chauvez realized the first of many risks to come had been taken. He felt certain that Piatra would have found this session far too cerebral for her taste, but perhaps her spirit would rest easier once the hoped for outcome was realized. He wasn't sure he believed in justice at all, much less some universal scales of reckoning that allowed for retribution in the name of justice. However, if such existed, he would toss Cabot's corpse into the pan opposite Piatra's and look for a leveling of the balance.

Chapter 17

A rush of cool air over his face awakened Forrester to his surroundings. The breeze was pungently laden with the clean smell of pine and heavy with the scent of fresh water and the forest floor. Flashes of sunlight played across his face and he could hear the faint calling of birds in the background. A husky voice in the distance was becoming increasingly clearer.

"I'm Bud, Doctor Forrester. You're back on Earth and we're nearing the reserve," the voice said in slow, deep tones.

Bud must be Arthur's friend, Forrester thought to himself. Bud, who Forrester could now see was a large blue-eyed man with coal black hair, helped him out of the burn tube and began peeling off the duraplast. Forrester eyed his surroundings. He was in a hopper flying at an extremely low altitude. The up and down motion of the craft suggested the autopilot had been set to conform the craft's flight path to just above the tops of the trees. His head cleared rapidly now. He knew Arthur would have used a short acting sedative whose effects would dissipate rapidly once the infusion terminated.

Still a little groggy, he nevertheless managed to pull on the clothes and boots Arthur had stuffed into a compartment of the burn tube.

Fully oriented now, a glance through the craft's blister port revealed a beautiful panorama of green and blue forest below.

"How far to the reserve?" He asked, turning to Bud .

"We'll be there in about five minutes. I'm going to drop you about one thousand meters from the shield portal, near a little stream. You can make your way to the portal by following the stream downhill. Arthur's instructions requested that I remind you to ask for Doctor Chen when you get to portal and identify yourself to the security guard," Bud replied as he moved back to the pilot's console.

Manipulating the controls, Bud slowed the hopper considerably and decreased their altitude until they flew only two meters above a small rocky stream as huge conifers rushed by on either side.

Forrester marveled at the beauty of the area as the forward motion of the hopper gradually slowed to a fast walk. Cabot and his people had done their homework. All the setting characteristics Forrester had speculated would feel right to the dominance deficient were in place. Forests of firs, clear rocky streams, mountainous terrain and weather cool to cold most of the year, these represented the meek's concept of heaven.

The hopper set down without a sound onto a small semicircle of water polished stones near the stream.

Bud nervously scrutinized the scanner screen while simultaneously activating the door release.

"OK Doc, this is it. Best of luck. I need to get my ass out of here before someone starts to wonder why a hopper has landed so close to the shield grid," he said with a hasty finality.

Climbing out of the hopper, Forrester experienced the sheer enjoyment of feeling the variegate textures, soil, rock and moss of mother Earth once again under his feet. Such a delightful contrast to the artificially smoothed surfaces of man made structures. The air felt clean and alive in a way no purifying and recirculating unit could ever mimic. The envelope of the forest emitted an inviting hum as the sounds of a million living systems in continuous interaction with one another intermingled on their common ground. Turning to thank Bud, he saw that the hopper was already two meters off the ground and the door was closing. Casting a wave to Bud, who gave him a thumbs up in response, Forrester watched the hopper rotate, skim just above the surface of the stream and speed away.

Assuming an observer stance he had cultivated as a child, stock still and hardly breathing, Forrester became part of the forest that surrounded him. Surveying the woodland beauty of which he now felt a nonintrusive part, he knew this was his natural home. Here was a setting filled with a host of self-verifying sensory experiences that summed together spelled peace for him. He knew the dominance deficient would feel at home here in a way they had never before experienced because he was one of them. Listening, not for anything in particular, he tuned his ear to the symphony of the greenwood. The basso thrum of the wind moving through the trees, the melody of the stream flowing beside him, the occasional staccato call of a bird were all but foreground for the amorphous and yet unmistakable background continuo of life that emanated from the great single organism was the forest. Quietly, and with absolutely certainty, it came to him, this setting was unique. Here, and only here, were his inner life and what he customarily perceived as the intrusions of the world around him, not two divergent cognitions, but a singular experience.

Intermittently, a shaft of sunlight struck his face as the branches of the trees moving in the wind above him momentarily parted to admit that orb's bright light. The piercing illumination awoke him to his purpose in being there.

He started off along the shoulder of the stream, walking with the current. The ground was damp but firm. Led by trailblazing gray lichens, colonies of moss scaled the rocks by the stream and their green carpet formed the cushioned paving of the path he trod. Bees, betrayed by the sound of their rapidly beating wings, went busily about their tasks, as a rabbit revealed her passage among the ferns only by the crinkling of a dry leaf under one paw. The sun told him it was midmorning as he rounded a bend in the stream and saw the shield portal about two hundred meters away.

On the other side of the portal stood a young woman clad in the black and silver uniform of Cabot's private security forces. She carried no weapon Forrester could discern, but she looked like she could handle whatever came her way. Nothing else occurring to him, Forrester elected the direct approach and marched in a straightforward fashion to the portal.

Mustering his best, I know what I'm doing manner, Forrester donned a smile and approached the guard.

"Good morning. I'm Doctor Nathan Forrester, here to see Doctor Chen," he announced.

She looked him over with the thoroughness and implicit suspicion that probably made her good at her job. Signaling the completion of her visual in-spection, she took several steps forward.

"And he is expecting you?" She asked in a questioning tone.

Caught off guard by a question he had not anticipated, he could hear Arthur's words ringing in his head about how he was the only one in the class of life who had failed deception 101. Arthur was right, Forrester couldn't bluff his way out of anything. If the sentry was good at her job, she'd catch any discrepancies between his nonverbal emotional signaling and his words. He elected to clothe himself in the holistic consistency of verbal and nonverbal demeanor that typically accompanied the truth.

"No, but he'll be anxious to see me," he responded.

Staring at him for what seemed like more than a minute, she reached down and activated her comm-link.

"Doctor Chen. Yes, this is the east portal sentry post. I have a gentlemen here who identifies himself as Doctor Nathan Forrester. He says he'd like to meet with you. Yes, Doctor .... I understand."

Terminating the link, she turned to Forrester and looked him up and down one more time with what appeared to be an even greater degree of suspicion. Then, she deactivated the portal shield and waved him in.

"Doctor Chen is flying here to pick you up," she announced.

Catching a whiff of ozone, accompanied by the soft crackle of the shield portal closing behind him, Forrester realized he was finally in Cabot's reserve. The sentry's eyes never left him until a hopper appeared over the trees and gently settled on the grass near the portal. Based on photographs he had seen of the slender young man who disembarked, Forrester instantly recognized Doctor Chen.

Ignoring Forrester, Dr Chen walked directly to the sentry and began to speak with her.

A breeze, driving a rustling in the pines, carried most of the conversation away, allowing Forrester to overhear only parts of what was said. From what he could gather, Doctor Chen ordered the sentry to expunge all records of Forrester's arrival. The sentry hesitated to do so, but then Chen said something about 'Cabot's orders' and the conversation ended. Chen, his face now wreathed in smiles, walked to where Forrester stood.

"My dear Doctor Forrester, it is a great honor to meet you in person. We had heard you died many years ago."

It was mind boggling how many times he had died on paper, Forrester thought to himself. He could only imagine that PP Natcorp had declared him dead after his suicide attempt and before they had retrained Arthur and him as physicians. But dead or not, he returned the greeting.

"My pleasure, I assure you, Doctor Chen."

Ushering him into the hopper, Chen activated the controls and they sped off over the tree tops. After a few seconds of flight, Chen activated the automatic pilot and leaned back from the console.

"Doctor, I can't tell you how exciting it is to meet the man whose work formed the foundation of this project. Your coming here provides me with the opportunity to show you the full realization of your research," Chen said as he swiveled his chair to face Forrester.

Momentarily taken aback by the effusiveness of the reception, Forrester hesitated before responding.

"You're ... you're very kind, Doctor Chen, but it was after all just a neuropsychological categorization technique."

Chen focused on Forrester with what could only be called an analytical smile.

"Your modesty confirms your identity," Chen replied.

Eating up distance with amazing speed, the hopper ride was brief and soon the craft hovered beside what Chen told Forrester was a service center. The cluster of single story buildings nestled into a natural meadow with a lovely alpine pond at its center. Pines, Spruce and Aspen graced the mountains looming all around. Scattered across the meadow were more hoppers than Forrester could count with deer and elk grazing unperturbed among them.

"They all seemed to know you were arriving this morning," Chen remarked.

"They?" Forrester asked.

"We call them the meek. They call themselves the people of the trees. Your research refers to them as the dominance deficient. They started arriving early this morning. When it got to be quite a crowd, I asked what the gathering was about, all they said was Forrester was coming."

"But, how could they know about me ... much less that I'd be arriving today?" Forrester stammered.

"Well, it's not because I told them, of that you can be sure. I think Doctor Forrester, you're in for quite a few surprises," Chen replied, his voice betraying considerable anticipation.

Settling the craft to the ground, Chen activated the door release and Forrester disembarked from the hopper. As soon as his feet touched the soft grass of the meadow, the people of the trees began to gather around him. Wholly absent from their behavior was the jostling or queuing so often seen in large gatherings. Individuals approached him one by one, presented themselves by name, shook his hand, and smiled, but otherwise said nothing.

If Chen was correct, Forrester thought to himself, then these were all left hemispherically directed individuals who, like Forrester, possessed little or no dominance strivings. He could not recall any event in his life wherein he had experienced such uniformly consistent feelings of warmth and peace in such a large crowd of people. These were all, like himself, individuals whose life lay within and whose existence in the world was merely coincidental to that inner experience. Individuals whose emotional life was dominated by tissue structures and biochemical processes exclusively devoted to positive cognitions and feelings surrounded him. The effect on Forrester was simultaneously exhilarating and calming. It was, in truth, security at a level he had never experienced before among his fellow creatures.

The long line of well wishers slowly shortened as they completed their introductions, scattered back into family groups and took flight in their hoppers. Chen, who had been standing to one side, came forward and motioned for Forrester to follow him to his office in the service center.

Preceding him into the office, Chen immediately produced a bottle of Piesporter Michelsburg, Spaetlese and poured a glass for each of them. Looking a bit askance at the bottle, Forrester accepted the glass of one of his favorite wines.

"I don't mean to offend, it's just that I read everything I could lay my hands on about you, including your favorite beverage," Chen said.

Sipping his wine, Forrester studied the large room. An extraordinarily detailed evolutionary time line of the human species incorporating all the relevant paleontological and DNA based markers that he had ever seen covered one whole wall. The opposite wall contained an equally immense genogram that he guessed represented the population of the reserve. Black capital 'R's' with a stroke through them noted under many of the families depicted caught his eye. At that moment, he felt Chen's eyes on his back and turned to face him.

"It's really quite an experience to be among them, isn't it Doctor Forrester?" Chen remarked, a hint of tension in his voice.

Forrester leaned forward and poured himself another glass of wine and took a quick sip.

"That's an astoundingly meager characterization of the feeling. I've only seen the dominance deficient, sorry, the meek, when they've been surrounded and completely outnumbered by their dominance driven fellows," Forrester replied.

Rotating the wine glass slowly in his hand, Forrester listened to the soft swish of the wind passing through the evergreens outside Chen's office window. He was momentarily lost in his memories of all the attempts he had made to teach social survival skills to his dominance deficient patients. He left his reverie behind and looked up at Chen.

"They are universally seen as dreamers and losers, individuals wholly submerged beyond any hope of rescue in a morass of incredible naiveté. The cognitive, emotional and behavioral functioning of the meek was always judged against the majority, namely the dominance driven, and found lacking. Some of the early researchers thought the dominance deficient actually represented a character disorder in which emotion had been completely sacrificed to intellect. However, the majority of clinicians simply considered them children who either hadn't grown up, or refused to do so," Forrester said.

"I've never had a clinical practice, but I could recognize the meek among my students. They had great ideas, but would cease to argue their points in class as soon as an antagonist raised his voice or asserted the irrational in human behavior as a given," Chen interjected.

Leaning back in his chair, Forrester no longer looked at Chen, he was just remembering.

"The reigning belief was that because they weren't consistently competitive or in other ways constantly striving for dominance over their fellows, they were losers. All kinds of theories were mustered to explain their truncated development, but every explanation led to the same conclusion, namely, that they never would become adult members of the species. Often their perspective on life was held to be so aberrant as to merit labels such as inadequate or asocial personality," Forrester remarked.

"Or immensely passive hysterical personalities," Chen added.

"I'm just working off a first impression of course, but here among their own kind, I mean of course those of like neuropsychological configuration, they seem to be confident and without a shred of arrogance. Their behavior in the crowd outside seemed to demonstrate a kind of cooperation not purchased at the cost of conflict and its retributive fallout," Forrester said quietly.

Leaning back in his chair, basking in the illumination of an intellect upon which he had patterned his career, Chen took it all in. He felt his eyes straying to the genogram of the meek on the wall and snapped his attention back to Forrester.

"Doctor Forrester, I envy your arrival at this point in the project. Changes are occurring in this population on practically a daily basis. Phenomena are presenting themselves that defy traditional scientific description. It's a hop, skip, and jump approach to cause and effect."

It was Chen's turn to lean back and stare at the ceiling as he continued.

"Everyday interactions with the meek make me feel more and more like a blind man among the sighted. The meek are very kind and try to help me understand what's happening for them. However, the more they explain, the more I've come to believe it's not a matter of comprehension as much as a phenomenological difference between their experience of the universe and my own."

What Chen was describing was not something that Forrester had foreseen in his research. To be sure, he had speculated that if the meek were allowed to live exclusively with one another that their lives would be more productive. In Forrester's mind, this would have been a straightforward function of not being forced to expend energy in endless defensive battles, large and small, with the dominance driven which, in principle, the meek could never win. His theory could not have predicted that new and perhaps materially unique abilities and forms of interaction would arise among them. The emergence of new forms of perception and social operations that were comprehensively different from those ways of interacting indigenous to the dominance driven was unanticipated.

Taking another sip of wine, Forrester glanced momentarily out of the window at the alpine meadow. Only moments before, the meek had gathered there to greet him. He wondered again how they knew he was coming. Hauling his focus back to the man who might be able to answer some of these questions, Forrester focused on Chen.

"What have you seen?" Forrester asked.

Chen took a deep breath, and resting his elbows on his knees, he responded.

"I don't know where to begin. It's a constellation of little things, like their independent development of the Senoi style of social interaction."

Forrester sat up straight. Here was a behavioral permutation among the dominance deficient that he had not foreseen. The Senoi apologized and made reparations for their dreams as though they had been real time breaches of social etiquette. How had the meek come up with that? It was, however, a perfect fit with a community in which dominance and conflict were considered bad form, if not clear evidence of a disease process.

"Really, you mean they apologize for unspoken and otherwise non-enacted feelings, thoughts and fantasies. Does that include dreams that, if realized, might have a negative impact on others?" Forrester asked.

"Yes, they seemed to hit on that way of interacting with each other right away. As to their current style of relating, well, I'm not sure how to describe it. They get together, say a few words to each other and everything seems understood. I don't know what to make of it. It's like substantive issues have become implicit to their nonverbal communication. Regardless of the mechanism through which their interactions function, there are no overt conflicts and no evidence of grudges among them."

Forrester paused, certainly the meek couldn't agree on everything. His research clearly indicated that a restless and insatiable curiosity resided at the heart of the dominance deficient's core personality. Pushing the envelope and challenging traditional views of the universe were intrinsic to curiosity's everyday application and such activities often caused opinions to collide.

"And disagreements, certainly there must be differences of opinion!" Forrester said.

Chen was delighted to become the teacher to a man who had always been his mentor in absentia. He did his best to conceal a shy smile as he prepared to respond.

"Ah yes, there are differences of opinion to be sure. But you'd be amazed at how diversity of perspective and opinion flowers and then merges into a factually, logically coherent, and unified view when competitive egos are not involved. The meek have realized in their everyday lives Shakespeare's prose as a functional means for interacting with each other: 'To thine own self be true and it follows as the day the night thou canst not be false to any man.' Of greatest value to each of them is an internal experience, uncluttered by self-deception and false facades created for others. This being their principal goal, relationships between them are not thwarted by the obstacle course of artifice and gile."

Forrester felt like a five year old kid who had gotten everything he asked for at Christmas and a mound of gifts he'd never expected to receive. Somehow, the meek had evolved a practical way of dealing with conflict that didn't involve adversarial approaches, much less bloodshed. He had anticipated they might find a new way of dealing with differences in opinion, but he had never given much thought to the practical procedures required to accomplish those ends. As he leaned in closer, he felt his heart rate rising.

"Yes, yes, but … but how does it work? What do they do and … and how do they do it?" He asked excitedly.

"It's difficult to describe. When there's an issue to decide, they meet together, everyone voices their opinion, and, this is what's so curious, then, there's a long silence. The silence can last for as long a twenty minutes. Then, a much smaller number of people from the total group will speak, each representing the principal points of difference among them. After this presentation, there's another long silence. The meeting ends with one person stating a synthesis of the views. Don't asked me how this synthesis is achieved, because it all occurs during the silence," Chen replied.

Noticing that the bottle of Piesporter Michelsburg was empty, Chen moved quickly to retrieve a bottle of Eiswein from a small refrigerator unit under the minibar.

"The last speaker always asks the same question, 'Is it sufficient?' In all the meetings I've attended, I've never seen anyone speak in response to that question. Something goes on during those periods of silence, but its nothing you or I can see or hear," Chen said as he refilled their glasses.

"What's your best guess, Chen? You've lived with a colony of pure left hemispheric processors. That's something I've only dreamed about. What do you think goes on during these periods of silence?" Forrester asked.

"Doctor Forrester, I can only speculate. My belief is that each person in the group, in the privacy of their own thoughts, looks at every other person's perspective and their own without a shred of ego investment," Chen replied and took another sip of wine.

Although staring at Chen, Forrester was, in truth, wholly occupied with a vision of the meek, who like Forrester, were all head journaling. In Forrester's vision, every member of the congregation of the meek could see into the journaling activities of their fellows. In the silence, a shared internal conversation took the place of an openly audible one.

"I hope you won't be offended if I sound like I'm pontificating. Imagine for a moment, a discussion among individuals whose feelings of individual security are not based on competitive ego enhancement and dominance striving with their peers, and then, it all seems pretty understandable. Each person looks just at the facts and the operations involved and makes a decision. No one tries to persuade anyone else, and no one is offended if their viewpoint is not accepted. Somehow, each and every one of them applies the scientific method, first to their own views, and then, to others' perspectives as reflexively as you and I draw breath," Chen concluded.

Forrester sat back in his chair, finished his wine and stared pensively into space as Chen refilled his glass. Forrester decided not to share his vision of the meek all head journaling to a happy consensus with Chen. If this young man hadn't come to that conclusion on his own, it was unlikely that he head journaled. Forrester elected to focus on the method rather than the meek's means of achieving a consensus.

"So, if you pull out the self enhancing component of ego function and the need to sway others to your view of the issue, what's left is the scientific method as the principal model of social interaction?" Forrester asked.

"Yes, precisely. It's all left hemispheric curiosity, not right hemispheric adventuring for the sake of some biochemical rush. For the meek, the desire to learn is an entity unto itself. Curiosity for these people is rather like having eyes and the very fact that you are so equipped means that when you lift your lids every morning you see. It's not the dry and staid curiosity of the laboratory. It's more like the curiosity of a child, positive and hopeful, always reaching out to know the universe in some small way," Chen said, smiling broadly.

Forrester framed his next question with full knowledge of the pain and devastation he had recently witnessed among Earth's defenders.

"So, knowing the universe is a positive experience for the meek?

"Yes, it is. Even though they are aware of Cabot's slaughter of their infants …" Chen said.

Chen felt a choking sensation as though someone had seized him by the throat. Instantly regretting his statement, he knew that he could not simply erase it from his mentor's experience. He decided to forge ahead.

"The infanticide was something we thought we kept from them, but even knowing, they remain positive in their outlook. I don't really understand their perspectives and attitudes. Their beneficence in the face of this horror strikes me as transcendental. It's like they're tapped into the universe in some very intimate way. Whatever this linkage amounts to, it allows them to trust that the outcome of individual events will merge seamlessly into some larger abstract and benign purpose."

Forrester's head whirled around the 'slaughter of the infants' phrase as he attempted to frame his question about the meeks' faith in the future in the face of such abominations.

"And they all seem to share this, I don't know what to call it, capacity, perspective?"

"Yes and no ... the children of these couples are a phenomenon unto themselves. The left hemispheric abilities of these kids are even more difficult to describe than those of their parents, and far superior to their mother's and father's. These kids have a connection to the universe that far outstrips that of their parents, " Chen said, as Crystal's face filled his mind.

"But how can that be? Some of the children, even those with two exclusively left hemispheric parents, would have to demonstrate right hemispheric neuropsychological configurations. You can't just sidestep the enormous momentum of an evolutionary genetic matrix that has been geared to churning out a preponderance of right hemispheric, dominance driven individuals for millions of years," Forrester said, holding Chen's gaze.

"Cabot gets around evolution ... like he gets around everything else, using the most direct route. In this case, the direct route cuts right through living tissue," Chen replied, avoiding Forrester's gaze.

Pausing a moment, Chen stared intently at the floor, obviously in the midst of some momentous decision. Standing up, he walked to the wall adorned by the genogram of the couples in the reserve. Turning to face Forrester, Chen pointed to the black capital 'R's' with slashes drawn through them.

"You kill every child born to the left hemispheric couples who carries a right hemispherically dominant imprint ... and if you're Cabot, you get a stooge like me to help you do it. Everyone of those 'R's' is a murdered child."

Chen stood motionless for a moment by the wall that illustrated the efficiency with which he had carried out his task before returning to his chair. He sat down and wearily, resting his elbows on his knees, he buried his head in his hands.

Forrester's thoughts echoed in a head that suddenly felt hollow as he sensed the blood draining from his face. Staring down at Chen, Forrester saw a man in agony. As Chen looked up, Forrester shared the despair of his student. Transfixed by the sea of 'R's" on the wall before him, Forrester wished for a moment that he, like Pontius Pilate, could call for a basin of water in which to wash away the blood of these innocent children. Before he saw it, he felt an entry from the scroll centering itself in his mind's eye.

> AS WITH THE PLANTS THAT ADORN THE
> GROUND AND THE INNOCENCE OF ANIMALS
> THAT GRAZE UPON THEM, LIFE, WHEN

YOUNG, IS SIMPLE. FOR MAN, AS WITH
THE FLOWERS AND BEASTS, TO BE SIMPLE
IS TO BE DIRECT. TO UNRAVEL THE KNOTS
OF ONE'S FELLOWS REQUIRES THE PATIENCE
AND WISDOM OF AGE. IN ITS YOUTH, MAN
SEVERS THE TWININGS WITH HIS OWN KIND,
NEVER SEEING THE TRAILING ENDS THAT,
WHEN LOOSED, REVEAL THE COMMON
THREAD BINDING THEM ALL TOGETHER.

What he saw on the wall refused to reconcile itself in his mind with the sea of bright and lively smiling faces that had greeted him his arrival at the reserve. However, the horrible depiction on the wall was consistent with the diarist's appraisal of the human condition as an infant species. Chen said that the meek were aware of the slaughter of their children. Forrester was the acknowledged expert on the dominance deficient, but, despite all of his efforts, he couldn't fit the smiling faces of the parents and the tiny broken bodies of their children together. In the midst of his slide down into an everlasting pit of guilt, Forrester suddenly felt a push propelling him at even greater velocity. It was a thought with the momentum of an avalanche that now plowed through his consciousness. The genetic probabilities favored that some of these slaughtered right hemispheric innocents would have carried Arthur's configuration. There was no avoiding the conclusion. His research had been instrumental in slaying an Arthur of the future, the very sort of individual who had run interference for Forrester's bumbling, stumbling voyage through life for the last three decades. Summoning up the remaining vestiges of his internal control, he redirected himself to the present.

"And this slaughter continues?" Forrester asked.

Unable to answer immediately, Chen continued to stare at the floor. He was fully engaged in an attempt to hold his own demons at bay. On this, his first meeting with his mentor, he had to confess a complete corruption of both his idol's contributions and more importantly his intent in making them. He composed himself enough to remove his hands from his face, but for the first time since meeting Forrester, he could not look him in the face.

"Yes and no ... over nearly four years we've slaughtered hundreds of infants. However, every year since we began, the number of right hemispheric births has declined and with it the butchery," Chen said softly.

"What has changed?" Forrester asked.

Chen turned and, for a long moment he looked out of the window where a few of the children of the meek played in the meadow and replied.

"About one year ago, all the women in the community began to experience spontaneous abortions before the end of the second trimester. Upon examination, all the aborted fetuses were found to be right hemispheric processors. What defies everything I know about genetics is that in the last six months, no right hemispheric children have been born. There have been no further spontaneous abortions and there's been no overall change in the population's birth rate. All the children born in the reserve now, without exception, are left hemispheric processors."

Forrester stared directly at him as Chen turned from the window.

"It's almost as if they knew … and … and just stopped conceiving right hemispheric fetuses," Chen stammered.

Utterly alone inside of his own head, Forrester was spectator to the demolition of the great edifice of facts, logical processes, and rational inquiry upon which his feet had firmly rested throughout his entire life. The sensory impact of the image was so profound that, for a moment, he felt as though he might fall into the bruising pile of rubble that represented his beliefs. Every attempt he made to fit this new phenomenon into his understanding of genetics proved unsuccessful. No matter how he permuted the equations in his head, there was no way to make it work. He didn't like the conclusion he was coming to, but he could see no other.

"There are only two possibilities. Either we are looking at a spontaneous mutation within the population of a kind we have never seen before, or we are witness to the application of some elemental force external to the inherent genetics of the population. In the end effect, it comes down to whether or not you believe that an organism possesses the power to transcend its essential, physical nature and how quickly it can do so," Forrester said.

"Doctor Forrester, your own research confirms that attraction is based largely on differences in hemispheric strength. Left hemispheric processors are attracted to right hemispheric processors. The exceptions to this fundamental law in the past have always favored the attraction of right hemispherically strong individuals to each other simply because they have always been in the majority in the general population," Chen said and paused.

"Yes, and …?" Forrester inquired.

Chen fidgeted with his wine glass and took a sip before he responded.

"The reserve is unique, in that its population is exclusively left hemispheric processors who, contrary to the premises of the theory, are attracted to each other. The attraction of left hemispheric processors to each other is in and of itself new, not to mention the fact that in the general population you would never find only left hemispheric couples living together in a community. This is an emergent phenomenon, and, therefore, something our genetic models could not account for as it has never occurred before."

"Doctor Chen, wasn't it implicit in your own research regarding the increases in Asperger's and autistic births that some fundamental changes were occurring in the species? Changes that, perhaps, were being driven by the burgeoning size of the human population and its global density?" Forrester asked.

"I wasn't aware you had read my publications. But, in answer to your question, I did assume that sheer numbers and density were forcing some kind of neurological splitting of the species," Chen replied, a measure of pride on his face.

It had been decades since Forrester had openly discussed his research with anyone and he had almost forgotten what it was like to converse with someone who shared a common substrate of knowledge and interest. Now that the opportunity was at hand, he realized how much he had missed it even amidst the horrors above and upon the Earth.

"I think, Doctor Chen, that your assumption is correct. Using it as a jumping off point, conventional genetic models direct us to the conclusion that the isolation of a species subgroup will hasten evolutionary changes in their ranks. However, I can add nothing to help us understand the most fundamental change in this whole process, namely, the attraction to and mating of left hemispheric processors with each other."

"There are evolutionary changes and *evolutionary changes*, Doctor Forrester. As soon as you meet one of the children of the meek, I think you'll see. When I look at these kids, I'm forced to think of evolutionary change in isolated groups as a matter of qualitative leaps in a continuously accelerating wave of mutation."

"Surely you must mean that the development of the children of the meek is simply accelerated?" Forrester said with some incredulity.

Suddenly, Chen's head was caught up in his interaction with Crystal. He knew there was no way he could describe what he had experienced in his interaction with her. Crystal was an existential event. Nevertheless, Chen decided that he would try to share the events with his mentor.

"Well, that much is certainly true. For example, I've had a number of extraordinary exchanges with a four year old girl with the stature of an eight to ten year old and the mental ability of a fully developed adult. But it's more than that, these children have perceptual and cognitive capacities that surpass their parent's in kind, not just degree."

"Are you describing a community in which the children form the leading edge of biological change while the parents are left in the evolutionary dust?" Forrester asked, betraying some concern in his voice.

"Of course, I can see how you would come to that conclusion, but it's not like that at all. All these new abilities come to flower in the children, but then they teach them to their parents. I don't know a more descriptive word than 'teach', but that word doesn't really cover what I've seen," Chen said as moved to the edge of his chair.

Taking another sip of wine, Forrester leaned forward in his chair unconsciously emulating Chen's posture. His movements in real time seemed to summon a conceptual stirring within as well. Scrolling upon a reserved area of his consciousness, another entry from the diarist's journal revealed itself.

FOR ALL LIFE THAT BEHOLDS AND COMPREHENDS, A MOMENT COMES WHEN A LEAP TO COMPLETE AWARENESS REQUIRES A STEP BACK INTO THE INNOCENCE OF CHILDHOOD.

The answer was there somewhere in the holistic fabric of what the diarist wrote. However, Forrester, cast upon his own resources, could only fall back on the well trodden step by step cognitive path laid down in his tissues.

"The only way I can conceptualize what you' re describing is to look at the children's capacities as nascent in the parents, but represented as fully realized potentials in the children. However, I know of no model of evolutionary mutation that allows for a change that reaches back into the preceding generation and drags them forward into the biological future. It's at odds with everything we know about what evolution has accomplished in the past. Now, instead of a mutated individual competing against it's predecessors and peers, it drags the rest of the species along for the ride," Forrester said, carefully measuring his words.

"I know this is going to sound like an intellectual escape hatch, but what I've been telling you can't be appreciated in a verbal exchange. Interacting with one of these children is a phenomenological … an experiential event. For example, there's a four year old girl here who …" Chen replied.

Chen's response was interrupted by a tiny knock at his office door. As he rose from his chair and walked to the door, it was almost as if he already knew who was there. His gaze reflexively fell as the door slid open and there, as he suspected, was Crystal.

Smiling at Chen as she entered, Crystal circled around him and strode directly to Forrester.

"This is Crystal, the four year old girl I was about to discuss with you,"

Chen said as he looked over at Forrester.

Approaching Forrester without the slightest hesitation, she took his hand and tugged, beckoning him out of his chair.

As he stood up, Forrester cast a quizzical glance at Chen.

"Once again, I envy you Doctor Forrester. Go ahead, we'll have plenty of time to talk later. Crystal knew you were to arrive today long before any one else in the community. It seems right somehow that you spend part of your first day here with her," Chen said, smiling warmly.

Feeling, and he was certain looking, somewhat confused, Forrester allowed himself to be led from the room. As they emerged into the soft sunlight of the alpine meadow and walked to Crystal's hopper, Forrester remember a phrase from an ancient text, "and a little child shall lead them." Maybe, the phrase was more than poetry, he mused.

Motioning him into the passenger seat, Crystal powered up the craft and positioned it on a heading toward what appeared to be the highest mountain peak in view.

As the craft rose into the air, Forrester could see Chen standing by the service center smiling and waving. The circumstances of his escape from the space station, his reception by the meek, and being flown over this beautiful sylvan sea by a young survivor of Cabot's holocaust, were all too surreal to be readily absorbed. Altogether in the moment, he was enfolded by a now familiar feeling of being carried along by forces and events that he neither understood, nor about which he could form a rational judgment.

Chapter 18

Sydes and Commander Tutunji divided their time between the flight simulator in the operations imaging room, and real time battles with left overs from the construction of the solar system in the asteroid belt. Von Strohheim brooded over them like new born chicks, constantly requesting feedback about the functioning of the Duo and their level of comfort with her. Regardless of the length of a test mission into the asteroid belt, when they returned Von Strohheim always waited, anxious to hear any critiques and suggestions they might have to improve the Duo's functioning.

It was the end of the third shift by the time Sydes and Tutunji established a parking orbit around the station. Sydes took note of Von Strohheim's absence in the receiving bay as a shuttle returned them to the station and mentioned it to Tutunji. Disembarking from the shuttle, they both agreed to go to the Paradise Bar and liquify their tension and fatigue.

Entering the bar, Sydes was the first to spot Von Strohheim seated by himself at a table clustered with bottles and generously set with a variety of hard to acquire delectables.

"It's momma Von Strohheim," Sydes said out of the corner of his mouth.

"You're just the son he never had, Sydes," Tutunji replied, wryly.

Von Strohheim rose from his chair as they approached. There was a genuine note of caring in his tone as he addressed them.

"Captain Sydes, Commander Tutunji … you have been out there a long time. I thought you might like some refreshment."

Sydes pulled up a chair, poured himself a drink and smiled at Von Strohheim.

"Thanks, Doc, and, before you ask, your lady performed like a dream."

"This is good, Jah, excellent. We must be ready, ready for when they come … soon.., perhaps …"Von Strohheim said, beaming like a school boy.

Finishing his drink, Tutunji began sampling the varieties of hummus that were scattered about the table. He found one particularly spicy mixture, filled a flat bread and munched it down. After sweeping some crumbs off of the table, he reached over and placed his hand on Von Strohheim's shoulder.

"Shaving that missile interval down to three seconds makes a big difference. Seen from the outside, the ship must look like a continuous fireball of destruction. Frankly, I don't see how anything could get through that wall of continuous nuclear destruction," Tutunji said, his voice filled with admiration.

"Doc, we did an experimental firing test today. We got into the thick of the asteroid belt and programmed continuous launches on all six missile towers. Then we ..." Sydes said.

"We launched missiles until the racks registered only one hundred in reserve in each tower," Tutunji reported, interrupting Sydes.

"And then we had to cease fire because ...." Sydes said picking up the story.

"Because the shields were weakening, yes?" Von Strohheim interrupted.

"Because the shields were weakening, no!" Sydes replied.

Von Strohheim looked startled at first and then, grimacing slightly, emitted a low chuckle.

"Ah, jah, yes, this he is a language joke."

"We had to cease fire, because the capacitors were fully charged and the reactors had been ratcheted down as low as they could go and still be on line," Sydes began again.

"Jah, I see, vell this will not do, not at all. We need more capacitors, but where to put them," Von Strohheim responded, unfurling his flat screen.

Moving his chair next to Von Strohheim's, Sydes studied the Duo's schematic portrayed on the flatscreen . After a few moments he put his finger on the flat screen.

"Lose this," he announced.

"Nein ... no, the escape pod, she is essential for crew safety," Von Strohheim replied in definitive teutonic tones.

Tutunji lifted his chair and moved it closer to Von Strohheim's side. He carefully examined the schematic and leaned back. Placing his hand on the little wizard's shoulder, Tutunji's tone was supportive.

"Doctor Von Strohheim, we're flattered that you're concerned for our safety, but the Duo is an attack ship in a desperate war. You built it to help us stem the tide of an alien invasion and that conflict may be decided by a single battle. If the human race loses that battle, where and to what could Sydes and I escape?"

"Yes, I suppose ... suppose that this is correct. I had not thought about losing. The ship is the best we can make it. It has to work. There can be no losing, everything, everyone would be gone. Nothing left of us, any of us," Von Strohheim replied.

Von Strohheim's expression assumed a solemn set. He was not looking at Sydes, Tutunji or the flatscreen. He was staring off into space, engulfed in a vision of some final species consuming holocaust.

"Hey Doc, don't worry about it. Just pull the damn escape pod. Look at it this way, if we get nailed really good in a fire fight, the Duo packed to the gunnels with reactors, fully charged capacitors and fusion missiles will go up like a supernova. No escape pod could save our asses from something like that," Sydes said, cutting through the gloom with bravado.

Busily making notes on the flatscreen, Von Strohheim was lost in his calculations and design considerations. The only audible evidence of his furious effort was a gurgling stream of fragmented mutterings in German.

Sydes poured another drink for Tutunji and himself and watched with satisfaction as the Doc reshuffled the Duo's innards to accommodate yet one more innovation. Dumping the escape pod meant the Duo could hang around in a fire fight longer and kill more of the enemy. He didn't mention it to the Doc, but he never would have climbed into that escape pod anyway.

"Yes, this is possible. With the escape pod gone, the conduits can be rerouted easily and we can add more capacitors from what we have in stores. The missile racks must be reloaded. There is much to do. The technicians can have this ready before the end of first shift," Von Strohheim's said, his head rising from his efforts.

"By first shift!" Tutunji exclaimed.

Von Strohheim looked up at Sydes and Tutunji. His expression had lost its aura of paternal concern and reverted to his more characteristic teutonic blank countenance as he spoke.

"We could do it in under four hours, jah, less than four hours. However, most of my technicians are elsewhere engaged."

"And what are the techs doing with their time Doc, building another Duo?" Sydes asked, chuckling through an astonished expression.

Von Strohheim's stoical expression was momentarily lost to a look of surprise as he stared intently at Sydes.

"Why yes, how did you know?" Von Strohheim asked.

"I didn't, Doc. It was just a joke," Sydes said, casting a glance at Tutunji.

"No, really, Doctor Von Strohheim … you're building another one of the big ships?" Tutunji asked.

Suddenly, Von Strohheim's expression suggested he was seeing something truly impressive, something not physically present in the bar.

"A big ship, jah she is very large. This vessel will be more than twice the size of the Duo. The framework is almost complete, soon, we install the propulsion units. The sum total of all of the Natcorps resources are now at our disposal, both men and materials. Much can be accomplished when we work together."

Still trying to assimilate the idea of another Duo class vessel, Sydes attempted a little humor. He leaned forward on the table and placed his elbows directly on Von Strohheim's flexible flatscreen.

"Yeah, but Doc, what are you doing with your free time?" he remarked in a jokingly sarcastic tone.

"My free time? What is this free time? I don't understand. There is so much to do," Von Strohheim said.

Then, looking up, he noticed the smiles on the faces of Sydes and Tutunji. Von Strohheim chuckled a bit, downed his drink, and deactivated his flat screen.

"Jah, I see, this 'free time', he is a joke. Vell ... I must go now and make use of my *free time*."

Rolling up his flatscreen, Von Strohheim rose quickly to his feet and left the table still chuckling and muttering to himself as he threaded his way through the crowded and noisy bar.

"Free time, unsinn, craziness, time, she must be full."

"What a guy! Hell, we're just the jockeys, he breeds the horses," Sydes said as he shook his head.

"I'm for a little sleep," Tutunji responded as he stifled a yawn.

"Sounds good ... you know I'm getting an increasingly bad feeling about this. It's been too quiet. I think we're about due for another little visit from those bloody bastards," Sydes said as he stood.

Rising from the table, Tutunji walked with Sydes from the bar, the two men parting as each moved off toward their compartments. Tutunji said nothing as they made their way to their rooms, but he shared Sydes' sense of foreboding about the imminence of another attack.

✥

Von Strohheim's techs had spent the last seven hours refitting and reloading the Duo. Commander Sadad felt a strong sense of relief when the technical crew informed him that the ship was again ready for action.

Summoning his Executive Officer to take over the bridge, Sadad entered the operations imaging room. He stood perfectly still for a moment until he became reaccustomed to the illusion. Once again, he was hanging suspended in the vastness of space created by the projectors. He took his place on the viewing plate next to the Operations Officer who had the imagers tied into feed from the scanners buoyed at extreme range from the station. He turned on the plate to the coordinates where he knew the station was positioned, but their was nothing to see. His visual perspective in deep space did not allow him to see the station at this distance.

"Anything?" Sadad asked the Operations Officer.

The Operations Officer responded without taking his eyes from the spherical view of the solar system's frontier.

"I don't know Sir. I'm getting some sporadic energy readings from this area. The source seems to be at the extreme limits of our scanners. It sort of comes and goes."

Then, he depressed a control on his remote and the area of space he had been studying became a tactical grid. In one quadrant of the grid, small points of light winked off and on at irregular intervals, shifting from one position to another.

"This is what it looks like on battle perspective. That's what I've been seeing for about half an hour. The scanner read out says it's a positive energy emission, not a reflection from some natural radiant source," the Ops Officer said.

"And why didn't you report this?" Commander Sadad said angrily.

"There's been no movement across the front sir. The emissions just appear and disappear. There's no evidence of any significant motion in our direction or any other. Whatever it is, it just seems to be …" the Ops Officer said, a trace of trepidation in his voice.

"Just sitting there … well, not anymore," Sadad said.

Prompted by a small motion sensor indicator blinking on the tactical display, Sadad turned back to the Ops Officer.

"Whatever those energy emissions are, they've just initiated a trajectory that will bring them in our direction."

Instantly activating the klaxon indicator on his remote, Sadad heard the echoes of the alarm as it sounded throughout the entire station.

"Transfer the image of that section of space to the main viewer on the bridge, "And I mean now, Mister," Sadad shouted as he headed for the door.

Jumping out of his bunk, Sydes wasn't certain what he had heard. In moments, he was on his feet, into his flight suit and already part way out of the door to his compartment when the clanging of the alarm finally registered in his head. Enroute, he met Tutunji and they entered the command bridge together.

"I guess this is it," Tutunji said with a hint of resignation.

"I certainly hope so. I'm tired of killing asteroids. I want something to play with that shoots back," Sydes retorted.

A blur of personnel scurrying from one end of the console to the other made the bridge complement look like they were being played at fast forward. Tutunji left Sydes and hurried into the operations imaging room. Sydes moved immediately to the main viewer, which was filled with points of light that were gradually taking on a bloody orange hue as they moved into the long range scanners focal range.

"How long until they get here?" Sydes asked as he joined Commander Sadad.

His fingers flying over the console's icons, Commander Sadad looked up only momentarily as he pointed to an event clock he had created on the viewer.

"If they maintain their current speed, they'll be in our laps in about an hour," Sadad replied.

Turning quickly, Sydes covered the few steps to the operations imaging room briskly. Entering the darkened chamber, he motioned for the Operations Officer to leave and stood on the plate next to Tutunji.

"Well, we guessed right. They weren't about to risk the mine field," Sydes said with a measure of satisfaction.

"Right, they're coming in along one of the routes we anticipated. I hope we haven't used up our entire allotment of luck for the day," Tutunji replied.

"You feel OK about running with our battle plan?" Sydes asked.

"Still looks good to me," Tutunji replied.

Sydes and Tutunji immediately approached Commander Sadad as they left the imaging room and entered the bridge.

"I assume that the battle plan remains as we formulated it. The Duo goes out on her own to confront the alien fleet. Behind her, at intervals of five hundred thousand kilometers, are three waves of one hundred strike craft each. One wave, plus reserves will be held here at the station as a last stand contingent," Commander Sadad said.

"Now, all the aliens have to do on their end is to cooperate and die," Sydes remarked.

"You have my complete confidence," Tutunji said as he placed his hand on Sadad's shoulder.

Tutunji knew it was the appropriate thing to say at that moment. It was easy to do, because he meant it. Sadad had come a long way since being designated as acting Commander.

"By the way, have you seen Von Strohheim?" Sydes asked Sadad.

"Not since last night. I saw him in the passageway. He was mumbling about building something in his free time. The bay Chief reported that Von Strohheim left the station, but that's all I know," Sadad replied.

Fleeting smiles passed over their faces as they considered the Doc's compulsive commitment. Then, expressions more consistent with their mission tightened their expressions as Sydes and Tutunji hurried to the shuttle that would carry them to the Duo.

Staring blankly at the empty bridge access portal for a moment, Sadad knew he was on his own now. In that moment, so many lives had become his responsibility and his alone. He didn't concern himself with doing his best, he knew he would do that. The question he couldn't answer until the crisis was upon them was, could he match the intensity of purpose of those in his charge, as well as, the aliens who seemed intent upon eradicating the human race?

⚜

Watching from a porthole, Arthur saw the Duo's thrusters flare as she ignited her engines. Slowly at first, then with a speed that took the big black ball rapidly from view, he followed her course as the principal hope of humanity disappeared into the void. He was glad Forrester was not here to see the beginning of this clash of wills. Nate would find some torturous way to construe the situation as his fault or fall into some horrifically dysphoric mood as he decried the irresistible need to dominate driving all sentient life.

Arthur understood and accepted the need to dominate and subdue all of creation as the central core of both the human, and apparently, the alien's character as well. As a result, he saw these events as but one more battle in humanity's struggle to survive. For Arthur, mankind's history consisted in justifying aggression in the name of defending, securing or preparing themselves to address enemies both real and imagined.

An external enemy would unify the human race to be sure, but only so long as the threat was in their face. As soon as the outside menace was gone, they'd get back to the business of subjugating and killing one another. Whether the enemy was the occupants of the blood ships or the guy next door was irrelevant. The whole point was to, in any way possible, localize the enemy in the not-me space outside of yourself, and conquer or kill it.

Damn, Arthur thought to himself, the inside of my head is beginning to sound like the outside of Forrester. He needed a drink and he needed it now. The bar was only a few steps away and he was already in motion.

⚜

Tutunji carefully studied the tight and orderly formation of alien ships as they became clearly visible in the viewer.

"They're tidy, you've got to give them that."

"Makes our job easier," Sydes responded.

Scrutinizing the spherical viewer carefully, Sydes assured himself that the tactical grid he had selected encompassed all the alien ships rushing headlong toward them.

Sydes watched as one after another of, the weapon's icons lit up on his board, reflecting Tutunji's preparations.

"Are you ready to deal some discouragement to these bastards?" Sydes asked.

"We're going to cut a path squarely through the middle of these bandits, right?" Tutunji replied.

"More like a hole than a path. When we get to within twenty-five thousand kilometers, I'm gonna kick this gal into hyperburn. As soon as we're within missile range, I want you to launch from the forward tower," Sydes responded.

"And if they disperse?" Tutunji asked.

"I don't think they'll get out of the way that fast. When I met them before, they worked hard to stay in formation. Real team players, no individual stars," Sydes replied.

"Maybe that's the way we get to them. If they hang together, we can plow through to the middle of their formation and blow them to hell from the inside out," Tutunji said hopefully.

"That's the idea. I want you to hold launches on the other five towers until we're in the thick of their formation," Sydes said with some gusto.

"Then, it's just blow them away up, down and all around," Tutunji said confidently.

"You got it," Sydes replied.

As the formation of alien ships loomed large in the surrounding viewer, Sydes prepared the ship for its plunge into the midst of the enemy.

"Bringing all launchers to ready status. What a ship! With these weapons and the shields eating the energy of everything they can throw at us, we can create hell, fly through it and come out the other end in better shape than we started. Dante will have to do a rewrite," Tutunji intoned with pride.

Bringing the ship to hyperburn acceleration as the bloody orange fleet completely filled the viewer, Sydes plotted a course through the exact center of the enemy formation as Tutunji commenced continuous missile launches from the forward tower.

The leading blood ship in the pack took five missile strikes and vaporized. The Duo was sustaining continuous laser fire from all ships in the alien formation within range. As they flew through the devastation they had wrought, Von Strohheim's shields absorbed the energy released by the detonation of the Duo's own fusion missiles, the enemy's laser fire, plus the releases generated by the exploding alien vessels. Enemy laser fire became less prolific and more selective as they entered into the midst of the formation. Sydes had been right, the enemy's shields were not up to the penetrating power of their own lasers.

Attending carefully to the readings on his console, Tutunji watched the capacitor indicators climb as the Duo's shields absorbed the vortex of energy in which she swam.

Despite Sydes' focus on flying the Duo, his activation of the broad beam drilling laser indicated he had noticed the rising capacitor status before Tutunji could mention it. The drilling laser ate energy like a starved shrew and the decreasing capacitor levels soon verified its voracious appetite.

All but one of the enemy ships were smaller by half than the Duo. The one that interested Sydes flew above and apart from the attack formation, and appeared twenty times larger than all the rest. He assumed it must be the equivalent of a battleship. That enormous vessel floating above them very likely served as a command and control center for the attacking fleet.

Targeting the huge craft, he locked the laser projector on an area of its hull near the propulsion units. Contrary to his expectations, the enemy vessel did not swerve or evade. Instead, the juggernaut continued steadfast on its course as the tunneling laser did its work.

Lighting up the darkness of space, the enemy laser fire doubled as soon as the Duo commenced its attack on the command ship. In response to the attack on their capital vessel, the enemy ships began tightening their formation around Von Strohheim's lady. Some of the enemy ships appeared to be coming to the aid of the large vessel Sydes had hooked and was drilling with the laser. However, Tutunji gave them a hard road to go with continuous launches from four of the Duo's towers.

Coursing straight down the middle of the fiery trail she had created, the Duo was almost clear of the enemy formation when the aft section of the enemy battleship Sydes had hooked with the main laser exploded. The detonation of the huge vessel clearly damaged two of the smaller alien craft that had come to its aid.

"We're coming around to cut another swath through the formation. What's the count?" Sydes asked as he reversed the Duo's course.

"We've launched about twenty-five percent of our missiles. All systems are on line and the capacitors register thirty percent of the total accumulation volume is energized. The computer scanned fifty enemy ships on approach, and twenty as we left the formation," Tutunji replied surveying his console.

Reflexively gripping the arms of the console chair as the universe spun around him, the Commander recognized almost instantly his bracing of himself as unnecessary. Sydes pivoted the Duo until the forward view revealed a huge cloud of fusion energy and debris beyond which they could not scan. However, it was safe to assume that the enemy formation was continuing its dogged trajectory towards the station.

Suddenly, the comm-link crackled to life. It was Commander Sadad.

"Outstanding work gentlemen. We show a sixty percent kill rate. Is the

Duo intact?"

"All systems nominal. We should be through the cloud in about ten seconds and in effective firing range in another half a minute. What's your situation?" Tutunji responded quickly.

"The enemy will be in our assault range about the same time they come into your effective launch radius. We'll have their ships in a box," Sadad replied.

Emerging from the fire fight cloud, the Duo's viewer revealed the enemy formation moving as a tightly clustered phalanx toward the first wave of one hundred strike craft.

"Damn! I have the awful feeling that I know why they fly that tight formation!" Sydes exclaimed.

Activating the link to the station, suddenly, the staid fighter ace was shouting.

"Sadad, disperse those strike craft, do it now!"

Comprehending the reason for Sydes' concern only moments before the enemy formation opened fire, Tutunji watched in horror as all twenty of the remaining blood ships activated their forward laser turrets simultaneously. Their beams were angled to coalesce at the dead center of the the strike craft formation. Seventy strike craft instantly vaporized as the huge singular shaft of energy lanced into the heart of the defending formation. Another ten to fifteen strike craft were crippled by debris hurled out by the explosions of their sister vessels. The first wave of strike craft was effectively obliterated.

As the Duo flew straight toward the heart of the enemy armada, Tutunji's range acquisition indicator lit up like a Christmas tree. Feeling Sydes' intensity as a tangible force, Tutunji punched in continuous fire on three of the Duo's six towers. He watched with satisfaction as missiles snaked out and homed in on the center of the enemy flotilla at the rate of one every three seconds. Following the missiles in, Sydes spurred the Duo toward the exploding center of the enemy formation.

"That's it, scatter the sons of bitches," Sydes shouted.

Climbing and spreading out, the remains of strike craft formation assumed a scattered spherical configuration around the beleaguered enemy squadron. Sadad had gotten Sydes message, Tutunji thought to himself.

Plowing through a fiery tunnel, the Duo was a singular source of devastation in the midst of the enemy formation. The targeting computer set for automatic selective fire, acquired enemy ships on all six of the missile towers and Sydes made good use of the tunneling laser. Emerging from the fire storm of missile explosions initiated by her own towers and the strike craft launches, the Duo remained unscathed. Keeping a close eye on the console, Tutunji noted the capacitors registered eighty percent accumulation.

Pivoting the Duo to face the growing fireball representing the alien armada, Sydes also noticed the capacitor accumulation.

"Sadad, get Von Strohheim on the line," Sydes barked.

"Working on that. But we've got another problem. I'm transmitting feed from the station's long range sensors to the Duo's viewer," Commander Sadad responded.

Instantly, the Duo's spherical view of the firestorm around them was replaced by an image of the area of space where they had first engaged the attacking enemy force.

The sight instantly drained all the accumulated energy of battle from Tutunji's body. There, in the viewer, was an unanticipated second wave of the alien attack force. The computer registered seventy five ships in this second battle group.

"Damn, look at that big bitch!" Sydes shouted.

"Damn, look at that big bitch!" Sydes shouted.

Then, adjusting the focal area of the screen to bring the image of a huge vessel in the center of the alien fleet into focus, he called out to Tutunji.

"We should feel honored, Tutunji. I think that big lady in red came to the dance just for us."

Feeling anything but honored, the Commander slumped a bit in his console chair as Sydes brought the Duo to hyperburn on a trajectory back through the clouds of fusion devastation toward the oncoming alien battle group. Perhaps Sydes' intuition was right. If the enemy's attack formation served their strategy of combined and concentrated laser fire then, that battleship had been brought up to hold their fleet and that strategy together. This battle wagon was three times the size of the vessel they had attacked and disabled earlier, which meant that the first capital ship they engaged must have been a heavy cruiser. The battleship probably had been included in this group expressly to defeat the Duo's capacity to disperse their assault formation. Clearly, their tactical approach was founded on a massed attack against significant numbers of equally tightly grouped opponents. The Duo, as a single well armed and equally well shielded ship, was not something they had in their play book.

Indicating an incoming transmission from the station, the comm-link icon blinked. It was Von Strohheim.

"Yes, Captain Sydes, the ship, she performs well?"

"The best date I had in years. Doc. She waltzes all her partners to death," Sydes responded.

"Jah, dances them to death ... very good," Von Strohheim said, chuckling.

"Listen Doc, is there any way to channel more power through this laser? Right now we're showing eighty percent capacitor accumulation and the only way to discharge the capacitors is through the tunneling laser. Maybe we can kill two birds with one stone. You know, get more firepower and no capacitor overload. Besides, I have the feeling that we'll need every bit of firepower we can lay our hands on," Sydes said.

"I'm in the operations imaging room and I think I see what you mean ... it's that big vessel. The capital ship in the second wave, she has to be fifty times the size of the fighters we've seen before. If I were building her, I would be certain that her shields could not be penetrated by fusion missiles," Von Strohheim replied.

"That was my thinking too Doc. So what about the laser? Can we jack up its output?" Sydes asked impatiently.

"Jah ... jah, this is possible. We had not anticipated this much energy accumulation in battle, but this we can correct," Von Stohheim responded.

"Yeah, yeah, Doc ... so, what do we do? We're gonna be in their laps in about three minutes," Sydes asked, his tone increasingly sharp and impatient.

"First, you must switch the console to schematic mode," Von Strohheim responded, quickening his pace.

"We're switched over Doc, what now?" Tutunji replied as he took over the conversation.

"You will scroll through the menu until you come to the capacitor relays schematic. You have this, yes?" Von Strohheim's asked.

"Got it," Tutunji responded.

"On the touchscreen, depress the master relay icon. Now, a conductance range indicator icon will appear. You see this, yes?"

Momentarily confused, Tutunji fumbled with the controls. Scrolling through menu after menu, he felt his hands begin to sweat.

"Just a second Doc ... OK, got it. It shows a range of conductance from zero to one hundred percent. The setting is currently at the fifty percent marker."

"OK, guys get it done. We'll be in their laser range in about a minute," Sydes snapped,

"This must be done correctly the first time or the energy in the capacitors turns on the ship itself. Now, Commander Tutunji, you tap the range of conductance indicator three times, no more or the energy stored in the capacitors will be channeled to the reactors and overload the system. Three strokes will direct one hundred percent of the energy in the capacitors to the laser. Four strokes will circuit that energy back to the reactors and, at the current capacitance load, detonate them. You understand, this, Commander?" Von Strohheim asked in an even scientific tone.

"Got it Doc, OK, here we go … one, two, … three," Tutunji counted aloud.

"All right guys! I show power output doubled on the laser display and we're still in one piece. Nice job," Sydes shouted.

"Good luck, I hope my lady does all you require of her," Von Strohheim added as he terminated the transmission.

Fully visible now, the ships of the alien battle group were so tightly grouped the bloody orange glow of their shields merged into a continuous aura of defensive strength.

Ablaze with the energy of a laser hit, the entire spherical compass of the Duo's viewer was momentarily useless. Range finding indicated the Duo was still beyond the reach of the enemy's lasers, which was probably why the first laser strike from the alien's capital ship caught them by surprise. Tutunji felt the ship being pushed backwards by the force of the blast as Sydes fought to acquire range on the fleet in order to focus the tunneling laser. Tutunji immediately looked down at the capacitor storage indicator. It read one hundred percent and the icon was blinking.

"Son of a bitch! That big lady has one long reach," Sydes muttered.

The capacitors' indicator incessant blinking had caught Sydes' attention as well. He instantly activated the Duo's tunneling laser and focused it on the battle wagon's main laser turret.

"Soften that bitch up," Sydes shouted to Tutunji.

"You're covered," Tutunji replied.

Tutunji immediately initiated continuous missile fire from the forward tower directed to the alien battleship's laser mount. A continuous river of laser energy burrowed into the battlewagon's shields as missile after missile added to the conflagration.

Capacitor levels rose and fell with incredible speed as the Duo's laser drew maximum power and fire from the vessels attending the capital ship, their lasers focused on the Duo, replenishing the capacitor's reserves. As the missile racks were ratcheting up one after another fusion bomb, Tutunji wondered how the aliens would react if they knew their defensive fire fed their attacker.

Shifting from red to brown, the shield coloration over the alien battleship's main turret signaled that Sydes' laser attack was picking its way through the lattice of energy that protected the huge vessel.

A lancing column of energy that propelled the Duo backwards with its force sprang from a second principal laser turret on the alien capital ship. Sydes ramped up the Duo's propulsion units to compensate. He knew he had to hold his ship within the tunneling laser's effective range to knock out the turret that had first engaged them. Strangely, the turret that continued to be the focus of his attention hadn't fired a salvo since the Duo's laser targeted it.

"I don't think their turrets can fire through their own shields when the laser projectors are under direct attack,"Tutunji called out to Sydes.

"Right, just keep hammering that forward laser turret. We're making headway," Sydes replied.

Shimmering and turning a dark brown, the shielding over the battleship's forward turret looked ready to collapse. Sydes was right, Tutunji thought as he directed a steady stream of fusion missiles toward the brown spot on the big ship.

Pendulating wildly, now under continuous fire from every alien ship in a position to target her, the Duo behaved much as a small boat might if its occupant had hooked too big a fish. The second turret of the capital ship fired on the Duo continuously, with supporting fire coming from the smaller ships gathered around her. The capacitor accumulation readings bounced up and down like a yo-yo on amphetamines as the energy expended by tunneling laser was quickly replenished by enemy fire. The enemy's capital ship was turning now, attempting to get out of range of the Duo's laser, or a least escape the beam's focus on her forward turret. The homing beacon incorporated into the laser projector, however, like some parasite permanently attached to the attack force's flagship, followed the battlewagon's every movement.

"Got you, bitch!" Sydes exclaimed .

Instantly, Tutunji saw what had Sydes so excited. The area over the forward turret had ceased to shimmer and the black plating of the hull of the capital ship, as well as, the silver barrel of the laser turret were plainly visible.

Under the withering fire of the tunneling laser, the laser mount on the forward turret of the battle wagon was disintegrating, and with it, adjacent areas of the hull.

The Commander launched five fusion missiles through the opening in the flagship's shields and watch as a series of detonations rocked the capital ship. These blasts were immediately followed by what seemed to be series of secondary eruptions. The fact that they were largely contained by the vessel's shields exaggerated the force of the explosions. The flagship heeled over and began a turn as the attendant ships parted to allow her withdrawal. Laser response from the flagship's turrets ceased entirely and the smaller vessels moving to her defense seemed less intent on attacking the Duo than interposing their craft between the Duo and their capital ship.

Dispatching five more missiles into the exploding flagship, which shook visibly from each successive hit, Tutunji monitored her closely as she limped away. Half of the attending vessels moved with her serving as a screen and shepherding her withdrawal.

Climbing on an attack trajectory toward the Duo, the remaining rearguard ships dispersed in a formation that portended an encircling and concerted strike on Von Strohheim's creation.

"They're learning. They've figured out the Duo isn't a fighter. Now, they're gonna try to harass us to pieces without presenting enough of a target to use our weaponry effectively. It's real clear they don't want us following their flagship," Sydes said in a quietly serious tone.

"We can't just walk away from what remains an effective enemy force. They might regroup and attempt to attack the station. Without our support, the strike craft losses will be enormous," Tutunji responded quickly.

Pivoting the Duo, Sydes activated the hyperburn drive and set a course to intercept the wounded flagship.

"Well, let's see what interests them most, "Sydes said.

Monitoring the aft portion of the spherical viewer as Sydes navigated the Duo toward the retreating elements of the alien fleet, Tutunji watched carefully to see what the alien vessels left behind would do. The rearguard squadron hung in space for a moment with its subcommander either waffling indecisively or awaiting orders from the retreating flagship. As the Duo ate up the distance between her and the withdrawing battleship, the rearguard made its decision. Tutunji ran a weapons check as the alien ships regrouped into their characteristic tight formation and initiated their pursuit of the Duo.

"Just as I thought, momma's boys. Let's see how good they are at protecting her ass," Sydes said wryly.

Diving towards the crippled flagship, Sydes ignored her battle group vessels as they clustered around the forward area where the battleship's shields had buckled. He had set his sights on the wounded battleship and would to be denied the prize. The rearguard ships were in hot pursuit, but could not arrive in time to prevent the Duo's first strike.

Sydes brought the tunneling laser on line the instant the Duo came within range. Threading the homing beacon through the maze of fighters that formed a protective wall around the wounded starboard section of the flagship, he opened fire.

Activating the independent homing option on the missile racks Tutunji initiated continuous launch against the rearguard pursuers from all six towers. The missiles detonated into multiple mushroom clouds of destruction as they met the pursuing alien craft. The last thing he wanted was to have the Duo caught between two fields of fire.

It was enormously gratifying to see how the Duo's laser, now functioning at one hundred percent efficiency, dispatched the fighters that tried to interpose themselves between Sydes' resolve and their injured mistress. As the alien fighter craft's shields and hull plating failed under the drilling laser's fire, the vessels disgorged their internal atmospheres, forcing out both occupants and contents. The Commander hoped the continuous video coverage of the Duo's engagements provided by the hull cameras would, upon digital pixel scrutiny, reveal something about the aliens, their atmosphere and perhaps their home world.

"This fighter screen is just so much annoying scrap and clutter. Now we're ready to finish this big bitch," Sydes snapped.

"Targeting the opening," Tutunji replied.

As Sydes widened the breach in the alien capital ship's armor plating with the tunneling laser, Tutunji directed a continuous stream of missiles from the forward tower into the ruptured hull.

The battleship slowly began to heel over, shuddering and reeling at three second intervals, as the fusion missiles struck their mark. Not a trace of defensive fire came from her turrets, a sure sign that the end was near.

Redirecting his attention, Sydes targeted the few remaining individual fighters with the tunneling laser as fusion missiles pounded the alien flagship. Concentrating on one fighter after another, he noticed the remaining shields around the flagship shifted to a brownish color as they ballooned out expansively into space around her hull.

"I think she's reached critical mass," he said called to Tutunji.

"Time to get the hell out of here!" Tutunji responded as he terminated all missile launches.

Initiating hyperburn and overflying the swelling shields of the flagship, Sydes aimed to put as much space between the Duo and the imminent explosion of the flagship as he could manage. Suddenly, the aft segment of the Duo's spherical viewer went white, as it was blanked by an enormous release of energy. The Duo rotated and tumbled as the shock wave of the blast struck her. The blast tested Sydes' considerable skill as a pilot as he fought to maintain the Duo's course away from the epicenter of the blast while avoiding being carried laterally along its curvilinear leading edge and out of range of the battle. The capacitors immediately shot up to one hundred percent accumulation and the warning light blinked frantically. Sydes instantly activated the tunneling laser and set it for random targeting in order to dissipate the stored energy.

Bobbing on a somewhat gentler sea of energy ripples as the the leading edge of the energy wave passed over them, Sydes regained control of the ship. As soon as the shields registered normal space at their boundaries, he pivoted the Duo to afford the broadest angle on the remains of the alien armada.

Gone was the flagship, except for what appeared to be a small portion of her aft section. Most of the fighters that had huddled around the flagship had been vaporized by the blast that signaled her passing and were now but a haze of particles drifting in space. The small number of rearguard ships that had survived moved cautiously toward the wreckage, perhaps looking for survivors.

In a jointly experienced silence, Sydes and Tutunji surveyed the scene of carnage they had wrought among the invaders. No danger now, neither man felt any need to attack the straggler enemy fighters who, in any event, showed no interest in the Duo.

"How's our lady feeling after the dance?" Sydes asked, breaking the silence.

Jolted out of a momentary interval of enjoying the fact he was still alive, Tutunji called up the diagnostic schematic on his console and studied the readouts.

"Apart from the fact that we're alive and under power, there are just one or two little problems. The shields are a little shaky. I think the energy conductance pathways will have to be reworked. Not even Von Strohheim could have anticipated the magnitude of the energy bursts we absorbed, much less the explosion of that battleship. The continuous readout on the shield to capacitor flow indicates that, at times, the shields were forced to deflect, rather than absorb, the energies directed against the ship. Another capacitor array might help. The main laser readout indicates it ran, beyond the maximum coolant capacity range at least half the time. Some additional coolant coils would certainly help there. Oh, and the missile racks are damn near empty, but that's to be expected," Tutunji said, leaning back in the console chair.

"The Doc did himself proud. Let's take this lady back to her daddy and get her all scrubbed and polished. We're a long way from home," Sydes said with a decided tone of satisfaction.

The devastation of the battle rapidly receded in the aft viewer as Sydes pointed the Duo back towards the station on hyperburn. Soon, they would be back among friends and well wishing comrades. Tutunji didn't particularly feel like being congratulated. They had killed hundreds, perhaps thousands, of an enemy they had never, and might never see face to face.

Battles in space lacked the remorse provoking horror of a battlefield strewn with the slain. There were no clouds of eye stinging smoke, no stench of burning bodies, or screams of the maimed and dying to drive home the reality of war. It was all too damn sterile and distant, Tutunji mused gravely. The horror and finality of destroying life had become much too easy to avoid and, if recalled, easy to dismiss. This disengagement from the tangible reality of war made the futility of destroying life a lesson even more difficult to learn.

Chapter 19

Unannounced and regular visits represented a new style of close order management for Cabot, who characteristically worked through intermediaries. With every report of another alien incursion, he paced the bridge of the ark, observing, encouraging and often prodding the supervisory team to work as rapidly as possible. On each successive visit, his words and manner communicated a sense of increasing urgency regarding the completion of the ark.

Saturated with his references to the alien invasion, Cabot's visits clearly revealed his concern with the incursions of the blood ships. Report of the combined Natcorps forces most recent victory over the alien invaders neither heightened his mood, nor the intensity of his commitment. Instead, Cabot's attention remained unflinchingly and narrowly focused on the losses incurred in the purchase of that victory. Cabot was not only a student of history, he was history. Having survived and prospered through nearly six hundred years of the parade of human endeavors, no assurances assuaged his basic suspicion. He was the acknowledged chess master of the pursuit of security through dominance conflicts. He knew the game of conquest, whether it was played among the refined trappings of a board room or with knives and baseball bats in a dark alley. History, from Cabot's perspective, was a stern and unflinchingly harsh schoolmaster that taught that a single battle seldom determined the outcome of a conflict and that a solitary ship, even one like the Duo, never won a war.

Consistent with Phil's expectations, Cabot moved Doctor Dvorak into a command compartment off the bridge of the ark shortly after that dark day aboard Nick's yacht. Dvorak, Chauvez and Phil worked together on a daily basis, cooperating in the automated refit of the vessel. The ark, which had been nearing completion before Cabot's meeting with Dvorak, now looked like a surrealistic melange of demolition and new construction. Most obvious in this revamp was the destruction of the technical crews' quarters to make room for Dvorak's huge automation assemblies and couplings. Clearly, Cabot felt much more comfortable with machines than people.

Confusion engendered by alternately tearing down and reconstructing areas of the ark tried all concerned. Nevertheless, a close working relationship between Dvorak and Chauvez had developed, in part, out of necessity given the close cooperation required in the refit.

Dvorak was leery of Phil. The automation genius saw Phil only as Cabot's number two man, a fact driven home by Phil's presence in Cabot's office when Cabot coerced Dvorak into helping with the project. Despite his lingering distrust of Phil, the two seemed able to function effectively with one another on their many overlapping tasks.

Chauvez had been supervising the placement of the exterior thruster baffles that formed the propulsion housing for the ark's drive system for what seemed like an eternity. As he watched the last of the major couplings drop into place, he looked up to see Dvorak waving him over to the console. Chauvez turned the job of sealing the couplings over to his technical chief and walked over to Dvorak's work station.

Dvorak hastily completed a series of instructions to his work crews in the technical recesses of the ark and turned to Chauvez.

"Has Cabot offered you a berth on the ark?"

Chauvez, although momentarily stunned by Dvorak's bluntness, elected the direct approach.

"Yes, he has."

"And Phil?" Dvorak asked as he glanced over his shoulder.

"Yes, I believe he has been offered a berth as well," Chauvez replied.

"So Cabot wants his top life sciences and technical people on board when he pulls out of here? Yes, that must be ..." Dvorak muttered as he stared into space.

A lifelong distaste for conversations in which the goal of the discussion was covert reminded him of why he found so much solace in engineering and mathematics. In these disciplines, definable operations were tied to tangible realities and led to concrete outcomes. At times like this, he yearned for Piatra and her remarkable directness. When she opened her mouth, every word she spoke was either a passionate affirmation or defamation of something or someone. In an exercise of will, Chauvez pulled himself back to the moment and a response to the uncertain direction of Dvorak's question.

"I understand from Phil that there is a top ranked physician from every medical subspecialty slated for a berth as well."

Chauvez took note of a slight twitching in Dvorak right eye as Phil's name was spoken.

"And where will all these people be housed?" Dvorak asked.

Dvorak's hard analytic tone was of a sort that Chauvez had not heard since he had heard it coming from the mouth of his 3-D chess instructor.

Leaning over the computer console, Chauvez called up a full schematic of the ark.

He surveyed the layout and then pointed to an area near the bridge. Several bulkheads separated the compartments he indicated from the generous suite of compartments Cabot had allotted for his own use.

"I believe here," he said pointing to the area.

"That was my feeling as well. Except for Cabot's suite, every compartment, including the ones you indicated, the bridge, and the large ecosectors in the ark have built in internal security measures. There are nerve gas ports, lasers built into the bulkheads and atmospheric bleeders to remove the breathable gases incorporated into every section. All the control leads serving these measures terminate in Cabot's apartments," Dvorak said.

Casting a nervous glance around the bridge, Dvorak's voice fell to a whisper as he stepped closer to Chauvez.

"This is a prison ship with Cabot as its warden!"

Some of Piatra's fire sprang to life in Chauvez's belly. Was it possible that Dvorak was ready for some decisive action against Cabot. Would he accept Phil? Chauvez decided he wouldn't risk that gambit here and now.

"Why don't we meet in my compartment after shift for some drinks and conversation?" He responded, matching Dvorak's low whisper.

Nodding his agreement, Dvorak moved back to his station at the console and the task of automating Cabot's ship.

The demands of schedule driven construction tasks made the shift pass quickly. Time went by even more rapidly after Dvorak left the bridge to personally supervise the installation of delicate couplings for the new automation equipment. Dvorak's absence from the bridge made it possible for Chauvez to share his interpretation of Dvorak's statements with Phil. Briefly discussing the issue of Dvorak's help in their plot against Cabot, Chauvez arranged for Phil to come to Chauvez's compartment at shift's end.

As the second shift crew arrived to start their daily tour, Chauvez left the bridge and made it back to his compartment in quick time. Feeling like the host of a seditious party, he pulled out bottles of vodka, cinnamon for Dvorak, orange for Phil, and some, tequila for himself. The transubstantiator unit kicked out some high protein munches and some salsa and chips for his soon to be assembled guests. Until the door chime snapped him back into reality, he remained in a murderously festive mood.

Entering the compartment, Dvorak looked around the room cautiously. Without offering a greeting, he produced a cube from his pocket that he placed on the table. As he depressed one corner of the cube, it rose into the air over the table and micro antennae arrays emerged from each of its six sides. The cube slowly made one full rotation, and then, the antennae disappeared into the recesses of the cube. Settling back onto the table, it began to emit a green pulsating light.

"The room is clean," Dvorak announced as he looked over at Chauvez.

"Neat gadget," Chauvez muttered.

Then, motioning Dvorak to a seat, Chauvez mixed a cinnamon vodka and soda for his first guest.

"I appreciate that your sweeping the room," Chauvez said as he handed the drink to his guest.

Dvorak, drink in hand, looked around the room as though he expected Cabot to pop out from behind the couch at any moment. Taking note of his guest's apprehension, Chauvez made a feeble attempt to relax the automation genius.

"Is the drink ... OK?" Chauvez asked.

Half the contents of the glass drained in one gulp, Dvorak's mood changed radically as he dove with gusto into an exposition of his opinions.

"The idea of the ark is fine. I have my own concerns about the war, and in particular, the radioactive zones it's producing in the solar system," Dvorak intoned, never looking at his host.

Quickly finishing his drink, Dvorak's gaze ranged suspiciously over the room again. Chauvez immediately snatched up and refilled his guest's glass. Staring blankly into space for a moment, Dvorak redirected his attention to a checklist of heretofore unexpressed feelings and ideas.

"I'm not convinced we're going to win this war. I've got the feeling we haven't yet seen the best the enemy has to offer. It's like they're probing our defensive capabilities to determine the level of force required to overrun us," Dvorak said.

Chauvez watched his guest carefully. Dvorak appeared nervous, but also anxious to share a raft of concerns. The automation expert paused a moment for another sip and went on.

"Sorry, I'm getting a little far afield. The ark is a good idea in any event. If we lose the war, something will be saved. If we don't, the ark represents the sort of long range colonization effort our species should have made a long time ago. No matter the outcome of the war, the ark has to sail ... but I think, without Cabot as her captain."

Relaxing back into his chair, Chauvez sipped his tequila. Clearly, Dvorak, despite his staid exterior, resembled Piatra more than either Phil or himself. Dvorak's head might be all circuitry diagrams, but his heart pumped the liquid fire of an uncompromising rebel. Heartened by this discovery, Chauvez decided to come to the point.

"Others feel exactly as you do. I count myself as one and Phil as another," Chauvez said in carefully measured tones.

"But, he's Cabot's right hand man!" Dvorak replied, his body stiffening.

All at once, Dvorak looked more than a trifle disoriented. A measure of suspicion began tracing itself in the lines at the corners of his eyes.

"Nevertheless, Phil and I started making plans to do away with Cabot before we decided to risk bringing you into our little project. He, as well as you, has my complete trust," Chauvez responded.

"If Phil is truly with us in this, I 'll know it when I look into his face," Dvorak said, holding Chauvez's gaze.

Chauvez paused a moment to depress a small icon on his link and looked up at Dvorak.

"You'll have that opportunity in just a moment. I've asked Phil to meet us here," Chauvez replied.

"You said nothing of this," Dvorak sputtered.

"Trust works both ways, Dvorak. Phil and I had to know where you stood before we shared plans that would certainly result, if discovered, in our deaths in one of Cabot's accidents," Chauvez retorted.

"Of course, trust must be a two party contract, or it is simple naiveté," Dvorak responded as his expression lost some of its suspicious edge.

Pausing a moment, Chauvez looked at Dvorak with eyes altered by his last statement. This was where Dvorak and Piatra parted company. Despite Piatra's brilliance, she had remained a perennial adolescent throughout her life. Her veritable flood of emotional fire had never been channeled and refined as was Dvorak's by the ability to appreciate perspectives and respect feelings other than his own.

Chiming, the compartment door announced a visitor. Chauvez pressed the door release. Entering, Phil looked first at Chauvez, who smiled slightly and then at Dvorak, who managed a grimace that mixed mild resentment and uncertain anticipation.

Selecting a seat closer to Chauvez than Dvorak, Phil sat down. Chauvez hurriedly mixed Phil's favorite concoction of orange vodka and lime, and handed him the glass.

"Well, where are we?" Phil asked, taking a quick sip of his drink.

"The question is, where are you? And what are you willing to do?" Dvorak said, fixing Phil with a stare.

"Where I am is with my coconspirators. What I'm willing to do is supply the roadmap that leads to Cabot's death," Phil replied, returning Dvorak's stare.

It was clear from his long pause that Dvorak had been taken back a bit by

Phil's directness. He continued to stare at Phil as if searching for some evidence of duplicity. Then, quite suddenly, as if someone had hit the kill switch, Dvorak's whole body seemed to relax and a smile spread over his face.

"So, how do we kill this bastard?" Dvorak asked.

Relieved, Phil felt the energy of a hundred negative outcome scenarios his imagination had conjured drain through the soles of his boots. Despite the fact they were discussing a murder plot, he felt somehow good about both the task and the company. The feeling of wholesome purpose that suffused his being seemed at odds with the content of the conversation, but Phil enjoyed it all the same. He took another sip from his drink and looked at each of the two men in turn.

"Cabot has a transceiver mastoid implant that keeps him in constant contact with his central computer. After two hundred years of watching failed assassination attempts on Cabot, I think that implant represents the only route to his death that stands a chance of succeeding," Phil said.

"Certainly, a frontal assault is suicide. I saw that the day I met with Cabot on his yacht. What happened there in space was no accident. He ordered the deaths of the people in those shuttles," Dvorak replied.

Taking a hard swallow of tequila, Chauvez paused a moment as visions of Piatra's death lived again in his mind's eye.

"My woman led that raid and paid for her passion with her life. I know that fervent ardor and a just cause are not sufficient. We must be careful and we must succeed the first time. There won't be any second chances," Chauvez said softly as he looked up at Dvorak.

An expression blending both shock and sadness instantly crossed Dvorak's face and fixed itself there. He hadn't been sure what to expect from this meeting, but the revelations about people who were only coworkers hours before just kept coming.

"I am sorry for your loss. I have a wife and two little daughters and I don't know how I could go on without them. That son of a bitch is holding their lives hostage until I automate the Ark," Dvorak offered, a quiet fire growing in his eyes.

Phil watched Chauvez shrink into his chair and suspected the engineer was reliving Piatra's death. Leaving Chauvez momentarily to his grief, Phil elected to pursue the particulars of the plan with Dvorak.

"We really think an electronic assault is the only viable route. Can you help us?" He asked turning to Dvorak.

Making no response, Dvorak stood and walked to the bar to make himself another vodka and soda. His mind raced, turning the problem upside down and inside out. Returning, drink in hand and still lost in his internal ruminations, he sat down hard. Then, just as abruptly as he had absented himself from the common reality of the meeting, he re-engaged in the discussion.

"How much information can you get me about the central computer and the implant?" Dvorak asked.

"Some, but not much. All the people who actually designed the implant and set the transmission frequencies and backups suffered Cabot style accidents. Cabot is very thorough when it comes to his personal security. One of the surgeons who did the implant was a close friend of mine. He mentioned before his 'accidental death' that the transceiver operated on a very narrow dedicated frequency," Phil replied, his tone fatalistic.

"That makes it a needle in an electromagnetic haystack proposition. On the other hand, the easiest way to find a needle in the straw is to burn down the haystack," Dvorak said pensively.

Regrouping his focus, Chauvez moved restlessly in his chair as he sent Piatra's fiery demise off into a dimly illuminated corner of his mind.

"So, how do we burn down this particular haystack?" Chauvez asked as he reached for his drink.

Suddenly animated, Dvorak's hands gesticulated in the air as though he were directing some great symphony of electronic interactions.

"I agree we'll have to do this electronically, but I would suggest incrementally. I can control all of that and cover the changes under the cloak of running repeated tests on the new automation systems, yes ... yes ..." Dvorak announced.

"I think I've got the broad strokes, but how will this work exactly?" Phil interrupted.

"I assume Cabot's people have laid down defenses and dead end viruses to defeat any direct assault on the dedicated frequency he uses to communicate with the central computer. The dedicated frequency is the needle. The haystack is that portion of the electromagnetic spectrum in which his personal frequency is nested."

"You're going to try to disrupt the whole electromagnetic spectrum!" Chauvez exclaimed in disbelief.

"No, his electronics experts would certainly have defended against something like a magnetic pulse that would wipe out the software. They would have planned for a momentary shut down of the link as the sensors in the implant detected the leading edge of a disruptive impulse," Dvorak replied.

His respect growing, Phil could see that Dvorak deserved his reputation as the leading expert in automation. Coming to Dvorak side, Phil refilled the engineer's glass.

"So, how then?" Phil asked.

"Incrementally, gentlemen, incrementally. The procedure is as old as the story about boiling a frog to death by increasing the temperature of his aquatic environment one degree at a time. Now, Phil this is crucial, do Cabot's travels take him anywhere except to and fro between the Ark and his yacht?" Dvorak asked as he sipped his drink.

"No, he does everything through other people. Last week, he tore out the entire cargo bay of the yacht and had the central computer's components brought up from the Urals. He's made sure everything he needs or wants is right here. I suspect he's preparing to pull out quickly if the war takes a bad turn," Phil responded.

Dvorak was on his feet, his eyes bright and his arms busily gesturing to his unseen symphony of electrons.

"Outstanding, then it will work!" He exclaimed.

"What will work?" Chauvez asked.

"It's unerringly simple, gentlemen. Phil, since you have the most intimate contact with Cabot, I'll provide you with a stealth equipped scanner to ferret out the range of the spectrum in which his dedicated frequency operates. We won't even try and locate the frequency itself. That would doubtless set off a series of sentinel programs and alert his computer's security systems," Dvorak said, his eyes brightening.

"You're sure his security scanners won't detect it?" Phil asked, looking a little worried.

"Absolutely certain, because I'll nest your stealth scanner frequency in the same subspectrum as his security scanners function. To his security scanners, the activation of your stealth scanner will look like a reflection of their own output. A very long time ago, I designed the basic unit that drives all security scanners. Believe me, you've got nothing to worry about," Dvorak said with supreme confidence.

"Cabot made one hell of a mistake in forcing you to work for him," Chauvez interrupted, a wry smile on his face.

"Once Phil gets me the subspectrum in which Cabot's dedicated frequency operates, I'll tune the automation equipment we're installing to slowly gener-ate a driver wave. That wave will initiate a cascade of electronically invisible feedback along that entire subspectrum," Dvorak said, smiling broadly,

"And that'll fry his brain," Chauvez said, diving in for the kill.

"Patience, patience, gentlemen. If we heat the water too quickly, the frog just jumps out and in this case eats us one and all. The automation equipment Cabot is having installed in the ark has the capacity to project a signal well beyond the confines of this ship," Dvorak said, his tone paternalistic.

"A sphere of electromagnetic radiation that will encompass the yacht as well," Phil interjected.

"Precisely! As long as Cabot remains in the space encompassed by his yacht and the ark, he will be continuously subjected to the signal produced by the automation equipment," Dvorak responded.

Chauvez felt a shiver as he was struck by the fear he had detected a fatal flaw in Dvorak's plan of attack.

"But, won't he notice something, some change, at least in the reception on his transceiver?" He asked.

"No! With our degree of technology, every bit of the electromagnetic spectrum available for transmission and reception is back to back and belly to belly with coded chatter. Cabot's link, dedicated as it is, couldn't function unless the central computer made constant corrections to keep the reception intact," Dvorak said emphatically.

"So the central computer will just systematically cancel out the input from your automation equipment," Chauvez interrupted.

"Not so much canceling the wave we'll be generating as isolating it. To cancel any frequency that fell within the subspectrum would require enormous power expenditures. More significantly, that sort of interference operation would advertise the band in which the dedicated frequency operates. Cabot's central computer will isolate the wave we're producing to preserve the link between itself and Cabot's implant," Dvorak said with no small amount of satisfaction.

"Won't the heuristic algorithms in the central computer recognize this attempt to squeeze down the range of the subspectrum in which the dedicated frequency is nested?" Chauvez asked, unwilling to let go of his doubts.

"I don't think so, " Dvorak responded.

"I agree. Cabot's not going to erect some huge wave interference sign that says look here for my dedicated frequency. Quite apart from that, he has always been more interested in defending his own personal interests than in governing outlying territories. Inasmuch as the fundamental engrams informing the basic functioning of the central computer are patterned after his own tissue, they'll probably reflect that same bias," Phil interjected.

"A wholly self-centered man married to a computer that represents a simple extension of his egocentric perspective. Incredible," Chauvez said, shaking his head in disbelief.

Phil sat back for a moment, seemingly lost in thought and then leaned forward and fixed on Dvorak.

"And as you ramp up and extrapolate the wave, the computer will be forced to isolate more and more of the input in that subspectrum," he remarked.

"Outstanding, exactly right Phil! As we adjust the output on the automation equipment to embrace more and more of the subspectrum, the central computer will be forced to isolate more and more frequencies until it is defending only the stream of impulses Cabot uses to send and receive," Dvorak said, almost gleefully.

"So the computer will eventually tell us exactly what frequency it uses to communicate with Cabot," Chauvez interjected.

"Yes, exactly. Precisely correct! And when we have that frequency, I will direct the entire power reserves of the ark through the automation relays and feedback a surge of power along his dedicated frequency that will fry Cabot to a cinder," Dvorak replied, his tone one of profound satisfaction.

"So we must be patient, until patience pays its dividend in definitive action," Phil said as he smiled at Dvorak.

"Yeah, and we boil the frog," Chauvez added.

Without warning, the excitement fled from Dvorak's eyes and his tone softened until it was barely audible.

"Yes, we boil the frog and perhaps make a future for humanity ... a future for my children and their children yet to come."

Sitting quietly for a few moments, the three conspirators, faces frozen in thousand yard stares, digested what they had planned with such great enthusiasm. Scientists all, they now had to come to terms with that most basic motivation of denial nurtured self interest intrinsic to the nature of their species, murder for the greater good.

"When can you have the stealth scanner ready?" Phil asked as he shifted in his chair.

"You'll have it by first shift tomorrow," Dvorak replied.

A somber silence followed Dvorak's reply. Chauvez, slumped down in his chair, pinned there by the vast quantity of tequila he had consumed. He looked up through half closed lids and added his own nearly poetic and entirely inebriated closing statement.

"I only hope that in murdering this Noah, we and our charges, whoever they may be, will be carried above the flood of this conflict to dry land somewhere ... it is the greater good, isn't it?"

In the throes of his drunken stupor, Chauvez had voiced the doubt central to every scientist who by nature, experienced an intellectual certainty far exceeding the emotional surety conferred by tribal confidence. There was nothing more to say and certainly no answer to Chauvez's question. Nodding to Chauvez, Phil and Dvorak filed from the compartment in silence.

Pouring another tequila, Chauvez didn't rise to see his guests out. He turned the notion of the greater good over and over in his head. The longer he thought about the notion, the less sense it made. Maybe the lesser of two evils fit the situation better, he mused. He poured yet another tequila and decided it was all bullshit. The bottom line was they were going to do murder. If any aphorism worked under these circumstances then it was 'the die is cast.'

Chapter 20

Piloting the hopper toward the mountain top with consummate skill, Crystal said nothing as they traveled. Forrester had worked with many children in his practice over the years, but Crystal impressed him as no ordinary four year old. He felt no need to engage her in conversation, much less a need to entertain her to maintain rapport as was necessary with most children this age. Crystal was quietly and comfortably at peace with herself. The sense of peace pervading the cabin of the hopper matched the tranquility of the scene below, but was at odds with Forrester's memories of the war's harvest of wounded and dying.

Electing to fill the silence with a question that had been troubling him since he learned of the existence of the reserve devoted to the meek, Forrester turned from the window of the hopper and toward his diminutive pilot. Engulfed by the hopper's instrumentation, she appeared even smaller than she had in Chen's office.

"What do you think of the war, Crystal?" He asked in quiet, cautious tones.

Eyes never straying from the hopper's console, Crystal responded in a cadence suggesting she had memorized what she was saying.

> TO HAVE LIFE IS TO KNOW ONLY IN PART.
> KNOWING ONLY IN PART, ALL ARE IN
> PAIN. IN THEIR PAIN IS FEAR AND RAGE
> AGAINST THAT FEAR. THE FIRES OF FEAR
> AND ANGER RAGING AGAINST THE PAIN
> OF LIFE WITHIN IS VENTED LIKE THE
> COOK STOVE'S SMOKE IN ANGRY
> DOMINATION OF THEIR FELLOWS.
> KNOWING NOT THE WHOLE, THEY BATTLE
> SHADOWS OF THEMSELVES IN THEIR
> FELLOWS.

Cadence and melody of language he believed up to now was known only to Arthur and himself rang in his ears. Forrester was still in a mild state of shock as Crystal maneuvered the hopper onto a pad by a beautiful home set amongst the trees on the slope of one of the highest peaks in the area. Crystal had quoted with perfect recall from the scrolls he had carefully buried on a mountain top in the region. His mind buzzed with questions, none of which could be immediately answered as the door of the hopper slid open. Through the portal, he saw a man and woman, presumably Crystal's parents, approaching the craft. The slender blue-eyed woman greeted him first.

"Hello Doctor Forrester, I am Esther. I'm Crystal's mother and this is Jacob, her father. We are honored by your visit. Crystal has told us so much about you."

Crystal had told them so much about him, Forrester repeated the phrase over to himself. He had never met this kid before. Gathering his thoughts, he managed a perfunctory response.

"It's very kind of you to have invited me into your home."

The family home appeared, from the outside, like a cross between Scandinavian and German Black Forest design set among towering pines. Jacob stepped out ahead and led the way as they entered the family dwelling. The interior featured vaulted ceilings and huge floor to roof windows that admitted light from every direction. In the center of the room stood an imposing conifer trunk that disappeared through an elastic seal in the roof. Around the base of the trunk, a pond with irregular boundaries was fed by a gurgling stream that entered from beneath the north wall. Bits of blond wood furniture and potted shrubs were scattered here and there. The overall impression created by the setting was that the best aspects of the outside had been brought inside. Jacob led the group to a large low set glass table on which stood a bottle of Piesporter Michelsburg and several long slender glasses. Indicating a chair, Jacob proceeded to pour the wine as Forrester sat down.

"I want to begin by apologizing if anything we have done or said has unduly startled or offended you. We feel somewhat awkward as we know so much more about you than you know of us," Jacob began.

"I guess it's the *how* you know what you do that intrigues me most?" Forrester responded hesitantly.

"That is very difficult to explain, but the longer you stay within our community, the more clearly you will grasp how things happen among us," Esther remarked as she reached for her wine glass.

Forrester watched as Esther took a sip of wine and turned her attention to a tree swaying in the wind just beyond the glass. Recalling what Chen had said about understanding the meek being an experiential event rather than something that could be verbally coded with any ease, Forrester elected to take another tack.

"Crystal quoted an entry from some ancient scrolls I discovered many years ago, how did she do that?" He queried.

Smiling in the most open and accepting fashion imaginable, Esther and Jacob beamed at Forrester and looked over at Crystal.

"The diary called to me in my mind and I brought it here for everyone to see," Crystal responded.

The feeling of his pupils dilating was a sensation Forrester could honestly say he had never noticed before this moment, although the roaring in his ears was familiar. He wasn't certain whether it was the phrase 'called to me in my mind' or the matter of fact manner in which Crystal said the words that was more astonishing to him. What was occurring in the reserve was clearly light years beyond anything he had imagined. He suddenly felt quite alone, wholly apart from the community he had been instrumental in bringing into being. Crystal seemed to sense this and reached out touched his hand.

"Without knowing it, you were the first of the people of the trees. You made us possible. You are the father of our community and will be with us always," Crystal said as she planted her hand in his.

Suddenly, the familiar feeling of invigorating clarity was there, traveling from that tiny hand to station itself in the comforting 'Y' position in his head. He saw things he could not explain to himself, while, in the background, an entry from the scrolls boomed loudly like the tolling of a bell whose pealing could not be escaped.

THE TIME DRAWING NIGH, THE LIGHT
WITHIN STRAINS AGAINST THIS VESSEL
OF CLAY. ARMED WITH BUT DIM RECALL
OF ITS FREEDOM, LIGHT UNTO LIGHT, IT
YEARNS AGAIN WITH ITS KIN TO ABIDE.

AS THE DAYS SUCCEED THE NIGHTS AND
THE SEASONS FOLLOW ONE ANOTHER, THE
FIRES OF THE CIRCLE'S BEGINNING
THAT BURN WITHIN INCREASE AS THE
FLESH, WHICH IS NOW BUT RAIMENT,
DIMINISHES.

LIGHT'S COMMUNION CALLS TO ITS OWN.

As Crystal released his hand, the diary entry faded away, but the 'Y' shaped feeling in his head continued. The continuation of that feeling was a first. In the past, the feeling had come and gone based on his contact with the scrolls or, occasionally, when he read a particular entry from the scanner. Under Crystal's touch, the 'Y' shaped feeling of invigoration seemed to spread throughout his brain, clarifying his thought processes and broadening their scope. The change in functioning felt stable, as if the phenomenon of invigoration had taken up permanent residence.

"What just happened?" Forrester muttered.

Esther, smiling like some kindly and beneficent earth mother, reached across the table and topped off Forrester's wine glass as she spoke.

"Crystal, like all the children born to this community, has gifts that she has shared with us and now shares with you. We all change together as a community, the succeeding generation assisting the preceding one. As the first of us, you were left alone at the beginning. Now that you have come, you may take your place among us."

Flowing like the wine into his glass, Forrester felt another entry from the scrolls suffusing his consciousness.

> KIN TO ALL, I AM A STRANGER WHEREVER I WANDER. IN VISIONS THAT SEAR THE SOUL, I SEE PEOPLE AND PLACES NOT OF THIS TIME. WHETHER THESE SPECTERS HAIL FROM MANY PASTS OR SUMMON FUTURES WITHOUT NUMBER, I KNOW NOT.
>
> ALTHOUGH BUT A PART, TRAPPED IN ONE PLACE AND TIME, I FEEL THE WHOLE OF LIGHT AND LIFE WITHIN ME STRUGGLING TO BE FREE. IF YEARNING BE THE MEASURE OF REFORMATION'S NEED, THEN COULD I TRANSFORM THIS PLACE I WOULD, OR FLEEING FROM IT, REST WITHIN THE REALM OF LIGHT.

Maybe that's the way it worked for the meek as well, Forrester thought to himself. The future, in the person of their offspring, strained in equal measure toward an illumined history to be while towing the past in the form of the living presence of their parents into a time not yet clocked. One thing was clear from both Crystal's intervention and her mother's words, no one was left behind among the meek.

"I believe that we have imposed upon the good doctor enough for one day," Jacob interjected.

Then, Esther cast a knowing glance at her daughter.

"Crystal, perhaps a walk in the forest is in order."

Time seemed to spin away before Forrester had the opportunity to formulate a response to all the questions vying for a hearing in his head. Sensing a pair of eyes on him, he looked up and saw Crystal standing before him. Taking his hand, she led him from the house into the forest that clustered protectively all about the dwelling. With Crystal leading the way, they climbed the steep hillside, weaving in and out among the trees until, they reached a clearing at the summit. Before them, in a broad expanse, lay the heavily forested mountain range dotted here and there with snow caps.

Stepping onto a smoothed rock so that her height nearly approximated his, Crystal swept her hand over the expanse before them. Then, she smiled and took Forrester's hand with the other.

"See that which is now," she said, squeezing his hand gently.

Forrester's gaze played over the panorama of forest, mountain and valley before him. He felt a twinge of confusion as he looked for whatever Crystal found so particular in the scene before them.

"Yes, I see the mountain range and the forest," Forrester replied.

"See the nows that were before." Crystal said as she closed her eyes to the vast sylvan tableau.

Staring at the vista stretched out before him, Forrester felt more than a little foolish. What was he supposed to see that he hadn't already looked at? Then, slowly at first but with increasing speed, he noticed changes in the scene he was observing. Day became night and day again with tachistoscopic speed until light and dark were only flashes. The bloom of spring was replaced by the snows of winter, and then, as the cycles of change accelerated, the trees and, finally, the mountains were gone, replaced by a shallow sea and flora he didn't recognize. The sea vanished to be replaced by a churning mass of molten rock and a sky as black as coal, graced only by a moon at least fifteen times larger than its current counterpart. The final view was one of deep space swaddled in spiraling clouds of dust with a globular mass of incredible brilliance at it's center. Then, as quickly as it had begun, he found himself staring once again at the view of the mountain range with which he had begun.

Looking down, he noticed Crystal had let go of his hand. A feeling of disorientation swept over him as if someone or something had just bumped into his sense of reality. He felt neither dizzy, nor faint. The disorganization was cognitive, not physiological. He could only guess he had seen some kind of compressed history of the Earth from the perspective of this particular mountain top. Then, it struck him that on at least one occasion during this temporal panorama, he had looked down to see himself standing in the airless black of space. Before his musings could carry him any further, Crystal took his hand.

"See the nows that are yet to come," she said in encouraging tones.

Bracing himself against the expectation of yet another trip through the temporal ether, Forrester fixed his gaze on the hills and valleys below. As before, days and nights merged together in a blur of light and darkness, but this time, Forrester noticed only the beginnings of one change of season followed by a brief glimpse of spring. Then, without any warning, the heavily forested mountains, valleys and lakes before him disappeared in a cloud of smoke and fire accompanied by a deafening explosion. Now the scene was dominated by clouds of black smoke driven by fierce winds that obscured the rapidly rising and setting sun. Through many cycles of dimly perceived day and night, the cloud of dust and smoke cleared revealing a mountain range with all evidence of life scoured away. A sky that only occasionally showed tinges of blue silhouetted the naked rock. Then, very slowly over rapidly accelerating cycles of change, bits of green appeared here and there in the valleys. The mountains gradually wore down into hills as vegetation scaled their heights against a sky that was once again painted in pastels of blue.

Inhaling deeply, Forrester looked down, noticing Crystal had released his hand. He was back. There before him was the expanse of blue and green forest, the mountains, valleys and lakes made all the more beautiful in the moments of twilight that signaled the end of the day. As he surveyed the view, some small part of him could still see flashes of what Crystal had called the nows before and the nows yet to come.

Smiling at him, Crystal seemed pleased with their adventure through time. It was a smile with which Forrester was familiar. He had felt that same smile cross his own face as a professor when a student had grasped a particularly difficult concept with but a single presentation of the idea.

Reaching down, Crystal carefully selected a white pebble with veins of quartz from among those scattered at her feet. She traced the veins of translucent rock for a moment with her finger and threw the pebble over the precipice.

"As the pebble travels in our now, it becomes part of the nows that were before and the nows that are yet to come. All of these together and all at once are the *NOW*. Soon, you will be able to see the NOW wherever you look, but the NOW comes only when the 'you' isn't there," Crystal said and turned to Forrester.

"The 'you'?" Forrester asked.

Watching a butterfly make its way among the flowers, Crystal extended her finger and the gayly tinted insect instantly alighted.

"The 'you' is the 'I' that does the talking inside your head. It's what says 'I' see, 'I' hear, 'I' feel, 'I' think," she replied.

She's talking about the ego, Forrester thought to himself. Perhaps, that's what got bumped out of the way when he felt his sense of reality jostled.

"Crystal, do you mean the 'I' that makes me an individual?" He asked.

Gently flexing her finger, the butterfly took flight. Then, her gaze fell to the ledge on which they stood. She studied the ground for a moment as if communing with the stones and low grasses at her feet and then looked up at Forrester.

"The 'I' that makes you an individual is separate and alone. It is what you're calling the ego," she remarked casually.

A roaring in his ears told him that, once again, he had fallen into his own personal whirlpool. In this swirling cognitive vortex, the number of questions completely overwhelmed the available store of answers. The churning spiral of confusion had become a familiar, but very uncomfortable refuge since he met Crystal. Had Crystal pulled that idea from his mind or was the word 'ego' part of her considerable word store? He knew this was a question that had to be set aside for the moment. Besides, he wasn't entirely sure he wanted to hear the answer to that particular query. Instead, he elected to pose an inquiry he hoped represented an attempt to stick to the point.

"So the 'I' that is separate and alone must go away before you can see the NOW?" He asked.

"The 'I' that is the individual is separate and alone. It is but a small part of the greater whole, yet it travels in darkness focusing on itself. This 'I' believes itself to be a whole. The 'I' that sees the NOW knows itself to be but a part of the whole. This 'I' knows that separation from the whole, from the LIGHT and from the NOW is an illusion. To know the LIGHT and the NOW is to let the illusion pass," Crystal said, directing her gaze over the mountain range and seemingly beyond.

Separate and individual, that was certainly the human condition, he thought. Separate or not, he was going to understand what Crystal was saying one piece at a time, no matter how ignorant it might make him appear.

"Crystal, what does it mean, let the illusion pass?" Forrester asked.

"The individual and separate 'I' that tries to force its way into the whole is the 'I' that, wandering in the darkness, believes itself to be a whole. This 'I' wants to dominate all that is. It is this 'I,' acting in the belief that it is the complete summation of thought and feeling, that wants to draw all things unto itself. This 'I' is an illusion that cannot see beyond its own edges," she said with uncharacteristic speed.

Pausing for a moment, she gazed at her feet, her expression suddenly cast in shadows of sadness. She reached down and picked a dry leaf from among those at her feet and crushed it in her hand. Opening her hand, the dry particles were carried away by the soft breeze and lost in the long shadows of the setting sun.

"So many of these 'I's, wandering in the darkness, each competing with all the others to become the whole," she said sadly.

Slowly filling with a calm wonder, Forrester felt at peace for no reason in particular he could characterize. He carefully studied this slight little girl who was physically present before him and yet, somehow existed as well in the dimensions of time she had shown him. In Crystal's words, he heard the central axioms of all the great religions presented, as they always had been, in metaphors approximating poetry. Here were the ideas, perhaps inspirations of Buddha, Christ, Confucius, Mohammed and so many more cast somehow in models vaguely reminiscent of the physics of the space-time continuum. Regrouping his scattered cognitions, Forrester focused his concentration on one last question, the answer to which would reveal either his insight or appalling stupidity.

"So, the universe cannot be forced to reveal itself. It must be joined in order to be understood?" Forrester asked and held his breath.

"Yes, yes, that's it. The 'I' that can see the whole, the LIGHT and the NOW is the 'I' that knows itself to be part of the whole. This 'I' knows it loses nothing by becoming part of the whole, for it is and always has been, a part of the whole. This 'I' gains itself and the whole universe by letting the illusion pass. The whole cannot be forced by the part, but in joining with the whole, the 'I' becomes part of everything," Crystal replied, smiling in open, innocent delight.

Quite without effort, the amorphous associational network in Forrester's feverishly overworked brain coughed up an idea he had not considered for years. An idea so bizarre he couldn't recall ever attempting to put it into words. Now, the ideas and their verbal codifiers seemed to come together with relative ease. Perhaps the future of the human race was nested in the perceptions, feelings and thoughts indigenous to childhood. Maturity, beginning at puberty was, at best, a bad cognitive and spiritual bargain in which so much of mankind's continuity with the universe was sacrificed to the mechanical and hormonal travesties necessary to ensure the continuation of the species. This little girl was the incarnation of an openness and comfort with a universe in which striving for egocentric dominance was wholly absent. It was difficult to imagine that nature's decree mandating the simple continuation of the species was so important as to necessitate banishing this perspective in every child who reached puberty.

Almost as if she had heard his thoughts, Crystal looked up and, in that moment, a passage from the scrolls came to him.

LIFE OF ITSELF BEGINS AND ENDS THE
CIRCLE OF LIGHT. TAKING BREATH IN
AIR OR WATER, ALL THAT LIVES YEARNS
TO SIGH AND INSPIRE IN THE GENTLE
WINDS THAT FILL THE SAILS OF THE
STARS. LIGHT'S CALLING, NOT GRASPED
BY THE EYE NOR SOUNDING IN THE EAR,
DRAWS ALL LIFE TO THE WOMB IT
REMEMBERS NOT.

DOES NOT ALL THAT LIVES BEGIN IN
THE SEED AND, GROWING TO MATURITY,
BECOME THE SEED AGAIN? THE FIELD
OF THE UNIVERSE WAS TILLED SO THAT
THESE SEEDS OF THE BEGINNING MIGHT
BE SOWN AND, RISING TO A FULL HEAD
RETURN AGAIN TO THE SOWER.

IN INNOCENT AWARENESS IS THE
GLORY OF THE LIGHT ENCOMPASSED
AND FULFILLED. THE RIGHTEOUSNESS
OF ETERNITY'S ILLUMINATION SLEEPS
IN THE UNBROKEN LINKS TYING TOGETHER
ALL THAT HAS LIFE WITHIN THE GREAT AND
ETERNAL NOW.

Perhaps the preservation of this innocent awareness in the face of the hormonal ravages of maturation represented nature's principal innovation among the meek. Only time and Crystal's development would tell.

Her movements drawing him from his reveries, Forrester looked down at the slight figure standing beside him. Like the little girl she remained in so many ways, she plucked a blade of grass from the ground at her feet and wound it around her finger.

"I'm hungry Doctor Forrester. A vegeburger with fries would be nice," Crystal said shyly.

Laughing aloud, his peals of laughter echoed back from the surrounding mountains. With this expression of mirth, he experienced a profound sense of release. It seemed even transcendence had an appetite.

"Sounds great," he replied as he took Crystal's hand.

Walking hand in hand down the mountain in the gathering darkness, Forrester noticed something that, given the events of the past hour, seemed only mildly surprising. His head now held every last passage in the scrolls. He could reel through them in memory in the same way he had by depressing the appropriate icon on his personal scanner, only faster. As they approached Crystal's house, one entry locked itself firmly into central focus.

IN THE STILL OF NIGHT, VENTURING
BEYOND THE VILLAGE WALL AND THE
CHATTER OF LIFE IT ENCLOSES, I PULL
ON THE CLOAK OF NIGHT AND AM
COMFORTED BY ITS LINING OF
SILENCE. BENEATH MY FEET THE
HILL'S HEAD, BEFORE ME THE RISING
MOON BLOTS OUT FAINT STARS. KIN
TO ITS COOL GLOW, I AM ONE STEP
CLOSER TO HOME.

THE HOSTS OF HEAVEN ARRAYED
BEFORE MY EYES ARE BEYOND
COUNTING, YET WITHIN, I SEE A
GATHERING OF LIGHTS THAT MAKES
FEW THE MULTITUDE OF STARS
CAPTURED BY THE COMPASS OF MY
FEEBLE EYE. GRASPING BUT IN PART,
I WOULD KNOW AGAIN THE WHOLE.

AS A CHILD EMERGING FROM THE
TINY VESSEL OF THE WOMB SEES
THE GREAT EXPANSE OF THE WORLD,
SO MY EYE WITHIN YEARNS AGAIN
TO BEHOLD THE NOW THAT IS THE
UNBROKEN CIRCLE OF THE LIGHT AT
THE BEGINNING OF THE UNIVERSE.

Perhaps, it was that simple. The meek, especially their offspring, were the very incarnation of wonder. Filled to overflowing with imagination, theirs was not the garden variety wish fulfillment mobilized in the service of the race's needs for security and dominance. This was wonder freed to fulfill its principal goal. The meek remained children who had been spared, not the need to reproduce, but the dominance motivations attendant to those drives. Optimistic curiosity, imagination, and wonder lay at the core of their perceptions. Forrester was only dimly aware of the aim of the meek's strivings that seemed to extend far beyond a simple exercise of their mental faculties. Like tiny tributaries reversing flow back to their headwaters, the meek's innocent perceptions led back to the beginning.

Finding the inside of his head was as busy as his feet in navigating the tangle of the darkening woods, Forrester was grateful when Crystal took his hand. Crystal's help as a guide in the darkness seem to have both transcendental, as well as, highly practical manifestations. On the mountain top, he had achieved a better understanding of the diarist's use of the word NOW. His own poor reading of the scrolls had made the 'NOW' into a symbol or perhaps an simple example of poetic license. Her compression of billions of years into a few moments of experience on the summit had translated a theory in physics into a personal sensation. What Crystal had shown him was no less than a snapshot of the continuity of space-time. Although he could not explain what had happened, neither could he deny its reality. A central part of the reality she shared with him was Crystal's ability to look into the past and the future as effortlessly as she might thumb through the pages of a picture book. He was also convinced, in a way he could not explain to himself, that the Nows with which Crystal had regaled him did not represent the NOW of the unbroken circle of the LIGHT of which the Diarist had so longingly written.

Hurrying through the darkness, Forrester could see the house with light spilling out of its many windows. The life of the forest's night shift began to announce its presence in soft calls and rustlings, while in the background, the gurgling of a small stream could be heard. Just then, he caught a glimpse of Jacob and Esther waiting on the terrace. Esther greeted them and led the way into the dining area of the house.

"You two must be very hungry," she said through her signature smile.

"Vegeburgers and fries, Mommy, please," Crystal said, impatiently jumping in place.

Nodding her approval of Crystal's request, Esther walked to the transubstantiator in the corner of the room and activated the requested settings.

Fatigue of a warm and comfortable sort directed Forrester to an inviting chair. As he sat down, Forrester picked up his glass of wine that remained where he had left it on the glass table and took a sip. It was absolutely delightful to watch this little girl, who only moments before had fulfilled the role of a transcendental guru opening his feeble brain to the mysteries of time and space, munch down her burger and fries.

"And for you Doctor Forrester?" Esther asked, catching his eye.

"Eggplant parmesan cooked in peanut oil with oregano risotto and peas prepared in Jaegermeister," Forrester said automatically.

Then, it struck him. He couldn't recall the last time he had taken a meal with a family and his manners were less than perfect.

"I'm sorry, I must have sounded like I was talking to a transubstantiator," he quickly added.

"It is of no consequence. You are among family now. Our basic rule is honesty and directness is never offensive unless it is intended to exalt the speaker or demean the listener. Besides your selection sounds delicious. I think I'll try it," Esther replied in a comforting tone.

"Sounds good to me too," Jacob added.

They all sat around a large glass table illuminated by a chandelier sheathed in copiz shells and broke bread together. The evening meal disappeared with amazing rapidity, accompanied by plaudits from Esther and Jacob for Forrester's selection.

"Dessert mommy, may I have ice cream?" Crystal asked as she jumped up from the table.

"What kind would you like, Love?" Esther asked as she smiled at Crystal's anticipation.

"I don't know," Crystal said, looking vacantly at the ceiling.

"How about some black raspberry? It's a dessert we used to make on the farm when I was a child. It was my father's recipe," Forrester interjected.

"OK," Crystal replied with some hesitation.

Fumbling in his pockets for his menu card, Forrester pushed aside the scanner that contained the scroll entries. He wouldn't need that anymore. His hand found the menu card and, in the touching of it, he felt a sudden sadness. He hadn't remember to bring it along, Arthur had made sure it was there. A good friend, Forrester thought and wished him there in Crystal's home to share in the joy of this family. Sentimentality, Forrester thought to himself, this was his notion of satisfaction, not Arthur's.

Sounding their approval of the selection of black raspberry ice cream, Esther and Jacob added coffee to the menu.

Empty dishes indicated everyone's approval of the dessert. As the adults sipped their coffee, Crystal drew pictures with a special marker on the glass tabletop.

Finishing his coffee, Forrester went for another cup. As he returned from the transubstantiator, he knew there was one more question, prompted by the last scroll entry, he had to raise before day's end. Drawing on the warmth and acceptance of this family and his own scattered bits of courage, he decided to chance it.

"Something puzzles me, who sees the NOW that is the unbroken circle of LIGHT?" He asked.

Sudden silence fell over the tiny assembly. The demise of the table banter that followed Forrester's question engendered a moment of anxiety in him. What if his question was verboten? Perhaps in anthropological terms he had broken some taboo among the people of the trees or trod on a patch of sacred ground. Forrester was greatly relieved when Jacob broke the silence.

"He who sees the NOW sees it all, no matter where he stands, worlds without number. In whatever now he sojourns, stars without end, he sees all for he stands in the unbroken circle of LIGHT," Jacob said and closed his eyes.

Immediately Esther and Crystal piously followed suit. Then, his eyes still tightly closed Jacob continued.

"He who stands in the unbroken circle of LIGHT is he who spoke from dust of centuries in the scrolls that you were chosen to find."

Before Forrester could initiate any effort to absorb the enormity of what Jacob said, the scroll entries began spinning in his head. The reels of passages came to an abrupt halt at an entry that he could see clearly in his mind's eye.

A NEW LINTEL FOR THE WINE MERCHANT
PRESSES MY SHOULDER DOWN AS STONES
WHOSE HEAT BREAD COULD BAKE PASS
BENEATH MY FEET. NAZARETH'S PATHS,
BLACK WITH FLIES, BUZZ MOREOVER
WITH THE COMMON STRIFE OF MAN
CROWDED UPON HIS OWN KIND. LIFE,
A SOJOURN EVER HOMEWARD BOUND IS
BUT A JOURNEY IN THE SOUL'S
REMINISCENCE, ENDING IN THE LIGHT.
YET, THIS MEMORY OF REDEMPTION,
FROM THE BEGINNING PERFECTED, IS
HOSTAGE TO THE TRIALS EACH DAY OF
LIVING BRINGS ANEW.

ALL STRIVE IN FEAR TO SUSTAIN BREATH
AND MOTION IN THIS BRIEF MOMENT OF
ETERNITY, KNOWING NOT THE LENGTH AND
BREADTH OF THEIR BEING. IN THIS STRUGGLE
IS MUCH LOST AND LITTLE GAINED.

THE DUST OF GALILEE CLOUDS THE EYE
AND STOPS THE EAR OF THOSE FEW WHO,
IN LISTENING, MIGHT HEAR AND, IN
LOOKING, MIGHT SEE. VISIONS THAT I
CLOAK IN WORDS TOO SMALL TO CONTAIN
ALL THAT IS THE LIGHT MUST LIE IN
THIS DUST UNTIL A NOW THAT IS YET
TO COME. OF ALL THE NOWS WITHIN
THE NOW, I AM HERE IN THIS DUST.

It was the carpenter of Nazareth, the lonely man who wrote for and to himself of whom Jacob spoke so reverently. Even with all he had seen, Forrester was uncertain he was ready to buy into this revelation. The people of the trees represented an extraordinary leap forward in the evolution of the species, but, just as he and Chen had discussed, somehow evolutionary genetics must account for the meek's abilities. He wasn't sure he was prepared to accept a deus ex machina pushing the buttons and steering the course of evolution. Despite the personally transforming events he had experienced before he came to know the people of the trees, he was uncertain. In the midst of this flurry of doubt he became aware that Jacob, Esther, and Crystal, all with eyes wide open, were staring at him.

"You were the first, but you were left behind at the beginning of our becoming. Your doubts are those of one who knows, but is not content in his knowing. Separated from the community of your own kind, you have journeyed alone. To be alone is to be in darkness and, in darkness there is always doubt and fear that you may lose your way," Esther said as she touched Forrester's shoulder.

Suspended in the moment, Forrester recognized Esther's remarks represented both an invitation and a challenge to resolve his own doubts.

"Stay with us, Doctor Forrester. If you find no light against the darkness in our community, it is not in our nature to persuade or constrain anyone," Jacob said as he extended his hand.

Before he could seriously entertain Jacob's offer, Crystal, seeming to sense

Forrester's indecision, stepped between her father and Forrester and took his hand.

"He is tired," she interjected.

Then, with a gentle tug she led Forrester from the living-dining area to an upstairs bedroom the family had prepared for him.

A soft click signaled the closing of the door to the guest room behind him. In the past, that sound had always created the illusion of security against the competitive confusion of a world in which people vied with one another for social ascendance. Now, the sound had a cold, hard and hollow ring that seemed to verify that he was alone. Not the comfortable alone that he had experienced all his life, this alone no longer felt like a fortress against a world of strife, or even appeared as a sphere of bright and sparkling cognitive diversion wherein insights played hide and seek with his analytic ability. This alone was dark and claustrophobic. The illumination that had always shone brightly within was in no way diminished, but now its radiance had a gloomy cast set alongside the light that he felt, and almost imagined that he saw, emanating from and clinging to the people of the trees. His experience among the members of this community amply demonstrated that light and darkness were relative terms defining their degrees of radiance in terms of the experience of the individual. A history of huddling by the tiny spark within himself, illuminating that private refuge from his more aggressive fellows, seemed but a faint candle compared to the full radiance of the sun in which the meek basked.

But Crystal was right, fatigue was folding over him like a warm blanket. He would sleep, falling swiftly into one last vestige of familiarity from his life as he had known it up to now, his nocturnal coma. Accompanying his descent into a welcome repose, an entry from the scrolls, serving as a lullaby, sang his way into the regions of slumber.

THE WOOD HAS WORKED ITS WILL ON
THIS FEEBLE SHELL OF CLAY AS, PAUSING
AT MIDDAY, THESE HANDS AND ARMS
LAMENT THEIR WEARINESS.

ESCAPING THE HEAT OF THE DAY, I SIT
BENEATH THE CANOPY OF SIMON THE
WEAVER, WHO IS MY FRIEND. NIMBLE
FINGERS, THREADS OF MANY COLORS,
BRAID TOGETHER UNTIL FROM MANY
COMES ONE. MANY COLORS AND MANY

TWININGS BECOME A COVERING THAT
SHEDS THE SUN OR DRIVES AWAY THE
CHILL OF NIGHT. IN THE WEAVER'S ART
IS THE LOVE OF SINGULARITY IN
DIVERSITY REALIZED.

WITHIN ALL THAT WHICH IS FAMILIAR
IS THE WHOLE OF THE UNIVERSE
REFLECTED. THE WOOL OF ALL THAT IS,
BECOMES MANY INDIVIDUAL THREADS,
EACH CARRYING ITS OWN TWIST AND
COLOR. UNDER THE WEAVER'S HAND,
EACH TWINING FIBER COMES TO KNOW
ITS PLACE IN THE TAPESTRY OF LIFE.
THAT WHICH LIVES IS THE WAKING
DREAM AND GLORY OF A UNIVERSE
THAT SLUMBERS, SAVE FOR THE
LIGHT AND LIFE IT SHELTERS.

Chapter 21

Maneuvering the Duo into parking orbit around the station, Sydes went over a mental checklist of modifications to be made in the ship. The Commander was in the middle of a post flight download on the console when Sydes called to him.

"I think Von Strohheim will be happy to see us," Sydes remarked.

"He should be. His ship performed magnificently," Tutunji replied.

"No, I didn't mean that. I meant he'll be happy because we have some upgrades for him to make in his lady … you know, something for him to do with his free time," Sydes said with a note of humor in his voice.

"Yes, I guess so. But as far as I'm concerned, the first job is to reload the missile racks. There's hardly anything left down there to shoot with," Tutunji said.

Suddenly, a voice broke in over the comm-link.

"Captain Sydes, Commander Tutunji, shuttle number twelve is standing by to transport you to the station."

"Copy that," Tutunji replied.

Releasing their restraints, the pilot and copilot floated from their console chairs up to the catwalk, where they took the tube to the shuttle receiving lock.

No conversation interrupted the pilot ferrying them back to the station. Tutunji's melancholy emerged as he observed the tractor shuttles towing some badly damaged strike craft to the receiving bays for repair. He knew there would be very few strike craft to repair and even fewer pilots coming back from the devastation that resulted from the alien's coalescing laser attack.

Landing gently in the receiving bay, the shuttle door slid open and they disembarked amid some of the damaged strike craft already under repair.

"Damn fine job, Sirs. I am to tell you Commander Sadad and Doctor Von Strohheim are waiting for you in the bar," the shuttle pilot said as he saluted.

A brisk stride took Tutunji and Sydes down the passageway toward the bar while receiving and returning salutes from several passing technical Chiefs.

"Damn convenient of them to meet us in the bar, eh?" Sydes remarked as they rounded the corner to the bar.

"Damn convenient or they just know us too well," Tutunji replied through a wry smile.

Entering the bar a large gathering of pilots and station personnel confronted them. Drinks were pressed into their hands as the assembled group raised their glasses in salute.

Commander Sadad stepped forward, smiling as he raised his glass.

"I give you two men and a solitary ship who stood against the enemy."

"And the many fallen, not among us," Tutunji quickly added.

Instantly, a silence fell over the large gathering as all drank deeply to the pilots the enemy had taken from their ranks.

Noticing Von Strohheim off to one side of the group, Sydes raised his glass to the Doctor.

"To the wizard of shields and lasers, the good Doctor and his formidable ship."

Those assembled saluted Von Strohheim who appeared mightily embarrassed by the attention. Then, Sydes and Commander Tutunji moved to Von Strohheim's side and, shaking his hand, escorted him to nearby table as the crowd dispersed.

"How did she perform?" Von Strohheim asked anxiously as he sat down.

"Like the great lady she is, but there are a couple of things we'd like to go over with you," Sydes replied.

Dipping into his pocket, Tutunji produced a scanner containing the download from his console and handed it to Von Strohheim. The Doctor immediately connected it to his scanner. In a matter of seconds he had downloaded Tutunji's recommendations.

"It looks like we need more efficient or, at least faster, conduction from the shields to the capacitors, more capacitors and more coolant capacity for the main laser. That's about it except for downloading the hull cameras and getting those records to the biological sciences people for study. We saw some alien's bodies drifting in space during the battle. I'm not sure, but maybe the bio guys can get something out of analyzing the digital replay," Tutunji said.

"We need those missile racks reloaded as soon as possible. I don't like our lady sitting out there empty. She's like a wasp without a stinger," Sydes said, his mood suddenly quite serious.

"The crews have already begun reloading the missile racks, but this will take two to three hours. We modified the missiles by adding an additional fusion tip assembly. They should now yield at least twenty-five percent more megatonnage of destructive power. These new missiles will also be supplied to the strike craft. And ... the other modifications you have mentioned can easily be made," Von Strohheim replied.

"That's great Doc. I have this nasty feeling there are more of those battle-ships out there and they're a tough kill," Sydes said.

Von Strohheim's expression clouded and his tone carried a quality of fore-boding Tutunji had not heard from this otherwise matter of fact engineer before.

"This same feeling, I have had also," Von Strohheim muttered.

"Visions of what could happen if the Duo is caught between two of those capital ships keep running through my head," Tutunji said.

"Yes, this is a problem. The strike craft can deal with the enemy fighters as long as we keep our forces dispersed. The last battle was a very expensive lesson, over ninety men and strike craft lost, gone in an instant … just to be instructed in their coalescing laser strategy," Von Strohheim replied.

Von Strohheim's gaze drifted over the bar, seeming to light on the face of one young pilot after another, before it returned to the table. A sad apprehension lace his voice as he turned back to Tutunji.

"Even if we keep our strike craft dispersed, my feeling is that we need a two to one advantage to break through the enemy shields. Only by assigning two of our fighters to every one of theirs can we hope to stop an enemy thrust into the solar system."

"Is there any way to beef up the strike craft?" Sydes asked hopefully.

"Nein … no, we have looked at this. The craft, they are simply too small. In order to make them more durable, we would have to start … from scratch. The strike craft are what we have. The fact that they are smaller and more maneuverable makes them a hard target for the enemy, but they are also much more fragile."

"How is work coming on the second Duo, Doc?" Tutunji asked as he took another sip of his drink.

"This will take some time. There is so much …." Von Strohheim replied in an apologetic tone.

Abruptly, the piercing sound of the klaxon interrupted Von Strohheim's response. The whole bar came alive with pilots charging toward the strike craft bays. Despite being dead tired, Sydes and the Command came instantly to their feet and started running toward the station's bridge.

Eyes glued to the bridge's main viewer, Commander Sadad supervised the mobilization of the station's strike craft force as Sydes and Tutunji entered the bridge.

"What do we have?" Sydes asked as he looked up at the viewer.

"The long range scanners indicate multiple explosions in the mine field," Commander Sadad replied.

Without exchanging a word, Sydes and Commander Tutunji immediately turned and entered the operations imaging room. The imaging Officer had already activated the long range scanner buoys stationed along the first attack route into the solar system used by the aliens. The huge spherical viewer revealed the radioactive cloud engineered to seal off this route was now alive with internal flashes of light.

"What the hell do you make of this Chief?" Tutunji asked the operations Officer.

"I don't know why Sir, but we have mines exploding along what appears to be a linear path through the center of the cloud," the Chief responded.

"Damn it! I think I know what they're doing. Those bastards are blowing a path through the mine field for their assault ships," Sydes interjected.

"There's only one ship we've seen in their fleet that could do something like that without destroying itself," Tutunji added.

"Yeah, another battleship class vessel ..." Sydes said, then shouted into his comm-link, "... find Von Strohheim, now!"

"Yes, Captain Sydes, and no, the Duo is not ready for action. All the modifications are on line and most of the missiles are loaded, but we still have to put everything back together. The Duo won't move for another forty minutes. Out," Von Strohheim responded.

Out of the corner of his eye, Tutunji glanced at Sydes who seemed to have shrunk in stature. This was the nightmare they both shared. Only the Duo that stood a chance against one of the enemy's capital class vessels, and the she wasn't going anywhere.

Tutunji watched the exploding radioactive cloud closely, hoping he would not see what he knew he would.

"Damn, it's got to be that big bitch," Sydes snapped.

Punctured by broad beam laser strikes and attended by the explosion of mines on all sides, the massive cloud began to resemble a large radioactive sponge. The energy from the continuous fire of immense laser projectors literally boiled away a broad, clear path through the cloud. Emerging from the haze of destruction she had created, the huge battleship was now fully visible. Slowing, her forward motion came to a stop just as she cleared the cloud.

"Why is she just sitting there?" The Chief asked.

"The bitch is guarding the gate," Sydes responded.

Leaving the operations imaging room at quick time, neither Sydes, nor Tutunji had to see what was coming next. They knew. As they entered the bridge, Commander Sadad was studying the developing battle front along the edge of the radioactive cloud.

Sydes was the first to see the multitude of faint outlines emerging from behind the battleship.

"Here they come," he growled through his teeth.

As the three watched, a steady stream of alien fighters emerged from behind the battleship and began to assume their tight attack formation in front of the capital ship. As the formation consolidated, Sydes estimated about seventy five fighters constituted the assault force.

"I have one hundred strike craft in the first sortie. They should arrive at the point of incursion in about eight minutes and the second wave of one hundred is forming up to follow them," Commander Sadad said, anticipating their questions.

Sweeping the viewer with one last quick glance, Sydes turned to leave the bridge.

In his peripheral vision, Commander Sadad caught sight of Sydes making for the bridge access.

"Captain Sydes, where do you think you're going?" Sadad snapped.

"To warm up the seat of a strike craft," Sydes replied, never breaking his stride.

"Hold fast Mister. That's an order! As commander of this station, I'm also commander of the combined defense forces and you will take my orders!" Sadad snapped.

Stopping dead in his tracks, Sydes, his eyes narrowing, slowly turned to face Sadad.

"You know I'm your best pilot. I've got to be out there. These kids don't know what they're up against."

"You're not only the best pilot we have, but the only one who can fly the Duo, which is precisely why you aren't going out there," Sadad responded.

Glancing over at Tutunji to garner some support for his mission, Sydes saw only a nod of affirmation for Sadad's position.

"I'm afraid I'll have to go with Commander Sadad on this one Sydes. No one else has a chance in hell of flying the Duo and you know it. If you go out there and get fried, we'll have this flying fortress sitting here, with not a living soul who can even maneuver her out of parking orbit," Tutunji said.

"You'll save more lives and do more damage to the enemy by directing the strike craft already out there, and you know it," Commander Sadad said in a tone suggesting that the discussion was over.

Another retort was on Sydes lips, but he said nothing. Instead, he indicated his reluctant agreement by returning to the command console.

"Captain Sydes, the operations console is to your left. You are now in command of all the strike craft," Commander Sadad said.

"And Commander Tutunji, if you would take position in the operations imaging room, we can coordinate this battle," Sadad said, turning to his old commander.

Nodding to Sydes in consolation as he passed, Tutunji exited to the imaging compartment.

Centered in the main viewer, as Sydes had predicted, the alien battleship remained at the edge of the cloud, guarding the attacker's escape route. Striking out along a trajectory which, if unchanged, would bring them into Mars' orbit, the alien fighters assumed the phalanx formation that served their coalescing laser strategy. This was the worst case scenario and Sydes knew it. Earth Force had moved the station in the vain hope the enemy would never risk the cloud and the mines. Now, the response time of the fighters to the alien incursion had tripled and the Duo couldn't even join the battle.

"This icon will connect you with all strike craft simultaneously. The name of the Captain of the first sortie is Natashe. She's a hell of a flyer, but takes too many personal risks. The second flight is captained by Swen, very steady, very methodical. He always gets the job done. These men and women have enormous respect for you Captain Sydes, use it," Sadad said, indicating the array on Sydes' station at the console.

Increasing velocity rapidly, the alien fighter assault group moved out and away from the position taken up by their battleship.

"Trajectory to Mars confirmed," Tutunji announced over the bridge speakers.

Sydes focused the main viewer on the arrival of the first sortie of strike craft moving rapidly into the alien battle group's firing radius. Opening the main link to the strike craft, the grounded pilot tried to filter the frustration from his voice as he donned the mantle of a commander and the unenviable task of sending others to their deaths.

"Sydes to strike craft. Stay a minimum of three hundred thousand kilometers from that battleship . Our previous engagement with one like her suggests that's the effective range of her lasers. And remember what the last engagement taught us about their fighters, don't bunch up!"

Tutunji watched the imager in horror as three tiny strike craft dove on the huge alien juggernaut.

"Sydes, you've got a loose cannon out there," Tutunji's shouted over the comm.

"Son of a bitch ... Natashe, pull those fighters out of there!" Sydes shouted into the strike craft comm.

"We're gonna give this big boy a bloody nose," Natashe replied.

Diving toward the target, the three strike craft appeared tiny against the backdrop of the alien capital ship as the station's command staff watched helplessly. The lead strike craft launched two missiles and then, overflying the battleship, disappeared into the radioactive cloud. The two strike craft flying wing positions, well behind the lead strike craft, released their missiles, but were vaporized only seconds thereafter by simultaneous, continuous fire from the battleship's two forward laser turrets. The missiles launched by the strike craft sortie exploded against the alien battleship, creating only a faint shimmering of her shields.

Mindful he was addressing the entire strike craft force, Sydes' voice became softer as he activated the strike craft comm.

"Natashe, we need sure kills, not losses. Let's concentrate on that battle wagon's fighter group. OK, everybody listen up. You all saw the videos of the coalescing laser the alien fighters generate, so no, and I mean no, frontal attacks. I want strike craft attacking as individuals, no wing attacks. We want these assholes to have to work to find targets. I don't want to see any predictable straight line assaults or overflights. Keep'em guessing … let's light up these bloody bastards."

"Sydes, what's an alien fighter group doing on a trajectory to Mars? I could understand that battleship cruising above Mars blowing holes in the real estate, but fighters?" Tutunji asked over the bridge comm.

"I don't know, but its certain they aren't here just to provide us with target practice," Sydes replied.

His frustration with flying the bridge console unabated, Sydes activated his personal comm-link and said a single name.

"Von Strohheim."

Von Strohheim's response was as immediate, as was his termination of the transmission.

"Twenty minutes, Captain Sydes."

"Damn, I hate this. I don't like someone else doing my dying for me," Sydes said, closing his comm-link.

Von Strohheim's new missiles were making a difference against the alien fighters. Natashe's group had already taken out twenty enemy ships. However, despite her superior fire power, Natashe had lost one third of her forces in the effort. Joining the battle, Swen's wing positioned themselves in a spherical halo around the alien sortie. As his wing made their individual runs, the enemy fighters seemed to tighten their formation, rather than rising to meet the oncoming strike craft.

Transmitting the imaging feed on the alien formation continuously to the bridge, the Commander took note of the closely packed clustering of the alien fighter force.

"Sydes, what the hell is this tight formation about?" He asked.

"I see it, but it doesn't make any sense. In their line of travel, the enemy fighters have nothing on which to focus their coalescing laser strategy, but they hang onto that bunched up formation," Sydes replied.

"The trajectory of those bastards is confirmed. They're vectored in on the main Martian installations. There are over three million civilians under those domes and only one poorly armed supply station in orbit over the ground complex," Tutunji said.

Commander Sadad's voice filled with incredulity as he used the main viewer's cursor to confirm the alien's trajectory to the Martian colony.

"They're going to attack planetary complexes ... civilians?"

"Yes, if their intent wasn't clear before, it is now. This is a genocidal war. They want us gone, every last one of us," Tutunji's said, his tone dark and foreboding.

"The bastards aren't very particular in their bloodletting, military or civilian doesn't make much difference. But even with their coalescing laser attack, they can't do that much damage against a planetary target. It's a bizarre strategy considering their losses," Sydes added.

"The enemy squadron is down from an initial force of seventy five to about twenty five ships. They must have something special in mind to take a beating like that, especially with that battleship just sitting there at the edge of the cloud," Commander Tutunji announced.

Sydes' brow furrowed as he watched two more alien fighters destroyed by strike craft missiles.

"It's a suicide mission. They're not even reaching out against the strike craft as they climb out from their missile runs. With the alien's tight formation strategy and laser tracking capacity, our fighters are an easy target. I don't get it. They're just plowing ahead towards Mars. It's a purely defensive strategy," Sydes said emphatically.

"But defending what?" Commander Sadad interjected.

Tutunji focused the feed from the big imager on the middle of the enemy fighter group. Then highlighting a single ship in the center of the formation, he transferred the image to the bridge viewer.

"Take a look at this. One ship in the nucleus of that formation that never fired a single laser burst. You see it, longer and more aerodynamic than the rest of the fighters," Tutunji said.

"Right, she's built for atmospheric entry. The damn thing's not a fighter at all. It's got to be a big mother of a missile," Sydes said.

Opening the comm to the strike craft, Sydes spoke at a feverish pace into the microphone.

"The ship in the center of the formation, the one that never returns fire, target and kill that bitch!"

The strike crafts' response was immediate as, one by one, the tiny vessels made runs on the ship protected by all the others in the enemy formation. With each diving attack, the enemy escorts interposed their vessels, taking missile hits intended for the projectile they were delivering. Then, as a unit, the entire alien fighter shield initiated nearly continuous laser fire against the attacking strike craft. Sydes watched as tiny strike craft became momentary flares in the darkness of the void.

"Now they're opening fire. Before, they just sat there and took it as long as that vessel in the center wasn't being threatened," Sydes said bitterly.

"We've seen this before. Sacrificing pilots and ships seems to be an integral part of their strategy and perhaps, their mentality," Tutunji interjected.

"Must be a hell of a military arm to serve in if its better to die than to fight back," Sydes responded.

"Or a whole society uncompromisingly devoted to achieving group goals at the expense of the individual," Tutunji replied as he watched the strike craft exploding in the void.

"Maybe that's why the Duo coming out by herself against them seems to fuck with their minds and slow their reaction time," Sydes remarked.

Flashes of light against the dark curtain of space marked the tiny strike craft vaporizing by the score under the enemy's withering defensive fire. Glad to be alone in the imaging room, Tutunji felt tears forming in his eyes. So many young men and women, humanity's repositories of confidence and courage, gone. The hand of his species stretched out against the darkness and the fingers of its youthful extension into the future were being brutally severed.

Enemy vessels took multiple hits before dropping out of formation. The alien fleet suffered masochistically startling losses. The huge formation of seventy five alien craft had been reduced to less than ten vessels as they approached the Martian orbital station.

Holding their tight formation, the skeletal remains of the enemy armada targeted the orbital station instantly vaporizing it using their coalescing laser attack. They turned once again to firing as individual units on the attacking strike craft.

"Son of a bitch. Damn them all to hell!" Sydes exclaimed.

Standing as a helpless witness millions of kilometers from the action, he watched as the enemy fighters peeled off from the vessel that formed the centerpiece of their formation. The solitary aerodynamic craft kicked into hyperburn and entered the thin Martian atmosphere on a heading directly toward the center of the domed civilian complex.

Diving on and destroying the remaining enemy fighters they now out-numbered by almost ten to one, the remaining strike craft completed the destruction of the enemy escort craft. A few strike craft hung at the edge of the thin Martian envelope of atmosphere. Despite the fact they had no atmospheric maneuvering capacity, one of their number dove after the aliens' flying bomb. In a matter of seconds, the strike craft spun out of control and was soon reduced to a flaming cinder. It's sister ships watched the bomb speed on its way, unwilling to fire their own fusion volleys after it for fear of adding to the force of the aliens' attack on the Martian colonies.

Moving at a speed that caused her hull to glow even in the thin Martian atmosphere, the alien missile struck the domed complex. Immediately upon impact there followed a blinding flash of light. The initial flash dissipated rap-idly, only to be succeeded by a series of detonations that marched outward in concentric circles from ground zero. Scanners revealed an incredible uplift of the planet's surface and an expanding crater around the center of ground zero with rippling waves of destruction spreading out over the Martian des-ert. The devastation was more than anyone on the bridge and in the imaging room could possibly have imagined possible from a single strike. The Martian landscape seemed to ruffle and roll like a vigorously shaken carpet. Billows of dust rising through the thin Martian atmosphere escaped the planet's gravity, obscuring the holocaust boiling on the surface.

Reorienting the imager, Commander Tutunji activated the battery of scanner buoys along the radioactive cloud to visualize the alien battleship. He watched as the huge vessel slowly turned and disappeared into the fusion mist. As Sydes had suggested, she had been stationed there to guard the gate and provide cover for her fighter group. No fighter craft would be returning and she was going back to her fleet.

"That juggernaut is retiring," Tutunji reported as he transmitted the feed to the bridge.

"Yeah, I see her going home. She never intended to join the fight. The mission was about the missile strike on Mars. I wonder what's next ..." Sydes responded.

"Captain Sydes, the Duo is flight ready," Von Strohheim said, interrupting Sydes.

"Yeah ... thanks Doc," Sydes replied.

Commander Sadad operated mechanically now to ward off the horror of three million deaths on Mars. He dispatched fifty of the station's shuttles to the planet to search for survivors and provide whatever aid they could. He had witnessed the primary and secondary blasts on the planet's surface and knew the rescue mission was pointless. However, he also knew that not making the effort would leave the station's personnel with a gaping loss and no way to fill the cold dark hole that had swallowed three million of their fellows.

After issuing a general recall to the strike craft wings, Sydes joined Tutunji in the imaging room. Opening his link, he called Von Strohheim and asked him to join them there.

Becoming quite a virtuoso with the imager, Tutunji acquired new scanner angles to circumvent the dust cloud that hung over what had once been a domed complex housing more than a million families. Quickly imposing a tactical grid onto the scene of the Martian devastation, Tutunji looked up from his efforts.

"How bad is it?" Sydes asked.

"The new scanner angles get us around the dust cloud. What they reveal is beyond belief," Tutunji replied.

Rapidly activating its several functions, Sydes used the remote to expand the tactical grid to the limits of the missile's zone of destructive influence. Where once a domed complex stood, housing over three million people, was now a crater five hundred kilometers in diameter. Beyond the crater, the Martian plain had been swept clean of any evidence of hills or even rocky prominences. In its place, there was an expanse of sand fused glass stretching out another one thousand kilometers around the crater. Transfixed by the image, Sydes didn't notice Von Strohheim as he entered the compartment.

"Mein Gott!" Von Strohheim gasped.

"What would it take for a single missile to inflict this degree of damage?" Tutunji asked as he handed the controller to Von Strohheim,

Concentrating on the sea of glass surrounding the main crater, Von Strohheim focused in on and magnified the image. He activated the scanner's elemental option and carefully scrutinized the readout projected along the borders of the image.

"A single missile did this?" He asked after a moment's study.

"Yeah, one missile approximately the size of one of their fighters. They spent seventy five of their ships making it sure it got to its mark," Sydes replied.

"And our strike craft losses?" Von Strohheim inquired.

"Considerably smaller than in any previous engagement, less than ninety strike craft lost out of a force of two hundred," Tutunji responded.

"A strategy of terror ... they wanted to show us what they can do to a planetary target, and what sacrifices they are willing to make in order to do it. But gentlemen, I fear this was just a demonstration," Von Strohheim said softly.

While his gaze was fixed on the Martian sea of glass, Tutunji's mind filled with a familiar blue-white ball far away.

"So the primary target is Earth," Tutunji murmured.

"Jah, I believe this is their goal. If each missile of this size can level an area of one thousand five hundred kilometers in diameter, it wouldn't take that many to make the Earth uninhabitable," Von Strohheim replied.

"Assuming that's the largest missile they have," Sydes interjected.

"I do not think this is a safe assumption. I believe they would have chosen a weapon to demonstrate, how do you say, the overkill on a relatively small target to make their point," Von Strohheim replied.

"And what the hell is their point? What do they think we're gonna do, just pack up and leave the solar system?" Sydes asked turning to Von Strohheim.

"That may not be far from the truth. The annihilation of the Martian colony is a way of showing us what they can do on a planetary basis without destroying what they actually want," Tutunji said as he stared off into the solar system.

"As insane as it is, this strategy can be understood. Break the enemy's will to resist and take the prize without destroying its value, perhaps as a colony," Von Strohheim remarked.

Sydes had heard that analytic tone in Von Strohheim's voice many times before. It always appeared when the doctor wanted to distance himself from the human variables in the equation and focus on the technical probabilities.

"So, they want the Earth intact. Do you think that means the aliens' needs are enough like our own, atmosphere and gravity, so they could live on the Earth like we do?" Sydes asked as he caught Von Strohheim's eye.

"I think this is a reasonable assumption. Biologically, they must be very much like us. If they wanted the Earth simply as a base for their forces, then, the kind of missile they launched against Mars would have already rained down on the Earth by the hundreds. There would be no need for an object lesson on Mars," Von Strohheim responded.

Tutunji desperately tried to shake his vision of the surface of the Earth reduced to a flattened plane of glass as he began,

"If the aliens are able to breathe something close to what's in our atmosphere and are comfortable with our gravity … damn, if they're like us in other ways as well, then, that means they don't know how or when to give up. They'll just keeping coming at us until they get what they want."

"Or we kill them," Sydes said quietly.

Von Strohheim was concentrating again on the elemental readout displayed in the borders of the image of the Martian desolation. He activated a link with the station's main computer and watched as a series of numbers flashed on the tactical grid's border.

It was obvious to both Sydes and the Commander that whatever Von Strohheim made out of the figures on the screen stunned him.

"The impact site shows clear evidence of a nuclear fusion detonation. But even multiple warheads housed in a single missile could not account for the enormity of the blast area. The weapon can only be a self-propagating fusion device. The initial nuclear detonation brings the materials at the impact site to a state of nuclear fusion. The fusion of these materials ignites matter surrounding the initial site, bringing it to the necessary temperature for a nuclear fusion reaction and the effect spreads. Somehow they have found a way to terminate this reaction or the release of energy from initially inert materials recruited by the original nuclear fusion reaction dissipates as the surrounding materials are ignited," Von Strohheim said, a slight tremor in his voice.

Fumbling with the imaging controller and the concepts that Von Strohheim was spitting out in rapid fire fashion, Sydes looked up at the Doctor.

"So, their fusion missile starts a reaction that, in turn, touches off the rocks and soil and whatever else until the whole system runs out of steam," Sydes said as his gaze fell.

"Yes, this is essentially correct. Even missiles the size they launched against the Martian colony ... mein Gott, if the aliens decided to launch enough of them simultaneously against the Earth, the detonations would have a planet wide effect, with each missile's nuclear fusion reaction feeding off the others. The attack on Mars is a demonstration. How do you say, showing off. The message they are sending us is clear, what they cannot have, they will destroy. The ancient Romans called this the scorched earth ... Jah, scorched Earth ... Alles ..." Von Strohheim stammered.

Listening intently, Tutunji tried to piece together a picture of the enemy's battle plan as Von Strohheim laid out the total obliteration of the human race.

"So, they want to destroy our defensive forces in space, keep the Earth intact, invade and then occupy the planet. And if the bastards can't check off every item on their menu, they'll burn the Earth down," Tutunji said as a look of despair enveloped his face.

"And if they invade instead of burning down the planet, what about the billions of our people on Earth?" Sydes asked.

"I imagine that what elements of the indigenous population they couldn't make use of would be liquidated," Von Strohheim said as the technical tone returned.

"Liquidated ... damn it Doc, that's the whole human race we're talking about!" Sydes exclaimed.

"All of which the aliens would already have accomplished if it weren't for the Doc and the Duo,"Tutunji retorted.

Sydes nodded and managed a slight smile as he turned to Von Strohheim.

"We all know that the next time they come it will be to finish the job. two or more of those huge capital ships will lead the attack. We did a descent job of finishing one off, but two battleships could grind us to powder between them," Tutunji said, his tone revealing his concern.

"Doc, is there anything ..." Sydes began.

"Yes, Captain Sydes. If I may, the second Duo is space ready, but no armaments have been installed, and that will take a great deal of time. As we completed the modifications on the Duo you suggested, it occurred to me that a second tunneling laser could be installed that would operate from the Commander's console. With the improved shield conduction to the capacitors, both lasers could be very effectively fed by enemy fire. I know this is not much, but it will give you a better chance in a simultaneous attack by two of their battleships,"Von Strohheim replied.

Then, Von Strohheim paused and looking down at the floor, an expression of deep concern enveloped his face.

"It is unfortunate, but I suppose unavoidable ... now that the aliens have seen the Duo's firepower in action, every alien ship in their task force will come directly at your ship ... and you, Captain ... and the Commander," Von Strohheim said, muttering to himself.

"So our job ... what we've got to do is to convince these bastards that destroying the human race comes at too high a price," Sydes said.

"If the aliens are as much like us as I'm beginning to believe ... then their strategists are probably sitting down right now thinking they have to convince us of the very same thing; namely, that resisting them is suicidal,"Tutunji said dourly.

"Yes, I believe this is what the corporate people call the cost-benefit analysis, but the cost is so much blood ... so many brave young people ... I just don't ..."Von Strohheim muttered and drifted off.

"Perhaps that is simply something we must accept ... all that counts is that someone survives to carry on,"Tutunji interjected.

Staring in complete silence, the three men stood, each lost in his own thoughts, as the image of the crater and the surrounding glassy plain filled the screen around them. The encompassing monitor vividly portrayed the only marker left to testify to the passing of three million men, women and children who died in an object lesson. Then, one by one, the men filed quietly from the imaging compartment, the specter of the Martian desolation on the viewer a silent witness to both their grief and their resolution.

Chapter 22

Frenzied but purposeful activity best described the increased productivity among the construction and technical personnel working on the ark and Chauvez knew why. News of the complete annihilation of the Martian colonies had galvanized the crews into speedy action with a renewed sense of purpose. The rate at which the work was proceeding showed an almost a thirty percent increase. Every man and woman in the huge construction force gave their best in the hope of completing what they imagined would be their new home before the aliens found their way to Earth and Cabot's moon base.

Cabot's devotion to the speedy completion of the ark came in the form of an engineer to replace Piatra in the number two supervisory position. The position had remained unfilled since Piatra's death and Chauvez had simply assumed it would remain so given that the ark was nearing completion. The replacement engineer was a young woman about Piatra's age whose name was Ashley. Although her credentials were impeccable, the most remarkable aspect of this new hire was her physical resemblance to Piatra. Certainly not a clone, she could easily have been Piatra's more docile sister. Ashley, possessing none of Piatra's rebellious fire was nevertheless a damn good engineer and easy to work with. Chauvez quickly came to rely on her expertise. Interactions with the construction crews demonstrated a management style radically different from Piatra's. Ashley listened to her staff, encouraged and praised their efforts, and pitched in to assist those on the front line when required. Piatra had always enjoyed the respect of her crews, but Ashley had both their respect and their affection.

A dramatic increase in the frequency of Cabot's visits to the ark matched the construction workers' intensely focused efforts. That Cabot found the news of the destruction of the Martian installations personally troubling was apparent by his presence for four hours of every day looking over plans and encouraging the supervisory staff. After one of these visits, Phil pulled Chauvez aside to relate his concerns about Cabot's increased attention and vigilance.

"In all the years I've known old Nick, I've never seen him so worried. He doesn't usually micro-manage and never deals with personnel that he doesn't directly control, much less something that has the catastrophic potential of an alien invasion," Phil said in a soft whisper.

Phil cast a suspicious glance about the bridge before continuing.

"Recently, Nick has been so distracted by the war and completing the ark I wasn't in the least concerned about using Dvorak's stealth scanner to get the frequency subspectrum of his mastoid implant. I have known Nick for centuries and, regardless of the pressure, he always remained cool, informed and in control. Now, he's as close to coming apart as I've every seen. If he were capable of having a heart attack, he'd probably have one now."

"No heart attack for Cabot, not until the ark is finished. Then, he can save us the trouble," Chauvez responded, chuckling in the throes of a bout of dark humor.

Taking note of Phil and Chauvez's conversation, Dvorak approached the two men with a flat screen in hand, a poorly suppressed evil grin on his face. He laid the flat screen on the console and pretended to show the two men something depicted on it.

"The horror at the Martian colony has worked in our favor. Cabot is spending much more time on the bridge, close to the source of the signal. The process is moving forward at a faster pace than we could ever have hoped. Once we have canceled out the subspectrum of frequencies in which his signal is nested, we can choose our moment," Dvorak said in a low whisper.

Phil pretended to be examining something on the screen as he spoke in muted tones.

"How long?"

"If Cabot continues to visit the bridge regularly, a week at the outside. After seven days, we can attack the link that ties him to the main computer and, then, his head explodes," Dvorak said, tracing an imaginary line on his flatscreen.

Marveling at the hate glowing in Dvorak's eyes, Phil pondered for a moment how long Dvorak would have lasted had he worked and lived as close to Cabot as Phil had. The answer was simple, not very long, despite the obvious talents he brought to the table. Cabot would have arranged an accident for Dvorak long ago. Phil's centuries of regret for his part in Cabot's many atrocities, large and small, was enormous and he couldn't simply dismiss it. However, his complicity had positioned him to do a favor for his species by severing the dark hand that reached out of the shadows to create so many of their troubles.

A raucous clanging of the bridge's proximity alarm abruptly terminated the exchange among the enclave of coconspirators and each quickly returned to their stations at the bridge console.

Discovering almost immediately what had tripped the alarm, Chauvez terminated the clanging. Climbing into orbit around the ark were two cruiser class gunships with Cabot's silver corporate logo emblazoned on their sides. The black hulled ships, about four times larger than corporate strike craft, were fitted with formidable laser turrets, as well as, fore and aft missile launch tubes. The size of the vessels suggested they were autonomous units designed to function without stationary bases such as the corporate strike craft required. The crews of these craft never had to leave their vessels except to reload spent missile racks, making these ships independently secure islands of firepower.

Hurrying to Chauvez's station at the console, Dvorak appeared anxious to share some information.

"I wondered what was going on. About five days ago, I got orders to redesign one of the shuttle bays in the ark to accommodate two large craft. Well, there they are," he announced with his usual measure of self-satisfaction.

"So, whatever purpose they're to fulfill now, they'll get tucked into the ark when she pulls out of orbit," Chauvez remarked.

"Exactly," Dvorak responded.

An entranced audience, the entire bridge complement watched as the two sleek cruisers took up positions about one hundred thousand kilometers from the ark. Chauvez's quick vector calculations placed the orbit they assumed directly between the ark and the likely trajectory of an attack by the alien armada.

Phil's intuitions were dead on, Chauvez thought to himself. Cabot was worried. More to the point, Ole Nick no longer seemed certain the Earth Defense forces could hold the line until he had completed his ark and made his getaway.

At shift's end Phil, Dvorak and Chauvez always made sure that they left the bridge at different times. They had no further need to meet even in the privacy of one of their compartments. Phil had provided Dvorak with all the information he could and Dvorak's frequency generators hummed along twenty four hours a day, absorbing the designated frequency subspectrum. Dvorak had planned well. If none of the coconspirators were alive to push the button that would channel the ark's reactor output along Cabot's dedicated frequency, then, a fail safe mechanism would do so automatically within twelve hours of achieving the target frequency.

No one knew better than Chauvez that no plan was fool proof. However, this operation qualified as a viable approach to the problem. The plan was simple and made efficient use of all information and resources available to the three men who were indispensable to Cabot and his project.

Fatigue rested on his shoulders like some ancient yoke, but Chauvez didn't want to go back to his compartment and spend hours with Piatra's ghost haunting his loneliness. Pausing a moment at a junction in the passageway, he decided to follow a small group of bridge personnel to a bar that had just opened in the executive recreational sector of the ark.

Magnificently appointed, natural dark woods and rare leathers adorned the bar wherever the eye fell. All this finery had been 'generously' supplied by the inhabitants of Cabot's many reserves on earth. Living plants were scattered about and several aquariums, bubbling merrily away, featured a rainbow of tropical flora and fauna. This was not an establishment for construction crews who did their drinking at the moon base. This bistro was for the supervisory staff who took the heat for everything and anything that went wrong on the ark.

Plagued by hunger as well as thirst, Chauvez elected to find a booth instead of sitting at the bar. Glancing at the lavishly appointed cubicles lining the walls, he noticed Ashley, his number two, sitting by herself. She smiled and waved him over. Her smile was much more appealing than the perfunctory collegial expression of passing approval typically exchanged among the bridge professionals.

Approaching the booth, Chauvez noticed immediately Ashley wore, not the standard black and gray disposable unisuit that Cabot issued to all of his employees, but a translucent white silk blouse and a knee length natural suede skirt. By both manner and attire she looked inviting. His decision to join her may have been driven by the fact that he missed Piatra or, perhaps, he simply didn't want to spend one more night alone. Whatever the reason, mustering his best smile, he strode the last few steps toward Ashley.

"Hi, mind if I sit with you?" Chauvez inquired.

"I was hoping you would. I don't like to eat alone," Ashley responded.

Arriving almost immediately, the waiter took their order. Ashley wanted a gin and tonic, while Chauvez ordered a triple shot carafe of special reserve tequila. They jointly decided supper could wait.

Well schooled, the wait staff promptly attended to the needs of the executive staff and, so, in moments the drinks arrived.

"The war has really got everyone on edge," Ashley remarked as she sipped her drink.

"I know. People are throwing themselves into the work to keep their minds off everything they can't control," Chauvez replied.

"But, it's exciting work. Just imagine, a real colonization effort. The ark is a first. It will carry so many people and a sampling of flora and fauna from the whole planet to a new start, somewhere out there," Ashley responded, her eyes brightening.

Staring analytically at this beautiful young woman whose appearance so mirrored Piatra's, he wondered how two individuals who looked so much alike possess such radically divergent perspectives on the same event. Piatra had been so cynical and direct, while Ashley was so naive and hopeful. A small enclave in his mind set about the task of trying to digest these discrepancies as he put away another shot of tequila.

"If the war continues to go badly, the ark might well represent all that's left of our species and its origins," he remarked.

"Such a sad thought. I'd rather focus on equally likely positive outcomes. So many brilliant people working so hard to save and disseminate our life form and culture. The ark represents the whole history of our technological progress focused on one single thrust into the galaxy," Ashley said as she took another sip of her drink.

Noticing his carafe was nearly empty, as was Ashley's glass, Chauvez ordered another round. As Ashley's gaze roamed over the patrons in the restaurant, Chauvez took the opportunity to study her face and compare the woman before him with the veridical image of Piatra in his head. Restricting her focus as much to the superficial as Piatra had always searched for dark and covert purposes in the most mundane of events, these two women were, apart from outward appearance, about as different as they possibly could be. Chauvez felt an attraction to this woman with whom he had no history, while, at the same time, he felt guilty for being so easily separated from his memory of Piatra. Yet one fact was undeniable, whatever he and Piatra had, she was gone and Ashley was here. Life is for the living, make the best of the moment, and many more self-serving aphorisms occurred to him as he dove into the conversation.

"Regardless of what happens, it will be a great adventure," Chauvez added, conforming his mood to hers.

"Oh yes, so many able people, like Phil, whose expertise has uprooted ecosectors thriving as though they are still on Earth and Doctor Dvorak, who has designed whole new technologies to manage the automation of the ark's systems. And, of course, you, designing and engineering the ark so everything functions as a unit," Ashley replied enthusiastically.

Feeling just a trifle off balance in the face of such praise, Chauvez remembered such ego enhancing statements were not something he was accustomed to hearing from Piatra, even on her best day.

"The real miracle is that everyone works together so well. Particularly on a project like this that's so complex and layered, with so many overlapping components," he remarked.

Upon the waiter's return to their booth, they decided on a sampler of appetizers including bread, cheese, oysters, shrimp and fruit. The waiter was back almost as quickly as the transubstantiator could spit out the order with the platter and refills for their drinks.

Seeing the food, his nose filled with the aroma drifting up from the plate of delectables, Chauvez's hunger reawakened and he dug into the oysters.

"You have any family at the moon base?" Chauvez asked between bites.

"No, just a mom and dad back on Earth. I had a someone special, but he was killed in an accident," Ashley replied.

"I lost my fiancee in an accident as well … not that long ago," Chauvez offered, his cautious demeanor drowning in a sea of tequila.

"I'm so sorry. I know how lonely it feels when you lose someone that close," Ashley offered.

Empty, the appetizer platter somehow reminded him he would be spending another night alone with Piatra's angry ghost. He decided to try a rewrite of his usual nightly script.

"Would you like to come back to my compartment? I just got a bottle of white chocolate brandy from a cousin in Venezuela," Chauvez asked.

Ashley's expression fairly glowed with the selfsame smile Chauvez had seen earlier when she waved him over to the booth.

"Oh, dessert. I must admit a weakness for sweets. That sounds great," she replied.

Unsteady as he and Ashley were on their feet gratis their alcoholic indulgence, the walk back to Chauvez's compartment nevertheless proceeded at a fairly rapid pace. Two chocolate brandies later they were a tangle in his bed. Ashley was much more vulnerable than Piatra, but no less passionate. Chauvez rated his own performance as mediocre, but he slept through until morning, something he hadn't done since Piatra's death.

Despite the relaxing nature of the previous night's activities, he awakened with a start and immediately noticed that Ashley had left. Dragging himself out of bed, Chauvez downed a cleaner capsule with the last of the chocolate brandy in his snifter and dragged himself into the sonic shower. Cleaned up and almost mentally oriented, he pulled on a unisuit and started for the compartment door. He passed his personal, computer console, which was stationed on the way to the door and immediately noticed the manual access was in standby mode. He thought it odd as he almost never used that feature, preferring voice access for its speed. He used manual access only if someone else was in earshot of the computer and he required privacy. He thought little more of it as he was already late for his shift.

Entering the bridge, Chauvez saw immediately he had picked a bad day to be late. Cabot was there surrounded by some of his security people with Phil and Dvorak standing at the periphery of the group. Cabot motioned impatiently for Chauvez to join them.

Pausing only momentarily as he passed Ashley, Chauvez asked her to take over his station at the console, and strode quickly to join Phil and Dvorak.

"I wonder if we could meet in the planning compartment?" Cabot said, wearing a concerned look.

Then, turning quickly, Cabot entered the compartment that adjoined the bridge, his entire security entourage in tow.

Chauvez shot Phil a questioning glance, but Phil just glanced down at the floor and gave a slight negative nod.

All of Phil's attention seemed focused on Dvorak, who appeared very apprehensive. Standing reassuringly close to Dvorak, Phil appeared to be saying something quietly to the nervous automation engineer.

In moments, everyone had found a place around the conference table. Cabot's security people stood at attention behind each person seated at the table. They maintained an anxiety provokingly close stance at the conference participants' backs.

"My security people indicate there may be a plot afoot to sabotage the ark," Cabot announced as he came abruptly to his feet, his eyes gleaming with a hard analytic glint.

Chauvez noticed beads of sweat beginning to appear on Dvorak's forehead.

"The three of you are in the best position to spot any anomalies in construction or operations that might suggest tampering. I'd like to know if you have seen or heard anything, no matter how apparently insignificant, that might indicate an attempt to undermine this project?" Cabot inquired.

"Everything seems to be ahead of schedule. The systems diagnostics we're running on a daily basis come out clean," Phil responded immediately.

"That's good, I suppose, but, I'd like the systems diagnostics run at the end of every shift instead of once every third shift," Cabot snapped back.

Taking note of Dvorak's growing apprehension, Chauvez decided to try and defuse the tension growing in the room.

"I have independent inspection crews running one shift behind every construction job, checking everything that's going into the project."

"Did I authorize that?" Cabot shot back at Chauvez.

"No Sir, you did not. I thought it an expedient precaution," Chauvez promptly replied.

"Very good," Cabot said.

Dvorak, shot a glance at Phil and Chauvez, took a deep breath and launched into his report.

"All the computers and servo's are online. Now, its just a matter of tying everything together and junctioning the circuits to the bridge and your compartments."

Dvorak paused and, producing a handkerchief, he mopped his forehead before continuing.

"Laying down over five billion circuits slowly and carefully takes one hundred percent less time than placing one incorrectly that will throw the whole electronic array into rolling chaos," he said in his best definitive tone.

"Point well taken, Doctor. Thank you for your time gentlemen and please don't think I'm not appreciative of everything you've accomplished thus far. I just want to be certain everything meshes nicely now that we're so close to completing the project," Cabot said almost deferentially.

Pausing for a long a moment, Cabot looked intently at each of the three men who were absolutely essential to the completion of his project, in turn. Then, accompanied by his security personnel, he briskly exited the planning compartment.

Functioning as a signal, the soft click of the compartment door sealing instantly prompted Dvorak to produce his electronic sweeper cube from a jacket pocket. Holding it under the table out of sight of the compartment surveillance cameras, he activated the mechanism, which suspended itself above the floor. Three of its six antennae remained extended and glowed fiery red. Dvorak produced another mechanism from his pocket and touched it to the cube suspended beneath the table. The three red antennae turned green and retracted into the cube.

"The room is clean," Dvorak announced.

Replacing the little electronic marvels in his pocket, he leaned back in his chair now visibly less anxious.

"I've redirected the signal from Cabot's surveillance devices to the bridge's digital storage. When his security people look at the microdiscs from the devices they've sequestered in here, they'll see an empty room. Synchronous readings from the bridge will show the three of us working in front of our respective stations at the console for this time interval. As soon as we're finished here, I'll make the adjustments in their spy scanners on the bridge to reflect a cross over between the planning compartment and the bridge surveillance devices. I'm the guy who created the state of the art surveillance circuits and I'll guarantee you his security people don't have them. If they catch it at all, which I doubt, they'll figure it was just a glitch," Dvorak said and smiled.

Phil got up from the table, tripped the security locks on the planning compartment door and turned to Dvorak.

"I'm impressed," he said.

Taking a moment to indicate his approval of Dvorak's competence in circumventing Cabot's security measures with a nod and a smile, Chauvez turned to Phil.

"So, what was that all about?" Chauvez asked.

"I've never seen Nick do anything like that before. Based on past performance, he typically says nothing at all and, then, one day there's a terrible accident and his concerns are alleviated. If I had to guess, I'd say he was trying to flush the game from cover," Phil said as he walked back to his chair.

"What the hell does that mean Phil?" Dvorak exclaimed.

"Nick's suspicious, but I'm reasonably certain he doesn't have anything concrete to go on yet. If he did, we'd all be dead and your subspectrum frequency generator would be so much junk floating in space," Phil replied as he looked down at the table and brushed away some dust that existed only in his imagination.

"So, he's trying to generate some panic?" Chauvez remarked.

"Exactly. He may believe he has something in hand or it may be just war jitters. I don't know. I'm just certain I've never seen Nick on a fishing expedition like this before. He usually gathers all his information covertly and, then, acts without warning," Phil replied.

"Could it be the subspectrum frequency generator is fucking with his brain?" Chauvez asked, pointing the question to Dvorak.

"No, I don't think so. I check those circuits daily for any changes in the feedback parameters from his central computer. No anomalies are registering. His central computer's diagnostic programs are more likely to target left over microwave radiation from the big bang than what we're up to," Dvorak replied.

"So there are only a limited number of possibilities. He's got something to fuel his suspicions, he wants to frighten us into showing our hand, or he's got nothing but generalized paranoia and he's fishing," Chauvez said.

"Got something or got someone?" Dvorak said as his gaze drifted to Chauvez.

Appearing startled, Phil turned abruptly to face Chauvez.

"Chauvez, yesterday, I saw your number two down in the automation section with what looked like an electronic scanner in her hand. I think she may have seen me because, by the time I got to where she was snooping around, she was gone," Dvorak said as he leaned toward Chauvez.

Sitting stock still, Chauvez suddenly felt as though any movement might cause his entire frame to fall to pieces. His midsection felt like someone had just detonated a fusion grenade in his gut as the aftershocks coursed through his body. The expression on his face must have betrayed something of what was

∽ 317 ∽

transpiring within, for as he looked up, both Phil and Dvorak stared at him.

"I'm your weak link. I should have known. It was all too easy, too perfect to be real," Chauvez said hesitantly.

"What the hell are you talking about?" Phil asked.

Taking a deep breath, Chauvez reflexively reached for a drink that wasn't there and, instead, began to draw interlocking circles on the table with his finger.

"My number two, her name is Ashley. She picked me up in the bar. Damn, she was so smooth and she looks so much like Piatra," Chauvez muttered.

"Then she's the one I saw in the automation section, yes … yes?" Dvorak said, his voice trembling.

"Yeah, that's her. She stayed the night in my compartment. In the morning I noticed that the manual standby on my personal computer was still active, but I didn't think much of it at the time," Chauvez replied.

"Now, this is important. Was there anything in that computer that could jeopardize our plans?" Phil said in a deadly serious tone.

Chauvez stared off into space as he took a moment to think through the contents of the computer.

"I don't think so. Just some schematics of the ark, technical stuff I work on after hours, and, and … damn, some journal entries."

Phil's eyes popped wide open as centuries of patience and diplomatic decorum fell away.

"Journal entries, shit! What's in the journal?" Phil snapped.

"Not much really, just some drunken ramblings about how much I missed Piatra and blamed Cabot for her death," Chauvez muttered.

"Not much … that's motive and Cabot knows that of all the people working on the ark … shit … the three of us are in the best position to destroy his creation, and … and … that's opportunity. It's no wonder Ashley was skulking about in the automation section. I'm the biggest threat to him. If Phil's ecosectors croak, Cabot can just dig up more of the planet, but if the automation section is sabotaged, the whole damn ark can go up. Hell, I'm a dead man!" Dvorak's shouted as he got to his feet.

"Relax, Dvorak. Just sit down. I think its pretty clear Cabot aimed Ashley directly at Chauvez. I've got the ecosectors and Dvorak has automation, but nothing really catastrophic could happen to the ark without Chauvez. He's in the perfect position to detect evidence of sabotage and, if he didn't report anything suspicious, he'd have to be part of the plot to make it happen. It's just like Ole Nick to pick the pivot point in a system to make his intervention. He must have gone to a hell of a lot of trouble to find a woman who looked so much like

Piatra," Phil said in deadly even tones as he looked directly at Chauvez.

"I don't think she got what she was looking for in the automation section. The feedback parameters were nominal last night and this morning. But you've got to know that if she's as bright as she seems to be, and has enough opportunity, sooner or later, she'll find something she knows shouldn't be there," Dvorak said as he regained some of his confident tone.

"Chauvez … damn it all … Chauvez. You know that we can't take the risk. Maybe its all coincidence, but we can't stake our lives on that gambit. I think the most convincing piece of evidence is her presence in automation. Nothing in her job description should take her down there," Phil said softly, his eyes dulled by a deep sadness.

"Listen Chauvez , she has to …" Dvorak began.

"I know … I know. She has to go. It's my fuck up and my job to clean it up," Chauvez interrupted, his voice heavy with resignation.

"You've never killed anyone before, have you?" Phil's asked in subdued tones.

"No," Chauvez replied, his eyes glued to the floor.

Chauvez's head felt so heavy he doubted he could raise it. Suddenly, it seemed as though the flow of the entire history of the universe had been damed by some bulwark that had been erected between his ears. Now, as if from a great distance, he could hear Phil's voice.

"I'm ashamed to say it, but, I know first hand Cabot has arranged the deaths of more people than I can count … and … God help me, I was there."

Phil paused for a moment, buckling under the weight of the words he was speaking and the memories they summoned.

"Ashley must die in a Cabot style accident and it must occur in the normal course of her duties. No one else must be involved in making it happen beyond us three and each one of us must be above suspicion."

His eyes remaining fixed on the floor, Chauvez saw there in its polished reflective surface, as if in an endless video loop, Piatra's shuttle impaled by one of Cabot's girders. The vivid memory was imbued with its own vigor. The energy of revenge burned away the feeling of helpless inertia that had paralyzed him. His eyes brightening, he looked up from the images his imagination projected on the deck and presented the plan forming in his mind.

"Next shift Ashley is scheduled to inspect the blow out seals in the bulkheads between compartments. The last seal she's scheduled to test is between an airtight compartment and one open to space. Despite repeated warnings, she never wears space gear during these inspections. The inspection requires her to activate the blow out option with the safety switch online. If I disable the safety switch, and adjust the relay so the icon indicates the safety switch is still active ... I guess the rest is obvious."

"Yeah, she gets sucked out into space and Cabot is forced to come up with another way to spy on us," Dvorak interjected.

"You know we're all in this together. Is there anything we can do to help?" Phil asked as he shot Dvorak a critical glance.

"Look, I'm sorry I was so blunt, but what we're planning for Cabot is like working with a sharp knife. When you cut, everything falls on one side of the edge or the other. I don't know why Ashley is doing this, maybe Cabot's leveraging her or maybe she volunteered. It really doesn't make much difference. If she succeeds, we die. And what's worse, our funerals mean Cabot gets to play God forever and ever," Dvorak said as he turned to Chauvez.

Chauvez's gaze was focused once again on the deck and his body rocked gently back and forth in his chair.

"Listen, I'll get you a relay that will do exactly what's needed in this situation. It will require all of five seconds to remove the original and drop the rigged one into place. The whole incident will look like it was caused by a bad relay that got by the factory inspectors," Dvorak said, his tone softening.

"Thanks, I'll install the relay at the end of the shift. I'm scheduled to do a walk through on that section anyway," Chauvez replied.

"There's no good way to do this. As long as there are Cabots, there will always be people of good conscience forced to destroy in order to preserve something greater than themselves. Its in our blood from the beginning, a symphony of destruction pointed by the need to dominate, and counterpointed by resistance to domination, with fear as the melody line," Phil said as he stood and placed his hand on Chauvez's shoulder.

Dragging himself out of the chair, Chauvez felt as though he were weighed down by some version of the chains of Marley's ghost in a Dickensonian reality.

Noticing Chauvez's uncertain steps as he rose from the table, Phil stayed by his side as they walked to the door. Dvorak brought up the rear, realigning and activating Cabot's surveillance devices as they left the planning compartment.

Striding immediately to his station at the bridge console, Dvorak made the necessary adjustments in the digital replay from the bridge surveillance monitors and then accompanied Chauvez as he exited the bridge.

"I'll meet you at the number twenty one junction in about fifteen minutes with the new relay," Dvorak said and disappeared down the passageway.

Trudging down the passageway at a rate much slower than his usual gait, Chauvez felt heavy and despondent. His mood approximated that of the accused in a capital punishment proceeding rather than Ashley's executioner.

It was worse than that, he thought, as images of Piatra and Ashley merged together in his head. What Cabot was to Piatra, Chauvez would become to Ashley. Perhaps what Phil said was correct, Cabot made all things like unto himself. To deal with power, you were eventually forced to use the tools and methods of the powerful. Power, its acquisition by the few, made the task of the many simply that of defending against the momentum of power's application. Regardless of one's role in this melodrama, the actions and motivations of all participants were gradually transformed into varying shades of gray. Issues, causes, injustices, retributions and, indeed, all other historical labels were but incidental to the savageries that themselves remained the only lasting testament to the history of human interaction.

As he rounded the bend in the passageway that would bring him to the number twenty one junction, Chauvez saw a man just ahead of him who looked from the back, very much like Phil. As he reached the junction, he saw his impression had been correct. Phil rounded up the construction crew working there and led them, amidst stories and laughter, away from the bulkhead area Ashley was to inspect. Pausing a moment, Chauvez considered how consistent this action was with his impression of the man. Phil made certain that there would be no collateral loss of life. Faint footfalls awakening him to someone approaching from behind, he turned quickly to face Dvorak who, with grim determination, pressed the relay into his hand and disappeared back down the passageway.

Moving purposefully to the bulkhead that interfaced between the airtight compartments of the section and the vacuum of space, Chauvez opened the control face plate. Quickly exchanging the relays, he closed the unit. How simple, he thought to himself, he had just extinguished a life without breaking a sweat or getting blood on his hands. The ease with which he performed his part in this deadly dance horrified him almost as much as the murder itself.

He made his way back to the bridge by another route with considerable haste. He was certain he couldn't carry this off if he met Ashley face to face in the passageway on her way to do the inspection. Passing several section Chiefs enroute, he failed to offer his usual greeting. His master motivation at the moment was to be on the bridge before Ashley reached the fatal endpoint in her inspection.

As he entered the bridge, Chauvez saw Phil and Dvorak giving a good impression of busying themselves at the bridge console. Approaching his own station, he noticed one console monitoring camera was trained on the bulkhead that was Ashley's last inspection stop. He vainly tried to focus his attention on supervising the realignment of some of the ark's internal supports, but found his eyes straying to the monitor tuned to the soon to be murder scene. The bridge seemed somehow darker than usual, but a check of the internal illumination indicators revealed they were set to the standard number of lumens. The darkness was within, not without.

Unconsciously managing to redirect his attention to the realignment operation, the sounding of the alarm caught him completely by surprise. A startle reaction, the magnitude of which surpassed anything he had ever felt before, almost caused him to lose his footing. His gaze snapped to the monitor just in time to see a body propelled from the bulkhead into the vacuum of space amidst a cloud of frozen atmospheric gases. Reflexively, hitting the magnification icon, he recognized what was left of Ashley's exploded remains.

Like a tidal wave quick frozen just before it broke onto the beach, the intervention of response protocols that long years of training caused him to activate automatically held the reality of the horrific circumstances of Ashley's death in abeyance. Dispatching a shuttle to pick up what little was left of Ashley and instructing crews to replace the seal in the bulkhead were all necessary actions that would support Chauvez's avoidance of the horror of what he had done. He would renounce his role in this tragedy as the villainous murderer and reemerge cloaked in his helpful and concerned administrative role.

Setting everything in order required all too little time and, once again, Chauvez's thoughts turned to Piatra. It was almost as if the image of Piatra's death formed a rampart between his vision of himself as a good man and the reality of his role in Ashley's murder.

Clustered like so many attentive hens clustered about a clutch of broken eggs, one shuttle assisted in the bulkhead's repair, while a second, holding the single largest part of Ashley's body in its manipulator arms, moved toward the receiving bay. The personnel division would have some remains to send back to Ashley's parents, which was more closure than Piatra's family achieved.

Backing away from the console, several of the supervisory Chiefs offering their condolences for the loss of his number two approached Chauvez. These expressions of sympathy prompted his realization that he could leave the bridge now and no one would think anything of it. As he took the few steps that would bring him to the bridge tube, he recognized that leaving was the safest course. He knew he couldn't vouchsafe his own words and actions if he remained among all those saddened by the loss. As he entered the transport tube and called out his level, he realized he would be returning to a compartment now haunted by the angry ghosts of two women, both of whom had just cause against him.

Chapter 23

The sun must have been shining in his face for some time given how close his bed was to the window. It's light had not disturbed him until now, and, now, looked very much like noon. Mentally, Forrester had been awake for some time, which was rather odd given his slow brain warming profile. He located himself physically sitting on the edge of what had turned out to be a very comfortable bed. Although his body desperately tried to resurrect itself from his nocturnal near death experience, the inside of his head was so busy he wasn't certain he could redirect enough energy to his limbs to rise from the mattress.

Like a jumble of ice floes piled by the spring thaw into an abstract representation of a mountain, the events of the past day presented themselves in a solidified tangle. The mass of interlocking factors so overwhelmed him that he didn't know where to begin even the most rudimentary form of analysis. He had witnessed phenomena among the people of the trees that scientific thinkers much more brilliant than himself had only dimly and incompletely conceptualized. Now, come to pass, the intimations of poets and mathematicians, ancient and modern, were in large part realities in this genetically isolated knot of humanity.

Names and paradigms streamed through his head, perhaps recruited by some recalcitrantly analytic portion of his mind to avoid the very conclusion for which he had for so long and so vainly searched. That conclusion now loomed like an insurmountable peak before him; namely, that a transcendent force stood behind all the ephemera of life.

Watson's ancient observations, coded as the hundredth monkey principle, suggested it was always the young who experimented with the novel in the environment. The children led the way and taught the adults. Certainly that fit Crystal. The fact the whole community of the people of the trees could now match Crystal's perceptions and abilities was the critical mass aspect of the phenomenon. According to Watson's observations, with the acquisition of an ability by the theoretical hundredth monkey, the new ability became universal in a species. The children were the hundredth monkey for their parents and for the entire community of the meek. But the transfer from child to parent incorporated more than learned behaviors. It was palpably apparent that sensory and cognitive abilities were also being passed back a generation. This was something the human species had never before achieved. Yes, species, Forrester thought to himself, that was the key. The people of the trees were a new species, humanity plus something. This assumption, appearing to follow from the facts and his experiences, seemed in every respect correct and, given that assumption, all the other pieces fell into place .

Sheldrake's hypothesis of formative causation and the theory's central notion of of morphogenic fields forced its way into Forrester's consciousness. A real mouthful for what most people saw as the simple manifestation of Zeitgeist, or the tendency for lots of people to independently develop the same idea at the same time. The concept was delicious, a nonenergic transfer of knowledge and perceptive ability across time and space within a species. There was no mechanical model for what Sheldrake observed during his lifetime, although he inferred a transcendent something that stood behind and within all that is this universe, as well as, yet undiscovered dimensions. Somehow, embedded in the ether, were blueprints for form, perception, cognition and behavior that governed learning and growth for a species and functioned to direct its evolution toward some continuing culmination.

His frenzy of ideas, theoretical models and mystical conjecture had reached its own version of critical mass. All the pieces fit together too fast for him to track. It was as though that part of Forrester that had experienced the transcendence of everyday reality evident among the people of the trees was trying to come to terms with the muddling, analytic component of his mind that had always determined his conscious experience of himself. The battle between transcendental experience and analytic reason had been fought to a stalemate.

Like a well deserved respite, reflexively taken from hard labor, his mind cleared. As had occurred so often before, Forrester simply stopped trying to reconcile the competing perspectives in his brain. On this occasion, the termination of this willful cognitive struggle represented a conscious decision on his part. He was prepared to accept, without any sense of personal defeat, that such battles were not a win or lose proposition. The battle itself was a signpost that pointed to itself and demanded a childlike openness to a new idea waiting impatiently in the wings.

The new idea came in the form of entries from the scrolls that positioned themselves implacably on center stage in his mind.

NONE OF THE EVERLASTING FIRE THAT
THE WORDS HERE SET TO PAGE MIGHT
IGNITE SHOWS UPON THE FACES AND

IN THE EYES OF THOSE MET UPON EACH
MARKET DAY. LIKE STONES STACKED
INTO A WALL, TIME MUST BE SET UPON
TIME UNTIL THOSE WHOSE LIGHT IS NOT
REFLECTED BUT SPRINGS FROM WITHIN,
LIGHTING THE COUNTENANCE AND FILLING
THE EYE RISE FROM THIS DUST AND JOIN
THEIR ILLUMINATION TO THE WHIRLING
DANCE OF TIME, LIGHT AND LIFE.

FROM THOSE AMONG WHOM I
SOJOURN, BLOOD INTERTWINING
OVER COUNTLESS GENERATIONS,
WILL ONE DAY COME SOME WHO,
IN LOOKING, SHALL SEE BEYOND
AND THROUGH THE HIGH TERRACES
THAT TIME BUILDS UPON THE BONES
OF ITS CHILDREN. THESE, ALSO IN
LISTENING, SHALL HEAR THE SINGLE
UNENDING REFRAIN THAT CHANTS
ITS WAY THROUGH ALL THAT HAD,
HAS AND WILL HAVE LIFE.

LIKE CHILDREN, OPEN AND TRUSTING,
THEY WILL KNOW, ENFOLD AND BE
ENTWINED IN THE WEAVE OF THE
UNIVERSE. RECEIVING IN THAT EMBRACE
THE STRANDS AND STREAMING OF THE
LIGHT THAT ILLUMINATES THE NOW.
WEAVING THEIR NEST OF THE LIGHT, THEY
WILL FLY UPON COMPASSION'S WINGS
UNTO A HAVEN WHERE STRIFE SHALL
FIND NO ROOT.

Illumination was the only word that even approximated what Forrester
felt at that moment. His analytic prowess had not been relegated to the dust
bin. However, a burgeoning belief that such analytic plodding represented the
long way around was lifted, in a single moment of self-verifying enlightenment, from the status of potential truth to tangible reality.

Words whispering through the millennia, the diarist's words were shattering to what Crystal had called Forrester's individual separate and alone 'I.' This simple message gently dismantled his little shelter from the woes of the world, his haven of private solace. In these scroll entries resided a view of the *now* through which Forrester and the people of the trees were passing. Of even greater significance, the words seem to point beyond themselves to a destiny that made this small planet seem even smaller. The people of the trees certainly seemed to fit the diarist's description of those 'who in looking shall see ... and who in listening shall hear.' However, Forrester had the feeling they and he hadn't seen or heard even the smallest portion of that which was to come.

Whether from within or without, he could not point to the direction from which his sense of assurance flowed, but with an increasingly calm certainty, he recognized that some transcendent force operated among the people of the trees. Even more personally significant was the fact that, to the extent that he was with and among them, he participated in some small measure in that transcendence. For the first time in a life of searching for that which stood behind the Platonic appearances of reality, he felt he had arrived at 'Start' in the game. Joining the game in which the meek were the principal players, provided him with no clear idea of, either how it was played, or the goal toward which it was directed. The only scrap of certainty he could muster resided in the assurance that this was a new game, one such as mother Earth and her long time dominant species had not seen before. Without benefit of knowing the source of his surety, he was convinced the board on which the meek's game was to be played extended far beyond this tiny planet sequestered in one remote spiral arm of the Milky Way.

Scrolling intrusively into his consciousness, another entry from the diary seemed to confirm his personal epiphany. This passage seemed to command the attention of every cell in his body. Like the roots of some great living tree, the 'Y' shaped sense of invigoration, now permanently resident in his head, seemed to extend its tendrils throughout his body in a network of energy and insight. He was no longer just a brain, fed by the convenience of a body to nurture and transport it about. He was being pulled together by an internal force with an external origin of which he had become a part. As before, but this time with greater depth of resonance, the Diarist's words boomed out and seemed to shake every molecule in his body.

SUFFERING, LIKE A BAPTISM IN COLD DARK
WATERS, SO CHILLS BODY AND SPIRIT THAT
HOPE IS SUSTAINED ONLY BY HUDDLING
NEXT TO THE FIRES WITHIN THAT COME

DOWN FROM THE FLAME OF ALL BEGINNINGS.
HERE ONLY, DO I SEE BEYOND THE
LIGHTLESS TOMB OF THIS WORLD TO THE
WARMTH THAT WAS AT THE START. THE
GREAT CIRCLE WHOSE BEGINNING IS ALSO,
IN ONE TIMELESS MOMENT, THE END CALLS
TO ME. I LONG FOR THE VISTA OF THE NOW,
FOR HOME.

THE NOW IS THE LIGHT BEYOND THE
RISE AND FALL OF THE STARS. THE
SPARKS OF AWARENESS FROM ALL
THE BEFORE AND AFTER EMBERS OF
LIFE MERGE INTO THE ONE GREAT
LIGHT THAT IS AT ONE MOMENT THE
EVERLASTING NOW.

IN THIS ONE ETERNAL MOMENT IS ALL
LIFE AND LIGHT CREATED AND, FOR
THIS CAUSE, IS THE UNIVERSE SPRUNG
INTO BEING. AT REST WITHIN THIS
CIRCLE OF ALL KNOWING, WOVEN
RIGHTLY TOGETHER, ARE SUBSTANCE
AND SPIRIT UNITED, BANISHING
FOREVER THE ILLUSION OF DIFFERENCE.
I YEARN ONCE AGAIN TO EMERGE
FROM THIS WOMB OF FLESH.

Revealed in these few modest words of the diary entry was the unbreakable unity of all living things, separated only by their manifestation in the persistent illusions of past, present, and future. The realization did not prompt Forrester to want to rush out and become a cleric. However, as a scientist, he was now prepared to embrace the great universal knowing embodied in all that had, now has or would have life. This trans-mortal awareness abolished all doubt it was life that was nested in the everywhere center of the transcendent NOW.

Given the small spark with which he was now imbued, Forrester could finally comprehend the yearnings of the Galileen carpenter who wished only to be freed from his prison of flesh. Finally, he understood. The sacrifice of the carpenter was not realized in his death on the cross, but in his birth. His entrapment in flesh represented the ultimate estrangement from the circle of light that was his rightful home. To be born was to be exiled to a tiny portion of the all encompassing NOW. It was to wander in darkness, having known the LIGHT. The symmetry implicit in this vision embodied a universal perfection. The whole, could for a brief flickering of time, become one of the parts as the carpenter so clearly illustrated in his private journal. However, as Crystal had dramatically shown Forrester, the individual and separate 'I' representing but a single spark from the eternal fire was destined to wander in darkness so long as it clung to the desperate belief that it was the whole.

Expanding his growing appreciation of the diarist's poignant sacrifice, another entry scrolled into view gently compelling Forrester's attention.

> BENEATH KINDLY SPRING SKIES, I OBSERVE
> THE SOWERS IN THE FIELD. HOW SIMPLE IS
> THEIR HANDIWORK. WITHIN THE SEED IS
> LIFE IMPRISONED, WHICH WATER FREES AND
> SOIL NURTURES. AS SPRING ROUSES THE
> SOWER, SO I AM CALLED BY LIFE, SCATTERED
> IN PIECES FAR FROM ITS BIRTHPLACE, TO
> GENTLY BECKON IT HOME.
>
> WHERE THERE IS LIFE, I AM SUMMONED
> TO VOICE THE FRAIL WHISPER OF BEGINNING'S
> REMEMBRANCE TO THE FORGETFULNESS OF
> FLESH. FROM ONE TO ANOTHER SWIRLING
> CONGREGATION OF STARS I JOURNEY, AGED
> BEYOND TIME'S COUNTING, YET, ALWAYS
> AND EVER NEWLY CRAFTED TO FINITE FORM.
>
> UNDER SUNS AND SKIES OF MANY HUES,
> I WITNESS IN PART TO THE WHOLE THAT
> CAN BE FELT BUT NOT SEEN. I AM IN THE
> BEGINNING OF THAT WHICH HAS NO END.
> I AM THE WHOLE OF ALL PARTS, I AM THAT
> WHICH BINDS THEM TOGETHER.

Echoing over and over in Forrester's head, the phrase, ' I am that which binds them together' seemed, by repetition to compel and confirm its significance. The diarist was a manifestation of the nexus that lay behind space and time itself, linking all of creation together. Not matter, not energy, nor space-time, not even the universe taken as a whole, but that which secured all those partial manifestations together at once and forever into a continuous and uninterrupted living fabric. Although he could not fully comprehend the concept that sang its way through three thousand years in the words of the diarist, Forrester recognized the music in the words pointed beyond this little planet and the galaxy in which it circuited to a larger universal symphony.

Something in the back of Forrester's head said, 'enough,' without actually forming the word. He was hungry, but more compelling than this fundamental drive was a newly forming sense of being separated from a community of which he had become a part. Before meeting the meek, to work and produce had been enough to round out his life. To be sure, there were invisible vacations that consisted in rejuvenating moments of turning inward to play in the endless universe of his thoughts. But, for a man who had spent his whole life creating niches to be alone with his thoughts, this sense of separation was novel. He would dispel this feeling of isolation. Pulling on his clothes, he hurried downstairs.

❦

Entering the living-dining area, Forrester immediately noticed the large glass table was laden with fruit, bread, cheese, cups and a large carafe of coffee. In that same moment, Esther, Jacob and Crystal entered from the terrace.

"Good morning Doctor Forrester," Esther said as she poured a cup of coffee for him.

His nose told him the brew that Esther was pouring into the cup, adding evaporated milk, to half its contents was orange cappuccino.

"How did you know?" Forrester asked pointing to the steaming cup.

"You are linked to our community now. Much, but not all, of what you need, feel and think is known to us," Esther responded.

Considerably less palatable than the steaming brew before him was the notion his inner life was common knowledge among the meek. With all of his abstract and transcendental visions of the linkages in the great universal fabric of space-time to which the meek were party, Forrester had overlooked one thing. He hadn't taken into consideration that one of the practical ramifications of this insight would have to be a complete transparency of thought and feeling among the members of this community.

"What does it mean when you say that you know much, but not all, of what goes on inside my head?" He asked.

"In time, none of this will require explanation. When we meet one another or just think about the community and its members, we see needs, feelings and thoughts as a panorama of colors. A person's needs are often displayed as red, orange, and sometimes brown. However, brown, only appears if that individual's needs are unmet. Emotions display themselves in a range of colors that include the yellow, green and blue part of the spectrum, while thoughts are represented by an iridescent white with a luster greater than the purest light you can imagine," Esther replied, an accepting smile on her face.

"So these colors are a lexicon of the contents of a person's internal experience?" Forrester asked.

"The colors act, not so much a lexicon as, a reference resource to the nature of the content. The intensity, distribution and volume of space within the person's aura the colors occupy tell us whether the person is concerned with needs, feelings or thoughts, and to what degree. The content of the person's needs, feelings and thoughts is imbedded in, but not wholly explained by, the colors," Jacob added as he continued the explanation.

Forrester finally felt as though he was getting a sense of what amounted to mind reading among the meek. Somehow, they actually experienced the feelings, thoughts and needs of others visually. More to the point of his own personal fears, it appeared each individual wore their inner experience as a kind of technicolor display. He suspected more than the obvious was subsumed by the word 'aura', but elected not to address that issue head on.

"So the colors tell you the category of experience, but not the particulars of the content?" Forrester asked.

"Yes and no ... within the community, we know each other so well that the colors also reveal the individual's need, feeling and thought content. That's because our familiarity with that person tells us what their particular color distribution and patterns have meant in the past. The continuity in the rainbow of their aura over time suggests what I guess you'd call their personality," Esther replied.

The specter of being completely transparent to those around him compelled Forrester to continue his investigation into the degree of privacy he could hope to retain in this community.

"I'm still stuck on the notion of the community knowing much, but not all, of what I think?" He asked.

"The phrase, 'not all,' refers to something we no longer experience in the community, although we did when we first gathered together. Now, it is something we notice only in a newcomer like yourself and in those who are not part of the community. Those needs, feelings and thoughts a person conceals from others are colored in grays and blacks. When we see those colors, we do not go there. Those who are not of the people of the trees are mostly gray and black, but sometimes tinges of red, orange and green appear in their auras," Esther replied.

Forrester decided to more thoroughly investigate the possibility of telepathic abilities among the meek. They were clearly a genetic branch that diverged from the mainstream of the human species and perhaps telepathy was one of the innovations evolution had thrown in for good measure.

"So, you can see into those not in the community, but they cannot see into you?" Forrester asked.

"No, that would be coercion, representing an attempt to dominate another person. When a person looks into another, this is accompanied by a simultaneous revelation of the seer's inner experience that in depth and intensity matches the sight into the other person in both kind and degree. This cannot be avoided. We cannot see into those not of the community, except to notice the colors they carry. We are unable to reveal ourselves to them because they are closed off from each other and from us. Each interaction among the people of the trees is a simultaneous exchange of the nature and content of what you would call our inner selves," Jacob said emphatically.

"Then, it's reflexive reciprocal empathy, not telepathy," Forrester muttered to himself.

"What were the words you said?" Crystal asked turning to Forrester.

A bit startled by Crystal's question, Forrester looked over at her. He had been only partially aware he had been thinking out loud.

"Reflexive reciprocal empathy ... I guess it means you automatically get only as much as you give," he responded.

"Good words," Crystal replied.

Then, with a delighted smile on her face, Crystal went back to eating her banana.

Forrester had a question he knew he had to ask. He was also aware that if he had correctly understood all he had been told, he would not necessarily get a direct answer.

"And what do you see in me?" Forrester asked.

Esther and Jacob smiled as Crystal put down her banana and took Forrester's hand in hers. The effect was immediate and dramatic. Forrester could see in and around Crystal a shining white light touched at the edges in hues of purple and light blue. He could also see himself transparently superimposed on her tiny body, mirroring that selfsame aura with a patch or two of gray positioned over the site on his head where, deep within, lay the locus ceruleus. That made sense, Forrester thought to himself, all sorts of obsessive thoughts and feelings ran in circles there.

Releasing his hand, Crystal stepped back but Forrester's 'seeing' continued. The auras he saw had a glistening transparent quality that in no way interfered with, but certainly added to, his understanding of his surroundings.

He turned his gaze to Esther and saw her dazzling white aura with hints of pink at the periphery. Those pink tinges at the edges of her aura evoked a memory. Then it struck him, the aura was the passive pink hue research done over a millennium ago had demonstrated evoked a calming and nonaggressive response from the beholder. The color registered in the eye and in the brain of the human species eschewing dominance and encouraging selfless cooperation. Jacob's sphere of light mirrored the sparkling white of his spouse's aura with the blue of loyalty and tranquility at the fringes of his orb of radiance. As Forrester glanced about the room, he noted everything that had ever been alive radiated its own unique aura. Everything that was once a plant, like the wood of the furniture, carried hints of blue, green and yellow. If the origin of the object had been animal life, like the leather covering the seat of an antique chair cushion, then, its aura contained faint orange and deep red hues.

Where life was still present, as in the plants scattered about the room, a glowing yellow-white, brushed with hints of blue, green and deep yellow, predominated. A fossilized trilobite resting on a shelf to one side of the room expressly drew Forrester's eye. Even this specimen of rock, which was but a mirror of a living form from the Paleozoic era, was haloed in a very faint bubble of orange. Given his brief exposure to the phenomenon, he thought that the aura of life must grow more faint with the passage of time, but, as the trilobite illustrated, it never entirely vanished. As this bit of rock so clearly showed, to have tasted life was to share in the illumination of all that had participated in the animation of the universe. Indeed, it appeared that to have enjoyed that peculiar confluence of molecules called life guaranteed permanent membership status in the fellowship of light.

Wholly enamored with the light show in continuous performance all around him and completely oblivious to Crystal's family, Forrester rose and took the few steps to the terrace. As he strode into the sunlit afternoon, the impact of the illumination coming from every direction momentarily overwhelmed him. Light streaming in myriad shades from the soil, plants and even the waters of the small lake below the terrace seemed to encompass him. He felt as though he were suspended in a sphere of illumination as life radiated its signature everywhere he looked. Beneath his feet, the wood of the decking shown in soft greens and yellows, while in the lake he could discern the silhouettes of plants and fish below the surface, each outlined in its own native aura of greens, blues and reds. Reflexively taking a few steps backwards, he reminded himself to breathe. All of this had always been here, a symphony of phosphorescent radiance playing for eons to a species, who, although sentient, was blind to the infinite carnival of beauty through which it sojourned. He felt a small hand in his and, turning, walked with Crystal back into the relative darkness of the room he had just before seen as so generously illuminated.

Forrester sat down. The energy of fascination seemed to drain from him. He was certain, although he could not see it, the expression on his face must have fit the definition of dazzled. As he surveyed the now comparatively gloomy interior of the house, something nagged at the back of his mind. He had an infuriating sense that something was missing. This feeling of lack of closure had represented a particularly vexing cognitive state for him all of his life. Then, quite unexpectedly, it came to him. In the vast palette of colors he had observed from the terrace, there was no illuminated purple.

Surveying the room yet again, he recognized the absence of the color purple here as well. To be sure, some flowers and fabrics carried that color, but nothing was encompassed by a purple aura. No living plant or person, nor indeed anything that once had life, was clothed in an aura with a purple hue save Crystal's and his own. He was in the process of framing a question about the purple auric inclusions when Esther answered it.

"That's correct Doctor Forrester, only you and the children of the people of the trees carry that color," Esther said, wearing a caring and solicitous smile.

As he prepared to ask what the purple hue indicated, Jacob began to answer Forrester's not yet fully crafted question.

"We believe, you and our children are part of some larger community. This community includes the people of the trees but extends so far beyond this place and time we cannot see its boundaries, if it indeed has such limits," Jacob said.

Had it been, in fact, intended to, the answer conferred no greater degree of certainty or content than Forrester had in formulating his question. The only light imparted by Jacob's response was inferential. His answer seemed to suggest purple pointed beyond itself and its wearer. Forrester correctly anticipated the single word that the associational network in his brain would cough up in response to Jacob's answer, namely, 'transcendence.' Purple was the signpost for transcendence. Then again, he wasn't at all certain what Jacob meant and it sounded like he wasn't either. Forrester now understood what Chen had mentioned about the silences he observed at the community's meetings. In this brief exchange with Crystal's family, it was apparent that audible speech was inefficient, distracting and largely irrelevant.

A simple glance at Esther and Jacob demonstrated they agreed with his last unspoken statement, but no words had been exchanged. Apparently, they had looked at his auric light show and understood his intention. Nevertheless, talking would be hard to give up altogether. Probably out of deference to his felt need, Esther and Jacob waited for Forrester to utter his next question, which had to do with the color gray. Since Crystal had made his seeing possible, he could almost feel the gray areas in his aura as cold spots in his head.

"What are the gray areas in my aura?" He asked.

"The cold gray areas of concealment are misunderstandings born of a truncated vision. You believe that in finding the scrolls and concealing them, you deprived your fellow man. This perceived wronging of your brothers you, in turn, believe has caused humanity to be visited with the terrors of the war and thwarted the mission of the diarist," Esther said, her tone kindly.

Forrester took a deep breath, knowing he wasn't exhaling. Esther could obviously read him, or more likely his aura, like a book. Exhaling, he looked up and saw Esther staring at him. She leaned forward as if to soften the blow of what she was about to say.

"To hold these things to be true, you must also imagine yourself as competent to unravel the tie that binds all of creation together. In truth, you have only done what you were called to do. Now, you are summoned to a new task. The first step of which is to lay down this exaggerated sense of personal responsibility and the last vestiges of your conviction of individual power that lie at its root," Esther said, her tone compassionate.

Swallowing hard, Forrester knew his alimentary reaction represented an outward sign of an inward process. As a neuropsychologist, he knew the psychodynamic connections Esther had delineated were coherent. Her insights were penetrating, but provided without a shred of condemnation. Forrester allowed the ramifications of her statement to spin out through his head with full knowledge that what he was thinking was obvious to those around him. Such cognitive-affective transparency, which should have represented a horribly disconcerting moment of stark naked emotional exposure, was instead an oddly freeing experience. The difference between the sense of comfort and peace he enjoyed in this moment and a life spent sequestered in the apparent safety of his own private cognitive fortress seemed a self-verifying miracle made personally manifest.

Wearing the onerous yoke of personal responsibility that always rested firmly on his shoulders regardless of what he did or failed to do was something he had experienced all of his life. With Esther's prompting, he could plainly see this collar had been crafted of raw materials mined from a deep and covert conviction of personal power and prerogative. An occult narcissism lurked in his psyche that at its foundations, denied the possibility of positive action by any agency greater than himself. A quiet and slyly unobtrusive monster of the id left over from a million childhoods stretching back to the first frightened cell huddled in upon itself against the hostile darkness was the culprit. This refractory vestige of the unconscious primitive, firmly entrenched in the mind of man, could not be slain, only entreated to leave. Certainly, no power existed within the upper echelons of the human psyche capable of casting out this primeval gargoyle. On his own an individual could accomplish no more than mixing the orange of desire and the black of negation to produce an enamel of the brown bile of denial to coat the limbically charged troglodyte. Suddenly, Forrester felt the gray blotches in his aura as palpable intrusions representing the talons of this chimera of primal instinct. He knew them now for what they were and desperately desired to be freed from their grip.

"These are not blemishes, but wounds received in conflict. They will heal more rapidly than you can imagine. You were the first of us, always alone and with no rational hope for the future. Soon, you will see you did no less and no more than what, without your knowledge, you were required to do," Esther said with a tone of comforting certainty.

"I say these things plainly because the gray of your pain distorts the feelings and thoughts of one who has been so wounded. He, whose hand touched quill to the scrolls, left a great record of words and deeds among those who journeyed with him in the flesh for all to see and study over these three millennia. They have their witness to the truth. The scrolls were left through you to us alone. All you have done and left undone is in keeping with that mission," Jacob said, echoing his spouse's sympathetic tone.

"Crystal only appears to be the first child born to the meek. Without parents from among them, you are the first child born to the people of the trees. You are Crystal's elder brother, and, at once, father to us all," Esther added.

In the midst of a cognitive revolution, Forrester felt he was undergoing a metamorphosis of his personality as well. The clash of past and present self-perceptions represented such a diametric contrast that it no longer concerned him that thoughts and feelings read like banner headlines to Crystal and her family. In childhood, Forrester viewed himself as a spectator upon, and, in adulthood, an investigator of, the human condition, but almost never as a participant in the parade of his fellow creatures' endeavors.

Jacob's sent a clear message, Forrester had always been an actor, albeit unwitting, in a drama he had no hand in writing. Now, the meek told him he had some role to play in their joint destiny and he didn't even have a script with which to study his part. His theological training coughed up the Biblical story of Jonah, with Forrester in the staring role. Except for Forrester, there was no ship to carry him away from the frightening mission of preaching Nineva's sins much less a rising storm to cause him to be cast into the mouth of a great fish. In any event, it didn't work out very well for Jonah and a replay with Forrester cast as the hapless Jonah would probably not turn out much better.

Right down to his toes, he knew he wasn't up to any quasi hero shit. They had the wrong guy. This job would take somebody, or more properly, a whole bunch of somebodies, with a hell of a lot more on the ball than he had going for him, or for that matter, ever had.

Practically in mid-thought, he felt a change in his body, accompanied by an increasing sense of clarity in his thinking. He felt warmer and somehow lighter. Instantly, he recognized he had been staring at the floor since Esther had spoken to to him. Looking up at the pillars of light that were Crystal and her parents, he moved his gaze from one to another and immediately saw his own aura superimposed on each of them. Pure white light, seemingly brighter now than before and crowned in purple hues surrounded his own image. He became a seamless pillar of iridescence without any patchy gray areas.

"Welcome Doctor Forrester ... welcome to the people of the trees. Welcome home," Esther said, her smile as inviting as her words.

Confronted by this little family of light, Forrester stood speechlessly before those who represented, both the means to an end, and an end in itself for his life. In sharp contrast to a lifetime of sojourning inside his head, he enjoyed his complete awareness of his surroundings. In that moment, he found himself completely immersed in the lights of life emanating from his own kind, as well as, all inhabitants of the biosphere, past and present. He became slightly disoriented by the feeling of being a solitary individual who drew sustenance from the great community of life, returning energy in kind at a cellular level. However, he also felt free and comforted in a way he had never before experienced.

"That your life's journey has always been upon a path leading to the *people of the trees* is foreshadowed in your name, Doctor *Forrester*," Esther remarked.

This revelation of the obvious tie between his name and that which the community had chosen to call themselves felt simultaneously comforting and frightening. Forrester had always seen himself as directing his life or, at the very least, cautiously picking his way through a maze of forces over which he had no control. Vainly perhaps, his thoughtful meanderings had always anticipated the arrival at some personal signpost of insight. Based on Esther's remark, he now had to factor in some meta-organic force that was summoning all the elements of his life, and perhaps those on the broader stage of history, to a final consummation of which he played but a small part. What was it that Crystal had said, something about the individual and separate 'I' going away before you could see the NOW. Well, it felt like his 'I' had just taken a permanent leave of absence.

"But Doctor Forrester, we have kept you too much to ourselves. It is time you met with the whole community," Jacob said as he took a sip of coffee.

The prospect of what he had been led to believe was to be a meeting with about one quarter of a million couples startled Forrester.

"The whole community!" He said.

"We'll meet at the service center. Many who living nearby will be there in person. Those who reside far away will attend holographically. The entire community will be in attendance and each one of them is very anxious to meet you," Esther offered.

Invested now with a better understanding of what that simple verb, to see, meant for the people of the trees, he could better appreciate what the rest of the community wanted to *see* in him. Glancing over at Jacob, Esther and Crystal, he saw his own auric outline superimposed on the several members of the family.

"OK, so, I guess they want to see is a purple adult," Forrester responded.

Quite unexpectedly, Jacob laughed. As he did, his aura expanded well beyond the limits of his body. The spreading globe of illumination scintillated as though the lights around him danced with merriment. Jacob's aura spread until it encompassed Esther and Crystal, who also began to chuckle.

As he watched this spreading aura of good humor, Forrester wondered whether the notion that laughter was contagious had its historical roots in an unseen, but somehow otherwise sensed, appreciation of this phenomenon.

"Yes, yes ... they want to see a purple adult. I did not mean to offend, Doctor Forrester, but even Crystal did not foresee your sense of humor," Jacob replied, finally controlling his laughter.

His remark hadn't been intentionally humorous, but its effect on what had otherwise been a very heady exchange was nevertheless welcome. Slowly, the waves of laughter subsided, providing him with the opportunity for another question.

"What will the community expect from me?" He asked.

"No one knows what to expect. That is why there is such anticipation in the community. No other adults have purple auras, you are the only one," Esther replied.

Forrester felt the teeth of performance anxiety gnawing at his gut.

"But, what am I supposed to do?" He asked.

"This is the most difficult part of the transition for you Doctor Forrester. Among the people of the trees, what you do is who you are, both as an individual, and as part of the entire community. Your purpose, what you do, will be revealed in interaction with the community," Jacob said.

"Are you ready?" Esther asked Forrester.

"I hope so," he replied.

Internally, Forrester recognized the 'hope' in his response provided the only beacon in an otherwise foggy appreciation of what was to come.

Walking to the large holographic transmitter built into the wall, Esther placed her hand on the identifier receptacle and the screen instantly brightened.

"All," she said.

Forrester watched carefully, but saw nothing more than the screen darkening as Esther turned to face the family.

"We can go to the service center now," she said.

Scurrying away in a burst of purposeful motion, Crystal left the room. In moments, the hopper stood at the ready in front of the house. Esther, Jacob and Forrester boarded the transport. Within minutes, the craft settled onto the turf in front of the service center. The green valley was alive with the meek, with many disembarking from their craft as more hoppers crested the trees preparing to land in the broad meadow.

Stepping out of the hopper and onto the grass, immediately Forrester was surrounded by a throng of children. It's the purple, he thought to himself. They hugged him and hung onto his knees while he waved to their parents, who smiled and nodded in response. Despite all the personally transforming events Forrester had experienced in the past few days, the attention and touch of these children was the most completely fulfilling. Although he had never had children, these children seemed to be his. Bright and hopeful, they represented a living beacon pointing to a now and future time of selfless confidence in a providential outcome for the species.

Crystal threaded her way among the other children and took Forrester's hand.

"It's time to go inside," she said.

Crystal escorted Forrester into the service center, waving to the throng of happy children as they dispersed to their parents.

As soon as he entered the service center, Forrester passed Chen in the lobby. He nodded and Chen smiled and nodded in return. Forrester felt a twinge of embarrassment as he noted Chen's aura was gray and green below his neck, with a dull white and blue showing around his head. Next to Chen stood Chandra, who Forrester somehow knew was connected to Chen in an intimate way. Very little light showed around Chandra. In fact, she appeared a uniform gray with large black and red splotches scattered within her aura and over her body.

❀

Instantly, Forrester knew why the people of the trees could not read the needs, feelings and thoughts of others. If, revealing one's inner self was an unavoidable prerequisite to reading the inner selves of others, no revelation of self was possible if the other party was, in largest part, invested in the gray of concealment and the black that represented the extinction of life and hope. Black, and to a lesser extent gray, represented either an indiscriminate mixture of all colors absorbing all light or simply the absence of light. Regardless of the definition one applied, the presence of black and gray in an individual's aura suggested most of that person's available energy was directed to concealment, rather than self-disclosure.

Holistic and reflexive confession of the self among the meek could speak only to its own kind. It became clear why the dominance deficient had always been victims among their fellows in the larger arena of human interaction. In some nascent form, this need for self-revelation had always been present among the dominance deficient, and was always accompanied by a reluctance to consciously deceive others. This lack of prowess in deception, coupled with the tendency to reflexive self-disclosure, had made them the foreordained prey of the dominance driven majority of humanity.

Concealment and deception were the strengths of the bulk of the meek's fellow travelers in the great journey of humankind. Concealment, growing out of a need for security, created separation, mistrust and therewith the need to control one's life space. In a relentlessly morbid line of reasoning, concealment generated the need to dominate or otherwise control one's own feelings, thoughts and actions, as well as, those of others.

Evolution's next great gambit was here before him in the person of the dominance deficient. For eons without number, evolution had favored the predatory majority of humanity and mandated survival of the fittest, entailing secrecy, duplicity and dominance. In the ascendance of the meek, there would be open and straightforward revelation of needs, feelings and thoughts, unavoidably and unmistakably portrayed in the auras of the people of the trees.

The great Darwinian experiment of raising the sheep with the wolves had failed. Self-disclosure and deception could not live side by side. All that remained of that four billion year old evolutionary venture were wolves feeding off of one another. The dominance driven had all but exhausted their supply of open and trusting prey within their own species. In the people of the trees, nature corrected that error, but how and what form this remedy would take remained a mystery to Forrester.

In moments, Forrester and the others entered a large and spacious hall that accounted for the bulk of the service center. Members of the community filled one quarter of the room, while three quarters began filling with holographic images of those who lived too far away to attend in person. Those present holographically appeared as three dimensional projections at every elevation within the hall, but demonstrated no aura. Forrester found this interesting. It appeared life could not be electronically scrambled and then made manifest in its most intrinsic and illuminating aspect.

"Doctor Forrester is among us at last," Esther announced as she rose and addressed the assembly.

"He has come as our children said he would. He is to be our lens, a focal point for that which we need, feel and think within the corporeal universe," Esther said, motioning for Forrester to stand.

Feeling the perfect fool, Forrester stood there not knowing what to do with his hands while Esther portrayed him in terms for which he had no referents in his personal experience.

"We may all now consider that which is to come," Esther announced and sat down.

Without fanfare or clamor, a spectacular view unfolded before him as the auras of those assembled in person seemed to brighten and expand until the whole assembly appeared as unified light source. The holographic representations crackled with static and flashes of light, finally merging into a single light source that, in turn, merged with that emanating from those physically present. It would seem, he thought to himself, that the force of life could supersede electronics with sufficient need.

Slowly, a single source of illumination that represented the entirety of the community formed itself into a sphere and rose from the floor, suspending its progress upwards midway between the floor and ceiling. The sphere contained streaks of light that seemed to originate from an infinite number of points within its voluminous interior. The bolts of illumination, impacted at almost every point on the internal surface of the orb, added their aggregate illumination to the radiant appearance of the sphere. The translucent globe of light, remarkably bereft of any trace of gray or black, seemed otherwise to contain generous pools of almost every tint and hue imaginable, save only purple.

Without any conscious consideration of his actions, Forrester stepped forward and touched the surface of the immense orb of energy. Simultaneous to his touch, Forrester saw beyond and away from himself and the sphere of light toward an image forming as if upon some great three dimensional screen suspended in space. The image gradually resolved into a great gray ball resting in a hand so black it seemed to bathe everything around it in ebony radiation. Traces of red appeared between the knuckles of the swarthy hand and, gradually, the fingers opened, releasing the ball to float freely in a star studded void. The ball suddenly took on an iridescent white glow and moved off, dwindling to a speck in the depths of the screen. Then, the screen was gone, as was the singularity of the meek's sphere's light that had filled the auditorium. In its place were the people of the trees, both in the flesh and those electronically transmitted.

"It is sufficient?" Esther asked as she rose to address the assembly.

No one spoke and no disturbance in the aura's of those assembled in the great hall occurred. The participants, who had resolved again into individual outlines of light, seemed, in a way that defied description, to emanate satisfaction.

"We are all enlightened by a vision of the now that is to come. We are grateful for he, who serving as our lens, has allowed us to see beyond this place and this now," Esther said, nodding to Forrester as she addressed the assembly.

Dumbfounded best described Forrester's state of mind. He had seen what everyone else had, but he in no wise perceived himself as involved in what had occurred. In fact, he wasn't even sure what had happened. It was compelling, whatever it was. As far as Esther was concerned, it was a view of the future, but a future event that would occur some distance from the service center in which they gathered. Perhaps that's what Esther meant by a lens, something, in this case someone, namely, himself, who could focus in on nows to come in distant places. To be sure, Crystal had shown him the past and future of a mountain range, but only from the solitary perspective of the ledge whereon they had stood. What happened in the service center reached far beyond the place they were all assembled.

It was tough enough to become accustomed to seeing people as light sources, now he was being hit with some kind of community generated clairvoyance. Frankly, he thought to himself, it was all a little too much.

<hr />

Quite unexpectedly Forrester found himself thinking about his university teaching experiences so many decades ago. Every new crop of graduate students got the same introductory speech outlining his research in axiomatic terms. He always uttered the same opening line. Right hemispheric processors, those who ran businesses, governments and fought wars, represented the majority of the human species whose first reflex was to act. Personal manifest destiny directed their actions with negative outcomes, resulting principally from the collision of mutually exclusive goals among the contenders. Any untoward consequences flowing from the actions of the right hemispheric processors were managed internally through denial and projection, while deception provided the ultimate tool for managing externally obvious misadventures. Misdirecting the minds of others from the negative outcomes of actions taken for the purpose of self-aggrandizement formed the core of all political successes. Finally, the right hemisphere maintained a tranquil psychic environment by forfeiting the welfare and lives of those who fell in the not-me category. All was expeditiously accomplished in the service of the greater narcissistic good.

Left hemispheric processors, of which the meek represented a pure type, had to make things right in their heads before they acted. An endlessly cycling loop in their minds was driven by neither dominance, nor self-interest. This perpetual strand of curiosity and service spiraled within each individual and, also, wended its way through the community of like minds. Curiosity, conscience and service bound the meek together in a quest for right intention as a prerequisite for action.

The extraordinary events Forrester had witnessed that day conformed to his model of left hemispheric functioning. The people of the trees were not looking for some way to alter the future. Representing lines already drawn on the map of space-time, the greater NOW, past, present and future was immutable. For the meek, altering the future would be to order the universe of space-time in a manner other than it was meant to unfold. Such actions would represent an attempt to dominate, indeed, to coerce the universe to their will. The people of the trees already perceived themselves as infinitesimal bits of the volitional nexus of the universe and, so, any attempt to alter the NOW would not only represent coercion, but redundancy. The dominance deficient simply wanted to understand and, through that comprehension, find their place in what must be.

The meek had always lacked, in a population top-heavy with their dominance driven fellow creatures, the narcissistic confidence with which the majority of the race was so richly favored. Evolution was in the process of correcting this oversight by granting the dominance deficient, in place of the gift of unbridled confidence conferred upon their brethren, an absolute vision of the expanse of space-time.

Nature created right hemispheric doers first. Forrester clearly saw this as essential to the survival of the species. The genetic code of doers, of necessity, entailed domination and, in particular, a mandate to manipulate, victimize and even destroy knowers. Perhaps 'slaying the dreamer' was more than a finely tuned bit of prose, he mused to himself. Eradicating the not-me knower gene pool became part of the basic programming meant to secure the future for the me-genes of doers. By isolating the dominance deficient from their doer fellows, Ole Nick had unwittingly served evolution's agenda. Cabot had created the structure evolution required to realize the maximum return on its investment in both the doer and knower elements of the human species. For the people of the trees, the knowers, this mechanism consisted in a sanctuary from their dominance driven fellows and the measure of genetic isolation necessary to realize their destiny.

For the people of the trees, knowing represented an end in itself. Even if their knowing amounted to no more than a single ray of the LIGHT of which the diarist had written, that knowing was their lifeblood. Maybe, Forrester thought to himself, just maybe, his research had unearthed a fundamental truth. Lefts change their minds to comprehend the universe, rights change the universe to conform to their needs and desires. Perhaps something foundational to the human condition was embodied in the old saying that those who can do and those who can't teach. Applying this aphorism to the meek required some modification. In the new reading of that old saw, those who don't do, the meek, learn and, serve and in those very acts of service, become teachers by example.

By now, Forrester recognized an upwelling of existential uncertainty was the natural consequence of the rigorous application of his analytic talents. It was almost as if the more incisive his analytic insights became, the more conviction undergirded his belief that his focus had become too narrow. What had he taught his students? Yes, that was it, simplicity evokes complexity and complexity summons simplicity. Personal doubts encompassing all that he had experienced, felt and thought began, like a drop of ink in the water, to pervade his consciousness and muddy the clean straight lines of analytic reasoning. Doubts, as they had on so many previous occasions, now summoned the ministrations of the scrolls. In response to his moment of uncertainty, an entry from the Diary instantly centered itself in Forrester's mind.

FROM THE BEGINNING, WITHIN ONE, TWO
HAVE BEEN SECRETED. IN MILLENNIA'S
COURSE, CLEAVING, THE TWO SHALL EACH
THEIR OWN SEPARATE DESTINY FULFILL.

TILLER OF THE SOIL AND CENTURION OF
ROME'S MIGHT TAKE THE FRUIT OF THE VINE

TOGETHER. THE GRAPE'S BLOOD, AS SWEET TO
BOTH, SETS THE HUSBAND OF THE EARTH TO
HARVEST SONG AND THE SOLDIER TO ANGER.
FROM A COMMON VINTAGE ARE TWO TEMPERS
BORN.

THOSE WHO KNOW AND ARE CONTENTED
BY THE KNOWING SHALL PART FROM THOSE
WHO DELIGHT IN THE STRUGGLE TO WREST
THE UNIVERSE TO THEIR WILL. IN THIS
PARTING, ONE SHALL BECOME TWO, EACH
TRAVELING THE PATH THAT HAS CHOSEN
THEM.

WHEN THOSE WHO CAN SUMMON THE
LIGHT AND ARE COMFORTED BY THE
NOW COME, THE PARTING BEGINS.

A lifetime of research had never afforded Forrester the quality of conviction he felt at that moment. Nudging its way into his consciousness, an old saying rang in his ears, 'the world is what we make it.' Odd, he thought. Perhaps a better characterization of that sentiment would be, the world is who we are ... and now it seemed there would be two worlds.

In that instant, he grasped the knowing of the people of the trees. It was a gentle assurance, like a cool wisp of a breeze, blowing over his face amidst the stagnant heat of an endless summer of need and greed. The meeks' knowing had none of the limbic heat and heart pounding arrogance of doer conviction, nor was it a knowing that inspired awestruck worship. This was an awareness born of the simple but compelling affirmation that one was personally and integrally included in the fabric of all that was, is, and will be. It was little wonder the people of the trees always had a trace of a smile on their faces reminiscent of Da Vinci's Mona Lisa.

✦

Responding to the faraway look in his eyes, Crystal walked out of the crowd and took Forrester's hand. He felt somehow suddenly better for no good reason.

"Time for lunch. Let's go home," she gently intoned.

As they left the service center, Forrester passed among the smiles and greetings of the people of the trees, sharing in the warmth of their presence. Forrester wondered, as he looked into the meek's eyes, how persons in the historical past, whose lives had also been touched by transcendence, reacted? Had they been emotionally affected by those events which for him had so completely overwhelmed mundane concerns? Did those in the distant past feel renewed on a moment by moment basis? Did they have lingering doubts. Did they get hungry, tired or even bored? Were the sacred chronicles from so many different lands and peoples expressly written to make transcendence appear as a continuing experience of rapture? Does a person grow accustomed to transcendence and, if so, did it still inspire awe?

Mingling with the brightly lit individuals surrounding him and seeing his own illuminated image superimposed on theirs, Forrester recognized immediately transcendence was not a simple novelty that would easily dissipate. Beyond the startling character of this revolutionary variety of perception was a quality of open, direct and effortless communion with others he knew would not quickly become usual and customary.

With gentle urgency, Crystal tugged at Forrester's hand, while, with her other, she waved her parents towards the hopper.

"I'm hungry. Let's go. Mommie has halbweiss bread, smearkase and apple-butter just for you and me," she said, smiling gleefully at Forrester.

Of course, Forrester thought. Crystal had sensed a specific craving in him even before he knew he was hungry for that particular childhood memory of the farm.

"Sounds great, Crystal," he said.

Musing aimlessly to himself as they walked to the hopper, Forrester wondered whether the notion of transformation was a good descriptor for the changes the meek had undergone. Transcendence's touch applied to the inertial momentum of evolution had created a new species, but one that shared a common form with its brethren. If transformation was the right label, then it represented a change proceeding by a process of kindly accrual rather than one that swept away the essence of the person and their store of memories.

In a few moments, the whole family had piled into the hopper and, as Crystal activated the controls, Jacob's face took on a peculiar contortion.

"Smearkase?" He said, wrinkling his nose.

The giggling began with Crystal, but, soon, Forrester joined her laughter until mirth and dancing scintillations of light filled the whole cab of the hopper with mirth.

Chapter 24

Emerging from the radioactive cloud, its bloody orange shields shimmering, the alien battleship returned without the seventy five fighter class vessels that delivered the planet wrecker missile. The fleet lay in the vast cold dark that was the immense volume of space between star systems. The operations base ship sat at the center of this immense flotilla. The command vessel was a thousand fold larger than the battleship that had just returned from her Martian mission.

The operations base ship housed the personnel that crewed the armada, as well as, the technical workshops and craftsman responsible for maintaining the enormous fleet. Clouds of fighter class craft and nineteen other ships, sister vessels to the battleship, formed a screen of defensive fire power around the operations base ship, which was adorned with its own banks of defensive weaponry.

The returning battleship's Captain had seen many campaigns in the service of this task force. Like many of his fellow officers, he had risen through the ranks by serving on several of the more than fifty exploratory armadas the empire fielded as part of its colonization outreach. Having been born in space, he had never seen his home world except in the form of holographic images. The birth place of his race was experientially no more or less alien than other worlds the task force visited with the goals of conquest and colonization.

Consistent with the other fleets on which he had served, this armada's mandate required the destruction of the capacity to resist and obliteration of indigenous populations on worlds that could support the empire's subjects. Once the military task force had accomplished its task, colony ships would follow, sometimes decades after the conquest. In the course of less than a century, these new colonies would be expected to participate in the expansion of the empire by building and crewing a fleet of ships to explore systems in their immediate neighborhood of the galaxy.

Genetically selected at birth for his profession as a warrior of the officer class, the Commandant had risen in the ranks on an unbroken wave of victories. His entire life had been divided between training, fighting and ordering others to their deaths. Although he had been conditioned to want nothing more, with the passing of the years, he sometimes felt the potency of the imperial conditioning waning. Yet, through his bureaucratic arm, the Emperor had ordained the Captain best suited to function as this specific cog within the great imperial machine and the Emperor was the empire.

Despite personal doubts about his place in the order of things within the empire, the Commandant knew that those who complained about their station in the vast imperial machine simply disappeared. The Emperor, who sat at the center of the ever expanding web of power that was the empire, was vested with the absolute power of life and death over his subjects. The Emperor, a single being with seemingly endless minions symbolized the irresistibility of his species' expansion throughout this small portion of the galaxy. No mere figurehead, the Emperor possessed both the absolute right and the power to eradicate the entire living genetic lineage of anyone who failed at a task set for them or who otherwise displeased him.

Already over one thousand years old, the Emperor would live, at minimum another one thousand years and, perhaps beyond. Relative to his subjects, who, at best, could be expected to survive only one tenth of the Emperor's current life span, he was immortal. Surrounded by endless layers of security forces whose family's lives were instantly forfeit should any harm befall him, the Emperor was untouchable. Rumor also held that he had over eight hundred concubines at his disposal, all of whom had been sterilized to preclude the appearance of any heirs to the throne or any the threat they might represent to his reign.

This particular Emperor had broken with a tradition so old no historian could locate its genesis in the history of their species. Imperial custom required the first born male heir must slay his parents and all his siblings upon achieving the age of thirty cycles. However, convention also required that before he was allowed to retire his entire family he first sire a son. The Emperor's birthday came and went, as did that of all members of his family, but no successor had yet drawn breath. The clerics raised an outcry, as did a few of the least savvy members of the court. The Emperor had the outspoken members of the court executed for treason and advised the clerics that a new doctrine was in the making. The clerics wisely held their peace. Advances in medical research that assured him virtual immortality informed the Emperor's unorthox stance. The biotechnical miracles that guaranteed his life were among the most closely held secrets in the empire. Immortality was a gift only the Emperor would receive and, with its receipt, he would become the last in the imperial line.

The gods of war demanded blood and victory. In their service, the Captain and this single imperial task force had erased the lives of billions of sentient life forms. Yet, the so-called powers of these mythic deities were but impotent apparitions as far as the old soldier was concerned. In reality the wrath of the fleet Overlord would certainly fall on a captain who had lost seventy five vessels, despite the fact that the objective had been achieved.

Easing slowly into its appointed orbit around the operations base ship, the Subcommander piloted the battleship with his usual efficiency. He had already ordered a ferry shuttle readied to transport them into the presence of the fleet Overlord. Boarding the ferry, the Commandant and Subcommander were brought speedily to the huge bustling complex that was the operations base ship.

Entering the main corridor of the vessel, they immediately mixed with hundreds of thousands of their fellows, each engaged in fulfilling his or her own particular task, the sum of which was the might of the empire. Making their way through the crowd, they passed armaments and propulsion technicians on their way to shuttles that would carry them to the battleships and cruisers in need of maintenance and repair. Color coded tunics of the numerous breeder females scurrying here and there indicated what genetic branch of the next generation they carried. The clear majority of the tunics were red, indicating a fetus that would become a warrior, with a scattering of blues representing the yet unborn destined to be technicians. Clerics representing the religion of the imperium were scattered among the throngs. Clad in orange-red tunics, they ministered to the spiritual needs of the people, although individuals at the level of the Captain's administrative rank knew the clerics were, in fact, imperial spies ferreting out low level sedition among the masses. Within minutes, the conveyors brought the Commandant and his Subcommander to the operations level.

Carried efficiently by a turbo tube from operations to the command level, security officers ushered them quickly through the command complex and, finally, into the immensity of the vessel's bridge. Here was the nerve center of the entire armada, where life and death decisions impacting the lives of millions were routinely passed down. Nowhere in this shuffle of busy midlevel command personnel was the fleet Overlord to be seen. A junior officer from the Overlord's personal entourage spotted them on the crowded bridge at almost the same moment they entered. Approaching the Commandant and Subcommander, he ushered them into the fleet Overlord's strategic planning chamber.

Passing through the well armored doors of the chamber, the Commandant glanced quickly about. He had been here many times before. Each previous visit had been a happy one. The task force group commandants had been

assembled to receive the congratulations of the Overlord on yet another victory. They had all received campaign medals and commemorative holo-orbs
depicting the planets that had been added to the empire. This campaign had not
been a successful one. So many vessels were already lost and an even greater
number of warriors had been canceled off the roster while the enemy fleet
remained a viable fighting force. One thing was clear, this summons to the
Overlord's privy chamber was not an occasion for celebration. Drinking in his
surroundings, the Commandant was fully aware these might be the last images
he saw in this life. In the face of the Overlord's displeasure, the odds of leaving
this audience alive had become slim to none.

One whole wall of the room was devoted to holographic images of the
worlds the task force had conquered and turned over to the colonization regime. Each planetary hologram was displayed with lines of light connecting
it to the home world of the empire. The seat of the empire was the point of
convergence in a huge web expanding outward and entrapping planets as it
spread. The Emperor sat atop this hub of power hungrily devouring worlds.

Displayed below each holographic image of a conquered planet were icons
representing the number of ships and crew members lost in achieving victory.

Approximately ninety-five percent of the planetary holograms carried no
iconic indicators representing losses sustained in their conquest. The former
inhabitants of these worlds had not yet achieved space flight and this category
represented the largest group of planetary conquests. Two types existed within
this cohort of technologically primitive civilizations. In the first and largest
group were all those worlds where life had not evolved to a level that constituted a threat to the empire's colonization efforts. On the second were those
planetary colonies that were supported by land based military garrisons whose
task it was to gradually eradicate any life forms that interfered with the success
of the colonies supported by these installations.

On worlds where a thriving sentient population existed and the technological progress of the inhabitants would make garrison driven eradication
expensive and time consuming, a more radical remedy was applied. The empire's policy on such planets was to seed the atmosphere with biological agents
designed to destroy only sentient life forms. The empire's methods were efficient and its science in this regard highly advanced.

Laboratories, staffed with hundreds of scientists and technicians on the
operations base ship could contrive a toxin to obliterate any sentient creature.
The discovery that sentience conferred a highly circumscribed vulnerability,
regardless of the species of life that achieved it, was one of the empire's scientific master strokes. The Captain, based on one visit there, could still see

the dark motto emblazoned over the entrance to the labs that read, 'Thought Kills.' However, the big ships that seeded these tailor made toxins were cumbersome, and possessed no armaments. This procedure for clearing the way for colonization only made sense if the inhabitants had no way to mount an effective resistance from space. The process of suffusing the atmosphere of a world with the seeds of death required time and left the planet unsafe for habitation by the empire's colonization ships for more than twenty years. Utilizing this procedure oftentimes got in the way of the colonization regime's schedule. On the whole, however, the empire preferred this approach to the cost in warriors and materials required to contend with a species competent to mount a defense of their planet from space.

Within moments the Commandant located, among the many depicted, the hologram representing the planet that was the focus of their current offensive. The underskirt of the hologram already contained icons indicating the destruction of nearly three hundred fighter craft and one battleship. The icons representing crew losses were too numerous to count. The Captain didn't have to review the other planetary holograms to recognize this campaign had cost the task force more than all their previous planetary conquests put together. This sad comment on the attack prowess of the empire's finest was the reason the Commandant and the Subcommander had been summoned into the Overlord's presence.

All heads turned as a portal to one side of the chamber slid open and the fleet Overlord entered. His bearing reflected that of the most successful task force leader in the empire, and his bearing indicated the pride he took in that status. The crew of the task force referred to him as Lord SS, referencing his tendency to say very little, 'silent,' while his record of victories, 'successes,' spoke for itself.

As tradition required, the Overlord was never without the baton of rank that signified his standing in the imperium. He strode directly to the wall of planetary holograms and touched each one in turn with his baton until he came to the hologram representing the task force's current objective. He stood there for a few moments, tapping the icon plate below the hologram of the blue-white planet with his baton of office. Then, turning suddenly, he pointed his baton in the direction of the Commandant and his Subcommander. A white hot laser beam lanced out of the tip of the baton and the Commandant watched as his Subcommander crumpled in death to the deck.

Resigned to his fate, the Commandant stood perfectly still waiting for a second blast from the baton that did not come. The Overlord moved instead to a console on a raised platform near the main viewer and touched a button located there. The spherical planetary icon representing the task force's current objective was immediately capped in a silver mantel that draped itself over one third of the planet's surface extending from one of its poles.

Pausing for a moment, the Overlord motioned to one of his aides to come forward. The Officer produced a battle baton topped with a finial shaped to represent the silver capped planet of the hologram. The Junior Officer strode toward the Commandant as two other aides removed the body of the fallen Subcommander. Placing the battle baton in the Commandant's hand, the Officer pivoted smartly and returned to his post by the Overlord's raised console. The fleet Overlord stared intently at the Commandant for a moment before the door behind the Commandant leading to the main bridge opened. Battle baton in hand, the Commandant saluted, and turning on his heel, hurried at quick time from the bridge.

As he heard the soft swish of expelled air as the door to the Overlord's chamber slid shut behind him, the Commandant breathed a guilty sigh of relief. He remained alive, but his Subcommander, a good officer and friend was dead. It was the way of the empire, a second in command often died for the failures of his commandant. Another failure would require the Commandant's life. Having received the battle baton meant he must plan and lead the assault against this planet. If he lost as much as one fighter, his life became forfeit. He studied the battle baton as images of the enemy's tiny ball of firepower utterly destroying his task force danced through his head. He was dead and he knew it.

Having reviewed the pictorials of all the battles with this recalcitrant life form more times than he could count, convinced the Commandant that the spiny ball of an attack craft this species had launched against the imperial fleet would exact additional losses before it could be destroyed. All he could realistically hope for was that the destruction of the planet would be reasonably swift and inexpensive in terms of crew and materials under his leadership. If the conquest of this species was not from this point forward, a cost-effective one, then, in addition to his own, the lives of his wife and family would be sacrificed to the fleet Overlord's displeasure in strict accordance with tradition.

In all of his years of service, the Commandant had never personally witnessed the vindictive wrath of the empire manifest in the complete and utter destruction of a planetary body that might serve as a viable habitation for the empire's subjects. Nothing would be left that could support life for the reigns of tens of thousands of emperors. He had read about such operations early in the history of the empire, when the technology of his race was still in its infancy, but no recent records existed of an attempted conquest that had failed to this extent. A devastated planet represented a loss to colonization, but if its position in the galaxy was a strategic one, it could still serve as a supply and operations staging outpost.

Faint glimmerings of an idea began to grow in his awareness. In a moment of hopeful optimism, the Commandant recalled the empire's conquests resulted in successes that were in no small proportion indebted to the appropriation of the technological genius of defeated species. The best scientists in the empire routinely did reverse engineering on captured weapons, propulsion and defensive technologies. The empire's fearful might had grown to its current proportions by stealing technology from those it swept out of existence. The procedure worked so well that, in the last several hundred years, the empire had not produced a single innovation that added substantially to its aggressive or defensive capability. The enormous imperial war machine had shifted from an innovative predatory to a parasitic predatory mode. As a parasite, the imperium had grown fat in its unchallenged arrogance. This otherwise unremarkable species had called into question the empire's presumption of invulnerability. Perhaps as much as the losses in personnel and material, the tenacious resistance of this species elicited the fear induced ire of the fleet Overlord and prompted his order to utterly annihilate this audacious race. The master of the fleet clearly wanted an absolute guarantee that the imperium would never have to face this enemy again. In his fever driven imagination, the Commandant saw this as the key. He could do nothing about the losses already sustained. However, if the Overlord's fear could not be assuaged then, possibly, his anger could be appeased. Perhaps, the Commandant thought he might still save his own life and that of his extended family.

Desperation driving his vision of the battle to come, the Commandant imagined he might capture the great spherical ship and the technology it housed. The secrets that lay behind the success this species had realized in the defense of their home world might represent the salvation of the lives of his family and himself. If this spiked ball of a ship could be made a prize of war, he would become the principal mover in an action that would simultaneously add to the armamentarium of the empire and the fleet Overlord's status.

Certainly, the technology built into the spherical vessel would be valuable to the empire, especially since that single ship had exacted such enormous losses among the imperial forces. The fleet Overlord might, offering only the technology that serviced the shields in that spherical ship, parley his position as task force Overlord into membership in the Emperor's privy council. Many on the privy council had achieved their station at the emperor's right hand in just that way.

Turning these ideas over and over again in his mind, the Commandant settled upon a course of action. In a very real sense, he knew he had nothing to lose by trying to capture the enemy ship. He could not realistically expect to conduct a campaign against this tenacious enemy without sacrificing personnel and vessels. If he sustained losses, his life and those of his family were forfeit. His only realistic choice was to throw something into the bargain to save his family and himself. That something would be the enemy's spherical ship. Somehow, he must find a way to destroy the home planet of this species while salvaging the enemy's formidable weapons system.

Returning as quickly as he could to his own bridge, the Commandant assembled the commandants of his sister battleships to a council of war, on what was now, the command vessel of the newly formed assault force. As custom demanded, he stood before the full complement of battleship captains holding the battle baton over his own head and that of those assembled, indicating his status and commission from the fleet Overlord. The officers of his task force saluted smartly in the hope that their newly appointed assault force leader had something up his sleeve that would save their reputations, careers and possibly their lives.

Surveying the familiar faces of friends and comrades before him, the newly appointed task force Commandant realized that he must now present the particulars of his daring and dangerous plan. Everyone in attendance had a life and death stake in the success of his strategy. In order to ensure their support, he knew he must invite their comment. He began outlining a formation consisting entirely of battleships. The assault fleet would not be accompanied by fighters, as these smaller craft were vulnerable to both the enemy fighters and the spherical craft that had inflicted so much damage on their ships in previous attacks. All twenty battleships would take part in the operation. Ten of these would provide the screen for a formation of self-propelled missiles that would target the planet. He didn't have to explain to these seasoned warriors why the fleet Overlord now judged the option of colonization too expensive in terms of personnel and materials to merit further consideration.

Ten battleships functioning as a spearhead would precede the group shepherding the planet wreckers to their destination. This lead formation of capital ships would engage the enemy's spherical craft. The plan called for the lead formation to diverge from their characteristic tight formation to a more open one that would invite the enemy's spherical ship to carry its attack into the midst of their battle group. Once the enemy's spherical ship moved within the confines of the formation, the battleships would resume their characteristic tight grouping and entangle the enemy's premier weapons' system within their overlapping shields.

A bold tactic it would require flawless coordination on the part of all the ships involved in the trapping maneuver. In particular, the technical considerations of manipulating the shields to net the prey would require close order collaboration among the vessels' commandants. The inner shields of the battleships would need to be hardened, utilizing near maximum power output, while the outer shields would be extended, resulting in a dispersion of the energy grid supporting them. The soft character of the outer overlapping shield barrier between the vessels would allow the enemy's spherical craft to fly into the middle of the formation. As soon as the enemy's spherical craft became centered within the battleship group, the inner and outer shield power grid distribution output would be equalized, ensnaring the enemy ship in interlocking fields of force.

Noting the restlessness among the assembled commandants as he laid out the plan, the Commandant explained the battleships could still utilize their main laser turrets through firing loops in their shields to disable the enemy craft. This seemed to quiet the unrest among his fellow officers. Then, he cautioned them again that the principal goal of this tactic was to capture the laser and shield technology incorporated within the enemy vessel intact, not to destroy the craft through concentrated laser fire.

The battle hardened officers clearly understood the value of capturing the enemy vessel intact. They had seen the pictorials illustrating the way this single spherical craft had stood off a whole battle group of fighters while simultaneously destroying one of their sister ships. They all wanted the technology that stood behind a laser that could cut through their shield defenses. No other race had ever penetrated the imperium's shields in numberless past campaigns and all the commandants wanted the technology that had accomplished that feat. They also wanted to give their engineers an opportunity to revamp their own shields to provide the seemingly impenetrable defensive power the little spherical ship possessed. In order to accomplish both of these goals, they had to capture the enemy craft with its shields and lasers more or less intact.

Based on past campaigns as well as this one, everyone knew the imperial shield technology could withstand multiple fusion missile strikes. The task force commandants could rest assured of this measure of protection for their vessels and crews. Their principal concern was the laser turret the little ball of a ship carried and how it incised their shields, allowing missiles to impact the vulnerable hulls of their ships. The assault Commandant pointed out that the enemy's spherical ship sported only one laser and could, therefore, engage but one ship in their formation at a time. This deficiency alone would allow the battleships adjoining the one under the enemy's laser attack to focus their own laser turrets on the enemy vessel, thereby disabling it.

Nods and smiles among the fleet commanders suggested his plan was well received The battleship captains and their families were as much at risk as he and his, but their analysis discovered no devastating oversights in his strategy. Dismissing the assembly, the Commandant spent a few moments exchanging greetings with some of the officers he had known for decades and, then, it was over. The officers of the capital ships gradually dispersed back to their commands leaving the Commandant in a solitary vigil against his own doubts and fears.

Now, there were duties to perform, some focused on life and far too many, directed to the real prospect of failure and death. He would have to choose a new subcommander and given what had occurred in the fleet Overlord's chamber, this position no longer merited an occasion for celebration for the prospective appointee. He planed to transfer his family to the operations base ship where he hoped their lives would be vouched safe by his victories against this obdurate enemy. If his task force suffered defeat, his wife and children would die aboard that ship at the hands of the Overlord's personal security operatives.

As custom dictated, he must also prepare a sealed message to all of his distant genetic relatives, most of whom were serving in lesser posts in the empire's many fleets dispersed throughout the galaxy. The message, a simple apology for his failure, should that eventuality arise, would be presented to his kin moments before imperial representatives executed them one and all.

The rewards of a military career in the Emperor's service provided status and real material benefit greatly exceeding any other non-political calling in the empire. However, the benefits were more than offset by the terrible price paid by individuals, men, women, and children genetically tied to the highest ranking members of the extended families should the officer fail.

The Commandant had taken the wager the fortunes of war forced upon him. How, many not present at the gaming table would pay the price if chance and cunning did not favor his gambit, he knew only too well.

Chapter 25

Apprehension flowed like a swollen spring stream among the personnel on the station. Arthur felt it. He didn't know what it was about, but he knew it was just as tangible as the bar on which he leaned. Arthur didn't like the intensity of the foreboding feeling gnawing at his innards, particularly when he couldn't link it to real events. In that instant, he decided to put that feeling to rest and find out what was going on. Noticing Captain Sydes sitting by himself at the bar, Arthur moved up the bar until he occupied the stool next to the ace pilot.

"Captain Sydes, everyone wearing an Earth Force uniform looks edgy. What's going on?" Arthur asked.

Sydes was well into his sixth drink which was about the only thing that made him feel talkative. Besides, he knew this guy. This was the buddy of the Doc who patched him back together.

"You're the friend of the Doc who fixed me up, aren't you?" Sydes said.

"The same," Arthur replied.

"I heard he died trying to save some construction worker who was in trouble," Sydes remarked.

"Yeah, a little while back," Arthur responded.

"Damn shame … he was good man, knew his stuff," Sydes said.

Ordering refills for both of them, Arthur returned to his original question.

"So what's up? The military looks like they just got some bad news," Arthur said, his tone careful but insistent.

"I guess … everyone will know soon enough," Sydes replied as he put away half of his drink.

"Know what?" Arthur asked.

"We launched a long range scanner probe along the route the aliens used in their last attack. Before the aliens blew it to pieces, we got some pictures of what's sitting out there," Sydes said in a tired tone of voice.

Noticing Sydes had finished his drink, Arthur ordered another round.

Listening to Sydes' tone and scrutinizing his expression, Arthur was not nearly as certain he wanted his question answered as when he first asked.

"So, what's out there that's got everyone so nervous?" Arthur asked.

"There's a whole fleet out there. About five hundred fighter and cruiser craft, twenty battleships and one big mother of a ship that looks like a central command vessel," Sydes replied.

Swallowing the rest of his drink, the gnawing in Arthur's gut disappeared. The sense of foreboding had been replaced, by what he hoped would be, the more manageable fear of a tangible danger.

"Apart from killing as many of us as they can, what the hell do you think they want?" Arthur asked.

"It's all guess work. The science boys went over the digital records of the battle coverage from the Duo's cameras. There were a few alien bodies blown into space during our attack on the formation led by one of their battleships. The biological sciences group analyzed the views of those bodies, pixel by pixel," Sydes said and then stared at the row of bottles on the wall behind the bar.

Lost in thought, Arthur didn't say anything immediately. Instead, he motioned to the bartender to bring yet another round. When the refills arrived, he posed his question to Sydes.

"So, what did they find?"

"The aliens are a carbon based life form like us. It looks like they breathe pretty much the same mixture of gases as we do and come from a planet with a gravity very much like Earth's. That's about as much as the science guys could be certain of with just the digitals from the Duo to go on," Sydes replied as he sipped his drink.

"So, they could live on the Earth like we do?" Arthur asked.

"Yeah ... when I saw the probe's transmissions of the size of the alien fleet, I knew they weren't here just to collect plant samples. I think their agenda is conquest. Since we're pretty sure they can live on Earth, this fleet must be the vanguard that clears the way for colonization," Sydes replied, staring into his glass.

Suddenly, Arthur recognized the foreboding pain in his gut had not adequately foreshadowed the seriousness of the situation. Despite his certainty as to the answer, he decided to ask the obvious question.

"But all of humanity has to go first?"

"I don't think they're interested in peaceful coexistence with us, if that's what you mean. And I'm pretty sure they won't be offering us reservation life on our own world like the white eyes did for my forefathers," Sydes responded.

Clearly recognizing the reference to the genocidal destruction of the American Indians in Sydes' remark, Arthur was savvy enough to let it stand. However, there was still a piece that didn't fit into this increasingly terrifying puzzle. He decided to see if Sydes had that puzzle piece in his pocket.

"If the aliens want to colonize, why in the hell did they destroy the complex on Mars?"

"Because they could? As an object lesson? Hell, I don't know. Maybe they just don't value that kind of artificial habitat. Whatever the reason, three million men, women and children are dead because we couldn't provide an adequate defense," Sydes replied.

Startled by Sydes' remark, Arthur suddenly realized this ace pilot was a much more complicated man than he had imagined. Sydes was a warrior-poet in the classical sense, a man of both courage and sensitivity. His calling was to protect people who couldn't protect themselves. Sydes obviously felt he had failed at a personal level. Arthur looked at the fighter pilot with new respect, in anguish at the bar beside him as he posed his next question.

"So what happens now?"

"We'll go out to meet them when they come. We can't defeat them, I'm sure of that, but maybe we can discourage the hell out of them. Sort of like a bear and a honey tree. A grizzly bear will tear down a whole tree to get at a hive, but if the bees sting him often enough on the nose and eyes, the bear may decide the honey's not worth the pain," Sydes said, his back straightening.

"And we're the bees," Arthur interjected.

"We sure as hell ain't the bear," Sydes replied as he dragged himself from the bar stool.

Noticing how unsteady the Captain was on his feet, Arthur reached into his pocket and produced a detox patch. Extending his hand to shake Sydes', Arthur pushed up the Captain's sleeve and slapped the detox patch on his arm.

"Something to help you plot your course," Arthur said.

Smiling, Sydes pulled down his sleeve and shook Arthur's hand firmly.

"Thanks, Doc. You'd make a good navigator," he remarked.

Then, Sydes turned and picked his way unsteadily through the crowd and out of the bar.

Arthur watched for a long moment as Sydes disappeared into the crowd. Then, he grabbed his glass, finished his drink and left the bar heading, for the compartment he had once shared with Forrester. He had one last duty of friendship to fulfill. He would let Nate know this was very likely humanity's last stand.

⚜

Entering the bridge, a considerably more sober Sydes noticed Von Strohheim in conversation with Tutunji and approached them.

"We were just about to call for you. I have seen the digitals from the probe we sent out to the alien fleet. This is not good. The Duo cannot hope to stand off all the capital ships in the enemy's armada. Many will certainly get through, and our strike craft are ineffective against the aliens' battleships,"Von Strohheim said as he turned to Sydes.

"Doctor Von Strohheim has recommended we evacuate the station of all but a minimum defensive force,"Tutunji added.

"Evacuate to where? We don't have the personnel or the ships to get them back to Earth," Sydes replied.

"The second Duo is being built in geostationary orbit around Mars. Because the construction installation is on the other side of the planet from the habitation domes, neither the ship, nor my base there, sustained any damage from the aliens' missile attack. The Martian base we use to house construction and technical workers could accommodate the stations' personnel. It would be cramped, of course, but, with a little effort, it can be done,"Von Strohheim responded.

"When the alien battleships mount their next attack, they'll almost certainly destroy this station. Even our multiple shielding layers won't hold up against the laser turrets of those capital ships,"Tutunji said, his tone solemnly realistic.

"What about Duo II?" Sydes asked expectantly.

Suddenly, Von Strohheim's expression altered to that of a school boy being chastised for not completing his homework.

"She will not be ready, I am sad to say. The propulsion units are functioning, but the shields and capacitors have not been tested. The tunneling lasers have been installed, but the entire missile launching assembly is still being constructed on the Martian surface. The Duo II is eighty percent an empty shell. It is the horror of science that the knowledge is there, but we cannot make what we know into a usable reality in time to make a difference. I am sorry Captain Sydes,"Von Strohheim replied.

"So, realistically, all that we have is the Duo to stand against some twenty battleships," Sydes said in a resigned tone.

"I fear this is so,"Von Strohheim responded.

Now, it was just a matter of when the aliens chose to attack,Tutunji thought to himself. The station would be obliterated, the Duo would be destroyed and, without Von Strohheim's ship, the strike craft stood little chance against the alien fleet. With Earth's space presence eradicated, there would be nothing to hold the line between the alien fleet and Earth.

Quite unexpectedly,Tutunji's mind filled with visions of a thousand generations of his family struggling to stay alive amidst the heat and sand. All those centuries of suffering, for what, he thought to himself. In a matter of moments, or at most days, the sum of his family's flesh and bone, indeed, all that was the living future of mankind, would be ash. Millennia of art, music and literature, as well as, the catalog of daily horrors each man visited upon his brother would have no more substance than a dream that flees with the morning's first light. He mourned for the children, for the water, for the bread and for the songs of his people.

⋪❖⋫

His frustration growing, Arthur had been working on the video transmitter for almost half an hour. He knew the transmitter's computer would not allow him to make a call to Earth using his personal clearance code, but even if he had a high enough clearance rating, he certainly didn't want the call traced back to him. There would be too many questions, particularly since he was attempting to place a call to one of Cabot's reserves. Finally, he hit on the idea of invading the residual files. Fumbling through his pockets, he found a jimmy card he had won from an electronics technician in a poker game. Arthur didn't know how the card worked, but he knew how to operate it. Inserting the card, he waited as the marvelously illegal gadget threaded its way through the computer's security measures. In less than a minute, he gained access to the residual files.

Scrolling through the listing of calls from the station to Earth over the past year, he noticed an identification number for a high ranking CC Natcorp division head. It was just the sort of priority clearance code that would allow him Earth transmission access and guarantee him a secure link. Activating the computer's search program revealed the division head no longer lived on the station. There was a good chance this would work, he thought, chuckling quietly to himself.

Beside himself with mischievous delight, Arthur activated the transmitter and typed in the division head's identification number. When the computer called for a retinal scan to verify the clearance number, Arthur made a few adjustments in the jimmy card and inserted it in the computer. The unit processed the input for ten seconds longer than usual, but finally gave Arthur access to initiate a transmission to Earth.

Entering a code provided by his friend Bud, Arthur initiated the transmission and waited. Bud said the code would access a Doctor Chen who was some kind of administrator at Cabot's Canadian reserve.

Completing the link, the vidscreen activated and a man who identified himself as Doctor Chen appeared.

"How may I help you?" Doctor Chen inquired.

"This is Arthur, Nate's friend. I arranged for Doctor Forrester to be smuggled to your facility. I would like to speak with him," Arthur said.

Instantly, a flood of reasons to terminate the link flooded through Chen's head. Although Cabot's policy allowed for a free flow of information into the reserve, that same policy sharply curtailed outgoing messaging. Glancing down at the console before him, he verified the link was secure. That much alone suggested a degree of informed discretion on the part of the caller and offered equal protection for Chen. Pausing only a moment, Chen accepted the man on the screen in front of him was Doctor Forrester's friend and, because Forrester was an important man in Chen's life, he elected to take the risk.

"I'm connecting you now," Chen said as he activated the link to Esther and Jacob's home.

Blanking momentarily, the screen exchanged Chen's face for that of an attractive woman in her late twenties who identified herself as Esther.

"I'm trying to contact Doctor Nathan Forrester," Arthur announced.

"I'll get Doctor Forrester for you," she replied.

In moments, Forrester appeared on the the screen. His expression shifted quickly from his characteristic matter of fact mien to one of genuine surprise.

"Arthur ... Arthur how are you?"

"OK Nate. How are things down there in the woods?" Arthur replied.

"A lot better than I could ever have imagined. I wish you could see this Arthur so much is happening. It's like ...." Forrester said, excitement in his tone.

"Listen up! I told you I'd see you again and this may be it," Arthur said curtly.

"What's going on Arthur?" Forrester asked, recognizing the gravity in Arthur's tone.

"Nate ... the war's going really badly and the next battle may be decisive. I just found out there's a huge alien fleet sitting outside of the solar system ready to swoop in for the kill. It doesn't look like we stand much of a chance. Captain Sydes, you remember Sydes, you treated him after his strike craft was destroyed?" Arthur asked.

"Yes, I remember him. Hell of a pilot," Forrester replied.

"Sydes believes, the alien's goal is to colonize the Earth for their species," Arthur said, his expression growing more somber.

In an instant, Forrester recognized he wasn't breathing. The first word that sprang to mind was karma ... lots and lots of karmic repayment for the sins of mankind. Taking a deep breath, he stated the obvious.

"That means all of us down here have to go to make way for them."

"I don't see any way around that conclusion, Nate. I think we're looking at the extinction of the human race," Arthur responded.

Forrester stared intently at the face of a friend who had stuck with him over all these years. More than any other single person, Forrester owed his presence among the meek and the wonders he had experienced among them to the man in the viewer before him.

"Damn, Arthur. What's gonna happen to you?"

"It's what's going to happen to all of us, Nate," Arthur said in a definitive tone.

"Does the military have any idea when the attack will come?" Forrester asked.

"If they know, they haven't told me. But frankly, I don't think they have any idea. We'll probably all know at about the same time … when those alien bastards blow us to hell," Arthur replied.

"So, this is it … altogether. What a waste … I mean … it's been good, Arthur, you stuck with me … you and I … I mean we've been …" Forrester stammered.

"Let it go, Nate. We've had a lot of time together and said more than enough to each other over the years. We don't need some kind of grand finale. I just wanted to say goodbye," Arthur said, graciously interrupting Forrester's verbal fumbling.

Staring at his best friend for a long moment, Forrester recognized Arthur said the simple truth of the matter. Then, he felt words forming that were not driven by simple hope but by an awareness he could neither localize in his experience nor explain.

"Goodbye, Arthur. Don't ask me how I know, but I think I'll see you again."

"Hell, who knows Nate. It would take an act of God to manage that sort of sleight of hand, but if either of us knows anything about that, it would be you. The only thing I'm reasonably certain of is that you and I are each where we're supposed to be. Goodbye, Nate," Arthur said and closed the link.

❧❖❧

Forrester felt a cold stiffness creeping through his body. Then, he came to himself sufficiently to recognize he had been sitting and staring at the blank screen for a very long time. He couldn't recall anything that looked as empty as that screen. This was an ending and, with his neuropsychological configuration, he knew, the one thing he hated was endings. Forrester, like the people of the trees, focused on the future, in particular, events to come that represented improvements over the past and present. To be left hemispheric was to be hopeful. Envisioning the best for the universe made them optimists, expecting the best from the bulk of their fellow human beings made them victims. Rob the lefts of the future and you have stolen their reason for living. Arthur, and those with even greater right hemispheric endowments, were better equipped to take any setback in stride. Denial was the key to their buoyant mood. How many times had Forrester, in more innocent times, instructed his students that denial preserved self-confidence at the expense of the facts, past and present. Then, without consciously recognizing it, Forrester became aware of Crystal and her family standing behind him.

⚜

"That which you told your friend is true. You will see him again, just as you did today," Esther said in soft but definitive tones.

"It was just a feeling, an emotion, Esther," Forrester responded as he turned around.

"A feeling is not always an emotion. Sometimes, we label an experience a feeling because it doesn't represent a clear cut perception easily traceable to some event we can point to in the environment. At other times, a feeling can be an event within us that isn't, as yet, under our conscious control. A feeling can be a gossamer finger that fills the mind, pointing insistently in the direction of some truth. However, because we cannot see the hand to which the finger is attached or cause movement in it, we call it a feeling," Esther said quietly.

"New abilities, like new skills, require practice in order for a person to become conversant in their use and certain of his competence," Jacob added.

"Yes, I suppose you're right," Forrester replied.

It never ceased to amaze him that what was so simple for him to assimilate in the abstract was so arduous to grasp experientially. But that was the nature of left hemispheric strength, there was always a ninety-nine percent loss in translation from the theoretical to the applied. The people of the trees were evolution's reactive amendment to nature's oversight among those with left hemispheric strengths. The meek's manner of 'seeing' was a direct response to that translational loss. They, and little by little, he, could plainly and effortless *see* the abstract realities that lay behind the mere forms and appearances of the so called material substance of the universe. Perhaps like truly insightful inhabitants of Plato's cave, the meek could see beyond the shadows to the primal forms that stood behind the silhouettes of the material universe.

"That's right. Soon you will be able to see for us and beyond us. You are the lens. You just have to practice. We will add to your light so that you can see our way," Crystal remarked.

"You are marked to summon the community at will. Just think 'All' and the light from all those who are the people of the trees will stream through you to focus on what all must see," Esther said.

Fully immersed in the throes of one of his dumbfounded moments, Forrester still tried to think in a linear fashion from known facts to general principles. Chiding himself, he recognized once again he had it backwards. The meek had provided him, in word and deed, with indisputable evidence the principles that permeated their awareness represented the governing dynamics of the universe. Their request was simple, think from general principles to specific outcomes. In the past, when he had doubted the perceptions of the people of the trees, he had always been wrong. This time he would endeavor to trust. He thought 'All'.

Saying the word 'All' felt like the most open invitation to the unknown imaginable. For a moment, he felt like a child. Once again he stood in the meadow by the creek in the warm twilight of a summer's evening watching fireflies rise from the grass. First, there were a few, then, hundreds and, finally, thousands of lights dancing in his mind. It should have felt overwhelming or at least confusing, but it didn't. Quite unexpectedly, he was struck by the immensity of the event in his mind. Somehow, the mental presence of a half a million minds had taken up residence in his consciousness in a way out of proportion to the size of his head. It seemed almost as if the collective cognition of the meek stood apart from the laws that governed the physics of three dimensional reality.

Swirling and sparkling points of blue-white light representing the community of minds that was the meek slowly formed a globe of surpassing brilliance in the center of his mind. Forrester recognized his own aura on the surface of the globe as a circular pool of purple tint. No wonder the people of the trees called it 'seeing', Forrester thought to himself. The presence of the community in his mind had taken on the shape of some great luminescent eye, with his own aura as iris. In the next moment, he became that iris and what he consciously thought and felt passed within the purple pool to become the lens of the community of the people of the trees, present somehow in his mind.

I am, no, we are seeing, he thought. Then, he felt himself disappearing as an individual into the experience of the meek, looking beyond this place and moment. Dimly at first, and then, with increasing clarity, we saw the whole of the Earth viewed from a great distance. In the blackness of space surrounding the Earth, hanging as if in attendance for some great event, were three small gray orbs. Then, a great haze enveloped the planet, obscuring its features from view. As the mist cleared, the sun's light struck the planet and the Earth shone like a great silver glass ball. The light reflected from the huge silver sphere, silhouetting the three tiny orbs against the darkness of space as the orbs turned and sped away into the void. Then, the seeing was over and Forrester felt himself increasingly alone as he watched the fireflies of light wink out of his consciousness.

Without knowing exactly how his question had been answered, he knew he would see Arthur again, in exactly the same way as he had seen him today. The community seeing had revealed so much more than what was required by way of personal assurance for Forrester regarding his old friend. However, the meaning of that 'so much more' was not immediately apparent. The community *seeing* did implicitly clarify one issue. In terms of an ancient aphorism, the medium was the message. Embedded within the seeing itself was an incarnation of the meek's optimism about the future far surpassing in significance the few images that the community had shared. Consistent with Esther's metaphor of the gossamer finger, the vision of the community revealed that to which the finger was pointing. Supporting and directing that finger, an entry from the scrolls centered itself in his mind's eye.

> AWAKE BEFORE THE SUN, I AM SENTRY AT THE
> GATES OF DARKNESS AS THE LIGHT SUPPLANTS
> NIGHT'S FEARS. THROUGH THE EYE OF THE SUN,
> I SEE A TIME WHEN ALL IS LIGHT, AND DREAD,
> LIKE THE EVEN'S SHADE, IS FOREVER BANISHED.
>
> WHEN THOSE COME, WHO IN LISTENING SHALL
> HEAR AND IN LOOKING SHALL SEE, A VISION
> CARRYING NOT BEYOND, BUT THROUGH THE
> DARK ILLUSION OF THE UNIVERSE TO THE LIGHT,
> WHICH LYING BENEATH THAT SHELL AND
> NOURISHING IT, SHALL BE THEIRS. SOULS
> ABIDING IN A TRUE VISION OF THE LIGHT,
> THEIR FLESH SHALL, NESTED WITHIN THE CRUDE
> MATTER OF ALL THAT IS, REMAIN AS LIVING
> WITNESS OF THAT WHICH, UNSEEN, SUPPORTS
> THE FABRIC OF THE HEAVENS.
>
> ALL THAT HAD, HAS AND WILL HAVE LIFE
> DWELLS WITHIN THE LIGHT. ITS COMINGS
> AND GOINGS IN THE DARKNESS OF THE
> UNIVERSE ARE BUT MOMENTS WITHIN THE
> NOW OF ALL TIMES.

THE LIGHT IS LIFE. LIFE MAKES MANIFEST
THAT LIGHT, RISING AS THE SUN IN THE
MORNING AND SINKING AT EVENTIDE, BUT
EVER THERE, SEEN OR UNSEEN BY THE EYE
OF MAN.

A GREAT LOOM OF LIGHT AND LIFE WORKS ITS
WOOF AND WARP IN THREADS OF MANY COLORS
BREADTHS AND LENGTHS. THE GREAT TAPESTRY
IT WEAVES IS NEVER FULLY REVEALED IN THE
FEW FIBERS THAT THE UNIVERSE DISCLOSES.

In the midst of his ruminations over the diarist's words, Crystal caught his eye.

"A big weaving machine. No matter where we are or when we are …"

Then, looking up at Forrester, she made a tying gesture with her fingers. "We're all tied together. It's just hard to see the knots," she said.

✢✦✢

She was right, the knots were hard to see. Yet, nested somehow in this communal seeing was life, dwelling above, beneath, and within the physical universe supporting, and sustaining it. This was life only partially revealed in the endless living forms with which any finite observer might be familiar. Here was life before the physical universe, a living force creating a material reality in and through which, in some fragmentary way, it might reveal itself. This wasn't life as a single strand wound within an individual gasping in the frightened turmoil of an isolated bloodstream to survive the next challenge. Neither was it the multiple loops of an entire species struggling in the hope of enduring in the monotony of their circular course. This was the continuous loom of life lying embedded within, but only faintly demonstrated in, all that which could be seen and felt.

Guiding the vision of the people of the trees was the absolute assurance that the loom of life came first in the beginning of all that is the cosmos. From the big bang through whole galaxies to the smallest particle of matter, the discernible universe merely provided a platform in and through which life manifested itself in an endless variety of physical forms. All that could be experienced as alive, without the seeing of the people of the trees, was little more than the stray threads of the weave of life poking their way into the physical universe.

"The weaver was the first row in the loom, entwining the pattern for the life of the tapestry," Esther said quietly.

"The weaver?" Forrester asked as he looked over at her.

"He who, as the oldest row in the tapestry, guides the weave and creates its patterns. The first sentient interlace of the fabric of life is also he whose diary you unearthed," Jacob said softly.

It was the carpenter and these were his children, carefully planned for eons. Now, they were here, gifted to *see* that from which they and all life had sprung. A dramatic manifestation of this tapestry of life, the people of the trees, themselves, represented an integral part of the weave. More importantly they knew and could see themselves as part thereof. In this knowing rested the genesis of their 'Mona Lisa smiles', the light of which seemed somehow to spread across the entirety of their bodies. Their expressions, as in the spheres of light that emanated from them, embodied the positive and indisputable assurance of the life they experienced within the tapestry of all existence. Both as individuals and in the body of the community these men, women and children swam in the light of life. In their *seeing* was a broad avenue leading to the life force that stood at the fountainhead and genesis of all matter. Entrained by space-time itself, the depth and breadth of their knowing made doing superfluous.

"Traveling from the light into darkness, life has come over the endless expanse of time closer to the light of its beginnings. The current, whose flow has driven us into the darkness of matter diminishes, while the voice that calls from the light strengthens. Still alive to the universe of matter, we are closer to home than when we first began," Esther said with quiet conviction.

Forrester finally got it. He grasped the nature of the unyielding drives so completely manifest in the dominance driven. These were motivations fully expressed in the churnings of an ancient, fully empowered and wholly uncompromising limbic system and its predecessor structures. This small knot of tissue conferred upon each and every one of the loom's strands of life the power to push its way into and contend with the forces intrinsic to an obdurate material universe. The fight for individual and species survival, driven by an uncompromising limbic system, had its roots in the power conferred on life to move from the light of the loom into the darkness of matter. The power granted to each of the loom's strands to obtrude into matter had, however, no off switch. Once the transition from light to darkness was accomplished, the strength of the drives remained unabated. The drive to dominance remained simply and inextricably bound up with the sense of individual self. In its most rudimentary form, then, dominance was no less than the ego's absolute insistence that all things be subject to itself. This uncompromising conviction, left over from the intrepid and enterprising thrust that propelled each soul through the arduous transition from light and warmth into the cold darkness of crude matter, was beyond the reach of reason.

Humankind's history was replete with examples of the intrusive character of these forces demanding the destruction of everything and everyone that stood between them and the fulfillment of their needs and wants. In each individual, the strength of these drives differed, but the greater the strength of the need to push from insubstantial light into the tangible darkness of matter, the more significant was the drive supporting individual survival at whatever cost. The dominance driven simply harkened back to those from a time before time whose capacity for struggle into and against the darkness of matter was uncompromising. Yet, from these same right hemispheric beginnings, the dominance driven carried the genes that would in the fullness of time produce the meek.

An endless catalogue of travesties perpetrated in the name of conveyance of one's own genes into the future fully represented man's history. All of this furthered the process whereby the threads of life's tapestry forced their way in the physical universe. A certain horrific symmetry existed in a process so invested with power that it could drive life and light into the darkness of the material universe wherein it could do no more than its intrinsic nature dictated. That which empowered birth set life on a course vectored towards egocentric struggle and death all around.

"It is the discipline of the loom and the patience of the weaver that all life should build upon the scaffolding erected by its own striving. Life constructs itself along a path that leads not up, but back, to its beginnings in the light," Jacob remarked.

Jacob had it right. The journey of all life's manifestations, large and small, travelled back to its beginnings, not forward to some imagined and illusory future. The future was the past. Having shared the meek's vision, one thing had become clear to Forrester. The phenomenon manifest among the meek didn't derive its significance from the content of what was seen, but from the momentary joining with the tapestry of all life. Evolution's gift to the people of the trees was vested in their communal capacity to achieve brief glimpses of that tapestry and the space-time continuum beyond the now through which material existence was currently passing. More lasting than these brief glimpses of light and life was the continuing feeling of assurance warranting that the participants had found their way home, if only for a brief visit.

Assurance was the irreducible and quietly unchallenged feeling that the *seeing* conferred on its participants. This feeling evoked Forrester's own child-hood memories of seeing the lights of the farm house as he trudged through the snow on a winter night. A sense refuge was there, a door opening to the light, warmth against the cold, good food and cheer in a place where he be-longed. He felt it, then, as now, he had come home. Home from the material substance that passed for reality to the warmth from which he and all other life had been extruded. It felt good to be home.

"To know how cold you feel, you must be able to remember how warm you were setting next to the fire," she said.

He heard Crystal's voice in the air, but also in his mind, a part of the conversation he was having with himself.

⌁❖⌁

Quite abruptly, thoughts of the diarist's plight, a man of sorrows and ac-quainted with grief interrupted the sense of profound comfort Forrester was experiencing. A big chunk of the underlying weave of life, according to Esther, the scribe of the scrolls was also a manifestation of the whole of the tapestry. Forever presenting himself in first one then another transient form at differ-ent times in the same place, his mission remained always the same, preaching light to the darkness. Whether sojourning on this blue-white ball or among the lights in the sky in forms alien to the human eye, he willingly entered into the sharp edges and unyielding surfaces of material reality just to let the parts know the whole existed. His was a nostalgic message. He preached of the light, home to all life, but a birthplace none could recall. Thrice distilled, all that he said and witnessed through his actions was that those who heard his words were only partially and momentarily estranged from the site of their illumined nativity. If there were an operational definition of love, this had to be it.

Unsummoned, an entry from the scrolls materialized word upon word in his mind. Forrester's epiphanous moment among the people of the trees claried what years of careful study had not. Words so often read and pondered, were no longer simply black marks upon a page. Now clearly revealed, they presented both history and prophecy joined in one great unbroken circle.

ESCAPING DROUGHT'S GRASP, A SOLITARY
DROP SUMMONS A DUSTY PLUME UPON
THE GROUND WHOSE GREATNESS OR TOWERS

THE SMALL RAIN BEAD'S BOUNTY. EACH
DROP JOINING TO ITS FELLOWS, BECOME A
RIVULET OF LIFE THEN A MIGHTY STREAM
THAT FEEDS THE HUNGRY SEA. THE MAIN
SATED YIELDS IT BOUNTY UNTO THE AIR,
ITS SEPARATE PARTS FALLING ONCE AGAIN
UPON THE THIRSTY GROUND. THE LIGHT
BEFORE ALL BEGINNINGS, AN OCEAN OF
LIFE SCATTERING ITSELF THROUGHOUT ALL
OF CREATION, CALLS BACK EACH DROP TO
THE MOTHER OF WATERS.

FROM THE WHOLE COMES EVERY PART.
KNOWING NOT THE WHOLE, EACH PART
BECOMES A WHOLE UNTO ITSELF. THEY
REAP SORROW AND TRAVAIL WHO WOULD
FORCE OPEN THE PORTALS OF LIGHT,
SEEKING TO MASTER THE WHOLE OF
WHICH THEY ARE BUT PIECES. IT IS THE
ANGUISH OF SEPARATION.

The travails of birth into the universe of matter were only superficially those of blood and pain. The separation as each strand was torn from the weave of life and thrust into the darkness was the real anguish. This separation, by its very nature, bred narcissistic self infatuation that, in turn, invited darkness rather than light into each individual's life. Birth was but the first step in a brief journey through an eclipsed valley in which the diarist's words were the only candle against the darkness.

More than any other ever to have trod the face of this planet, the diarist knew this anguish most acutely. Railing against the pain of separation, he spoke against fear, hate, and the illusion of security purchased through domination of others. Domination, rather than a bulwark against these lonely horrors and rages was, instead, the very incarnation of them all. He denounced the specters of pain encountered on our brief transit through the dark room of matter as shadows whose lively power was only an illusion created as the darkness fled from the small light carried within each individual.

In a manner that trannscended the simple detection of vibrations in the air called hearing, Forrester felt Esther's entry into his internal conversation.

"Set within a vessel, the light, no matter how resplendent, shines only as brightly as the lattice of the lantern allows," she said, her voice trailing off.

In the neuropsychological parlance of Forrester's training, the words of the scrolls required that the reader surmount the darkness into which all life had been thrust. The calling and the mission of each sentient life rested in rising above the demands of the limbic vehicle that armed individual survival within and against the darkness. The diarist called upon us, one and all, to recall that which was beyond individual memory. He told stories and spoke in parables, vainly attempting to awaken in all who heard the memory of a time, before time was measured in which all was light and that light was life. His rendered a ministry of the whole to the parts who could not recognize their separateness from something greater than themselves. Forrester felt saddened by the diarist's pain, but thankful and gratified by the sacrifice embodied in his birth. The message of the diarist was deceptively simple. Recall that which the head could not recollect but the heart could remember and see life's sojourn as but a path leading back to the source of all light and life.

Chapter 26

Devoid of solace, save for that which had flowed from a half empty bottle of tequila, Chauvez sat crumpled, as if against the cold, in a chair facing the wall. Sadness, guilt and alcohol drove his thoughts into dark places. Perhaps the adversarial foundations of the legal system represented more than a collection of historical precedents, he mused. Maybe a law library provided a more honest repository of human nature than the best psychology had to offer. As far as Chauvez could tell, divining justice in human affairs was neither a mystical, nor a factual, exercise. In truth, it seemed little more than a fist fight. The most deceptive, the strongest, the ones with the most friends and money inevitably won. These victors formulated the 'truth' of the contested matter for the public, at least as much truth as humanity was ever likely to know. Darwin's simple insights had never been meaningfully challenged in the daily give and take of life. Survival of the fittest governed human dynamics, but what the English naturalist may not have foreseen was the psychopathic nature of the fittest.

As an unrepentant murderer, Chauvez was a man who was systematically and at times, even eagerly plotted to kill again. He knew this simple truth could not be justified, rationalized or by stint of any other self-deception, avoided. This less than ennobling status he now shared with Cabot. Somehow, becoming just another member among so very many in this wholly conventional human club didn't make it any less distressing.

As a denomination of human endeavor, murderer was a crowded category. Often understood as an individual act of passion, such examples, in fact, represented only the smallest percentage of murderers. By far the greatest proportion of slayings resulted from the so-called just wars of nations, the plagues of prejudice including racial and religious slaughter, the successful competitive acts of corporations, and the selective elimination of opponents in squabbles over political fiefdoms. It was, to be sure, an arena of endeavor with room for all.

Chauvez, who had previously been little more than a spectator at the carnival of carnage that passed for human history, now found himself a fully vested participant. There were no more *theys* in his view of the murderous universe of human endeavors, he had joined the ranks of *them*. Becoming in deed what

Piatra had only managed to plan, he wondered whether Piatra would be proud of him? Sensibilities blunted by his new found status as a fully enfranchised member of a murderous species, he wasn't sure he cared any more how she would have felt.

Interrupting Chauvez in the midst of his alcoholic self recrimination, the chiming of the compartment door announced visitors. Phil and Dvorak appeared as the door slide open, but neither said a word as they entered the compartment until Dvorak had completed his surveillance sweep of the room. Dvorak replaced the sniffer cube in his pocket and looked up at his coconspirators.

"We're ready. The subfrequency monitors have isolated the frequency Cabot uses to communicate with his central computer. The twelve hour failsafe mechanism is activated and counting down. If something happens to any of us …" Dvorak said as he checked his chronometer. "… then, in ten hours, the entire power output of the Ark will be automatically channeled for a few seconds through Cabot's mastoid implant."

"What kind of damage do we anticipate to Cabot's central computer? I don't want to be picky here, but that computer contains the sum of human knowledge. Cabot has invaded every library computer on the planet over the centuries to make certain he has accumulated everything the human race has ever committed to computer storage. What's housed in that unit is nothing less than a compendium of human knowledge," Phil said.

"We are simply amplifying a frequency already being transmitted by the central computer," Dvorak responded as he leaned back in the chair.

"Yes, but the Ark's total power output will be channeled along the frequency. Won't it fry the central computer as well as Cabot?" Phil countered.

"It is very unlikely. In the circuit we've created, Cabot will be a better ground than the computer. He's dead meat unless he suddenly starts walking around wearing a five hundred pound insulator on his back," Dvorak remarked.

"Where's the central computer now? I heard Cabot brought it up from the Urals and installed it on his yacht," Chauvez asked.

"It was moved to a bunker adjacent to Cabot's private apartments in the ark two days ago. The central computer compartment is so well shielded I think the sun could go supernova and the computer would survive intact," Phil replied.

"That's good. I've heard about Cabot's library and I know its probably the greatest treasure he or, hopefully soon, the human race possesses," Dvorak remarked.

"It'll be his contribution, a little payback for all he's …" Chauvez said.

Dvorak gestured for Chauvez to hold his peace as the automation genius racheted forward in his chair.

"Hold on ... I've been so focused on isolating the subfrequency that I forgot. I should have passed this along before. Yesterday, I was working on the central computer, finishing up the connections to all the automated functions installed in the ark. It was so crowded with Cabot's technicians and security people you could hardly turn around. With everyone's eyes on me I wasn't allowed any more access than absolutely required to do the job. I did take the opportunity to look around a bit and recognized some of the basic designs of the unit. The firewall and front line security units are sound. I recognized the basic designs as those of one of my old teachers. In addition, the computer has invasion bulwarks, surge and feedback protections that defy belief. There's even an automatic isolation program that cuts the central processor off from all outside electronic input in the event of a burst of electromagnetic radiation that overwhelms the surge protectors. The computer is perfectly safe from anything we do to Cabot. It's like ..."

"Apart from the central computer, how much collateral damage can we expect to the surroundings when all the ark's power momentarily flows through Nick's implant?" Phil interrupted.

"Yeah, if Cabot is on the bridge of the ark when we fry him, does the whole bridge console melt down? Does everyone in his immediate vicinity become a cinder?" Chauvez asked, joining his concerns to Phil's.

"Frankly, I don't know. It's only a three second surge, but an incredible amount of energy. We can't afford to use less power because we have to be certain we overwhelm whatever safeguards are built into Cabot's implant on the first attempt. The power flowing along that frequency also has to be sufficient to cut through his personal shield grid so we can be certain he grounds to something," Dvorak responded hesitantly.

"It's that grounding part that bothers me. I don't think we can afford to burn him down while he's on the ark. We are, after all, trying to save this vessel," Chauvez remarked in a dubious tone.

"The only way to be certain we attain both objectives, killing Cabot and preserving the ark, is to attack while he's on the yacht," Phil said.

"I agree," Chauvez responded.

Phil leaned back and considered the exchange. Initially, the only matter of significance was Cabot's death. Now, the library had to be saved and the whole issue of collateral damage to the ark and her personnel had to be sorted. It was an entirely human phenomenon, enough was never enough.

"Sounds reasonable. To be certain we get the job done with minimum risk to the ark and her personnel, I'll have to activate the relay the next time we're sure Cabot is on the yacht," Dvorak responded.

"I think it's a little more complicated than that. The ark is nearly ready to launch. The closer we get to completing the ship the more time Cabot is spending here on the bridge taking personal control of every aspect of the finishing touches," Phil interjected.

"So he has to live just long enough to complete what he started," Chauvez responded with a dark twist to his tone.

"Exactly. If we take him out of the equation before the Ark is ready to launch, we'll have chaos. For example, in the next twenty-four to thirty six hours Cabot is transporting more than a half a million people from Earth to the ecosectors. Imagine trying to accomplish that in the midst of a coup d'etat. I could take over most of what Cabot has left to do, but there's his personal security force," Phil replied.

"Inasmuch as his personal security people always huddle around him like a football team around a quarterback, the surge that takes Cabot out is likely to barbecue them as well," Dvorak added.

"I agree that the timing is important. Work on the ark is essentially complete, except for loading Cabot's passengers. I know for a fact that all the construction crews have been terminated and are partying down at the moon base on Cabot's tab. Tomorrow is payday and everyone down there is drinking and discussing how they'll spend their wages and bonuses. All that's left on the ark now are the three of us and a few technical supervisors," Chauvez remarked.

"With all the automation relays up and running, we don't really need any more crew than the few that are here, but I did wonder why it felt so empty on board," Dvorak added.

"Maybe everyone's pretty much gone because that's the way Cabot wants it. His security people are here, but that just for his protection. Now that its finished, he's clearing out the ship. Maybe ..." Phil said, his tone ominous.

Chauvez blanched and his eyes widened as he reflexively took a deep breath.

"He wouldn't! I mean it would be just gratuitous mass murder if he ..." Chauvez said in a frantic tone,

Sounding like an exclamation point at the end of Chauvez's statement, the bridge alarm blared over the ark's intercom system. Punching a hole in their discussion, it caused a generalized startle reaction. The three men jumped to their feet and, exiting Chauvez's compartment, entered the bridge in a matter of moments.

Moving to the console, Chauvez terminated the alarm as soon as he saw what had tripped it. A proximity motion sensor had detected Cabot's two battle cruisers as they broke out of their defensive orbits around the ark. The sleek craft overflew the ark on a trajectory that would bring them over the moon base far below. Watching in horror, the three men saw the cruisers set up for strafing runs over the huge lunar complex housing hundred of thousands of construction workers.

"No," Chauvez said through gritted teeth.

As a helpless observer, Chauvez watched the fusion missiles lance out from the cruisers and reduce the lunar base to a plume of fire and dust.

Struck momentarily speechless, Phil stood an impotent witness to the deaths of the many who had slaved to build Cabot's little kingdom in the sky.

"Damn you Nick, damn you to hell," Phil muttered.

Making one additional pass over the moon base, the cruisers appeared to be scanning for anything or anyone they might have missed. Apparently satisfied they had totally obliterated their target, they climbed back to their defensive orbits beyond the ark.

Shaking uncontrollably, Phil grasped the console unable to take his eyes from the destruction below. Once again, time and timing had made him complicit by omission in one of Cabot's atrocities.

In a flat tone suggesting he was desperately trying to put some distance between his emotions and the horror he had just witnessed, Dvorak added his impression.

"I guess this is the surest sign Cabot is ready to set sail."

In the past, before he had donned the cloak of murderer, Chauvez might have been offended by Dvorak's insensitive remark. Now, he just stared at the holocaust below on the moon's surface, shrouded in plumes of destruction. The scope of the atrocity was too incomprehensible to appreciate in terms of the hundreds of thousands of individual lives that had been unceremoniously snuffed out of existence.

"Yes, I suppose that's what it means," Chauvez replied.

The hypnotic power of such atrocities to rivet an observer was a primal form of shock and, perhaps, the closest man came to sharing the despair and death of his fellows. Phil was immobile. No matter how much he wanted to look away, he could not take his gaze from the scene of devastation below. So much of his life had been spent in Cabot's service, so much living, so much standing passively on the sidelines while Cabot coerced and assassinated his way to the personal convenience of nearly absolute power. If Phil had any vestigial doubts about murdering Nick, they had been swept away by the fuel dump fed firestorm that continued to ravage the shattered domes of the lunar base.

After a few seconds of silence, Phil spoke in slow, carefully measured tones.

"There will be a moment … a moment when the population of the ecosectors will be entirely ensconced … a moment before Nick transfers his security force and personal effects from his yacht to the ark … that is when we must kill him."

"Why do we have to wait for Cabot's handpicked passengers to show up? If he picked them, they're probably as depraved as he is. Let's kill the son of a bitch now!" Chauvez said, his voice laced with anger.

"I agree with Chauvez. The sooner we act the better our chances of success. Besides, its natural to assume Cabot would pick those of like mind and temperament to serve with him on this voyage of the damned. The moon base villainy convinces me Cabot always intended the ark to be an amalgam of pirate ship and Flying Dutchman," Dvorak said.

Studying Dvorak and Chauvez intently in turn, Phil knew anger contaminated their reasoning. The situation reassured him that a discussion and clarification of the matter of the ecosector's inhabitants was required. Such a discussion might also serve to distract them from the profligate destruction of human life they had just witnessed.

"Your reasoning is sound but incomplete. Nick's whole life has been about exercising control over people. It's no more complicated than that. In order for Nick to be the only member of the species that no one controls, he has to be the person who controls everyone else. If he populated the ark with a half million people like himself he could never achieve that goal," Phil said in a subdued tone.

"But hasn't Cabot already achieved absolute control over the human race through the centuries? I mean he answers to no one and he's untouchable," Chauvez said in rebuttal.

"Power is the ultimate and possibly defining addiction of the human species. For those like Nick who are profoundly addicted, every door opened to a vista of power also reveals an infinite number of portals beyond it that promise even greater dominion," Phil said in a world weary tone.

"If you're right about power being the fulcrum of human motivation, then who the hell is Cabot ferrying up here to fill those ecosectors, sheep?" Dvorak responded.

"In a metaphorical sense that's exactly what Nick has in mind. Decades ago Nick stole the research of an insightfully, creative neuropsychologist that extolled a theory in which a small proportion of humanity represented just that, sheep. Cabot translated those theories into fact in a large reserve in western Canada exclusively populated by those 'sheep,' " Phil replied.

"So if Cabot is going to stock the ark with human sheep, what does that make the rest of us, wolves?" Chauvez asked bitterly.

"I guess if you want to extend the metaphor, that's exactly what the majority of the human race represents. Like those predatory pack animals, we take care of each other, care for our young with considerable solicitude and enforce pack solidarity through a dominance hierarchy. Except wolves don't destroy their own habitat or engage in killing for its own sake. Unlike the wolves, it is human nature to exploit one another to an even greater extent than we abuse the environment that spawned us. As an older and evolutionarily more refined species, wolves no longer have a lot of our infantile, self-destructive traits. They ..." Phil replied.

"So does that make Cabot the big bad wolf of humanity?" Chauvez interjected.

"I don't know. But, he is certainly a *bad* wolf, as wolves go. He's divorced from the pack, cares for no pack member but himself and routinely makes kills that don't serve his survival needs or those of the pack. Yes, I'd say that he's ..." Phil replied.

Fidgeting in his chair; Dvorak finally gave expression to his exasperation.

"Hell, I'm lost. Who are these people Cabot is shipping up here?"

"The neuropsychologist who did the research called them the dominance deficient. They represent an incredibly small, indeed shrinking, proportion of the population. They differ from the majority of the human race in that their strengths are largely left hemispheric. Despite considerable evidence of ability and an incredibly strong intrinsic work and service ethic, they inevitably end up being victimized by their more dominance driven peers," Phil replied.

Dvorak became increasingly frustrated with the lack of a definitive answer to his question.

"So what's this left hemispheric crap?" He asked.

"OK, the short version ... the right hemisphere is what has kept us alive for millions of years. It houses all our visual-spatial strengths, hunting instincts, reflexive reactions to threat, as well as dominance and procreative drives to ensure our personal and tribal survival. It's the oldest part of what you might call the thinking brain," Phil replied.

"OK, I've got that, but what about the left?" Chauvez said.

"The left hemisphere, well language to be sure, but language principally in its symbolic rather than concrete aspects. The left hemisphere is about abstraction, about positive energy directed to constructive means and their natural ends. The left focuses on the future as completely as the right hemisphere is wedded to the present and the past. Cabot's interest in this group comes down to one attribute they all possess, its the characteristic for which they're named the dominance deficient, or, as Cabot's inner circle calls them, the meek," Phil responded.

"So they're losers. Cabot wants to take off into the galaxy with a whole shipload of docile, smilingly hopeful losers," Dvorak said spontaneously.

"Losers, yes, that's a pretty good comparative descriptor. If you contrast the meek's behavior to the majority of their dominance driven fellows in the human species whose stated or covert goal in every interaction is winning ... that's operational ... yeah, that works," Phil replied.

"OK, let me get this straight. We fry Cabot to a cinder and if we're lucky, we take out his private security force and the whole fucking yacht to boot," Chauvez said.

"That's a possibility," Dvorak interjected.

"So for the sake of argument, we've gotten rid of Cabot, the ark pretty much runs itself and what it can't do for itself the three of us can handle. The ecosectors that account for seventy-five percent of the ship are filled with losers, who do what? I mean, do they just mill about bleating contentedly while thinking happy thoughts?" Chauvez continued.

"Damn good question. What the hell do we do once we've loaded a human cargo that was handpicked by a man who is dead and gone? I mean, hell, I have no desire to become some kind of half-assed sun king to a bunch of losers who can't do shit for themselves," Dvorak chimed in.

Chauvez became more agitated as he considered the price so many had paid to bring them to the point of freeing the ark from Cabot's grasp.

"I don't know if I relish the idea of firing up the ark and pulling out of here with a boatload of the least successful examples ... of ... of humanity evolution ever coughed up for parts unknown because the war is going against us ... and, and leaving the better half of humanity ... behind," Chauvez sputtered.

Listening carefully to opinions he fully expected to hear, Phil's ear, tuned by two hundred years more experience than either Chauvez or Dvorak, heard nothing unanticipated. Grooved by the study of living systems rather than the mechanical relationships Chauvez and Dvorak's technical training had provided, Phil heard the fear and frustration that always accompanied too tight a focus on a very large and as yet unrevealed picture. He knew that what he was listening to was utilitarian reasoning and logical inferences proceeding from input-output equivalencies. Nowhere in their analysis did they recognize the simple fact that creativity was the exclusive and intrinsic property of living systems and that the passengers of whom they spoke, the meek, were a living system.

Phil allowed Dvorak and Chauvez's emotional crescendo to wind down for a moment before he spoke.

"I mentioned that Nick chose them expressly for their dominance deficiency. As always, Nick culls people out of the general population solely for attributes he perceives will fill his needs. But Nick is no biologist. For him, people's lives are a means to his ends. Underestimating the potential inherent to an individual life, much less the force of evolution as it is manifested in the population of over a half a million, is always foolhardy."

"So, you think there may be more to these people than the fact that they're dreamers?" Chauvez asked.

"Yes, a great deal more. The left hemisphere is the newest functional addition to the thinking machine we call the brain. We just don't know what left hemispheric thinkers can do when they're isolated from the competitively hostile environment created by the dominance driven right hemispheric majority. It is highly unlikely that whatever they can do will amount to a simple redundant extension of right hemispheric abilities. I just don't ..." Phil said.

Demonstrating his characteristic impatience with anything that could not be reduced to a circuit schematic, Dvorak interrupted.

"What's your best guess?"

"The only thing I'm certain of is that the genetics of evolution dictates mutations never occur in isolation," Phil replied.

"What the hell does that mean?" Chauvez retorted.

"It's an old medical rule of thumb. If you find one, look for two, if you find two, look for three, if you find three, look for a whole bunch," Phil replied.

"Shit, Phil ... is this your Zen master routine? What the hell are you talking about?" Dvorak said impatiently.

"Nick misapplied a technical-business paradigm to an evolving, living system. He picked the meek as worshippers because of their dominance deficiency as that was the only attribute interesting to him. But that dominance deficiency is tied up with abstract symbolic competence, that's two. Then, there's these people's positive outlook that demands that both the means of achieving a goal and the resultant ends be constructive, that's three. If we fall back on the old medical rule of thumb, I mentioned before, then three makes a whole bunch. That suggests there may be a whole constellation of attributes embedded in these people that we haven't yet discovered or abilities vested in their nature that simply haven't fully declared themselves," Phil said, smiling ever so slightly.

"Wait a minute. It just struck me what your medical rule of thumb amounts to," Dvorak exclaimed his eyes brightening.

"What's that?" Phil asked.

Suddenly, Dvorak's face was wholly contorted into a self-congratulatory expression as he leaned forward and launched into his explanation.

"Hell, it's the Fibonacci sequence. You know, the old rabbit propagation model. You put one male and one female rabbit in a field with no predators and over time how many rabbits do you get. Come on, you guys know this. The rate of increase in rabbits goes, 1, 1, 2, 3, 5, 8, 13, 21, and so on. The damn sequence is part of every living system on the planet."

"You're right. I'd just never thought about it that way. If the meeks' mutation has released a cluster of genetic changes that follows the Fibonacci sequence, then the number of their new abilities may outstrip anything I imagined," Phil replied.

"It still seems to me we're gonna pull out of orbit with an evolutionary pig in a poke on board," Chauvez remarked.

"Or, based on what you're saying Phil, maybe the evolutionary future of humankind. Sure as hell, they don't sound much like the rest of us. I think I'm beginning to get it. These meek, whatever, are like a quantum circuit that can alter itself, but you can't tell how many directions it might take off in simultaneously. The future of humanity, what a notion," Dvorak said in a more serious tone.

"I guess the future of any life form is always a pig in a poke. Creative unpredictability has always been a defining characteristic of all living systems. In any event, we'll be onboard, as well as our families, representing the majority of our dominance driven and murderous kind. In my opinion, we don't have a lot of choice. Cabot has arranged for the meek to be ferried up here and I don't think we have the time to start over again from the beginning. Besides, how would each of you chose a half million people to fill out the ship's complement out of the billions on the planet?" Phil added.

"If the scuttlebutt I've heard about the war represents anything close to the truth, we could have anything from minutes to days before those alien bastards climb down our throats," Chauvez said as he folded his hands and stared at the floor.

"I agree. We've got to go with what's in place. We can't reinvent the wheel at this late date. Phil and I have already arranged for our families to be ferried up with the first load of ... sheep ... meek, whatever. What about you, Chauvez?" Dvorak asked.

"My immediate family is gone. All I had was Piatra, and then ... Ashely, but she wasn't ..." Chauvez replied sadly.

Dvorak, demonstrating a degree of insensitivity his colleagues had come to accept with good humor, interrupted Chauvez's soliloquy.

"Don't worry Chauvez, I've got a couple of real knock out female technical supervisors in mind for you. You'll be all right."

Attempting to stifle a grin, Phil looked away momentarily. Dvorak was so predictable, always to the mechanical heart of the matter. Chauvez glancing up, noticed the half embarrassed smile Phil tried to conceal and the wholly genuine expression of solicitude on Dvorak's face.

"Whatever," Chauvez said, turning to Dvorak.

All smiles, Dvorak seemed pleased with the success of his matchmaking intervention into Chauvez's state of conjugal solitude.

Broadening smiles appeared on the faces of Chauvez and Phil which opened into raucous guffaws. Without knowing why, Dvorak joined in their expression of joviality.

Gaining control over his bout of laughter, Phil sat back and watched the two men laughing in an ever escalating cascade of uproariously good humor. A release of pent up tension, he thought to himself. Here were two very different men sharing a common moment of happiness in which neither understood the other's motivation to mirth. In the microcosm, it was a lesson in the relative insignificance of motivation. Each of his friends was laughing at something different, or at nothing at all. It made no difference, the outcome was beneficial to both. It was a lesson hard in the learning for a species equally enamored with both motivations and outcomes to recognize that for the mainstream of humanity there was no necessary connection between the two.

In this brief interlude, Phil realized that the transient moment of good humor between two friends, was different only by degree from Cabot's global scheme for himself and humanity in that order. In both instances, there was no compulsory cause and effect relationship between motivation and outcome, save only in the arrogance of human contrivance. Perhaps the meek had it right. Nothing could be vouched safe except by insisting on the rightness of both means and ends. Damn his own analytic penchant. Phil could see problems with espousing either the congruity or incongruity of motivations and outcomes. One thing was clear, congruity of intention and its expression in action only worked if everyone involved played by the same rules. Maybe, he wondered, that's what the meek were about, everybody actually and consistently playing by a rule book that mandated righteous intentions as well as righteous outcomes.

Regardless of how this venture unfolded, Phil was increasingly convinced that the sum of the beliefs, feelings, and motivations of all those concerned, including himself, would have little to do with the outcome. As for Cabot and the grandiose plans he would never live to see realized, well, it wouldn't be the first time in human history that a malevolent motivation produced a beneficial outcome. He listen to that thought reverberate in the vault of this cranium, and desperately hoped that it represented more than a naive fantasy.

Chapter 27

Awakened by a gentle knocking, Forrester rose from his bed, donned his robe, and went to the door already knowing it was Crystal who had roused him. He felt very satisfied with himself as he opened the door to Crystal's smiling face. He was getting better at comprehending the meek and how they made their way in the world. At its root, this seeing-knowing ability resulted from a conscious decision to perceive the world without falling back on the five physiological senses, sort of like being asked to make sense of a woodland scene by closing your eyes. Suddenly, you could hear the stream gurgling, the birds singing and the insects humming about you. You could feel the sun on your skin and smell the difference between the grass growing along the bank of the stream and the turf prosperiing on the hill.

"Good morning Doctor Forrester. It's time for breakfast," Crystal said, a happy lilt dancing in her voice.

Transfixed for a long moment, Forrester was captivated by the purple and blue hues dancing in Crystal's aura. Then, for reasons he couldn't explain, it struck him that he wasn't seeing that aura with his eyes. It felt like vision, but when he closed his eyes for a second, Crystal and her aura persisted. He had never tried that before and so he hadn't recognized that the *seeing* of the meek occurred without benefit of the physiological pathways associated with vision. Then, pulling himself away from the excitement of yet another epiphany, he responded to Crystal's invitation.

"Good morning Crystal. Breakfast sounds great."

"Old paths are well traveled and feel safe. New paths are harder to walk, but there are more things to see," Crystal said as her expression warmed to beneficence.

Then, placing her hand over the center of her forehead, she gestured for Forrester to do likewise.

Positioning his hand over his own forehead in imitation of Crystal's placement, he noticed a marked difference. The perceptual impact immediately failed as his vision of Crystal and her aura dimmed. His field of vision for what the ancient Indian Yogis would have called his third eye was obscured. When he removed his hand, Crystal and her aura sprang back with perfect clarity. The seeing he experienced was a physical manifestation of the brain's activity that proceeded without benefit of any externally discernible sensory organ.

Analytic relays closing with perfect left hemispheric precision, he deduced this ability had been latently present to greater or lesser degrees in the human gene pool for eons. The perceptual phenomenon sometimes called second sight, but more frequently referred to as the third eye, was said to see beyond the material to the spiritual. Amidst hordes of pretenders, a few shamen and holy figures seemed able to characterize mortal men as surrounded by halos of light or auras they perceived emanating from the human body. A much larger group of people with well documented synesthesia saw colors inherent in people and objects, but to which they attributed no particular spiritual significance. Clearly, the precursor fragments of the seeing of the people of the trees had been around a long time.

"Breakfast," Crystal said as she tugged on his hand.

With Crystal in the lead, they marched down the stairs and onto the terrace where Esther and Jacob were setting the table in the bright sunlit expanse of the morning. Crystal immediately grabbed a glass of orange juice and sat down.

Forrester had no difficulty finding his place at the table, marked as it was by a large glass of brown and frothy apple cider. Exchanging greetings with Esther and Jacob, he felt his appetite rising as Esther set a plate before him containing a filet of eggplant resting on a bed of saffron rice. It was marvelous to have your desires read before they reached the plateau of verbal conceptualization. As they all sat down to eat, intrusively, the quiet of the woodland was shattered by the roaring passage of a large spacefaring shuttle passing over head. Forrester was the only one at the table to look up.

"They're gathering additional animal specimens for the ecosectors on the ark," Esther remarked without glancing up.

Jacob looked up and over the terrace railing to the lake that lay only a few hundred meters from the house. He spoke, but his gaze remained fixed on the azure blue surface of the lake.

"Soon, it will be our turn. It will be difficult to leave all this."

Esther offered Crystal a napkin to dab away some syrup that had found its way onto her cheek.

"Have you started your packing, Honey?" Esther asked.

Crystal nodded without looking up from her waffles and corn syrup.

"Daddy, I don't think Doctor Forrester knows. You know, about going away," she said, looking up at her father.

Jacob set his fork down onto the bed of ginger, black rice and honey on his plate as he turned to Forrester.

"I'm sorry Doctor Forrester. I should have recognized you are still hesitant to see into others without a specific invitation to do so," Jacob said apologetically.

"Yes, I guess that's so. There are quite a number of things I haven't figured out and even more with which I'm not yet comfortable," Forrester replied, taking a sip of cider.

"We received a message over the reserve's holosystem early this morning that the entire community will be transported to Mr. Cabot's ship in the next day or so. Each of us will be allowed to take two containers of personal effects with us on the transfer," Jacob remarked.

"We still have plenty of time to get ready because the shuttles are beginning their pickups at the western edge of the reserve," Esther added.

Consummately satisfied that he didn't have to look at his own face as it expressed yet another variation of confusion and disorientation, Forrester cast a glance about at the idyllic landscape. He was just becoming acclimated to the reserve and now they were moving to Cabot's ark, a vessel he had heard about only by way of snatches of gossip on the space station.

"So, what's this all about?" He asked, looking over at Jacob.

"We have all seen the visions of what must be. The map of space-time shows the way … that which will be, already is," Jacob responded, wearing a puzzled expression.

A vortex that refused to resolve into a coherent focus churned inside Forrester's head. His mental panorama was a jumble of images, fragments of physiological perceptions and bits of *seeing*. His linear analytic prowess was not up to the task of justifying this confusion into a series of neat branching programs. More telling, however, was the sinking feeling he must have appeared like the paradigmatic doubting Thomas to Jacob.

Detecting his confusion, Crystal reached out and placing her tiny hand into his, gently squeezed his fingers.

"To see is not always to notice," she intoned almost melodiously.

Coincident to her touch, the confusion within Forrester's mind ebbed. Slowly, the whirlpool of sensory fragments jelled into two distinct images. The first image displayed a huge ball, at first gripped in an ominous black hand and, then, glowing with a blue-white light, it sped off into the void. The second image portrayed the Earth transformed into a glass ball. Then three spheres that instantly took flight into a field of stars entered the scene.

Forrester was the pupil now, and Crystal was teaching him how to perceive the 'seeing.' It was a lesson he had taught generations of graduate students. Sensation was the raw material, perception was the cognitive process that made sense of it. The seeing was not magic, but a new sensory experience. Learning how to manipulate and categorize this sensation made it comprehensible, made it a perception.

Looking down, Forrester noticed Crystal had released his hand. He leaned over and kissed her lightly on the top of her head.

"Thank you, Crystal," he said.

Smiling at Crystal, Forrester turned to her parents with a slightly embarrassed expression on his face.

"I apologize for being such a slow learner."

"No apology is ever required for learning. The community has learned together as a unit for a long time. Your absence at the beginning has forced you to learn on your own what we discovered together," Esther replied.

"Doctor Forrester, I've been a student of your work from a time long before we came to the reserve. And, if you'll forgive me Sir, your commitment to factual analysis is commendable, but it prevents you from gathering the fruits of speculative extrapolation toward which your own work so clearly points," Jacob said, traces of a sheepish expression on his face.

"Gently, gently, Jacob. The Doctor's work made all of this possible. The fact that we are together in this place and enjoy the opportunity to see and learn all that we have begins with him. In order to accomplish that for us, he has lived his entire life among the right hemispheric majority," Esther interjected.

Jacob smiled at Esther and turned to Forrester, speaking in softer and more conciliatory tones.

"You have always experienced yourself as a second rate person compared to the right hemispheric majority of the human race. You could not effectively compete with your right hemispheric peers in wresting from the world that which they held to be of value. The right hemisphere, as you know only too well, is perfectly attuned to the visual-spatial realities of the material world. That half of the brain is tasked with subduing, dissecting and wringing meaning from that which can be seen, heard and touched. The right brain quests endlessly for significance in the dirt and, when it cannot find that which satisfies its soul, it destroys the very ground upon which it stands."

"The right brain is the mother of our survival, but she appreciates only her own needs and desires while striving ceaselessly to remove obstacles to their fulfillment. She is a relentlessly vigilant parent whose obedient offspring seek, by subduing the whole of creation, to quiet the unrest they feel within," Esther said as she tenderly grasped Jacob's hand.

"In us, nature is searching for another avenue through which the universe may know itself. We are nature's next step in her endless quest for less cluttered and more direct avenues through which the universe may come to greater self awareness. We are a grand boulevard paving over the path the right hemisphere has beaten over the millennia, just a fork that divides the common highway of humanity. We are called as seers to the material universe so it may better comprehend the loom of life that spawned and supports it," Jacob remarked as he intertwined his fingers in those of his spouse.

"As with all new life, we remain fragile. But stepchildren of the right hemisphere. nature makes the way for us to travel, but, in truth, she knows us not. Were it within her power, she would sort us out of the litter and drown us to preserve her own lineage. To survive, if survive we will, a separate path chooses us," Esther said, staring off across the lake.

"And that separate path is Cabot's ark?" Forrester asked looking intently at Jacob.

"Yes," Jacob replied.

"But, by all reports; Cabot is a person wholly committed to himself, a man who regards others as but means to his ends. Why would he save the people of the trees? If Cabot is the man he appears to be, who will rescue the people of the trees from the man who is delivering them?" Forrester asked, as he fired off a string of definitive analytic questions.

"These are worthy questions for which we have no worthy answers. We know only that what we have seen is what must be. Our assurance rests in knowing that what must be serves life for its source is the first row in the weave of all that lives. In this hope we remain. What Mister Cabot is, what he thinks, feels and does is already part of what must be," Jacob replied.

"To be of the people of the trees is to know that all the threads of life return to the loom from which they were loosed. With each fiber of life that returns to the weave, the loom becomes more aware of what it has created in fashioning the physical universe," Esther said, a reverent tone in her voice.

Desperately trying to assimilate everything he had just heard, Forrester suddenly became aware that Crystal was staring at him. Then, turning her gaze to the lake and hills surrounding the terrace, she carefully recited a passage from the diarist's scrolls.

> WE ENTER LIFE KNOWING ONLY LIFE.
> THOUGH WE SOJOURN IN DARKNESS,
> WE HOLD IT TO BE LIGHT, OUR EYE
> DIMMED BY THE SHADOWS. OUR
> JOURNEY FROM BEFORE TO NOW AND
> TO BEFORE AGAIN IS A TIMELESS
> SOJOURN FROM LIGHT TO DARKNESS
> AND DARKNESS TO LIGHT AGAIN.

THROUGH ALL THAT HAS LIFE WILL
THE LIGHT KNOW THE DARKNESS
THAT SPRANG FROM IT. AS THE
CHILD BECOMES A MAN, SO THE
DARKNESS GROWS WITH EACH
TWINKLING OF LIFE TO THE
MANHOOD OF LIGHT.

WHEN THE LIGHT, THAT MADE
THE DARKNESS, GATHERS IT ONCE
AGAIN UNTO ITSELF, THEN, SHALL
ALL BE LIGHT AND ALL THAT IS
LIGHT SHALL BE LIFE.

⁂

Forrester had not yet completely appreciated the implicit faith of the people of the trees. Nevertheless, he felt the quiet power of their conviction in which not the tiniest shred of proselytizing need resided. In Crystal's recitation of the diarist's words, Forrester suddenly saw the reality within the poetry. A culmination was coming. In some timeless moment, the loom of light and life would so completely perforate the physical universe with pathways for living threads of itself that the shell of material reality would simply crumble back into the life force that had created it.

Despite the transfiguring changes he had experienced in his perception and physical being, he was still a step by step thinker. Perhaps it was this attribute, which so fully governed his cognition, that made him an adequate lens for the seeing of the people of the trees. Like a man laying paving stones for a path, Forrester had always pieced bits of fact and inference together in a straight line driven by the naive faith that the path would lead to some great insight. So very often, he thought to himself, that straight line had proliferated into an endless branching network of ideas and speculations. His investigations had managed only to add to the growing edge of each branch so that over the years, like some great tree, his thoughts spread outward with most cognitive limbs and twigs terminating in the thin air of the unknown.

In becoming the lens for the people of the trees, the flow of his personal thinking style reversed. Now, he became the trunk that gathered all the twigs, branches and limbs of the meek together in a joint cognition of what must be.

Forrester knew in an instant that sliding down the trunk of this arborescent met-aphor had evoked the image he required to understand the vision of the black hand clutching the sphere. Blood had dripped between the knuckles of that dark hand as it released the sphere. The hand that crafted the ark would be severed, allowing the people of the trees to follow the path that had chosen them.

Gradually, he became aware of Crystal's and her parents' stares. Looking up, he saw their faces wreathed in expressions of satisfaction.

"Sorry, I tend to drift off like that," he said, fumbling with his napkin.

"You are set among us to be the trunk to our branches. But, you are also clad in the purple of childhood and, as a child, you climb into the branches and slide down the trunk of the tree that is the thought and seeing of the com-munity. All of our children will one day frolic in the boughs of this tree and your thoughts reveal the games they will play," Esther said, her face warming with delight.

Feeling foolish for what seemed an interminable moment, Forrester re-membered. Of course, they *could* see his thought process. It was difficult to keep that in mind while he muddled about in the labyrinthine maze that passed for his brain.

"I sort of get lost trying to figure things out. Sometimes I'm just lost, and sometimes, on rare occasions, I find something I didn't even know I was looking for in a place I wasn't even searching," he said, not knowing exactly what to say.

The moment he stopped speaking, a blindingly simple insight rose from a dusty corner in his mind. Perhaps, not all of his thoughts were his own. 'Trunk to our branches' Esther had said. Maybe all those years of piecing together his own thoughts into branching programs of fact and inference served as but preparation for providing that selfsame service to the community of the meek. One thing was clear, at least at this point, they could see into his head better than he could see into their minds. This fact alone suggested some of the input he juggled might be coming from them. Even more amazing than this phenom-enon was the fact that, as the thoughts wandered through his head, they all felt like his own.

Crystal and Esther had referred to him as a lens for the community. A lens gathered light and focused it on a single point. Up to this point, he had understood his function in that regard in terms of the community's need to see beyond their current time and place in the stream of space-time. Now, it occurred to him this lens business might be a twenty-four-seven occupation. Maybe the inside of his head acted like kind of a cognitive town hall where the thoughts of the meek congregated.

"It is the gift of the purple to look into the mind and not be afraid. You show us how to follow whatever path presents itself and are the complete manifestation of a belief in life that only a child of the trees may own. Yours is to know when complexity must give way to simplicity, and when simplicity is but the gateway to greater intricacy. You follow the light amidst the darkness even when you have only your belief that it shines around the next turn in the path to carry your steps forward and we follow you," Jacob said.

"Vested in the right hemisphere from the beginning of our race is the courage to confront the dangers of the material universe. The valor of the left is to follow wherever thought leads with only the flickering flame of curiosity to light the way. That most fundamental and irreducible quality of thought and feeling is the trusting curiosity of childhood. At the center of the loom of life and representing the seed of its genesis, this positive striving existed from before the time when the dark blanket of the universe unfurled. This singular quality, which arises in the youth among those who seek dominance but ebbs with maturity, is the flesh and bone of the meek at any age," Esther said, reaching to take Forrester's hand.

A gentle smile lighting her face, Esther held Forrester's gaze as she continued.

"We are now and forever the hopefully curious children of humankind. It is no accident that the diarist's scrolls came to you or that you came to us," she said with a gentle finality.

Feeling the weight of this onerous responsibility to the people of the trees pressing down on his frame, Forrester slumped visibly in his chair. Yet, his crumpling posture was a mere token of the whirlwind of dire musings churning within. The horror that spun feverishly in the midst of his mind turned on the prospect of making some error in his thinking that might jeopardize the entire community.

"Doctor Forrester, what you do for us is fully represented in who you are.

Who you are has brought you to us, to this place, and to this time. Your own doubts notwithstanding, everything is as it should be," Jacob's said, interrupting Forrester's cognitive distress.

"We are gathering," Crystal said as she stood.

Practically at a run, Crystal moved toward the hopper. Following their daughter's lead, Esther and Jacob rose from the table and hurried toward the hopper with Forrester in tow. With all onboard, Crystal activated the hopper, which rose and, in minutes, alighted amidst many of its kind on the grassy expanse surrounding the service center.

A large crowd of the meek had already gathered around Chen and Chandra when the hopper carrying Forrester and Crystal's family arrived. Adding to Forrester's feeling of embarrassment at what he perceived as wholly unmerited attention, several members of the crowd nodded and smiled deferentially at him as he passed among them.

Chen raised his hand and the crowd directed their attention to him.

"As I am sure you are already aware, you will all be transferred to Mister Cabot's ark in the next fifteen hours. Please bring only two containers of personal effects. In the ark you will find your homes within the largest of the ecosectors that has been appointed with the native flora and fauna of this region. The other ecosectors of the ark, representing most all of the major ecospheres of the planet, are uninhabited except for their native animal and plant species. These are open for you to visit at any time," Chen said, a hint of sadness in his voice.

"You must all be ready when the space shuttles arrive at the service center. There are many people to transport and delays will not be tolerated," Chandra added, her tone as dark as her expression.

Taking a few steps toward the crowd, Chen appeared to be distancing himself from Chandra and the harsh and uncompromising melody carrying her words.

"You will all be notified in time to board the shuttles," Chen said, smiling.

Then, looking down at the grassy expanse at his feet, Chen paused for a long moment before returning his gaze to the sea of faces before him.

"It is the ... the crowning achievement of my life to have lived among you. I have been witness to ... I have been honored to witness ... a new birth in the future of the human species and for that I am grateful. I wish you well on your journey," Chen stammered as tears appeared in his eyes.

Moving forward in small groups, many among those assembled were anxious to shake Chen's hand and say their goodbyes. As the well wishers dispersed, Forrester, whose mood had been lifted by Chen's outpouring of affection toward the meek, walked over to where he was now standing by himself.

"Doctor Forrester, how nice of you to come by. You look well, happy," Chen said as he looked up.

"I take it from your remarks that you won't be accompanying the community?" Forrester said, shaking Chen's hand.

"No, I wasn't invited," Chen replied hesitantly.

Then, exercising obvious effort, he gathered his composure and continued.

"I'll wrap up some paper work here at the reserve and then, well, I don't know. Maybe, I'll look for another university position. The experience of working with the meek should make it easy for me to land a full professorship. I'm sure it will all work out, but nothing is ever going to compare to working with and living among the meek."

"Everyone among the people of the trees is convinced I'm going with them, but, I'm not so certain that Mister Cabot would be pleased to see me," Forrester said.

"I'm positive he wouldn't. Cabot generally doesn't tolerate anyone in the trenches who has a more complete picture of how one of his projects works than himself. In particular, he would exclude someone like yourself who is the acknowledged instigator of the research that forms the foundation of this effort. You'd be seen as a source of dangerous ideas and, therefore, a threat to Cabot's agenda. For that reason alone, I feel it is essential you accompany the community. Someone who understands the meek as something other than a means to an end must be there to defend their interests," Chen replied emphatically.

In that moment, it became clear to Forrester that Chen's affection for and commitment to the meek was more than simple lip service. However, Chen, like the meek, grossly overestimated Forrester's ability to advocate for them.

"The word is that the space shuttle crews are checking identification chips as they board passengers. I don't have an identification chip anymore since I'm dead, at least, according to the official records," Forrester said.

A sly smile crept across Chen's face as he responded to Forrester's concerns.

"I've thought of that. From the day you arrived here, I've been resurrecting a child we slaughtered in the early days of the project. This child's parents never saw him. Once we have an entity in the computer records, it's only a matter of a few key strokes to adjust the age to reflect your current status."

An awful pall of darkness settled over his thoughts as Forrester met Chen's gaze.

"So I'll have the identity of a little boy murdered to satisfy Cabot's evolutionary agenda for the meek. An agenda he drew directly from my work."

"With all respect, Doctor Forrester, you cannot rationally take responsibility for every action Cabot took after stealing your research. You saw the dangers inherent in your work and did your best to suppress your discoveries because of that concern. You'd be on firmer logical ground to feel culpable for the prehistoric progenitor who killed a competitor to get the woman who stands at the head of your genetic line than to carry a cross for these atrocities," Chen retorted.

For a moment Chen sounded like Arthur, Forrester thought to himself. Despite the fact Chen had known Forrester only a brief period of time, Chen was right. Forrester's old guilt reflex had reawakened to its full vigor by the startling necessity of the circumstances.

"So in the stead of whose son do I stand?" Forrester asked.

Then, without consciously realizing it, he reflexively stepped back as if to cushion the blow of the upcoming revelation.

Taking note of Forrester's physical withdrawal, Chen's altered his tone from the chiding note he had just taken to a nearly apologetic softness.

"Based on the operations necessary to get around the computer safeguards there was only one good fit. You will bear the identity of Esther and Jacob's first born."

Noticing he had taken yet another step back from Chen, Forrester heard a snap in his head as if another piece of some gigantic puzzle being assembled there had fallen into place. What was it that Esther had said to him, 'You are Crystal's elder brother and at once father to us all,' Forrester had assumed the reference to be a poetic one, now he wasn't so sure.

"Thanks, Chen. We've known each other for only a short time, but you've been a good friend," he responded.

"In all truth Doctor Forrester, it's not that difficult to be your friend. Besides it's been my pleasure. Very few professionals get the opportunity to pay back a mentor. But ... there is one thing you could do for me," Chen said.

"If it's within my power," Forrester replied.

"The meek, how does it come out? What do you see? Are they the future of humanity?" Chen asked as he ushered Forrester toward his office.

"I really don't know. I suspect they're one experimental branch in the future of the human race. The bulk of humanity will continue pretty much as we've known them throughout history," Forrester responded.

"So if evolution is sending them off in a separate direction from the majority of the tribe, what makes them fundamentally different from the mainstream of humanity?" Chen asked as they entered the office.

Suppressing a smile as he pondered the question for a moment, Forrester recognized something very familiar about Chen's repetitive linear questioning. He was left hemispheric to be sure, but likely he had some right hemispheric strengths as well. Maybe Chen was more like Arthur than Forrester had initially suspected.

"I'm reasonably sure I haven't seen even ten percent of what they will eventually be able to do, but what I have seen is pretty remarkable. It's difficult to explain because, like you said when I first arrived, knowing the meek is an experiential process. Physiologically they have the ability to see beneath the appearance of material reality. They can apply that same sensory capacity to seeing both into each other and into the future, which they believe is fixed to the same extent as the past," Forrester replied.

"I've suspected for some time there was something more than sociological change going on in this community. Just separating the prey from the predators wouldn't account for all the things I've seen. A new sensory avenue through which to experience the universe, what's it like?" Chen asked, his anticipation growing.

"I'm just speculating, you understand, but I think the meek represent a nearly complete frontal lobe ascendance over the driver mechanisms of the limbic system. The right hemisphere was the first cognitive step up from the reflexive drives intrinsic to the limbic system. Over eons, the limbic-right hemispheric enmeshed nexus consistently ensured our survival through the meanderings of our evolutionary history right up to the present time. However, the right half of our cerebral powerhouse has provided that security at the cost of an ensanguined, dominance goaded history ever since," Forrester replied.

"And the left?" Chen asked.

"The left hemisphere comes along full of words, abstractions and ideals but armed with no intrinsic survival drives. In particular, the left half of the brain has no rough and ready peer dominance reflexes, hence, the lefts become, of necessity, the meek. What's happened among the people of the trees is the frontal lobe gets recruited by the left hemisphere and, in this process, the physiological ability to see the abstract as reality emerges."

"So they project their own unfulfilled needs to see everything come out OK onto the universe at large?" Chen interjected.

"No, I don't think projection plays a role in the meek's psychic economy. You and I both know you can't get the meek to lie and their commitment to the Senoi practice of revealing their dreams and fantasies to each other suggests they can't repress or deny much of anything. It would appear they can't even think if their mental landscape is cluttered with unfinished business," Forrester replied.

"Got it," Chen responded. "If there's nothing simmering on the mental back burner, there's nothing to project."

"We both know people often hallucinate or see visions that represent unfulfilled desires. Now, the meek see visions to be sure, but they don't experience visions the way the dominance driven routinely report seeing things. The dominance driven right hemisphere hallucinates its own limbic demons and then projects them onto the canvas of other people's lives. The right's visions often have a prima facia validity because most of their fellow travelers in the general population are right hemispheric processors like themselves.

Seeing one's own needs in action in the life of someone put together just like oneself is no great feat. The endemic error among the dominance driven has always been to see their needs and motivations as operating within the meek, who in one form or another have been fellow travelers in the population for at least three thousand years," Forrester said.

Leaning back, Forrester seemed lost in his own thoughts for a moment and then, sitting up again, he looked directly at Chen.

"For the right hemispherically dominance driven majority, wants and needs have always had primacy over circumstances. All the rights accept that as 'normal' in each other. In the meek, nature has perfected a clear vision of present and future circumstances while simultaneously muting limbic demands. It is by virtue of the meek's prescience that needs and wants no longer play a potentially conflictual role with circumstances in the human equation. The meeks' visions reveal events in future space-time and are notably impersonal. Whether what they envision amounts to our notions of the present or the future isn't particularly relevant to the meek, as time and space are all of one simultaneous and unbroken piece for them. Given all this insight, yet, it is the meek's ability to see the fundamental abstraction that underlies material reality they prize most," Forrester said as he leaned back again.

"And what is that abstraction?" Chen asked, a slight trembling evident in in his frame.

"Life ... not just what is alive, but what was alive and will be alive and whatever supports all that life. I guess in a nutshell, what they see is the life force that predates the space-time continuum ... you know, the physical universe, if that makes any sense. For the meek, the cosmos didn't give rise to life, life created the universe," Forrester responded.

"Actually, physiologically seeing the primal life force. What an evolutionary jump. You know, once I thought I saw something like that. It was when Crystal discovered what I now know to have been the scrolls and took them back to her family. There was a sort of light all around them. At the time, I figured I was just tired and imagining things," Chen said excitedly.

"That's part of it," Forrester responded.

"Can you do it, I mean, see those lights?" Chen asked.

"Little by little, I'm getting the hang of it," Forrester replied.

"Surely, the emergence of all these abilities can't be a simple function of the meek being isolated from the pressure their predatory peers in the human species have applied over the millennia?" Chen said, his tone skeptical.

Feeling on uncertain ground, Forrester was in the curious position of knowing exactly what Chen was asking, as it represented the same line of inquiry he would have pursued himself. He pondered the issue for what must have been many uncomfortable moments of Chen listening to utter silence.

"You're looking for tissue changes," he said looking Chen directly in the eye.

"Precisely! We did routine three-dimensional body imaging on the left hemispheric infants that were allowed to live and all of them showed some subtle departures from the norm in the rostral medial prefrontal cortex. The selfsame area in the right hemispheric infants was, in every respect, normal," Chen replied.

"And what did you make of that?" Forrester asked.

"I suppressed the findings, and refused to allow any follow-ups on the kids as they matured. I was afraid if Cabot got wind of some anomalies in the left hemispheric births, he'd soon be slaughtering all of the children born to the community, not just the right hemispheric infants," Chen replied quickly.

"You're a good man, Chen. A fine scientist to be sure, but more importantly a good man," Forrester said as he gripped Chen's shoulder.

Chen, wrestling with his own guilt, attempted to tilt his shoulder out and away from under Forrester's grip.

"I don't know about that. I was here, and, and in charge when all those newborns met their deaths," Chen replied.

"We were all there in one way or another, Chen. Do you have a portable three-dimensional imager available?" Forrester asked as he let go of Chen's shoulder.

"Yes ... I believe here ... somewhere in this pile of clutter that passes for my desk," Chen replied rummaging through his desk drawers.

"More than anyone, you have protected and nurtured these people. You did what you could to defend this community. You are entitled to know what you've been safeguarding," Forrester said.

"Now what?" Chen asked, having retrieved the imaging scanner.

"Point it right here and tell me what you see," Forrester replied as he indicated the center of his forehead.

Chen aimed the scanner where Forrester indicated for a few seconds and, then, attached the imager to, and activated a holographic projector on, his desk. Instantly, a three dimensional image of Forrester's brain sprang to life, floating above the disarray of Chen's desk.

"The rostral medial prefrontal area of the cortex appears to be well delineated from the surrounding neural tissues. The area is expanded well beyond normal, but the tissues don't appear pathological, just different. And look, there's some reduction in the bone density of the skull anterior to the expanded area," Chen intoned, his voice and eyes full of a wonder.

Smiling at Chen's excitement, Forrester directed his gaze deeper into the structures represented in the hologram of his brain slowly rotating over the desk.

"Anything else?" He asked.

"Oh, yes ... I see what you mean. This can't be ... but it is, my God. The limbic system seems to have undergone a reduction in size. This new frontal structure appears to be as large as , if not a tad larger than, the limbic assembly," Chen replied.

"It's a new sensory organ with other undeclared functions that have nothing to do with sensation, but only time will tell us what they may be. One thing is certain, however, in this new structure, nature has found a way around the limbic override that has bloodied the history of our species for millennia. In the past, the master passions of the limbic system have supported us, but they have also predestined our species to routinely set aside reason in favor of one or another variety of lust. In this new cerebral configuration, at least, reason has an even chance to be heard over the roar of our master passions and maybe better than even," Forrester intoned softly .

"Then, this must represent an undeclared latent ability in all pure left hemispheric processors. Using this imaging procedure and the comparative values it generates, it should be simple to locate more of these evolving left hemispheric processors in the general population and replicate Cabot's experiment without all the bloodshed. Hell, I'd be a shoo-in for a Nobel. I'll show all those academic bastards who dumped me like so much psychotic baggage," Chen responded.

"Yes, I suppose you could," Forrester replied.

Counter-dominance, Forrester thought to himself, as he watched the color rise in Chen's face. It was the need for revenge, one of the oldest of the monsters of the id, rising from the primordial slime within his new friend. Here was the man who would make good Forrester's escape ensnared within the grasp of one of the most ancient and powerful motivations to which humankind was subject, the need for pay back.

"Thanks. This is the second time you've provided me with a professional life goal. Now, I've got to see to the arrangements for shuttling everyone out of here. By the way, here's your identification chip. Good luck," Chen said, shaking Forrester's hand.

Hurrying away, cloaked in his patchy gray aura, Chen appeared a man with a renewed professional mission. Watching Chen disappear through the door, Forrester knew this new friend was going to dig the requisite two graves the pursuit of revenge demanded. Turning from a vision of the tattered aura of his friend, Forrester walked through the service center toward what he knew would be the blended shinning aura of Crystal's family waiting by their hopper. He knew part of him wanted to save Chen from himself or at least from his agenda. However, he also knew Chen's frontal lobes were, at this very moment, losing yet another battle to an older and more wiley limbic antagonist. Trying to save Chen from himself would entail persuasion if not some more blatant form of coercion. Forrester knew he could not help Chen win this particular battle, even if his current state of mind would allow Forrester to undertake the motivational convolutions requisite to that campaign. The text of the next step in evolution, the lesson taught in the very tissue of the people of the trees, was that from conception to implementation coercion brought one no closer to the source of life and light.

Soon the space shuttles would carry the meek from their birth place, far from the beauty of Earth's mountains and trees to an iron ball clasped in the cold, black hand of space. They would leave behind Chen and the bulk of the race that had spawned them. Those left behind, as well as those participating in this exodus, shared perhaps an equally uncertain fate. For Forrester, this ascent from mother Earth into the heavens felt like both an ending and a beginning.

Pocketing the identification chip, Forrester strode from the service center into the beauty of the meadow beyond. The sun shone brightly and the trees, resplendent in blues and greens, seemed at peace with their lot. Then, it struck him, the trees' auras didn't shimmer like those of human beings. Perhaps the trees were truly at one with their surroundings. These leafy sentinels demonstrated no striving and no reaching out to fill needs, they were complete within themselves. The meek must have seen this long before Forrester took notice. The meek had named their community for an attribute they shared with the towering foliage surrounding them, 'the people of the trees', a community at peace within itself.

Movement in his peripheral vision caused Forrester to look off to his left just in time to see Chen board a hopper which, rising, disappeared over the ridge. Again, he was leaving behind a good friend, just as he had left Arthur. Two good men, both embroiled in losing battles with themselves. Two men's lives, as indeed his own before the intervention of the meek, were microcosms of the losing battle with limbic passions that the species had contested and failed to surmount over countless millennia. In the meek, nature had elected to weigh reason over survival driven, security focused and dominance targeted motivations to the same degree she had favored reflexive survival drives over reason at the outset of human existence.

His sense of obligation was a testament to the debts of gratitude he owed to these two men. However, Forrester was more than aware he was indebted to a host of kindnesses many had shown him that he knew he could not repay. It seemed his life was devolving into a veritable morass of unpaid and unpayable liabilities. There was Arthur who had supplied decades worth of protection and support, Chen facilitating his continuing fellowship with the community, and, of course, the meek themselves who had quite literally given Forrester a new life.

Try as he might, Forrester knew he could never break even with the new life that had been thrust upon him. Just maybe, he thought, this was what it meant to be part of the whole. Embodied in these experiences was the personal recognition that, as one of the many tiny parts of life, his existence was bound up in a continuing cosmic dynamic of reciprocal indebtedness. Perhaps the contrary of striving for dominance was not behaving meekly, but consisted rather in the daily recognition that the interlocking and freely undertaken obligations of the parts constituted the whole.

Losing Arthur and Chen were personal forfeitures that cut to the quick. Although rapidly becoming one of the meek, Forrester, in so many ways, still stood at the fork in the road between old and new routes the human race was taking into the future. He was sure that, given time, he would incorporate the competencies, perspectives and attitudes of the meek. However, he was equally certain that some part of him would always remain connected to the mighty stream of humanity that had brought them all to this momentous division. Evolution had set him the task of walking a razor-edge between her ongoing experiments with the old and 'new' brain. He wasn't sure he wanted to spend whatever years he had left walking that narrow border between two species, but a part of him knew the decision wasn't his to make.

Rising within him, he sensed changes that heralded the appearance of an entry from the scrolls in his mind. As so often before, the words came unsummoned in response to a need which he neither fully felt nor could adequately describe. The words of the entry reeled onto the screen of his mind over a background of purple tint instead of the infinite black upon which they had appeared in the past.

IN THE DEW OF MORNING, I BEHOLD THE
SOWERS GO OUT INTO THE FIELD. THOSE
WHOSE ART IS HEAVY WITH AGE SOW
UPON THE HILLS WHERE THE GROUND IS
SOMETIMES HARD AND STONEY. YOUNG
HUSBANDS OF THE SOIL CAST THEIR SEEDS

UPON THE BANKS OF STREAMS WHERE THE
SILT IS SOFT AND DEEP. THE AGED SOWERS'
YIELD IS SPARSE BUT THEIR HARVEST,
ALTHOUGH MODEST, IS AN ASSURED
INCREASE FROM EVERY KERNEL STREWN
UPON THE RAGGED SLOPES. UNTUTORED
BY THE WISDOM OF MANY SEASONS'
PASSAGE, THE YOUTHFUL SOWERS' SEEDS
ARE OFTEN BY THE FLOODS OF SPRING'S
PASSION, SWEPT AWAY AND WITH THESE
WISPS OF LIFE, THEIR HOPES.

BETWEEN LIGHT AND DARKNESS LIKE THE
AGED SOWER I TRAVEL. AT HOME IN THE
LIGHT, BUT NEEDED IN THE DARKNESS, I
TREAD THE HARDENED GROUND. THE
SEEDS OF LIGHT MUST BE SOWN WHERE
THEY ARE NEEDED, BUT IN ROCKY SOILS
ABOUNDING WITH STRIFE, MOST CHOKE
AND DIE. IN A NOW TO COME, NEW SEEDS
STREWN IN GROUND UNDARKENED BY
WARS OF THE HEART AND WELL WATERED
WILL SWELL TO AN INCREASE IN PEACE
UNBEGOTTEN BY PRIDE. I AM THE SOWER
WHOSE HARVEST COMES NOT UNTIL THE
FIELD IS WHITE WITH LIGHT.

The diarist who had begun in the light was journeying into and planting seeds of light in the darkness of matter. When the day of gleaning came in the dark soil of matter, he would realize a harvest of living energy. A conscious decision to descend from the heights of pure energy and omnipresent awareness into the dark confines of finitude was very different from Forrester's attempts to climb out of the mire. Forrester was trying to drag himself out of the darkness into the light, while the diarist was attempting to suffuse the darkness with radiance. In his shaky housing of clay, Forrester did, however, share, if only to a shadow's depth, a measure of the unequal traction experienced by the diarist in his constantly shifting interface between the darkness and the light.

Chapter 28

Juan had worked for four decades for CC Natcorp in Peru. His job was not demanding, but he considered it an important one. Juan conducted the final inspection of all transubstantiator units before they were shipped to outlets across the world. In forty years, not one of the units he had scrutinized had been returned for a factory fault. Juan was proud of his work. He had refused promotion many times over the years choosing instead to instruct new workers in his craft. Juan's joy in the work came in the execution of its intricacies not in the status that flowed from greater management authority.

An amiable and quiet man, Juan counted very few as friends and had never married. Saving scrupulously for fifteen of those forty years with CC Natcorp, he had purchased the one acre of land and constructed a small house. He enjoyed the solitude of his life, communing best, as always he had, with the elements of wood, water, and the plants who were his most steadfast and trustworthy companions. Building his home from native woods and stone, he had carefully crafted each part of his dwelling. He loved the warmth and rich texture of the wood and had used it for the few pieces of furniture scattered throughout its several rooms. He had gathered native rocks, carefully chosen for their colors and intricate pattern of faults, and built a wall of stones around his property. Juan's great love was his garden. It was as if the house were just an afterthought, constructed so he could eat and sleep close to the trees and plants he tenderly cultivated. In the midst of a population of millions, Juan had created solitude among the unquestioning stones, warm woods and plants whose only utterances came in the form of silent prayers to the sun and soil.

Hurrying home from work to take full advantage of the bright sunlight of a beautiful spring afternoon, Juan was only at peace inside his garden wall. He was anxious to do some ornamental pruning on a few of his dwarf fruit trees, and to see if any of the tomatoes in the garden had ripened sufficiently to serve as his supper. Of course, he could always get fresh tomatoes from the transubstantiator unit, but those plump red fruits just weren't the same as those he had coaxed to life with his own hands.

Pruning came first, as it was the least rewarding of the tasks of the garden. After depositing the twigs and branches on the compost pile, he allowed himself the reward of looking at the tomato vines. Juan had always disciplined himself to save the best part of any job for last. As he had hoped, several of the tomatoes shone a dark, soft red in the sun. They were ready to eat. He marveled at the large and fully ripened fruits that demonstrated extraordinary growth for this early in the season. Looking about, he realized he must have accomplished a great deal in a short time as he noted the sun still shone brightly on the fruit, the surrounding trees and budding vegetables. Then, breaking with his customary nontemporal mindset while in the garden, Juan looked down at his watch. It read nine p.m. He looked again, yes, he had seen it correctly, nine o'clock, but why was the sun shinning so brightly at this time in the evening? Juan pondered the sun's odd behavior for a moment and picked up the basket of fruit. It was of no consequence, the tomatoes were ripe and he had the sun to thank for that blessing and his evening meal.

⚜

Doctor Chung had worked for twenty years in a small hospital on the outskirts of Peking. Although trained as a physician, his work was more of a ministry than simply a calling to heal the sick. The older members of the community knew Doctor Chung had previously been a full professor at a medical school where he had trained many able and famous physicians. What no one knew is why one day he simply quit his post and founded a small clinic to serve those who could not afford the miracles of modern medicine.

In a tiny refurbished house which served as his clinic was bed upon bed of dying patients whose only obstacle to a life of full vigor was money. Despite millennia of medical advancement, the rules of economics had remained unchanged. In this epoch, one percent of the population controlled ninety-nine percent of the wealth, and those elite few used their enormous resources to purchase a disease and disability free existence that stretched out for centuries. The majority of the population lived and died as had their forefathers in eras long forgotten. Doctor Chung did what he could, but most of his patients would die of conditions and diseases for which cures had been perfected centuries ago. He made those without hope comfortable and even facilitated the recovery of a precious few.

Years of twelve to fourteen hour days had begun to take their toll on Doctor Chung. He took more breaks, as now, stepping out onto the little porch of the clinic to enjoy a glass of tea, that his only nurse and spouse had prepared for him. Looking up at the sky, he noted how bright the sun was for this late in the day, curious, he thought to himself. Doctor Chung's mind was elsewhere and the long light of evening did not hold his attention. He would lose two young people to bone cancer tonight, and he wasn't sure he could keep them pain free to the inevitable end. Doctor Chung didn't like pain, especially the nonconstructive agony that preceded death. Finishing his tea, he turned to enter the clinic when his nurse met him at the door. For a woman whose demeanor made the word stoical an understatement, she was beside herself with excitement as she explained that all the patients had refused their pain medications and were demanding to be released.

Walking back toward the door to the clinic, Doctor Chung focused his thoughts on his wife. She was a good nurse and a fine woman who had simply snapped after too many years of emotional overcontrol. Entering the clinic, he was immediately greeted by all thirty of his patients out of their beds doffing their gowns and pulling on their street clothes. The group of happy ex-patients included the two bone cancer patients he was certain would be dead before morning. He dipped into the pocket of his smock and produced a diagnostic scanner. It was the only luxury he had afforded himself from the small inheritance left by his mother. A quick sweep of each patient revealed no evidence of disorders of any kind. Doctor Chung stood half dazed in amazement as each patient vigorously shook his hand and exited with a sprightly gait from the clinic. Over the years, Doctor Chung had observed a number of spontaneous cures, but overnight remission of bone cancer had never been among them. Although he had just run an systems check on the diagnostic scanner, he ran it again. There was not doubt, it was in perfect working order.

Without the vaguest notion of what had happened, suddenly, he was out of business. Standing by the open door of the clinic, he watched as the jostling mob, laughing and hugging one another, reached the sidewalk and dispersed along different routes to homes where they would soon be greeted by astonished relatives. Unexpectedly, Doctor Chung felt empty. For the first time in forty years, he had no one to serve. The feeling persisted until, encircling his waist with her arm, his wife drew him back into the clinic and onto the side porch.

Having prepared more tea, she shared a cup and a rare moment of conjugal solitude with her husband. Husband and wife, now with no lives to serve except their own, stood on the porch, marveling at the light which, filling the sky, showed no sign of waning.

⌐✦⌐

Uri had been chief financial agent for FF Natcorp in Moscow for ten years. A decade of striking hard and fast deals for the corporation was on the verge of paying off. The head office in Lucerne was considering him for advancement to the international finance committee level, however, he knew that he needed one more big deal to put him over the top. That deal was in the works, but he had his doubts that all the pieces would fall into place. The pain in his gut seemed to confirm his feelings of trepidation. A refinance offer for some antigravity units to the CC Natcorp's international representative was on the table that would net FF Natcorp some truly obscene profits. Uri was betting CC Natcorp couldn't get replacements fast enough to keep their own bottom line healthy and would be forced to refinance their existing units.

Two high pitched beeps followed by a low pitched tone told him it was about two o'clock in the morning. He had closed the blinds in his office a long time ago. He didn't want to be reminded of how late it was. Pacing up and down waiting for a call from halfway around the world, Uri knew this next conversation would make or break his career. Despite a consistent run of money making transactions for the company, he knew corporations had very short memories. All that counted as far as head office was concerned was what have you done for us lately. Out of the corner of his eye, he noticed light filtering in between the slats in the blinds. Walking to the window, he activated the blind riser. Sunlight poured in, filling the room with its yellow brilliance. He was shocked, but only momentarily. The sun was up at two o'clock in the morning, so what, he didn't want to see the light, he wanted to hear the vidscreen chime.

Like every good gambler/financier, Uri believed in sympathetic magic. He'd shave in preparation for the video conference and, in so doing, he would summon the call and the positive outcome he desired. He moved the sonic shaver over his face in brisk strokes quickly finishing the job as thoughts of a huge chateau overlooking Lake Lucerne coursed through his head. A quick comb through his hair and a straightening of his collar provided the last ingredients in the evocative ritual. As if on cue the vidscreen chimed and his opposite number in CC Natcorp brusquely acquiesced to the refinance deal. Uri maintained his best poker face until the vidscreen went blank and then leapt into the air and danced about his office, thoroughly enjoying his moment of conquest.

Deciding not to notify the head office personally, he elected to be reserved about the deal. At the head office in Lucerne, they'd know in less than a half hour when CC Natcorp deposited the funds in the FF corporate account. This was it. He could feel it. He was on his way to the top. If he made the right moves, in another ten years he'd be running the outfit. As far a Uri was concerned, the sun was out in the middle of the night to celebrate his coup.

Following in her father's footsteps, Arindi raised wild animals in Kenya for the elite of the world to hunt. These wealthy and powerful trophy hunters never took the meat. All they wanted were hide, hoof, and horn. Left with the carcasses, Arindi started a side business selling the meat to local restaurants that specialized in real game meals for the tourists. Functioning as a wholesale butcher provided funds that supplemented her hunt fees and allowed her to live comfortably. Her father's legacy was a healthy chunk of fenced veldt that served as a hunting reserve. Her inheritance also included breeding stock and the pens that housed them until they were released for her patron's sport.

Arindi's feelings of regret, watching the animals she raised slaughtered for a few moments of an oftentimes drunken hunter's safe excitement, were tempered by the knowledge that the fees she collected kept a few species alive that would otherwise have passed into extinction.

Chores finished for the day, her boots kicked up tiny plumes of dust as she made her way back to the big house. Looking up through the branches of one of the ancient spreading trees near the verandah, she noticed that the sun was not where it should be, close to the horizon. There was no chronometer on her wrist to verify the hour. Her activities were governed by the rhythms of the veldt not by some mechanical contrivance. As a gamekeeper, she knew where the sun should be at any moment in the day and by now a quarter of its shimmering bulk should have disappeared below the horizon.

Although there had been no hunts on the schedule, it had been a long day full of chores and she was tired as she arrived at the door of the main house. Looking over her shoulder at the bush as she opened the door, the position of the sun in the sky continued to puzzle her. It seemed stuck up there like a big yellow ball in a child's drawing of the sky. Climbing the stairs of the old house, she reached the observation terrace on the roof and poured a gin and tonic. This was her favorite time of the day. All the animals were safely contained in their electronically surveilled pens and corrals surrounding the old house. The recently installed security measures on the property had been necessitated when poachers had become more active in her area. The large block of fenced savanna was empty now except for the brush and trees punctuating the expanse of grass. She sipped her drink and allowed her eyes to roam aimlessly over her well preserved portion of the veldt where no other dwellings interrupted the primal scene.

Her glass was half empty when she noticed the first movement among the trees and brushy growth of the plain. First, a giraffe's head poked through the tree tops. Then, one, two, no, ten elephants were working their way through the bush. She came to her feet, drink still in hand. A large pride of lions rested peacefully in the tall grass as gazelle picked their way among them. Where there should be nothing but native plants, the grassland was alive with animals, cheetah and hyena lying down with zebra and wildebeest.

These animals shouldn't be there, she thought to herself. The huge fenced savanna should be empty. Shifting her weight from foot to foot, she looked at the pens by the main house where her stock still rested peacefully in the endless afternoon sun. Turning her attention back to the bush teeming with animals, she noticed more than one species she knew to be extinct. Even more remarkable than the appearance of the animals from Africa's distant past on the veldt were the mixed clusters of predators and prey lying placidly next to one another. She looked down into her half full glass, no she hadn't even put away her customary two drinks, only half of one. Tilting back the broad brim of her hat, she looked up and there was the sun, still stuck in the same place in the sky where she had marked its position two hours ago. Sitting down with a thump, she wasn't sure whether she should have another drink, or swear off spirits altogether.

Electing to refill her glass, she decided to take in the teeming panorama of life gracing the plain. How her father would have rejoiced to see the veldt alive again. Raising her glass to an unseen presence, she toasted 'Da', as she had always called him, and drank in both the spirits and the veldt's past on parade before her.

✯

Krishna, was a holy man in an India, that had long since dispensed with that niche in the social order. He spent his days in prayer and meditation, accepting only meager support from the family of his older sister. She had always been there since the death of their mother when he was but five years old. At first, his sister saw to his upbringing. Now she provided for his sustenance in old age. From early childhood, Krishna's eyes had mirrored a soul whose travels were in, but not of, this world. His neighbors knew him as a man whose anachronistic hours of meditation and prayer were accepted, not so much for their religious significance, as for the ambiance of historical continuity they conferred on the community.

His fasting, prayer and meditation verified his role as a holy man but his status as a good man derived from the attention and care he provided to his nephews and nieces and, indeed, to all of the children of the community. He taught them the old ways, the ancient chants and songs and told stories whose origins were lost in the history of the continent.

Every child in the community knew Krishna's schedule and all would seek him out once he'd completed his daily meditations. A sea of youngsters would form around him, ebbing and flowing, faces coming and going as he told stories and sang the ancient songs. The parents of the community never objected to Krishna's small ministry as he never required anything of their children. His role and practices in the community did not earn him reverence as a purveyor of religious and cultural instruction, instead the community accepted him as a trusted, mystical baby sitter who entertained and kept their children safe.

Owning nothing, Krishna desired no ties to the impermanence vested in the universe of material possessions. Housed in his own frail body while communing with the familiar ghosts of solid matter, he saw this life as but one among many of his soul's excursions in the desert of illusion. His was a spiritual pilgrimage marked by ceaseless and sincere efforts to transcend the material.

Rising long before the sun, he desired always to be on his feet to greet the light that dispelled the darkness. As the first light began its task of pushing back the night, Krishna experienced a feeling of great anticipation filling his tiny frame. Something was coming. He knew not what, save that it represented a fulfillment of his otherwise insignificant sojourn through this life. The feeling danced through his body in a frenzy, but he didn't allow its whirling and swaying to excuse him from his meditations. Not owning a timepiece, he unconsciously judged the passage of the day by the transit of the sun across the sky and the length of the shadows it cast. Today, his internal clock told him the time of meditation was over, but the angle of the sun on his closed eyelids disagreed. In the distance, he heard the shouts and laughter of the children milling their way through the town in his direction. His spiritual clock was right and the children were right but the sun was wrong.

The dance in his soul, which had begun with the sun's rising, had become a glowing circle of swirling lights. In the midst of the circle, the makings of a spiritual fire made their appearance. Like embers long smoldering, something in the center of the circle, something inside Krishna, burst into a tongue of flame. It was nothing of the body, over those processes he had complete yogic control. This was an awakening of the spirit. He looked up directly into the sun fixed in the sky as if stopped in its course across the heavens by some great unseen hand. He felt no pain in his eyes and experienced no reflex to turn away. The sun was as bright as it had always been, but its light was soft and caressing, not piercing. Then, about the great circle of the sun's rim, Krishna saw the wheel of life. It was not the great wheel of all lives, but the wheel of his life. The wheel balanced on its rim, a seemingly endless parade of births, deaths and rebirths that was the journey of his soul. Krishna saw therein the consummation of his many lives. His own slender form, clad as he found himself there in the marketplace, emerged in a burst of light from the wheel. Rejoicing, he knew he was finally freed from the cycle of birth, death and rebirth. He felt fulfilled and released in a single moment. The children gathered about him now, and filled with a peace he had never before known, he began the great chant of beginnings and endings.

Doctor Clarke had spent most of his life pursuing a career as an astrophysicist. The small circuit of his life's entrances and exits had turned in little rooms whose space was contrived to serve electronic expediency, not creature comfort. For what seemed like the forever of his existence, he had watched equations and vectors live out their brief moment of significance on computer screens forty centimeters from his nose. Decades at the Hawking observatory on the moon and an equal number of years peering at the feed from the great orbital radio telescope array of the Strazinski astronomical outpost in orbit around Mars had narrowed his life. Nearly a half a century living in the crowded quarters of a head full of equations, all demanding to be fed with measurements reflecting the nature of the universe, had made him claustrophobic within the confines of his own mind.

Somewhere along the way, he had lost the magic. The stars and galaxies, the red shifts, and the advances in technology had all dulled the enticing sparkle and splash of his own inexhaustible fount of curiosity. His youthful self image as a quester after the nature of the cosmos had yielded over time to a view of himself as little more than a cartographer of places upon which he would never set foot.

After sixty years of committed study, Doctor Clarke had come up empty. His wife had left him thirty years ago. His two sons, enamored only with financial success, worked for FF Natcorp. The stars as his only companions, he found himself alone among stacks of reprint discs representing years of scholarly investigation. The ageless stars no longer beckoned with the warmth and excitement they had embodied in his youth. Now, those selfsame points of light were just cold, hard dots staring back at him, filled with the predatory sheen of reptilian eyes. Doctor Clarke had tried to wrest meaning from the universe, but the universe wasn't having any of it.

In his eighty-fifth year of life, Doctor Clarke became Brother Thomas in a monastery near Jerusalem. Very few monastic orders remained on the planet to choose as a place of retreat. This one, in particular, appealed to him because of what he had heard about the brotherhood. Locals referred to it as the 'numbers order.' Members of this anachronistic group were largely, but not exclusively, disenchanted scientists with professional backgrounds that bespoke mathematical prowess. There were physicists of every flavor and an equally diverse collection of engineers, mathematical modelers and one radiologist. These were all men who, if having nothing else personally in common, had all come to the conclusion that although mathematics held the promethean promise of magical revelation, it was, in the end effect, little more than measurement.

The brotherhood made few concessions to technology. One of these was a transubstantiator programmed to render only water. All the brotherhood shared the common task of cultivating their food. Considerable acreage lay within the walled boundaries of the monastery and the brothers raised what they ate. The simplicity of their life was, perhaps, the spiritual medicine that most benefitted men who had lived under the unyielding tyranny of numbers all of their lives. They all felt a common calling to prepare the way for the unfolding life locked within the plants that sustained them. This profession was a calling different in kind from coercing the universe into yielding up her secrets in the form of numeric sequences. Perhaps for just this reason, they all willingly participated in cultivating the garden that offered sustenance for both the body and the soul.

Brother Timothy awakened Brother Thomas in what should have been the middle of the night. Brother Thomas slowly rubbed the sleep from his eyes. Bright sunlight was pouring into his cubicle. Brother Timothy, an erstwhile nuclear physicist, held the monastery's only clock in his hands and pointing excitedly at its face. Brother Thomas assured himself it was indeed the middle of the night and glanced at the sunlight dancing on the sill of his only window. The laws of physics simply didn't allow for this sort of absurdity, he thought to himself.

Donning his robe, Brother Thomas followed Brother Timothy to the chapel where the entire brotherhood had assembled. This was not a pious gathering, but a lively discussion of possible extrapolations of existing theoretical mathematical models that might account for the solar phenomenon. The clamor of voices gradually subsided as Brother James, the senior member of the group, attempted to sum up the divergent views. His précis was simple and straightforward. All the theoretical extrapolations represented equally likely possibilities, but only that, possibilities. The most probable explanation was that natural law had been superseded. A long silence spread among the brotherhood. Then nods of affirmation consolidated the heads of those assembled into a wave of agreement.

Accompanied by Brother Timothy, Brother Thomas left the chapel for the garden, while many of the brotherhood remained in the chapel to pray. Brother Thomas knelt down by a small sweet pea plant that had just broken the rough surface of the soil, and brushed away the clods of dirt that impeded the tender plant's passage into the light. The fledgling shoot might make it without his intervention, but it would carry the scars of its struggle into the time of full flower. He could help this single life navigate a few of the trials of living. He hoped, in a way wholly inconsistent with his training as a scientist, that someone or something would do the same for him.

꧁❖꧂

Claude Matisse, chairman of the United Nation's board of directors, was a man overwhelmed by a deluge of unique information for which his training and experience had in no wise prepared him. He was receiving reports from reliable scientific sources across the planet informing him that the sun's position everywhere on the globe approximated mid afternoon. Frankly, he wasn't sure what he could do about the curious behavior of the solar body, much less the bewilderment that reigned in the scientific community.

People across the face of the Earth were troubled, but, strangely enough, there was no panic, just generalized uncertainty. Matisse made calls to the Earth Defensive Force Headquarters to ascertain whether the alien invasion force was behind the planet wide phenomenon. Commander Sadad, responding from the orbiting operations station, had assured him the alien fleet was not even in the solar system and was not responsible for the curious phenomenon. Matisse would have preferred to hear an explanation that involved an invading alien force, something of tangible consistency, something he could address.

At this point, Matisse fell back on the one tried and true axiom of political life, when in doubt form a committee. He immediately called for a joint meeting of the board of directors and the general assembly. The representatives could gather quickly as most of them were already in the greater New York area in preparation for the first meeting of the assembly tomorrow. Matisse's aides informed him that many of the members were already collecting in the smaller antechambers of the building, anticipating that U.N. action would be necessitated by the planet wide event.

As Matisse moved through the corridors making his way to the immense assembly hall and the podium, he didn't have the faintest idea of how he would begin his address, much less what recommendations he would make to the delegates. Entering the great hall of assemblies, he mounted the dais. His eyes told him what the delegate counter under the podium confirmed, he was experiencing a first in his tenure as chairman, every representative was in their seat. He activated the gong that called the delegates to order and the multitude of voices fell silent. Looking down at a podium on which no notes or prompts of any kind lay, he lifted his head to speak.

Before the first uncertain word could pass his lips, a general rustling and murmur among the delegates captured Matisse's attention. His gaze followed the upturned faces of the delegates to the ceiling of the assembly hall, which was gradually assuming the pale transparent blue of a springtime sky. Some few of the delegates began to look down at their feet, where the great auditorium's floor was slowly passing from its white marble tones to the deep blue of the open sea. Even the air seemed different. No longer the heavy, the stuffy atmosphere that marked large gatherings, it instantly became cool, fresh and carried the scent of flowers and pine. If Matisse didn't know what he was going to say when he ascended the dais, his mind was now wholly bereft of words.

Out of the corner of his eye, Matisse thought he saw movement to his right on the dais. A quick glance at the assembled delegates confirmed his impression, all faces were directed to his right. Suspended in a cone of brilliant white light stood a man with flowing hair and a full beard clad in a simple white robe. Without even a flicker of doubt passing through his mind, Matisse knew this was the carpenter, the itinerant preacher from Nazareth.

Abdul, the chief delegate from what was once the nation state of Iran, saw a turbaned figure dressed in loose fitting robes with full beard he knew to be the prophet Muhammad.

Noha, sitting but a row behind Abdul, from the territory once known as Israel, saw an imposing figure surrounded by tongues of golden flame that he recognized instantly as the prophet Elijah.

Raad, seated directly in front of the figure on the dais, saw Lord Krishna, eighth avatar of Vishnu, bedecked in ceremonial attire.

Chi from the expanse of the area formerly known as China saw the Lord Buddha seated in a lotus position and suspended in midair, his beneficent smile directed solely at Chi.

Simon Walking Bear representing what used to be northwestern United States, saw only wisps of sacred smoke he knew to be a manifestation of the great spirit that moved in all things.

Each delegate saw what represented the sacred, or at least the fullness of the good in life, in accordance with his or her experience and their deepest, often unspoken, beliefs. Some saw parents, others beheld grandparents. A few found themselves staring at a field of stars and galaxies, while others perceived an infant untouched by the vicissitudes of living and glowing with health.

Suddenly, all those assembled observed a dynamic flow of motion in their personal perception of that which occupied the dais with Matisse. Attending that perturbation, each delegate was straightway transformed from within by an irresistible feeling of well being. The images and sensations differed from one person to the next, with the only common theme encompassing somehow the notion of going home. Even among those for whom home had never represented a refuge of love and safety, an idealized reality replaced the horrors of the memories retrieved by that concept.

Then, as precipitously as it had begun, the event terminated. Matisse watched as first, the robed figure and, then, the cone of light that contained him gradually faded away. Somehow, Matisse knew he would not be required to say anything. The delegates rose from their seats and filed without speaking from the great assembly hall. Matisse stepped down from the dais with a perfect conviction that he was going, home. His chauffeured hopper awaited him on the roof and, in less than fifteen minutes of flight, he alighted from the craft at his home in the mountains to the north of the city.

Looking at least ten years younger, his spouse came down the walk to greet him. She excitedly told him his aged and ailing mother had left her sick bed and was preparing his favorite soufflé. His two young daughters hugged him as he entered the house and, doffing his coat, he proceeded to open a fifty year old bottle of Eitelsbacher- Karthaeuserhoefburg Riesling Auslese a German friend had given them several Christmases ago.

Gathering around the huge vidscreen in the living room, the entire family watched the most extraordinary series of newscasts the world had ever witnessed. Reports were coming in from every sector of the planet. To Matisse's surprise, that to which he and the assembled delegates could attest, was seen by every inhabitant on the face of the Earth. Individuals disputed with one another on the global stage of the news media what each had individually seen, but the quarrels were wholly without rancor. Indeed, the time honored, common fare of the news conflict, was altogether absent from the reports of each and every commentator, regardless of the location on the globe from which they broadcast.

Of most extraordinary significance, hospitals and prisons released patients and inmates respectively healed of their ailments and assuaged in their anger and discontent. The entire family sat nearly immobile before the parade of good news on the vidscreen. Only Matisse's mother, who was busy serving soufflé to everyone, seemed unimpressed. Her family fed, she stood back from the vidscreen and noted simply, and in a tone most matter of fact, that the sins of the world had been forgiven. A poetic reference, Matisse thought to himself. Her words, even if they were only a function of the ravages of one hundred years of living on her delicate brain, nevertheless represented a fitting summation.

Matisse smiled at his mother as she brought him another portion of soufflé. Perhaps her artless characterization of the situation was at once the most encompassing and direct way of understanding this unique event in the history of the world. Matisse looked away from the vidscreen for a moment to examine his chronometer. He had been awake now for over twenty hours, but he felt no fatigue. Perhaps like the sun or even time itself, he and the rest of humanity were firmly rooted in this one timeless moment of complete satisfaction.

Chapter 29

Climbing rapidly through the atmosphere, the shuttles soon left behind all but the most diaphanous traces of the Earth's protective envelope. Forrester watched first the reserve, then the face of the North American continent dwindle in size and finally disappear behind the clouds. Crystal's face was glued to one of the shuttle's ports as the whole of the Earth became visible. The craft climbed steadily toward the moon and the ark in orbit around it. Despite his feeling of uncertainty, Forrester found that, like Crystal, he couldn't take his eyes off the gradually shrinking blue ball that was the birthplace of their species.

Crystal was the first of the passengers to verbalize what all staring out the shuttle's ports could clearly see.

"It's daytime everywhere," she said excitedly.

A singular view, the image of the Earth illuminated from every angle was dramatically compelling. No evidence of a day/night terminator demarcated the planet that now seemed so far away. No astronomer, but as far as Forrester could tell, the Earth, sun and moon were all about where they were supposed to be relative to one another. Everything he knew told him half the planet should be in light and the half turned away from the sun should be in darkness. Yet, no night, existed anywhere on the globe. The orb of the Earth shone in sun from the perspective of the shuttle, and, looking beyond, he could see a halo of light projecting from the far side of the planet as well. Forrester looked away from the port for a moment and Esther caught his eye.

"The Light of the diarist has come," Esther said, reaching down and touching a case that rested by her seat.

Her hand rested upon a case, that he instantly recognized as the container in which he had placed the diarist's scrolls. For a moment, overwhelmed by memory, Forrester smelled the dust on the desert wind and saw the glowing oval from which he had retrieved that private, and poignant journal. He watched closely as Esther snapped open the case. The instant the lid came up the shuttle's cabin filled with a brilliant white light. Extaordinarily, the illumination filled every recess of the cabin, and, as so long ago in the hut amidst the desolation, cast no shadow anywhere. What Forrester recalled as a white light tinged in blue now shown with the purest incandescent white, filling the cabin covering everyone and everything within the confines of the craft like a fluid. It was a light like no other he had ever witnessed. Caressing the skin with its warm glow, it engendered no painful glare in the eye and carried with it the stillness he had first experienced upon the scrolls' discovery so long ago.

Reaching into the case without glancing at its contents, Esther drew out a single scroll still sheathed in its leather quiver. As she touched the scroll, an illumination that flowed over her skin as a if it were a liquid immediately drenched her hand and arm. She passed the scroll through the hands of several of the members of the community. Each person's hand instantly glowed as if immersed in the white light until the scroll reached Forrester.

As Forrester slid the scroll from its quiver, he watched in amazement as the scroll unfurled, quite of its own volition, to a passage that seemed to glow with its own letter by letter radiance. The words of the passage were plain and translated effortlessly. As he read, Forrester knew the whole of the community of the people of the trees would be perusing the passage with and through him.

> I WANDER WHERE CURRENTS OF LIVING
> WATERS MEET THE DESERT WASTES. HERE,
> LIFE'S FLOW TOUCHES THE GROWING EDGE
> OF SCORCHING DEATH. IN THIS WORLD OF
> FAINT KNOWING, WHAT LIVES IS BEHELD
> AS FRAIL, YET, IN ALL THAT PARTAKES OF
> LIFE'S QUICKENING IS STRENGTH BEYOND
> MEASURE. THE DWELLING WHEREIN LIFE
> NESTS IS BUT RAIMENT WHICH, WHEN
> CAST ASIDE IN THE CONSUMMATION OF
> ALL CREATION, WILL BE REVEALED AS
> BUT A VAIN AND BEGUILING HABIT.
>
> WITHOUT THE ATTIRE OF MIGHT, I
> SOJOURN AMONG THESE WHO ARE MY
> BROTHERS IN THE QUICKENING OF THE
> CLAY THAT IS LIFE. I SPEAK OF LIFE'S
> MARROW, YET, THEY SEE ONLY THE CLOTH
> OF FLESH AND BONE. SOUNDS UPON THE
> WIND, MY WORDS MINGLE AND ARE LOST
> IN THE HUM OF DARK CLAY'S CLAMOR
> UPON THE EARS OF THE SOUL. EYES

TUNED TO THE BRIEF CLAIMS OF THE
CLAY UPON THE SPIRIT, THEY SEE FORM
ONLY. MEN'S FRAIL MEMORY OF CLAY
CANNOT HOLD FAST THE REMEMBRANCE
OF THOSE FIERY THREADS THAT
ENLIVENED THEIR BEGINNINGS.

THE ASCENT OF LIFE FROM UNSEEN WRITHING
SPECKS IN WATERS SLOWED BY THE REEDS
TO THAT WHICH BEHOLDS THE ORDER IN THE
HEAVENS IS BUT SAND SWIRLING IN THE
WILDERNESS. THE SOLITARY WAYFARER SEES
THROUGH THE ARROGANCE OF HIS NEEDS
THE SHIFTING GRAINS FORM SHAPES THAT
MAKE THE DESERT'S SHINING SEA A
UNIVERSE RECONCILED TO HIM ALONE.

THAT WHICH IS NATURE, THAT WHICH
MOVES IN ALL LIFE IS THE LIGHT. LARGE
AND SMALL, SEEN AND UNSEEN, EACH
SPARK IS ENLIVENED TO STRUGGLE AGAINST
THE BONDAGE OF THE CLAY AND RETURN
AGAIN TO THE FIRES OF CREATION FROM
WHICH IT SPRANG.

I AM COME AS CLAY. I SHALL COME AGAIN
IN THE GREAT CIRCLE OF LIFE AS LIGHT TO
ENLIVEN THE WORLD. IN JOY, THE DUST
OF THIS WORLD WILL BE SUMMONED HOME,
BUT NOT ALL. TWO STREAMS SHALL ISSUE
FORTH INTO STARRY FIELDS FROM THE BLUE
WOMB OF WATERS. ONE SURGING OUT IN
A GREAT FLOOD OF CONQUEST, THE OTHER, A
TRANQUIL RIVULET BEARS ONLY A TAPER,
ITS FLAME KINDLED BY THE LIGHT OF
CREATION.

Without thinking and without analyzing, Forrester knew that he was but a
drop in the rivulet flowing out into the universe upon which the small candle

carrying the fires of creation sailed. Clearly, there was a place for the dominance driven in the plan, a great flood of conquest played out on the material facade that concealed the primogenital light of all life.

Rolling up the scroll, he replaced it in the leather quiver and sent it through many reverent hands back to Esther and the case from which it had been drawn. Esther replaced the scroll in the secure case and the glowing white light slowly dissipated as she closed the lid.

Turning his gaze once more to the shining globe enveloped entirely in the light of day, Forrester wondered what the population of that tiny blue ball would make of the phenomenon. Without the message of the scrolls and the evolutionary miracle of the people of the trees, he knew that every other inhabitant of the Earth would remain puzzled and confused. Esther was right, the Light of the diarist had come. The words of the scroll were exquisitely to the point of the Light's visitation. The dust of this world, over eons beyond counting, made man would be summoned home. If the *seeing* of the community was preternatural and the words of the scroll precognizant, it would be a devastating homecoming for the planet below and those who dwelt there.

Soon the Earth, bathed everywhere in the radiance of a spring afternoon, would disappear from his view as the shuttle climbed into stationary orbit with Cabot's Ark behind the moon. A dark, nostalgic feeling fell over him as the community's vision of a bright silver and featureless ball filled his mind, substituting itself for the life generating blue planet below.

Assuming docking trajectory, the shuttle occupied by Forrester, Crystal's family and many others from the eastern district was part of the last group of craft completing the evacuation of the Canadian reserve. As the shuttles rounded the moon, Forrester got his first look at the ark. It was larger, by far, than he had ever imagined. He was not the best judge of size and distance, but to Forrester the disparity in size between the ark, and the moon almost appeared to be proportionate to the differential between the moon and the Earth. The shuttles began their docking approach to the ark which now seemed as large as a small world. The craft carrying the last of the people of the trees seemed so tiny in comparison to the immense sphere that would soon be their home. Forrester felt a growing sense of foreboding as the dark gaping expanse of the shuttle bay swallowed up the covey of shuttles. He and the whole of the community of the meek were now trapped in the great iron ball of their vision, tightly grasped by the cold black fist of space. As the tiny shuttles entered into the ark's dimly lit interior, an entry from the scrolls, also seemingly shrouded in the darkness of a despair shared by Forrester and its author, displayed itself across the tableau of Forrester's apprehensions.

THE DIARY

GROUND DOWN BY THE WEIGHT OF TODAY
AND WHAT I KNOW MUST COME, I FEEL
THE DARKNESS FILLING EACH FOOTPRINT,
AS I FLEE FROM SUNRISE TO SUNSET.

⤙❖⤚

Phil monitored the last of the shuttle arrivals from the bridge of the Ark. Soon all of the meek would be tucked away in the ecosectors that could easily serve as habitation for the half a million of their number for centuries to come. Phil had not met with any of the meek since they had been transplanted into the reserve and he was anxious to see what had become of them. Inasmuch as Cabot had destroyed ark's builders with the exception of a handful of supervisory technicians, very few would know the vessel well enough to help the meek find their homes in the ark's immensity. Phil decided to lend a hand in the process of settling in the last members of the community to leave the Earth.

Boarding the high speed tube that would carry him from the bridge to the ecosectors, Phil's mind studied the contrast between visions of the pacifistic meek and the ruthless machinations of their 'benefactor,' Cabot. An odd set of bedfellows, he thought to himself. Cabot, representing the worst example of psychopathic behavior the species had spawned, had unwittingly becoming the savior of what might represent the best of humanity.

Even with the improvements Dvorak had made in this system, Phil knew it would take the tube car several minutes to reach the center of the ark. The size of the ark only became apparent when you traveled through the tubes that connected its internal levels. It seemed even larger now that the construction crews were gone. In the solitude of the tube, Phil mulled over the phenomenon of global daylight. Remote scanners positioned beyond the visually hindering bulk of the moon revealed the entirety of the Earth in sunlight, an event that clearly defied the laws of physics.

In the solitude of the tube, a recurrent theme reasserted itself at the edge of Phil's consciousness. Although Cabot appeared to be the prime mover in the enormous undertaking encompassing the reserve, the meek and the ark, while he, Chauvez, Dvorak seemed to be only pawns in some cosmic 3-D chess strategy, that might not be the whole truth of the matter. Pieces moving on four levels made 3-D chess so much more challenging than the ancient game played on a single plane and introduced a random variable into the game. As the tube door opened, Phil, although not a religious man, considered that, perhaps, a fifth level of play existed where the hand of an unseen grand master of the game prompted the movements of both the levels of reality and the men who fleetingly occupied them.

The tube deposited Phil in a passageway leading from the shuttlebay to the ecosectors. The meek, crowded the corridor smiling, and helping one another carry their few containers of personal items to their new homes. To Phil, they looked like any other collection of humanity in transit and, yet, they didn't. It may have been a trick of the light in the narrow corridor, but the outline of their bodies seemed somehow indistinct. Their frames sort of blurred at the edges by an illumination that became unmistakably obvious when they stood against a bulkhead. The radiant blurring was also accentuated when, in the tight confines of the walkway, their bodies came into contact with one another. At the points of contact, the members of the group seemed to merge into a shared globule of glowing indistinctness. It was almost as if this single unit of luminescence was the true representation of their individual natures.

Moving to the head of the group of new arrivals, Phil anticipated helping these latest additions to the passenger list find the hoppers that would convey them to their predesignated dwellings. Arriving at the ecosector portal, he discovered the meek who had come on earlier shuttles had already taken over the job of ushering those at the head of the group into hoppers with pre-programmed destinations.

Taking a step back from the crowd, Phil recognized there was really nothing for him to do. As he surveyed the last of the new arrivals appearing through the ecosector portal, he thought he saw a face he recognized. He strode briskly toward the man.

"Is it possible? Are you Doctor Nathan Forrester?" Phil asked as he extended his hand.

Turning to face a voice that called his name, a name that could make actual his paperwork demise, Forrester wondered if the black hand of the meek's vision was preparing to snatch him up.

"Yes, it is you. I recognize your face from the holographs I've seen. At one time, you were an extremely important topic of discussion in Cabot's inner circle of advisors. I'm Doctor Philip Lawless, a great and steadfast admirer of your work," Phil said.

Forrester, expecting that the other shoe, that might well contain his death warrant could drop at any moment, decided to take the risk.

"Yes, I'm Forrester," he replied.

"Don't be concerned Doctor Forrester. I was saddened by the report of your death and now I am extremely pleased to see that the report was in error and that you made it to the reserve and here to ark," Phil responded.

Feeling reassured by Phil's greeting, Forrester took a moment to look more closely into the face of Doctor Lawless. Served for once by a clarity of memory, Forrester recognized the man from pictures and publications.

"I am pleased to meet you. I have admired your work as well," he replied.

"Do you have a place to stay in the ecosector?" Phil asked.

Esther stepped forward protectively interposing her body between Lawless and Forrester.

"Doctor Forrester will be staying with us," she said.

"Well then, that's settled." Phil responded as he stepped back.

"You have quite a supporter in this young woman," Phil said.

Then, a broad smile enveloping his face, Phil grabbed Forrester by the arm and ushered him in the direction of the transport tube.

"I'd like to show you the bridge of the Ark and have you meet some friends of mine. After all, this whole project has more to do with you than Cabot."

Tracked by Esther's wary gaze, Phil moved toward the tube entrance with Forrester in tow.

"In a very real sense, you are the reason all this exists. The meek, the reserve, the ark, all of this is a direct outgrowth of your research," Phil said.

"I certainly never envisioned this sort of response to the simple notation of some consistent differences in what was otherwise perceived as a monolithic characterization of human behavior," Forrester replied.

"That's the nature of the momentum generated by living systems, beginnings seldom fully predict endings. It's a model that fits new ideas particularly well," Phil replied as the tube door opened.

"I suppose that's so," Forrester replied.

Forrester recognized that no matter the source, he would never become accustomed to all this attention, much less adulation. As he scrutinized this man, Forrester knew that, although Doctor Lawless was an unknown quantity, the man gave every appearance of someone who could be trusted. His aura was replete with a host of patchy gray areas, far more than Forrester's had when he first came to the reserve. Despite these cold spots of pain, blue white illumination largely enveloped Phil's form. Forrester took note of what appeared to be almost a fraying about the edges of Phil's aura. Although he could not be sure, Forrester imagined these small tatters might be evidence that Phil's life span had been artificially extended.

Propelled by the antigravity units in the carrier capsule, the tube ride seemed to go more quickly for Phil with Doctor Forrester as companion. Phil took the opportunity to fill Forrester in on a few of the high points of the ark's construction, carefully excluding any reference to the wholesale slaughter of those who had built her. As the doors to the bridge opened, Phil saw Dvorak and Chauvez at their console stations and quickly escorted Forrester over to meet his coconspirators.

"Doctor Forrester, these are Doctors Chauvez and Dvorak," Phil announced.

Dvorak stepped forward and shook Forrester's hand vigorously.

"So, I finally get to meet the idea man behind all this. I'm the wiring guy," Dvorak said.

"Very pleased Doctor Forrester. I guess, I'm the construction foreman," Chauvez said.

Like it or not, Forrester could clearly see the auras of the two men to whom Phil had just introduced him. Doctor Dvorak exhibited a busy sphere of largely white light, punctuated by constantly shifting zones of orange and yellow. Differing from Dvorak's and Phil's, Chauvez's aura consisted largely of yellow luminescence surrounded by greens and blues. Both men were generously supplied with zones of gray, but no black or red hues were evident in either. Staring at Chauvez for a moment, Forrester imagined a tiny representation of a female figure at the periphery of his orb of radiance whose greatly expanded aura was a deep blood red. Quite unexpectedly, he felt a sense of shame and embarrassment rather like a peeping tom whose unknowing victims had given him a genuinely warm reception. With a conscious exercise of will and a curious sense of relief, Forrester pulled himself back to the comparatively barren domain of verbal communication.

"You're very kind, but all I did was run neuropsychological tests on people and feed a computer. The reserve, the meek, and particularly the ark, these are all tangible realities that you have created," Forrester responded.

Phil was about to verbally beat the drum for ideas as the beginning point for all tangible realities when the bridge chime announced a shuttle arrival. Looking up at the console, Phil saw Cabot's shuttle docking at the private receiving bay located adjacent to the bridge.

Looking at each other warily, Phil, Dvorak and Chauvez then centered their attention on Forrester. They all knew there was no time to get this little surprise off the bridge before Cabot appeared among them.

As the door between Cabot's private apartments and the bridge slid open, Phil strode quickly to meet Cabot.

"Nick, glad you dropped by. I was just about to transmit the data showing the full complement of the reserve on board," Phil said, grabbing a flatscreen as he hurried past his console station.

Glancing briefly at the flatscreen Phil offered, Cabot immediately looked past Phil directly at Forrester. He studied Forrester's face intently for a moment and, without the slightest change in his facial expression, he returned the flatscreen to Phil.

"You're Doctor Nathan Forrester. My sources indicated you had perished in an accident on the Earth Defense Force's command station," Cabot said.

Forrester desperately searched for some believable scenario to offer for the fact that he was alive, but all that came out was a single word.

"Well ..."

"No matter, we're glad to have you on board," Cabot said in a business like tone.

Experiencing no prompting to reply, Forrester was overwhelmed by what he saw before him in the person of Cabot. The aura of this master of both the Earth and the ark shown with the darkest blood red Forrester had ever seen in years of medical practice. So deep was the crimson over the outline of his body that the man's features were barely discernible. More remarkable than the russet overlay of his form was the zone of darkness that surrounded his person entirely. Cabot combined the intolerable red heat of passion with layers of bone chilling blackness overlaid. Even more so than the fraying about Phil's aura, Cabot's bubble of black light showed long trailing tears rent in the periphery of his aura. He must be ancient, Forrester thought to himself. Even more than great age, the shredding of the boundary of Cabot's aura suggested an erosion of the light of life by the darkness in which it was immersed. So overpowering was the vision of this implementer of Forrester's scientific speculations that he stepped back as if to gain greater emotional distance from the red and black of mankind's basest strivings. The vision recruited a little chant from memory that one of Forrester's high school chums had, in singsong fashion, repeated every time Forrester decried the injustices of the world, 'there is no right or wrong, just weak and strong.' It seemed a fitting melodic accompaniment to the oppressive light show of Cabot's aura.

Taking only passing notice of Forrester's withdrawal, Cabot turned abruptly to Phil and fixed him with a penetrating and indicting stare.

"I'll be docking the yacht in the apartment receiving bay as soon as I clean up a few details. My readouts indicate we're ready to leave orbit. Is that correct?"

Phil turned slightly and received affirming nods from both Chauvez and Dvorak.

"That's right Nick. Everything is nominal. The engines are on line and at stationkeeping, all that's required is a course heading."

Shining with a cold and predatory glint, Cabot's eyes came to a tight focus as he slowly swept his gaze over Chauvez, Dvorak and Forrester, finally coming to rest on Phil.

"Phil, I'd like you come over to the yacht so we can go over a few things before I dock with the Ark," Cabot said in chillingly, measured tones.

In a flash of horrific realization that Phil short-circuited before it registered on his face, it became clear to him Cabot was expecting some eleventh hour action against him. Forrester's presence on the bridge had only confirmed Cabot's suspicions. Phil knew with absolute certainty he was being invited along as a hostage.

"Sure Nick," Phil replied, mustering his most unrevealing vocal tone.

Pivoting smartly, Cabot, accompanied by his security guards, exited the bridge as Phil lagged just a few steps behind the group.

Insuring he was the last man through the hatchway, Phil paused momentarily and with his hand held close to his side, he made an emphatic button pushing gesture.

Both Chauvez and Dvorak saw the gesture but said nothing until Cabot's shuttle had left the receiving bay.

Swiftly extracting his surveillance sniffer cube from his pocket, Dvorak activated the mechanism. Examining the cube's readings, he moved directly to the console where he made some adjustments to the bridge security system.

"We're clear. Everything is diverted to replay of existing records of bridge activity showing just you and I at the console," he said turning to Chauvez.

"Phil wants us to do ... do it now?" Chauvez asked staring down at the deck.

"I don't think there's any other way to understand his gesture. You could see it in Cabot's eyes, he suspects something and knows it involves the three of us. That's why he took Phil along as security against any action we might take," Dvorak replied.

"So to take out Cabot, we have to slaughter Phil, too?" Chauvez asked as he looked up.

Watching in horror as Chauvez and Dvorak discussed the death of Cabot and the collateral of Phil's demise, Forrester recognized he had left the Sinai of optimistic abstraction and entered the valley of the shadow of real time death. Based on the community's *seeing*, he knew Cabot must die. However, that was a visionary abstraction. In the halting cadence of this moment in time, the reality of sweat and blood assassination was in the offing.

"We're out of time. It has to be now before Cabot's yacht begins its approach to the ark. With all the nuclear armament Cabot has on that barge, we can't risk damage to the ark and the half a million people we've boarded. Phil knew before he left the bridge what had to be done … he knew," Dvorak replied, his tone absent its usual bravado and passion.

Chauvez watched as Dvorak produced a small activator module from his pocket.

"Damn!" Chauvez spat out.

Transfixed in the moment, Forrester smelled both the fear and desperate resolve of these two men. Even more dramatically, he saw the patchy gray areas in their auras merge into uniformly gray bubbles surrounding each of them. The dancing fringes of light that had marked the edges of their orbs of life had disappeared. Quite suddenly, they had been replaced by a narrow margin of darkness. Here was the moment of prophecy's fulfillment but there was nothing grand or culminating about it. With the push of a button, they would sweep away the darkness in Cabot and with it the light of their comrade. The visions of the meek might represent the future, but their view had been sanitized of the heart pounding terror of human doubt and despair.

❧❀❧

As the shuttle docked with Cabot's yacht, Phil matched Nick's marching stride as they approached and entered the huge central section of the luxurious craft that served as his office. The enormous hologram of the ark, already activated, rotated slowly in the middle of the immense office. Nick walked immediately to the image, examined it closely while producing something from his pocket which he rubbed vigorously. In the reflection of the mirrored wall across from Cabot, Phil could see it was Nick's talisman, the combination ankh and sword. Nick, detecting Phil's surveillance of his actions in the mirror, quickly replaced the object in his pocket and turned to face Phil.

"So what's on the agenda, Nick?" Phil asked.

"You know damn well what's going on. You don't think I've survived all these centuries by ignoring my gut. I've suspected the three of you were plotting my death for some time now. You confirmed my suspicions with Ashley's accident and telegraphed the timing with Forrester's presence on the bridge. If I hadn't needed the three of you to complete the ark, you'd all be floating out there in space with Chauvez's girlfriend, Piatra. The only thing I don't know is how you intend to do me in, although I expect something quite sophisticated given the triumvirate of brain power you gentlemen represent," Nick said, fixing Phil with an unblinking raptor's stare.

"I'm sure I don't know what you're talking about Nick," Phil responded, holding Cabot's steady gaze.

"I expected a more straight up answer than that Phil. By the way, how does it feel to have Ashley's blood on your hands?" Cabot said.

Through the deck plates of the office, Phil felt the slight thrum of the yacht's engines coming on line. Cabot's crew was making ready to dock the vessel with the ark. He knew Chauvez and Dvorak would have to act now, before the yacht began its approach to the ark. Entertaining one last picture of his family safely ensconced in the ark, he gave a moment's consideration to the wonders they might see on their journeys. The vision of his children and grandchildren playing among the stars comforted him in what he hoped to be a valiant ending to a less than heroic life. Like Moses who had killed an overseer his complicity in Ashley's murder would prevent him from crossing over into the promised land with his family. Then, the little boy inside Phil's three hundred year old head demanded an opportunity to let Nick know what was coming and to have the last word between them.

"Nick, you remember our 3-D chess match in the tourney ... I let you win," Phil said, a smile crossing his face.

Nick's face started to redden but Phil knew Cabot's rosy complexion was not an indication of rage or embarrassment. Tiny sparks leapt from Cabot's boots, arcing through his personal shielding to the deck plates. Then, swelling to enormous proportions, his head exploded like a melon with an fissionable core, his entire body rapidly reduced to ash as bolts of energy lashed out in all directions from what was left of his extraordinarily durable mastoid implant. The release and grounding of the ark's momentary burst of power ignited every surface as it arced into the cabin.

Standing amidst the blaze of energy that was now Nick's office, Phil's last thoughts were of absolution. His dying hope was that this fiery sacrifice might weigh in the balance against his years of complicity in Cabot's horrors. He closed his eyes against the flames, graced by a perfect conviction that the blast would remove the last threat to the ark.

❧❖❧

His gaze never straying from the ark's main viewer in which Cabot's yacht was centered, Dvorak watched as the yacht first yawed and then spun, finally disappearing in a enormous explosion followed by a cloud of fire and debris.

Dvorak slowly turned and looked at Chauvez and Forrester.

"It's done," he said solemnly.

Transfixed by the swirling mass of wreckage that was once Cabot's yacht on the main viewer, Chauvez felt the tension flow from his body as he crossed himself.

"Thanks Phil. Rest in peace," he muttered in a tone just above a whisper.

Ever so slowly, the fires of the yacht's destruction winked out. Where there was once a magnificent ship that housed a man who was arguably the master of the world, only fragments of metal remained. Where human envelopes of life once busied themselves pursuing individual destinies culminating in brief moments of good and evil, only a cloud of insensate molecules marked their passing. The wrappings of the gift of life lay in shreds in the midst of the void, but the gift had returned to the giver. Phil's loss was real to Forrester, although he had known him only briefly. This man's courage had saved them all. The loss and the waste created an emptiness within Forrester that mirrored the void in which the ark swam.

Reaching down, Dvorak terminated the proximity alarm that sounded in response to the fragments of the yacht spinning about the ark. He had turned to say something to Chauvez when the alarm sounded again drowning out his voice.

Turning to the console, Chauvez activated the proximity scanner's directional finder on the main viewer and the two cruisers keeping watch over the ark immediately snapped into central focus. The viewer showed them speeding toward the ark at flank speed.

"I think we've got another problem," Chauvez said as he turned to Dvorak.

"They're a wild card to be sure," Dvorak responded.

A flickering light called Chauvez's attention to the hailing icon on the panel, indicating a request for ship to ship communication. He activated the channel and the Captain of the lead cruiser appeared in the viewer.

The Captain, a swarthy man with fiery eyes came directly to the point.

"What happened to Mr. Cabot's yacht?" He asked.

"We're not entirely certain. There was an explosion on board and then the whole ship went up," Chauvez replied,

"Was Mister Cabot on board?" The Captain queried.

"Yes, he had just left the ark to maneuver the yacht into her berth here," Chauvez replied.

Pausing for a moment as if he were considering his options, the Captain looked to one side, cut the audio feed to the ark and appeared to be in voice communication with the commander of the second cruiser. After a few moments of apparent consultation, he turned to face the viewer and reactivated the audio transmission.

"Our allegiance to Mister Cabot was a corporate contract. With his death, that contract is terminated. We have decided to join our craft to the fleet of the Earth Defense Force. We wish you best speed, Captain Chauvez," the Captain said.

As the Captain terminated his end of the transmission, the main viewer reverted to a long range scan. Chauvez watched as the cruisers came about on a trajectory that would take them out of lunar orbit.

Breathing a sigh of relief, Chauvez sat down hard in the console chair.

"Nothing like rising in the ranks, eh, Captain Chauvez," Dvorak said as he began chuckling.

"I've never thought of myself as an officer, that's for certain," Chauvez replied.

Swiveling the chair closer to the console, Chauvez appeared momentarily bewildered as his hands played aimlessly over the controls.

"Now that we've succeeded, what happens? Getting rid of Cabot has been the central focus of my life for so long I haven't thought much about what we'd do once ole Nick was out of the way. The ark's a finished product, Cabot's gone, and I don't know, I sorta feel like I'm out of a job. And Phil, Phil's gone … he was sorta like, I don't know Socrates' ghost … seemed to know where it was all going," Chauvez said.

"Well, one thing's certain, we can't follow the cruisers example and join the fleet. The ark has only minimal defensive weaponry. I really don't think it makes any sense to sit here in orbit around the moon, but, on the other hand, I don't have any idea where we should be going," Dvorak replied.

Everything moved pretty fast for Forrester, but in the back of his mind a certain conviction of what came next arose. The only problem was he couldn't trace that conviction to any fact or series of inferences.

"The time of departure and the course to be set will be determined by your human cargo. I know that sounds silly given everything you've accomplished … and sacrificed to bring all of us to this time and place. I don't know, I guess, you'll just have to trust me on this," Forrester said, without any careful premeditation.

"I'm in the mood to believe almost anything after watching continuous daylight on Earth for more than thirty-six hours. There may be bigger and better circuits activating the servos in this situation than I've ever seen or could imagine," Dvorak responded.

Gazing at the two men, Forrester's thoughts centered on Phil, who had given his life to bring those on the bridge and all those in the ark below to this juncture in the history of space-time. We're all parts, he thought to himself, pieces of a puzzle crafted by a force glimpsed only dimly and fleeting by the people of the trees. He would return to be among those who were now his people and patiently await the illumination that experience had taught him would surely be forthcoming.

Noticing Forrester's slight movement towards the tube access, Chauvez turned and studied this man he had just met with eyes filled with sad resignation. Chauvez was ready for someone else to take responsibility for all the lives encompassed within the ark.

"Just let us know where to go and when. That's enough for me," he said in a tone of quiet acceptance.

"I think we should go and drink Phil into the hereafter in style," Dvorak interjected.

Although Dvorak's tone betrayed his usual bravado, his eyes glistened as though he were on the verge of tears.

Nodding his approval, Chauvez watched with Dvorak as Forrester walked to the bridge access to the conveyer tube.

"Phil was a good man. Have one in his memory for me," Forrester said without turning around.

Entering the tube, his feelings of sadness were oddly supplanted by a sense of confidence. He was more certain he could deliver on what he had promised to these brave men than of anything he had experienced in his life. It was not a vain conceit arising within him, but, rather, a force flowing through him and the people of the trees. A certitude that had its wellspring in a source he could neither measure nor analyze, it inspired a feeling of complete assuredness.

As the closing of the tube door left him alone, Forrester was comforted by an entry from the scrolls. The few lines provided a perspective that valued Phil's sacrifice and supplied a more encompassing dimension to the momentary horror of his death.

THE WEAVER'S ART, MORE THAN THE
CARPENTER'S CRAFT, REVEALS THAT FIRST
LIFE THAT BROUGHT ALL CREATION TO
PASS. THE FIRST ROW SETS THE PATTERN
FOR THE WEAVE. ONCE COMPLETE, EACH
FIBER LOOSED FROM THE TAPESTRY OF ALL
LIFE MUST FIND ITS WAY BACK TO THE
PLACE APPORTIONED TO IT. BEARING THE
DYES AND TWISTS OF ITS PILGRIMAGE,
FROM EACH THREAD'S RETURN, A NEW
PATTERN BORN OF BOTH REDEEMED
MORTAL PAIN AND JOY IS WOVEN.

IN PERFECT KNOWLEDGE THAT IN EACH
PART IS THE WHOLE CONTAINED SHALL
THE TRUE INHERITANCE OF THE MEEK
BE CONFERRED.

IN STRUGGLE'S BLIND CONFLICT IS LIFE'S
BEGINNING. ITS FOREVER FUTURE, PURE
AND COMPLETE, IS WHOLLY SWALLOWED
UP IN CONSCIOUSNESS. FOR ALL OF LIFE,
LIGHT AND THOUGHT ARE WITHIN EACH
AND EVERY STRAND, AT ONCE ETERNAL.
ALL THAT IS LIFE RETURNING THREAD BY
THREAD TO THE LOOM, PERFECTING BY
ITS PRESENCE, ROW UPON ROW, THAT
WHICH IS THE TAPESTRY OF CREATION.

Chapter 30

A taut anticipation permeated the atmosphere of the bridge as Commander Sadad began his watch. Everyone knew what was coming. The general consensus among the crews was that the outcome for the Earth Defense Force would be catastrophic. Grim determination seemed to be the median response among those Commander Sadad knew intimately, but a few of the young pilots had a 'go out in a blaze of glory' mind set. The influence of the natural intoxicants of youth, he thought to himself.

Entering the bridge, Sydes quickly inventoried the level of activity among the command staff, looking for any evidence of panic and then went directly to Sadad's side.

"Have the stealth scanners picked up on those bastards scurrying around out there?" Sydes asked as he surveyed the console.

Sadad punched up a time lapse option on one of the scanners and beckoned Sydes over.

"Take a look at this," he said.

In a continuous readout, the screen chronicled the activity of the enemy fleet over the past ten hours. The movement on the screen clearly indicated a reformation of the alien fleet. Twenty battleships, originally clustered around the huge central vessel slowly regrouped into two separate battle formations. The lead battle group was made up of only battleship class vessels, while the second formation of battleships clustered around what appeared to be a large group of fighter class craft. The time lapse option played out. Sydes recognized he was now looking at real time transmissions.

"Not very pretty, is it?" Sadad said in a dark tone.

"Not at all. Is there any way to get a closer look at that second battle group? I especially want to see what looks like a fighter craft in the center of those battle wagons," Sydes responded.

"The only way I know to do that would entail sacrificing one of the stealth scanners. I can remote fire the maneuvering engines on the scanner that has the best angle on the second battleship sortie and bring it in for a closer look, but the instant I fire those engines, the enemy will locate and destroy the scanner," Sadad replied.

"Do it. Ignite the scanner's maneuvering engines at maximum acceleration and burn up the entire fuel reserve in a single thrust. As soon as the fuel is spent and the engines shut down, they'll have a hell of a time trying to track it. The momentum will carry the scanner over and past that second battle group and give us the view we need," Sydes said emphatically.

With a nod Sadad, moved to the console. He considered this to be one of Sydes' most admirable characteristics. Sydes never wasted human life, but he'd sacrifice any amount of material to get the information he needed to save lives. Making the necessary adjustments in the scanner's engine programming, he increased the digital focus on its cameras to maximum.

"We're ready," Sadad reported.

"Light it up," Sydes responded, his eyes fixed on the main viewer.

Appearing on the viewer only momentarily as a tongue of flame, the stealth scanner instantly vanished. Almost simultaneously, paired bolts of laser energy leapt from the battleship closest to the site of the scanner's engine ignition. The streams of destructive light coursed harmlessly through the position where the scanner had fired its engines, but the stealth camera unit was no longer there. Momentum propelled, it was already cruising silently and undetected past the first and then the second alien battle group, dutifully sending back visuals of everything in the range of its cameras.

Sydes intently scrutinized the feed from the scanner until it passed beyond the fleet into the depths of interstellar space.

"Beautiful," he remarked.

"Playback?" Sadad asked as he looked over at Sydes.

"You bet," Sydes replied.

Sadad adjusted the feed and commenced a replay of the scanner's journey.

"There! Hold it there. Center and enhance the fighter group in the middle of those battle wagons," Sydes snapped.

Sadad centered the fighter group on the viewer and instructed the computer to enhance the image. He knew he was looking at the same image as Sydes, but he also knew he wasn't noticing the same things as the veteran pilot.

"Son of a bitch," Sydes hissed through clenched teeth.

"Isolate and enumerate the smaller craft in central focus," Sydes instructed the computer.

"One hundred smaller craft," the computer's mechanical voice responded.

"Damn it," Sydes muttered.

"What?" Sadad asked.

"Damn them to hell," Sydes murmured.

"What do you see?" Sadad asked again.

"Those are not fighters. No laser turrets, no communication arrays, just propulsion units in perfectly aerodynamic shells. They're missiles capped with planet wrecker warheads, only larger than the ones they used before. Those craft are the same as the one the last alien sortie escorted down to the Mars' colony. Those alien bastards are escorting one hundred of those killer missiles in the second formation," Sydes replied, placing his finger on the viewer over the smaller craft.

"What possible strategy could be served by that kind of massed attack? Those missiles have no offensive weaponry and limited maneuverability. If the Mars attack is any indicator of how the aliens use them tactically, then those missiles have to be shepherded to their mark and then guided to their targets. Those kinds of weapons would be useless against our fighters, the station, and, certainly, the Duo," Sadad asked.

"That's not the target of the second battle group," Sydes replied, his expression growing darker by the moment.

"Then, what is?" Sadad asked.

"The Earth," Sydes said in almost a whisper.

Unable to clearly hear what Sydes had uttered, Sadad asked again. What?"

"The Earth!" Sydes said loud enough for the entire bridge crew to hear.

"The ..." Sadad began.

"Those sons of bitches plan to pilot that missile group to Earth. Just one missile, smaller than these, destroyed the whole Martian colony and laid waste to one thousand kilometers of surface. With a sortie of one hundred missiles and what Von Strohheim said about multiple missiles feeding off each other's self-propagating fusion reactions ... they can lay waste to the whole surface of the planet," Sydes said.

"What would be the point?" Sadad asked.

"Because they can! Because they're pissed off that we put up such a fight and cost them so much in personnel and materials. Hell, I don't know," Sydes replied.

As he studied the freeze frame of the alien missile group on the main viewer, Sadad felt the life ebb out of him. He felt the rage radiating from Sydes like a hot wind blowing in from the desert. He didn't understand this retributive aspect of human motivation or at least refused to accept it. Spite, vengeance, irrational malice, bad blood, parched earth, whatever verbal flag was flown, it was the ultimate testimony to the seductive power of the mindless savage living in the basement of every human brain. Now, if Sydes evaluation was correct, that the same raging primitive occupied the cellar of the aliens' cerebrum as well. Perhaps, an easily aroused and vindictively malevolent infant permanently resided in the hearts of all sentient life, no matter how technologically advanced or biologically evolved.

Activating the personnel search code in the computer, Sydes located Von Strohheim in the bar.

"Here's Von Strohheim's flat screen code. Send the scanner's flyby data to his unit," Sydes said.

Then, stepping away from the bridge console, Sydes turned and exited the bridge at a pace just short of a run.

His gaze still fixed on the image of the alien missiles on the viewer before him, Sadad wondered if his old commander had been right. Perhaps he should have been a medic. He might have been better suited to manipulating the universe of biological forces within an individual than being confronted with decisions significant to the survival of his species on the larger stage of the cosmos.

⚜

Sydes spotted Von Strohheim and Tutunji seated at a quiet corner table having a meal and hurried towards them. Threading his way through the crowd, he passed among the denizens of the bar, including Arthur who raised his drink in salute. Nodding slightly in response to Arthur's greeting, Sydes hurried on.

"Captain Sydes, I received your transmission from the bridge," Von Strohheim said pointing to the flat screen.

"So, what do you think?" Sydes said as he motioned to a waitress to bring drinks.

"I see, what I'm sure you must as well. The second alien battle group is a defensive formation meant to deliver fusion propagating missiles of the type used on the Martian colony. This second battle group can have only one strategic target, Earth," Von Strohheim replied.

"Then, what's the mission of the first formation of battleships?" Tutunji asked as he took his drink from the waitress.

"The first formation will clear the way for the second," Von Strohheim responded after taking a sip of his drink.

"We're what's in the way ... the fighters, the orbital stations and the Duo," Sydes snapped.

"And all the men women and children on them," Tutunji added.

"Yes, this is an important consideration. There are four stations still operational, not counting the command center in which we find ourselves. All these must be evacuated. They are primary targets with no ..." Von Strohheim responded.

"Chance in hell against those battleships. What about the Duo II?" Sydes interjected.

Von Strohheim fell silent for a moment. Then staring at the flatscreen before him, he began to do something on the screen that looked like an engineer's version of doodling.

"She will not be ready for battle in time," Von Strohheim said without looking up from the flatscreen.

Sydes stared at Von Strohheim as a deathly silence fell over the table. Then, he reached out and put his hand on the Doctor's shoulder.

"You've worked more than your share of miracles Doc. We'd all be dead now if it weren't for the Duo."

"If the Duo II can't be battle ready in time, could she be used to evacuate the stations' personnel?" Tutunji asked.

"Yes, this is possible," Von Strohheim replied, his mood brightening.

Von Strohheim's gaze falling to the flatscreen, he pondered what he saw there for a few moments.

"Ninety percent of her hold is empty except for structural supports. It would be a small matter to fabricate living space and we have the transubstantiators to service the needs of the people. Yes, yes, this can be done," Von Strohheim said as, reaching into his pocket he produced a small communicator.

"Hans, reconfigure the Duo II's interior to accommodate habitation for several thousand people. You have two hours. Out," Von Strohheim ordered.

"They can do that in two hours?" Tutunji said an expression of complete disbelief crossing his face.

"Yes. Living space is nothing compared to metric tons of automated missile firing assemblies," Von Strohheim replied.

"Are any of those missile assemblies ready?" Sydes asked.

"A few … but as I said they are not installed, and …" Von Strohheim replied.

"I think, I see where you're going with this, Sydes. If the Duo II could tow those assemblies back here …" Tutunji interjected.

"We could install them in the remaining stations," Sydes interrupted.

"Yes, this much we can manage. There are enough completed assemblies to install one in each of the stations. Each assembly can be loaded with eight hundred fusion missiles," Von Strohheim said.

"We can evacuate the personnel to the Duo II, install the missile assemblies in the stations, and, then, … then, we turn out the lights." Tutunji said, fingering his worry beads.

"Turn out the lights. What the hell does that mean?" Sydes asked.

"We shut down all power on the stations, except the instant remote activation relays on the missile assemblies. There will be absolutely no power emanations for the enemy sensors to read," Tutunji said, a cheshire grin on his face.

"Got you ... so when the alien battle groups' approach brings them into scanning range of the stations, they'll look dead, abandoned," Sydes responded.

"This is, jah, brilliant, Commander Tutunji. Perhaps we can apply some explosive charges to the stations' exteriors and do some cosmetic damage as well. What you call, ice the pie," Von Strohheim remarked.

"Ice the cake ..." Sydes said, "Ice the cake, Doc."

"Good idea ... if we're really lucky, the alien battleships won't see the stations as targets. The enemy fleet captains may well assume the stations have been deserted, and not waste the time and energy to fire on them," Tutunji chimed in.

"It's a gamble but its the only chance we've got. My guess is the range of the alien battleships' laser projectors exceeds the effective reach of our missiles. So, if they don't fall for this ruse and blow the stations to hell, we've got nothing but the Duo," Sydes added.

"But if they do fall for it and we disperse our fighters so the battleships have to target them one at a time, the missile barrage from the stations could create a few openings in the battleships' shields through which the fighters could launch their missiles," Tutunji said.

"I think this is a workable strategy. The Duo has to do as much damage as she can to the first battle group, but her primary target must be the second formation that is escorting the missiles. In order that we can ..." Von Strohheim remarked.

"If the Duo raises a little hell with the first alien sortie and there's a cloud of fighters providing harassing fire, that first formation might just ignore the stations because they look non-operational anyway," Sydes interjected.

"Also, jah, I think then this is workable. So we use the Duo II to evacuate the personnel, put the automated missile assemblies in the stations and scar their exteriors, ein bischen, excuse me, a bit, and shut them down. Then, its up to the Duo and the fighters," Von Strohheim said.

"That's about it Doc. Now, we got to empty these stations. You know, I think I've got just the guy to ramrod this evacuation. A real talker, he could convince anyone of anything, any time," Sydes said as his eyes roamed over the crowded bar.

"I'll coordinate with Sadad. This is going to be difficult for him. We're asking him to abandon his first command to the enemy," Tutunji added as he rose from the table and made his way through the crowd.

In a flurry of motion, Von Strohheim, giving all the appearances of a man delinquent in his cerebral checklist, sprang from his chair.

"I have much to do," he muttered as he scurried off, elbowing his way through the crowd.

Sydes remained at the table and ordered another round of drinks for himself and his anticipated guest. He scanned the bar until his gaze lit upon Arthur. Sydes waited until he caught Arthur's eye and waved him over.

Although in the midst of telling a story to an enrapt knot of pilots, Arthur noticed Sydes beckoning him to the table. Excusing himself to his audience, Arthur moved nimbly through the crowd towards Sydes.

"Well Captain, what can I do for you?" Arthur said as he sat down and grabbed a drink off the table.

"Funny you should ask. I've just logged you into the bridge's record of commissioned officers as the Commandant of evacuation for all five orbital stations," Sydes said with a broad smile.

"Well, I ..." Arthur stammered.

"Now, don't be modest Arthur, this is something you're suited for. I want you to start here on the command station and get everyone but the pilots and bridge personnel to pack one container and get ready to evacuate," Sydes said, the broad grin still fixed on his face.

Arthur sat stunned by the fact Sydes was playing the role that Arthur typically filled in his interactions with his old friend, Forrester.

"Where to?" Arthur asked.

"The Duo II will be along in a bit. Load everyone on that ship and, then, accompany the ship to each station in turn and evacuate all personnel," Sydes said.

"I'm not sure that I can ..." Arthur said, fumbling for words.

"Listen up Mister, you've been conscripted into a commissioned rank in the Earth Defense Forces. Now Commandant, and this is an order from your commanding officer, report to the bridge. Well, snap to it!" Sydes said emphatically.

Quite without thinking about it, Arthur found himself on his feet and headed toward the bridge. For the first time in his life, he wasn't sure how he had come to the place in which he found himself in the order of things.

As the doors of the bridge opened, all the command officers except Sadad saluted Arthur. He faked his best imitation of a salute in response. The only thought in his mind was that things were moving too fast for him to get to know the players and the behind the scenes' agenda.

"Welcome Commandant," Commander Sadad said, shaking Arthur's hand.

Thank you Sir," Arthur replied.

"I have placed ten station security personnel under your direct command. I'm informed you know what to do. The Duo II will dock at the station within the next two hours. Please have everyone ready to board her. Dismissed," Sadad said.

Reflexively, Arthur found himself saluting Commander Sadad and, turning on his heel, he left the bridge. As Arthur heard the door seal behind him, he had but one thought, Sydes, you son of a bitch. The bastard had enjoyed every minute of sticking him with this toy soldier bullshit.

Jolted out of his one minute hate, the appearance of ten uniformed security personnel, all of whom were offering a salute confronted Arthur. Of all the insanity, one of them had a uniform in hand that he was offering to Arthur. Damn that Sydes, Arthur thought to himself as he returned their salute.

"We'll meet … at … in … the conference room in … in fifteen minutes," Arthur said haltingly as he took the uniform.

Then, exchanging another half-hearted salute with his new charges, Arthur headed for his compartment.

❦

Hastening toward the anonymous refuge of his private compartment where the door would close out all this insanity, it occurred to him that this must be how Forrester felt all the time. All Arthur wanted was step out of the spotlight and gather his thoughts.

No sweeter sound had ever met Arthur's ears than the compartment door closing behind him. He went immediately to the bar and poured himself a drink. He stared at the glass for a few moments and set it down on the bar. He was stuck with being in charge, and he didn't like it, but he couldn't do the job, detox patch or no, carrying a cargo of alcohol.

Stripping off his clothes, Arthur considered how successful he had been in living out the role he imagined he had consciously chosen for himself. Always the guy who knew what the people in charge were thinking and doing, he never had to pick up the baggage of responsibility they carried. He shared in the excitement of the lives of the powerful and charismatic without the twenty-four-seven concerns that came with their status. Always in the know, Arthur never had his head on the block when the ax fell.

The stiff shell of the uniform straightened his posture so he felt like he was standing on his own for the first time in his life. He had spent decades following Forrester around acting, as Nate's sometimes critic and source of gossip, while Nate wrestled with the issues and their consequences. Now, Arthur had to make the decisions, not big ones to be sure, but he had to make them, while someone on the sidelines would play critic and rumor monger to his performance. Finally, pulled together, Arthur presented himself before the mirror, looking at a uniform and the man in it with as little a sense of familiarity with the costume as with the man now so attired.

A flurry of things he'd like to say to Forrester blew through his mind like so many dry leaves in the wind. They were all things that needed saying if Nate were here now or, more properly, things Arthur preferred to retract, most particularly, a lifetime of glib remarks. But Arthur knew what Forrester would say, it's OK Arthur. Forrester, despite all of his research, never did understand the bulk of humanity very well. Arthur knew he fell into Forrester's dominance driven category, although he wasn't an extreme example of the breed. Arthur required the stiff arm of another member of his tribe, of the dominance driven, firmly planted in his back to accomplish life goals. Forrester was a good friend, but as one of the meek, he could not consistently wield the confrontational scalpel required to cut through Arthur's line of bullshit.

Poor Nate just wasn't endowed with the limit setting reflexes, that, skillfully applied, put the competitive majority of the human race on notice that actions and omissions, not erudite denial, were the standard of truth and integrity. Wandering in a wilderness of motivations and intentions, Forrester never could bring himself to flatly and unequivocally tell someone they were out of line. Nate was always seeking to understand what in the neurology of the dominance driven caused them to take, or persistently avoid taking, some action. If such investigations proved fruitless, Forrester would focus on why those committed to dominance spent the bulk of their energy denying or rationalizing the obviously negative outcomes of their actions. Good old Nate just couldn't accept the simple and unimpeachable fact that the majority of humanity just wanted what they wanted and they wanted it now. In the end, everyday dealing with the dominance driven came down to a simple binary, either give them what they demanded and risk an escalation of their demands, or say no and deal with their angry disappointment and retaliatory reflexes.

Straightening his uniform, Arthur turned to face the door of the compartment. Forrester should have confronted him, Arthur thought, called him on his excuses and hit him square between the eyes with his avoidant life style. Arthur stopped dead in his tracks, his hand on the door switch. There it was, he thought, the core of the dominance driven configuration. I'll do what I feel like doing and I won't do what doesn't feel good to me at the moment and, if no one calls me on it, then, the consequences are their fault.

"Hell! It sounds like a spoiled adolescent babbling and bitching about being held to the most meager of adult responsibilities," Arthur said aloud.

He knew Nate would say that well rationalized narcissistic avoidance was just one of the traps in Arthur's neuropsychological configuration. As far as Forrester was concerned, every configuration had its own unique landscape, replete with pinnacles of power and bottomless abysses of despairing weakness.

Hitting the door activator with a force ten times more than necessary to trigger it, Arthur stood looking out into the passageway. Just like Nate had always said, you can only think along the lines your neurology allows. Well, what Sydes had done to and for Arthur was proof of that axiom. For the dominance driven, integrity flourished only in the thorny maze of social checks and balances. For the meek, an internal decision process authenticated against the burning bush of individually embraced standards did the job.

The dominance driven, the strong, required confrontation by their fellows to grease the competitive machinery. In order for the strong to get anything done, the voice of another competitive cerebrum screaming at them to wake up and fly right was required. The whole system ran in circles, competition kept everyone on their toes, but dominance was competition's hidden agenda. The short version was fear held the whip hand and greed pulled the cart of the strong.

"Fuck, trapped in the hall of the mirrors of your own brain," Arthur muttered to himself as he stepped into the passageway.

Being sly just wouldn't cut it anymore, Arthur thought to himself as he hurried down the passageway to confront his troops. Now being, 'in the know' would include 'being on the spot' for his own actions and those of others. What a bitch. It was a hell of a leap, but, as Nate would doubtlessly point out, that was the only way you got right hemispheric types to do anything. Fate, life, but more properly their fellow travelers, had to force them to bite off big challenging chunks all at once and, most importantly, swallow them whole. Arthur felt himself reflexively swallow as he hurried down the hall. Maybe he could choke this down, he thought to himself as he quickened his pace along the passageway.

Chapter 31

Sleep as an idea, much less a need, hadn't tugged at Matisse since the Earth's sun had failed to set. He couldn't remember when last he had slept or given even passing consideration to his responsibilities at the United Nations. Remarkably, no fatigue hung on his shoulders. Even the simple need to close his eyes was notable by its absence. His mother was, as he remembered her from his childhood, constantly in motion, preparing food, cleaning up and soliciting the welfare of everyone in the household.

Looking out across the terrace to the tree studded lawn, his eye, directed by his ear, caught the sight and sound of his girls giggling amongst the flowers. The next generation, in the person of his two daughters whose grandmother had found them some red balloons to bat, about laughed and played amidst the greenery. Putting his arm around his wife, she snuggled up to his side. The scene laid out before him, the flood of positive reports carried by the news media, and the events at the United Nations all represented a cascade of peace and contentment that simply too idyllic to be sustained.

"You're favorite," his mother said as she offered him a pastry.

Taking a seat, she poured herself another glass of wine and watched her granddaughters play in the sunlight.

"It is the garden of ..." she offered, never separating her gaze from the children.

"What mama?" Matisse asked.

"It is the garden of Eden, in this place, and in our time. It is fitting that the ending should be as the beginning," she said in an entranced tone.

"Garden of Eden, whatever do you mean mama?" Matisse asked as he turned to face her.

"Soon, I will feel your father's arms around me and see my papa," she replied.

A smile coming to her face, she leaned her head back and stared into the translucent blue of the afternoon sky.

Seeing her in that sunlit moment of comfort, he recognized how much she had loved his father. It was the wine, he thought to himself, inhibiting thought and disinhibiting feeling across three generations. His mother had always fancied herself as some kind of clairvoyant, a fact to which his earliest childhood memories testified. She was wrong ninety percent of the time but that didn't seem to trouble her, then or now.

Sliding closer, his wife rested her head on his shoulder as they watched the girls skipping their way out of the garden toward them. His mother's poetic references to Eden were beautiful, but she was wrong of course, he thought scooping the shining, giggling faces into his lap. There were no children in the garden of Eden.

⚜

As the chief obstetrician for the intercorporate medical conglomerate, Doctor Reitan was at a loss to explain the data that flooded his computer console. It showed a veritable deluge of pre-term births of fully mature and healthy neonates. If a woman was short of the first trimester, the pregnancy simply disappeared. If she was in the second or third trimester, a fully developed, self-sustaining infant was born. There was no explaining it.

Leaving his office, he knew he had to witness this phenomenon first hand. Hurrying down the stairs to a delivery suite, he observed the birth of an infant in the second trimester. The child was delivered quickly and in the full bloom of health. Having witnessed a wholly nontraumatic birth for both mother and child, he completed a routine examination of the neonate and checked the chart three times. No doubt about it the period of gestation was less than five months, yet, before him lay an infant fully expressing nine months of intra-uterine development.

More startling than these healthy premature births were the eyes of the infants themselves. They seemed awake, conscious, and surveyed their admirers and the hospital surroundings with a steady gaze. These infants showed none of the confusion he had seen in the tens of thousands of births he had witnessed. These infants were aware. It was as if birth, in and of itself, had conferred a life time of conscious experience on these newborns. They seemed to know where they were, and, in a way Doctor Reitan could not explain, they appeared to know why they were here as well.

To Doctor Reitan's chagrin and that of the nurses, the newborns seemed perfectly content. They required nothing beyond the opportunity to bask in the sunlight that poured in through the nursery windows. When removed from its benevolent stream of rays, they became agitated and full throated crying signaled their dismay. Inconsolable through feeding, changing or even their mothers' cradling touch, they continued to express their discontent until returned to the compass of the sun's amber rays. Failing any other recommendations, he left instructions to maintain the infants in the unabating light of the afternoon sun.

Doffing his gown, Doctor Reitan hurried to the elevator, which carried him swiftly to the roof where he activated his hopper and pointed its nose towards home. Skylanes nearly devoid of hoppers, he would arrive home in record time. No more than three minutes into the flight, the voice of his spouse activated the comm-link. She excitedly told him their four year old son, afflicted for two years with a devastating and incurable strain of childhood dementia was up and about. Miraculously, he was talking, laughing and playing with his sister. Dr. Reitan shared her joy in response to this truly inexplicable turnaround in his son's condition and, closing the link, increased the hopper's velocity to maximum.

Possessed of a single conviction, the scientist, physician, and the man within him knew that whatever was happening violated the laws of nature. The cascade of improbable events since the sun refused to set suggested to him a bit of clinical lore that warned that the speed of onset of a change in functioning predicted the rapidity of the patient's termination. If the old axiom applied here, then he had very little time to enjoy his son's new bloom of health, the comfort of his family and the more general benefits of the world wide transformation before the planetary patient expired. He was going home where he would burn his diploma, play with his children, look at his wife with a young man's eyes and have a drink.

⨲⟐⤳

Werner's ancestral home in the Swiss Alps represented a profound anachronism in the age of space flight, transubstantiators and cloned organ replacements. He had lived alone among these mountains' rocky crags, spring flowers and deep winter snows his entire life. Last in a family line that had dwelt in this lofty chalet, he had committed to memory a lineage that wound its way back almost two thousand years. Having little to do with those whose lives wandered to and fro in the holes and flats of the earth below, his only concession to progress was an old transubstantiator unit that drew its power from the sun.

In centuries past, his family had made their living providing water to travelers from a spring near where the family's founder had chiseled a chalet into the mountain. The chalet had stood the test of time with walls of hewn native granite more than a meter thick and a roof of slate that disappeared into the mountain. At one time, the terraces cut into the mountain's face centuries ago had pastured goats that provided milk, cheese and skins for his progenitors' sustenance. Later, these pastures and the narrow paths that connected them had been trod by flatlander tourists up for a day in the mountains.

Werner was proud of his family's millennial sojourn of persistence, endurance and stubborn self-sufficiency in the isolation of their alpine homestead. The history of his family stood above and apart from wars, changing jurisdictional entities and the international corporate conglomerates that now governed the planet. Ruling classes came and went, but his family endured. Werner's little clan had never wanted anything from those who fought for territory and power on the flats and so remained securely aloof from the churning dominance driven strife below over the centuries.

Members of his family had always been extremely long-lived even before medical science made such longevity more commonplace. Werner himself had lived over three hundred years without ever consulting a physician. The family mythos attributed their lengthy tenure to the eternal spring, as they called it, that bubbled out of a small grotto in the mountain's face near the chalet.

In millennia, the flow of this fount of waters had neither ebbed in winter, nor surged with the spring thaw. Its source deep in the granite heart of the mountain, was rich in rare minerals and microscopic life forms not found in the streams and wells of the valleys. Scientists had come centuries ago to study the freshet's constituents, but their research revealed only that his clan's longevity represented a marriage between the family's genetics and the peculiar components of the waters. The spring conferred its blessings only on those who had tended it over generations. However, the spring's flow had ceased over forty years ago and all of Werner's excavations could not coax it back to life.

Thirty six hours of daylight made Werner's body restless and disquieted his mind. His daily hike about the top of the mountain was best enjoyed near twilight, but now there was nothing but the afternoon sun of spring. As he returned to the chalet from that daily constitutional, his keen ear detected a sound he had not heard for what seemed half a life time. He heard the unmistakable gurgling of the eternal spring flowing again from the mountain grotto. Quickening his pace so his eye might confirm what his ear told him, he arrived at the grotto. There, bubbling out of the mountain as it had for untold time before his family ever discovered it, the spring flowed clear and cold from the hidden vaults of the mountain. He cupped his hands and drank deeply of the refreshing waters.

Having slaked his thirst, Werner sat down on the stone bench carved into the mountain next to the spring's mouth so many centuries ago. He listened to the music of the spring, looked at the chalet and the hundred mile vista beyond it. He felt completely content, as though something in his life had come full circle. The sun played tag with some quartz crystals embedded in the far wall of the chalet and Werner thought he saw a figure emerging from behind the pillar that contained the family cornerstone. He came quickly to his feet. In a visionary moment, his father, mallet and chisel in hand, approached Werner, a mere lad watched as his father carved the family crest into the cornerstone.

That scene had occurred was more than three hundred years ago, Werner thought to himself. Yet, there he was, just a youth admiring his father's skill as the mallet rang against the chisel chipping away the excess rock to reveal the flourishes and mythical creatures that made up the family coat of arms. It was an emblem still visible in the pillar, signifying service to an ancient chieftain whose bones and name had long since passed to dust.

Then, his father became the figure of the boy and Werner's grandfather was instructing Werner's father in paving the path to the pasture with cobble. One father to son transformation followed another in a seemingly endless parade back through the centuries with only a telltale family resemblance revealing the faces of progenitors for whom no photographs or paintings existed in the chalet.

Finally, there was no pasture, no cobbled path and no granite chalet, just a broad and sturdy ledge jutting out of the mountain. A solitary, roughly clad figure stood against the wind on the outcropping, his long hair flowing out behind him. As the figure turned, Werner recognized many of his own features in this bearded man's face. Instantly, Werner knew, this man was the beginning of his family line, a man who had emigrated from Scandinavia to live among these mountains. The winter garbed man picked up a large rock and placed it on the ledge where, so much later, the column of the chalet's cornerstone would stand.

A winter wind of millennia past played over Werner's face despite the glowing sun and cloudless sky that constituted his personal reality. The specter of the first of his nordic forebearers looked directly at Werner for a long moment and a glimmer of recognition passed over his craggy, bearded face. He smiled and then, beckoning to Werner, the begetter of this alpine bloodline, his garment of skins wrapped tightly around him against the cold, faded gradually from view. In that moment, Werner knew what was coming. He understood the vision's purpose in revealing the line of his people and its founder.

Gradually emerging from and finally superimposed upon the granite wall of the chalet was a vision of himself, a boy again, standing solemnly by his grandfather's death bed. There he stood, head bowed, grieving for the passing of his own and his father's teacher and protector. Werner recalled with perfect clarity the patriarch's final words before he was wrapped in the cold pall of death. In homage to two thousand years of family struggle and in the hope of a reunion with the line that had lived and died among these granite precipices, Werner recited them now. It was the old Norse prayer of passing, handed down unchanged from father to son over countless generations.

> TRAVELERS ON MOUNTAIN PASSES
> UP FROM MISTY FIORDS THEY COME
> THE SKEIN OF MY PEOPLE WOUND
> TOGETHER AS ONE.
>
> THE STRAND OF MY FATHER
> THE THREAD OF MY MOTHER
> FIBERS OF BROTHERS AND SISTERS
> ALL CALL TO ME TO TWINE WITHIN
> THE BRAID OF OUR BLOOD.
>
> WOVEN TOGETHER WE JOURNEY
> BACK TO THE STARRY LOOM OF LIFE
> TO FEEL AGAIN THE WEAVER'S HAND.

Despite its poetic beauty, Werner wasn't certain that he could subscribe to the symbols of the herdsman and weaver that lay at the nordic roots of the prayer. Yet, from the crown of his head to the soles of his feet planted in the rocky soil of that same ledge claimed by the sire of his clan so long ago, he desired the final consummation of being gathered to his people.

❦

Franz, it must be recognized, was not a composer of note. He had striven all his life to emulate the genius of Bach, Handel, Mozart, and Beethoven without ever discovering his own voice. His colleagues considered him out of touch with his time. A musician stuck in a past now considered ancient, Franz was simply not attuned to the beat driven cacophony that intoned victory, money, sexual striving, and the quest for power. His muse was a blithe spirit that lead him to tempos of quiet beauty, sublime passion and devotion.

Having striven in vain with his oratorio, writing and rewriting both words and music times without number, Franz could not bridge the gulf between his vision and the notes that appeared on the score. The work was a hymn to the firmament of heaven and an affirmation of life, but, more than that, it was a vision of a universe alive with purpose. From his earliest childhood, Franz had heard a majestic vibration in the whole of creation. It was a sound generated by an invisible striving towards a great becoming that extended beyond his few rooms and the small planet which had spawned him. Although an overriding passion within him, the music of the spheres eluded his key strokes.

Rising abruptly from a computer console that mimicked the best piano ever crafted, he poured a glass of Black Tower. He stared at the score which had for so many years mocked his attempts to set down his sense of the life force that sustained and supported the mere clay that was the visible universe. Drinking the wine quickly, he poured another glass. His eye strayed from the score and was caught by the sunlight streaming in through the window. It seemed even nature was conspired against him in that the now constant day permitted no shadow in which to shroud his incompetence. In a fit of rage, Franz hurled his glass to the floor with a tinkling crash. He instantly regretted it. Retrieving another glass from the shelf, he filled it and vowed to exercise more control over his frustrated child within.

Having plumbed the depths of his well of personal inspiration and finding it dry and dusty, Franz was dying of thirst in a desert into which no musical muse would venture. If he were to believe his old teacher, this was the time to compose. In that moment, when the last little bit of his self-centered ego was fully erased, only then could he finally hear the song the universe had always melodiously chanted.

He seated himself at the keyboard, placed his fingers on the keys, and waited. At first there was nothing. No motion in his head meant no movement in his fingers. Then, he felt a slight pressure on the top of each finger and watched as his hands struck out a simple plaintive melody. He wanted to pause a moment and assimilate the progression of tones his fingers described, but his hands continued their course. The oratorio wrote itself. It unfolded like an endless series of Fibonacci spirals coursing through his hands, summoning the sounds he had always striven to hear and inscribe.

A work in progress, the oratorio possessed the clean mathematical cadence of Bach, the inspirational flights of Handel, the playful genius of Mozart and the brilliant, wrenching passion of Beethoven. But the medium through which it flowed was wholly generated by a hope and vision, previously locked within Franz that was now freed to soar and sing. As he struck each chord the computer dutifully transcribed every sound to the notes of a printed score. Oblivious to the passage of time as he played, he somehow knew when the oratorio was complete. Neatly stacked in the printer bin were sheet upon sheet of the score. Words long since penned were finally fully fused with the music in a perfect union.

Review of his work was unnecessary. Something inside finally told Franz that what lay before him fully realized his vision. He had transcribed the melody he had heard only in snatches since childhood. Here lay his completely consummated hymn to life. He activated the printer which instantly produced four copies. He wanted scores for each of his friends and supporters, including his old mentor.

Franz rose from the console, walked to the antique shelf, pulled down a large ceramic of Black Tower, and poured himself another glass. He stood for a moment watching the flashes of sunlight play across the room, dancing with a lyrical frenzy over the paintings of his musical heroes hanging on the wall behind the computer console. The paintings seemed so enlivened by the scintillations of the streaming daylight that he imagined the four greats stepping out of their enclosures in full figure to the floor beneath their framed images. Rubbing his eyes, he felt certain that somehow they had actually materialized. Bewigged and clad in the livery of their times, their chests rose and fell as if drawing breath for the first time in centuries. Greeting one another as though they had forgotten all past rivalries, they ceremoniously straightened their attire and then directed their gaze toward the computer console. As one man, they strode confidently toward the printer and the stack of scores resting there.

Bach was the first to pick up a copy of the score. Exercising great care, he leafed through page after page, occasionally smiling as he hummed a portion of the score. Handel was next in line, scanning each sheet studiously before carefully placing them face down on the table in order when he had finished. Mozart had found the Black Tower and poured a glass for himself and Beethoven. Handel could not be bothered with the wine, waving Mozart off, but Bach smilingly accepted a glass. Mozart picked up a copy of the score, moving through page after page so rapidly that sheets, once dropped were scattered all over the table. Handel seemed somewhat perturbed at the disruption of the orderly stack, but good humor prevailed. Beethoven rapidly read through the score dropping pages at his feet as he went. His left hand, moved in concert with what he saw, directing what he read, as the fingers of his right hand moved purposefully through the stack.

Oddly enough given their divergent styles, the four great composers finished reading the score simultaneously. Upon their joint completion, Handel took a glass of the Black Tower as Bach, Mozart and Beethoven refilled their goblets. Thereupon ensued a lively discussion among the four that Franz could not understand, his German being more than a little rusty. Franz was, however, able to gather that the conversation revolved around his composition. Then, quite abruptly, the conference among the great composers ceased. Refilling their glasses, they turned and, as one, looked at Franz. Raising their glasses in salute, they drank deeply and simply faded away in a bout of renewed conversation.

Franz looked down at his hand and noticed he had been gripping the chair by the computer console so tightly during the course of the apparition that his knuckles had been drained of all color. Setting down his wine glass, he rubbed his hands together to restore a bit of feeling and circulation. Then, leaning back in his chair, he basked in the afterglow of his wish fulfillment fantasy. How marvelously compliant the brain was in hallucinating the fulfillment of life long desires when lubricated by a good German white wine. Indeed, as daydreams went this was certainly the most ego enhancing one Franz had ever experienced.

Walking to the table he absentmindedly began to pick up and order the pages of the score scattered on its surface and the floor beneath. The score that Mozart literally flew through had a roughly drawn caricature of a dour Bach sketched in the margin. Franz recognized he'd have to reprint that page before he passed the copy onto his mentor. In the midst of this display of compulsive ordering activity, Franz stood straight up and stared at the four empty wine glasses and the disarray of paper in which he found himself. Then, he looked again at Mozart's attempt at cartooning. He was cleaning up after hallucinated figures from the history of music who, emerging from the mystical rays of the sun, had created a symphony of tangible disorder in his small room.

As his gaze tracked across the balance of the room, his eyes told him the other meager accoutrements to his surroundings were as he remembered them in the moments before he had completed the score. No psychologist, but Franz, nevertheless, didn't believe that hallucinations behaved like care- less children leaving isolated and tangible disarray in the wake of their passing. Suddenly, Franz no longer had any desire to tidy up after his guests. He went back to the console, sat down and sipped his wine, reveling in the palpable, albeit littered evidence of this extraordinary visitation.

Franz never knew how long he sat there sipping his wine and enjoying the play of light across the aftermath of his master's examination. Whether his convic- tion of the reality of these titans' materialization was wholehearted, he could not say, but he felt fulfilled. Perhaps the sun's streaming light, which had only hours before brought condemnation, had in the end effect conferred a benediction.

<hr />

The meek were gone and even Cabot's security forces had been with- drawn leaving the reserve empty except for Chen and Chandra. With little left to do, they spent their time watching the broadcasts that described the marvels occurring everywhere on the planet under a sun that refused to set. The media coverage presented an endless parade of testimonials to personal encounters with some form of transcendent visitation, all of which seemed to have bypassed Chen and Chandra.

It was a marvel to be sure, Chen thought to himself, but even more curious was the fact he and Chandra had been excluded from an event that appeared to have been universal to their species. Both a momentous occurrence and a note-worthy exclusion, he mused. These thoughts held his attention only briefly. Chen had more important things on his mind. Currently, he was focused on setting down the thoughts and observations derived from his last conversation with Forrester. He could already feel the excitement of vindicating himself to the staid academics who had condemned him. He wanted to see those pomp-ous, textbook writing assholes eat crow.

Some hastily scribbled notes that had secreted themselves somewhere in the creative disarray of his desktop were the current object of his frantic search. As he rummaged through the bits and pieces of fragmented thought, shoving aside the detritus of dead ended ideas, he came across what he knew must be Forrester's scanner. The case was well worn and carried a barely discernible 'N.F.' engraving. He had known Forrester just long enough to recognize that his scanner's presence amidst the clutter of Chen's desk was no oversight. The fact that the security lock on the scanner registered as open verified Chen's impression. Forrester had left his personal scanner on the desk expressly for Chen to find.

Upon closer examination, Chen discovered an extensive catalog of en-tries in Aramaic among the scanner's contents. The display panel indicated a translator option and Chen activated it before lighting the screen. It became immediately clear the scanner had been preprogrammed to present a specific entry to the viewer. Chen watched as the entry centered itself on the screen in translated form.

> THE UNIVERSE OF LIFELESS CLAY,
> LIKE THE MARKETPLACE CAUGHT IN
> THE HEAT OF THE NOONDAY SUN,
> TRADES ITS WARES IN KIND. FOR
> GOODS OF WORTH GIVEN, GOODS
> OF WORTH ARE RECEIVED.
>
> OFTEN IN THE CONCOURSE OF MEN,
> GOOD IS REQUITED WITH EVIL AND

THE DIARY

FOR EVIL, GOOD IS EXCHANGED. IN
THIS COMMERCE, THE SOUL, EVIL FOR
GOOD RECEIVING, IS NOT INJURED.
THE WORTH OF THE BARTER LIES IN
THE HEART OF THE SELLER. MERCHANTS
ALL TO OUR FELLOWS IN VENDING EVIL
VEILED AS GOOD, WE ENFEEBLE THE
LIFE AND LIGHT WITHIN.

IN DECEPTION, THE DECEIVER IS
DECEIVED. FOR EACH FALSENESS
QUELLS THE SMALL SPARK DRAWN
FROM THE FIRES OF CREATION THAT
HAVE FROM THE BEGINNING
QUICKENED BOTH DECEIVER AND
DECEIVED ALIKE.

THE SPARK OF THE DECEIVED
FLICKERS NOT WHEN EVIL IS
RECEIVED FOR GOOD, WHILE
THE EMBER OF THE DECEIVER
SMOLDERS, RETREATING FROM
THE LIGHT TO THE COLD
SOLACE OF DUMB CLAY.

A LIFE DARKENED BY THE SHADE
OF MASTERY OVER OTHERS IS
ESTRANGED FROM THE LIGHT. THE
TRADERS OF COMMERCE EXCEL IN
THEIR DOMINANCE OF OTHERS, BUT
NOT IN THE GENTLE WISDOM OF THE
LIGHT. THE MARKET PLACE REWARDS
THOSE WHO ARE HER MASTERS.
RECOMPENSE IS THEIRS IN KIND,
CLAY FOR CLAY.

TO RETURN EVIL FOR EVIL JOINS
EACH TO THE TRIBE OF CLAY
WHERE CREATION'S LIGHT DAILY

RENEWED IN THE EYES OF THE
MEEK DWELLS NOT.

BARTERING IN THE LIGHT
BENEATH THE DARKNESS, THE
MEEKS' EXCHANGE FANS THE
SPARKS OF CREATION'S FIRE,
TRADING IN AN EXCHEQUER
WHERE GIVING IS GETTING.

MEN DIFFER ONLY AT THEIR BEST.
OVERCOME BY DOMINION'S
IMPASSIONED ENTREATY, THEIR
COMMON CLAY IS OF ONE MIND
AND SPIRIT.

Reading the entry several times, Chen was struck by the simplicity of the message. There was only one possible source for this material. The scanner must hold a record of the content of the scrolls he had helped Crystal excavate so long ago. Considering the enlivening sensation Chen experienced as he read, he now better understood the envelope of light he had seen form around Crystal's family as they received the scrolls in the dusk of that summer's evening.

Fully assured Forrester had selected this entry specifically for him, Chen read it again. Upon this reading, he focused his attention on discovering what he knew must be a personal message Forrester had left in his selection of this particular passage.

Despite the metaphors of the time in which it was written, the message seemed to be that the physics of the material and insensate universe was, simply put, cause and effect on a scale beyond imaging. However, the dynamics governing the interaction of living systems clearly differed from the action-reaction Newtonian model governing matter. The entry seemed to suggest that each sentient life form represented an isolated cause and effect universe within itself. Nested in each individual's perception was the self-destructive illusion that, through the expression of their own malevolent thoughts, feelings and actions, they were injuring another person. The dark tides of each person's internal life and external actions were, in fact, causes that produced negative effects principally within him or herself. Attempts to materialize maleficent thoughts, make real destructive feelings or fulfill wholly self-serving needs and wishes in the material universe represented a descent into darkness, disappointment and despair. Negative feelings and thoughts were forever trapped within a bubble that wholly encompassed their originator's life. Such externalizations, indeed projections of individual arrogance, devolved one to the mindset of the primal tribe. Mankind huddling in the darkness, surrounded by mastodons or transubstantiators, remained forever a fearful and angry species that relied on one another only when faced with a greater threat emerging from beyond the circle of the campfire's glow.

Leaning back in his chair, Chen remembered how the meek had spontaneously rediscovered and instituted the spiritual cleansing practices of the Senoi. All negative thoughts, feelings and even dreams directed against another were confessed to the party concerned and reparations made. The entry from the scrolls enlightened his understanding of the necessity for this curious style of interaction. No individual member of the meek wanted dark or self-serving thoughts trapped inside them. In the words of the scrolls, such self-deceptions 'enfeebled the life and Light within.'

The people of the trees, the dominance deficient, were evolution's response to the primacy of the dominance driven tribal mentality, proceeding unchanged from the murky past to the 'enlightened' present of human interaction. The meek's inbuilt capacity for a self-revelatory, continuous, and wholly communal dialogue made the dynamics of dominance directed to both physical control of the group and enforcement of a shared tribal vision entirely superfluous. But, more than superfluous, the dynamics of enforcement leading to tribal consolidation lay at the heart of all that was destructive in the human character. To be sure, much good had been accomplished by the motivations, both consciously and unconsciously experienced, that drove and enforced consolidation of group effort. However, the benefits to those concerned were experienced principally when something with long teeth invaded the campfire's bulwark of light, threatening all rather than just one member of the group.

More tangibly than ever before, Chen grasped the evolutionary leap that the meek represented. They represented a new biological paradigm wholly unmoved by dominance dynamics prompting the individual to subjugate his fellows, untouched by the group pressures of the tribal ascendancy over other tribes, and completely oblivious to the driving need to subdue the environment that sustained them all. The meek were fully individuals and yet completely communal in thought, feeling and action. Their focus entirely eschewed dominance as nonsensical within the shared fabric of their cognitive and emotional experience. Without exception, the meeks' focus was directed to that which tied creation together, not on dominating one or another facet of some grand illusion that suggested the universe was but a collection of disparate parts.

Drawing a deep breath, Chen pushed his chair back from the desk and exhaled. He felt as though he were expelling the musty air that had welled up from an ancient text provincially written to defend the proposition that man stood at the center of the universe. If the small portion of the scrolls he could grasp was any indication, what the meek comprehended of nature, indeed of the cosmos, must be truly astounding. What he could only read and understand in part, represented the meeks' reality. In their universe of interaction, they moved freely amidst the unsullied light of creation. They experienced every vision of one another as a perfect revelation of who they were, every word as the simple unself-serving truth, and every event as consistent with what must be.

Looking up from his study of the entry and the rush of revelations that had come in its train a knock on his office door interrupted, Chen's musings.

"Come," he called.

The door opened, revealing Chandra silhouetted in the sun's constant light. For a moment, Chen imagined he could see an outline of darkness around her form, but reconsidering, he judged it to be a simple contrast effect produced by backlighting.

Moving toward the desk, Chandra surveyed the room as though she had never visited Chen's office before. Her gaze finally came to rest on the scanner that occupied a central and relatively uncluttered position on his desk.

"What's that?" She asked.

"You remember those scrolls I told your about?" Chen replied.

"Yeah," Chandra responded, a sneer contorting her face.

"This is Doctor's Forrester's scanner. It contains all the entries in the scrolls he discovered," Chen said, his eyes brightening.

"So," Chandra retorted.

"They foreshadow the evolutionary development of the meek more than three thousand years before it occurred. And that suggests that either the scrolls embody clairvoyance, or the hand that wrote them is working behind the illusion of natural law prompting a new unfolding of the biological destiny of the human species," Chen said, excitement rising in his voice.

"Sure, whatever," Chandra retorted.

Reflexively retreating from the bitterness emanating from Chandra, Chen slowly moved his chair farther from the desk. It seemed as if her interaction with the community of the meek during her tenure at the reserve had deepened her acerbic temperament. Although the door to his office had been closed shutting out the sun's light, he imagined he could still see a zone of darkness around her.

"What's the matter Love?" He asked.

"I just can't get very excited about some moldy ramblings extolling losers as evolution's final word on the human species," Chandra said.

Her bland tone and the venomous undercurrent it carried shocked Chen. It seemed a timbre usually reserved to the amygdala driven adolescents of the race.

"What happened to you? You've moved from not understanding the meek to hating them. I don't get it. They've always treated you well," Chen said.

"They're a bunch of pampered children. Everything is handed to them, and they sit around thinking good thoughts with those lobotomized smiles plastered on their faces. You and I both know why Cabot picked them. He wanted sheep to herd about in his own little kingdom in space," Chandra replied, anger growing in her tone.

"You never knew them the way I did. They worked hard, science, art, music. They were always in a full on creative mode. And they shared their work and insights with anyone who cared to look or listen," Chen retorted.

"Terrific. So where are these tangible contributions that made life better for everyone, if they worked so damn hard," Chandra replied.

"They gave everything away over computer linkages to anyone who showed an interest," Chen replied.

"Then they're damn fools! If you have nothing, you are nothing. This is the real world, not some kid's left hemispheric fantasy of magical transformations. No real change is possible without a power base. Cabot may be a bastard, but at least he makes a difference," Chandra spat back.

"OK, let's say that all you propose is correct. Every last one of the meek are hysterically fixated five year olds. Same question, what did they do to injure you?" Chen asked.

Sitting in silence for almost a minute, an expression of embarrassment crossed Chandra's face before she directed her gaze to the floor.

"They seduced you," Chandra replied in a barely audible tone.

"They what?" Chen asked, unable to make out what Chandra had said in her tiny, little girl's voice.

"You love them more than me," Chandra blurted out.

Chen watched in amazement as Chandra sank into the chair, pulled up her legs and curled her frame into a close approximation of a fetal ball. Suddenly, he was struck by how small and fragile she appeared. Needy was too meager a word to describe her. The little girl who sat before him was a cosmic black hole of unrequited narcissism. How could he ever have imagined he would be able to fill the needs of a woman who required a psychic servant? Her wants might be sated by some mythical creature who anticipated Chandra's real and imagined requirements before she sensed them herself, but Chen was in no position to do so.

⚜

Intellectually, Chen knew his attraction to Chandra was involuntary. It was a matter of opposing but complementary neuropsychological configurations and immunological strengths meant to benefit the next generation. Nature had never intended their affinity for one another to smooth the emotional way between them. These basics of genetic dynamics had been more than adequately demonstrated in Forrester's research on attraction. If Chen's makeup represented left hemispheric infatuation with abstraction and governing dynamics, then Chandra's must be right hemispheric and focused on taking and keeping. To be sure, she was nurturing. There were more than enough examples of that in their relationship over time. However, hers was not a nurturance informed by left hemispheric good will, its anatomical and evolutionary origins were older than that. Chandra's nurturance was reflexive, arising in the amygdala and unrefined by the so-called higher centers in the brain. As such, her care-taking was a protective-possessive nurturance, narcissistically jealous and expectant of exclusive allegiance from the object of its 'affection.'

I guess, he thought to himself. He had never recognized how faltering the emotional path between them might become or how many rocks might litter it. Then, halted in mid-rant, the words of the entry Forrester had marked for him intruded into the wave of disappointment and recrimination that dominated his mood.

> TO RETURN EVIL FOR EVIL JOINS
> EACH TO THE TRIBE OF CLAY
> WHERE CREATION'S LIGHT DAILY,
> RENEWED IN THE EYES OF THE
> MEEK, DWELLS NOT.

Suddenly, he recognized rising within himself the very emotional, indeed physiological, propensity to return evil for evil. It was the right hemisphere's inbuilt reflex to defend and attack that prevented his entry into the community of the meek. His personal demon was no less than a manifestation of the most primal striving of all living systems, the need to ensure individual survival. Whether the attack was physical and life threatening, or merely emotional and ego deflating was indistinguishable to this simple cellular cluster.

The mechanism was a primitive binary switch with just two options; run away from, or reflexively attack, the perceived attacker.

Absent from the primordial programming of this reflex, that was clearly intended to ensure physical survival was a well defined and discriminating off switch. The reflex itself did not spell out a counterattack sufficient to resolve a personal hurt, just as the magnitude of the defensive reaction was unprescribed. The whole system of individual defense was open-ended and, therefore, subject to the individual's experiential and circumstantial interpretation in the moment of perceived threat. To be sure, a frontal lobe inhibition represented a moment's pause for rational reflection, but the history of the human race amply illustrated that reason had never been an effective counter to rage. The reflexive personal defense valve was incapable of metering flows large and small; it was a river carrying individuals forward in a torrent of self-defense that merged insidiously into unprovoked attacks on others. An endless parade of humanity had been borne through history on this flood, buoyed up by justification, rationalization, and denial of the horrific consequences of their 'self-defensive maneuvers.'

Having lived with and studied the people of the trees, Chen knew beyond all hope of rationalization that his own thoughts and feelings condemned him as an outsider. He could not simply wish away the fully automated and wholly irrational need to defend himself built into the very fabric of his tissues. What he could do, and would do in this moment, was exercise his own frail version of control over this ancient and uncompromising monster programmed to ensure individual survival.

⚜

"I'm sorry my actions lead to confusion between scientific enthusiasm for the meek and my attachment to you," Chen said in soft and appeasing tones.

"I didn't want to be left behind. You always had your work, I ... I just had you. My own work never enthralled me the way yours did you. I wanted you to be as excited about me as you were about your job. Now the meek are gone, I'm here, and you're still talking about them," Chandra responded as tears formed in her eyes.

All the adrenaline driven physical changes that attended the need to defend his position by attacking Chandra surged within him. Like Cabot, what Chandra wanted was a degree of devotion that was tantamount to worship. She also shared Cabot's monotheistic demand that he have no other gods before her. Amidst his own biochemical avalanche of retaliatory feelings, Chen empathized with her sense of being left behind. He was, after all, here on the

Earth and the meek, well, the meek were in the heavens with a destiny among the stars he could only guess at. Chen swallowed hard as he regained that little bit of control necessary to continue the exchange.

"For me, there's no you and I, there's just us. I've never had those feelings about the meek."

Then, reaching out, he took her hand. With the instant of his touch, the tension in Chandra's body gradually dissipated and a trace of a shy smile appeared on her face.

"I guess I knew that, but I needed to hear it," she said.

Perhaps it was a fancy of his imagination, Chen couldn't be certain, but as Chandra relaxed under his touch, he felt a palpable drain of energy from his body. The sensation presented a sharp contrast to the influx of excitement and sense of hope he always felt when dealing with the meek. Interaction with the meek energized him, perhaps that was one of their gifts. The animation the meek inadvertently conferred was not a frenetic one, but rather like that associated with the blue end of the visual spectrum, far reaching, calming, accepting and invigorating. Perhaps at a fundamental level it was a simple matter of physics. The meek, at their own expense, conferred energy on others, while the dominance driven drew energy from those around them and utilized it for their own purposes.

Rising from his chair, he walked from behind the desk and encircled Chandra in his arms rocking her gently. He would try to be for her what the meek had been to him, a source of energy and hope. He knew now why Forrester had marked that particular entry for him. Somehow, the old man knew what Chen needed to hear to take the first faltering step out of the darkness toward the light.

⚹❖⚹

He would not, nor could he, tell Chandra what he had seen in the 3-D imager hologram of Forrester's brain. But Chen was convinced that what he saw there was likely evident in the cerebrum of everyone of the meek. Having turned the imager on himself, he knew that the fully developed structure he saw in Forrester brain, Chen possessed in only its most rudimentary form. He didn't have to scan Chandra to confirm what he already knew from her behavior and emotional state. He would see frontal areas as normal as those of any of the right hemispheric infants they had euthanized.

Almost as if the light of creation had momentarily kindled to flame the small spark within Chen, he knew what Chandra required from him now was what he had received from the meek. In order to progress toward the light, she needed a personal beacon of energizing illumination in the gloom of her rage and disappointment, not passion's dark response in defensive kind. Chen had to surmount his own need to defend or withdraw from the darkness in which Chandra was lost, not founder himself in the limbic mire. He could not ascend into the heavens with the people of the trees, of that much he was certain. Nevertheless, he could pull himself up by his own bootstraps to a level where he could actually see, instead of simply noticing, the stationary sun shining beneficently on the Earth and thrill in the wonder of its light. Perhaps that was as much illumination as his level of evolutionary development would allow.

The last passage in the entry Forrester had selected for him sprang to mind with renewed force and clarity.

> MEN DIFFER ONLY AT THEIR BEST.
> OVERCOME BY DOMINION'S
> IMPASSIONED ENTREATY, THEIR
> COMMON CLAY IS OF ONE MIND
> AND SPIRIT.

To differ at his best in dealing with the darkness in Chandra was Chen's sincerely sought for consummation. He would chip away at the dark obstacles the timeless mechanism of attraction had, with clockwork indifference, strewn upon the path between them.

A warm and accepting smile on his face, Chen reached out and took Chandra's hand. Reluctant at first, she returned his grasp and smile. Then, hand in hand, doubts and differences in tow, they stepped together into the seemingly endless afternoon of the sun's warm glow. For Chen, the warming rays conferred a calming acceptance. He was not one of the meek, but he felt better about working with what he had. It was the old saw that ontogeny recapitulated phylogeny - what you were at conception represented the evolutionary line from which you sprang. He had maximized his evolutionary potential. No one could realistically expect to do more than that. In a curious sort of way, so had Chandra. Despite her brilliance, she had stretched her hand as far as her emotional reach would allow. For him to expect more from her than that was both unrealistic and unforgiving.

"It will be all right," he said as he squeezed her hand.

He said it because he meant it, but also because he knew it was precisely what she needed to hear. Listening to the tolling of his own motivation, Chen quite unexpectedly recognized the telltale discordance produced by a right hemispheric primate sounding a troop alarm in some faraway jungle canopy.

That primate progenitor, crafty and proficient at mobilizing others needs in the service of his own, still dwelt comfortably within Chen's own psyche. Clearly the right brain conferred compassion and the left brain housed conscience, but the right hemisphere also reveled and indeed excelled at the oldest game known to the human species, manipulating the needs and emotions of others.

Crossing the meadow surrounding the service center toward the wooded hillside, the couple's stride seemed solely guided by a need to move in unison. Chen recognized the conscious effort on his and Chandra's part necessary to produce this synchronous gait. Conscious volition was required to produce such cooperation among the dominance driven. For the meek, cooperation flowed in their veins and fed every cell in their bodies. Chen realized that although he could understand the description of the meek in the scroll's entry, he could, in truth, neither feel, nor live it.

> BARTERING IN THE LIGHT
> BENEATH THE DARKNESS, THE
> MEEKS' EXCHANGE FANS THE
> SPARKS OF CREATION'S FIRE
> TRADING IN AN EXCHEQUER
> WHERE GIVING IS GETTING.

'Where giving is getting,' fine words, simple words and fully comprehensible, but he knew they represented more than meaningful sounds transcribed to paper. The meek didn't just believe those words, their lives were those words. Evolution had created in the tissues of the meek a continuing existence which, before their advent, was only to be found in the yearnings of poets and mystics. The frontal lobes of the meek consistently generating what could be as what will be, were fulfilling the yearnings of millennia of humankind's transcendental strivings. In the meek, mankind became as naturally and unquestioningly giving as the teeming mainstream of the dominance driven majority of their species had for ages without number greedily taken from mother Earth and each other. Not mankind's only future, the meek were nevertheless a grand experiment of the master geneticist. In the meek, there would be individuality, without dominance and strife. Like many before him, Chen was blessed with a vision in which he could not participate. Perhaps for the first time in his life, Chen fully appreciated the feelings that lay behind the term 'bittersweet.' The meek might be right, Chen thought, words are experiences and so must be carefully chosen.

Entering the living canopy of the forest, the comfortable synergy of life all around him enveloped Chen. Curiously, he felt himself an alien invader in this benign living organism, beset as he was by a nagging self-centered question that would not be dismissed. Why had the whole world beheld an image of their life's fulfillment except Chandra and himself? Why single out poor Chen for exclusion from this unique, transcendental event? He heard the same self-pitying narcissism in his queries he so readily recognized in Chandra's whining. He didn't like it. Nevertheless, the question would not be dismissed. Then, as if summoned to the resolution of his existential doubt, he heard a voice so clear and resounding he looked about to locate its source. In a fashion he could not explain, he recognized the voice did not read from the scrolls but came from their scribe. He attended closely to the basso resounding in his head although he realized that no cognitive operation beyond listening was possible amidst the booming resonance.

THE WRATH OF GOD ABIDES ONLY IN THE CONJURING OF MENS' GUILTY RAGE AND SORROW. UNWILLING TO YOKE THEIR OWN PASSIONS, THEY LOOK TO THE HEAVENS FOR ANOTHER TO DO SO. THE DAY OF JUDGMENT WAS CRAFTED, NOT IN THE LIGHT, BUT IN THE CLAY OF MAN'S TERROR. THE HORROR OF A DAY OF RECKONING SPRINGS FROM MINDS DEVOTED TO MASTERY, RAGE AND RETRIBUTION. THE LIGHT AT THE BEGINNING OF THE UNIVERSE SOWS NOT THE DARKNESS OF FEAR AND RAGE, BUT REJOICES IN THE ILLUMINATION THAT DAILY RISES IN THE BRIGHT GARDEN OF THE SOUL.

MAN IS HIS OWN WRATH AND JUDGMENT. THE WEAVER'S LIGHT IS WISDOM AND LOVE IN EQUAL MEASURE. KNOWING THE FLAWS OF EACH FIBER AND STRAND OF CREATION, HE SEEKS ONLY THAT THE FINAL WEAVE OF LIGHT'S CONSUMMATION FILL ALL THAT IS WITH BRILLIANCE.

'Humbled,' that was the word best used to describe how he felt. Despite all his infantile and short-sighted whining, he knew he had received what no other on the face of this teeming planet had succeeded in getting, a direct personal revelation. Simply put, each man was vested with the power of creating his own daily hell or engineering his own moment by moment salvation. The realization was horrifying. In the face of that horror, Chen chose the truth.

He knew, with perfect and uncluttered clarity, he could not reflexively live in that reality which was the inheritance of the meek alone. Forrester's last testament was one left hemispheric processor's gift to another, an understanding of a future Chen would not see. For the now in which he was perhaps for the first time fully present, there was green grass beneath his feet, the shade of ageless conifers and the love of a woman who gave as much as she was able. It was a feast tailored to fit his appetites and modest capacity and it was enough.

Chapter 32

Conferencing for an amazingly brief period of time, Sydes, Commander Tutunji and Sadad had all agreed. Their unanimous decision sent Von Strohheim and his technical staff back to the Martian base where the Duos I and II had been constructed.

Protesting mightily against being removed to a safe location, Von Strohheim had made a good argument for being immediately available to deal with any technical problems that might arise in the course of the coming battles. Nevertheless, his well reasoned arguments availed him naught. Sydes adamantly insisted that the core of Earth Forces' technical genius be out of harm's way.

All in readiness, the strike craft had been mobilized, the Duo fully armed, and the stations equipped with the automated missile assemblies originally intended for installation in the Duo II. Five hundred strike craft stood at the ready, either in the receiving bays, or in orbit around the command station. At the first indication of the alien's approach, the strike craft would be dispersed along the enemy's flight path to harass their thrust into the solar system. Everyone knew the effectiveness of the strike craft depended on how well the Duo's tunneling lasers did at punching holes in the enemy's shields. Without the breaches in the alien battleship's shields that only the Duo could create, the strike craft would be no more deadly than gnats to a cape buffalo.

On board the Duo II, Arthur had completed the evacuation of the last station on his list and was docking once again with the command station. Here, he would pick up the last of the military personnel with the exception of the strike craft pilots. He had also been directed to pick up the three dimensional viewer. That eye on space had already been dismantled into its component parts for removal from the command bridge as the Duo II arrived. It would be reassembled and installed by a few of Von Strohheim's staff in the Duo II.

Arthur's travels made him aware of the total population of the five stations. A rough count suggested he had taken about one hundred thousand men, women and children on board. Despite the large number of displaced people and the confusion associated with the uprooting of so many families, settling the frustrated and frightened souls in the Duo II's prefabricated hold had been less trouble than he anticipated.

Disembarking from the Duo II, he docked with the command station's receiving bay in a shuttle sent to receive him. Activating the shuttle's comm link to Sydes, he began his report.

"All personnel accounted for, Sir. We've returned for the final pick up," Arthur announced.

"Are all the stations armed and blacked out?" Sydes asked.

"Yes, Sir. The stations are completely powered down and the missile assemblies are on line with autonomous power sources set to instantaneous remote activation from the Duo II's main console," Arthur replied.

"And the explosive charges?" Sydes inquired.

"Attached to the stations' hulls where they won't do any damage to the missile assemblies or shields," Arthur responded.

"Well done. Report to the bridge Mister," Sydes said.

"Yes Sir," Arthur replied.

Leaving the receiving bay, he made his way at quick time toward the command station's bridge. He ducked into a side hall as bridge personnel hurried by carrying the last few components of the three dimensional imager to the Duo II. Arthur knew Earth Force was effectively blind until that imager was up and scanning from its new home on the Duo II. As the door to the command bridge slid open, the alarm klaxon began to ring. The sound sent a chill down Arthur's spine.

"What the hell ... they can't be that good, to be on us the minute we take down the imager," Sydes said as he scanned the control console.

"It's the station's proximity alarm," Commander Sadad said.

Then, he terminated the klaxon and activated the directional scanner on the main viewer.

"Cruiser class vessels, two of them, but I don't recognize the insignia," Tutunji said after studying the main viewer for a moment.

"They look like basic Earth design, but they're not ours. Give them a fighter escort," Sydes said emphatically.

Ordering a squadron of strike craft to surround the two cruisers, Commander Sadad opened a communication link to the approaching vessels.

"This is Earth Defense Force Command to unidentified cruisers. Hold your position or you will be fired upon."

In response to the hail, an isolated videoframe opened to the left of the image of the cruisers on the main viewer. A man clad in a black and gray uniform appeared on the screen. Standing stiffly erect, his otherwise stoical presentation was fragmented here and there by poorly controlled signs of apprehension.

"I am Captain Merkson, late of Mister Cabot's defense force," the uniformed figure reported.

"I thought I recognized the insignia on those ships. These guys are part of Cabot's little private army," Arthur said as he stepped up to the viewer.

"What are your intentions Sir?" Commander Sadad snapped.

"To join in your defense against the alien incursion Sir," Captain Merkson's replied.

"And what does Mister Cabot think about that Captain?" Sydes retorted.

"Mister Cabot is dead Sir. Our corporate contract to serve in the defense of his holdings terminated with his death. The officers and men of these vessels, now free to make their own choice, are united in our commitment to serve in the cause of Earth's defense," Captain Merkson said with a note of finality.

"Hold your position Captain," Sadad ordered as he closed the transmission.

"Do you think it's some kind of trick?" Sydes asked turning to Arthur.

"No, I don't think so. Cabot wouldn't have anything to gain by sabotaging our efforts here," Arthur replied after pausing for a moment.

"I agree. Cabot obviously built these vessels to protect his interests against the alien invasion. These ships are cruisers, too large and not maneuverable enough to be effective against corporate strike craft. They look more like ships constructed to defend a base or perhaps a larger vessel," Tutunji added.

"The Ark. I bet they were built to defend Cabot's floating planet ... ah ... Sir," Arthur interjected.

"I agree with the Commandant. This Captain Merkson may be just what he seems to be, a man without a flag. Besides, he's sitting on some firepower out there that might be useful to us," Sydes said, smiling at Arthur.

"We could assign these cruisers as escort to the Duo II," Sadad suggested.

"Good idea. If it turns out that this is some kind of trap Cabot is laying for us, the Duo II can hold off these two cruisers with her shields and dispatch them with her tunneling lasers, if need be," Sydes responded.

"That plan would free up the strike craft we had intended as escort to the Duo II for use here," Tutunji remarked, fumbling with his worry beads.

"That works for me. Cabot's crews haven't had any flight experience with our squadrons. They haven't been battle tested against the alien craft and have no knowledge of our tactics. They'd be worse than useless in a fire fight," Sydes said.

"We are in agreement then," Sadad said as he opened a link to the cruisers.

"Captain Merkson, the operations staff has decided to accept your offer. You are, from this moment, under the command of the Earth Defense Force," Commander Sadad announced.

"Thank you Sir," Captain Merkson replied as he visibly relaxed.

"There are two large spherical vessels in orbit about this station. When ordered to do so you will accompany the larger of the two as escort. The vessel you will be defending is the Duo II," Sadad instructed.

"Just so there are no mistakes, Captain Merkson, the Duo II has the firepower to vaporize both of your vessels," Sydes added, stepping up to the viewer.

"Yes sir. I understand. Sir. Trust is a commodity always purchased in installments," Captain Merkson replied, his face tightening.

The Captain's image fading, the viewscreen now contained only the two cruisers completely encircled by strike craft.

"I think we can live with this guy," Tutunji said to Sydes, who nodded his agreement.

Turning quickly toward the sound of the security door sliding open, Sydes watched Von Strohheim bustling onto the command bridge with his usual efficiency.

"The three dimensional imager is now operational on the Duo II," Von Strohheim said as he tried to avoid Sydes' gaze.

Sydes glared at Von Strohheim with an expression of feigned disapproval.

"Doc … I thought I told you to stay at your Mar's base?"

"Yes, this is correct. However, military prerogative must give way to the gods of engineering necessity. I supervised the installation of the missile assemblies in the stations and did additional habitation refit on the Duo II while she was underway," Von Strohheim replied.

Then, Von Strohheim smiled and chuckled as he toyed with his Phi Beta Kappa key.

"And … in my free time since we arrived at the station, I got the technicians started on the installation of the three dimensional imager. By the way, what are those cruisers doing out there?" He asked.

Shaking his head in disbelief, Sydes, a slight smile on his face, looked over at Tutunji who began to chuckle quietly.

"Is that all?" Sydes asked, feigning a questioning expression.

"Ah … yes … that is all …," Von Strohheim replied, appearing a little disappointed.

Then, Von Strohheim's gaze roved over the broadening smiles on the faces of the bridge crew.

"This is the joke, yes?" Von Strohheim asked.

"Yes, this is the joke. And the cruisers represent new recruits that will function as your escort," Sydes responded.

"Also, yes … I see these are cruisers from … from Cabot's people. I know his engineers, all fluff, no stomach stuff," Von Strohheim remarked, a drop of distaste in his voice.

"Stomach stuff?" Sydes asked, a smile already beginning on his face.

"Jah, lousy shields, no reliable weaponry, just pretty hulls and shiny logos. No stomach stuff," Von Strohheim replied with greater emphasis.

"Oh, I gotcha. No guts, you mean, no guts," Sydes said, allowing himself a slight chuckle.

"Jah, no guts, this is it," Von Strohheim repeated.

His face etched in a smile that revealed the fond regard in which he held the good Doctor, Tutunji turned to Von Strohheim.

"Well, maybe we can get you to fix them up for us," Tutunji said.

Holding up his hand, Arthur attempted to get the group's attention.

"Sirs ... Sirs ... Sirs, it is time to evacuate all personnel to the Duo II," Arthur said, his volume rising.

A silence fell over the bridge as all eyes turned to Arthur, who suddenly felt slightly embarrassed.

"If you please, gentlemen," Arthur added.

"All right, *gentlemen*, you heard the Commandant, let's move it!" Sydes snapped.

With a rustle of uniforms and the hard cadence of boots on the metal decking, the entire bridge crew disappeared through the bridge access on their way to the Duo II. As Von Strohheim and Arthur followed the bridge crew through the portal, Tutunji, remained by the console, nodding at Sydes on his way to the Duo.

Tutunji quietly watched Sadad who stared at the main viewer and toyed with the controls. Sadad slowly flipped through one after another view of space around the station. After a few moments, Tutunji stepped up along side the acting Commander and placed his hand on Sadad's shoulder.

"It's always hard to leave your first command. In this case, it's especially difficult because you know it's likely that the station will be destroyed," Tutunji remarked.

"As long as she punches some holes in those bastards, it'll be OK. I don't like to think of her going out as just a practice decoy for the alien's big ships," Sadad replied.

"Well, she's a decoy with a hell of a sting. I'm sure she'll give a good account of herself," Tutunji responded.

Patting the console lovingly, Commander Sadad turned and followed Tutunji from the bridge. The two erstwhile Commanders of the now abandoned station had just reached the shuttlebay when the klaxon sounded.

Arriving at the access door to the last shuttle bound for the Duo II, Sadad stopped momentarily on the ramp. Turning smartly, he saluted his old Commander.

Returning Sadad's salute, Tutunji took one last look around the bay. In the blink of an eye, he reviewed nearly a decade of memories that called to him from his old command and entered the shuttle to the Duo.

As the two shuttles carried their passengers to their respective vessels, the strike craft began to move out from the station, setting a course supplied by the now operational three dimensional imager on the Duo II. The time of preparation was over.

～❖～

Entering the expanded bridge of the Duo II Commander Sadad was met by Von Strohheim. The Doctor directed Sadad's attention to the scene on the main viewer, which was receiving feed from the three dimensional imager installed in the hold below.

"The alien fleet, she is in motion. There are two separate formations of ten battleships each. The first formation is the spearhead and the second formation is shepherding the planet wrecker missiles. Extrapolating a vector based on their current course heading, the alien armada is on a trajectory that will carry them right through the heart of our armed stations directly to Earth," Von Strohheim said.

"The U.N. security council should be notified," Sadad said as he reached for the long-range comm-link.

"To what end?" Von Strohheim asked as he placed his hand on top of Sadad's.

"They have the right to know what's coming," Sadad replied, pulling his hand from under Von Strohheim's.

"Und, what would they do, if they knew? All of Earth's armed defense forces are here. Either we stop the alien incursion in space, or the Earth is destroyed. There is no third alternative," Von Strohheim remarked.

"Maybe, some of the population could take refuge under ground. I don't know?" Sadad responded, anxiety tingeing his tone.

"There is no refuge from the alien's planet wreckers, Commander. Based on the aftermath of the attack on the Martian colonies, we know the detonation of these missiles will fuse the surface of the planet. I am sure the blast will strip the Earth of her atmosphere. Underground facilities will provide no protection as the enormous heat and shock waves generated by multiple missile explosions and ignition of materials on the Earth's surface will set off rolling volleys of earthquakes, perhaps even tectonic plate movements, and may awaken volcanoes. All that can be done, must be done here, by us," Von Strohheim said, his cadence slower and his voice softer.

Sadad looked down at the console. A feeling of despair evoked by the scene Von Strohheim described threatened to swallow up all of his hopes. Then, squaring his shoulders and setting his jaw, he transmuted his despair into a hardened resolve to prevent this unimaginable catastrophe.

"Best possible speed to our designated position," Sadad snapped, as he turned to his chief engineer.

Sadad felt the big engines of the Duo II come on line. Best possible speed would get them to their observation and coordination position rapidly. Despite the difference in size, Von Strohheim had constructed the Duo II to have the same speed and maneuverability as the Duo. The two cruisers serving as escort might have some trouble keeping up even though they were built as attack craft.

As soon as the ships of the Earth Defense fleet achieved a safe distance from the command station, Sadad activated the explosive charges that had been placed on all five stations. In the viewer, he saw a chain of small fiery tongues leap out into space in response. All stations now bore the cosmetic scarring that would add to their abandoned and helpless appearance.

Von Strohheim tapped Commander Sadad on the shoulder and directed Sadad's attention to some icons newly installed in the command console.

"This first relay activates intraship communication. This second one is a conference communication link. Once the conference link is activated it remains open, connecting you to all of the strike craft, the cruisers and the Duo, and they to you just like an open-ended conversation," Von Strohheim said.

"That's good Doc," Sadad responded.

"It should speed up the flow of information … just as long as everyone doesn't try to talk at once," Von Strohheim responded.

⚜

On board the Duo, Sydes had the ship straining beyond the fringes of maximum acceleration in an attempt to intercept the alien fleet before the first formation entered the solar system.

"It's in our laps now," Sydes remarked without looking away from the viewer.

"Right. Now I know what it feels like to be part of a last stand … well … if what's going on in my gut is any measure … then, all the visions of glory that are written after the fact must be the ramblings of drunken adolescents," Tutunji replied as he activated the weapons systems.

"Glory ... after your first battle, you never use that word again," Sydes said quietly.

Then, Sydes activated the Duo's end of the conference communication link.

"Operations, what's our status?" Sydes requested.

"You should have a visual on the lead formation in the enemy fleet in about two minutes," Commander Sadad responded.

"What's the strike craft disposition?" Tutunji queried.

"The first formation of two hundred fighters is one hundred thousand kilometers to your rear, all well dispersed. The second formation of two hundred strike craft are one hundred thousand kilometers behind them and the home guard of one hundred vessels is fifty thousand kilometers outside of extreme Earth orbit. Good hunting," Sadad replied.

Suddenly, the spearhead formation of alien battleships centered itself in the Duo's viewer.

"They're ahead of schedule. That first group of battleships is really widely dispersed. That's a real departure from their usual tight formation," Sydes said.

"Looks like an invitation to fly right through the middle," Tutunji remarked.

"It's got to be some kind of trap, but let's not disappoint them," Sydes said, matter of factly.

Angling the the ship toward the center of the battleship formation, Sydes slowed the Duo's acceleration to attack speed as he and the Commander brought their tunneling lasers on line.

"The Doc's second laser should come as a real surprise," Tutunji said wryly.

"I sure as hell hope so," Sydes replied.

Plunging toward the alien formation, the Duo's imminent attack drew no defensive fire from the battleships' laser projector batteries.

"Yep, it's a trap. We've been in range for almost five seconds and they haven't even spit at us. They want us in there," Sydes said.

"Maybe we should stay outside of the formation, pick a couple of those battle wagons and start drilling," Tutunji suggested.

"Nope, that would make it too easy for five or six of those big ships to wheel around and focus their laser projectors on us simultaneously ... and you know what that looks like. Let's just play the game as they've set it up," Sydes responded.

"But by our rules, right?" Tutunji replied.

"Definitely," Sydes said.

Guiding the Duo between two of the battleships in the center of the formation, Sydes instantly found the ship's forward motion slowing to almost a standstill. Regardless of the direction in which he turned, he found his attempts to maneuver the Duo were met with very sluggish reactions. As the Duo lost her forward momentum, the two alien battleships closest to her began to close the distance between each other and the Duo.

"Nice trick, sticky shields. Let's apply our rules and see how they fit with whatever game they have in mind. You want the left?" Sydes said, a tinge of excitement in his voice.

"The left sounds good to me. Uncommonly decent of them to decrease the range to target like this," Tutunji replied.

"Uncommonly decent?" Sydes retorted as he activated his tunneling laser.

"Sorry, a phrase out of an old book I've been reading," Tutunji replied.

His eyes glued to the viewer, Sydes felt a smile tugging at the corners of his mouth as his laser turned a reddish orange area on the battleship's shields a faint shade of brown.

"Oh, this is better than I expected. They won't fire on us for fear of hitting their sister ships and their shields can't stand up to our lasers," Sydes said, a snide chuckle in his voice.

"There's only one possible justification for a tactic that places their ships in this kind of jeopardy. They want the Duo intact as a prize of war," Tutunji replied as his laser began tunneling.

"Wouldn't Von Strohheim be proud. They're willing to take this kind of punishment just to get at his shields and lasers," Sydes replied.

Despite the withering fire inflicted on them by the Duo's lasers, the two battleships gradually decreased the distance between them and the Duo until, by space flight standards, it became negligible.

"OK, I've got a hole burrowed in her hide. Give me ten right down the homing beacon," Sydes announced as he opened a breach in the enemy's shields.

Logging the count into the weapon's console, Tutunji activated the missile launchers on towers three and four. Nose to tail, two groups of five fusion missiles followed the trail of the laser's homing beacon through the breach in the battleship's shields.

Detonations merging one into another, the battleship shuddered and heeled over as all ten missiles tracking along the laser's homing beacon found their mark. The force of the blast captured within the forcefield surrounding the alien juggernaut quickly exceeded its containment strength, ripping the balance of the battleship's shields away. The tidal wave of destructive energy released by the explosion propelled the Duo squarely up against the surface shields of the ship the Commander was still drilling.

"Quite a ride. Give me ten more birds into this big bitch," Sydes said, excitement rising in his voice.

"Ten for you and ten for me," Tutunji replied.

Tutunji broke through the shields of the ship he had been lasing and instantly dispatched ten missiles into the well he had dug in the alien battleship's shields.

"Hell, I'm so close on this side I could get out and shove them in by hand," Tutunji added.

"Keep the lasers open, we're about to overload the capacitors," Sydes shouted.

Simultaneously, twenty fusion missiles detonated against the naked hulls of the two battleships that had performed the entrapping maneuver. In that instant, the Duo found herself in the middle of a fusion sandwich as both alien battleships belched fire and debris. Then, the two alien behemoths slowed to a dead stop in space as the balance of the formation moved steadily forward. The geyser of energy produced by concurrent detonation of the alien juggernauts squeezed the Duo out from between them with enormous velocity to a position high above the alien formation. For the first time since the engagement began, the Duo, unencumbered by the alien's interlocking shields, swam free in space high above the attacking formation.

"Just like being popped out of an old fashioned toaster," Sydes remarked.

"Yeah, but look at that battleship formation now. I think they've junked plan A," Tutunji replied.

Tightening the viewer's focus on the alien formation of battleships they had just attacked, Sydes saw Tutunji was correct. The spearhead enemy formation had closed ranks and the sensors indicated a slowing in forward velocity.

"Hell, they've slowed to a crawl," Sydes observed.

"Sydes, Commander Tutunji ... the second formation of battleships is accelerating," Sadad said, his voice sounding over the conference comm.

"Plan B ... the first battle group will wait for the second and form up with it," Tutunji offered.

"That means they'll have eighteen battleships functioning as a screen for the planet wreckers they're shepherding toward Earth. Son of a bitch!" Sydes spat out.

"OK, now its strictly guerrilla warfare. Slash 'em, bleed 'em and run. Let's do the sitting duck targets first," Tutunji said, his tone hard and unyielding.

"Copy that. We can punch some holes in the shields of that first formation of battleships. That'll give the strike craft something to shoot through," Sydes replied.

"You know if they've decided they can't capture us ..." Tutunji remarked.

"Yeah, I know, they're gonna have to kill us," Sydes shot back.

Choosing a spiraling trajectory toward the first formation of alien battleships, Sydes began targeting the ships most widely dispersed at the rear of the group. As soon as the Duo came within range, the laser projectors of four of the battleships fired simultaneously. Sydes had chosen an attack vector and velocity that made it impossible for their beams to coalesce, but all four bolts of laser energy struck the Duo individually and at nearly the same moment. Instantly, the Duo jerked back and pushed smoothly and consistently backward and away from the alien formation as Sydes fought to maintain a firing angle on the battleships for the Duo's lasers.

"Shit! This isn't working. Under this kind of barrage, I can't get us in close enough to do any damage with the tunneling lasers," Sydes snapped.

Ablaze with laser light, the viewscreen was of little use. However, oblivious to that portion of the electromagnetic spectrum that the laser energy occupied, the targeting computer for the tunneling lasers functioned perfectly.

"Let's take a page from their book and see if we can ..."Tutunji began.

Von Strohheim, who had been listening to the plight of the Duo, broke into the conversation.

"Commander ... Commander, switch the tunneling laser targeting feed from circuit A-1-2 to A-1-1."

"What the hell will that do, Doc?" Sydes asked.

"Both tunneling lasers will come to a singular focus and the effective firing range at the junction point will be increased by thirty-two percent. The new setting will activate both lasers from your console, Captain Sydes," Von Strohheim replied.

Tutunji quickly made the necessary adjustments in the lasers' targeting circuits.

"Got it. You're on line Sydes, let's punch some holes,"Tutunji said.

Activating the tunneling lasers, Sydes looked warily at the capacitor readouts which showed levels of energy that spelled detonation unless expended. The levels began dropping immediately as the two laser beams lanced out toward an alien battleship at the rear of the formation. The two tunneling beams coalesced into a single shaft of energy about five thousand kilometers before impacting on the battleship's rearward shields.

"It is unfortunate, but this laser feed configuration is forty percent less energy efficient than the original because of the collimating function where the beams join," Von Strohheim said.

"Not a problem, Doc. The enemy's lasers are supplying much more energy than we need to carry on this fire fight,"Tutunji responded.

If the Doc only knew, Tutunji thought to himself. The Duo's main viewer was a patch work of enemy laser fire, affording only occasional glimpses of the alien flotilla. Sydes had the Duo's thrusters set at maximum acceleration just to hold their position against the repulsive force of the continuous fire from the battleships' huge projectors. The Duo's shield capacitors hovered consistently around the ninety-nine percent level as enemy blasts refueled what the tunneling lasers expended.

"That's more like it. Put some Christmas gifts down that chimney, Tutunji," Sydes exclaimed as the red orange glow of the battleship's shield faded to brown.

Feeling a renewed sense of optimism, Tutunji dispatched five fusion missiles along the homing beacon of the newly combined tunneling lasers.

"It just so happens, that I have some left in my bag. Ho, ho, ho," Tutunji said in sotto voce.

"Ho ... what?" Sydes asked.

"Nothing, bad joke," Tutunji replied.

Flying true along the homing beacon toward their mark, of the five, only the first two missiles found their target. Laser fire from the battleships' immense projectors tracked and destroyed the remaining three. Sydes watched as the alien battleship reeled under the detonation of the two fusion missiles that made it through the laser barrage.

"Now, that's fucking disappointing. We just wounded her," Sydes said.

"Perfect, something for the strike craft to scavenge," Tutunji replied.

"Yeah, I guess you're right. But I like to see those big bitches go up," Sydes replied as he focused the tunneling lasers on another battleship.

"Sydes, Commander ... the second formation of battleships will be on top of you in less than three minutes," Sadad called over the comm.

"Let me know when they're in range of our fusion missiles," Tutunji responded.

"Give me five more," Sydes shouted as he saw the shields fail on his latest target.

Launching five more missiles along the homing beacon, Tutunji watched as the enemy's lasers destroyed four of the five. The single missile that found its way through the gauntlet of fire appeared to damage the drive section of the big ship.

"They're getting better at this," Tutunji remarked.

"Yeah and it breaks my heart. By the way, what the hell are we gonna do about the second bunch?" Sydes asked as he focused the Duo's lasers on yet another target.

"I have an idea, but I'll have to run the details by Von Strohheim first,"

Tutunji replied.

"Yes, Commander." Von Strohheim responded instantly over the conference com.

"Doc, can I launch these missiles with a delayed detonation?" Tutunji asked.

"Yes, this is possible but it requires some reprogramming," Von Strohheim responded.

"What do you have in mind?" Sydes asked.

"A little confusion to the enemy. As the second battleship formation approaches, I'll fire fifty missiles at them head on to create a burst of light and an energy shock wave. Hopefully, it will disrupt, or at least cloud, their sensors for a few seconds. At the same time, we drop four hundred missiles dead in their path at zero acceleration and move the Duo to the head of the first battle group," Tutunji replied.

"I love it. Hell, they'll think we're retreating. They may even get sloppy enough not to pay close attention to what they're flying through. By the way, give me five more missiles down this hole," Sydes responded.

"Nein, launch these five missiles, yes, but at irregular intervals. Three seconds, two seconds, eight seconds ..." Von Strohheim interrupted.

"Got it, Doc." Tutunji interjected.

Quickly reprogramming his console, Tutunji began to launch the missiles at staggered intervals.

Sydes smiled with satisfaction as three of the five missiles found their mark, disabling two of the target battleship's laser projectors.

"Thanks, Doc," Sydes said.

"Jah, jah," Von Strohheim replied.

Von Strohheim had no time for expressions of gratitude as he turned to the task of helping Tutunji alter the missiles' programming.

"It will be simplest to reprogram the first one hundred missiles on four of the towers and then fire the fifty missile disruption burst from the remaining two towers. Call up the four towers you have chosen and cancel the homing function on the first one hundred missiles in each. An icon should appear that says select detonation. You see this, yes?" Von Strohheim asked.

"A real pretty green light, Doc. I've got it," Tutunji replied.

"You will depress this icon once and it will show manual detonation. Then, pressing the lock icon next to it, you will see a pretty red light, yes?" Von Strohheim continued.

"We're in business. Thanks ..." Tutunji responded.

"The second battle group is within your missile range in three, two, one, now," Sadad interrupted.

Actuating the programmed launch protocol, Tutunji dispatched a fifty missile flight directly toward the oncoming enemy formation.

"OK, lay your eggs and lets get the hell out of here," Sydes said.

Turning his attention back to his quarry, Sydes focused his laser directly on one of the alien battleship's laser projectors that was firing on the Duo. To his surprise, the laser mount instantly exploded. As a respectable chunk of the big ship's shields were torn away, exposing its unprotected hull, the alien vessel dropped out of formation.

"Brilliant!" Von Strohheim remarked as he followed the visual transmission of the Duo's strike.

"Yeah ... but what the hell happened?" Sydes asked.

"The tunneling laser must follow the least energetic portion of their laser beam down to its source through the firing loops in their shields. Himmel, this I had not expected, wunderbar!" Von Strohheim exclaimed.

At that moment, fifty fusion missiles struck the forward shields of the second battle group with a flash of energy that momentarily blanched the Duo's scanners white. Tutunji watched the spreading conflagration as he counted slowly to himself. Reaching five in his count, he dropped the four hundred fusion missiles dead in the path of the oncoming alien formation.

"Eggs in the nest, let's go," Tutunji called out.

"OK, now we have to look like we're running to save our skins," Sydes replied.

Maneuvering the Duo out of range of the first formation of alien battleships' laser projectors, Sydes overflew the first battle group at maximum velocity. Tutunji adjusted the viewer to focus on, and magnify the approach of, the second formation of enemy dreadnoughts.

"The lead alien battle formation will be within attack range of the first flight of strike craft in thirty seconds," Sadad's voice announced over the conference comm.

"We're sending them four intact battle wagons and four wounded. We'll see if we can wound a few more before the strike craft take up the fight," Sydes responded.

"It is the second formation that must remain our principal concern, Captain Sydes," Von Strohheim interjected in a uncompromising tone.

"Yeah, yeah, I know Doc, but I hate to serve up four battle wagons to the strike craft without a nick in them. It'll be murder. Then we've got this other bunch coming up and ..." Sydes responded.

"This war, you cannot win him by yourself Captain," Von Strohheim retorted.

"We're about to do something about that gentlemen," Tutunji interjected.

Carefully monitoring the movement of the second formation of battleships and the position of the missiles he had dropped in their path, Tutunji jammed the manual detonation control icon definitively. As he watched, four hundred fusion warheads detonated simultaneously among the lead vessels in the second formation of alien battleships.

Instantly, a blinding flash of light ensued that wiped the Duo's viewer clean of her vista of space even though the ship was removed from the site of the blast by considerable distance. Slowly the Duo's viewer came to life, revealing the scene of devastation she had wrought. The lead battleships in the second alien battle group could be seen yawing in the midst of the firestorm. Their shields were a light show of shifting spectral colors, changing from orange to dark red and then to brown. Then, slowly, the battleships' shields reverse shifted their spectrum from brown to their characteristic reddish orange color. Only one of the alien capital ships showed evidence of significant damage to a forward port shield.

"Damn, I was hoping for a hell of lot more than that," Sydes said.

Watching in dismay, the Commander saw the second formation of alien ships regrouping and merging with the four intact and four damaged battleships that represented the remains of the first battle group. The four wounded battleships took up positions within the screen of their intact sister ships. Now, the new battle group consisted of eighteen alien capital ships, all protectively surrounding their sortie of planet wrecking missiles.

"We've got to open a hole in that formation," Sydes said.

Activating the tunneling lasers, Sydes put the Duo into a steep dive toward one of the undamaged battleships in the newly formed enemy battle group.

"Here comes the first flight of strike craft," Tutunji announced.

As planned, the strike craft made individual runs against the enemy battle formation. The tiny craft quickly took up positions in a widely dispersed halo around the alien formation of juggernauts. Then, Earth's fighters selectively targeted the battleships that showed evidence of the Duo's attack. Diving, they launched their missiles at the brown spots on the alien battleships' shimmering aura, marking areas where the Duo had penetrated their shielding.

Sydes targeted the lead battleship in the formation. As the Duo's tunneling lasers began their deadly work, he was surprised to find that no fire from the big laser projectors of the fleet directed at the Duo. Instead, the battleships concentrated their fire against the strike craft as they dove and launched their missiles.

"What the hell kind of strategy is this?" Sydes remarked.

"I don't know, but it makes me nervous,"Tutunji replied.

Resolution of Sydes' and the Commander's confusion materialized almost instantaneously as six laser beams from as many battleships lanced across and through the Duo's tunneling lasers flow of coherent light.

"Kill the laser generators,"Von Strohheim shouted over the comm the instant he saw the alien's maneuver.

Moving faster than he imagined they could, Tutunji's fingers found and hit the master kill switch to the laser generators, but it was already too late. The battleships' intersecting beams had created an interference wave of laser energy that backtracked toward the Duo at incredible speed.

Sydes immediately activated the five second emergency acceleration option and backed the Duo away from the ball of energy that flowered into a sunburst of highly energized photons. The wave of energy struck the Duo, pushing it away from the fleet at incredible speed while simultaneously spinning it like a top.

Images of the stars and the alien armada smeared together on the viewer as Tutunji reactivated the tunneling lasers and Sydes fired them randomly into space. The continuous firing of the lasers decreased the capacitor's load as the ball of energy bombarding the Duo's shields gradually dissipated. Sydes skillful manipulation of the Duo's propulsion units slowly brought the ship to a stationkeeping standstill.

"The second wave of strike craft is joining the attack. One minute until the alien fleet comes into range of the orbiting stations' missiles and ... and three minutes to Earth," Sadad's voice sounded over the conference comm.

Diving over and over on the alien fleet, the Earth Force pilots had managed to destroy two of the battleships the Duo had wounded, and to cripple two more by launching missiles directly at the alien vessels' laser projectors. The cost of these small victories had been high as small flashes in the night of space winked out of existence indicating another life lost.

The tabulator function on the imager caught Commander Sadad's eye. What he saw there was slightly blurred by a film of water marginally short of overflowing into tears. Try as he might, Sadad could not see the battle as an engagement of nameless forces. Each twinkling of light represented a strike craft, each spark extinguished was a life. Men and women, who only hours ago were joking and laughing with one another, full of spoken and unspoken plans for the future, were gone. Four hundred strike craft had gone out to meet the enemy and less than two hundred remained visible in the imager. The enemy fleet still had twelve intact battleships and the planet wrecking missiles the big ships guarded remained snug and undamaged within the confines of the screen of capital ships.

"Captain Sydes, Commander Tutunji, you … you are all right?" Von Strohheim inquired, his voice betraying some apprehension.

"We're OK Doc," Sydes replied.

"The tunneling lasers, these … they can no longer be fired from a stationary position. The next time, we may not be so lucky. The enemy will now try to cross your laser beam closer to the Duo's projectors. The feedback along your energy stream will ignite the laser generators and destroy your ship. You must make rapid passes over the fleet using course changes they cannot predict," Von Strohheim said.

"We're on it," Sydes replied.

His fingers flying over the console, Sydes set the Duo's course to overfly the alien fleet.

"It looks like the aliens have no interest in the space stations. That means you have thirty seconds before all attacking craft must pull back from the battleship formation as we initiate simultaneous launch of the combined stations' missiles," Sadad interjected.

"All strike craft, follow us in and launch along the line the Duo's lasers trace on the enemy's' shielding. And keep them guessing about your attack vectors," Tutunji announced to the remaining complement of strike craft.

"We're gonna have just enough time for one pass," Sydes said.

Activating the lasers, Sydes accelerated the Duo in a serpentine course over the enemy battle group.

As one, the laser projectors on the alien battleships illuminated the darkness with continuous fire as the Duo approached. None of the enemy gunners were able to intercept the Duo's shaft of laser energy as Sydes swerved and turned, often a right angles over the enemy flotilla. The strike craft followed, launching missiles at the line the Duo's lasers etched in the enemy's shields. Two of the aliens' capital ships heeled over and dropped out of formation as fusion missiles penetrated weakened areas in their shielding.

Accelerating the Duo to maximum speed, away from the alien fleet, Sydes led the few remaining strike craft not destroyed by the pass through the battleships' defensive laser cannonade out and away from the invading armada.

"Missiles away," Commander Sadad announced over the conference comm.

With an expression of grim determination on his face, Sadad pressed the remote activation switch and sent four thousand missiles from the five stations head on into the enemy armada. The gambit worked. Now, his first command would have her opportunity to bite back.

Flying swiftly and true, the stations' flight of missiles caught the alien fleet by surprise as they struck the lead ships in the armada. In an instant of time, the entire solar system lit up as though witnessing the birth of a second sun.

Thrown back almost ten thousand kilometers, the Duo spun and tumbled but remained unscathed by the holocaust, The blast incinerated twenty of the fifty remaining strike craft accompanying the Duo as escort.

Sadad and Von Strohheim, eyes unflinchingly fixed on the imager's viewer initially blanked by the blast, now watched anxiously as the screen slowly resolved into a view of the enemy fleet. The two lead battleships had been shattered into several large burning fragments and the two ships flanking these, severely damaged, dropped out of formation. The six remaining capital ships, seemingly undamaged, accelerated at half again their previous velocity on a course that would bring them into Earth's orbit in less than sixty seconds.

As he pushed the Duo to maximum acceleration, Sydes' only thought was to catch up with the remains of the alien fleet as it sped toward the little blue ball in space. The thirty remaining strike craft attempted in vain to keep up with the Duo's progress, but were soon left behind.

Moving up next to Sadad and Von Strohheim at the imager, Arthur watched the home guard of over one hundred strike craft dive on the six alien capital ships and their flock of planet killers closing in on the Earth. One strike craft dove directly into the lead battleship, its fusion ordinance obviously set to explode on impact. Another of the little fighters followed him in with a second suicide detonation, weakening the battleships shields sufficiently to allow the third strike craft's sacrifice to detonate the forward section of the alien capital ship.

"Let's chew up this bitch," Sydes said.

Activating the Duo's lasers, Sydes focused the fiery beams on the rear guard alien battleship.

"It's now or never," Tutunji murmured.

Tutunji programmed an attack that would pave the way before her as the Duo pursued the remnants of the alien fleet. Then, he pressed the icon for continuous fire on all six of the Duo's towers. Just shy of four thousand missiles were pumped out in a continuous stream toward the five remaining alien battleships and their covey of planet wrecker missiles. The combination of the Duo's laser and the detonations of the fusion warheads took out the rearguard battleship and badly damaged another.

Continuous laser fire emanated from the remaining three intact battleships, providing a seamless screen of death around the planet wrecker missiles as they approached the atmosphere. One after another of the strike craft dove on the planet wrecker missiles the remaining alien battleships protected only to be incinerated by the huge vessels' laser barrage.

Sydes locked the tunneling laser on one of the three remaining battleships as he attempted to open a breach that would allow the Duo and the strike craft to fire directly on the formation of alien missiles. He watched intently as the battleship's shielding spotted brown under the Duo's laser and soberly as four strike craft dove on the area of weakened shielding. The explosion of their vessels' impact on the alien behemoth's hull tore away the aft section of the battleship.

"Damn it to hell! Those last two battle wagons are going in with their missiles!" Sydes exclaimed.

All eyes were glued helplessly to the viewers as the last two alien battleships entered Earth's atmosphere, glowing first red, then white, with friction's heat. The few remaining home guard strike craft not incinerated by the enemy's continuous laser fire followed the battleships and their complement of planet wreckers into the atmosphere, launching their missiles at the alien ships before incinerating in the atmosphere.

"Mein Gott," Von Strohheim gasped.

Unable to look away from the imager, Von Strohheim watched as tongues of flame leapt from the planet wrecker missiles, propelling them in a widely dispersed pattern across the face of the planet.

Hanging alone in the darkness beyond the envelope of the Earth's atmosphere, the Duo and the two men who sat helplessly at her controls knew firsthand the inevitability of what must follow. The strike craft were gone. The alien battleships were but flashes of burning wreckage deep in the stratosphere and the missiles had vanished from view beneath the churning clouds of humanity's birthplace.

Tutunji detected the first evidence the planet wreckers had struck their mark. The Earth seemed to grow in size, expanding in every direction, as the planet's atmosphere rushed towards the Duo.

"Reverse course," Tutunji shouted.

"Christ!" Sydes exclaimed as he spurred the Duo to maximum acceleration.

Detonation of the planet wrecker missiles propelled, first clouds of water vapor, then fragments of the stations, in close orbit around the planet past the Duo at incredible speed. The shields took the punishment as the Duo's engines, coupled with the force of the blast, propelled the ship into an increasingly extreme orbit of her maker's home.

Finally coming to rest, the Duo swam in and through the thin skin of the Earth's living surface as it gradually passed beyond the ship and out into the cold, lifeless void of space.

In place of the blue and white mottled globe of striving life that had been their ancestral birth place, there now hung a bright silver ball of fused elements, tongues of flame licking about her circumference. Sydes and the Commander said nothing. They had failed in a way that made any defeat previously sustained in the long and bloody history of their species wither into insignificance. Billions had perished without warning in a blinding flash of light and heat. A whole species wiped clean from the chalkboard of the universe in a single stroke except for the few meager strands of DNA sealed in steel spheres drifting despairingly in the otherwise sterile void.

Chapter 33

The light heralding Earth's demise momentarily illuminated the entire solar system. Although hidden behind the moon, the ark's smooth skin took on a silvery glow as streamers of radiance from the blast, reflecting from surface to surface, struck it.

Deep within the confines of the great sphere, the meek, as one, stopped what they were doing and looked up. Esther, her eyes wet with tears, stared at the firmament of the manmade sky and the wisps of clouds traveling across it. Then, bowing her head as if in prayer, she stood with her eyes closed for several minutes.

"The birthplace of man is become a sea of glass and all those upon that sea are loosed from dark matter's cinch. May they be woven anew into the loom of light that gave them life. Orphaned by the death of their planetary mother, only two brothers of that ageless family she has nurtured remain. These two, the meek and the strong, although of common nativity, are now parted. Brothers, reared together, are now chosen to follow separate circuits among the stars. Seeded among the stars as Earth's final legacy, kinsmen of common blood and divided destiny are scattered among the lights of heaven," Esther said softly and reverently.

Forrester felt an immobilizing instant of overwhelming fear and pain as billions perished, then, nothing. Something inside of him twisted in agony. The suffering of millions of years was gone in a blazing moment of finality. All the striving as life moved from inorganic molecules to creatures that could think in terms of inorganic molecules had ended in a flash of light. The destruction and waste could not be grasped by any single thought or feeling. Good people, men, women and children, were simply gone and Forrester was still here. Survivor's guilt was too small a concept to encompass the feeling that coursed through him.

"It is the vision," Jacob said as he placed his hand on Forrester's shoulder.

"The destiny of the people of the trees lies in tasting the pain and anguish of others. Although shielded from the despair of the nows that came before, we are touched by the agony of the now that is upon us and feel as muffled pangs the travail lurking within the nows that are yet to come."

"Yes ... the pain ... of course," Forrester replied, haltingly.

He could see with perfect clarity that to which Jacob referred; the huge silver ball of the Earth hanging suspended in space and three much smaller orbs, indeed vessels, speeding away from the desolation. The vision, when first he had seen it, was cloaked in pain. Though not a pain of the body, it was nevertheless a palpable ache in the soul. Somehow, all that had been embodied in the vision, but only now had he experienced it as personal anguish. At the time of the vision, he thought of the sensation as an indication of his failure to have fully participated in the conviction of which the meek seemed so completely possessed. Never mentioned it to anyone, he realized now that the pain he associated with that first vision was, in fact, a verification of his membership in the community of the people of the trees.

At different times and in so many ways stretching back into his childhood, Forrester had felt that pain. This selfsame ache had always visited him, appearing as a constant companion to his global realization of the implacable pattern of repetitive horrors man visited upon his fellows. A pain that would not be quelled, it was fully recharged as each succeeding generation pursued with renewed vigor the sins of their fathers. This pain was more piercing to the soul than ever he could have experienced in the tangible execution of these acts of horror which the abstraction so completely embodied. He had always seen it as a weakness to weep more for the general depravity of the human condition than for its specific manifestations. Now, rightly or wrongly, he saw this empathy for the pain his race routinely inflicted upon itself as one of the defining characteristics of the meek. A portion of the mission to which the meek were called was to weep for mankind.

"Visitors," Crystal said as she approached her father and Forrester.

Looking up and over Crystal's head, Forrester glimpsed Chauvez and Dvorak. He waved to the two men as they walked up the gently sloping grassy knoll to Esther and Jacob's house.

"I don't guess you can help us out with what's going on here? Our Earth side drone cameras were destroyed by something accompanied by a big flash of light," Chauvez said.

Suddenly, Forrester experienced a strange feeling of personal embarrassment for which he had no explanation. His tone was that of an individual providing a personal apology for some unspeakable transgression as he prepared to respond to Chauvez.

"The Earth ... the Earth is gone," he stammered.

"What do you mean gone?" Dvorak asked in a deadly serious tone.

"Wiped clean of all life," Forrester replied, his mood darkening even further.

"The alien invasion … they must have had a weapon that could destroy a whole planet. The whole of the Earth, all its peoples, all its children, all … all gone?" Chauvez asked, his eyes glistening with as yet unshed tears.

"Then we've lost the war," Dvorak said, speaking the words ponderously.

"I won't even ask how you know all this. Are we … we the only survivors?" Chauvez asked as he regained his composure.

"No, there are others," Esther said as she joined the group.

"Where?" Dvorak asked.

"There is another ship containing one fifth our number that has survived," Jacob responded.

"Same question, where?" Dvorak asked, his tone increasingly irritated.

Crystal walked up to Dvorak and tugged at his jacket.

"What?" Dvorak snapped.

In response, Crystal simply pointed up to the ark's artificial semblance of the sky.

"What the hell is that supposed to mean?" Dvorak asked, his frustration merging to anger.

"If Crystal says that's the vector along which you will find the other ship, I'd believe her if I were you," Forrester said as he smiled at Dvorak.

"So, you are expecting me to swallow that we've got a boatload of psychics on our hands?" Dvorak asked, his face wrinkling into a sardonic sneer.

Chauvez's gaze playing over Forrester, Esther, Jacob and lighting on Crystal, he studied the little girl carefully for a moment.

"I think you're supposed to believe we have a boatload of psychics," Chauvez responded in a soft and thoughtful tone.

He could hear Phil's voice in his head explaining and applying the old medical rule of thumb to the latent abilities of the meek. Where there's one, look for two, if there's two, look for three, if there's three, then there's a whole bunch. Apparently, Dvorak had forgotten his own realization of the extraordinary genetic potential inherent to the meek. That was interesting, inasmuch as Dvorak had been the one to point out that the profusion of the meek's unfolding abilities might well follow an extrapolation of the Fibonacci number sequence. Chauvez decided to allow Dvorak to continue to indulge his cynicism, if only to discover what was driving the brilliant designer's bitterness.

"Right … do they read palms, too?" Dvorak asked snidely.

Producing a small scanning projector from his pocket, Chauvez looked first at Dvorak and then, allowing a self-satisfied smile to cross his face he glanced over at Crystal.

"Crystal would you please point to the other ship again?" Chauvez asked politely.

"There," Crystal replied and pointed again in the direction she had before.

Activating the scanning projector resulted in the production of a small scale holographic model of the ark around the tip of Crystal's finger. The model rotated slightly as Chauvez adjusted it to reflect the ark's current orientation in space. Then, depressing a small icon, a line traced its way from the tip of Crystal's finger through the ark's hull and beyond. Chauvez depressed one more icon on the unit and a series of coordinates appeared at point where the line extended beyond the hull of the holographic Ark.

"Let's go see. If Crystal's right, a tight transmission along these coordinates should put us in touch with a ship," Chauvez said as he turned to Dvorak.

"Or some galaxy far, far away," Dvorak retorted in a smirking tone.

"Come on, Truth Seeker," Chauvez said.

Beckoning to Dvorak, Chauvez ushered the cynical automation engineer away. Casting a glance over his shoulder, Chauvez waved goodbye to Forrester and Crystal's family. Exercising some effort, Chauvez maintained a good-natured demeanor with Dvorak as they walked toward the tube that would carry them to the bridge. Once they had passed out of earshot of Crystal's family, Chauvez whispered a single word to Dvorak.

"Fibonacci," Chauvez said.

"What?" Dvorak snapped, his tone still abrasive.

"You're the one who pointed out that the meeks' abilities might expand in accordance with the Fibonacci sequence. You know, 1, 1, 2, 3, 5, 8, 13, 21, 34, 55 ..." Chauvez remarked.

"Yeah, yeah, I know the damn sequence. I use it everyday in designing intelligent circuits," Dvorak responded angrily.

"Well, we discussed with Phil how the meek might have abilities that haven't as yet declared themselves," Chauvez said.

"So?" Dvorak retorted.

"So, why's it so hard to believe Crystal might know where another ship is that we neither see, nor know for certain exists?" Chauvez queried.

"My daughters," Dvorak replied, his tone barely audible.

"What?" Chauvez asked, completely surprised by Dvorak's response.

"My two daughters. They're both within a couple of years of Crystal's age. What will happen to them? How in the hell will they ever compete with kids like Crystal, who just know things. My God, Crystal is an offspring of just the first generation of the meek. What will succeeding generations be able to do? If she's right, about the location of this ship out there ... what will my kids grow up with ... omniscient playmates? Just think of it. The kid one ecosector over on the ark who just knows everything, no instrumentalities, no chain of reasoning, nothing observable or quantifiable ..." Dvorak said as his gaze drifted off toward the hills of the ecosector.

"I don't think its a matter of competition. It's just two entirely different ways of knowing. The meek know the 'what' of the universe, but that doesn't mean they know the 'how.' The meek live in accordance with the 'what' they know. The 'how' of that 'what' is our job and that of your daughters. The 'how jobs' represent the tasks that make what we know of the universe run. It's great for the meek to know the significance of cosmic events, but someone has to fix the plumbing or the meek and everyone else goes down the drain," Chauvez replied.

"Maybe, but it still scares me to think of my kids growing up with seers who are the genuine article. How do my kids see themselves as anything but second rate human beings?" Dvorak replied.

"Well, you, me and lots of people like us and their kids back over the millennia created the technology that made this ship possible ... and this ship is the only reason the meek are alive," Chauvez said quietly.

"Yes, I suppose you're right," Dvorak replied.

"I don't know ... I'd be a fool to say that I knew what you were feeling because I don't have any children. However, of this much I'm certain, the kindly way the meek treat and care for those around them has no correlates in the history of human interaction. Show me any epoch in human history, before the meek came on the scene, when competition and exploitation of one another wasn't the rule in both individual and tribal exchanges. There ain't any. Among us, the non-meek, well, we don't have the first idea of what it would look like if we weren't constantly trying to beat the other guy to the punch. I know that it isn't much, but I have the feeling that without competition and the aggression it entails, things may all work out very differently," Chauvez said.

"Could be, but it would have to be a whole lot different from human history as we've known it up to now," Dvorak remarked.

Wholly at odds with his well controlled facade, Chauvez's mind rushed off to another place and time. His brain was running an independent program of panoramic views of everything he had ever seen on the Earth. Mountains, plains, desert expanses, the shores of blue-green seas were all catalogued in their native splendor. But, perhaps most of all, there were the faces of people he'd known, as well as, those simply glimpsed in his travels. Each memory jostled the other for a moment in the spotlight. Now it was all part of galactic history, a planet that was. He suddenly felt alone in a way he had never experienced before. Like the myth of the flying Dutchman, he was imprisoned in a ship destined never to touch the shores of home again.

⚜

Watching as Chauvez and Dvorak disappeared through a grove of trees on their way to the bridge, Forrester saw what they could not, the darkening of their auras. Forrester knew the eclipses shading their globes of light signaled a full realization of the loss suffered by all those who had survived the obliteration of their birthplace. It suddenly struck him that, felt or unfelt, the auras of the surviving human race registered the fate of all of their kind. The dimming of humankind's light cast a shadow within the illumination of every man.

"What happens now?" Forrester asked, turning to Esther.

"Look and see. You are the eye of the people of the trees. We see what you look for," Esther said as she looked at him quizzically.

With Esther's words, Forrester suddenly felt his mind filled with the comforting presence of each individual in the community of the people of the trees. At one moment, he could sense both the cognitive characteristics of each of the over one half million individuals, as well as, the synergistic energy of the group. The feeling became an image of five-hundred thousand points of light all connecting to one another and to the interior surface of a great translucent sphere housing them all. Then he *saw*.

In that which was now his greatly expanded mind's eye, stood a pillar of light exuding a sense of presence such as no previously evolved physiological sensory organ had ever mediated. From this supra-existential vision emanated a column of light that proclaimed both assuredness and reassurance in equal proportions. Then, as quickly as it had begun, the vision was over.

"This will be soon," Forrester said, looking over at Esther.

"Yes ... soon the diarist comes," she replied.

⚜

Forrester recognized this vision represented a near time event and felt immensely pleased with himself as always he did when he learned something new. He knew that what he had seen for the meek was close at hand because the expenditure of energy in seeing it was so meager. The first visions had been of events further along on the map of the space-time continuum and were accompanied by a feeling of greater individual energy expenditure. The energy consumed by this most current seeing seemed negligible, suggesting it was but a miniscule step forward on the cosmic scale of the space-time atlas.

Quite unexpectedly, his mind blazed with the bright light of intellectual excitement. Its advent left no shadows anywhere, even in the deepest recesses of his thoughts. The *seeing* was clearly a physiological event, it consumed energy. The farther you saw along the spatial-temporal nexus of the universe, the more energy you burned. Then, he caught himself in the midst of his own internal dialogue. The energy was replenished too quickly to have its origins solely in the metabolism of mortal clay. Seeing drew energy from the individual and the group to be sure, but somehow it must also tap into the light and energy that drove the space-time continuum itself. Seeing consisted in both receiving information and energy from some cosmic source, as well as, drawing on personal resources. The conclusion was inevitable. The *seeing* of the people of the trees tapped into energies flowing from the very wellspring of space-time itself.

The meek were evolution's response to the timeless material estrangement of the individual threads of consciousness from the loom of life. After countless eons of striving, life had found a shortcut back to its origins. The people of the trees expended personal energy to maintain their connection to the underlying light and life that engendered the physical universe, but they also drew foresight and energy from it.

As if awakening to the outside world, Forrester slowly became aware of Esther's presence and the fact she was staring at him. He made a conscious effort to externalize whatever it was that did his thinking from the inside of his head to his surroundings. Suddenly, there was no doubt in his mind, he was one of the meek. Evolution had finally coughed up a human subspecies congenitally detached from the five senses that tied the bulk of humanity to the universe of matter which they esteemed to be all that was, is and will be.

⚜

"Yes, Esther, what is it?" he asked, returning her gaze.

"Thank you Doctor Forrester for doing what you do best. You are both student and teacher for us all. Your thoughts and investigations become our own even as you think them," Esther replied.

"What your mind calls 'head journaling', little of which you have ever spoken aloud, now becomes a conversation with the whole of the community. You speak within, we listen and respond. Soliloquy has become colloquy," Jacob interjected.

⚜

Initially feeling a bit startled, Forrester recalled his cognitive wanderings had an audience of over a half a million of the meek. He was, for the first time, relieved rather than embarrassed. Wending the labyrinth of his speculations would no longer be a solitary expedition. Were his attachment to the physical surroundings of what most held to be reality more durable and his compulsive need to know less demanding, he might not have given free rein to his analyses and extrapolations with such a host of onlookers. Strengthened by the mandate of the meek, he would explore fact and fantasy as he had from childhood. Led by hope, curiosity pushing from behind, the meek by his side and insight the goal, they would travel together.

Herein lay one of the defining characteristics of the meek, he thought to himself. The light of life was always brightest within. For the meek, attachment to the sensory feed that bound the majority of the human species to the material universe was tenuous at best. The daydreaming, arcane ruminations and infatuation with abstraction indulged in by so many dreamers over the eons, all of these represented evolution's neuropsychological heralds of the meek. As was faintly foreshadowed in their genetic forebearers, so now risen to full flower among the meek, abstraction was raised to the nth power. All limits removed, wonder now strove ceaselessly to reach beyond material reality and the senses evolved to discern it.

The whole of human history lay there, all of it presaged in the broad strokes of the evolutionary developmental activation of several major divisions of the brain. First, in the order of the evolution of consciousness, came the limbic system with its red and black decision making apparatus. Next, the limbic system's close cousin, the right cerebral hemisphere, tinted in tones of black, brown, red, and green with yellow emerging. Yoked together beyond any cleaving, the limbic system and right hemisphere constituted both the reflexive and conscious decision making apparatus of the dominance driven.

Left hemispheric activation followed in the evolutionary scheme, its muted yellows, greens and blues emblematic of the spectral distance achieved from the fiery reds and black engines of its limbic predecessor. Here was the placenta of the meek. Largely detached from nature's mandate to conquer the material universe and spread the genes of domination over all that could be seen, heard and touched, the left hemisphere represented something new.

Activating still later in the evolutionary timeline, the left frontal area carried tints of receding and nurturant blues and violets intoning a retreat from the limbically driven universe of material domination. In this area of the brain lay the fountainhead of energy devoted to abstractive outreach. These cool but highly energetic wavelengths of blue and violet represented as much power in conceptual perception as the right hemispheric reds and oranges demonstrated in aggressive outreach to material mastery.

It was the paradox of the electromagnetic spectrum. The colors of the meek were cooler, receding into the distance according to the human eye, shorter in wavelength, yet more energetic. The tints borne by the dominance driven emerged from the longer wavelengths, and although warmer and more aggressive were less energetic.

Quite unexpectedly, he recognized a thought within his mind that he recognized was not his own. Its contours, instead, bore the distinctive cognitive and emotional lineaments of Esther's mindfulness.

"Two designs separately conceived but interwoven from the first spinning of Earth's fabric of life. Each design individually composed, thread upon thread, by the weaver's patient hand and sown within the first entwining of life," she said.

It was as if the simple truth had been there all the time, awaiting only Esther's words to catalyze its explication. In their material expression, the threads were genes. The weaver of genetics had, from the beginning, been preparing two final expressions of the human genome; the genes of domination directed to the task of mastering the material universe, and the recessive genes of knowing and more particularly of pure abstraction. The first would finally, after having triumphed over all, be forced to turn to the conquest of themselves. The second recessive genes required billions upon billions of years to migrate through numberless matings into the conglomerate of tissues and abilities that were the meek. In this process, basic cellular struggle and dominance striving were refined away in the meek and set aside as dross, leaving the enormous energies fueling these ancient drives open to other applications. Harnessed by a new amalgam of abilities, these primal energies now served the meek's ability to see into each other and trace their path upon the chart of space-time.

Here was a symphonic process, carefully orchestrated by an illumined hand, sorting and resorting through the dynamics of attraction and attachment over millennia to midwife the emergence of a new sensory organ in the meek. Perceptual tissue tuned only in part to the physical universe, the process was more specifically evolved to divine what lay beneath and supported material creation. Nature had achieved in tissue what physics had yet to comprehend. In this new sensory organ lay the capacity for isochronal existence in two dimensions, the material universe from which it sprang and the loom of life which preceded and engendered all that could be seen without the third eye. At the same time and in the same place, the meek were set with one foot in the darkness of the universe all could see, while the other rested within a realm of light in which all of time and space existed in a singular moment.

Forrester could not know the particulars of how this new organ of extrasensory awareness came into being. However, his previous experience with Crystal suggested it operated out of the mid forehead and Chen's scan of Forrester brow seemed to confirm the organ's existence. Crystal's simple demonstration was founded in physical reality. The third eye, so often mentioned by the ancient mystics, was an outgrowth of the rostral medial prefrontal cortex. That small area of tissue contained the neural map for enlightened integration of emotion, and, most startlingly, the prediction of events which had not yet occurred. Perhaps of greater historically abiding significance this area mediated one of the purest examples of thought-feeling integration of which the brain was capable, namely, that perfection to which all other forms of art aspire, music.

Quite abruptly, Forrester's focus returned to the meadow where Esther, Jacob and Crystal patiently waited. Forrester had been playing in the light again, or as Esther's words had suggested contemporaneously learning and teaching.

⁂

"Well, how was it?" Forrester asked tentatively.

"It was like looking at a family tree, ancestors seen and known, and those who toiled in anonymity to prepare the way," Esther replied, her eyes glistening with emergent tears.

"I liked the lights and colors," Crystal added enthusiastically.

Considering Crystal's remarks for a moment, Forrester could see that, in some ways, his thought processes were words, but her statement reminded him that a great deal of what went on in his head was manifested in swells of light, color and motion.

"Yes, lights and colors," he replied smiling at Crystal.

⁂

On the bridge of the ark, Dvorak busily entered Crystal's gestural coordinates into the communications computer as Chauvez smiled and looked on.

"What the hell are you grinning about?" Dvorak snapped.

"Oh, I'm just looking forward to the expression on your face when someone answers on the other end of that transmission," Chauvez said playfully.

His preparations complete, Dvorak glowered at Chauvez and activated the communication array.

"Any ship, this is the ark." Dvorak announced.

Although his tone was definitive, Dvorak's expression suggested his attempts were driven more by a need to placate Chauvez than any belief his call would be answered.

A long silence ensued during which Dvorak leered at Chauvez. Chauvez simply nodded and pointed insistently to the communication console.

"Any ship, this is the ark ... please respond," Dvorak transmitted again.

"Ark, this is the Duo II of the Earth Defense Force. What is your status?" Von Strohheim responded.

Dvorak muttered something about "dumb luck" under his breath and responded to Von Strohheim.

"This is the ark, in orbit on the dark side of the moon, carrying five hundred thousand passengers, what's going on?" Dvorak asked.

"A half a million ... so many saved, wunderbar! This is Doctor Von Strohheim on the Duo II, carrying a complement of one hundred thousand souls. The Earth is destroyed and we are not sure of the enemy's intentions beyond that. Do you require assistance?" Von Strohheim inquired.

"Thank you Doctor Von Strohheim. We require no assistance at this time," Dvorak responded.

"Very good. We are currently engaged in monitoring the balance of the enemy fleet and addressing the needs of our wounded. Perhaps we can contact you later. Von Strohheim out."

"I still think it's a combination of dumb luck and guesswork," Dvorak said, closing the link.

Mustering his last vestige of bravado, Dvorak turned about and looked over at a still smiling Chauvez.

Chauvez now smiled so broadly that the corners of his mouth hurt.

"Oh, you're probably right. How about a drink?" Chauvez asked.

Chauvez chuckled as he put his hand in the middle of Dvorak's back and gently pushed him toward the bridge access and the bar beyond. As he accompanied the somewhat confused, but considerably more credulous Dvorak, to the bar, Phil's words rang once again in his head, 'Where there's three, there's a whole bunch more.'

❧❖❧

A leisurely lunch gradually drew to a close as Forrester, Crystal and her parents noticed a large crowd forming in the immense open meadow between the stream and the house. Forrester didn't have to ask why the meek were gathering. He knew the flow of space-time had nearly caught up with his vision of the pillar of light. Rising from the table, Esther, Jacob and Crystal immediately joined him. How much like a family, Forrester thought, as the four walked together to the meadow in the dimming light of the ecosector's artificial eventide.

Arriving at nearly the center of the meadow, Forrester could smell the moisture laden air that rose from the grasses at the passing of day's light. Glancing about the hills surrounding the glade, he saw the community of the meek literally blanketing the hills and rocky outcroppings that formed a natural amphitheater around the meadow. The whole of the people of the trees assembled in the flesh, waiting. There would be no holographic representations for this event.

They're all here, he thought to himself. Then he heard Crystal's thought in his head saying, "Yes, they're all here." It was a curious cognitive event, not intrusive, almost as if her thought took up no space in his mind at all. The thought was uniquely Crystal's, more recognizable than her facial features or the identifying timbre of her voice.

A perfect stillness pervaded the meadow and the hills, broken only by the gurgling flow of the stream. So many people gathered in one place and not the faintest echo of a human voice could be heard, even from among the children. Then, declaring itself in his mental landscape, he felt a driving organic process that not unlike a countdown, nevertheless lacked the cogwheel precision that characterized mechanical denominations. It was as though the vision he experienced earlier had formed a watershed in space-time toward which the passing moments were tending. He felt that watershed fill to the brim and, then, looked up.

In the midst of the meadow, appearing without the slightest perturbation of air or shadow, was the pillar of light Forrester had seen earlier in the community's vision. Roughly the height of a tall man, but without a discernible face or limbs, it suspended itself but a few meters above the heads of the assembled. The pillar's light shown with the purest white, but within the column danced tiny orbs of the most brilliant purple Forrester had ever seen. The tiny globes were neither red violet nor blue violet, but a pure, cool color. The myriad of violet spheres constantly traversed the shaft in ever changing patterns. Experiencing the most holistic wave of self-verifying certainty he had ever known, Forrester realized this was the diarist in his purest form. An envoy from the loom of life, he was manifest in the confines of this now and fully present in the dimension that housed the material universe.

A sense of well being emanated from the resplendent pylon which, reflecting its intrinsic nature through those radiations, conferred the gift of peace freely on all those assembled. The most dramatic accompaniment of the insistent illumination was a compelling sense of coming home that went beyond the remembrance of any tangible place or loving family. It was a yearning for something so dimly recalled as to be little more than a lilting wisp in the mind. The skeleton of a memory, it spoke of light without darkness, illumination without glare or shadow, a place of warmth, a realm of belonging so perfected that strife and rejection were not ponderable within its boundless extension. Then, like the slowly swelling crescendo of some indescribable symphony of continuous creation, came a melody, ever changing and all encompassing, that perfectly transformed knowledge into wisdom. Softly, but insistently, like lyrics to accompany this quietly reverent oratorio of the spheres, came the words of the diarist. The words were new, but the voice was familiar and heard by each of the meek in their personal cognitive sanctum and yet, by all together in their communal awareness, at one moment.

THAT WHICH WAS ONE IS NOW
TWAIN. THE NEST OF LIFE IS TORN
BY THE WINDS OF STRIFE AND TWO
FLEDGLINGS MUST TAKE WING. ONE
TO HEROIC CONQUEST AND THE
REVELATIONS OF FRUSTRATED PASSIONS,
THE OTHER TO CONTEMPLATION OF THE
LIGHT BENEATH THE DARKNESS OF
THIS UNIVERSE.

FOR EARTH'S ORPHANED CHILDREN
OF THE LIGHT THERE SHALL BE NEW
HEAVENS AND A NEW EARTH. THERE
AMIDST HER GARDENS SHALL BE A
GENESIS IN AND OF THE LIGHT. FROM
THIS NEW BEGINNING SHALL A BRIDGE
ARISE THAT ALL MAY CROSS UNTIL
EVERYWHERE IS LIGHT AND THE
DARKNESS OF MATTER IS FOREVER
BANISHED.

FOR EARTH'S CHILDREN OF BLOOD
AND FEAR, THERE WILL BE CONQUEST

ENOUGH TO SATE THE VAINEST
STRIVINGS OF THE HUMAN HEART.
WORLDS WITHOUT END, ENEMIES
WITHOUT NUMBER, UNTIL ALL
SUBDUED, THEY SEE THE WREATHS
OF VICTORY AS BUT EMPTY CIRCUITS
OF THEMSELVES.

AS THE INHERITANCE OF THE MEEK
IS GREAT, SO MUCH IS REQUIRED.
TO YOU IS GIVEN LIGHT'S SIGHT
BEYOND ILLUSION'S IMPERMANENT
DARKNESS. ABIDE, THEREFORE, IN
THIS LIGHT. WINNOW ALL KNOWING,
SHARE THE GRAIN OF TRUTH FREELY
WITH ALL THAT HAS LIFE AND, IN
PATIENT SERVICE BE STEADFAST. I
AM WITHIN YOUR EYE'S SHINING.
I AM THE STILL SMALL VOICE
COUNSELING LIGHT IN THE MIDST
OF STRIFE'S DARKNESS UNTIL THE
DARKNESS IS NO MORE.

Bathed in an illumination of body and spirit, Forrester and the people of the trees watched the pillar of light assume the shape of a flattened sphere and spread at forehead level across the assembled multitude. Passing over and through each of them, the dancing bundles of light dispersed until the light was no more. Folded within the ripples of its passing, Forrester beheld a fleeting glimpse of what he would, now and always, hold to be the loom of life. Threads of pure energy that glowed with a benign and nurturant light such as he had never beheld. Ever in motion, it was a moving web that shifted its shape, manifesting in all things that grew and reproduced in the universe of clay. The impact of the vision was physically exhausting but mentally invigorating. The experience attested to the impermanence of their clay vessels and celebrated the everlasting nature of the light they contained. The encounter provided its own verification of the final collapse of matter and darkness into the light and life of the loom that had woven it.

In its wake, the diarist's passing left a sense of mission to all who had witnessed the manifestation. The fully revealed destiny of the meek was not to do something but to be something. They were the cartographers of the space-time map and, in seeing ahead, would become part of its unfolding destiny. They would foresee, learn, and impart that knowing freely to any who desired it. Their revelations were to be offered without comment or inducement. They would not compete with, threaten, coerce or even persuade those who crossed their path as to the interpretation or application of the fruit of their *seeing*. They would be the voice of the loom of life, a race of investigators and seers who offered their counsel freely, but, having done so, would leave the freedom and destiny of choice to those who heard. "*See, share* and *serve*," the message was parsimonious, but, then, most great truths were just that, simple.

Dispersing into the gathering mists, the people of the trees had received the imprimatur of that which had, over unfathomable expanses of time, prepared their way. In that moment, it was plain to Forrester that the second coming was not an ending but a new beginning. Two divergent routes had been opened for the human species, each course was charted indelibly on the map of space-time, and with its own company of travelers chosen through an imprint in their tissues. For the dominance driven, there would be worlds without end, enemies and conquests without number. For the meek, there would be new heavens and a new Earth. Differing directions and contrasting destinies for two peoples drawn from a single root. Forrester, without benefit of any special vision, was suddenly overtaken by a premonition that the ark would carry the meek far from the tragedy that had befallen their birthplace and even farther from their dominance driven brethren.

Chapter 34

One hundred thousand, remnants of humanity from among the billions lost, now called the huge hold of the Duo II home. Commander Sadad had made many visits to the habitation amphitheater since first going there to announce the destruction of the Earth. The initial response of Earth's orphaned survivors had been stunned silence. Then, there were questions, lots and lots of questions. Some wept openly, others refused to believe that the Earth was gone, and many wanted revenge against the invaders.

Waves of confusion and anger made it more than expedient to mobilize the agitated energy of loss among his charges into something they could see as constructive. In response to this need, Sadad recruited Von Strohheim's technicians to undertake additional habitation refitting tasks in the hold, but as supervisors and instructors not as workers. Despite some initial reluctance, soon, an ever increasing number of the survivors were busily learning about and working on the many small tasks that went into enhancing the refit of the Duo II's hold.

Standing on a small catwalk near the bridge, Sadad watched the activity below. There were still a lot of people milling about aimlessly, but the numbers joining the clusters of technician led work details were increasing.

Climbing onto the catwalk from the bridge, Von Strohheim joined Commander Sadad.

"This is a very good idea. There is a great deal still to do, and my people seem to enjoy being publicly acclaimed experts instead of always working behind the scenes," the Doctor remarked as he observed the activity below.

"Yes, I think its safe to say that most people enjoy being appreciated for their talents," Commander Sadad replied.

"I have come personally to get you. The Duo is docking with us at the emergency access port of the bridge," Von Strohheim said.

Turning toward Von Strohheim, Sadad's expression suddenly became quite somber.

"We have a lot of decisions to make, the most important of which is what to do next," Sadad said, turning and starting toward the bridge.

Taking one last look at his technicians working below, Von Strohheim smiled dotingly as he watched a new generation of apprentices learning the craft. Gut, sehr gut, he muttered to himself as he turned and followed Sadad onto the bridge.

⚜

Catching a glimpse of Sadad and Von Strohheim leaving the catwalk high above, Arthur busily put people back together as he moved from one patient to the next. He had elected to break himself in rank from Commandant of evacuation back to physician as there was more to do for the wearer of that hat than for the former.

Anxiety reactions abounded and incipient depressive episodes were well represented, but they were easy. Arthur passed out neural stimulators on all sides. When applied at the correct position on the scalp over the right hemisphere they would prevent the biochemical cascade that produced significant symptomatology. The people would do the rest for themselves. They'd talk to each other, share their fears, despair, and finally their hopes for the future. Arthur knew that was about as much as he could do. Certainly, clinical lore provided little insight into dealing with the magnitude of post traumatic stress that would arise in reaction to the destruction of an entire home world.

Principal and most pressing of his concerns were the few strike craft pilots shuttles were ferrying in from the devastation of Earth's last stand. These young men and women's strike craft had sustained only glancing strikes from the alien's laser projectors. Those whose fighter vessels had suffered direct hits wouldn't be coming back. Arthur wasn't sure of the exact counts, but the few unscathed pilots he had talked to indicated that five hundred had gone out to meet the enemy and less than twenty five craft remained space worthy. It was a quirk of the mind and Arthur knew it, but somehow a ninety five percent loss among the strike craft force, the survivors of which he could see and touch, was a more dramatic measure of the horror inflicted on the human race than the deaths of unseen billions on the Earth.

The shuttle was offloading some twenty odd wounded pilots. As Arthur moved quickly from one to another triaging for his med techs, he knew all he could do for over half of them amounted to little more than quelling the pain of their ending. Although he had never told anyone of his distress, the immediacy of one human being breathing their last breath into your face had always troubled Arthur. He wished Forrester were there to help. Nate had a way with terminal patients.

⚜

Entering the Duo II's bridge, Sydes and Commander Tutunji stepped quickly aside as several of Von Strohheim's technicians brushed past them enroute to the Duo to assess the damage.

Two men who had gone into battle with but one mind and heart now returned from the devastating outcome they had committed their lives to prevent. The faces and carriage of each clearly represented two radically different reactions to a horror that was the death of hope for both.

Tutunji appeared somber, his facial expression and movements suggested an individual on the brink of a depressive episode of clinical proportions. His head slightly lowered and characteristic military ramrod posture slumping, he appeared every inch a man weighed down by the guilt of some great and unforgivable transgression.

Sydes, although likely motivated by the same sense of guilt, had transformed that feeling into anger. His movements were quick and decisive and his eyes shone with a hate that would never be quelled by a well reasoned discussion of the facts of their defeat or praise for his valor. Everyone gave him a wide berth as he marched, more than walked, to the bridge console and stared at the viewer.

Spinning about, Sydes faced the assembled bridge crew. His face, dark with anger, was that of a young man who had become ageless in the matter of a few hours. His jaw set, his words came out as well articulated hisses.

"I want payback. Not one of these alien bastards is going home to report any kind of victory."

"We have very little to work with Captain Sydes. The Duo and perhaps twenty-five strike craft are flight worthy, but all of these vessels must be rearmed. None of this can be accomplished here. All the stores and technical resources to accomplish rearming and repair are at my base on Mars," Von Strohheim said, breaking the silence that followed Sydes declaration.

His head rotating with mechanical precision, Sydes' penetrating gaze came to rest on Commander Sadad.

"Well Commander, let's get under way. The Duo can be out of here in five minutes. The strike craft, the Duo II and those cruisers can follow."

Scanning each of the principal architects of Earth's failed defense gathered on the bridge in turn, Sadad saw the verdict on their faces. Sydes' passion for revenge reflected in their eyes. From Sadad's perspective, there were one hundred thousand good reasons in the Duo II's hold not to subscribe to Sydes' plan to take on the aliens again. Although he understood his primary responsibility was to the few remnants of humanity carried by his ship, Sadad recognized that those on the bridge supported Sydes' need for revenge and that that need likely would be applauded by the thousands of angry and frightened people below as well. Perhaps Sadad's responsibility to keep his charges safe might best be fulfilled in the relative safety that Von Strohheim's base afforded. Maybe this plan could satisfy both Sydes' need to strike back, as well as, Sadad's desire to preserve a vestige of humanity. In terms consistent with Sydes' heritage, Sadad had become council chief while Sydes was clearly the war chief of this tribe.

"We can be at Mars base in twenty minutes Captain Sydes," Sadad replied, holding Sydes' gaze.

Unfocused, Tutunji's eyes played over the scene on the bridge. He considered how many times this sort of drama had been played and replayed over the eons of his race's existence. Blood for blood, with only some mindless and insatiable primitive in the crypt of the species' brain keeping the tally. He knew reason was too frail a levee to hold back passion's tide. Tutunji would flow with the rising waters of Sydes' need for revenge. Rage against the other, rather than well tempered judgment, had always been the glue that held the tribe of man together.

"Doc, I'd like you to come with Tutunji and me on the Duo," Sydes said looking at Von Strohheim.

"Make all preparations for getting under way. Inform the cruisers and the strike craft that our destination is Von Strohheim's Martian base." Commander Sadad barked to his number two.

Sydes, Tutunji and Von Strohheim quickly boarded the Duo, which Sydes eased slowly away from the Duo II . The three architects of Earth's defense fell silent as the viewer revealed a starry display which seemed strangely empty. Tutunji expressed what they all felt.

"So dark ... cold ... billions of living lights missing out there."

Sydes nodded and punched in maximum acceleration. The Duo sped quickly away from the Duo II which, in the company of the cruisers and the strike craft, would follow at a slower pace.

"Do you have the missiles to rearm the Duo?" Sydes asked Von Strohheim after setting an automated course to the Martian facility.

"Yes, and many more. We made preparations to arm and rearm the Duo II several times. That would have required many more missiles than the Duo could carry," Von Strohheim replied.

"I want that alien operations base ship. I want it blown to bloody pieces, or at least crippled to the point that it can never return home," Sydes said, his tone venomous.

"Her screen of battleships is gone. Before the battle, our drone cameras indicated the alien fleet had twenty capital ships. They committed all of them to the Earth's destruction. We know we destroyed most of them and left the rest so crippled they'd be lucky to make it back to the operations base ship," Tutunji responded.

"Yes, but, we don't have a count on their fighters. Hundreds of them may remain operational and ready to defend the operations base ship," Von Strohheim added.

"What's your best guess Doc. Do you think the aliens have faster than light speed engine capability?" Sydes asked.

Somewhat surprised by the question, Von Strohheim paused for a moment. Leaning back, he began pulling together all the bits and pieces of information he had gathered about the invaders.

"It is all speculation, you understand, but given everything that we've seen, I think it very likely. The probabilities suggest a task force of this size was fielded for extended voyages of conquest. Even so, the operations base ship, as immense as it is, still is not large enough to sustain a reproductive population that could supply warriors for all their battleships and fighter craft over millennia. If all they could manage was sublight speed it would have taken them those millennia to get here from any distant planetary system that looks like it might sustain carbon based life forms. And, we know that they are looking for planets that can sustain carbon based life forms since they wanted the Earth. This assumption is also supported by our digital analysis of their bodies and their ships' expelled atmospheric gases. Since we know from astronomical surveys there are no planetary systems nearby that could support their life form or ours, that means they cannot be from our sublight neighborhood. Jah, I believe they are from far away … so far that the capacity to meet and exceed the speed of light would be required in order for them to fulfill their mission."

Sydes stared off into space, his expression suggesting he was deep in thought. Von Strohheim studied Sydes' face for a moment and then, fumbling with his Phi Beta Kappa key, he turned to Tutunji.

Herr Doktor Professor Einstein understood so much about the universe, but in this, excuse me Herr Doktor, I think he was wrong … the speed of light she can be surpassed, "Von Strohheim said in a respectful tone.

"Then those battleships must have light speed capacity as well. Even as big as she is, it's unlikely the operations base ship could house twenty capital ships in her bays. Those battle wagons must have been built to keep pace with her at light speed," Tutunji added.

"That assumption is consistent with this line of speculation," Von Strohheim replied.

"But the smaller fighter class craft could be housed in the operations base vessel," Sydes added.

"That seems reasonable. Again, this is all speculation, but I think it unlikely the fighter craft would have engines sufficient for faster than light speed velocities. For them, as for us, at some point it becomes a matter of power generation, the bulk of the engine and the size and maneuverability of the vessel. I do not believe you can cram all of that into a craft designed to be a small target and a highly maneuverable interceptor ship," Von Strohheim responded.

"I think I see where you're going with this Sydes. If the alien fighters can't match the velocity of the battleships and the operations base vessel, she must house them in receiving bays in her guts," Tutunji said.

"Exactly! If we can get in there fast and destroy, or at least clutter up the launch platforms of those fighter bays, then ..." Sydes said emphatically.

"Then we've trapped their fighters in the belly of that mother ship," Tutunji interjected.

"The Duo should have an easier time of it with the operations base ship than what she went through with the battleships. As big as she is, the operations base vessel is only one ship and she can't possibly maneuver as well as the battleships. We're also less likely to get caught in a crossfire engaging a single ship because the laser turrets have only a limited circumference of fire. It's not like getting pinned by three or four battleships vectoring in at you from different trajectories," Sydes continued.

"All of that sounds tactically sound, but why should the operations base ship still be there? After all, the alien fleet has achieved their objective?" Von Strohheim said.

"I'm not sure they did. I think they wanted the Earth intact. Destroying a planet they can't occupy may be dictated by some insane conquest and colonization policy. On the other hand, it may just be a way of insuring there's no one at their back with the firepower to make their lives miserable as they continue their exploration of the galaxy," Tutunji responded, his tone analytic.

"I think its simpler than all that. Hell, human history is full of examples, but they all come down to the same thing, if they can't have it no one else will," Sydes retorted.

"So, you believe that its more a matter of spite than tactics?" Tutunji asked.

"Absolutely, and any son of a bitch who's going destroy something just because he can't have it is gonna have a look-see at his handiwork ... if only to gloat," Sydes replied.

"They're beginning to sound frighteningly human, but I'm forced to agree. I expect they'll send a small sortie of fighters to Earth to get some pictures to send home," Tutunji said.

"What we need then is intelligence gathering on the operations base ship. I still have a few stealth camera drones at the Mars base. We could send them out to the operations base ship's last known position to do reconnaissance," Von Strohheim added.

"No! For this plan to have any chance of succeeding, the attack must come as a complete surprise. The alien's scanners might spot the stealth drones as we maneuvere them into position," Sydes responded emphatically.

"This is possible," Von Strohheim said.

"When that alien surveillance squadron makes for Earth, all I want them to see is a ravaged planet, wrecked strike craft, and what remains of the abandoned stations. I want every bit of destruction they run across to tell them they've achieved a complete victory," Sydes continued.

"Give them what they expect to see, or hope to see," Tutunji added.

"Exactly," Sydes replied.

A small icon on the console sounded, indicating the Duo had reached Martian space. Sydes turned to the task of establishing the Duo in orbit above Von Strohheim's technical construction base.

"Doc, there's something that's been bothering me since we talked about the alien's likely capacity for light speed travel. If they have the technology to propel their ships at velocities exceeding the speed of light, why weren't their weapons vastly superior to ours?" Tutunji asked.

"Well, first, I must say that my response cannot be as good as your question. On the one hand, the answer may be quite simple. In their exploration and colonization thrusts they may not have run across any species that could mount as effective a challenge to their current level of weapons development as we have. There is no rule I know of that says all life forms across the galaxy must achieve the same level of technological prowess in the same epoch. What it is, in English, necessity is the mother of invention, yes, that's it," Von Strohheim replied.

"That would certainly explain why they took such a beating trying to capture the Duo. If they are accustomed to easy victories, when they didn't achieve an instant and definitive triumph, they'd want to know the why and how," Tutunji responded.

"Jah, und this might be another reason they wouldn't just leave after destroying the Earth. They would want to know what happened to the Duo. Yes, in their position, I would want to do some reverse engineering on the Duo's shields and tunneling lasers," Von Strohheim said pensively.

"I hadn't considered that. I think you're right, but it still doesn't answer my question. If they've achieved faster than light travel, a trick that has eluded us, wouldn't that technology, in and of itself, just sort of bring along weaponry we can't even imagine?"Tutunji asked.

"This is really two questions. First, faster than light travel has not eluded us. The Natcorp consortiums were making too much money supplying the consumer needs of the Earth and Martian based populations to concern themselves with anything outside of the solar system. I've tried many times, year after year, but they couldn't see any, what did they call it, jah, near term profit, coming out of a research investment in faster than light speed propulsion,"Von Strohheim replied, his voice tinged with a trace of uncharacteristic anger.

"The aliens weapons, Doc?"Tutunji asked again.

"Yes, yes, of course. As you can see, this is a difficult subject for me. If they had given me the funds twenty years ago, the Earth ... the Earth would still be there ...."Von Strohheim said as his mood rapidly shifted to grief. "... my father, meine mutter, der Schwarzwald, alles ..."

"I'm sorry Doc. I didn't know you had family on Earth,"Tutunji said in a comforting tone.

Then, with an almost audible snap, Von Strohheim regained his characteristic teutonic composure.

"I'm sorry, this is jah, inexcusable."

"It's OK, Doc. We've all relied on you so much that none of us has even thought about the personal losses you might have experienced,"Tutunji replied.

"The alien weapons, light speed capability ... yes ... vell ... there are many parallels in Earth history. The Chinese had gunpowder and used it for entertainment, rather than conquest. The Inca civilization had an incredible system of roads, but the only use they found for the wheel was on their children's toys. Applications are often best seen retrospectively. The alien's self-propagating fusion weapons may have come out of their faster than light propulsion research, but I doubt it,"Von Strohheim said, having fully regained his professorial-engineering composure.

Quite abruptly, Von Strohheim stared off into space, seemingly studying a vista only he could see.

"Science has always been better at understanding the pieces than how to put them together. We make most of the really important unifying discoveries in science when we're looking for pieces to fit into smaller puzzles. What is the whole and what is only a part ... these have always been difficult concepts. Often, a part has been mistaken for the whole and umgekehrt ... the other way around. It is ..."Von Strohheim said.

"Doc, your base is hailing you," Sydes interjected.

"Von Strohheim here. Make ready all shuttles and available personnel to rearm the Duo," he responded over the comm link.

"Doc, have you had a chance to take a look inside those cruisers that came over from Cabot's security forces?" Sydes asked.

"No, there has been no time," Von Strohheim replied.

"While your technicians are rearming the Duo, I'd like you and a couple of your best people to take them apart. I'd like to know if you can fit our fusion missiles into their launch bays, drop in some of your shield generators and capacitors, and maybe rework their lasers," Sydes said.

"If they are as large as they appear, this may be possible. Some of the reserve components for the shields and the tunneling lasers that have already been fabricated for the Duo II might fit. It's just a matter of throwing out what's installed in the cruisers and wiring in what's on hand at the base," Von Strohheim replied.

"Commander Sadad, what's your time of arrival?" Sydes asked opening the link to the Duo II.

"About seven minutes Captain Sydes," Sadad responded.

"Advise those cruisers to prepare to be boarded by Von Strohheim and his crew. Tell Captain Merkson and his crews to provide all possible assistance to our technical people as we will be attempting a weapons refit. And, Sadad, pick two of your best flight commanders to take over those vessels. We'll need someone on board each of those cruisers who knows our battle tactics and who we can trust," Sydes said in rapid fire order.

"Consider it done," Commander Sadad replied.

✦

For the next five hours, over two hundred of Von Strohheim's technicians from the Martian base labored to rearm the Duo, tearing apart Cabot's cruisers and improving the habitation facilities on the Duo II. As the refit of the cruisers neared completion, the space around the two ships became increasingly cluttered with parts jettisoned to make way for weapons and shield components originally intended as backup parts for the Duo II.

"Captain Sydes," Von Strohheim called from the lead cruiser.

"Go ahead Doc," Sydes replied.

"I believe the cruisers are ready for battle. We have torn out the crew's quarters and automated a number of navigation and weapons functions," Von Strohheim responded.

"Everything fit?" Sydes asked.

"Yes. I wouldn't have been worried about installing the components prepared for the Duo II if I had known the cruisers were built to be self-sustaining.

There were crew quarters, bathrooms, transubstantiator kitchens and even an entertainment center. Once we threw all that out there was more than enough room for the shield generators, capacitors and the tunneling lasers," Von Strohheim said excitedly.

"Captain Sydes, Doctor Von Strohheim … we're getting feed from the imager. It looks like a squadron of alien fighters are retracing the course the battleship formations used to reach Earth," Commander Sadad said over the conference comm.

"Son of a bitch, I knew those ghoulish bastards would have to survey their handiwork. OK, who's our man on the lead cruiser?" Sydes asked, bringing the Duo's engines on line.

"Anna Krekora, Sir," Sadad replied.

Pausing a moment, Sydes opened the comm-link to the cruiser.

"Commander Krekora, I want you to lead those two cruisers on a course that will bring you in on the flank of the alien operations base ship. Your job is to provide a diversion. They'll send fighter craft out to meet you. Keep 'em busy, but do not approach the operations base vessel. I'm transmitting the course coordinates. Any questions?"

"No Sir, Captain Sydes. Draw off the enemy and kill the bastards. Seems pretty straight up," Commander Krekora replied.

"I want you to get under way immediately. And Commander, you've got Duo style shields and armaments at your fingertips now, make good use of them," Sydes said with a tone of grim resolution.

"Yes Sir, we'll try and leave something for you to shoot at," Commander Krekora replied.

"Good hunting Commander. Doc, you've done an outstanding job. Now, get the hell off that vessel and back to the Martian base," Sydes replied, a slight trace of a smile on his face.

"Of course Captain Sydes. But you know it's a shame I never get to see my toys in action," Von Strohheim replied.

Sydes chuckled softly, his good humor mirrored in Tutunji's expression.

"Yeah, I know Doc, but we need you and your people to make all of this work. Now, get the hell out of there," Sydes responded.

Slowly detaching from the lead cruiser, the shuttle carrying Von Strohheim and his crew spiraled on its solitary course back to the Martian base. With the shuttle's departure, the cruisers' engines sprang to life and the two vessels moved off along the coordinates Sydes had supplied.

"We'll wait about five minutes and then follow on a slightly different course," Sydes said to Tutunji.

Completing the preflight checklist, Tutunji brought the weapons console to ready status.

"So, we want to arrive after the base ship has dispatched some of her fighter craft to deal with our cruisers?" Tutunji inquired.

"Right. I figure the operations base ship should still be oriented so that her launch bays face us. We'll fly straight in at maximum acceleration and focus our attack on those launch bays. Between monitoring the transmissions from their vulture squadron over Earth and the diversion supplied by the cruisers, we should get a few seconds of grace," Sydes responded.

"Captain, Commander … confirming all four vessels interlinked on conference comm. Good luck and good hunting," Commander Sadad announced.

Breaking the Duo out of orbit, Sydes set her course toward the object of his vengeful feelings as Tutunji released the firing locks on the weapons' systems.

Knowing the motivations of those involved in Sydes' attack group and the odds against succeeding, Sadad fixed his gaze on the Duo as she dwindled to a dot on the main viewer. Surprise would be their most formidable weapon. What was left of the alien armada would hardly anticipate retaliation in the face of the destruction of his species' home world.

"Keep a close eye on that alien fighter squadron enroute to Earth. I want to know the minute they reverse course back to their base ship," Commander Sadad barked to his number two.

Within minutes, the alien operations base ship was centered in the Duo's viewer. The alien commander had committed only twenty fighters to the incursion by the cruisers and the cruisers dispatched them with extraordinary speed and efficiency.

Taking considerable delight in watching the cruisers' engage and dispatch the enemy fighters, Sydes pushed the Duo to maximum acceleration on a course vectored directly at the launch bays of the operations base ship.

"Krekora's pretty damn good," Sydes remarked.

"Gutsy lady," Tutunji remarked as he activated the weapons system guidance.

"Damn, maybe we finally caught a break. There the naked bitch is … and she's dropped her shields on the launch bays to field additional fighters against Krekora's cruisers. Are we in range?" Sydes shouted excitedly.

"Missiles away," Tutunji responded.

Tutunji set a total complement of five hundred fusion missiles for continuous fire targeted on the two launch bays of the alien base ship and released his birds. The huge laser projectors of the operations base ship were ablaze with deadly light, but they were too late to intercept any but the last one hundred missiles. Four hundred of the deadly projectiles found their mark, completely obliterating the yawning mouths of the two launch bays and at least fifty fighters in the process of launching. The huge vessel reeled under the detonations of the Duo's missiles and the secondary explosions of the fighter craft in her belly.

"Captain Sydes. Sorry to report, Sir, but we've run out of aliens to kill," Commander Krekora's called over the conference comm.

"Damn shame, but since you've done such a good job, you can come over here and play. Use your tunneling lasers and fire directly on the base ship's laser turrets. Let's pull her teeth," Sydes responded.

"The base ship's forward laser turrets are out of commission," Tutunji said.

Tutunji immediately launched another volley of two hundred missiles targeted on the carrier ship's fighter bays. The missiles were no sooner on their way than the base ship's flank turrets caught the Duo in a coalesced stream of laser energy.

"Son of a bitch, I've got to pay closer attention," Sydes said.

Sydes instantly activated the Duo's combined tunneling lasers against one of the base ship's laser projectors. As the Duo shuddered under the impact of the aliens' coalescing laser beams, Sydes maintained the tunneling lasers' focus on the base ship's turret. Going dark, the laser turret dissolved into a puddle of molten metal, and the coalescing impact of two of the base ship's turrets firing on the Duo simultaneously was gone.

Yawing under the impact of the second missile launch, the alien ship began to drift. Tutunji watched with some satisfaction as the base ship began to slough off some of her skin when her shields disintegrated. The whole forward half of the big ship, now completely devoid of electromagnetic shielding, fragmented with huge pieces of her hull spinning off into space.

Firing tenaciously on the big vessel's flank laser turrets, one of the cruisers was caught in four intersecting shafts of energy from the base ship's aft turrets. Unable to withdraw, the cruiser's capacitors overloaded and she vaporized in a cloud of energy.

"Damn, those miserable bastards! We've got to kill this big bitch's brain," Sydes said.

"I'd say the bridge is in that superstructure just aft of the second laser projector array," Tutunji suggested.

"Looks right to me," Sydes replied.

Spurring the Duo to maximum acceleration, Sydes initiated a dive toward the bank of laser turrets protecting what appeared to be the nerve center of the operations base vessel. The six smaller laser projectors protecting the bridge lit up as one, but the Duo's rapid dive had brought her in too close for the shafts of energy to coalesce.

Keeping a close eye on his console, Tutunji watched nervously as the Duo's capacitors fluctuated between ninety-nine and one hundred percent capacity. The Duo's tunneling lasers were focused at maximum output on the base ship's bridge and there was nothing more to be done to dissipate the energy her shields were absorbing from the laser barrage of the six enemy turrets.

Hanging suspended in space, the Duo fired continuously on the base ship as six turrets returned her fire. The Duo moved neither forward, nor back as she absorbed and returned enemy fire. Dynamically frozen in position, the Duo's propulsion units maintained an effective range against the base ship as her tunneling laser bored through the big ship's bridge shielding. Von Strohheim's lady was trapped by her own attack.

"We won't hold together much longer with this kind of punishment," Tutunji reported, an edge of apprehension in his voice.

"Well, soften this bitch up a little bit. The shielding around the bridge is about twice as tough as everywhere else," Sydes retorted.

"We're in too close for a fusion detonation, especially with the capacitors running at one hundred percent. We'll go up with her," Tutunji replied.

Sydes fought to stabilize the ship under the withering laser fire from the alien base ship while applying every bit of his many years of experience as a pilot to keep the tunneling lasers in range and on target.

"We're dead either way. I know the capacitors haven't budged from one hundred percent. I suspect they're carrying more than that but the gauges just don't register any higher. If the capacitors go off line or detonate, the Duo goes up either way. At least with a fusion blast we have a chance of just being shoved out of the way. Von Stohheim designed these shields to sustain a few seconds of hell bent energy better than the continuous barrage we're getting from these laser turrets," Sydes snapped.

"So you'd rather be blown to pieces from the outside in, than from the inside out," Tutunji replied as he made preparations for a missile volley.

"That's about it. Now, get these bastards off my back," Sydes said as he managed a slight chuckle.

Calling up a barrage of five hundred missiles, Tutunji launched them at the big ship's bridge. The base ship's gunners must have seen them coming as they attempted to wheel their turrets away from the Duo toward the incoming projectiles, but they were too late. All five hundred missiles hit home along the tunneling lasers' targeting beacon. The resulting explosion completely disengaged the bridge from the rest of the huge vessel while simultaneously igniting the laser turrets and cutting the immense base ship in half.

Blanking the Duo's viewer, the blast propelled the ship away from the wreckage of the base ship at incredible speed. Sydes maintained the tunneling lasers' at full output as the Duo's shields and capacitors vainly tried to absorb and dissipate the enormous energy of the fusion detonations. Despite his best efforts, the Duo bucked and spun resisting Syde's attempts to bring her under control.

"We've lost two capacitors. The energy overload is shunting to the reactors. If I don't take them off line, she'll blow," Tutunji shouted.

"Do it," Sydes shouted back.

Shutting down the reactors, Tutunji channeled the energy from the remaining overloaded capacitors to the propulsion units Sydes needed to control the vessel. Slowly, Sydes regained control of the spinning ship.

Looking up from his console, Tutunji noticed the main viewer had come back on line. There, dead center in the screen, was Commander Krekora's cruiser. Her ship was on an attack trajectory toward the alien fighter squadron returning from their surveillance mission over the devastation their fleet had rained down on the Earth.

"Commander Krekora, what the hell do you think you're doing?" Sydes shouted over the conference comm.

"Just clearing some undesirables out of the neighborhood, Sir," Commander Krekora replied.

"What's our status?" Sydes asked Tutunji impatiently.

"Two capacitors fried, the rest are at forty percent and the reactors are shut down," Tutunji replied.

"Can we get under way? That cruiser is gonna need some help." Sydes asked anxiously.

"What remains in the capacitors can't feed both propulsion and weapons systems. It will take two minutes to bring the reactors back on line," Tutunji responded in a somber tone.

"So, we can either shoot or move, but not both. Shit, that makes us fucking useless spectators. Damn, I hate this!" Sydes snapped.

Relegated to the stands, Sydes and the Commander could only watch as the lone cruiser, tunneling laser firing, dove directly into the squadron of alien fighter craft. The cruiser launched several missiles but was hit on all sides by the enemy's laser turrets. The cruiser began to spin and heel over but she continued to exact a heavy toll on the enemy. Of the twenty enemy fighter craft that had engaged her, only twelve remained, but that was more than enough to finish the cruiser.

"How soon on the reactors?" Sydes asked, his frustration barely contained.

"Another minute," Tutunji responded.

"That's about fifty seconds too long," Sydes replied.

Sydes watched in angry dismay as the cruiser, taking heavy fire on her thrusters, lost navigational control and began to drift, her laser firing randomly.

"Well, look at this! There at four o'clock starboard," Tutunji said excitedly.

Sydes saw it immediately, two shafts of the bright yellow energy that could only have been produced by tunneling lasers. The beams cutting a path through the night of space struck and cut two of the alien fighter craft in half. Then, two more of the enemy fighter craft came under fire.

"We got tired of sitting on our hands. Besides, the Doc was pestering me to death. He just had to see his toys work in person," Commander Sadad called from the bridge of the Duo II.

Staring in absolute amazement, Tutunji watched as the tunneling lasers of the Duo II dispatched the remaining enemy fighter craft in a matter of seconds. Each burst from the Duo II's laser projectors vaporized an enemy fighter almost the instant it struck the enemy vessel.

"Well Doc, that's your biggest and best toy yet. Those tunneling lasers must be twice the capacity of the Duo's," Tutunji exclaimed.

"5.378 times the capacity, to be exact. But this is wunderbar Captain Sydes. You have saved for me the propulsion section of the alien base ship," Von Strohheim replied with obvious and growing anticipation.

"We aim to please Doc," Sydes responded.

"Commander Krekora, what is your status?" Tutunji inquired.

"We're not ready to throw a housewarming party over here, but the crew is in one piece," Commander Krekora replied.

"I've already sent for shuttles to tow you back to Mars base. So just hang on," Commander Sadad interjected.

"Reactors on line," Tutunji announced.

"Let's see what's left of that base ship," Sydes said.

His mood now unmistakably brighter, Sydes activated the engines and set a course back toward what remained of the alien flagship.

"You cannot possibly leave me here. I must examine the propulsion units on that ship," Von Strohheim said in a petulant tone.

"OK Doc. But first let Tutunji and me inspect what's left of this big bitch for signs of life," Sydes replied.

"I'll call in half of the strike craft force from Mars base to support your survey of the base ship and hold the Duo II here," Commander Sadad responded.

"Sound plan. And by the way Commander, good job. You saved our ass," Sydes replied.

THE DIARY

As the Duo sped toward the now darkened wreck of the alien base ship, Commander Sadad took a deep breath and thought to himself, thanks Captain Sydes. It was the first time Sadad felt as though he was in truth what his rank suggested, a commander.

The Earth was gone, only a frayed remnant of her teaming billions survived locked in tiny orbs of steel, but the battle was won. As he heard himself think it, Sadad marveled at the human psyche's ability to fabricate cognitions with that degree of absurdity. Perhaps this measure of irrationality represented the fundamental saving grace of the species, namely, the ability to wrench hope out of the clutches of the most soul destroying of defeats.

Chapter 35

Although no longer physically present, the pillar of light signifying the diarist's visitation had taken up permanent residence in Forrester's mind. More than a memory, the vision of assuring illumination was alive and renewing itself from moment to moment in his awareness. If the current course of events were indeed what the ancients had called the second coming, then the manifestation of the light at the beginning of the universe left a permanent imprint and a continuing presence behind. In an instant of clarity, Forrester recognized that, for the meek, of which he was now a part, transcendence was not a historical footnote but an ongoing experience.

Finishing his coffee, he looked up and saw Crystal entering the terrace even as her parents still slept. Without any audible exchange, Forrester recognized she shared his desire to venture into the scrapbook of the Earth that the ecosectors represented. Driven by a singular motivation to experience the beauty of a birthplace that was no more, they climbed into the family hopper and set off to survey the menu of environments Cabot had unwittingly preserved from the holocaust.

Whatever his motivations, Cabot had done a magnificent job of recreating the world in a bottle. Forrester and Crystal's hopper excursion through two of the ecosectors had not offered them a view of even one percent of the environments the ark had to offer. The hopper was returning now, passing silently over the Canadian woodlands of their home. Gently settling on a grassy expanse on the simulated north side of Jacob and Esther's house, Crystal and Forrester disembarked.

"Those were really big doors," Crystal remarked to Forrester as she activated the door closure on the hopper.

"Yes, really big, but they opened and closed very quickly," Forrester replied.

Crystal referred to the portals and forcefield panels that separated the ecosectors and preserved the environmental conditions necessary for each. Phil had done a magnificent job Forrester thought to himself. It was painful to remember Phil had given his life as seal to his work.

"He tried very hard to be a good man. His courage at the end ... kept all of us safe," Crystal responded, her expression tinged with sadness.

Once again, Forrester was reminded there was no such thing as a private thought among the meek.

"Yes, it did," Forrester replied.

"For thoughts that are secrets, the meek build a green wall all around one place in their minds. Then, they think their thoughts inside the emerald circle. No one will try to look in," she said.

"You mean no one can look past the green wall?" Forrester asked.

"I don't know if they can, but no one would try," Crystal replied.

"How does the community react to members who put up green walls?" Forrester asked, fully engaged in one of his discovery fevers.

"You just sort of look around them. Adults, but just the first ones, sometimes have them. Children never do. For the first ones, walls come and go," she responded.

"The first ones?" Forrester asked, bewildered by the reference.

"Our parents, the ones who first came to the reserve," Crystal replied.

"Do I have the green walls?" He asked.

"No. There was some green in your aura at the beginning but never a wall," Crystal responded.

"Well, Crystal, that sounds right to me. From early childhood everyone said they could see right through me. As my good friend Arthur put it, I failed deception 101," he replied, embarrassment tingeing his expression.

Reaching up, Crystal took Forrester's hand as they walked together into the house. Entering the sunlit interior of the great room, Crystal paused momentarily and looked up at him.

"You are the eye of the people. I don't think you can make green walls," she said, mirroring her mother's kindly smile.

Crystal's comment seemed to strike a chord. Maybe she was right. Maybe it was a can't do thing for him rather than a conscious act of will not to deceive others. Certainly his history of getting in trouble every time he opened his mouth would support the can't do hypothesis.

His mind was still busy as they walked hand in hand through the house. Then, he detected a wave of fatigue washing over him. It was the sort of mental weariness he had experienced as aftermath to one of his analytic exploratory fevers since childhood. The drain on his energy felt familiar. Then, he recognized its signature. It was of a kind he experienced after an instance of *seeing*, but of much greater magnitude. A greater drain on his energy must be the result of his own feeble powers being the only source powering these personal explorations. Then, an odd thought occurred to him, perhaps his bouts of curiosity driven exploratory fevers were genetic precursors to the visions of the meek. Somewhere within the snarls of tissues that passed for his brain, evolution had laid down a structure meant to tap into the loom's underlying source of energy. However, before the timely emergence of the meek, this structure was energized solely by his own personal resources. His realization of the genesis and significance of the fatigue seemed, in a most curious fashion, to dispel it.

Moving through the great room and onto the terrace, Forrester saw Chauvez seated there in conversation with Esther and Jacob. Esther rose immediately and hugged Crystal.

"Captain Chauvez has some questions for you Doctor Forrester," Esther remarked as she turned toward him.

"We've lost touch with the Earth Defense Force ship we contacted earlier. Dvorak says I'm crazy, but I thought I'd come down here to find out if you had any idea of what's going on," Chauvez said as he set down his glass of guava juice.

⋇⋄⋇

Initially startled by Chauvez's request, Forrester suddenly felt a gathering energy inside his head. In a very curious fashion, the sensation he experienced felt just like the head journaling he had been prone to since childhood. However, this sensation felt magnified by a factor of infinity. Pausing a moment, he recalled that his training analyst repeatedly told him one of his greatest weaknesses was a reflexive tendency to answer every question put to him. With the best of intentions, his analyst had preached, persuaded and attempted to cajole Forrester out of this practice without success. The kindly old clinician had explained that questions were not always simple requests for information. He noted interrogatives just as often functioned as probes intended to supply the questioner with a tactical advantage in the dominance driven warfare of conversation.

Fumbling with his napkin, Forrester stared at Chauvez. Well, there was the reflex again, but this time its emergence seemed to fit into his job description as eye to the people of the trees. Perhaps a long wave genetic process drove his lifelong and wholly intractable reflex to respond to questions. An automatism that had been present since early childhood may have been constitutionally mandated so he could fulfill his current role among the meek.

Commendable as Chauvez's patience was in the face of Forrester's long bout of silence, Forrester felt pressed to do something. Then, as if on cue, the energy in his head reached a clarifying fullness. The phenomenon resolved itself into a three dimensional image so compelling he felt, for a moment, as though he were suspended in the cold void of space. In an instant, he saw the wreckage of the alien fleet, the remaining ships of the Earth Defense Force, and recognized feelings of relief and vindication at their victory. For the first time, he discerned that the significance of the images was greatly enhanced by an underlying commentary derived from the mean emotional response of the battle's survivors. It occurred to him that, with this event, the *seeing* had occurred often enough to permit a leap from simple sensation to perception. Simply *seeing* an image had given way to a reflexive analysis of its constituents. Then, the vision began to fade.

With the vision's termination, it occurred to Forrester that this was yet another instance in which he had *seen* without any felt assistance from the community of the people of the trees. Further, he detected no personal energy expenditure such as he had experienced on all previous occasions of viewing in the Now. Given his past experience and the physiological constraints of the sensory experience of *seeing*, his vision must have been directed to the immediate Now. What he had seen had just occurred or was a continuing event in the present.

The conclusion was obvious, *seeing* contemporary events at a distance was an energic freebee. Cutting across the spatial aspect of the spatial-temporal map required no corporate or individual energy expenditure among the meek. It was the temporal dimension that ate up calories. The temporal continuum gave back energy when *seeing* was enacted, nevertheless, there was a small net loss to the individual and the community.

Momentarily, casting a glance at his audience, Forrester recognized that Crystal, Esther and Jacob were party to his thoughts, but Chauvez, well, the man's patience could only be characterized as glacial. Despite his need to respond to Chauvez's question, Forrester could feel that the ramifications of the vision had not yet spun themselves out to completion.

Fascinating, Forrester thought to himself, the physiology of this newly evolved sensory organ was completely at odds with the mechanics of all previous human sensory experience. In mundane existence, time simply passed without any effort on the part of those who found themselves carried along in its wake. Space, on the other hand, required effort to traverse. Within the meeks' organ of *seeing*, these relationships were reversed. Mentally traversing contemporary space was effortless, but visions that penetrated time required exertion.

Although he recognized it as the purest speculation, Forrester suspected the evolution of the organ of *sight* among the meek represented an assembly of tissue that existed somehow in two dimensions of reality simultaneously. The organ was clearly here in the domain of the material universe, sitting behind the forehead of every one of the meek. However, in some way Forrester couldn't even begin to conceptualize, it simultaneously existed within the loom of life and light that supported the crude matter of the cosmos.

In the strata of the eternal, below that which was universally accepted as reality, the game must be played differently. Perhaps, in that dimension, time and space were simply two sides of a coin called motion. Time was, conceivably, just faster motion when considered in isolation. Perhaps, it only seemed slower when compared to moving from here to there in space because time carried the entirety of the universe on its back. Although Forrester couldn't vouch for the physics of his speculation, the differential energy drain on the meeks' dimensionally intersecting organ suggested some support for his hypothesis.

Drifting slowly out of the fully illumined playground in his head into the relative darkness of shared reality, Chauvez's face once again came into focus. Smiling at the master of the ark, Forrester knew he would relish this pronouncement. He had always enjoyed the role of the bearer of good tidings.

✦

"The Earth Defense forces have achieved a complete victory over the invading alien fleet. There is a permanent base on Mars and, when their ships return to it, they will contact you," Forrester relayed in tones of confident satisfaction.

"Dvorak will never buy this. But for me, its more the source than how much sense the information makes that's convincing," Chauvez remarked, leaning back with a sly smile on his face.

Feeling his face flashing through a mixture of expressions reflecting the spectrum from satisfaction through embarrassment, Forrester said nothing.

Chauvez drained his glass and stood up.

"Thanks Doc. If I come up with any more questions, I'll be back," he said.

As Chauvez walked down the hill toward the tube that would carry him back to the bridge, his remarks about the source being intrinsically convincing really stuck with Forrester. He had always lived by the standards of demonstrated proof and logically coherent argument. To have his words accepted, well, because he was some kind of oracle was disquieting. The sense of discomfort seemed to derive principally from the fact that Chauvez was not one of the meek. The discrepancy in constitutional ability between Chauvez and Forrester was troubling. The potential for abuse of the power resident in the evolutionary gift of *seeing* clearly existed. The ability to *see* the Now was a source of extraordinary comfort and solidarity when exercised among his peers. However, it could easily be perverted to a darker purpose when employed outside the community of the meek. Although he may have had his doubts before, the words of the diarist now rang clear and true.

> THOSE WHO KNOW AND ARE
> CONTENTED BY THE KNOWING
> SHALL PART FROM THOSE WHO
> DELIGHT IN THE STRUGGLE TO
> WREST THE UNIVERSE TO THEIR
> WILL. IN THIS PARTING, ONE SHALL
> BECOME TWO, EACH TRAVELING
> THE PATH THAT HAS CHOSEN THEM.

A complete and perhaps permanent separation of the meek from their brethren in humanity's mainstream appeared to be in the best interests of both.

As the reflexive prey of their dominance driven, the meek could not survive, much less flower, in their midst. On their part, the dominance driven could never fulfill their destiny in conquest, and the ultimate realization of its futility, if they were allowed to control and use the *seeing* of the meek to further their shortsighted ends. For the strong, an ultimately redemptive outcome could only be realized when all that was conquerable had been subdued. Only in that fleeting moment of complete victory could they recognize its futility and, turning within, see the Light always resident there outshining all of their triumphs.

"A good man whose past darkens his present," Forrester remarked.

Then, Forrester recognized his characterization of Chauvez encompassed those few not of the meek who had remained onboard the ark.

"A companion whose openness and value will increase with time," Jacob added.

Something about Jacob's statement seemed to take root in Forrester's brain. Apart from the meek, there was Chauvez, Dvorak's brood, Phil's family and a few techs left on the ark. Perhaps their presence among the meek was not an accidental inclusion in the broader topography of the space-time map Forrester could not yet see.

Saying nothing, Esther studied the path of Chauvez's passing long after he disappeared among the trees and then turned her attention to Crystal, who was sitting at the table coloring a long strip of paper.

"So, you're making another one of those," Esther remarked as she stroked Crystal's head.

"This one is almost finished," Crystal replied as she looked up and then returned to her coloring task.

"She's probably made over a thousand of these since she was two years old," Esther said.

"Crystal, what is it you're making there?" Forrester asked, leaning over to look at her handiwork.

"I don't know ... just something pretty," Crystal replied.

Knowing that Crystal, despite her young years, seldom did anything without some purpose, Forrester began to study the narrow strip of paper more carefully. It was about two centimeters across and twenty four centimeters long. The strip was divided into two centimeter segments that Crystal had colored individually. Almost in the center of the strip, the segment was colored yellow, to the right each segment in turn had been colored yellow-orange, orange, red-orange, red and red-violet. To the left of the center yellow, the segments showed yellow-green, green, blue-green, blue, blue-violet and violet. The narrow strip was colored on both sides in the same order of colors.

"It's very pretty," Forrester remarked.

"Just about finished," Crystal replied.

Then, grasping the strip, she twisted it into the shape of a Mobius band (∞) and fastened the two ends together. She held it up for Forrester to see.

"It goes round and round, always changing and always the same. This one's for you," she said and handed the tiny Mobius spectrum to Forrester.

"Thank you Crystal," Forrester responded.

He marveled at the simple beauty of the spectrum of visible light bent back upon itself and joined in a continuous and unending loop.

"If the band could move around like the links of a bicycle chain real fast it would make white," Crystal said.

Then, she produced a color wheel she had made with the colors arranged in the same order in pie shaped wedges from circumference to center and spun it like a top on the table's surface.

Always fascinated by the simplest demonstrations in science, Forrester observed Crystal's experiment as the colors on the wheel merged to white and then became separate wavelengths in the light spectrum again as the wheel slowed.

"That's right, if it goes fast enough, all the parts merge together into white," Forrester remarked.

"All it takes is enough energy to keep it going and the separate bits join together to become part of the whole again, the white light," Crystal said as she spun the color wheel once more.

A glimmering awareness of impending insight slowly illuminated the theater of Forrester's mind. He was head journaling again. This little band of color evoked all the trappings of a symbol in his mind, suggesting that Crystal's handicraft represented more than a delightful entertainment. Something had awakened below the level of verbal consciousness when Crystal was two years old, her crafting of one thousand iterations of this simple strip of color was its way of manifesting itself. Crystal was teaching without fully comprehending the lesson she was instilling.

More than a handful of experiences, with the internal changes preparatory to the *seeing,* now allowed Forrester to feel it coming. There was a fullness in his head accompanied by a fomenting sense of energy. It was one of his analytic, exploratory fevers but, on this occasion, driven by more than his own personal energy. He could also feel the supportive presence of the community of the meek, within his mind, overshadowing his own sense of being and the manifestation of the community's life, there was something else. It was an eidolon, a perfect image of all that could be intuited and thought, and a source of seamless, benign energy, unbounded by the viewer's cognitive and experiential horizon. He knew it. He could feel it. This was more than a vision. This would be a revelation.

Centered in the mist of an unfolding panorama was a wholly animated and perfected realization of that which Crystal's Mobius strip was only a dumb and incomplete copy. Here was the reality which she had tried, vainly, in over one thousands attempts to mirror. For but the briefest instant, Forrester felt himself like Ezekiel who had beheld the wheel's unassisted turning.

There, before him in all its revelatory splendor and burgeoning with life, the living Light of creation slowly unwound until it was a vertical axis of color segments. Along side the red-violet and red bottommost end of the strip, Forrester saw a whole universe of one cell and multicellular creatures, some of which he recognized and others, which must have come from environments quite different from Earth's, were wholly unfamiliar. Ascending along the strip through the yellow and green segments, he saw an endless variety of fish, reptiles, birds and mammals, including man. There was warmth and feverish activity in the column of life adjoining this segment of the strip. The column of aggressively vibrant light, progressing from red through green, seemed to engender striving and struggle. Here was a palpable wrestling with material existence for individual survival and dominance, both within and across species. Of singular purpose, each idiosyncratic collection of genes competed to establish and disperse itself across the breadth of creation.

As life stacked itself upon life, upwards along the vertical axis of the strip of colors through blue-green, blue, blue-violet and violet, the intensity of the light diminished, but its penetrating clarity seemed to increase. A continuum seemed apparent, with struggling masses of life decreasing as red became blue along a spectrum in which translucent clarity and definition increased as blue and violet emerged.

The cooler blue and violet portion of the spectral band, lacked the boiling mass of living forms layered one upon the other seen in the warmer regions of color. In this cooler zone of light, life forms were sparingly broadcast here and there in tiny knots of social convocation. Each individual icon of life had a more distinct outline despite the fact that all represented here seemed to be receding into the background rather than pushing themselves to the fore.

A reversal of background-foreground clarity and definition along the strip was the most singular component of the vision and contrary to all laws of visual perception with which Forrester was acquainted. Here, life forms seen at an apparently greater distance possessed greater visual definition while those closer to the observer, blurred, seemingly merged together. It suggested that the clustering of those in the background of the blue and violet range of the spectrum was volitional. Involuntary merging, driven perhaps by limbic tribal forces, was evident at the red end of the spectral strip. In the blue-violet and violet bands of light, Forrester saw the people of the trees, wearing a particular radiance, their beautiful violet children, offspring of the meeks' congress with one another.

Then, just as Crystal had completed the prototypical strip of Light, life and color, upon which she had unconsciously patterned her efforts, reattached itself end to end, in the shape of a figure eight so, slowly at first, and then with increasing speed, the living Mobius strip began to move, each light segment following the next as though traveling on some unseen and endless conveyer. Faster and faster it spun until it shown only as a figure eight of dazzling white light. The Mobius of brilliant, living energy blurred into a unified form, rotating to a fully vertical presentation and suddenly filling with tiny orbs of violet light dancing about its length and breadth. It was the diarist. Here were all the colors of life merged into one, ever cycling, forever energized by the loom of life and facilitating animation in the darkness of matter. Here was all life, large and small, primitive and evolved, sentient and barely aware. Each and every fleck of protoplasm was incorporated as an equal and necessary part of the whole that was not just all life, but life summed up. It was the forever of life's compendium cycling in unity in one place and at one time. Revealed in this simple but compelling symbol was the first life, and indeed all life, that had and continued to precede and support the material universe. Forrester was finally graced to see the whole that was life. Here was the emergent force of life and light, revealed in its unbroken unity, where before all that could be grasped was its many and diverse parts.

⊱❖⊰

Abruptly terminating, the image of a little girl replaced the vista of this great revelation. It was Crystal, upon whose finger a butterfly had settled.

"We are both just different colors in the ribbon of life," she remarked, staring at the multicolored wings of the monarch.

"Yes, I'm sure that's exactly what it means," Forrester replied.

"All life stands upon itself, foot upon shoulder in a great circle until head meets head. No part can be removed, lest the whole circle falls to pieces," Jacob remarked.

"The circle of color is the pillar of light. Mother and father to all that has, is now, and will have, life," Esther added.

⊱❖⊰

Then, like a gentle breeze coming upon the heels of a great storm, words whispered in the quiet wake of the vision. Words spoken before in many tongues by forms both familiar and alien to human experience, in places comfortingly near and distant beyond imagining, were heard now with a clarity of intent only the vision could reveal. These were words spoken over and over in the time and space of the universe of matter, but whose heretofore unseen origins lay in that which enlivened all of creation. It was the diarist, manifest both in the pillar of circulating white light, as well as, in the strip of encompassing colors, representing all that was the ordering and replicating dynamic of life.

> I AM THE BEGINNING AND THE END.
> I AM THE LOWLIEST AND THE LOFTIEST
> OF LIFE BECOME ONE IN AN ENDLESS
> CIRCUIT OF LIGHT.
>
> I AM BORN AND BORN AGAIN, LIVING
> IN AND DYING TO WORLDS WITHOUT
> END. IN MANY FORMS, AT MANY TIMES,
> CLOTHED IN THE FLESH OF THOSE UPON
> WHOM I CALL, I AM EVER THE SAME.

I AM THE ASCENT OF LIFE. I AM ITS
STRUGGLE IN THE DARKNESS AND ITS
REPOSE IN THE LIGHT. FOREVER IN
THE NOW, I JOURNEY FROM THE
LIGHT TO LIFE'S CLAY LANTERN AND
TO THE LIGHT AGAIN.

TO THE LOOM'S FRAGILE LOOPS I AM
THE FIRST OF ALL ROWS AND THE
ARCHETYPE OF ALL LIFE'S PARTS. THE
DARNER OF THE LOOM, I PASS IN AND
THROUGH LIVING ROWS, INTERLACING
ALL LIFE UNTIL THE TAPESTRY OF TIME
IS WOVEN WHOLE AND COMPLETE.

While the tolling of the words was finished, the resonance of their meaning continued to echo in Forrester's head. As the echoes slowly faded, the vision continued.

The spectral strand of life's light slowed its revolutions to a complete halt and, detaching end from end, it straightened to its full extension and descended into an infant human form. Over many years of maturation to adulthood, the strip slowly turned and twisted until head and tail rejoined into the Mobius loop.

Slowly at first, the multicolored hoop began its revolution until, in a blur of white light, it burst free from its corporeal prison. What had all the appearance of death, upon rough hewn tree boughs in the darkness of the material universe, was a liberating passage through brilliant portals into the dimension that is the loom of life.

In rapid time succession, the scene repeated, each new view illustrating the descent of a straightened rainbow of the living Light into sentient forms so diverse as to defy description. In each incarnation, the spectral rainbow twisted, recoupled and transformed itself into that selfsame pillar of white light the whole of the community of the meek had witnessed. Then, the vision ended and Forrester found himself once again in the company of Crystal's family, among the trees and hills of the ecosector.

❧❀❧

"It is the great vision that we have awaited. It demonstrates the fullness of the loom of life's ministry to the darkness in which our race has wandered for so many ages," Esther said as she stepped forward and hugged Forrester.

Crystal, a smile of knowing innocence that might well be called enlightenment shinning on her face, slowly turned her hand, allowing a half finished Mobius strip to flutter down onto the table.

As Forrester looked at her and the small scrap of colored paper resting there, he knew she had no need to make another.

The scrolls, the visions and moments of en-Lightened insight, all of these were but catalysts spurring the meek to a broader vision of that which enlivened all of creation. In the simple lyrics accompanying the music of this revelation was the ultimate in reconciliation of theology and biology. Life did not begin in the terror and confusion of a single cell's struggle for existence. The words were simple and clear, '**I am the first of all rows and archetype of all Life's parts.**' The diarist, a single incarnation of his many manifestations, was Life complete. All that could be discerned as alive was but a partial incarnation of the fullness present from before what any finite being could conceive as the beginning of time. From the lowliest bacterium to the beings more advanced than imagination could conjure, we were all but parts broken from this original template and scattered amidst the nooks and crannies of the material universe.

Deep within the multicolored recesses of all that was alive lay a misty awareness of a separation from the wholeness and the perfection at the beginning. The restlessness of life was not a measure of the intensity of its struggle to survive in a hostile universe, but an unspoken recognition of its separation from the whole of which it was once a part.

The threads of light strained to return to the loom from which they had been loosed. These living genetic filaments, only dimly recalling the pattern of the weave of all beginnings, wished only to to take their place once again in life's universal tapestry. Representing the fullness of space-time spun by the loom of existence before the birth of matter, life was not new but older than the smallest quanta.

Cerebral venues, derivative of his simian origins, were simply insufficient to encompass the enormity of the knowledge pouring into his brain. The part cannot contain the whole, that much was clear. What little he grasped could not be subsumed under the sensory denominators of 'felt', 'heard' or 'seen.' These fragmentary senses could not begin to circumscribe the synergy of all life. He and the meek were party to the truth of abstraction, devoid of sensory descriptors and mediated by a prefrontal organ for which the human species had no vocabulary. Forrester was tired, but it was a good tired. He had done his job. He had served as eye to the meek even when his gaze fell upon that which no finite being could comprehend, and he had survived.

In a curious amalgam of the now dwindling human voice in his head and the illumined utterance of the meek, he heard the simplest of answers to a question that had plagued humanity since their first guttural conversations. Cast in the ongoing conflict between science and religion, the question was always, at its core, one of primacy. Did, as science would have it, the material universe set the stage for life or, as piety would hold, was life the playwright for the cosmos? The argument was over sequencing or in common parlance, a means-ends confusion. The meeks' appearance clarified this controversy. Life, all at once in the Now of space-time, created the universe to variegate and experience itself. A cosmic stage of wonders and sensory delights was created as an infinite schoolyard, but it was also well stocked with scraped knees and bullies. Material existence was the middle school of darkness between the light at the beginning and the light at the end. Each of life's delicate filaments, after a hard day of serious study and play, got to go home. Forrester felt it, he could see the lights of his farm house home shinning as beacons in the chilling darkness of a winter's night.

Chapter 36

Holding the Duo II at a safe distance from the debris strewn scene, Commander Sadad surveyed the tangible evidence of humanity's vengeance on their invaders. The aliens had been a vindictive and merciless enemy, but in humanity they had confronted a species of superior tenacity and a highly developed, if unreasoning, appetite for revenge. Perhaps without firsthand knowledge of the species they were attempting to supplant, the aliens intuitively knew that they could not leave humanity at their backs. The destruction of the Earth had been an act of desperation meant to rid themselves of an implacable enemy they could not otherwise defeat. It was a strategy that had failed and perhaps floundered in a way they would come to regret in the centuries that stretched out before the few remnants of the human race.

However, at the moment, Sadad's most trying responsibility stood beside him in the person of Von Strohheim. The good Doctor was insistent in his request to be ferried over to the what was left of the alien operations base ship. The Duo II's main viewer and the conference comm kept them in constant contact with the Duo, which was circling the wreck of the alien base ship, but in this much Von Strohheim was correct, it was not the same as being there.

Onboard the Duo, Sydes and Tutunji approached the wreck of the alien operations base ship cautiously. There were no overt signs of life from the vessel and no lights shown on the hull or from her interior. Sydes decreased velocity to a crawl and toured the remains of the alien's operation base ship in a close circuit. He intended to be very thorough in scanning for any energy emissions coming from the hulk of the alien ship.

"We're gonna just creep around this beast, or what's left of her. I don't want any surprises, particularly if Von Strohheim wants to clamber through her innards," Sydes said.

"Right, we could afford to lose a whole bunch of somebodies, rather than him," Tutunji replied.

"Present company included," Sydes replied.

Sydes guided the Duo in tight to the hull of the shattered alien colossus, watching the energy sensor scanners closely.

"She looks pretty dead. I can't find one electron running in circles laid down for it by any mortal being," Tutunji noted.

"Sounds like that monster is pretty well spent," Commander Sadad remarked over the conference comm.

"Yeah, but I want to make one more sweep to be sure. You can get space gear ready for everyone who's coming over to what's left of this alien monster. Make sure the strike craft pilots who are going to assist in this little expedition are issued mini-scanners and side arms. With these spiteful bastards, I wouldn't be surprised at anything we might find," Sydes responded.

"Do you really think there's anyone or anything left alive on that hulk?" Tutunji asked.

"When it comes to these bloodthirsty bastards, I don't think at all. I expect the worst and haven't been disappointed yet," Sydes remarked.

An image of the surface of the Earth blowing by the Duo in space had assumed center stage in the Tutunji's mind. The prospect of another holocaust lurking within the bowels of this last remnant of the invading force that could liquidate the balance of the human race seemed all too real.

"Yes, I guess its best to err on the side of caution," Tutunji replied.

"So Captain Sydes, when do I get to start my investigation. I have six of my best engineers ready to go and we are all anxious to open our Weihnachten … ah … our Christmas presents," Von Strohheim announced over the conference comm.

Even in this dark moment, Sydes still derived some small measure of amusement from Von Strohheim's childlike excitement and anticipation.

"Just hang on Doc. We're finishing up the second sweep right now. We want to be sure Santa hasn't left anything explosive for you under the tree," Sydes replied, suppressing a chuckle.

"Order the strike craft to take position near the hulk and to remain at stationkeeping by what's left of the aft section until they receive further orders," Commander Sadad said to his number two.

Facing the Duo II's main viewer, Sadad surveyed a scene he had never expected to see when the conflict began. The invading alien fleet lay in ruins before him. The vestiges of wrecked battleships devoid of light and life, the immense body of the operations base craft cut in half during the attack, and fragments of alien fighters and cruiser craft all adrift in space. And there was the Duo. She looked so tiny as she circuited the remains of the gargantuan alien command vessel that had directed the murder of his home planet. The victory over the invading armada was small compensation for the slaughter of the billions who had perished in a momentary flash of light. His father's summation of the human condition flooded into his mind as he contemplated the scene, 'when nothing constructive can be done, something destructive is called for.'

Sydes watched as fifteen strike craft flew in perfect attack formation enroute to the Duo's position.

"This team works well together," he remarked.

As the Duo completed her second sweep of the huge alien hulk, Commander Sadad waited as the little sphere of fury stationed herself by the gaping hole that opened to the base ship's remaining aft section.

"All strike craft assume position along side the Duo," Commander Sadad ordered over the conference comm.

As the tiny strike craft approached in a perfectly synchronized formation, Tutunji studied their disciplined maneuvers carefully.

"Wholly independent individuals guided by a single purpose, remarkable," he murmured.

Tutunji thoughts, however, were centered on the terrible price humanity always paid to achieve the unity of tribal mind and purpose, evident in both its greatest achievements and most grievous barbarisms.

"What?" Sydes queried.

"Nothing … I just thought those strike craft looked pretty good coming in …"Tutunji replied.

"Yeah … well, I'm gonna suit up and lead those pilots in reconnoitering that beast's insides," Sydes said as he released the restraints on his console chair.

"I don't think that would be appropriate Captain Sydes," Commander Sadad responded over the conference comm.

"What the hell do you mean? I killed this bitch, the least you can do is let me conduct the postmortem," Sydes retorted.

Sorely tempted to verbally support Commander Sadad's position, Tutunji thought better of it. He'd let Sadad handle this one.

"You're absolutely right Captain Sydes. If anyone is entitled to lead this exploratory team, it's you. But, as before you're stuck with being the only pilot we have who can handle the Duo. If that alien mother ship has any surprises left in her, well, you can't fly the Duo from the hold of that wreck," Sadad responded.

"Son of a bitch! Damn it! I'm really fed up with this indispensable bullshit. You know I don't like to sit on the bench when the ball is still in play. So what am I supposed to do if this beast rises from the dead while our people are still in there? Blow it and them to hell?" Sydes snapped back.

"That is exactly what I will expect you to do Captain," Sadad replied solemnly.

"So what's gonna happen? Are you leading this hike Sadad? " Sydes asked as he coupled his restraints and leaned back in his console chair.

"No, that would be equally inappropriate. I'm personally responsible for over one hundred thousand people. As exciting as the prospect of seeing the workings of that ship sounds, I can't just walk away from my command responsibilities," Commander Sadad replied.

A smile of near paternal dimensions spread across Tutunji's face as he considered how much his erstwhile number two, Commander Sadad, had grown into the job.

Tutunji activated the console icon that shifted weapons control to Sydes' instrument panel and loosened his console chair restraints.

"Gentlemen, I believe that leaves me as the most expendable command officer," he interjected.

"That's a hell of way to put it," Sydes responded.

"But true nevertheless," Commander Tutunji replied.

Then, Tutunji climbed out of the console chair and, floating up to the catwalk, began to don his space gear.

"Sydes, it's nice to be indispensable, but like everything else in life it has its drawbacks. Besides, we need one old man to share the risk with all these hot shot strike craft kids," Tutunji said as now, fully suited up, he headed for the access hatch.

"Very well, all strike craft pilots evacuate your ships and join up with Commander Tutunji on the alien vessel. I want your helmet scanners activated as soon as you're out of those cockpits. We'll monitor from both the Duo II and the Duo," Commander Sadad announced.

"No disrespect intended Commander Sadad, but my group should go in with them," Von Strohheim said.

"The whole point of this expedition is to get you and your people in there to scavenge the alien technology. But, my job also includes making sure that you come out alive with what you find. I expect you and your technical team to monitor the transmissions from the expeditionary group's scanners as they go," Commander Sadad replied.

"They have the beacons, yes?" Von Strohheim inquired impatiently.

"You mean locater beacons?" Commander Sadad responded.

"Yes, I want them to place the beacons as markers where we see something interesting," Von Strohheim said.

There was an edge to the good Doctor's voice that was considerably more insistent than his customary detached scientific tone.

"Everyone copy that? Wherever Doctor Von Strohheim indicates, place locater beacons in areas he wants to investigate when he and his people get over there. Remember, securing that wreck is your primary task," Commander

THE DIARY

Sadad announced over the conference comm.

Sydes had long since passed envy on his menu of emotions as he adjusted the Duo's main screen. He carefully brought the tiny band of explorers swimming in space at the edge of the yawning mouth of the remnants of the aft section of the alien base ship into focus.

"OK, we're going in. All helmet and scanner lights on," Tutunji said.

As Sydes watched sixteen suited figures fire their suit jets and move into the alien hulk, he remembered the battle. Images of the multiple barrages of fusion missiles the Duo had launched against the alien vessel still replayed in his head. The last thing he wanted to add to those pictures were visions of the exploratory party fried by residuals of the Duo's victory.

"Watch the background radiation readings," Sydes warned.

"Looks tolerable and the space gear provides some protection, but I wouldn't want to take an extended vacation here," Tutunji responded.

Casting a wave in the direction of the Duo, Tutunji and his charges, lights and scanners active, disappeared into the darkness of the gaping wounds in the alien vessel.

Startling views of the alien ship's interior filled both the Duo and the Duo II's main screens. Sixteen separate images were blocked out across the screens, one from each scanner in the exploratory party. All of the views revealed various aspects of the incredible devastation within the wrecked vessel. Warped bulkheads and twisted shards of metal were visible in every direction. Even though scorched by the fires of multiple explosions, the walls and floors of the giant ship revealed the same red-orange tint her shields had once projected. Remnants of alien bodies were visible at every turn as the team moved through the wreckage. Even though most of the corpses had been reduced to pieces by explosive decompression or horribly burned, it was clear they had two arms and two legs like the species they had attempted to displace.

As he tracked the feed from the pilots' helmet scanners, Von Strohheim's attention was captured by one view that reflected a young Lieutenant's interest in a more or less intact alien body. Even in the uneven illumination of the helmet lights, the body had clear hominid characteristics. Von Strohheim guessed he was looking at a male of the species whose head seemed disproportionately large given the body's size. This impression was principally informed by the alien's massive lower jaw and brow ridges that protruded well beyond homo sapiens' norms. Although the creature's physiognomy appeared primitive by human standards, Von Strohheim reminded himself these invader's possessed the technology to destroy the Earth and very likely had mastered faster than light travel.

Leading the way, Tutunji was at the head of the group that was picking their way through a twisted labyrinth of passageways. Stopping abruptly, he focused his scanner on a small relatively intact form sprawled half way out of a side compartment. Another larger figure held the smaller one in an embrace that death had frozen into a tableau of futile protective sacrifice. Both figures were badly charred, but the significance of the two ashen forms clutching one another could not be dismissed.

"Damn, I didn't have to see this," Tutunji muttered.

"What?" Sydes asked.

"Nothing," Commander Tutunji replied.

Tutunji quickly shifted his scanner away from the horror of the last moments of what may well have been a mother and child forever joined in life's final chapter.

As the group moved forward, the passageway divided into three corridors. Tutunji proceeded along the main passage with three of the pilots and split the remaining personnel into two groups to investigate the side branches.

Lieutenant Ravich led the group that went to the left. Picking his way along the darkened and cluttered passageway, the Lieutenant was the first to come upon a large concave hemisphere of metal forming the end of the corridor.

"Very interesting, Lieutenant … Lieutenant?" Von Strohheim remarked as the hemisphere caught his attention.

"Lieutenant Ravich, Sir," the Lieutenant responded.

"I think this is a door, Lieutenant. The shape of the door suggests that it was designed to contain an explosion that might occur inside the chamber that lies beyond. Any detonation on the other side of such a hemispheric door would seal it even more tightly. This may be an armaments storage compartment. Is there anything that looks like a control panel on the bulkhead surfaces around the door?" Von Strohheim asked.

Ravich swept his gaze over the surrounding area with his helmet lights and scanner.

"None that I can see, Doctor Von Strohheim," Lieutenant Ravich replied.

"Excellent. Then this is a pivot door. Despite its size, the door should open very easily. Apply pressure to the right side of the door and step back," Von Strohheim instructed.

Despite the Lieutenant's doubt that the huge door could be opened with such minimal force, he did as Von Strohheim instructed. Ravich's gentle push against the lip of the huge hemisphere caused the right side to swivel inward, pivoting on an unseen center post set in the floor of the entry. His helmet lights revealed an immense room with mechanisms on waist high supports scattered all about. The compartment was so large the helmet lights of the team could not completely illuminate it.

His gaze fixed on the Duo II's viewer, Von Strohheim studied the images transmitted from the helmet scanners of the six members of the exploratory team as they swept over the cavernous room.

"Halt ... stehenbleiben, jah, jah ... stop there ... number three scanner, wie heisst er ... Lieutenant Olafson, yes, Lieutenant, please move closer to that large red cylinder on the supports to your left," Von Strohheim barked.

Moving to his left, Lieutenant Olafson played his scanner over the entire length of the large red cylinder.

"Place a beacon there. Someone take a reading. What is the background radiation in this compartment?" Von Strohheim asked.

"Place a beacon there. Someone, take a reading. What is the background radiation in this compartment?" Von Strohheim asked.

"It's forty percent higher than in the passageway, Doctor Von Strohheim," Lieutenant Ravich responded.

"Thank you gentlemen. Now, I suggest you proceed back to the main corridor with some haste. And seal the door to this compartment as you leave," Von Strohheim said, urgency in his tone.

Staring at the viewer, Von Strohheim watched carefully as the team exited the compartment. His gaze remained fixed on the image until the huge door pivoted to its closed position.

"I think this is an armaments machine shop. The size of the compartment suggests it may have served the needs of the entire fleet. The long red cylinder may have been one of the fusion loads used in their planet wrecker missiles. Examining this fabrication facility may help us to understand the self-propagating fusion reactions incorporated into their warheads," Von Strohheim said as he turned to Commander Sadad.

"Even if it served the whole fleet, still, that was an enormous amount of space. I mean we couldn't see where it ended," Commander Sadad said.

"I believe that this suggests, as we have suspected, that the fleet is self-sufficient. It may never have to return to its home port for resupply. What is of even greater concern is that so many of the components of the vessel we've seen thus far are so uniform and repetitive. Such perfect replication of bulkheads and fixtures may indicate some enormous ship building yard somewhere. There is perhaps a fully automated facility based on their home world that does nothing but stamp out whole fleets of vessels," Von Strohheim replied.

"So, you think there may be other whole fleets like this one roaming around out there?" Commander Sadad asked.

"I fear that this is likely," Von Strohheim replied.

"More ... whole fleets like this one ... maybe ... coming to finish the job," Sadad muttered under his breath.

"I doubt that we can anticipate another fleet arriving any time soon, Commander. It is more likely that fleets as enormous as this one are each assigned whole quadrants of the galaxy to conquer," Von Strohheim responded.

"I wonder what happens when one doesn't report in?" Sadad said.

"This is a troubling but good question, I ..." Von Strohheim replied.

Then, his eye caught by a flash of metal in one of the scanner frames, Von Strohheim quickly turned back to the viewer.

"Lieutenant Rommel, there at your feet to the right, something that shone silver in the light," Von Strohheim snapped.

Lieutenant Rommel picked up a slender silver baton with a black handle and held it in front of his scanner for Von Strohheim to examine.

"This, Herr Doctor Von Strohheim?" The Lieutenant replied.

"Jah, this is it. Are there any control features on the black handle?" Von Strohheim asked.

"Jawohl, Herr Doktor," Lieutenant Rommel replied.

"Please to hold it only by the handle. Extend it away from your body, point it at the bulkhead and then activate the control," Von Strohheim instructed.

"Of course, Herr Doktor," Lieutenant Rommel responded promptly.

The Lieutenant activated the handle control and a reddish-orange glow enveloped the silver shaft of the baton.

His fingers toying with his Phi Beta Kappa key, Von Strohheim studied the phenomenon for a moment.

"Please deactivate the device Lieutenant. You will be so kind as to bring this with you ... and thank you," Von Strohheim said.

"Of course, Herr Doctor Von Strohheim," Lieutenant Rommel replied as he slipped the baton into a loop in his space gear.

✦

"So, what is it?" Sadad asked as he turned to face Von Strohheim.

"Of this I cannot be certain but I believe it is an instrument for what is called ... wie sagt man ... das ... crowd control. The mechanism generates a force field not unlike their shields, but the harmonics of this field are very likely tuned to inflict pain," Von Strohheim replied.

"Must have been a tough ship to serve on," Sadad remarked.

"Yes, with what little we have witnessed of the aliens' philosophy of life, I would imagine that discipline was enforced exclusively through fear and violence. Such a system is effective and efficient, but inevitably self-destructive. Based on the individual's fears, each punishment becomes an object lesson to the group of the price paid for breaking the rules. It is this mindset that informed their destruction of the Martian colonies. Having witnessed a demonstration of their might, I think they expected us to surrender," Von Strohheim replied.

"And then what?" Sadad asked.

"The 'then what' would have been the systematic slaughter of humanity in a way that would have spared the Earth for them to colonize," Von Strohheim replied.

"How long have you known this?" Sadad queried.

"Known … not known, but I have suspected this since the obliteration of the Martian domes," Von Strohheim said.

"Well, regardless of the contradictions inherent to their social order, judging from our most recent experience, they do a lot of damage before they go under," Sadad retorted.

"This is unfortunately true," Von Strohheim responded, his tone somber.

"Doctor Von Strohheim, this is Lieutenant Botswala with team three. Can you see this?" The Lieutenant announced.

Indicating the section of the main viewer receiving feed from Lieutenant Botswala's team, Commander Sadad directed Von Strohheim's attention to the images transmitted by the team's scanners. The views illuminated by the team's bright helmet lights revealed line upon line of transparent cases three meters in height and one meter in breadth and depth. Each of the cases contained what was once a living being. In most of the cases, the beings appeared to have hominid characteristics, but there were wide differences in the physiognomy of the bodies. The display cases filled the room in row upon row of a gruesome collection that extended far beyond the illumination of the helmet lights.

"My God, they look like specimen cases," Commander Sadad said in a horrified tone.

"I believe you are precisely correct, Commander. Notice at the top of each case there is an insignia. The insignia remains the same for four cases in a row and then a new emblem appears. The bodies in the first two cases are always larger, and in next two much smaller," Von Strohheim remarked in a dark but matter of fact tone.

"No. Those bastards! They couldn't. Do you really think these are … are families?" Commander Sadad said, his voice filled with shock and pain.

"I fear so Commander. My guess would be that the aliens collected at least one family group from each planet they conquered and preserved them here.

Perhaps as trophies, perhaps for scientific study, this I do not know … and I am not sure that I want to know," Von Strohheim responded as he lowered his eyes from the viewer.

"Sir, the scanner readings suggest the cases are intact and are maintaining cryogenic interior environments," Botswala reported.

"Mein Gott! Then they are not trophies. These are living specimens frozen for later study, perhaps even for medical and genetic experimentation," Von Strohheim exclaimed.

"Those fucking, soulless bastards," Sydes interjected.

"Jah, that to be sure Captain Sydes. I have suspected this for some time, but now I am certain that this race is very methodical in everything they do. The repetitive elements in the ship's construction and, now, this chamber of horrors. Everything they do seems to point to a very orderly and systematic mindset. Having destroyed a whole race, they would want to preserve elements of the gene pool of the vanquished species … perhaps for use in research focused on enhancing their own genome," Von Strohheim replied.

"Enhancing their genome?" Commander Sadad said.

"Jah … the genetic dynamics of a species can best be understood in a genetically linked group, and so, they would want whole famlies," Von Strohheim remarked.

"That's why they wanted the children …" Commander Sadad murmured.

"Yes … the interaction of the parent's genetic material would be best understood by studying their offspring. Perhaps the aliens wanted to add the genetic endowments of vanquished races to their own … for reasons that are not immediately clear. Regardless of their intentions, it is clear that, in all they do, there is evidence of a methodical and orderly mindset," Von Strohheim said.

"Yeah Doc, and all that do it by the numbers bullshit is what got 'em burned out of the sky. Your little ball of fire just ate 'em alive by not playing according to their neat little set of rules," Sydes interjected.

"I suppose this is true. Guerrilla warfare was our only option given their superior technology and numbers. But look at all of these display cases, stretching far beyond what the helmet lights show us. The alien's strategy has obviously been a successful one. They must have obliterated hundreds of races and colonized as many worlds. And I fear that this battle group represents but one among many task force fleets this species has fielded to colonize the galaxy for their species," Von Strohheim replied.

"I bet there are some cases in here chilling down for us," Lieutenant Botswala remarked to one of his men.

"That's enough Lieutenant Botswala. We're here to do a security sweep.

Nothing in this compartment represents a threat," Commander Sadad declared.

Sadad knew all he wanted to know about the horrors the aliens could inflict. The deaths of nine billion on Earth were still fresh in his mind. The aliens' souvenir gallery would wait until Von Strohheim got the technology for which they had come.

"Mark the area with a beacon and then get your team the hell out of there," Sadad barked, summoning up his best command voice.

✲✲✲

Commander Tutunji and his group, working their way down the main corridor, busily cleared away shafts of twisted metal and threaded their way through bulkheads bowed out by detonations in the side compartments. Emerging from the tunnel of twisted metal into a relatively unscathed patch of corridor, the Commander could see light flooding through a large portal directly ahead.

"Teams two and three, follow us up the main corridor," he announced over the conference comm.

Clearly illuminated by intact lighting that seemed to emanate from the walls themselves, the next twenty paces of the corridor was clutter free. The walls, floor and ceiling were obviously made of more durable material than they had encountered earlier as hardly any interior damage was evident. Huge arches of metal were evident overhead and the wall panels were overlapped with massive metal supports and bracing.

Tutunji swept his scanner over the scene illuminated by the helmet lights of his team.

"See this Doc," Tutunji said.

"Yes, I see Commander. This is more structural support than we have seen anywhere else on the ship. It may have something to do with why this section of the vessel survived relatively undamaged," Von Strohheim replied.

"But why here, so deep in the ship's interior?" Tutunji queried.

"I think to protect her heart. See, look ahead there. Jah, wunderbar, der ist es!" Von Strohheim exclaimed.

At that moment, Tutunji's team emerged into a huge open compartment of the vessel. Extending horizontally for two hundred meters about midway between the upper and lower plates of the ship's hull was a glowing shaft of energy, the confining circumference of which was nearly transparent. The shaft of light, which was about ten meters in diameter, seemed to be pulsing with a restless energy along its entire length.

"This is the drive section ... und der drive. Mein Gott, this could only be the energy source for the faster than light engines. Gott in himmel, the power source, it appears still to be active,"Von Strohheim said, his words tumbling out.

"How can that be, Doc? Our scanners read a dead ship," Sydes broke in.

"The scanners cannot read a form of energy we have never seen before. Now Commander Sadad, this you cannot forbid, my team and I must go over there,"Von Strohheim responded excitedly.

"I see no reason ..." Commander Sadad began.

Von Strohheim abruptly leaned into the viewer, his gaze fixed on Tutunji's party,

"Touch nothing!"Von Strohheim shouted frantically over the comm link.

Spinning about, Von Strohheim turned to his coterie of engineers.

"This is jah wunderbar. I expected only to find the wreckage of their engines. This system ... she, she may still be operational."

"Operational?" Sydes interjected.

"Jah, it is possible that the light drive of the ship still works. I must get my space gear. Is there a shuttle ready? Touch nothing! We must go ... jetzt ... now, right now,"Von Strohheim replied.

"Everything is in order, Doctor. The gear is in the shuttle and the shuttle is waiting for you and your team in the receiving bay," Commander Sadad replied.

Then, an amused surprise painting his expression, Sadad watched as Von Strohheim and his team left the bridge at a dead run.

"I've never seen the Doc run before. He's not a bad sprinter," Sadad remarked with a slight chuckle.

Standing in awe of a shaft of energy that defied Einstein's speed of light constant, Tutunji marveled at the technology that allowed living beings to traverse the interstellar night. The glowing shaft of power terminated in a huge wedding cake configured structure rising over forty meters above the decking of the cavernous compartment. He imagined this structure might be the control console that harnessed and directed the restless energies confined within the glowing shaft. Controlled as it was behind the shields that contained it, the energy within the shaft seemed benign. At the same moment, he realized that, unleashed, it had driven the immense ship and its occupants over the barely comprehensible distances between the stars.

Surveying the immensity of the drive compartment, Tutunji was struck by the uniformity of the plating and the many other components that constituted it. He felt a mild shudder creeping its way up his spine. Without any way of proving it to anyone, he had to agree with Von Strohheim. This huge vessel had to be but one of many commissioned by some incredibly vast empire. Not unique, this colonizing juggernaut, and, very likely many like her, were committed to appropriating, or failing this option because of the technological prowess of the resident species, destroying all worlds suitable for life forms that might compete with their own. Even more horrifying was the obvious conclusion that humans and these as yet unnamed invaders were destined by virtue of similar physiology to be forever enemies of the blood in endless battles over habitable environments. He could clearly foresee centuries of unrelenting warfare over planetary bodies equally accommodating to both species.

Loud and lively conversation coming from Von Strohheim and his engineers as they made their way through the wreckage of the ship, intruded on Tutunji's black thoughts. They were making good time, he thought, and moving quickly through what his teams had already cautiously explored.

"Mein Gott, alles unbeschadigt ist. It is all in one piece still, undamaged!" Von Strohheim exuberantly exclaimed as he entered the drive compartment.

It was the glow of childlike enthusiasm in full bloom, Tutunji thought to himself as he saw the expression of exuberance on Von Strohheim's face.

Unceremoniously pushing his young engineers in front of him toward the pulsating shaft of energy, Von Strohheim was singularly focused on the beam of energy.

"Ion power source, enclosed within an electromagnetic bottle," he said excitedly.

Losing all patience with the pace his engineers were setting, he quickly detoured around his group of disciples. Von Strohheim was now nearly jogging toward the alien power plant while gesturing at the huge shaft of energy.

"Just as I imagined so many years ago. Und, this must be the control console." he exclaimed.

Without any warning, Von Strohheim and his disciples clambered up the tiers of the wedding cake structure at the head of the energy shaft.

"Be careful Doc! These bastards didn't exactly invite you for a tour of their engineering section. The damn thing could be booby trapped," Sydes cautioned over the comm link.

Oblivious to Sydes' warning, Von Strohheim and his crew achieved the top tier of what appeared to be the drive console. There, they were confronted with a seemingly endless array of raised icons on the control faces. Busily examining everything in detail, the small knot of Earth's engineering talent was suspended in a moment of scientific rapture. Their conversation now proceeded entirely in German and was therefore incomprehensible to the balance of the exploratory party.

Suddenly, something that looked suspiciously like an warning system activated. Lights flashed everywhere in the drive section while Von Strohheim and his engineering crew stood stock still staring at the console.

"Gott in himmel! We touched nothing!" Von Strohheim exclaimed.

"Maybe that's the problem. It may be a security clearance protocol. When you mount the control rostrum,

"So close ... almost within our grasp ... the whole galaxy open to us ..." Von Strohheim muttered, his face and voice falling simultaneously.

Tutunji was the first to notice it. He could feel a vibration emanating from the deck plates working its way bone by bone up his body. The pulsation was taking on a regular cadence and the lights in the engineering section were flashing in rhythm to the pulses he could feel traveling through his boots.

"Sydes is right. It's a countdown to detonation!" Tutunji shouted into the conference comm.

"Look!" Von Strohheim shouted as he pointed to the energy shaft.

The two hundred meter long shaft of energy had ceased its regular pulsations and begun to produce undulating waves of intensifying energy traversing its length from the control console to the terminus at the propulsion units. The whole vessel shuddered each time an energy wave met the regulators that interfaced between the column of energy and the thrusters.

"If this system overloads and detonates, it will wipe space clean for five million kilometers," Von Strohheim declared, his voice trembling.

"Sadad, get the Duo II out of here! We can't have these huns reaching out from the grave to finish the job of exterminating us," Tutunji shouted over the comm.

"Copy that. We're under way, but five million kilometers, I don't think we're gonna make it," Commander Sadad responded.

"Do what you can," Tutunji replied.

"I can swing around and fire on the thrusters. Maybe that will release the build up in the reactor column," Sydes broke in.

"Nein, no, no! That will detonate the the reactor prematurely," Von Strohheim shouted.

Watching the pulsating warning lights in the engineering section carefully, Tutunji knew the time for idle conversation was over. Both the intensity and frequency of flashes increased with alarming speed.

"Sydes, get the Duo out of here! The Duo II will need an armed escort wherever she goes. We're finished here," Tutunji snapped.

"Not a chance in hell," Sydes responded.

"Do it! You're all that's left to defend one hundred thousand people," Tutunji said.

"Fuck!" Sydes spat out.

Pivoting the Duo, Sydes spurred her to maximum acceleration and set a course to catch up with the dwindling dot of the Duo II.

Almost mesmerized by the warning lights that had reached near stroboscopic frequency, Von Strohheim decided some intervention was required.

"Gentlemen, we have nothing to lose at this point," he said.

Reaching down, he attempted to depress one of the raised icons on the control face before him. The icon could not be budged, nor could any of the others on the control face. They all appeared to be locked. Instantly, his engineers scattered about the panel's housing. Their investigations revealed no way into the seamless control console.

"It is all we can do and it is not enough," Von Strohheim said, his voice heavy with resignation.

All about him, the warning lights flashed so fast they now appeared to emit a steady glow. The deck plates shook with a vibration that felt like a constant drum roll on his feet. This was how it ended, Tutunji thought to himself. Even at this distance he could see Von Strohheim's expression of grim acceptance through his lighted face plate. The most Tutunji could hope for at this moment was that the Duo II and Sydes could clear the blast area in time.

Quite suddenly, almost as if some great switch had been thrown somewhere, the frenzy of the warning lights and the shuddering of the ship came to an abrupt halt. With the cessation of the ship's vibration, Tutunji felt a great quieting peace flow over him. Instantly, the fear induced stench permeating the recirculated air in his protective suit was transformed into the clean and fresh balm of a spring breeze. He felt his heart slow from its panicked beating and his breathing relax to an even and serene pace. The shaft of energy that was the ship's reactor resumed its slow and steady pulsation and a soft but brilliant light filled the immense engineering hold.

Suspended above Von Stohheim and his engineers on the control rostrum was a pillar of the purest white light Tutunji had ever seen. Within the pillar circulated sparkling tiny violet orbs whose motion seemed to mimic the action of a blood supply. It hung motionless about ten meters above the rostrum, and then, all within the hold felt a wave of overwhelming reassurance wash over them. In the peace following that wave, each man heard a quiet voice within. The voice spoke the same words to each, but to every man the words tolled in the language of his rearing.

FEAR NOT. THOUGH YOU ARE FEW,
MANY SHALL YOU BECOME. AS
ONCE YOU TROD UPON THE BREAST

OF YOUR MOTHER, NOW SHALL YOU
WAYFARERS BE AMONG THE LIGHTS
OF THE FIRMAMENT.

OF CONQUEST AND DEFEAT, YOU
SHALL, IN THE SIFTING OF TIME'S
SAND, EQUAL MEASURE RECEIVE.
YET, IN CONFLICT WITH MANY
WHOSE IMAGE REFLECTS NOT YOUR
OWN, SHALL KINSHIP'S KNOT BE
TIED. WHEN VICTORY'S SHALLOW
PROMISE GIVES WAY TO GRACE
IN SELFLESS UNITY WITH THOSE
NOT OF YOUR OWN TRIBE THEN
WILL PEACE BE VOUCHED SAFE
TO YOUR SEED.

THE GIFTS OF LIGHT'S FLIGHT ARE
YOURS SO THAT SOJOURNERS AMONG
THE EMBERS OF CREATION YOU MAY
BECOME. USE WISELY THAT WHICH,
WITHOUT PETITION, YOU HAVE BEEN
GRANTED. AS YOU HAVE RECEIVED,
SO GIVE.

THAT WHICH WAS YOUR BIRTHPLACE
IS NO MORE. ALL THAT IS THIS GALAXY
HAS BECOME YOUR LEGACY. LEARN
JUSTICE, PRACTICE HARMONY WITH
ALL THAT HAS LIFE, GROW IN WISDOM,
AND IN PEACE AND MERCY PROSPER.

Then, as suddenly as it had appeared, the pillar of light was gone. There were no voices on the conference comm for what seemed like an eternity. Tutunji's gaze still focused on the space above the heads of Von Strohheim's party where the pillar of light had appeared. He was certain of only three things, what he had seen, what he had heard, and that the self-destruct protocol had been terminated.

"What just happened?" Sydes called over the conference comm.

"I'm not entirely sure. But whatever it was makes us and those alien bastards look pretty damn insignificant,"Tutunji replied.

"I disagree. Whatever happened here today makes me feel that something or somebody thinks our fumble fingered species is worth saving," Commander Sadad retorted.

"Ich versteh es doch,"Von Strohheim interjected.

"English, Doc, English," Sydes responded.

"I understand the icons. I can read the control panel as though it were marked with German abbreviations. Here is the main release for the panel's icons and here is the static test controller for the reactor,"Von Strohheim said with mounting excitement.

"How in the hell is that possible?" Sydes asked.

"Nein, nicht, hell, es ist himmel geschenkt, jah, heaven sent. Mein opa, grandfather, always said every scientist is a child and a believer,"Von Strohheim replied reverently.

Your question … I don't know how I know, but … but … this is, jah, child's play,"Von Strohheim replied .

The elated engineer moved quickly down the length of the panel depressing first one and then another icon. Slowly, the pulsations in the huge column of energy increased in frequency and stabilized at the higher setting.

"Steady on Doc, you don't want that wreck to wake up and try to achieve light speed," Sydes said.

"Nein, no, of course not,"Von Strohheim replied.

Quickly adjusting the settings on the immense power plant, he brought it back to its ready operational status. Then, Von Strohheim stood back and stared at the console with a smile on his face that broadened to a nearly face splitting expanse of childhood pleasure.

"Do you grasp the significance of this moment, Captain Sydes? I can understand the alien language, just as if I had been reading it all my life. We have only to find their central computer, or perhaps even a library, and I can translate all of it. There will thousands … tens of thousands of years of scientific progress … ours … for the taking. This technology will open the galaxy to our exploration … and allow us to secure our people against any future alien attack."

"I mean, I know you're bright and all that, but how's it possible Doc?" Sydes asked.

"How is anything that's happened here in the last few minutes possible? The laws of physics, they are suspended. Cause and effect … she becomes poetry. There is light where no light can be and purpose speaks prophecy. For an explanation of this you need a holy man, not an engineer,"Von Strohheim replied.

"Suffer the little children ..." Sydes' muttered.

Nodding reflexively in response to Sydes' words, Tutunji said nothing. He had never imagined he would be in attendance when natural law as he understood it was transcended. This was the burning bush of the year three thousand and he was there. He had witnessed a force of nature in action, no, it was more than that ... it was *the force of nature*. Of all the wonders he had seen and heard in that moment, it was what he felt, the wave of reassurance, that was most significant and most personally compelling.

He would remember what had happened here the day the human race was redeemed and he would make certain that others remembered. It would become his personal mission to make certain that generations to come knew the human race was given a second chance in the belly of an alien ship bent upon their destruction. For those who had neither seen, heard, nor felt the singular presence emanating from the pillar of light suspended there in the ravaged hulk of an alien vessel, he would become the future's memory of this atoning moment.

Chapter 37

Perhaps it was the cool air wafting through the window or just a pleasant sense of business in his mind, but whatever the precipitating cause, Forrester was up early. He pulled on some clothes and made his way through the spacious interior of the house to the terrace of Esther and Jacob's home.

Softly illuminating the clouds, the lights in the dome of the ecosector were just beginning to glow, mimicking the rising sun. Although there was no single sun-like orb in the sky, the effect was nevertheless quite spectacular. What amounted to the artificial east of the sky was brightening and the intensity would grow as the light panels in the dome lit up in succession, progressing towards the west over the course of the day. The climate readout panel on the wall of the terrace indicated rain at two o'clock this afternoon and the clouds that would yield that precipitation were already forming high in the dome. The lush greenery of this ecosector needed watering and the streams that cut through the landscape had to be kept brimming.

Servicing his need for the first dose of caffeine of the day, the transubstantiator rendered up a tall glass mug of the steaming brew. Forrester leaned back in his chair, gazed at the sky and sipped his orange cappuccino. For a brief moment, he could imagine himself back on an Earth that no longer existed. Feeling a cool breeze on his face and saturated by the comforting bouquet of the trees and grasses in the surrounding landscape, he was seduced by the illusion.

Phil had done a magnificent job. Even the birds and insects approved as they busily went about their daily tasks, seemingly oblivious to their transplantation. The ecosector was so well designed that it was difficult to imagine that it rested deep within a huge metal ball hanging in the freezing vacuum of space. Although he knew it to be true, Forrester had difficultly accommodating himself to the stark reality of the Earth's utter destruction. It was particularly difficult to make that fact real to his awareness, tucked away, as he was within this idyllic botanical envelope. The contrast between the security of the ark, the beauty that surrounded him, and the unimpeachable specter of the death of the world set a new course for his thoughts.

Somehow, his selection for life in the face of a holocaust that dwarfed anything in human history was unsettling. There was no charitable way to evaluate the fact that he was alive from the perspective of the billions of decent human beings who were ashes. Even passing consideration of the prospect made him feel shabby and grasping. Issues of cosmic consummation be damned, he was alive, and billions were dead, and there was no way to skirt that horrific fact. If there were a level playing field somewhere in this grand design, he sure as hell couldn't see it. A word he had committed to memory decades ago sprang to mind, daseinsberechtigung. A real German mouthful. Simply translated it meant, justification for living. Well, he just couldn't get the scales to balance, his life in one pan and nine billion in the other.

⚜

Sitting back in his mind, he felt the mental quill in hand and saw his head journal opening. As Forrester observed this exercise in self flagellation, he attempted to balance it against the hopeful insight he had experienced among the meek. In the wings, yet another mental homunculus in this crowded cognitive venue functioned as spectator to both perspectives. If he were to acknowledge Esther's evaluation of his functioning, then it was this capacity for a three party exchange in his head that, in part, accounted for his ability to function as eye to the community. It was hard to believe that this committee of divergent perspectives was anything more than a source of troubling ambivalence.

Facing straight on into a cognitive corner in his mind, he saw no way to rationally turn around and walk out. Reconciling the issue of his life, the life of the meek, and a handful in the Earth Defense Force against nine billion didn't work. No matter how he juggled it, dead was dead. Then, in the midst of his obsessive crisis, he saw himself scrabbling against the walls of a dark corner in his mind and watched as a luminous hand reached into the theater of his mind and gently turned him toward a warm and beckoning glow. In a curiously familiar way, he knew what was coming. Having dead ended himself, a bail out was in the offing. However, this was not one over which he had any control. Then, as they had so many times in the past, the words of the diarist flowed through his mind.

> NO TILLER OF THE EARTH COUNTS HIS
> SEEDS IN THE DARKNESS, LEST, FALLING
> INTO THE SHADOWS, THEY ARE LOST TO
> THE PROMISE OF THE LIGHT. RATHER
> HE GAZES UPON EACH KERNEL IN FULL
> ILLUMINATION AND JUDGES HOW MUCH
> FRUIT IT WILL BRING FORTH.

THE LIFE OF THE CORN IS IN THE LIGHT,
BOTH IN ITS COUNTING AND ITS
INCREASE. THE DARK OF THE EARTH IS
BUT A BRIEF RESPITE FOR THAT WHICH
MUST GROW INTO THE LIGHT.

LOCKED IN THE KERNEL IS A MEMORY
OF THE LIGHT AND, SPROUTING, IT STRAINS
TOWARD THAT WHICH IT RECALLS. TWISTING
WITHIN DARK MATTER'S GRASP, EACH
SEEDLING OF LIGHT'S FULLNESS STRUGGLES
IN ANGUISH AGAINST THE HARD EDGES OF
ITS CONFINEMENT. YET EVEN WHEN
WEDGED IN THE DARKEST CREVICE, ALWAYS,
LIFE REACHES TOWARD AN ILLUMINATION
GLOWING ONLY IN MEMORY'S FAINT HOPE.

CRAFTED AT THE BEGINNING BY THE
LIGHT, DARK MATTER'S IMPERMANENCE
IS VOUCHSAFED AS BUT A BRIEF
SHADOW IN THE SOJOURN FROM LIGHT
TO LIGHT. CRUDE MATTTER'S CREATION,
FROM THE TINIEST MOTE TO THE GREATEST
STAR, EVER DYING AND REBORN, TURNS
LIKE A WHEEL WHOSE HUB, LIFE, IS THAT
WHICH REMAINS FOREVER ITS
STEADFAST ANCHOR AND GUIDE.

Simple and clarifying, the words evoked another perspective. His doubts, confusion and despair were those of an untutored farmer counting his seeds in an unlighted hut. Life was not a means to an end, it was an end in itself. Neither the means, nor the ends of life could be realized in the darkness of matter, but only in the loom's light from which it came and to which it must return. Despite its occasional moments of joy, life in the material universe was nothing more than a brief vacation in a bog of darkness. So, why bother with a marshy cruise through the moor of a material universe so consistently fraught with fear, rage and pain? Forrester immediately recognized this as a pivotal question to which he had no elegantly simple answer. Then, into his wilderness of doubt came the diarist's words. A particle of illumination never inscribed in the scrolls, but echoing insistently now in his thoughts, came in the form of an answer he had not anticipated.

> A TAPER BURNING IN THE NOONDAY
> BRIGHTNESS CASTS NO SHADOW, NOR
> CAN ITS POWER TO ILLUMINATE THE
> DARKNESS BE KNOWN, SAVE IT BE
> THRUST INTO THE WOEFUL GLOOM
> OF A MOONLESS NIGHT.
>
> TO RECOGNIZE ITS RADIANCE, EACH
> OF LIFE'S EMBERS MUST JOURNEY IN
> THE DARKNESS. ABIDING ALWAYS
> WITHIN THE WOMB OF CREATION'S
> FIRES, NO SPARK CAN KNOW ITS
> TRUE NATURE.
>
> THE SPARK OF LIFE HOLDS ITS OWN
> BRILLIANCE DEAR ONLY WHEN
> SWALLOWED BY A DARKNESS THAT
> THREATENS TO QUENCH THAT FIRE.
>
> ALL SEPARATE, THE LIGHTS OF LIFE
> JOURNEY WITHIN THE DUSK OF
> MATTER. EACH A SINGLE BEAM,
> YET ALL SUSTAINED BY HOPEFUL
> MEMORY OF THE FIRES THAT
> KINDLED THEM, THEY TURN
> EVER TOWARD REUNION WITH
> THE GLOW OF ALL BEGINNING'S
> TO WHICH ALL LIGHT MUST
> NEEDS RETURN.
>
> UNSEEN, YET EVER WITHIN AND
> SURROUNDING EACH EMBER FROM
> THE BURST OF LIFE THAT WAS THE
> BEGINNING, I AM THE WIND THAT
> DRIVING THE STARS EVER OUTWARD,
> FANS YOUR SPARK IN THE DARKNESS.

A FAITHFUL GUIDE AND COMPANION
IN EVERY PLACE AND AT THE SAME
MOMENT, I LIVE IN EVERY MOTE OF
LIFE'S MARROW AND AM ALL LIFE
SUMMED TOGETHER.

So the doctrine of recognition by contrast was not simply a function of human perceptual-cognitive idiosyncrasy. The diarist's dimension also included, as part of its heuristic menu, the validating experience of life within a tension of opposites. Everything, Yin and Yang, synthesis and antithesis was in part defined by its contrary. The revelation implicit to these words was that the opposite of life and light was not death, but darkness, or more simply put, the absence of light. Death as mankind knew it didn't enter into the equation, representing as it did only a passing illusion.

Overtaken in that moment by a sense of his own frailty, Forrester was embarrassed by the sticky web of doubt in which his mind had become entangled. He was the spider in the shrunken web of his own life busily spinning shortsighted silk into a snarl of utter incompetence. How frail we are, he thought, how easily adversity collapses us into ourselves. Like an amnesic seed, he had forgotten from whence he had come and whither he was destined to go. Then, as if in answer to a question as yet unasked, the words of the diarist suffused his consciousness.

THAT WHICH OPENS AND AWAKENS THE HEART
TO THE LIGHT OF CREATION, ALSO DRIVES THE
WHOLE OF THE UNIVERSE TO ITS SHINNING
FULFILLMENT. IN ONE LIFE IS ALL AND ALL
MAKE THE MEASURE AND FULFILLMENT OF
CREATION.

WISDOM, FLOWS NOT, FROM THE REFINED
MEASURES OF THE MIND, BUT FROM THE SPIRIT
THAT INSPIRES THOSE SMALL AND FALTERING
STEPS TOWARD THE TRUTH IN WHICH ALL THE
AWAKENING EMBERS OF LIFE PARTAKE.

IN MAN'S HEART ARE BOTH THE PRINCE OF
DARKNESS AND THE PRINCE OF PEACE
CONTAINED. THE BATTLE FOR ALL CREATION'S
CULMINATION IS WITHIN, NOT WITHOUT.

BE OF GOOD CHEER, FOR TO LOVE LIFE IS TO
JOIN IN THE CREATION OF THE UNIVERSE.

IN THIS END OF TIMES AND NEW BEGINNINGS, I
WILL SHARE WITH ALL WHO CAN HEAR, THE
MYSTERY OF CREATION. IT IS LOVE, GIVEN FREELY
AND WITHOUT PRICE, THAT DRIVES CREATION
TOWARD THE LIGHT OF FULFILLMENT FOR ALL
WHO HAVE RECEIVED THE GREATEST GIFT THE
UNIVERSE MAY OFFER, LIFE.

IN THAT FINAL MOMENT OF CONSUMMATION,
ALL WHICH LIVES, LOWLY AND KNOWING
WILL BE GATHERED TOGETHER AND SHARING
THEIR GIFTS WILL BECOME MORE THAN ALL
THEIR PARTS.

IN THIS GREAT BECOMING, ALL DARK
MATTER IS CONSUMED AND ONLY
LIGHT, LIFE, REMAIN.

IN LOVE THERE IS LIFE AND IN LIFE IS THE
CONSUMMATION OF THAT FOR WHICH
PURPOSE IS THE UNIVERSE CREATED
FULFILLED

Then, slowly, the world of the ark and Esther's face, which was fully embracing an expression of querulous concern, came into focus.

<hr/>

"Without this doubting, you are neither the eye of the community nor him who is both student and teacher for us all. You stand within and cannot escape the layers of feeling and thinking that evolution, over endless millennia, has used to mold the mind of man. To see and feel this, without setting any part of it aside, is to become the portal through which the meek may enter and gather in your mind. Of one mind with the meek, you also stand between that which was and that which will become humankind," Esther said, her voice containing no hint of condemnation.

"There is so much weakness and pain in that place," Forrester replied quietly.

"To be of the people of the trees is to know pain. Although of the light, we dwell in the darkness with our stronger brethren who are not of the community of the meek. As one of us, you share in the blind agony of the darkness but know that matter's very gloom reminds us that our work is here. Be content, the congregation of the meek is always within and about you even in those dark places where wends the map of space-time," Esther replied, matching his quiet tones.

Pain and confusion, yes, certainly that, Forrester thought, but not isolation. The ferocious reality of the physical universe could not be dismissed with a good thought, but seeing it as a part of something more fulfilling helped. The meek were the incarnation of a quiet conviction in beneficial outcomes for all life. As the eye of that community, Forrester's job was to make sure that their faith was not blind.

Hearing a slight shuffling noise over his shoulder, Forrester turned in his chair. There, entering the terrace, were Jacob and Crystal each carrying platters laden with the makings of a hearty breakfast.

"Good morning Doctor Forrester. We've brought breakfast," Crystal said cheerily.

"And more cappuccino," Jacob added as he set the tray on the table.

"We wanted to hear the news," Crystal said anticipation sounding in her voice.

"News?" Forrester asked.

"News about the others, what happened to them," Crystal replied as she snatched a waffle off the tray.

Then it struck him, Crystal was, in a very nice way simply asking him to do his job as the eye of the meek. In a moment of near panic, Forrester wasn't sure how to make it happen. In the past, a question put to him had automatically triggered an instance of *seeing*. Now, nothing was happening. Then, ever so quietly, the means came to him in the form of two interactions he had had with his new family over time. He remembered the question he had put to Crystal at the reserve during his first introduction to *seeing*: The 'I' that is separate and alone must go away so that you can see the NOW? The affirmative answer he received from Crystal seemed to suggest his current course of action. The particulars necessary to initiate the vision had been provided by Esther in her simple statement: Just think 'All'.

Leaning back in his chair, Forrester closed his eyes and visualized the night sky. Then, removing the stars from the image, he allowed himself to disappear into the void already visualized and thought 'All.' Almost instantly he felt an energy building within his body that came to rest in a 'Y' shaped focus in the center of his forehead and he *saw*.

Before him lay a scene of great devastation. The ships of the alien fleet had been torn to pieces and their dead crews were scattered amidst the wreckage. Tiny lights illuminating their way, the remnants of humanity now possessed the great ship of the alien armada. Their explorations triggering a holocaust, the strong, brethren of the meek stood but moments from their final extinction. In the midst of their desperation, the diarist appeared, a blazing pillar of light redeeming the strong of his creation and provisioning their separate path. Then, the vision faded.

Opening his eyes to the smiling faces of Esther, Jacob and Crystal, Forrester felt no personal energy drain. The events he had seen were a fait accompli having occurred in the continuing present of the Now.

"The strong branch of the tree of humanity is preserved as was promised," Jacob said.

"Many are lost, but that which is now two human branches of the same tree, the meek and the strong are saved," Esther added.

"A visitor," Crystal said, without glancing up from her plate of waffles swimming in butter and syrup.

Experiencing no need to turn around in his chair anymore than Crystal had to look up from her plate, Forrester knew that Chauvez was coming up the hill.

"Good morning Doctor Forrester. What a beautiful day you're having down here. Phil was one hell of a craftsman," Chauvez said as he mounted the terrace.

"Indeed, he was ... and a landscape artist of the first water. He shall be missed," Forrester replied.

"Phil ... I wish he could have seen all this. He was so invested in making this all work for you and your people," Chauvez remarked, a note of sadness in his voice.

Unexpectedly, Forrester felt Crystal's eyes on his back. Turning about, he looked into her eyes and heard her voice in his head. Snatching a napkin off the table he hastily wrote down the coordinates that Crystal's voice dictated.

"Yes and Phil's last gift to all of us is needs to be collected," Forrester said.

"What's that?" Chauvez asked.

"Phil promised to save Cabot's computer ... and somehow he managed it," Forrester replied.

"I'm afraid that was destroyed when Cabot's yacht went up. An incalculable loss … it contained the sum of human knowledge and history," Chauvez said.

"I think you'll find it's perfectly safe in a well shielded section among the debris at these coordinates," Forrester said as he held up the napkin.

Pausing a moment as if lost in thought, Chauvez nodded. Appearing to compose himself, he sat down at the terrace table and accepted the napkin Forrester passed to him.

" I'll certainly check this out when I get topside. You know, I told you I'd be back when I had more questions. Well, here I am," Chauvez remarked.

"What's on the agenda?" Forrester asked.

"Dvorak is up there on the bridge losing his empirical mind. The computers have been running nonstop for the past two hours and were still churning out data when I left the bridge. It's an endless feed of equations and technical schematics that Dvorak believes represent the recipe for a faster than light propulsion system. To say that he's excited has got to represent the understatement of the century," Chauvez said.

"It's a gift," Crystal remarked as she pushed aside her plate.

"A what? What did she say?" Chauvez asked leaning forward in his chair.

"A gift," Forrester replied.

"I don't know what that means, but I'm telling you, Dvorak is getting fringy. Ever since the data started rolling in, he has been trying to find a transmission source for the feed that's driving the computers," Chauvez continued.

A smile tracing its way across his face, Forrester reached across the table and placed his hand on top of the ark's Captain's. Forrester felt the now familiar flow of energy, beginning in his head, course throughout his body.

"He won't find it," Forrester said.

"You know, my gut level reaction is to believe that," Chauvez replied as he politely withdrew his hand, looked at it curiously, and smiled.

Returning his smile, Esther refilled Chauvez's cup.

"Now, where was I? Ah yes, when I left the bridge Dvorak was shouting something like, it's coming from everywhere in general and no place in particular. You ought to see him. He's running around activating every tracer circuit on the console and driving the technical supervisors to distraction," Chauvez said.

Smiling, Forrester knew this was a first. He had just done for Chauvez what Crystal's touch had done for him on so many previous occasions. He had passed along a tiny particle of illumination to one who was prepared to receive it. It wasn't necessary to look at Crystal, Esther and Jacob, he could feel the smiles on their faces. The meek grasped what was happening. The diarist was parceling out the means to travel the universe evenhandedly to the two, now fully divergent, branches of humanity.

"I suspect that 'everywhere and no place in particular' is the best description anyone is going to come up with," Forrester responded.

"You want to know what the real kicker is? The feed is coming through the computers in English. I mean the whole thing has already passed beyond the pale for me, but Dvorak is still trying to make linear sense of it," Chauvez said, a knowing smile growing on his face.

Studying Chauvez's face carefully, Forrester knew that before him sat a man who was prepared to simply accept what he couldn't understand in terms of his own narrow view of reality. He would be an interesting companion in the years to come.

"So, are we to give credence to the technical feed that's filling the memory banks up there?" Chauvez asked.

"Yes. In time this propulsion system will become part of the ark," Forrester replied.

"Ah hell, I won't tell Dvorak that, it'll drive him over the edge. How's about I say that it's something we can verify technically?" Chauvez responded.

"That sounds good. I suspect he can get behind that kind of challenge," Forrester replied.

"You know Doc, that's a good idea. A challenge, yeah, once the data feed stops, we can take the stuff we've received and create an engineering modeling program in the computer. Then, I guess, we'll just plug in what we've got and see if it works. Oh, and I'll check out these coordinates as well," Chauvez said as he held up the napkin.

"That would certainly go a long way toward Dvorak regaining his empirical sanity," Forrester remarked, a slight trace of a smile on his face.

"Oh damn, I almost forgot. There's someone trying to contact you. The signal sort of fades in and out, but I can pipe it down here and boost the power when I get back up to the bridge," Chauvez said.

"I'd appreciate that," Forrester replied.

Setting down his cup, Chauvez rose from the table, turned and walked down the knoll, pausing only briefly to turn and wave goodbye as he disappeared below the crest of the small hill.

"I'd like to see the stars of home before we leave," Crystal said as she stood up.

"I think that can be arranged," Jacob replied as he rose from the table.

Somewhat mystified for a moment, Forrester watched the family move as a unit toward the living room. Grabbing his mug of coffee, he got up from the table and followed Jacob, Esther and Crystal into the house. As he entered the living room, Jacob was already activating the holographic projector and tying it into the ark's external viewers. Esther was moving furniture away from the center of the room and Forrester pitched in and helped her with the job. Then, he took a seat around the large circular expanse of the now uncluttered center of the living room with Crystal's statement still ringing in his head, '... before we leave.'

With unerring accuracy, Crystal stood in the exact center of the open space created in the living room when the hologram snapped to life. There she stood among the stars of the milky way, smiling and pointing to first one and then another part of the galaxy as seen from the ark's perspective. The moment seemed right somehow to Forrester, here was a child of the humanity's future at home amongst the stars. It was almost as if Crystal were creating a memory to carry with her into a future in some faraway place. What faraway place, Forrester wondered. If he was supposed to be the eye of the meek, why didn't he know, and if she did what did that make Crystal?

Father and daughter were actively engaged in naming stars and constellations when the vidscreen in the adjoining room began to chime. Coming rapidly to her feet, Esther walked quickly toward the sound.

"It's for you Doctor Forrester," she said upon her return.

Leaving his seat, Forrester walked carefully around the Milky Way and toward the vidscreen. As he sat down before the holographic transceiver, he saw Arthur's face, wreathed in smiles, filling the monitor.

"Damn Nate, it's good to see you. I thought I'd catch you up on the news. We lost the planet, but we've won the war, and from what I hear, we got a hell of a lot of new technology in the bargain. So how's by you?" Arthur said with no small amount of exuberance.

"It's good to hear from you Arthur. Thanks to you, I'm here on the ark with the people from the reserve. I'm so glad to hear you're safe as well," Forrester responded.

"What's left of us are going back to Von Strohheim's Mars base where that crafty old kraut is gonna build us a ship that can travel faster than the speed of light. Can you imagine that? Hell, we can travel all over the galaxy looking for another Earth or maybe a bunch of them, who knows," Arthur said.

"That sounds exciting Arthur," Forrester responded.

"So what are all you little Buddhas doing over there?" Arthur asked.

"Pretty much what you'd expect, sitting around waiting for enlightenment," Forrester responded, suppressing a slight chuckle.

Quite abruptly, Arthur's effervescent mood turned serious and his face assumed a somber cast.

"I'm not gonna see you again am I Nate?" He asked in a rhetorical tone.

Forrester felt the full stinging sensation in his nose that heralds the onset of tears. Holding back the avalanche of emotion, Forrester tried to respond.

"No Arthur, I ... don't think so. Arthur, you saved my life more than once and ... you're the best friend, I've ever had .... I ..."

"Hey, hey, Nate, calm down," Arthur quickly responded.

Quickly donning his best stoical expression, Forrester composed himself.

"Look, I'm not gonna do melodrama and I won't allow you do some kind of half-assed eulogy over our friendship. I didn't call to say anything in particular, except goodbye. If there were more time, there are some smart ass things I've said that I'd like to take back, but hell that's old business. You're doing what you're supposed to do and me, well, as usual, I'm just doing. Hell, if all that mystical, transcendental crap you're always talking about is true, we're bound to meet up again somewhere. The universe is a big place, but I've got the feeling it funnels down to a real comfy little spot somewhere down the line. If I get there before you, I'll ice up a good German white wine for you."

"Thanks, and I expect you're right Arthur," Forrester replied.

The two old friends stared at one another over the vast expanse of space for a long moment. Each silently recognized that at some unspoken level of awareness their life paths were diverging both cosmically and personally. Arthur broke the silence.

"Well old buddy, gotta go. Lots of things to do. Hell, I'm military now, a fucking Commandant at that. No rest for the wicked. See you Nate ... and Nate, wherever you're going, well ... good luck."

Before he could respond, the vidscreen went blank. Forrester continued to sit before it for a moment as the image of the dig in the desert, so many years ago, refused to budge from center stage in his mind. Whether he or Arthur knew it at the time, that find signaled the beginning of their paths' insidious divergence.

"Goodbye old friend," he said, placing his hand on the screen.

Lost in remembrance for a long time, his head was full of more than thirty years of sounds and images. Always at center stage in this nostalgic review were he and Arthur working together through the best and the worst of it. It was one thing to recognize the evolutionary expediency of dividing the human race into two branches with very different destinies, it was quite another to see that partition run down the middle of the only real friendship Forrester had ever experienced.

After hours of high speed transmission, the data flow into the computer's memory banks had finally terminated. Chauvez busily helped Dvorak create an interface to integrate the new data set into the engineering modeling function of the main computer.

"I still don't like the idea of feeding this data into the modeler when we don't know where it comes from. The whole business is too hocus pocus for my taste," Dvorak said suspiciously.

"The computer modeler has its own built in safeguards. The data set and schematics either hang together and show us a workable propulsion system or they don't. What could be simpler?" Chauvez replied.

"I'll be honest with you Chauvez," Dvorak said. "I'm more worried about the possibility that the damn thing works than I am about the modeler spitting it out as nonsense. I've never liked reaching a goal without knowing how I got there."

"I know what you mean. But I have it on good authority that it's gonna work," Chauvez replied as a smile traced its way about the corners of his mouth.

"Ah, shit … you've been consulting with the fortune tellers down in the hold again, haven't you?" Dvorak spat back.

"Yep. By the way, the modeler is ready to go. Do you want to push the button or shall I?" Chauvez asked.

"Hell, let's not make a ceremony out of it," Dvorak said as he activated the unit.

The big screen of the computer modeler sprang to life in a blur of equations and schematics. Within seconds, the unit generated a succession of orderly construction and flow diagrams illustrating the operation of the propulsion unit.

"Holy mother of … the damn thing works. Look at that, according to these readouts, once you achieve twice the speed of light, there's no limit to how fast you can go. It's just a matter of how much power you can generate. Pretty simple really, once you see it, but it never would have occurred to me to go at the problem this way … never in a million years!" Dvorak exclaimed.

"I've been waiting for this all day, Dvorak. Now, tell me again about the fortune tellers down in the hold," Chauvez said, his smile broadening.

"Screw you!" Dvorak replied with no small amount of emphasis.

Now, with renewed resolve, Chauvez was intent on shoving the clear evidence supplied by the computer modeler down Dvorak's throat.

"Has it ever occurred to you that all that mystical, magical hocus pocus might just be another route to the same destination, namely, knowing how things work? For a man of science, you've got a bad case of hardening of the categories."

"Yeah right," Dvorak said sullenly.

"Shit man, one of your heroes, Einstein, was practically a mystic in his personal life. Look at the history of science, our understanding of nature always starts out simple, then gets complex and then progresses to a new level of simplicity. Did it ever fucking occur to you that there may be a whole different way of perceiving the universe that represents a legitimate shortcut to our empirical muddling? Maybe there's a way of seeing and doing things that looks mystical to us just because we just don't have the biological equipment to see it as anything but spiritual hocus pocus?" Chauvez said.

"All right, enough with the spiritual already, I get the point. My head may be full of physics, engineering schematics and circuits, but my mother told me when I was just a kid that I had a soul and my mother never lied," Dvorak replied in exasperation.

Then, Dvorak turned about and, gazing fondly at it, he patted the housing of the computer modeler with almost loving tenderness.

"Besides, whatever the source of the input, the damn propulsion system works and opens the way for an altogether different sort of future for the human race," Dvorak said quietly.

"Oh, just one more thing," Chauvez said.

"What now?" Dvorak asked.

"Here are the coordinates for Cabot's super computer," Chauvez said as he handed Dvorak the napkin.

"The one that was destroyed when the yacht blew up? And I guess I'm supposed to believe the coordinates are scribbled on this napkin?" Dvorak asked.

"Yep," Chauvez replied.

"Don't tell me ... you got this from the mystics down below," Dvorak said. Chauvez smiled.

⋆⊰◆⊱⋆

Still reeling from the loss of his friend, Forrester made his way back to the living room where Esther, Jacob and Crystal continued engrossed in the hologram of the milky way.

"We are sorry for your loss, but your friend was right. You are not forever separated from one another," Esther said as Forrester sat down beside her.

Crystal, playing happily among the holographic stars, suddenly stopped and turning about looked directly at Forrester.

"It's time for you to go," she said emphatically.

Not even a shadow of uncertainty lurked in Forrester's mind as he stood up. Growing in his mind with each passing second was the gathering presence of the people of the trees. Leaving the terrace, he walked down the knoll toward the tube that would carry him to the ark's central control compartment. There on the bridge, he would fulfill yet another aspect of his role among the meek, envoy to the strong.

In a relatively brief period of time, the tube would bring Forrester to the bridge. The time of transit was filled with visions of what was to come and the small role he had to play in it. As the tube doors opened and he entered the command compartment, Chauvez, Dvorak, and a bevy of technical supervisors were huddled around the computer modeler engaged in a lively discussion.

Knowing generally what was going to happen, Forrester didn't have the first idea of exactly what he was going to say to this band of technical talent that would help them make sense of it. Dvorak solved the problem by being the first to notice Forrester's presence on the bridge.

"Doctor Forrester, are you and your people responsible for this mathematical wizardry?" Dvorak asked as he pointed to the computer modeler.

"It is not our creation … but it is here because we are here," Forrester replied.

"I don't know what the hell that means. But there it is, the key to exploring the universe, and it works," Dvorak said as he gestured again to the computer modeler.

Having studied Forrester's face intently since he entered the bridge, Chauvez leaned back against the console. An expression indicating a new awareness had been awakened by Forrester's touch showing on Chauvez's face, he caught Forrester's eye.

"You're here for a reason, aren't you Doctor Forrester?"

Swallowing hard, Forrester tried to gather his thoughts. Then, quite unexpectedly, it all seemed rather simple.

"In a few moments something rather extraordinary is going to happen. I am here to, as best I can, help you feel comfortable with what will transpire."

"Well, after getting a faster than light propulsion engine as an anonymous E-mail, I may be a little hard to shock," Dvorak remarked.

"That's good. In a matter of moments, the ark will begin her maiden voyage," Forrester responded.

Looking a bit askance at Forrester, Dvorak, after a moment's consideration, turned to the console and began to activate some of the controls.

"In that case, I suppose I'd better bring the engines to ready status," Dvorak cast over his shoulder.

"That won't be necessary," Forrester responded quietly.

"Well, the ship's not going to move without them, that's for sure. With all respect Doctor, I think you'd better stick to psychology and let engineers deal with what makes things go," Dvorak responded.

"Where are we going Doctor Forrester?" Chauvez asked, interrupting Dvorak.

"I only know we will be leaving this galaxy," Forrester replied.

"The galaxy!" Dvorak exclaimed.

"I had a feeling it would be something like that," Chauvez said.

Then, with a quiet smile and nod of his head, Chauvez turned about and faced the ark's huge main viewer expectantly.

"What is this, the ship of fools? It would take us years even at light speed to reach the nearest star cluster in this galaxy, much less the millennia a voyage to another galaxy would require. This has gone beyond crazy," Dvorak said as he looked squarely at Forrester.

Light filling every corner of his mind, Forrester felt the energy of the community of the meek building within him. Yet completely overshadowing the rising tide of the meeks' corporate cognitive input was a power and an illumination beyond the capacity of any concept to encompass.

Transfixed before the main viewer, Chauvez called to Dvorak.

"Dvorak, come here. If you think what Forrester said is crazy, then this will blow your tight little mind."

Joining Chauvez and Dvorak at the main viewer, Forrester saw what he knew he must. However, he instantly recognized that the real time reality surpassed any and all visionary expectations. There, on the screen silhouetted against the darkness of the void, stood the diarist. A pillar of perfect white light, tiny orbs of violet circulated through its height and breadth like so many corpuscles enlivening a spectral bloodstream.

"Holy ..." Dvorak exclaimed.

"Exactly," Chauvez replied.

As eye of the people of the trees, Forrester concomitantly absorbed and transmitted the incredible vista portrayed on the viewer before him. The brilliant white light of the diarist expanded from a solitary form into an envelope that wholly encompassed the immense expanse of the ark. A shimmering cloud of luminescence filled with violet corpuscles dancing all about the ark seemed to buoy the vessel up and above the mundane space in which it swam. Then, slowly at first, the ship began to move. Its speed increasing exponentially, the ark left lunar orbit in seconds and the solar system in even less time. The speed of the vessel constantly increased and the stars elongated into streaks of light through the viewer as the ship moved ever faster.

Dvorak tore his attention from the viewer long enough to look at the velocity indicator on the console.

"It's off the scale," he said.

He immediately busied himself inputting a continuous calculation program to extend the velocity indicator's range of registration.

Unflinchingly, Forrester stared at the viewer. His mind was alive with the hope and an overwhelming sense of fulfillment flowing from the corporate presence of the meek in the hold below. His role, as theirs, was to stand as witnesses to this miracle. Transfixed by wonder, he watched as the fiery light of the Milky Way's billions of suns was left behind. The ark, aglow with the light of life, plunged with constantly increasing speed into the vast emptiness of intergalactic space.

Dvorak, his face drained of color, looked up from the command console.

"The computer says were moving at one thousand times the speed of light and accelerating. I've checked the program three times, based on everything I been taught, we should have reached infinite mass some time ago."

"Let it go," Chauvez said as he smiled calmly at Dvorak.

Leaving the viewer for a moment, Chauvez stepped to the console and hauled Dvorak over to the screen.

"Come and enjoy what no member of our species has ever experienced. This is the stuff of millions of years of dreaming. Ever since the first hairy bastard stood erect and noticed the points of light in the night sky, we've all wanted to be here," Chauvez intoned.

Darkness spread out forever in the void between galaxies. Sailing as the sole point of illumination in this empty sea was a tiny bubble of light that was the ark. Forrester watched as the light of many galaxies faded, wholly swallowed up by the infinite blackness. The only illumination came from the diarist, both encompassing and preceding them through the darkened ocean of space-time. The fragment of an old verse crept into his mind, "…and a pillar of fire by night." History repeats itself, he thought, although the scale of this wilderness dwarfed the experience of those who participated in the first exodus.

Noticing the ark's gradual bending toward a particular pool of swirling light, Chauvez grabbed Dvorak's shoulder and pulled him closer to the viewer. Nudging Dvorak, Chauvez, his face wreathed in smiles, pointed to a spiral galaxy that grew in size at an incredible rate.

"I think that's our destination," Chauvez said.

The corporate presence of the meek within Forrester confirmed Chauvez's observation. This was to be their new beginning and their new home. Forrester could feel a host of images filling his mind, new worlds and life beginning anew upon them. A young galaxy, just starting up the ladder of evolution. A lush garden burgeoning with newly formed flora and fauna engaged in the struggle for existence. It was to this raw beginning that the meek were called as caretakers to a new and emergent history of life. It was not the promised land, but it did represent the promise of work and the meek were built to work. Here was the blank slate of nature to which the meek, whose very tissue disallowed coercion, would gently apply a form of constructive effort directed solely to harmonious interaction among all life's parts. Their mission was to discover if the history of life could be written with the quill of reason and the ink of compassion rather than the spear of dominance and the blood of conflict.

The illumined ark slowed now. The viewer was ablaze with the light of suns without number. The whole of the new galaxy could no longer be seen. The viewer was now crowded with but one of its spiral arms. As the ship moved among the fiery stars of its destination, deeper and deeper into the galaxy's embrace, Forrester felt the intent and plan of the diarist as both suffused the community of the meek. This was indeed the great experiment, mankind newly equipped and reseeded in this raw garden of Eden.

Here amidst stars to which man was a stranger, a new definition of evolution would be crafted. Here, tissue change would flower in perfect accord with the mandates of the loom of life's inner spark and produce life without strife. Relegated to the past was the time in which the forces intrinsic to insensate clay, which only briefly contained the light of life, would dictate, through bloody struggle, its unfolding. The universe of matter as stepparent to life had fulfilled its obligation. Over billions of years, this harsh taskmaster had shaped a capacity for survival among the vessels of light within the confines of its own hard and unyielding surfaces. This next step in the celestial order would address the light that the earthen vessels served only to contain. Now, the loom of Light, which lay beneath and had given rise to the darkness of matter, would take a direct hand in the rearing of its children. In this new and ongoing genesis, the lights of life would be fanned to a blaze that would eventually consume the vessels that had for so long both sheltered and confined them.

The great ship's approach slowed until it came to rest within the confines of a solar system governed by a brilliant yellow star that was its sun. Gently guided by the diarist's orb of energy, the ark nestled comfortably into orbit around a blue-white planet whose position ranked third from the sun. As the great ship slowly circled that which would become the new home of the people of the trees, Forrester felt an all encompassing peace emanating from the community of the meek in her hold.

Regaled in a light that paled the sun, the diarist stood before them as the envelope of brilliant white energy that had surrounded the vessel, gathered itself back to its maker. The pillar of light who had penned the diary unearthed so long ago, now hung suspended in space between the ark and the promise of the blue-white planet below.

Softly, but with a depth of resonance that sounded across the canyons of time and the infinity of space, the words of the diarist pervaded the bridge and filled the minds of the meek ensconced within the ark.

FOR NEW WINE, A FRESH SKIN IS FOUND.
GUIDED BY THE LIGHT WITHIN, LAMB
AND LION, SHALL LYING DOWN TOGETHER,
KNOW NOT THE STRIFE IN WHICH YOUR
BLOODLINE IS ROOTED. HERE SHALL LIFE'S
LIGHT, FROM ITS FIRST STIRRINGS, SHINE
THROUGH THE LAMP'S DULL CLAY
WHEREIN IT BURNS.

A NEW EARTH SHALL BE BOTH YOUR
TEACHER AND SIT AT THE RIGHT HAND
OF YOUR COUNSEL. THROUGH AGES
BEYOND COUNTING HAVE THE MEEK BEEN
PREPARED, WITHIN THE VESSEL OF STRIFE,
TO KNOW CONTENDING NO MORE.

HIDDEN WITHIN AGES OF ENMITY,
SLAUGHTER AND PAIN, THE MEEK LAY AS
BUT FRAGMENTS WITHIN MAN'S LOINS.
NOW GROWN UNTO THIS FIRST FLOWERING,
THE FULL BLOOM LIES YET BEFORE YOU.

NUMBERED IN MILLENNIA, LIFE'S FULL
MEASURE OF YEARS SHALL BE YOURS, AND
OF YOUR LINEAGE MORE.

YOUR OFFSPRING SHALL, STANDING UPON
THIS WORLD, YET KNOW ALL OF CREATION.
IN THIS KNOWING, SHALL THEY SERVANTS BE

TO ALL LIFE NOT OF YOUR SEMBLANCE. IN
CHILDHOOD'S INNOCENT COMPASSION, THEY
WILL TEACH PEACE TO THE STRONG. UNTO
ALL THE HEAVEN'S FIERY EMBERS SHALL
YOUR ISSUE, GIRDED ONLY WITH THE SPIRIT'S
MIGHT, LIFE'S EMISSARIES BE.

KIN TO ALL PRESENT AT THE ETERNAL
NOW OF CREATION, YOU ARE CALLED TO
SEE BEYOND LIFE'S SHADOW INTO ITS
MARROW. YOURS IS TO KNOW THAT
SIMPLICITY IS BUT REASONING IN
LOVE FOR ALL THAT HAS LIFE.

WHEREFORE, A NEW COMMANDMENT
I GIVE YOU, BE YE THEREFORE SIMPLE.

BEHOLD, YOU ARE GIVEN NEW HEAVENS
AND A NEW EARTH. YOU ARE CALLED TO
HUSBAND THE SEEDS HERE PLANTED, TO
TEND THE NEW SHOOTS, TO MINISTER TO
AND WATCH OVER THE LIFE THAT SPRINGS
FROM THIS GARDEN.

THE LIGHT OF CREATION THAT BURNS
BEYOND THE CLAY OF THIS UNIVERSE IS
YOUR LEGACY. AS CHILDREN OF THE LIGHT
BE THEREFORE GUIDED BY IT. AS YOU ARE
BORN TO PEACE, SO PEACE SHALL FLOW
FROM YOU TO THE VERY ROOT OF LIFE'S
UNFOLDING UPON THIS ISLAND OF LIGHT
ADRIFT IN A SEA OF DARKNESS.

THOUGH I GO FROM AMONG YOU, YET
AM I WITH YOU ALWAYS EVEN UNTIL
ALL DARKNESS SHALL BE SWALLOWED UP
IN THAT LIGHT WHICH IS THE LIFE OF ALL
BEGINNINGS.

Then in a shimmering of brilliant white light and an effervescence of purple orbs, the diarist disappeared and only the blue-white planet glistening in the sun of a new beginning remained. Yet, at the instant of the diarist's evanescence, Forrester felt within himself and the community of the meek in attendance in his mind, a sparkling effulgence that spread to every one of the meek. A direct line had been opened from the loom of life to each of the meek and to the people of the trees as a community. Beyond a stream of continuous revelation, this was a reliable flow of the undiluted energy of the loom of life which was from the beginning. The diarist had left something behind. It was an open line to eternity. Forrester felt the flow of relentless but gentle energy and knew it to be a resource sufficient to the great task that lay before them all.

As the energy of the diarist's parting gift flowed through his body, Forrester suddenly found himself in the midst of what felt like a mandatory remembrance of that which had brought him to this place in time. What had begun so many years ago with his disenchantment with himself and the human condition had led to the discovery of the diary, the destruction of the Earth and the division of humankind into two independent and self-sustaining branches. For the meek, their gifts of imagination would guide their destiny in the light, while among the strong, for whom sensation was the whole of perception, wrestling with matter would fire their efforts. Now dreamers and realists had gone their separate ways to exercise gifts that would create very different futures for each.

Somehow this great sojourn had cut a path directly through his life. Was it foreordination? It didn't feel like it. The meek saw the goal toward which space-time was tending and consciously chose to flow with those tendencies. Their faith, not fate, dictated those choices. The strong chose to experience the crude matter of the universe and bend it to their will. Their faith rested finally in themselves.

For the strong, it was the same old galaxy. For the meek it was a new genesis, complete with a garden planted in strange heavens. In this Eden, evolution would proceed without dominance striving and life would unfold without the whiphand of the survival of the fittest to drive it. A bold experiment indeed, which Forrester reckoned Augustine would find familiar, but Darwin would not recognize.

Here, at last, was the opportunity for man to remain within the garden of Eden. The knowledge of good had been gifted in greater measure than that of evil. That dowry of pure benefaction precluded the need to be driven out of paradise to subdue a new Earth or be subdued by it. The meek were tasked with tending a garden without ever resorting to coercion. No weeds would grow here because nothing was a weed and no life required uprooting.

For Forrester, however, the truth of the moment lay in his feelings. Forrester no longer felt alone. He was but a single shaft of light and life among many, and yet, all of these summed to one. It was enough. His sojourn in the desolation of conflict was at an end, he had come home.

A distant echo in his head, a passage from the scrolls, incomprehensible on dusty parchment, but now clarified by events in which transcendence had become the bread and butter of reality, asserted its meaning.

> BEHOLD, YOU ARE GIVEN NEW HEAVENS
> AND A NEW EARTH. YOU ARE CALLED TO
> HUSBAND THE SEEDS HERE PLANTED, TO
> TEND THE NEW SHOOTS, TO MINISTER TO
> AND WATCH OVER THE LIFE THAT
> SPRINGS FROM THIS GARDEN.
>
> THE LIGHT OF CREATION THAT BURNS
> BEYOND THE CLAY OF THIS UNIVERSE IS
> YOUR LEGACY. AS CHILDREN OF THE
> LIGHT BE YE THEREFORE GUIDED BY IT. AS
> YOU ARE BORN TO PEACE, SO PEACE SHALL
> FLOW FROM YOU TO THE VERY ROOT OF
> LIFE'S UNFOLDING UPON THIS ISLAND OF
> LIGHT ADRIFT IN A SEA OF DARKNESS.
>
> THOUGH I GO FROM AMONG YOU, YET
> AM I WITH YOU ALWAYS EVEN UNTIL
> ALL DARKNESS SHALL BE SWALLOWED UP
> IN THAT LIGHT THAT IS THE LIFE OF ALL
> BEGINNINGS.
>
> ENDINGS ARE THE PROVINCE OF MAN'S
> VANITY AND FEAR. THE LIGHT OF LIFE IS
> OF, AND AT, THE BEGINNING, WHICH IS
> ALSO THE FINAL HOME OF EACH AND
> EVERY MOTE OF EXISTENCE. THE CRUDE
> MATTER SHELL OF ALL THAT FROM LIFE'S
> THREADS DID SPRING, WAS OF LIFE'S
> MAKING. IT'S FIRST ILLUMINED SPINNING,

THE DIARY

LIFE WOVE THE MANYFOLDED AND
TEXTURED FABRIC OF THE UNIVERSE.

BE AT PEACE, FOR THAT WHICH
STRIKES TERROR SOUNDS UPON THE
HOLLOW OF AN IMPERFECT VESSEL THAT
IS QUICKLY REDUCED TO SHARDS THE
GROUND CONSUMES. ALL LIFE IS WOVEN
TOGETHER BY LOVE. ONLY THAT WHICH
RENDS THIS CARING WEAVE CAUSETH
A WAVERING OF CREATION'S FLAME THAT
BURNS WITHIN.

Epilogue

The home world of the alien imperium was also the seat of power of the empire. It was one continuous city inhabited by the wealthy and powerful whose daily fare consisted in scheming to achieve yet more wealth, influence and power.

A planet completely surrounded by orbiting assembly platforms where ships of the imperium were constantly under construction, the home world contained within its orbit all the means necessary to conquer the galaxy. Huge transport ships made regular calls at these platforms, bringing the raw materials needed for the construction of more fleets of ships. The ores of the home world long since exhausted, the raw materials now came from planets the empire had conquered as colonies for their species.

Governance of the empire was elegant by virtue of its simplicity. The Emperor made all decisions of significance, and a bureaucracy, immense and complex beyond all reason, carried out his mandates. The Emperor's advisors assisted in the task of managing an empire that spanned over three hundred worlds and their loyalty was guaranteed by their lives and those of their extended families. A universal law known to the imperium was that trust, the most scarce and therefore most valuable commodity in any system of governance based upon dominance-striving and fear, had to be vouched safe by the ultimate penalty. A complete understanding of this simple mandate necessitated the creation of technological means and social networks of constraint to make up for the dearth of this increasingly rare medium of exchange.

Reliable information, as well the Emperor knew, is the life blood of any form of government. To this end he maintained an immense network of spies in each of whose bodies the equivalent of a lie detector mechanism was implanted. This device insured the accuracy of his covert agents' perceptions of others and the reliability of their reports to the Emperor. Trust is the currency of power and the Emperor's financiers were his spies. Of these agents there were only two varieties, those who the lie detecting mechanisms in their bodies reported they could be trusted and the dead. As justice was swift and efficient in the Emperor's intelligence network, so it was for all of his subjects. There was only one crime, disloyalty to the Emperor, and only one punishment, death.

The Emperor had recently received a report from the Lord of the seventy eighth fleet that the destruction of a world that appeared to be an excellent candidate for colonization was required. For the Emperor to be deprived of such a prize simply by virtue of the enormous opposition the natives mounted was unacceptable. The Emperor was displeased and sent word to his agents aboard the operations base ship that the fleet Lord was to be assassinated. The message was a clear one and would be readily understood by the second in command who would ascend to the rank of fleet Lord subsequent to his superior's fatal retirement.

The message dutifully transmitted to the seventy eighth fleet over thousands of light years received no response. The Emperor was concerned. This sort of thing had never happened before. The absence of a response suggested all manner of possibilities, none of which were to the Emperor's liking. In counsel with his imperial cabinet, he decided to dispatch six heavy cruisers to investigate the seventy eighth fleet's failure to respond and to act decisively relative to whatever they found.

⚜

In this place and for this race it was the fullness of time. Into a world that had dwelt for millennia in the shadow of fear, in which domination was the measure of worth and where the lives of others were valued as but a means to some personal end, the diarist would come.

Here, he would begin again his ministry of light to the darkness below. His visitation would be to those from whose reach he had snatched two small remnants of a previous ministry. The internal energies constantly revolving within the pillar of perfect white light slowed as the pillar uncoupled and extended to become the perfect realization of Crystal's tiny Mobius strip of light's spectrum. It was only by rendering up his unity that the diarist could enter into matter. Detaching end from end, the spectral strip descended to dwell for a time in a vessel of clay. Here, as but a discontinuous fragment of himself, he would walk upon this planet as witness to a reality greater than any empire that might span the galaxy's breadth.

Freely entering into the bonds of matter was the envoy of the loom of life to complete the sacrifice of drawing breath once again. Here, he would mature confined within a tiny sea of biochemical tides and eddies whose currents defined this species' struggle for existence. Upon his own person, he would translate a perfect knowledge of the nature of the universe into those few fragments of insight that this race of vessels could contain.

Achieving corporeal sympathy with this life form, he would come to know first hand the strength of the forces that drove them. In eating their bread and drinking their wine, he would be one of them, experiencing the exaltation of their joy and the depths of their despair. He would speak of the Light and minister in compassion to these who had so fully embraced the many transient illusions of matter. Some few would hear, understand, and remember, but most, inured to the transactions of fear and greed, would turn away.

A man of sorrows and acquainted with grief, in their fear and rage at a message that dismissed all that they held dear, they would free him from his material incarnation. Dead to matter, he would rise again, shuffling off the finite mortal coil that had contained the infinite for less than two score passages about their sun.

The sojourn of sacrifice and estrangement from the beginning's light done, he would be free once again to wander among the stars as the living emissary of the loom of Light and life.

The cycle of death to the Light and rebirth to its indivisible resplendence had begun again.

> LIFE'S LORD AND FIRST ROW IN THE
> TAPESTRY OF EXISTENCE IS, IN
> IMAGINATION'S FLIGHT, A WEAVE
> TINTED IN BRIGHT SPIRALING HOPES
> AND ENTRAINING ASPIRATIONS. YET
> THROUGH MANY TRIALS IN THE DARK
> CLAY OF LIFE THAT GLIMMERING FIRST
> ROW IS WARPED GENEROUSLY WITH
> DARKLY KNOTTED FEARS AND TWISTED
> SORROWS BORN OF LIFE'S SOJOURN
> IN MATTER'S NIGHT. SCHOOLED BY
> ENDLESS INCARNATIONS, ITS FIBERS
> ARE DYED FAST BY THE LONGINGS
> AND TRAVAILS OF ALL LIFE'S TOILING
> STRANDS.
>
> UNCOUNTED LIVING THREADS LOOSED
> FROM CREATION'S LOOM AND YEARNING
> FOR HOME GAZE IN AWE, EACH
> THROUGH THEIR OWN TINY TANGLE
> OF CRUDE MATTER'S CONSTRAINING
> LATTICE, AT HEAVEN'S FIELDS WHITE
> WITH LIGHT.

THE DIARY

OF THESE MANY SINGULAR THREADS,
SEVERED FROM THE LOOM OF LIFE'S
WHOLE CLOTH, A SINGLE WISP, THE
TRIBE OF MAN, BESET STILL WITH
UNCHARITABLE DIVISIONS, IS BUT
ONE.

The End

Dr. Nathan Forrester: The Man

After a quarter of a century of clinical research, Doctor Nathan Forrester pronounced his work a singularly resounding failure. He had set out to show that challenge, conflict and hard won insights could produce changes, indeed improvements, in the basic form of an individual's personality. Instead, he had succeeded only in relating genetically hardwired brain structure to personality and that immutable framework to every man's tendency to make the same mistakes over and over again. In his eagerness to be of service to humanity, Dr. Forrester had managed only to prove that the redemption of the human condition had never been, and would ever be, a function of man's ability to change himself.

In a single sweeping of his arm, he cleared the desk of empty coffee cups, scraps of notes and all the salubrious adolescent hopes for humanity he had nourished for many decades. All denial fled. He hoisted a pencil and began the task of confronting himself with line item proof of his failure to contribute to the well-being of his fellow creatures.

I. The fundamental personality of individuals does not change.

Five year old kids whom he had evaluated a quarter century ago, whom reassessed as adults, thought,felt and behaved exactly as they had at the age of five, except they were now in a better position to enforce their will. Nature clearly eclipsed nurture. Hardwired neuropsychological structures molded perception, and perception was fact to the individual. Shared perceptions among individuals became socially actionable realities.

II. Fundamental personality traits increasingly dominate individuals' thoughts and actions as their feelings become more intense.

Like the deepest channel in a river, the seething waters of emotion fill the narrows of an individual's fundamental personality first and to the greatest depth. Old brain emotional demands are uncompromising and yield ground only to the application of power from outside the individual.

III. The pursuit of personal 'security' inevitably leads to subjugation, domination, or death.

Lurking in the brain's subbasement, the ageless limbic system and seat of emotion exercised the blunt force dynamics meant to insure personal, tribal and progeny survival. Survival security, like a powerful vehicle with no brake pedal sped down the road of life where caution and stop signs erected by society acted only as momentary distractions. The unchecked quest to secure personal survival always leads to the subjugation of ones' fellows, unless thwarted by the action of superior survival and dominance drives in others. The uneven stride of evolution and the march of human history notwithstanding, little had changed. Strength was admired and sought after, weakness was despised.

IV No one wants to change to accommodate the needs of others. It always '*Them*' who were supposed to do the changing.

Twenty five years of doing psychotherapy with the rich and powerful, the 'wanna-be' nobility of wealth, scholars, scientists, children and dreamers, was now simply a blur of complaints that the world hadn't yet molded itself to the fulfillment of their fantasies.

V Homo sapiens, evolved from right brain processing simians and who had stumbled around only about one third of the game board from the point marked 'Go' on the playing surface for their species were lost.

Seventy percent of the human race remained as right brained as their evolutionary predecessors and their proportionate representation among the family of man was increasing. Evolution looked like it was on rewind.

VI. For the past three thousand years, the human race had been consistently segregated into right and left brain thinkers.

The right brain thinkers (70% of the population) wanted tribal solidarity, power and prerogative, preferably right now.

The left brain thinkers (30% of the population) wanted to be left alone to pursue the endlessly beckoning muse of their curiosity, nourishing a hope of discovering some rational order in all of creation. Their numbers were shrinking.

VII Right brain humans are predators. Left brain humans are pets at best, prey at worst.

The 7/10ths of the human race that is right brained negotiated an uneasy truce with one another on the battlefield of interpersonal relations.

The inequities of power and dominance among them became the generally accepted measure of morality.

The diminishing 3/10ths of the race that is left brained victimized themselves by shrinking back from the conflict inherent to competition. Secreted within their tissues from the first ascendancy of that half of the brain was Kant's dictum: if you cannot universalize your actions to every man in similar circumstances, your actions are immoral.

VIII As the number of right brained predators in the population increased and the number of left brained prey decreased, predators must, of necessity, prey upon each other.

In a downwardly spiraling moral cascade, whatever one person got away with became the new mean morality for everyone in the game. Each innovative breach of trust or physical atrocity set a new mark for the hunting pack.

IX. The best scientific minds could account for only ten percent of the stuff that made up the universe yet had come to conclusions relegating life to a relatively small quantitative amendment to the space-time-matter mix. They could be wrong.

It was a leap of faith and Forrester knew it, but he believed life was the point; and space, time, and all the rest were just means to that end. Indeed, when raptured by Beethoven's ninth symphony, he was almost certain that life had come first and the universe was just stage dressing.

X. If the hand of God operated in history, then clearly His mitts were in his pockets. Perhaps nonintervention was the essence of divinity, or maybe He was just waiting for man to engineer his own mass extinction.

Man preying upon himself was not an open-ended game. A society rapidly progressing to the status of a club for predators could not sustain itself for long.

If Moses was right, then clearly Forrester was wrong. Both men had come up with ten admonitions. Moses was into 'thou shalt not' as both a remedy for mankind's ills, and a means to their eventual reconciliation with God. Forrester's Sinai experience, although not as dramatic, was equally compelling and more on the order of 'thou might as well forget it.' The divine plan, if there be such, fulfilled the concept of 'cryptic' more completely than anything Forrester had ever encountered. From Forrester's less than omniscient perspective, it looked more like humanity was going to 'hell in a hand basket.' The words of this phrase had very little real meaning for him, rather it was the image of his grandfather speaking them that imparted their significance.

In spite of the dark colors on his palette of the future, as a left brain thinker, Forrester was not yet willing to succumb to his own fatalism. He would step back from both his myopic perspective on man's simian brain and from a view of humanity informed by the single historical epoch in which he resided. He had made his decision. He would undertake a new direction in his life, one that might provide a broader cosmological perspective. Regardless of how far back he had to go, he was determined to discover the method and, hopefully the ends, that lay behind God's tinkering with the human brain.

The Diary ~ Journal entries
in order of presentation

Page 15 JAMES, BROTHER AND FRIEND, ALWAYS
QUIETLY THERE. THESE WORDS, FOR
YOUR EYES ALONE WILL BE DELIVERED
UPON MY DEATH. WRITTEN IN THE
VANITY OF SOLITARY PAIN AND AS
SERVICE TO THOSE YET TO BE BORN,
I COMMIT THEM TO YOUR KEEPING.
SHOW THEM TO NO OTHER. BURIED IN
THE SHIFTING DUNE OF TIME THEY
WILL BE REVEALED BEFORE EARTH'S
MANTLE IS SHED.

Page 15 I SET DOWN THESE WORDS, TRAPPING
THEM IN THE SCROLL, EVER IN THE
HOPE OF BANISHING SPECTERS FROM
A HEART AND HEAD THAT LIKE A
NOISY MARKET PLACE OVERWHELMS
THE EYE AND EAR. LOOSED FROM A
FEVERISH BROW, I YIELD THEM UP
TO AGES BEYOND THE HORIZON OF
THESE TIMES.

Page 16 THE NIGHT IS THE WORST, A TIME OF HALF
DREAMS AND VISIONS. WITHIN THE
FIRMAMENT MOVE SHADOWS CAST BY
MESSENGERS WITHOUT NAMES WHOSE
CHARIOTS FILL THE HEAVENS. SPECTERS OF
PEOPLE AND PLACES COME, WHICH NOT

OF NAZARETH, BRING FIRE AND FURY EVEN
THE ROMANS CANNOT CONJURE RENDING
THE CLOAK OF DARKNESS.

Page 17   CRAFTING THE WOOD BUSIES THE
HANDS AND FREES THE MIND TO
WANDER. PERHAPS MINE WANDERS
TOO FAR, TOUCHING ON LIFE WHERE
IT CANNOT OR WILL NOT CHANGE. THE
BOUNDARIES SET UPON THE SOUL BY
THE BODY IN WHICH IT DWELLS ARE
KNOWN ONLY TO ITS CREATOR.
SECRETED IN THE TWINKLING OF ALL
BEGINNINGS, A RECEPTACLE ONLY,
THE CLAY CONFINES THE RANGING OF
THE SOUL NESTLED WITHIN.

Page 19   THE MALLET AND CHISEL CANNOT
TAKE BACK WHAT THEY HAVE DONE,
NOR CAN THE WOOD, ONCE STRUCK,
BE WHOLE AGAIN . IF CERTAINTY IS
ACTION, IS DOUBT THE CHIPS ON THE
FLOOR THAT ARE SHORTLY SCATTERED
BY THE WIND?

AT LIFE'S ENDING WILL I HAVE
CRAFTED SOMETHING OF VALUE
OR WILL ALL THAT I AM BE BUT
SHAVINGS TRODDEN UNDER
COUNTLESS FEET IN TIME'S
RELENTLESS MARCH?

Page 22   DOES THE LION BIRTH A LAMB OR
THE JACKAL SUCKLE A GOAT? THAT
WHICH IS OF THE WORLD IS
BLOODIED BY FEEDING UPON
ITSELF.

MAN IS BOTH LION AND LAMB
UNTO HIMSELF. NEVER LORD OVER
HIS OWN PASSIONS, HE SEEKS
POWER OVER HIS FELLOWS AS
RECOMPENSE FOR HIS WEAKNESS.
EACH FAULT COMMON TO THE FLESH
IS SEEN BY EVERY MAN IN HIS FELLOW.
JOINTLY DISCERNING EVIL WITHOUT,
THEY EACH AND ALL STEP BACK INTO
THE DARKNESS WHERE UNBEKNOWNST,
SAVE AS ENEMIES, THEY SLAY ONE
ANOTHER.

Page 23
THE TREE WILL BE HEWN TO A YOKE TO
CARRY WATER TO THE THIRSTY OR TO
PRESS DOWN THOSE WHO FALL TO THE
WILL OF CONQUEST.

THE PURPOSE OF ITS LIFE IS FULFILLED
IN THE TREE'S GROWTH AND FLOWERING.
THE INVENTION OF ITS CARCASS REVEALS
THE CRAFTSMAN'S INTENTION FOR GOOD
OR EVIL.

CUT INTO EACH SOUL'S GRAIN IS A
BROAD CHART OF ITS TRAVELS. YET,
IN LIFE'S JOURNEY, NONE CAN SAY I
AM OBLIGED TO THIS PATH OR THAT
BYWAY.

Page 24
I FEEL LIKE A MAN AFOOT WHO HEARS A
CHARIOT IN THE DISTANCE, THAT HE KNOWS
WILL OVERTAKE AND CARRY HIM WHERE
HE WILL NOT GO. I AM NO LONGER THE
CARPENTER, NOR EVEN THE PLANE, I AM
BECOME THE WOOD.

FIBER AND GRAIN, READIED FOR THE
CUT, I AM SET UPON THE BENCH OF LIFE'S

TRIALS. YET TO BE SHAPED TO A PURPOSE,
I AWAIT THE CRAFTSMAN'S HAND.

Page 25   THE MESSAGE WITHIN IS CLEAR AND
WILL NOT RELENT. THE FAULT IN MAN
IS DOMINION, BUT NO ONE LISTENS
UNLESS I SHOW POWER. I FEAR THE
LOCK OF HUMAN LONGING ACCEPTS
ONLY ONE KEY.

Page 25   OFTEN MY WORDS, OPENLY SPOKEN,
ARE WELL AND TRULY RECEIVED. THE
LIGHT IN THE EYES OF THOSE WHO
HEAR PLAINLY MARKS A QUICKENING
OF THE MIND AND SPIRIT WITHIN.
YET, WITH ONE SUN'S SETTING AND
RISING, THEY ARE LOST LIKE A SOLITARY
KERNEL AMIDST THE CHAFF IN THE
NOISY RUSTLE OF LIVING THAT SIGNALS
THE MORNING.

LIKE DUST FROM THE DESERT, FAITH
CAN BLOT OUT, IN A MOMENT OF
RAPTURE, ALL THAT IS FAMILIAR. YET,
WHEN IT SETTLES EVENLY ONTO THE
BOWL OF STRIFE AND CUP OF FEAR
THAT COME TO HAND EVERY DAY,
IT PASSES FROM SIGHT.

Page 28   TOO MUCH SAID IS OFTEN TOO LITTLE
HEARD, WHILE ONE WORD WRONGLY
GRASPED CAN UNDUE A GREAT WORK.

UNBIDDEN, WORDS COME SPILLING INTO
MY HEAD. THEN, FALLING FROM MY
LIPS, THEY ARE NOT MY VOICE, YET THEY
RING OF TRUTH MOST HARSH. I MUST BE
WARY.

Page 44   SLAVE AND MASTER ARE YOKED
          TOGETHER, EACH KNOWING HIMSELF
          THROUGH THE OTHER. DEATH DRIVES
          THIS UNEQUAL SPAN OVER ROCKY
          GROUND INTO A PIT DARKENED BY
          THEIR LOATHING ONE OF ANOTHER.

          THE FRUITS OF THIS CULTIVATION
          ARE BITTER TO BOTH. ITS INCREASE
          A CONFLAGRATION THAT CONSUMES
          BOTH OWNER AND OWNED.

Page 45   THROUGH AN EYE OF CLAY, THE SOUL'S
          VISION IS MUDDIED, IT'S EAR SOUNDING
          ONLY TO BLUNT BLOWS MADE UPON
          UNSTRETCHED SKINS. BRIEF FLESH IS
          SWADDLED IN MUFFLED SHADOWS.

          THE STRIVING OF ALL LIFE SEEMS BLIND
          ONLY TO HIM WHOSE SPAN IS BUT A
          SINGLE DROP IN THE OCEAN OF TIME.

          THE HERB'S FULL FLOWER CANNOT BE
          SEEN IN THE KERNEL FROM WHICH IT
          SPROUTS, NOR CAN IT BE SAVORED IN
          THE WATERS THAT NOURISH THE DARK
          SOIL FROM WHICH IT SPRINGS.

          OF ONE WEAVE, EACH THREAD OF LIFE
          TWISTS WOOF AND WARP AMONG ITS
          FELLOWS TO FIND THE PLACE CHOSEN
          FOR IT IN THE TAPESTRY THAT IS THE
          UNIVERSE. NEITHER THE THREADS
          LOOSED UPON THE FLOOR, NOR THE
          FRAMEWORK OF THE LOOM, REVEAL
          THE MIND OF CREATION'S WEAVER.

Page 47   THE DARK HUB OF ALL DESPAIR IS
          BUT MEMORY LOST OF WHENCE WE

HAVE COME AND TO WHITHER WE
SHALL RETURN. UPON THIS AXIS
TURNS THE WHEEL OF DOUBT,
CHURNING UP DUSTY SPECTERS OF
FLESH'S PERIL AND SUMMONING
DEFENSE.

DOES DOMINION GOAD FEAR OR FEAR
DOMINION? IS A WHEEL ITS RIM OR
SPOKES? DOES NOT THE WHEEL OF
STRIFE, RIM AND SPOKES, GOUGE AN
EVER DEEPENING FURROW INTO THE
HEART OF MAN.

ONCE CUT, THE FURROW BECKONS
TO ALL WHOSE WILL FOLLOWS THE
ANGLE IN WHICH THE GROOVE IS
WENDING. THE COLUMN OF MAN,
THROUGH THE HILLS OF TIME
TRAVERSING, BRINGS WITH IT THE
FEET OF SONS TREADING IN THEIR
FATHERS' STEPS. THE FURROW
THEY GOUGE DEEPENING CREATES
A CHASM FROM WHICH NONE
ESCAPES.

Page 50   EVER A YOUNG AND TENDER FLOWER,
GOODNESS IS SOON WILTED BY FEAR,
WHICH LIKE THE RAYS OF THE
NOONDAY SUN, LEAVE NO SHADE
OF FAITH IN WHICH IT MAY PROSPER.
EVEN SO, SERVICE IS A REED SET
AGAINST THE STAFF OF DOMINION,
THE OUTCOME IS CERTAIN.

Page 52   THE COURSE OF A SINGLE LIFE
MIRRORS THE WANDERINGS OF
MAN ACROSS THE AGES. EACH
IS ALL, AND ALL ON PILGRIMAGE

THROUGH TIME'S WILDERNESS
SEEK THEY KNOW NOT WHAT.

A DROP OF WATER MAY NOURISH
A SINGLE SEED, OR JOINING A
FLOOD, BRING LIFE TO THE FIELDS
AND DEATH TO MANY IN THE
DELUGE.

Page 58   DEATH IS A MOTHER WITH TWO FIERCE
SONS, FEAR AND DOMINION. A FAMILY
OF DARK VESTMENT, THEY ARE THE
CONSTANT COMPANIONS OF MAN'S
TRAVELS THROUGH TIME AND THE
BLOODLETTING THAT IS HIS HISTORY.

WAR IS ALL THAT IS UNCLEAN, MOTHER
DEATH JOINED IN INCEST WITH FEAR
AND DOMINION. TOGETHER THEY LAY
WASTE TO THE EARTH, HERALDING ITS
CLOSE.

Page 71   IN ALL BEGINNINGS ARE THEIR ENDINGS
CONTAINED. EACH OF LIFE'S DANCERS
ARE NOW AND FOREVER JOINED TO THE
OTHER IN A WHIRL OF COMINGS AND
GOINGS.

DEATH IS IN THE FLOWER OF THE WHEAT
THAT MAKES OUR BREAD AND IN THE
BABE OF THE EWE IS THAT WHICH
NOURISHES OUR CHILDREN. GRIEVING
THE DEATH OF OUR OWN, WE SLAY TO
LIVE.

HOLDING OUR OWN LIVES DEAR, WE
KNOW NOT THAT WHICH CAME BEFORE
OR THAT WHICH ARISES AFTER OUR

THE DIARY

BRIEF MOMENT OF EATING, DRINKING,
JOY AND PAIN.

WE AWAKEN IN A STREAM NOT KNOWING
IT HAS FLOWED BEFORE WE ROUSED. AS
OUR PASSAGE ENDS, CLUTCHING THE HOPE
THAT THE TORRENT OF LIVES WILL ENDURE,
WE SINK BENEATH THE SURFACE.

Page 73   THE DUST RISES AND DEATH IS
CARRIED ON THE WIND. A GUST
FILLING EVERY LIFE'S SAIL
THRUSTS EACH INTO THE DARK
DOLDRUMS OF THE GRAVE.
ENTERING UPON THIS MOMENT
OF COMPLETE STILLNESS, ALL
HOPE TO BRIDGE THAT INSTANT
OF ENDING, STRIVING TO A
BRIGHTNESS OF HOPE PRESERVING
THE BEST STRENGTHS OF APPETITE,
HEART, AND MIND BEYOND THE
CHAINS OF TIME, THE COLD
DARKNESS FOLDS SOFTLY OVER
THEM.

ALL THAT THE EYE BEHOLDS OF
MAN IS BUT A DRIFTING HAZE UPON
THE FORGETFUL WINDS OF FOREVER.
WITHIN THAT UNSEEN GAIL, OUR
RUDDER IS FAITH, AND OUR PILOT
THE SOUL. THE PILOT'S INVISIBLE
MATE, HOPE REMAINS HIS
ONLY STEADFAST COMPANION.

Page 79   WE ARE, EACH TO ONE ANOTHER, THE
MEAT THAT CANNOT BE EATEN. IN VAIN
STRIVING TO REPLENISH A PART TORN
FROM OURSELVES, WE SLASH AT OUR
BRETHREN IN RAGEFUL HOPE OF

RECOVERING A LOST PORTION OF THE
COMMON FLESH IN WHICH WE ARE
ALL ARRAYED.

THE DARKNESS THAT REIGNED BEFORE
THERE WAS LIGHT, IN SECRET CHAMBERS
OF THE HUMAN HEART DWELLS THERE
STILL. SOUNDLY NOURISHED, IT DINES
UPON THE MEAT OF HATE AND DRUNK
WITH THE BITTER WINE OF VENGEANCE,
IT PROSPERS. TAKING UP RESIDENCE
IN THIS ABODE FROM BEFORE THE STARS
WERE A SOURCE OF WONDER, IT PLOTS
AND SCHEMES TO UNDO THE LIGHT OF
CREATION.

EVERY MAN PROWLS THE WORLD, HIS
OWN SCALE OF JUSTICE IN HAND. FOR
EACH, THE RAGE AND GUILT OF HIS
FELLOWS WEIGHS MORE HEAVILY THAN
HIS OWN AND CRIES FOR REQUITAL. THE
KILLING ENDS ONLY AS THE LAST OF THE
SLAYERS PASSES BACK TO THE DUST
FROM WHICH ALL MEN SPRANG.

Page 80   ONLY WHEN ONE MAN'S PAIN BECOMES
THE AGONY OF ALL WILL THEY CEASE TO
INJURE ONE ANOTHER. LIFE, TO WHICH
END THE WHOLE TAPESTRY OF CREATION IS
WOVEN, CANNOT IN PART BE INJURED SAVE
THE WHOLE ANGUISHES AND BLEEDS. THE
MAKER KNOWETH THAT THE RIVING OF
BUT A SINGLE STRAND WEAKENS THE
WEAVE UNTIL THE WHOLE FABRIC IS RENT.

BORN SOLITARY OF HEART AND MIND,
MAN SEES NOT THE MANNER IN WHICH
HE IS BOUND TO ALL THAT LIVES. IN THIS
BLINDNESS IS COMPASSION'S WANT.

Page 112   WORDS ARISE IN THE MIND OF MAN ONLY
IN THE TWILIGHT OF THE DAY WHEREIN
EDEN IS MORNING'S FIRST LIGHT. TO SWAY
THE SOUL, THEY MAY HAVE POWER, BUT
TOUCHING NOT THE BODY, THEY REMAIN
UNREVEALED BY THE ACTIONS OF THE SOUL
THAT DWELLS WITHIN.

IT IS ONLY IN THE HEART OF THE HEARER
THAT WORDS ARE QUICKENED TO ACTS.
THE MESSAGE CALLS TO THE SPIRIT OF
HE WHO HARKENS AND NONE ELSE.

IN THE MORNING OF LIFE, FROM ONE
COME MANY. IN THE NOONDAY, MANY
BECOME ONE. AS THE DARKNESS OF DAY'S
END GATHERS, ONE BECOMES TWO. FROM
THIS BRANCHING SPRINGS A BOUGH OF
THE SPIRIT, AND A LIMB OF THE FLESH. OF
COMMON ROOT AND FLOWERING UNTO THE
LIGHT, THEY GROW BY SEPARATE PATHS,
BENDING FINALLY BACK UPON THEIR
BEGINNINGS.

Page 138   THE BRIGHTER THE FLAME OF A THOUGHT'S
BURNING, THE DEEPER THE SHADOW IT CASTS
UPON THE SOUL'S FOUNDATION. LIGHT,
THE FIRST CREATION, AND SHADOW, THE
SECOND, EACH MARK THEIR OWN CIRCUIT
UPON LIFE'S STRAINING REACH.

IN THE BEGINNING IS LIFE, WHICH PASSING
FROM THE LIGHT INTO DARKNESS AND TO
THE BRIGHTNESS AGAIN, FULFILLS ITS ROUND.

THE SPARKS AND SHADOWS OF THESE
THOUGHTS, MADE PLAIN, JOINS THEM
AND ME TO A DARK PATH AT WHOSE
ENDING DWELLS THE LIVING LIGHT.

Page 138   THE TEARS OF SUFFERING EONS, A CLOUD
OF DESPAIR CREATE THAT FILLED TO
OVERFLOWING, POURS OUT IN A RAIN
OF TORMENT UPON THE LAST GENERATION.
THE WATERS OF AFFLICTION DESCENDING
UPON A WEARY EARTH BECOME GREAT
RIVERS OF PAIN, FLOWING INTO A SEA OF
SORROW.

THE SORROWFUL SEA, KINDLED AND
OR'FLOWING ITS BRIM, STREAMS OUT
IN FIRE CONSUMING THE WHOLE
WORLD, PREPARING THE WAY FOR NEW
HEAVENS AND A NEW EARTH.

Page 144   NEVER WAS DARKNESS THE SOLITARY
LORD OF ALL THAT IS. IN THE MIDST
OF ALL BEGINNINGS' GLOOM, EVEN
SO, THERE WAS LIFE'S TWINKLING,
WHOSE VOICE, STILL AND SMALL,
SAID, LET THERE BE LIGHT.

THE BLAZE OF LIFE HAS BURNED FROM
BEFORE THE UNIVERSE DONNED HER
ROBES OF LIGHT AND TO THE STARS
GAVE BIRTH. TO LIFE'S PURPOSE IS
THE WHOLE OF CREATION SET IN
EVER RENEWING MOTION.

EACH SOUL A SPARK FROM GOD'S
ETERNAL FIRE, A DYING EMBER UPON
THE HEARTH OF LIFE'S TRAVAILS MUST
BECOME. NO EMBER SPEWED FROM
THE BLAZE OF ALL BEGINNINGS CAN
LONG SURVIVE APART.

Page 146   THE LIGHT OF THE UNIVERSE, A CIRCLE
UNBROKEN BY TIME'S ILLUSION, TURNS
UPON EACH LIFE, LARGE AND SMALL. FOR

LIFE'S PURPOSE AND IT ALONE ARE THE
ENDLESS STARS OF HEAVEN SET TO DEATH
AND REBIRTH. IN EACH SPECK OF DUST,
SWEPT UP IN STARRY PASSAGE, IS ALL THAT
IS, PART AND WHOLE, COMPREHENDED.
EVERY MOTE, A LONELY SOJOURNER IN THE
VOID HAVING FINALLY OF LIFE TASTED,
CREATION SHALL AS ONE DRAW ITS FIRST
BREATH IN JOY

IN ONE LIFE IS ALL THAT LIVES CONTAINED.
YET, NO ONE SPARK'S SOLITARY GLOWING
CAN SHOW FORTH THE GLORY OF CREATION'S
FIRES.

Page 163   IN THE HEAT OF THE WORKSHOP, DUST
DANCES IN THE AIR LIKE GUESTS AT A
WEDDING FEAST. THE WINE OF SWEAT
STAINING THE WOOD TO A DEPTH ONLY
THE PLANE CAN REMOVE, ADDS TOIL TO
THE DAY'S LABORS. THE HANDS MOVE
ACROSS THE FACE OF THE BOARD GUIDED
BY YEARS OF WATCHING, FAILING AND
FINALLY CRAFTING, WHILE WORDS THAT
PENETRATE THE HEART OF MAN WITH NO
LESS BITE THAN THE AWL UPON THE JOINT,
FILL MY HEAD.

LIKE AN IMAGE IN THE MIND THAT
RESISTS THE CARVER'S SKILL TO FIND ITS
FORM IN THE CURVES OF THE WOOD, MY
WORDS SHAPE NO BEAUTY IN THE TIMBER
OF THIS WORLD. NO MATTER THE ANGLE
OF THE BLADE OR THE CARE GIVEN TO THE
STRIKING OF THE MALLET, THIS WOOD
SPLITS ONLY ALONG THE GRAIN OF POWER.
I AM ALONE.

Page 164

THE MIGHT OF ROME SHUFFLES WEARILY
THROUGH THE COOL OF EVENTIDE, PAST THE
OPEN WORKSHOP DOOR. CLAD IN DUSTY
RED WITH SHARP METAL HUNG ABOUT
THEIR LOINS, THESE MASTERS OF THE WORLD
ARE BUT THIS DAY'S EMBLEM OF DREAD'S
VICTORY OVER FAITH.

SACRIFICE IS KNOWN TO THOSE AMONG WHOM
I WANDER ONLY IN DEFENSE OF SEED, TRIBE
OR TERRITORY. WHERE NO TERRORS LOOM,
THEY FALL UPON ONE ANOTHER SPURRED BY
GREED, AGGRIEVED BY OFFENSES OF THE
HEART, AND IN ENDLESS QUEST FOR BADGES
OF OFFICE.

ONLY TERROR AND REWARD SPEAK TO THE
BLOOD AND BONE OF THOSE RISEN FROM
THIS DUST. UNGOADED BY THE THREAT
OF LOSS OR THE PROMISE OF POWER, THEY
ARE UNMOVED. I AM ALONE.

Page 165

I FIND NO PLACE TO BEGIN. THE DYER OF
RAIMENT, WHOSE VATS STAND BEYOND MY
WORKSHOP DOOR, CANNOT HEAR EVEN THE
VOICE HIS CHILDREN GIVE TO THEIR
SUFFERING, HIS EARS BEING STOPPED. A
FRIEND OF MANY YEARS, WITHOUT WORD
OR MOTION, HEAL I HIM AND HIS SEED.
YET, STILL HE HARKENS NOT AS I SPEAK
OF THE LIFE AND LIGHT FROM THE
BEGINNING. HIS EARS OPEN AND EYES
BRIGHTEN ONLY WHEN I PRATTLE OF
GOODS AND TAXES. MADE WHOLE, THE
BODY'S ROUGH HUSK STILL ARMORS THE
SOUL AGAINST THE TRUTH.

IMPRISONED IN THE BODY'S DARK CELLAR,
THE SOUL GLIMPSES POORLY AND SELDOM

THE DIARY

THROUGH THE LATTICE OF THE FLESH,
GRASPING BUT FEW SHAFTS OF THE LIGHT
FROM WHICH IT SPRANG. WHEN WORDS
ARE LENT TO THIS VISION OF ALL BEGINNINGS,
THE REVELATION IS OFT SEEN AS MADNESS.
THE MEMORY OF ALL BEGINNINGS IS LOST TO
TIME, TRAVELING IN BLOOD AND BONE. STILL
FRESH AT BIRTH, IT WANES IN MANHOOD,
ACHIEVING BRILLIANCE AGAIN ONLY IN THE
MOMENTS BEFORE DEATH AS THE SOUL IS
SET UPON ITS JOURNEY HOME.

THE CHILDREN OF THE VILLAGE AND THOSE
WEIGHED DOWN BY YEARS ARE MY GREATEST
COMFORT. FRAIL FLESH'S BEGINNINGS AND
ENDINGS ARE CLOSER TO THE LIGHT, WHEREIN
LIES MY SOUL'S LONGING AND RELEASE.

WHEN I AM BECOME BUT A CHANNEL
FOR THAT WHICH ENLIVENS THE WHOLE
OF CREATION, THEY LOOK NOT TO THE
SOURCE OF THAT QUICKENING FIRE, BUT
ARE FIXED ON THE FEW SPARKS THAT
TOUCH THEIR LIVES. WERE I TO OPEN
THE VISTA OF ALL CREATION, YET I FEAR
THEY WOULD REMAIN UNMOVED. I AM
ALONE.

Page 167 IN A MOMENT OF REST, I WATCH AS THE DYER
OF RAIMENT EMPTIES HIS VATS. STREAMS OF
COLOR SINKING INTO THE DUST ARE CARRIED
AWAY ON THE SANDALS OF THOSE WHO PASS
THIS WAY. TROD UNDERFOOT, BOTH BEAUTY
AND THE TRUTH IT REFLECTS ARE FOREVER LOST.

LIKE THE DYE THAT FASTENING NOT TO THE
STRANDS OF THESE LIVES IS WASHED AWAY
IN THE WATERS OF DAILY USE, SO MY WORDS
ARE BLANCHED BY TIME TO THE COMMON

COLORS OF THIS CLAY. SURVIVING THE DUST
OF CENTURIES, WHAT WAS SAID ABIDES,
WHILE WHAT IS MEANT PERISHES. I AM
ALONE.

Page 168 FEVERED BY DREAMS AND VISIONS, I GO
ALONE TO THE WORKSHOP THERE TO DRINK
IN THE STILLNESS OF A NIGHT IN WHICH
EVEN THE ANIMALS QUIETEN THEIR CRIES.
THROUGH THE LATTICE I SEE THE STARS
THAT SEEM MORE A HOME THAN THIS
DARK AND DUSTY ABODE IN WHICH MY
FEET ARE PLANTED. MY MIND GRASPS
LIVING LINES BINDING THEIR FIERY
BODIES TOGETHER THAT ARE BY THE
EYE UNSEEN, YET ENTWINE ALL PARTS
INTO A LIVING WHOLE. IN THOSE TRACINGS,
THE MAP OF ALL CREATION, SUSTAINED BY
AND FOR LIFE, IS SEEN.

DRAWN UP INTO THE WEB OF THE
FIRMAMENT'S LIVING BODY, I AM
QUICKENED IN THE SPIRIT, OR MADE
MAD BY THE WINE OF ITS GRANDEUR.
FROM THE ARC THAT BEGINS THE
THE CIRCLE, I HAVE, AM NOW, AND
WILL EVER AGAIN TURN UPON THIS
WHEEL UNDER SUNS WITHOUT
NUMBER IN FORMS MANY AND
VARIED.

I SPEAK AND GO UNHEARD, UNVEILED
AND GO UNSEEN, TRANSFORMED AND
AM UNCHANGED. ON WORLDS
WITHOUT END, I AM THE WAYFARER
OF THE LIGHT, TILL THE DARKNESS
SHALL PASS INTO THE LIGHT OF ALL
GENERATION. I AM FOREVER THE

STRANGER IN A STRANGE LAND. I AM
ALONE.

Page 199   TWILIGHT STEALING INTO THE GARDEN,
THE QUARRELING VOICES OF NEIGHBORS
RISE ABOVE THE WALL AS THE SINKING SUN
YIELDS TO THE NIGHT. THE COOL OF DAY'S
LAST LIGHT, HEATED BY SUCH STRIFE, WILL
FAN THE EMBER OF THEIR RAGE UNTO THE
MORROW'S LIGHT.

ALL LIFE AND LIGHT EMERGES INTO
AND IS EMBEDDED IN, DARKNESS.
THE BRIGHTER THE LIGHT OF
DISCERNMENT, THE MORE THE
DARKNESS, IN ENVY, ENCROACHES
UPON AND SEEKS TO EXTINGUISH IT.

THE GREATER LIFE'S ILLUMINATION,
THE MORE DARKNESS IT DISPELS.
THE DOMINION OF DARKNESS SO
CHALLENGED, RISES, IN ITS IRE, TO
WHOLLY QUENCH THE OFFENDING
FIRE.

Page 202   THE LABORS OF THE DAY ARE NOT BURDEN
ENOUGH TO SMOTHER ME INTO DREAMLESS
SLEEP. NOT AT REST, MY SPIRIT ARISES
AND WANDERS, TOWING A SHUFFLING
BODY IN ITS WAKE. BODY AND SOUL
RETRACE A PATH TO WHERE MEMORY OF
THE DAY'S TOIL COMPELS ITS COURSE.
IN THE COLD SHADOWS OF THE WORKSHOP,

WHILE THOSE I CALL KIN SLEEP, I AM ALONE
AWAKENED BY VISIONS THAT ROUT SLEEP.
ACROSS THE MARCH OF CENTURIES, I SEE
THAT CHRONICLE OF MY WORDS AND ACTS,
WHICH SURVIVING MY PASSING, PRESSED

MORE TO EVIL THAN TO GOOD. YET, SPEAK
I MUST, AND ACTIONS FOLLOW IN THE DAILY
COURSE OF LIVING. I CANNOT UNDO WHAT I
HAVE NOT YET DONE, NOR CAN I STEP ASIDE
FROM THE PATH APPORTIONED TO ME.

Page 202　　SCRIBING THESE WORDS WHERE NO ONE
CAN SEE IS A TESTAMENT IN VAIN. YET,
WHAT CANNOT BE SAID FOR LACK OF EARS
IN THE MARKETPLACE TO HEAR, MUST
TAKE FORM, IF ONLY IN COMFORTLESS
MARKS UPON THESE FLATTENED REEDS.
THE SOUL GUIDES THE FLESH TO SEE
THAT WHICH IT KNOWS THROUGH HANDS
OF CLAY TO EYES OF MORTAL DUST.

SANDALED FOOT TREADING AMONG MY
FELLOWS, MY VOICE VAINLY SEEKS TO
WRITE IN THE CLAY OF LIFE FROM WHICH
WE ARE ALL ASSEMBLED, BUT IN THESE
ACTS OF LIVING, THERE IS NO SOLACE FOR
THE SOUL. SCRIBING IN BOTH WORD AND
DEED UPON THE VERY DUST IN WHICH
MAN HAS HIS LIFE, MAKES THIS A GOSPEL
OF MEAN CLAY THAT TURNS NOT TO MY
WORDS BUT EVER BACK UPON ITSELF. THE
FIERCE TIDINGS THAT TIME, UPON
BLOODIED SHOULDERS WILL BEAR ACROSS
THE CENTURIES YET TO COME WILL THE
EPISTLE OF MAN'S NATURE BE, AND NARY
THE MESSAGE OF MY WORDS.

Page 207　　ENTERING THE WORKSHOP, THEY WANT HERE
A TABLE, THERE A CHAIR. FROM THE GLOOM
WITHIN, EVERY MAN FRAMED BY THE DOOR
AND LIT BY THE SUN IS REVEALED. IN THIS
DISCERNMENT, I BEHOLD IN ALL WHO
COME A DIVISION.

IN EACH WHO COMES UPON THE THRESHOLD
TO PURCHASE MY SKILLS ARE TWO PARTS
EQUAL RESIDENTS. ONE OF THE SEA, THRICE
REMOVED, AND ONE OF STARDUST, ONCE
REMOVED FROM THE FIRES OF THE
BEGINNING. FIRE AND WATER STRIVE
WITHIN THIS HABITATION OF CLAY,
YIELDING ONLY THE VAPORS OF DOUBT
AND DISCONTENT.

THE TRIAL OF LIFE IS NOT BY FIRE BUT
BY WATER. BREAKING THE WATERS, WE
STRUGGLE UPON THEIR SURFACE AND
SUBMERGE AGAIN AT OUR VOYAGE'S
END. BORN IN THE FIRES OF CREATION
BEFORE THE FIRST WATERS OF MORTAL
LIFE FLOWED, WE EACH AND EVERY SOUL
LONG, WITHOUT RECALL, TO RETURN TO
THAT WARMTH AND LIGHT. EVER ABIDING
IN FAINT HOPE OF REUNION WITH THE
FIRST GENERATION'S RADIANCE, WE ARE
BECKONED HOME.

Page 210 GRIEVING NOW THE DEATH OF HIM WHO
WAS FATHER TO ME, I SEE ONLY MY HANDS
UPON THE WOOD. TO THOSE WHO NOW COME
A TALENT TO PURCHASE, THEIR EYES FOLLOW
THE CRAFTING OF EVERY PIECE TO SEE IF THE
FATHER'S SKILL HAS COME DOWN TO THE NEXT
GENERATION.

THE WORTH OF THE APPRENTICE CANNOT
BE JUDGED WHILE THE MASTER YET LIVES.
PASSING THE CRAFT BEGINS IN THE HANDS,
JOURNEYS THROUGH THE HEAD, AND RESTS
IN THE HEART. THE LIGHT'S ARTISAN, I
CAN GUIDE THE HAND, AND REFLECT
WITHIN THE MIND'S EYE, BUT THE HEART

OF THE APPRENTICE MAY BE ILLUMINED
ONLY BY A FLAME FROM WITHIN.

Page 218   MY MINISTRY, BUT A BRIEF DAY AS
WITNESS TO THE LIGHT, IS UPON ME.
OPENLY I WILL PASS AMONG THOSE OF
THIS WORLD KNOWING THAT LITTLE OF
THAT WHICH HERE IS WRITTEN CAN I
UTTER. THE LIFE AROUND ME REMAINS
A DRAMA OF ENDLESS REPETITIONS, AS
ONLY PLACE AND PLAYERS CHANGE AND
ARE CHANGED AGAIN. THE BEST OF WHAT
I MAY SAY WILL NOT BE HEARD, AND SO,
MUST GO UNSPOKEN. IN TIME'S
RECKONING, THE SHADOW UPON THE
SUN'S DIAL IS PATIENCE AND IN THIS
STILLNESS OF PURPOSE IS WISDOM.

OF THOSE WHOSE EYES CAN SEE AND
EARS CAN HEAR THE WORDS HERE SET
DOWN, THIS GENERATION PRODUCES
TOO FEW. A RACE, YOUNG AND FULL OF
LIFE, THEY SEE NOT BEYOND THEMSELVES
TO THAT WHICH WAS LIFE BEFORE EVER
THEY GLIMPSED THE FEW STARS ARRAYED
ABOUT THIS TINY WORLD. UPON THESE
FEEBLE REEDS THEN, IN FUTURE'S HOPE,
I SET AND SEAL THIS SCRIPT OF MY SOUL.

JAMES, BROTHER AND FRIEND, BURY
THESE MY THOUGHTS UNTO MYSELF
DEEP AND WELL. LONG AFTER WHAT
YOU HAVE SEEN OF ME AND I OF THEE
IS CRUMBLED TO DUST, THEY WILL
SPEAK AGAIN. IN THE TIME THAT
IS TO COME, THE HAND THAT SWEEPS
THE DUST FROM THESE PAGES IS
ORDAINED SO TO DO.

Page 224 DEATH IS LIFE'S LEVEL. YET, THE
LEVEL REVEALS ONLY THE WOOD'S
OUTER SHELL, NOT ITS TRUE NATURE.

KNOWING WHEN AND HOW I MUST
SHED THIS MOMENTARY RAIMENT OF
CLAY GIVES LEASE TO THE NEEDS OF
THE FLESH. VISIONS OF WHAT
BRIGHTNESS AWAITS BEYOND THE
TRIAL MAKES THE FEAR AND PAIN NO
LESS REAL. HOW EASILY DOES THE
BODY'S FRAIL DESPERATION MASTER
THE SOUL.

DYING TO THE DESPERATE 'I' OF WANT
AND NEED EXTINGUISHES NOT THE GLINT
OF LIFE, RATHER, FREED FROM A LANTERN
OF CLAY, THE SPIRIT'S LIGHT MAY WANDER
AGAIN AMONG THE STARS FROM WHICH
IT SPRANG. IT'S WHOLENESS IN FREEDOM
FINALLY PERFECTED, LIFE'S LIGHT MAY
DELIGHT IN THE FULFILLMENT OF THE
SOUL ETERNAL'S QUIET YEARNING.

Page 245 AS WITH THE PLANTS THAT ADORN THE
GROUND AND THE INNOCENCE OF ANIMALS
THAT GRAZE UPON THEM, LIFE, WHEN
YOUNG, IS SIMPLE. FOR MAN, AS WITH
THE FLOWERS AND BEASTS, TO BE SIMPLE
IS TO BE DIRECT. TO UNRAVEL THE KNOTS
OF ONE'S FELLOWS REQUIRES THE PATIENCE
AND WISDOM OF AGE. IN ITS YOUTH, MAN
SEVERS THE TWININGS WITH HIS OWN KIND,
NEVER SEEING THE TRAILING ENDS THAT,
WHEN LOOSED, REVEAL THE COMMON
THREAD BINDING THEM ALL TOGETHER.

Page 249 FOR ALL LIFE THAT BEHOLDS AND COMPREHENDS,
A MOMENT COMES WHEN A LEAP TO COMPLETE

AWARENESS REQUIRES A STEP BACK INTO THE INNOCENCE OF CHILDHOOD.

Page 279 TO HAVE LIFE IS TO KNOW ONLY IN PART. KNOWING ONLY IN PART, ALL ARE IN PAIN. IN THEIR PAIN IS FEAR AND RAGE AGAINST THAT FEAR. THE FIRES OF FEAR AND ANGER RAGING AGAINST THE PAIN OF LIFE WITHIN IS VENTED LIKE THE COOK STOVE'S SMOKE IN ANGRY DOMINATION OF THEIR FELLOWS. KNOWING NOT THE WHOLE, THEY BATTLE SHADOWS OF THEMSELVES IN THEIR FELLOWS.

Page 281 THE TIME DRAWING NIGH, THE LIGHT WITHIN STRAINS AGAINST THIS VESSEL OF CLAY. ARMED WITH BUT DIM RECALL OF ITS FREEDOM, LIGHT UNTO LIGHT, IT YEARNS AGAIN WITH ITS KIN TO ABIDE.

AS THE DAYS SUCCEED THE NIGHTS AND THE SEASONS FOLLOW ONE ANOTHER, THE FIRES OF THE CIRCLE'S BEGINNING THAT BURN WITHIN INCREASE AS THE FLESH, WHICH IS NOW BUT RAIMENT, DIMINISHES.

LIGHT'S COMMUNION CALLS TO ITS OWN.

Page 282 KIN TO ALL, I AM A STRANGER WHEREVER I WANDER. IN VISIONS THAT SEAR THE SOUL, I SEE PEOPLE AND PLACES NOT OF THIS TIME. WHETHER THESE SPECTERS HAIL FROM MANY PASTS OR SUMMON FUTURES WITHOUT NUMBER, I KNOW NOT.

ALTHOUGH BUT A PART, TRAPPED IN
ONE PLACE AND TIME, I FEEL THE
WHOLE OF LIGHT AND LIFE WITHIN ME
STRUGGLING TO BE FREE. IF YEARNING
BE THE MEASURE OF REFORMATION'S
NEED, THEN COULD I TRANSFORM THIS
PLACE I WOULD, OR FLEEING FROM IT,
REST WITHIN THE REALM OF LIGHT.

Page 287   LIFE OF ITSELF BEGINS AND ENDS THE
CIRCLE OF LIGHT. TAKING BREATH IN
AIR OR WATER, ALL THAT LIVES YEARNS
TO SIGH AND INSPIRE IN THE GENTLE
WINDS THAT FILL THE SAILS OF THE
STARS. LIGHT'S CALLING, NOT GRASPED
BY THE EYE NOR SOUNDING IN THE EAR,
DRAWS ALL LIFE TO THE WOMB IT
REMEMBERS NOT.

DOES NOT ALL THAT LIVES BEGIN IN
THE SEED AND, GROWING TO MATURITY,
BECOME THE SEED AGAIN? THE FIELD
OF THE UNIVERSE WAS TILLED SO THAT
THESE SEEDS OF THE BEGINNING MIGHT
BE SOWN AND, RISING TO A FULL HEAD
RETURN AGAIN TO THE SOWER.

IN INNOCENT AWARENESS IS THE
GLORY OF THE LIGHT ENCOMPASSED
AND FULFILLED. THE RIGHTEOUSNESS
OF ETERNITY'S ILLUMINATION SLEEPS
IN THE UNBROKEN LINKS TYING TOGETHER
ALL THAT HAS LIFE WITHIN THE GREAT AND
ETERNAL NOW.

Page 288   IN THE STILL OF NIGHT, VENTURING
BEYOND THE VILLAGE WALL AND THE
CHATTER OF LIFE IT ENCLOSES, I PULL
ON THE CLOAK OF NIGHT AND AM

COMFORTED BY ITS LINING OF
SILENCE. BENEATH MY FEET THE
HILL'S HEAD, BEFORE ME THE RISING
MOON BLOTS OUT FAINT STARS. KIN
TO ITS COOL GLOW, I AM ONE STEP
CLOSER TO HOME.

THE HOSTS OF HEAVEN ARRAYED
BEFORE MY EYES ARE BEYOND
COUNTING, YET WITHIN, I SEE A
GATHERING OF LIGHTS THAT MAKES
FEW THE MULTITUDE OF STARS
CAPTURED BY THE COMPASS OF MY
FEEBLE EYE. GRASPING BUT IN PART,
I WOULD KNOW AGAIN THE WHOLE.

AS A CHILD EMERGING FROM THE
TINY VESSEL OF THE WOMB SEES
THE GREAT EXPANSE OF THE WORLD,
SO MY EYE WITHIN YEARNS AGAIN
TO BEHOLD THE NOW THAT IS THE
UNBROKEN CIRCLE OF THE LIGHT AT
THE BEGINNING OF THE UNIVERSE.

Page 291 A NEW LINTEL FOR THE WINE MERCHANT
PRESSES MY SHOULDER DOWN AS STONES
WHOSE HEAT BREAD COULD BAKE PASS
BENEATH MY FEET. NAZARETH'S PATHS,
BLACK WITH FLIES, BUZZ MOREOVER
WITH THE COMMON STRIFE OF MAN
CROWDED UPON HIS OWN KIND. LIFE,
A SOJOURN EVER HOMEWARD BOUND IS
BUT A JOURNEY IN THE SOUL'S
REMINISCENCE, ENDING IN THE LIGHT.
YET, THIS MEMORY OF REDEMPTION,
FROM THE BEGINNING PERFECTED, IS
HOSTAGE TO THE TRIALS EACH DAY OF
LIVING BRINGS ANEW.

THE DIARY

ALL STRIVE IN FEAR TO SUSTAIN BREATH
AND MOTION IN THIS BRIEF MOMENT OF
ETERNITY, KNOWING NOT THE LENGTH AND
BREADTH OF THEIR BEING. IN THIS STRUGGLE
IS MUCH LOST AND LITTLE GAINED.

THE DUST OF GALILEE CLOUDS THE EYE
AND STOPS THE EAR OF THOSE FEW WHO,
IN LISTENING, MIGHT HEAR AND, IN
LOOKING, MIGHT SEE. VISIONS THAT I
CLOAK IN WORDS TOO SMALL TO CONTAIN
ALL THAT IS THE LIGHT MUST LIE IN
THIS DUST UNTIL A NOW THAT IS YET
TO COME. OF ALL THE NOWS WITHIN
THE NOW, I AM HERE IN THIS DUST.

Page 293   THE WOOD HAS WORKED ITS WILL ON
THIS FEEBLE SHELL OF CLAY AS, PAUSING
AT MIDDAY, THESE HANDS AND ARMS
LAMENT THEIR WEARINESS.

ESCAPING THE HEAT OF THE DAY, I SIT
BENEATH THE CANOPY OF SIMON THE
WEAVER, WHO IS MY FRIEND. NIMBLE
FINGERS, THREADS OF MANY COLORS,
BRAID TOGETHER UNTIL FROM MANY
COMES ONE. MANY COLORS AND MANY
TWININGS BECOME A COVERING THAT
SHEDS THE SUN OR DRIVES AWAY THE
CHILL OF NIGHT. IN THE WEAVER'S ART
IS THE LOVE OF SINGULARITY IN
DIVERSITY REALIZED.

WITHIN ALL THAT WHICH IS FAMILIAR
IS THE WHOLE OF THE UNIVERSE
REFLECTED. THE WOOL OF ALL THAT IS,
BECOMES MANY INDIVIDUAL THREADS,
EACH CARRYING ITS OWN TWIST AND
COLOR. UNDER THE WEAVER'S HAND,

EACH TWINING FIBER COMES TO KNOW
ITS PLACE IN THE TAPESTRY OF LIFE.
THAT WHICH LIVES IS THE WAKING
DREAM AND GLORY OF A UNIVERSE
THAT SLUMBERS, SAVE FOR THE
LIGHT AND LIFE IT SHELTERS.

Page 324 NONE OF THE EVERLASTING FIRE THAT
THE WORDS HERE SET TO PAGE MIGHT
IGNITE SHOWS UPON THE FACES AND
IN THE EYES OF THOSE MET UPON EACH
MARKET DAY. LIKE STONES STACKED
INTO A WALL, TIME MUST BE SET UPON
TIME UNTIL THOSE WHOSE LIGHT IS NOT
REFLECTED BUT SPRINGS FROM WITHIN,
LIGHTING THE COUNTENANCE AND FILLING
THE EYE RISE FROM THIS DUST AND JOIN
THEIR ILLUMINATION TO THE WHIRLING
DANCE OF TIME, LIGHT AND LIFE.

FROM THOSE AMONG WHOM I
SOJOURN, BLOOD INTERTWINING
OVER COUNTLESS GENERATIONS,
WILL ONE DAY COME SOME WHO,
IN LOOKING, SHALL SEE BEYOND
AND THROUGH THE HIGH TERRACES
THAT TIME BUILDS UPON THE BONES
OF ITS CHILDREN. THESE, ALSO IN
LISTENING, SHALL HEAR THE SINGLE
UNENDING REFRAIN THAT CHANTS
ITS WAY THROUGH ALL THAT HAD,
HAS AND WILL HAVE LIFE.

LIKE CHILDREN, OPEN AND TRUSTING,
THEY WILL KNOW, ENFOLD AND BE
ENTWINED IN THE WEAVE OF THE
UNIVERSE. RECEIVING IN THAT EMBRACE
THE STRANDS AND STREAMING OF THE
LIGHT THAT ILLUMINATES THE NOW.
WEAVING THEIR NEST OF THE LIGHT, THEY

WILL FLY UPON COMPASSION'S WINGS
UNTO A HAVEN WHERE STRIFE SHALL
FIND NO ROOT.

Page 326 SUFFERING, LIKE A BAPTISM IN COLD DARK
WATERS, SO CHILLS BODY AND SPIRIT THAT
HOPE IS SUSTAINED ONLY BY HUDDLING
NEXT TO THE FIRES WITHIN THAT COME
DOWN FROM THE FLAME OF ALL BEGINNINGS.
HERE ONLY, DO I SEE BEYOND THE
LIGHTLESS TOMB OF THIS WORLD TO THE
WARMTH THAT WAS AT THE START. THE
GREAT CIRCLE WHOSE BEGINNING IS ALSO,
IN ONE TIMELESS MOMENT, THE END CALLS
TO ME. I LONG FOR THE VISTA OF THE NOW,
FOR HOME.

THE NOW IS THE LIGHT BEYOND THE
RISE AND FALL OF THE STARS. THE
SPARKS OF AWARENESS FROM ALL
THE BEFORE AND AFTER EMBERS OF
LIFE MERGE INTO THE ONE GREAT
LIGHT THAT IS AT ONE MOMENT THE
EVERLASTING NOW.

IN THIS ONE ETERNAL MOMENT IS ALL
LIFE AND LIGHT CREATED AND, FOR
THIS CAUSE, IS THE UNIVERSE SPRUNG
INTO BEING. AT REST WITHIN THIS
CIRCLE OF ALL KNOWING, WOVEN
RIGHTLY TOGETHER, ARE SUBSTANCE
AND SPIRIT UNITED, BANISHING
FOREVER THE ILLUSION OF DIFFERENCE.
I YEARN ONCE AGAIN TO EMERGE
FROM THIS WOMB OF FLESH.

Page 328 BENEATH KINDLY SPRING SKIES, I OBSERVE
THE SOWERS IN THE FIELD. HOW SIMPLE IS
THEIR HANDIWORK. WITHIN THE SEED IS

LIFE IMPRISONED, WHICH WATER FREES AND
SOIL NURTURES. AS SPRING ROUSES THE
SOWER, SO I AM CALLED BY LIFE, SCATTERED
IN PIECES FAR FROM ITS BIRTHPLACE, TO
GENTLY BECKON IT HOME.

WHERE THERE IS LIFE, I AM SUMMONED
TO VOICE THE FRAIL WHISPER OF BEGINNING'S
REMEMBRANCE TO THE FORGETFULNESS OF
FLESH. FROM ONE TO ANOTHER SWIRLING
CONGREGATION OF STARS I JOURNEY, AGED
BEYOND TIME'S COUNTING, YET, ALWAYS
AND EVER NEWLY CRAFTED TO FINITE FORM.

UNDER SUNS AND SKIES OF MANY HUES,
I WITNESS IN PART TO THE WHOLE THAT
CAN BE FELT BUT NOT SEEN. I AM IN THE
BEGINNING OF THAT WHICH HAS NO END.
I AM THE WHOLE OF ALL PARTS, I AM THAT
WHICH BINDS THEM TOGETHER.

Page 343   FROM THE BEGINNING, WITHIN ONE, TWO
HAVE BEEN SECRETED. IN MILLENNIA'S
COURSE, CLEAVING, THE TWO SHALL EACH
THEIR OWN SEPARATE DESTINY FULFILL.

TILLER OF THE SOIL AND CENTURION OF
ROME'S MIGHT TAKE THE FRUIT OF THE VINE
TOGETHER. THE GRAPE'S BLOOD, AS SWEET TO
BOTH, SETS THE HUSBAND OF THE EARTH TO
HARVEST SONG AND THE SOLDIER TO ANGER.
FROM A COMMON VINTAGE ARE TWO TEMPERS
BORN.

THOSE WHO KNOW AND ARE CONTENTED
BY THE KNOWING SHALL PART FROM THOSE
WHO DELIGHT IN THE STRUGGLE TO WREST
THE UNIVERSE TO THEIR WILL. IN THIS
PARTING, ONE SHALL BECOME TWO, EACH

TRAVELING THE PATH THAT HAS CHOSEN
THEM.

WHEN THOSE WHO CAN SUMMON THE
LIGHT AND ARE COMFORTED BY THE
NOW COME, THE PARTING BEGINS.

Page 365   AWAKE BEFORE THE SUN, I AM SENTRY AT THE
GATES OF DARKNESS AS THE LIGHT SUPPLANTS
NIGHT'S FEARS. THROUGH THE EYE OF THE SUN,
I SEE A TIME WHEN ALL IS LIGHT, AND DREAD,
LIKE THE EVEN'S SHADE, IS FOREVER BANISHED.

WHEN THOSE COME, WHO IN LISTENING SHALL
HEAR AND IN LOOKING SHALL SEE, A VISION
CARRYING NOT BEYOND, BUT THROUGH THE
DARK ILLUSION OF THE UNIVERSE TO THE LIGHT,
WHICH LYING BENEATH THAT SHELL AND
NOURISHING IT, SHALL BE THEIRS. SOULS
ABIDING IN A TRUE VISION OF THE LIGHT,
THEIR FLESH SHALL, NESTED WITHIN THE CRUDE
MATTER OF ALL THAT IS, REMAIN AS LIVING
WITNESS OF THAT WHICH, UNSEEN, SUPPORTS
THE FABRIC OF THE HEAVENS.

ALL THAT HAD, HAS AND WILL HAVE LIFE
DWELLS WITHIN THE LIGHT. ITS COMINGS
AND GOINGS IN THE DARKNESS OF THE
UNIVERSE ARE BUT MOMENTS WITHIN THE
NOW OF ALL TIMES.

THE LIGHT IS LIFE. LIFE MAKES MANIFEST
THAT LIGHT, RISING AS THE SUN IN THE
MORNING AND SINKING AT EVENTIDE, BUT
EVER THERE, SEEN OR UNSEEN BY THE EYE
OF MAN.

A GREAT LOOM OF LIGHT AND LIFE WORKS ITS
WOOF AND WARP IN THREADS OF MANY COLORS

BREADTHS AND LENGTHS. THE GREAT TAPESTRY
IT WEAVES IS NEVER FULLY REVEALED IN THE
FEW FIBERS THAT THE UNIVERSE DISCLOSES.

Page 369 ESCAPING DROUGHT'S GRASP, A SOLITARY
DROP SUMMONS A DUSTY PLUME UPON
THE GROUND WHOSE GREATNESS OR'TOWERS
THE SMALL RAIN BEAD'S BOUNTY. EACH
DROP JOINING TO ITS FELLOWS, BECOME A
RIVULET OF LIFE THEN A MIGHTY STREAM
THAT FEEDS THE HUNGRY SEA. THE MAIN
SATED YIELDS IT BOUNTY UNTO THE AIR,
ITS SEPARATE PARTS FALLING ONCE AGAIN
UPON THE THIRSTY GROUND. THE LIGHT
BEFORE ALL BEGINNINGS, AN OCEAN OF
LIFE SCATTERING ITSELF THROUGHOUT ALL
OF CREATION, CALLS BACK EACH DROP TO
THE MOTHER OF WATERS.

FROM THE WHOLE COMES EVERY PART.
KNOWING NOT THE WHOLE, EACH PART
BECOMES A WHOLE UNTO ITSELF. THEY
REAP SORROW AND TRAVAIL WHO WOULD
FORCE OPEN THE PORTALS OF LIGHT,
SEEKING TO MASTER THE WHOLE OF
WHICH THEY ARE BUT PIECES. IT IS THE
ANGUISH OF SEPARATION.

Page 387 WE ENTER LIFE KNOWING ONLY LIFE.
THOUGH WE SOJOURN IN DARKNESS,
WE HOLD IT TO BE LIGHT, OUR EYE
DIMMED BY THE SHADOWS. OUR
JOURNEY FROM BEFORE TO NOW AND
TO BEFORE AGAIN IS A TIMELESS
SOJOURN FROM LIGHT TO DARKNESS
AND DARKNESS TO LIGHT AGAIN.

THROUGH ALL THAT HAS LIFE WILL
THE LIGHT KNOW THE DARKNESS

THAT SPRANG FROM IT. AS THE
CHILD BECOMES A MAN, SO THE
DARKNESS GROWS WITH EACH
TWINKLING OF LIFE TO THE
MANHOOD OF LIGHT.

WHEN THE LIGHT, THAT MADE
THE DARKNESS, GATHERS IT ONCE
AGAIN UNTO ITSELF, THEN, SHALL
ALL BE LIGHT AND ALL THAT IS
LIGHT SHALL BE LIFE.

Page 399   IN THE DEW OF MORNING, I BEHOLD THE
SOWERS GO OUT INTO THE FIELD. THOSE
WHOSE ART IS HEAVY WITH AGE SOW
UPON THE HILLS WHERE THE GROUND IS
SOMETIMES HARD AND STONEY. YOUNG
HUSBANDS OF THE SOIL CAST THEIR SEEDS
UPON THE BANKS OF STREAMS WHERE THE
SILT IS SOFT AND DEEP. THE AGED SOWERS'
YIELD IS SPARSE BUT THEIR HARVEST,
ALTHOUGH MODEST, IS AN ASSURED
INCREASE FROM EVERY KERNEL STREWN
UPON THE RAGGED SLOPES. UNTUTORED
BY THE WISDOM OF MANY SEASONS'
PASSAGE, THE YOUTHFUL SOWERS' SEEDS
ARE OFTEN BY THE FLOODS OF SPRING'S
PASSION, SWEPT AWAY AND WITH THESE
WISPS OF LIFE, THEIR HOPES.

BETWEEN LIGHT AND DARKNESS LIKE THE
AGED SOWER I TRAVEL. AT HOME IN THE
LIGHT, BUT NEEDED IN THE DARKNESS, I
TREAD THE HARDENED GROUND. THE
SEEDS OF LIGHT MUST BE SOWN WHERE
THEY ARE NEEDED, BUT IN ROCKY SOILS
ABOUNDING WITH STRIFE, MOST CHOKE
AND DIE. IN A NOW TO COME, NEW SEEDS
STREWN IN GROUND UNDARKENED BY

WARS OF THE HEART AND WELL WATERED
WILL SWELL TO AN INCREASE IN PEACE
UNBEGOTTEN BY PRIDE. I AM THE SOWER
WHOSE HARVEST COMES NOT UNTIL THE
FIELD IS WHITE WITH LIGHT.

Page 414 I WANDER WHERE CURRENTS OF LIVING
WATERS MEET THE DESERT WASTES. HERE,
LIFE'S FLOW TOUCHES THE GROWING EDGE
OF SCORCHING DEATH. IN THIS WORLD OF
FAINT KNOWING, WHAT LIVES IS BEHELD
AS FRAIL, YET, IN ALL THAT PARTAKES OF
LIFE'S QUICKENING IS STRENGTH BEYOND
MEASURE. THE DWELLING WHEREIN LIFE
NESTS IS BUT RAIMENT WHICH, WHEN
CAST ASIDE IN THE CONSUMMATION OF
ALL CREATION, WILL BE REVEALED AS
BUT A VAIN AND BEGUILING HABIT.

WITHOUT THE ATTIRE OF MIGHT, I
SOJOURN AMONG THESE WHO ARE MY
BROTHERS IN THE QUICKENING OF THE
CLAY THAT IS LIFE. I SPEAK OF LIFE'S
MARROW, YET, THEY SEE ONLY THE CLOTH
OF FLESH AND BONE. SOUNDS UPON THE
WIND, MY WORDS MINGLE AND ARE LOST
IN THE HUM OF DARK CLAY'S CLAMOR
UPON THE EARS OF THE SOUL. EYES
TUNED TO THE BRIEF CLAIMS OF THE
CLAY UPON THE SPIRIT, THEY SEE FORM
ONLY. MEN'S FRAIL MEMORY OF CLAY
CANNOT HOLD FAST THE REMEMBRANCE
OF THOSE FIERY THREADS THAT
ENLIVENED THEIR BEGINNINGS.

THE ASCENT OF LIFE FROM UNSEEN WRITHING
SPECKS IN WATERS SLOWED BY THE REEDS
TO THAT WHICH BEHOLDS THE ORDER IN THE
HEAVENS IS BUT SAND SWIRLING IN THE

WILDERNESS. THE SOLITARY WAYFARER SEES
THROUGH THE ARROGANCE OF HIS NEEDS
THE SHIFTING GRAINS FORM SHAPES THAT
MAKE THE DESERT'S SHINING SEA A
UNIVERSE RECONCILED TO HIM ALONE.

THAT WHICH IS NATURE, THAT WHICH
MOVES IN ALL LIFE IS THE LIGHT. LARGE
AND SMALL, SEEN AND UNSEEN, EACH
SPARK IS ENLIVENED TO STRUGGLE AGAINST
THE BONDAGE OF THE CLAY AND RETURN
AGAIN TO THE FIRES OF CREATION FROM
WHICH IT SPRANG.

I AM COME AS CLAY. I SHALL COME AGAIN
IN THE GREAT CIRCLE OF LIFE AS LIGHT TO
ENLIVEN THE WORLD. IN JOY, THE DUST
OF THIS WORLD WILL BE SUMMONED HOME,
BUT NOT ALL. TWO STREAMS SHALL ISSUE
FORTH INTO STARRY FIELDS FROM THE BLUE
WOMB OF WATERS. ONE SURGING OUT IN
A GREAT FLOOD OF CONQUEST, THE OTHER, A
TRANQUIL RIVULET BEARS ONLY A TAPER,
ITS FLAME KINDLED BY THE LIGHT OF
CREATION.

Page 417 GROUND DOWN BY THE WEIGHT OF TODAY
AND WHAT I KNOW MUST COME, I FEEL
THE DARKNESS FILLING EACH FOOTPRINT,
AS I FLEE FROM SUNRISE TO SUNSET.

Page 427 THE WEAVER'S ART, MORE THAN THE
CARPENTER'S CRAFT, REVEALS THAT FIRST
LIFE THAT BROUGHT ALL CREATION TO
PASS. THE FIRST ROW SETS THE PATTERN
FOR THE WEAVE. ONCE COMPLETE, EACH
FIBER LOOSED FROM THE TAPESTRY OF ALL
LIFE MUST FIND ITS WAY BACK TO THE
PLACE APPORTIONED TO IT. BEARING THE

DYES AND TWISTS OF ITS PILGRIMAGE,
FROM EACH THREAD'S RETURN, A NEW
PATTERN BORN OF BOTH REDEEMED
MORTAL PAIN AND JOY IS WOVEN.

IN PERFECT KNOWLEDGE THAT IN EACH
PART IS THE WHOLE CONTAINED SHALL
THE TRUE INHERITANCE OF THE MEEK
BE CONFERRED.

IN STRUGGLE'S BLIND CONFLICT IS LIFE'S
BEGINNING. ITS FOREVER FUTURE, PURE
AND COMPLETE, IS WHOLLY SWALLOWED
UP IN CONSCIOUSNESS. FOR ALL OF LIFE,
LIGHT AND THOUGHT ARE WITHIN EACH
AND EVERY STRAND, AT ONCE ETERNAL.
ALL THAT IS LIFE RETURNING THREAD BY
THREAD TO THE LOOM, PERFECTING BY
ITS PRESENCE, ROW UPON ROW, THAT
WHICH IS THE TAPESTRY OF CREATION.

Page 444 TRAVELERS ON MOUNTAIN PASSES
UP FROM MISTY FIORDS THEY COME
THE SKEIN OF MY PEOPLE WOUND
TOGETHER AS ONE.

THE STRAND OF MY FATHER
THE THREAD OF MY MOTHER
FIBERS OF BROTHERS AND SISTERS
ALL CALL TO ME TO TWINE WITHIN
THE BRAID OF OUR BLOOD.

WOVEN TOGETHER WE JOURNEY
BACK TO THE STARRY LOOM OF LIFE
TO FEEL AGAIN THE WEAVER'S HAND.

Page 448 THE UNIVERSE OF LIFELESS CLAY,
LIKE THE MARKETPLACE CAUGHT IN
THE HEAT OF THE NOONDAY SUN,

THE DIARY

TRADES ITS WARES IN KIND. FOR
GOODS OF WORTH GIVEN, GOODS
OF WORTH ARE RECEIVED.

OFTEN IN THE CONCOURSE OF MEN,
GOOD IS REQUITED WITH EVIL AND
FOR EVIL, GOOD IS EXCHANGED. IN
THIS COMMERCE, THE SOUL, EVIL FOR
GOOD RECEIVING, IS NOT INJURED.
THE WORTH OF THE BARTER LIES IN
THE HEART OF THE SELLER. MERCHANTS
ALL TO OUR FELLOWS IN VENDING EVIL
VEILED AS GOOD, WE ENFEEBLE THE
LIFE AND LIGHT WITHIN.

IN DECEPTION, THE DECEIVER IS
DECEIVED. FOR EACH FALSENESS
QUELLS THE SMALL SPARK DRAWN
FROM THE FIRES OF CREATION THAT
HAVE FROM THE BEGINNING
QUICKENED BOTH DECEIVER AND
DECEIVED ALIKE.

THE SPARK OF THE DECEIVED
FLICKERS NOT WHEN EVIL IS
RECEIVED FOR GOOD, WHILE
THE EMBER OF THE DECEIVER
SMOLDERS, RETREATING FROM
THE LIGHT TO THE COLD
SOLACE OF DUMB CLAY.

A LIFE DARKENED BY THE SHADE
OF MASTERY OVER OTHERS IS
ESTRANGED FROM THE LIGHT. THE
TRADERS OF COMMERCE EXCEL IN
THEIR DOMINANCE OF OTHERS, BUT
NOT IN THE GENTLE WISDOM OF THE
LIGHT. THE MARKET PLACE REWARDS
THOSE WHO ARE HER MASTERS.

RECOMPENSE IS THEIRS IN KIND,
CLAY FOR CLAY.

TO RETURN EVIL FOR EVIL JOINS
EACH TO THE TRIBE OF CLAY
WHERE CREATION'S LIGHT DAILY
RENEWED IN THE EYES OF THE
MEEK DWELLS NOT.

BARTERING IN THE LIGHT
BENEATH THE DARKNESS, THE
MEEKS' EXCHANGE FANS THE
SPARKS OF CREATION'S FIRE,
TRADING IN AN EXCHEQUER
WHERE GIVING IS GETTING.

MEN DIFFER ONLY AT THEIR BEST.
OVERCOME BY DOMINION'S
IMPASSIONED ENTREATY, THEIR
COMMON CLAY IS OF ONE MIND
AND SPIRIT.

Page 454   TO RETURN EVIL FOR EVIL JOINS
EACH TO THE TRIBE OF CLAY
WHERE CREATION'S LIGHT DAILY,
RENEWED IN THE EYES OF THE
MEEK, DWELLS NOT.

Page 457   MEN DIFFER ONLY AT THEIR BEST.
OVERCOME BY DOMINION'S
IMPASSIONED ENTREATY, THEIR
COMMON CLAY IS OF ONE MIND
AND SPIRIT.

Page 458   BARTERING IN THE LIGHT
BENEATH THE DARKNESS, THE
MEEKS' EXCHANGE FANS THE
SPARKS OF CREATION'S FIRE

TRADING IN AN EXCHEQUER
WHERE GIVING IS GETTING.

Page 459 THE WRATH OF GOD ABIDES ONLY IN THE
CONJURING OF MENS' GUILTY RAGE AND
SORROW. UNWILLING TO YOKE THEIR OWN
PASSIONS, THEY LOOK TO THE HEAVENS FOR
ANOTHER TO DO SO. THE DAY OF JUDGMENT
WAS CRAFTED, NOT IN THE LIGHT, BUT IN
THE CLAY OF MAN'S TERROR. THE HORROR
OF A DAY OF RECKONING SPRINGS FROM
MINDS DEVOTED TO MASTERY, RAGE AND
RETRIBUTION. THE LIGHT AT THE BEGINNING
OF THE UNIVERSE SOWS NOT THE DARKNESS
OF FEAR AND RAGE, BUT REJOICES IN THE
ILLUMINATION THAT DAILY RISES IN THE
BRIGHT GARDEN OF THE SOUL.

MAN IS HIS OWN WRATH AND JUDGMENT.
THE WEAVER'S LIGHT IS WISDOM AND
LOVE IN EQUAL MEASURE. KNOWING THE
FLAWS OF EACH FIBER AND STRAND OF
CREATION, HE SEEKS ONLY THAT THE FINAL
WEAVE OF LIGHT'S CONSUMMATION FILL
ALL THAT IS WITH BRILLIANCE.

Page 493 THAT WHICH WAS ONE IS NOW
TWAIN. THE NEST OF LIFE IS TORN
BY THE WINDS OF STRIFE AND TWO
FLEDGLINGS MUST TAKE WING. ONE
TO HEROIC CONQUEST AND THE
REVELATIONS OF FRUSTRATED PASSIONS,
THE OTHER TO CONTEMPLATION OF THE
LIGHT BENEATH THE DARKNESS OF
THIS UNIVERSE.

FOR EARTH'S ORPHANED CHILDREN
OF THE LIGHT THERE SHALL BE NEW
HEAVENS AND A NEW EARTH. THERE

AMIDST HER GARDENS SHALL BE A
GENESIS IN AND OF THE LIGHT. FROM
THIS NEW BEGINNING SHALL A BRIDGE
ARISE THAT ALL MAY CROSS UNTIL
EVERYWHERE IS LIGHT AND THE
DARKNESS OF MATTER IS FOREVER
BANISHED.

FOR EARTH'S CHILDREN OF BLOOD
AND FEAR, THERE WILL BE CONQUEST
ENOUGH TO SATE THE VAINEST
STRIVINGS OF THE HUMAN HEART.
WORLDS WITHOUT END, ENEMIES
WITHOUT NUMBER, UNTIL ALL
SUBDUED, THEY SEE THE WREATHS
OF VICTORY AS BUT EMPTY CIRCUITS
OF THEMSELVES.

AS THE INHERITANCE OF THE MEEK
IS GREAT, SO MUCH IS REQUIRED.
TO YOU IS GIVEN LIGHT'S SIGHT
BEYOND ILLUSION'S IMPERMANENT
DARKNESS. ABIDE, THEREFORE, IN
THIS LIGHT. WINNOW ALL KNOWING,
SHARE THE GRAIN OF TRUTH FREELY
WITH ALL THAT HAS LIFE AND, IN
PATIENT SERVICE BE STEADFAST. I
AM WITHIN YOUR EYE'S SHINING.
I AM THE STILL SMALL VOICE
COUNSELING LIGHT IN THE MIDST
OF STRIFE'S DARKNESS UNTIL THE
DARKNESS IS NO MORE.

Page 517   THOSE WHO KNOW AND ARE
CONTENTED BY THE KNOWING
SHALL PART FROM THOSE WHO
DELIGHT IN THE STRUGGLE TO
WREST THE UNIVERSE TO THEIR
WILL. IN THIS PARTING, ONE SHALL

BECOME TWO, EACH TRAVELING
THE PATH THAT HAS CHOSEN THEM.

Page 521 I AM THE BEGINNING AND THE END.
I AM THE LOWLIEST AND THE LOFTIEST
OF LIFE BECOME ONE IN AN ENDLESS
CIRCUIT OF LIGHT.

I AM BORN AND BORN AGAIN, LIVING
IN AND DYING TO WORLDS WITHOUT
END. IN MANY FORMS, AT MANY TIMES,
CLOTHED IN THE FLESH OF THOSE UPON
WHOM I CALL, I AM EVER THE SAME.

I AM THE ASCENT OF LIFE. I AM ITS
STRUGGLE IN THE DARKNESS AND ITS
REPOSE IN THE LIGHT. FOREVER IN
THE NOW, I JOURNEY FROM THE
LIGHT TO LIFE'S CLAY LANTERN AND
TO THE LIGHT AGAIN.

TO THE LOOM'S FRAGILE LOOPS I AM
THE FIRST OF ALL ROWS AND THE
ARCHETYPE OF ALL LIFE'S PARTS. THE
DARNER OF THE LOOM, I PASS IN AND
THROUGH LIVING ROWS, INTERLACING
ALL LIFE UNTIL THE TAPESTRY OF TIME
IS WOVEN WHOLE AND COMPLETE.

Page 539 FEAR NOT. THOUGH YOU ARE FEW,
MANY SHALL YOU BECOME. AS
ONCE YOU TROD UPON THE BREAST
OF YOUR MOTHER, NOW SHALL YOU
WAYFARERS BE AMONG THE LIGHTS
OF THE FIRMAMENT.

OF CONQUEST AND DEFEAT, YOU
SHALL, IN THE SIFTING OF TIME'S
SAND, EQUAL MEASURE RECEIVE.

YET, IN CONFLICT WITH MANY
WHOSE IMAGE REFLECTS NOT YOUR
OWN, SHALL KINSHIP'S KNOT BE
TIED. WHEN VICTORY'S SHALLOW
PROMISE GIVES WAY TO GRACE
IN SELFLESS UNITY WITH THOSE
NOT OF YOUR OWN TRIBE THEN
WILL PEACE BE VOUCHED SAFE
TO YOUR SEED.

THE GIFTS OF LIGHT'S FLIGHT ARE
YOURS SO THAT SOJOURNERS AMONG
THE EMBERS OF CREATION YOU MAY
BECOME. USE WISELY THAT WHICH,
WITHOUT PETITION, YOU HAVE BEEN
GRANTED. AS YOU HAVE RECEIVED,
SO GIVE.

THAT WHICH WAS YOUR BIRTHPLACE
IS NO MORE. ALL THAT IS THIS GALAXY
HAS BECOME YOUR LEGACY. LEARN
JUSTICE, PRACTICE HARMONY WITH
ALL THAT HAS LIFE, GROW IN WISDOM,
AND IN PEACE AND MERCY PROSPER.

Page 544 NO TILLER OF THE EARTH COUNTS HIS
SEEDS IN THE DARKNESS, LEST, FALLING
INTO THE SHADOWS, THEY ARE LOST TO
THE PROMISE OF THE LIGHT. RATHER
HE GAZES UPON EACH KERNEL IN FULL
ILLUMINATION AND JUDGES HOW MUCH
FRUIT IT WILL BRING FORTH.

THE LIFE OF THE CORN IS IN THE LIGHT,
BOTH IN ITS COUNTING AND ITS
INCREASE. THE DARK OF THE EARTH IS
BUT A BRIEF RESPITE FOR THAT WHICH
MUST GROW INTO THE LIGHT.

LOCKED IN THE KERNEL IS A MEMORY
OF THE LIGHT AND, SPROUTING, IT STRAINS
TOWARD THAT WHICH IT RECALLS. TWISTING
WITHIN DARK MATTER'S GRASP, EACH
SEEDLING OF LIGHT'S FULLNESS STRUGGLES
IN ANGUISH AGAINST THE HARD EDGES OF
ITS CONFINEMENT. YET EVEN WHEN
WEDGED IN THE DARKEST CREVICE, ALWAYS,
LIFE REACHES TOWARD AN ILLUMINATION
GLOWING ONLY IN MEMORY'S FAINT HOPE.

CRAFTED AT THE BEGINNING BY THE
LIGHT, DARK MATTER'S IMPERMANENCE
IS VOUCHSAFED AS BUT A BRIEF
SHADOW IN THE SOJOURN FROM LIGHT
TO LIGHT. CRUDE MATTTER'S CREATION,
FROM THE TINIEST MOTE TO THE GREATEST
STAR, EVER DYING AND REBORN, TURNS
LIKE A WHEEL WHOSE HUB, LIFE, IS THAT
WHICH REMAINS FOREVER ITS
STEADFAST ANCHOR AND GUIDE.

Page 546   A TAPER BURNING IN THE NOONDAY
BRIGHTNESS CASTS NO SHADOW, NOR
CAN ITS POWER TO ILLUMINATE THE
DARKNESS BE KNOWN, SAVE IT BE
THRUST INTO THE WOEFUL GLOOM
OF A MOONLESS NIGHT.

TO RECOGNIZE ITS RADIANCE, EACH
OF LIFE'S EMBERS MUST JOURNEY IN
THE DARKNESS. ABIDING ALWAYS
WITHIN THE WOMB OF CREATION'S
FIRES, NO SPARK CAN KNOW ITS
TRUE NATURE.

THE SPARK OF LIFE HOLDS ITS OWN
BRILLIANCE DEAR ONLY WHEN

SWALLOWED BY A DARKNESS THAT
THREATENS TO QUENCH THAT FIRE.

ALL SEPARATE, THE LIGHTS OF LIFE
JOURNEY WITHIN THE DUSK OF
MATTER. EACH A SINGLE BEAM,
YET ALL SUSTAINED BY HOPEFUL
MEMORY OF THE FIRES THAT
KINDLED THEM, THEY TURN
EVER TOWARD REUNION WITH
THE GLOW OF ALL BEGINNING'S
TO WHICH ALL LIGHT MUST
NEEDS RETURN.

UNSEEN, YET EVER WITHIN AND
SURROUNDING EACH EMBER FROM
THE BURST OF LIFE THAT WAS THE
BEGINNING, I AM THE WIND THAT
DRIVING THE STARS EVER OUTWARD,
FANS YOUR SPARK IN THE DARKNESS.
A FAITHFUL GUIDE AND COMPANION
IN EVERY PLACE AND AT THE SAME
MOMENT, I LIVE IN EVERY MOTE OF
LIFE'S MARROW AND AM ALL LIFE
SUMMED TOGETHER.

Page 547 THAT WHICH OPENS AND AWAKENS THE HEART
TO THE LIGHT OF CREATION, ALSO DRIVES THE
WHOLE OF THE UNIVERSE TO ITS SHINNING
FULFILLMENT. IN ONE LIFE IS ALL AND ALL
MAKE THE MEASURE AND FULFILLMENT OF
CREATION.

WISDOM, FLOWS NOT, FROM THE REFINED
MEASURES OF THE MIND, BUT FROM THE SPIRIT
THAT INSPIRES THOSE SMALL AND FALTERING
STEPS TOWARD THE TRUTH IN WHICH ALL THE
AWAKENING EMBERS OF LIFE PARTAKE.

THE DIARY

IN MAN'S HEART ARE BOTH THE PRINCE OF
DARKNESS AND THE PRINCE OF PEACE
CONTAINED. THE BATTLE FOR ALL CREATION'S
CULMINATION IS WITHIN, NOT WITHOUT.

BE OF GOOD CHEER, FOR TO LOVE LIFE IS TO
JOIN IN THE CREATION OF THE UNIVERSE.

IN THIS END OF TIMES AND NEW BEGINNINGS, I
WILL SHARE WITH ALL WHO CAN HEAR, THE
MYSTERY OF CREATION. IT IS LOVE, GIVEN FREELY
AND WITHOUT PRICE, THAT DRIVES CREATION
TOWARD THE LIGHT OF FULFILLMENT FOR ALL
WHO HAVE RECEIVED THE GREATEST GIFT THE
UNIVERSE MAY OFFER, LIFE.

IN THAT FINAL MOMENT OF CONSUMMATION,
ALL WHICH LIVES, LOWLY AND KNOWING
WILL BE GATHERED TOGETHER AND SHARING
THEIR GIFTS WILL BECOME MORE THAN ALL
THEIR PARTS.

IN THIS GREAT BECOMING, ALL DARK
MATTER IS CONSUMED AND ONLY
LIGHT, LIFE, REMAIN.

IN LOVE THERE IS LIFE AND IN LIFE IS THE
CONSUMMATION OF THAT FOR WHICH
PURPOSE IS THE UNIVERSE CREATED
FULFILLED

Page 561   FOR NEW WINE, A FRESH SKIN IS FOUND.
GUIDED BY THE LIGHT WITHIN, LAMB
AND LION, SHALL LYING DOWN TOGETHER,
KNOW NOT THE STRIFE IN WHICH YOUR
BLOODLINE IS ROOTED. HERE SHALL LIFE'S
LIGHT, FROM ITS FIRST STIRRINGS, SHINE
THROUGH THE LAMP'S DULL CLAY
WHEREIN IT BURNS.

A NEW EARTH SHALL BE BOTH YOUR
TEACHER AND SIT AT THE RIGHT HAND
OF YOUR COUNSEL. THROUGH AGES
BEYOND COUNTING HAVE THE MEEK BEEN
PREPARED, WITHIN THE VESSEL OF STRIFE,
TO KNOW CONTENDING NO MORE.

HIDDEN WITHIN AGES OF ENMITY,
SLAUGHTER AND PAIN, THE MEEK LAY AS
BUT FRAGMENTS WITHIN MAN'S LOINS.
NOW GROWN UNTO THIS FIRST FLOWERING,
THE FULL BLOOM LIES YET BEFORE YOU.

NUMBERED IN MILLENNIA, LIFE'S FULL
MEASURE OF YEARS SHALL BE YOURS, AND
OF YOUR LINEAGE MORE.

YOUR OFFSPRING SHALL, STANDING UPON
THIS WORLD, YET KNOW ALL OF CREATION.
IN THIS KNOWING, SHALL THEY SERVANTS BE
TO ALL LIFE NOT OF YOUR SEMBLANCE. IN
CHILDHOOD'S INNOCENT COMPASSION, THEY
WILL TEACH PEACE TO THE STRONG. UNTO
ALL THE HEAVEN'S FIERY EMBERS SHALL
YOUR ISSUE, GIRDED ONLY WITH THE SPIRIT'S
MIGHT, LIFE'S EMISSARIES BE.

KIN TO ALL PRESENT AT THE ETERNAL
NOW OF CREATION, YOU ARE CALLED TO
SEE BEYOND LIFE'S SHADOW INTO ITS
MARROW. YOURS IS TO KNOW THAT
SIMPLICITY IS BUT REASONING IN
LOVE FOR ALL THAT HAS LIFE.

WHEREFORE, A NEW COMMANDMENT
I GIVE YOU, BE YE THEREFORE SIMPLE.

BEHOLD, YOU ARE GIVEN NEW HEAVENS
AND A NEW EARTH. YOU ARE CALLED TO

HUSBAND THE SEEDS HERE PLANTED, TO
TEND THE NEW SHOOTS, TO MINISTER TO
AND WATCH OVER THE LIFE THAT SPRINGS
FROM THIS GARDEN.

THE LIGHT OF CREATION THAT BURNS
BEYOND THE CLAY OF THIS UNIVERSE IS
YOUR LEGACY. AS CHILDREN OF THE LIGHT
BE THEREFORE GUIDED BY IT. AS YOU ARE
BORN TO PEACE, SO PEACE SHALL FLOW
FROM YOU TO THE VERY ROOT OF LIFE'S
UNFOLDING UPON THIS ISLAND OF LIGHT
ADRIFT IN A SEA OF DARKNESS.

THOUGH I GO FROM AMONG YOU, YET
AM I WITH YOU ALWAYS EVEN UNTIL
ALL DARKNESS SHALL BE SWALLOWED UP
IN THAT LIGHT WHICH IS THE LIFE OF ALL
BEGINNINGS.

Page 564   BEHOLD, YOU ARE GIVEN NEW HEAVENS
AND A NEW EARTH. YOU ARE CALLED TO
HUSBAND THE SEEDS HERE PLANTED, TO
TEND THE NEW SHOOTS, TO MINISTER TO
AND WATCH OVER THE LIFE THAT
SPRINGS FROM THIS GARDEN.

THE LIGHT OF CREATION THAT BURNS
BEYOND THE CLAY OF THIS UNIVERSE IS
YOUR LEGACY. AS CHILDREN OF THE
LIGHT BE YE THEREFORE GUIDED BY IT. AS
YOU ARE BORN TO PEACE, SO PEACE SHALL
FLOW FROM YOU TO THE VERY ROOT OF
LIFE'S UNFOLDING UPON THIS ISLAND OF
LIGHT ADRIFT IN A SEA OF DARKNESS.

THOUGH I GO FROM AMONG YOU, YET
AM I WITH YOU ALWAYS EVEN UNTIL
ALL DARKNESS SHALL BE SWALLOWED UP

IN THAT LIGHT THAT IS THE LIFE OF ALL
BEGINNINGS.

ENDINGS ARE THE PROVINCE OF MAN'S
VANITY AND FEAR. THE LIGHT OF LIFE IS
OF, AND AT, THE BEGINNING, WHICH IS
ALSO THE FINAL HOME OF EACH AND
EVERY MOTE OF EXISTENCE. THE CRUDE
MATTER SHELL OF ALL THAT FROM LIFE'S
THREADS DID SPRING, WAS OF LIFE'S
MAKING. IT'S FIRST ILLUMINED SPINNING,
LIFE WOVE THE MANYFOLDED AND
TEXTURED FABRIC OF THE UNIVERSE.

BE AT PEACE, FOR THAT WHICH
STRIKES TERROR SOUNDS UPON THE
HOLLOW OF AN IMPERFECT VESSEL THAT
IS QUICKLY REDUCED TO SHARDS THE
GROUND CONSUMES. ALL LIFE IS WOVEN
TOGETHER BY LOVE. ONLY THAT WHICH
RENDS THIS CARING WEAVE CAUSETH
A WAVERING OF CREATION'S FLAME THAT
BURNS WITHIN.

Page 568   LIFE'S LORD AND FIRST ROW IN THE
TAPESTRY OF EXISTENCE IS, IN
IMAGINATION'S FLIGHT, A WEAVE
TINTED IN BRIGHT SPIRALING HOPES
AND ENTRAINING ASPIRATIONS. YET
THROUGH MANY TRIALS IN THE DARK
CLAY OF LIFE THAT GLIMMERING FIRST
ROW IS WARPED GENEROUSLY WITH
DARKLY KNOTTED FEARS AND TWISTED
SORROWS BORN OF LIFE'S SOJOURN
IN MATTER'S NIGHT. SCHOOLED BY
ENDLESS INCARNATIONS, ITS FIBERS
ARE DYED FAST BY THE LONGINGS
AND TRAVAILS OF ALL LIFE'S TOILING
STRANDS.

THE DIARY

UNCOUNTED LIVING THREADS LOOSED
FROM CREATION'S LOOM AND YEARNING
FOR HOME GAZE IN AWE, EACH
THROUGH THEIR OWN TINY TANGLE
OF CRUDE MATTER'S CONSTRAINING
LATTICE, AT HEAVEN'S FIELDS WHITE
WITH LIGHT.

OF THESE MANY SINGULAR THREADS,
SEVERED FROM THE LOOM OF LIFE'S
WHOLE CLOTH, A SINGLE WISP, THE
TRIBE OF MAN, BESET STILL WITH
UNCHARITABLE DIVISIONS, IS BUT
ONE.

CPSIA information can be obtained at www.ICGtesting.com
Printed in the USA
BVOW02s1551060813

327772BV00002B/15/P